D0535496

THE OXFORD
ILLUSTRATED DICKENS

MASTER HUMPHREY'S CLOCK

AND

A CHILD'S HISTORY OF ENGLAND

THE OXFORD ILLUSTRATED DICKENS

Charles John Huffham Dickens was born on 7 February 1812 at Landport near Portsmouth, where his father was a Navy pay clerk. His family moved to London in 1815 and in 1817 to Chatham, where Dickens spent the happiest time of his boyhood. This was followed by a period of misery during which his father was imprisoned for debt in the Marshalsea and Dickens was withdrawn from school and, at the age of 12, sent to work in a blacking warehouse. These experiences deeply affected him and his future work. He returned to school, and left at 15 to become a clerk, a shorthand reporter in the law courts, and a reporter of debates in the Commons. In 1833 he began contributing articles to periodicals, which were later reprinted as *Sketches by Boz* (1836–7); these led to an approach from publishers, resulting in the creation of Mr Pickwick and the publication in monthly numbers of *The Posthumous Papers of the Pickwick Club* (1836–7). In 1836 he married Catherine Hogarth; they had ten children over the next 16 years. Dickens began to publish *Oliver Twist* in 1837 in *Bentley's Miscellany*, a periodical of which he was the first editor. *Nicholas Nickleby* followed in 1838–9. *The Old Curiosity Shop* (1840–1) and *Barnaby Rudge* (1841) were intended for *Master Humphrey's Clock*, a weekly written by Dickens, but he eventually abandoned 'Master Humphrey'.

Dickens's visit to America in 1842 resulted in *American Notes* (1842) and an American section in *Martin Chuzzlewit* (1843–4). He lost readership with the latter but regained it with 'A Christmas Carol' (1843), the first of his five *Christmas Books*. In 1844 he visited Italy, and contributed 'Pictures from Italy' (1846) to the *Daily News*, a paper he founded. *Dombey and Son* appeared in 1846–8 and *David Copperfield* in 1849–50. In 1850 Dickens began the weekly journal *Household Words*, incorporated in 1859 into *All The Year Round*, which he edited until his death. In these appeared essays later issued as *Reprinted Pieces* (1858) and *The Uncommercial Traveller* (1861), and his *Christmas Stories*. A *Child's History of England* was published in 1851–3, *Bleak House* in 1852–3, *Hard Times* in 1854, *Little Dorrit* in 1855–7, *A Tale of Two Cities* in 1859, *Great Expectations* in 1860–1, and *Our Mutual Friend* in 1864–5. In 1856 Dickens bought a country house, Gad's Hill Place, near Rochester, and in 1858 he and his wife separated. He threw himself into public readings of his works, which were greatly successful but draining. His last work, *The Mystery of Edwin Drood*, was left unfinished when he died suddenly on 9 June 1870.

The Frontispiece to Volume I of the first edition of
Master Humphrey's Clock *in book form, 1840*

MASTER HUMPHREY'S CLOCK
AND
A CHILD'S HISTORY
OF ENGLAND

By
CHARLES DICKENS

With Twenty-nine Illustrations by George Cattermole
'Phiz', Marcus Stone and F. W. Topham
and an Introduction by
DEREK HUDSON

OXFORD   NEW YORK   TORONTO   MELBOURNE
OXFORD UNIVERSITY PRESS

Oxford University Press, Walton Street, Oxford OX2 6DP

Oxford New York Toronto
Delhi Bombay Calcutta Madras Karachi
Petaling Jaya Singapore Hong Kong Tokyo
Nairobi Dar es Salaam Cape Town
Melbourne Auckland

and associated companies in
Berlin Ibadan

Oxford is a trade mark of Oxford University Press

Master Humphrey's Clock was the title of a periodical wholly written by Dickens which was issued both as weekly and monthly parts from April 1840 to November 1841. The entire work was also published as a book in three volumes, the first volume dated 1840 and the other volumes dated 1841. The greater part of *Master Humphrey's Clock* consisted of two serials, *The Old Curiosity Shop* and *Barnaby Rudge*. These are published as separate volumes in the Oxford Illustrated Dickens (known before 1966 as The New Oxford Illustrated Dickens). The remaining contents of the periodical are presented in this volume.

A Child's History of England appeared serially in *Household Words*, January 1851 to December 1853, and was first published as a book in three volumes dated 1852, 1853, and 1854.

The illustrations to *Master Humphrey's Clock* have been taken from the three volumes of 1840 and 1841. The illustrations to *A Child's History of England* consist of the frontispiece to Volume I of the first edition in book form, 1852, and of the engravings provided for the Illustrated Library Edition, 1861–74.

In the Oxford Illustrated Dickens this volume was first published in 1958, and reprinted in 1963, 1966, 1974, 1978, 1981, 1987, 1989, 1989, 1991.

Published in the United States by Oxford University Press, USA

This volume: ISBN 0 19 254520 5
21-volume set: ISBN 0 19 254522 1

Printed in the United States of America

INTRODUCTION

by DEREK HUDSON

ALTHOUGH the two works included in this volume cannot be judged, by themselves, of much literary importance, they have a considerable biographical interest for the student of Dickens and his times. Neither *Master Humphrey's Clock* nor *A Child's History of England* can be properly appreciated without some knowledge of the circumstances in which they were produced. Both derive from experiments in periodical journalism.

*   *   *

,Dickens's popularity as a novelist had been firmly established by *Pickwick Papers*, *Oliver Twist*, and *Nicholas Nickleby*, when, at the age of twenty-seven, he outlined to John Forster for submission to Chapman and Hall the scheme for 'a new publication consisting entirely of original matter' which took shape in April 1840 as *Master Humphrey's Clock*. Dickens was the sole author of this weekly miscellany, and its plan was simple. The reader was introduced at the outset to a kindly old gentleman, Master Humphrey, whose most cherished possession was his 'cheerful, companionable Clock', and to a small company of friends who foregathered with him regularly to read manuscripts which they had previously deposited in the clock-case.

That Dickens intended these interpolated stories to have an historical and antiquarian trend is shown by his invitation to George Cattermole, who specialized in 'costume', to collaborate with 'Phiz' in the illustrations. Nothing could have been 'nearer to the heart of Dickens', as G. K. Chesterton has said, than 'his great Gargantuan conception of Gog and Magog telling London legends to each other all through the night'. But this prospect remained unfulfilled; after yielding the Elizabethan story of Hugh Graham, 'a bold young 'prentice who loved his master's daughter', the colloquy of the Giants was not resumed. For the second historical tale, the unmasking of a black-hearted villain of Charles II's reign, the Giants bore no responsibility.

It is with the entrance of Mr. Pickwick that *Master*

Humphrey's Clock, in its present form, takes on its chief
interest. Even the most self-possessed reader must feel his
pulse quicken as Mr. Pickwick trips across the garden towards Master Humphrey's seat, 'with his hat in his hand,
the sun shining on his bald head, his bland face, his bright
spectacles, his fawn-coloured tights, and his black gaiters',
Although he maintained later that he had no intention 'of
re-opening an exhausted and abandoned mine', the temptation to revive some of his most famous characters proved,
for the first and last time in his work, too much for Dickens.
It must be admitted that *Pickwick redivivus* is something
of a disappointment, a shadow of his former self. He sponsors
a Jacobean tale of witches, a lonely gibbet and a secret
burial in a city church; but he has little to say in his own
right. The Wellers make a more convincing reappearance.
Mr. Weller, senior, expatiating on his grandson, or helping
Mr. Pickwick into his great-coat ('Right arm fust—now the
left—now one strong conwulsion') is capital; while Sam, in
the tragic little story of the hairdresser's dummies, has
material worthy of his gift as a *raconteur*:

. . . the gen'lmen vith blue dots for their beards, wery large viskers,
oudacious heads of hair, uncommon clear eyes, and nostrils of amazin'
pinkness; the ladies vith their heads o' one side, their right forefingers on their lips, and their forms deweloped beautiful, in vich last
respect they had the adwantage over the gen'lmen, as wasn't allowed
but wery little shoulder, and terminated rayther abrupt in fancy
drapery.

Meanwhile, however, the future of *Master Humphrey's
Clock* had been casually determined by the appearance in
the fourth number of the first chapter of *The Old Curiosity
Shop*, originally intended to be no more than one of the
'personal adventures' of Master Humphrey, and not
necessarily a long one at that. There was, however, beside
Dickens's growing interest in the story and its characters,
a pressing reason for providing a regular serial: the sales of
the *Clock*, after reaching nearly seventy thousand copies
with the first number, had fallen away alarmingly when its
readers found that it offered no continuous tale. Therefore,
having appearéd intermittently for some weeks, *The Old
Curiosity Shop* took entire charge of the *Clock* from its
ninth chapter and henceforward was published week by
week until the story was finished.

The original plan of the miscellany was never resumed.

We may, however, read an interesting 'bridge passage', following the conclusion of *The Old Curiosity Shop*, in which Master Humphrey, who had obviously begun the story in the character of the old bachelor, is made to reveal that he was in fact 'the younger brother, the single gentleman, the nameless actor in this little drama'—a revelation that surprises us as much as it surprised Master Humphrey's friends. And this same passage is memorable for Dickens's evocation of London at night, and his conception of St. Paul's clock as London's Heart.

> Heart of London, there is a moral in thy every stroke! as I look on at thy indomitable working, which neither death, nor press of life, nor grief, nor gladness out of doors will influence one jot, I seem to hear a voice within thee which sinks into my heart, bidding me, as I elbow my way among the crowd, have some thought for the meanest wretch that passes, and, being a man, to turn away with scorn and pride from none that bear the human shape.

After a few more paragraphs Dickens introduced a new serial, *Barnaby Rudge*. It is Master Humphrey's rumination over the conclusion of *Barnaby Rudge* that follows next and is suggested by Phiz's illustration. Little remained but to record the death of Master Humphrey and to disperse his company of friends; 'the chimney-corner has grown cold; and Master Humphrey's Clock has stopped for ever'.

What we have here, then, is, from one aspect, only a collection of sketches and tales which formed the original setting for two great novels. These papers do not derive from the higher levels of Dickens's inspiration; yet they are characteristic of his work, both in comedy and tragedy, and contain much that is rewarding. They reflect the trend of his interests and the cast of his mind. They give us an intimate understanding of the young author-editor as he seeks to win public favour for his first magazine. When Dickens announced to his readers the termination of *Master Humphrey's Clock*, in September 1841, he did so with considerable relief, because he had found the weekly publication of his serials 'perplexing and difficult'. But he still looked forward to further experiments as an editor. Sentiment that might seem insincere in another must be accepted from him: 'To commune with you, in any form, is to me a labour of love'.

*   *   *

Dickens first mentions his intention of 'writing a little

history of England for my boy'—his eldest son Charles, then aged six—in a letter to Douglas Jerrold of 3 May 1843, in which he congratulates Jerrold on an historical article in the *Illuminated Magazine*, and adds: 'I don't know what I should do if he were to get hold of any Conservative or High Church notions.' He refers to the project again when writing to Miss Coutts in August 1843, and emphasizes his desire that Charley 'may have tenderhearted notions of War and Murder, and may not fix his affections on wrong heroes, or see the bright side of Glory's sword and know nothing of the rusty one . . .'.

The idea did not take active shape until 1850, when Dickens began to edit a new weekly journal, *Household Words*. The spirit of the age was didactic; the Great Exhibition, with its strong educational pre-occupation, influenced patriotic minds long before its opening in May 1851. When *A Child's History of England* began to appear in *Household Words* in January of that year, few can have doubted that this was a sound journalistic decision.

There was every reason, moreover, for Bradbury and Evans, his new publishers, to be interested in publishing Dickens's history in book form. The demand for informative children's books increased yearly. Peter Parley, Felix Summerly, and J. O. Halliwell were to be found in every nursery and schoolroom; while two highly successful histories 'for the use of young people' adorned Mr. Murray's list—Mrs. Markham's famous *History of England*, and *Little Arthur's History of England* by Lady Callcott, which was overtaking it in popularity. 'Lady Callcott's style is of the right kind', the *Examiner* had said, 'earnest and simple'. Dickens did not disdain such qualities, but by preference he was masculine and radical; he prepared to try conclusions with the mild gentility of these ladies.

The history appeared regularly in *Household Words* throughout 1851, 1852, and 1853, being forwarded by instalments to W. H. Wills, Dickens's sub-editor, as and when Dickens found time to produce them. 'I send the "History of England"—with a very pretty bit in it, describing the drowning of the son of Henry the First', he wrote from Broadstairs during the summer of 1851. 'I don't think I can finish the "Child's History" in one morning', was a comment in December 1852, 'for I have got my favourite ruffian Henry the Eighth to deal with'. And

when the sheets of the last volume in book form were coming
from the printer in October 1853—for the three original
volumes were published at yearly intervals—Dickens asked
Wills to insert a reference to James I's treatise on witches,
'in whom he was (as such a wrong-headed Dolt ought to
have been) a strong believer'. This failing of King James
had already been noticed by Dickens in 'Mr. Pickwick's
Tale' in *Master Humphrey's Clock*.

Dickens's attitude to his history was not flippant, as
these remarks to Wills might suggest, though its composition was only a side-line for him during a period which saw
the conclusion of *David Copperfield* and the writing of *Bleak
House*, while the general pressure of his editorship continued.
The greater part of the *Child's History* was dictated to his
sister-in-law, Georgina Hogarth, but he wrote long passages
in his own hand. There is autograph manuscript, heavily
corrected, in the Victoria and Albert Museum for Chapters
II and III, for Chapter IX, and for Chapter X down to the
death of Robert of Normandy. It is satisfying to find
Dickens giving his full personal attention to that great
Victorian hero, King Alfred, whose thousandth birthday
celebrations in 1849 had been organized so zealously by
Martin Tupper at Wantage, where an ox had been roasted
'by the aid of Mr. Charles Hart's Steam Engine' and 'the
polka and waltz were kept up till a late hour'. Nowhere in
this book does Dickens better reflect an enlightened Victorian view of history than in what he writes of Alfred:

I pause to think with admiration, of the noble king who, in his
single person, possessed all the Saxon virtues. Whom misfortune
could not subdue, whom prosperity could not spoil, whose perseverance nothing could shake. Who was hopeful in defeat, and
generous in success. Who loved justice, freedom, truth, and knowledge. Who, in his care to instruct his people, probably did more to
preserve the beautiful old Saxon language, than I can imagine.
Without whom, the English tongue, in which I tell this story might
have wanted half its meaning. As it is said that his spirit still inspires
some of our best English laws, so, let you and I pray that it may
animate our English hearts, at least to this—to resolve, when we see
any of our fellow-creatures left in ignorance, that we will do our best,
while life is in us, to have them taught . . . .

Elsewhere there is much that is deplorable to modern eyes
in *A Child's History of England*. Unlike Scott or Thackeray,
Dickens had no patience with history as such, and deeply
mistrusted 'the good old days'. He made no claims to be

a dispassionate historian; there was little allowance for changed circumstances; Dickens saw everything in black and white (mostly in black). Chivalrously concerned for Joan of Arc or Lady Jane Grey, he regarded Henry VIII as 'a blot of blood and grease upon the History of England' and said that 'Bloody Queen Mary' would 'ever be justly remembered with horror and detestation'; James I ('His Sowship') was 'like the Plague, and everybody receives infection from him'. Much of this 'cockney History of England' (as William Allingham called it) is as crude in its humour as in its violence, and at times recalls the anti-clericalism of Victorian *Punch*. For Swinburne its 'cheap-jack radicalism' made it the 'only one book which I cannot but regret that Dickens should have written'. It is not the history that Lewis Carroll would have chosen for Alice.

When all this has been said, there is something to be added. It would be a mistake to regard *A Child's History* as typical of the Victorian approach to schoolroom history— Mrs. Markham, Lady Callcott, or Charles Knight (whose illustrated history began publication in 1856) are much more typical. As a Dickens manifesto, however, it is highly significant. Frankly, it is a boy's book, founded on a strong sense of social justice, with nothing of Little Lord Fauntleroy about it and with no cosy dialogues beginning 'Pray, mamma, do tell us'. There are, certainly, a number of passages, especially in the first half of the book, where Dickens is ready to reassure his young audience—as when, after describing some disagreeable habits of the Druids, he thoughtfully adds: 'It is pleasant to think that there are no Druids, *now* . . . and of course there is nothing of the kind, anywhere.' Nevertheless, as the book went on, the children at Dickens's knee were given an unsparing picture of pro-longed wickedness in high places, exposed with lurid detail and much rough sarcasm. The justification for the book, if it can be justified, must be that, speaking generally, Dickens's moral values were true and lasting. G. K. Chesterton believed that the 'mere common-sense of Dickens' gave 'a plainer and therefore truer picture of the mass of history than the mystical perversity of a man of genius writing only out of his own temperament, like Car-lyle or Taine. . . . This black-and-white history of heroes and villains; this history full of pugnacious ethics and of nothing else, is the right kind of history for children.' A

debatable verdict; for some of the children may be put off
the study of history altogether, and if ever a history book
was written out of an author's own temperament, surely
this one was ? Dickens says of Cromwell, 'The whole country
lamented his death'; he does not quote Evelyn's remark
that at Cromwell's funeral 'there were none that cried but
dogs'. Yet, despite his ignorance and his prejudices, on the
whole Dickens's emphasis was sound. His heart was in the
right place. He revived his horrors only to condemn them.
His narrative was vigorous and purposeful. He made
English history, in parts, read rather like one of Fitzball's
melodramas at Astley's, but there was still genius in his
limelight.

Dickens undertook no original research. John Lingard
may have been one of his sources, but he seems to have relied
largely for his facts on Thomas Keightley's three-volume
History of England (1839). In his own copy of Keightley
many passages are marked, comparisons between the two
books sometimes suggesting a cautious paraphrase, though
where Keightley gave him promising romantic material
Dickens would often briskly elaborate it with dramatic
gusto. Neither his own enthusiasm nor the sales of *Household Words* encouraged him to take the account beyond
1688, however. In the autumn of 1853 he rapidly rounded
it off, saluted Queen Victoria, and departed for a holiday
in Italy with Wilkie Collins and Augustus Egg.

The *Child's History* was dedicated by Dickens 'To My
Own Dear Children whom I hope it may help, by and by,
to read with interest larger and better books on the same
subject.' Better books? Well, yes. But this, whether we
like it or not, is Dickens's book.

MASTER HUMPHREY'S CLOCK

CONTENTS

I

II

III

IV

V

VI

LIST OF ILLUSTRATIONS

By GEORGE CATTERMOLE

By HABLOT K. BROWNE ('PHIZ')

CHARACTERS

THE DEAF GENTLEMAN, a cheerful, placid, happy old man; an intimate friend of Master Humphrey.

GOG, one of the Guildhall giants.

HUGH GRAHAM, a bowyer's apprentice, in love with his master's daughter.

MAGOG, one of the Guildhall giants.

WILL MARKS, the hero of a tale submitted by Mr. Pickwick.

MASTER HUMPHREY, the founder of a Club holding weekly meetings in his chamber for the purpose of hearing original tales read by its members, the manuscripts having previously been deposited in the case of a quaint old clock.

MR. OWEN MILES, a wealthy retired merchant, of sterling character.

MR. SAMUEL PICKWICK, the hero of 'The Pickwick Papers'.

JOHN PODGERS, a character in Mr. Pickwick's tale; a stout, drowsy old fellow, and uncle to Will Marks.

JACK REDBURN, the inseparable companion and factotum of Master Humphrey.

MR. SLITHERS, a bustling, active little man, and Mr. Pickwick's barber.

JOE TODDYHIGH, an old playmate of the Lord Mayor-elect.

SAMUEL WELLER, Mr. Pickwick's faithful servant.

TONY WELLER, THE ELDER, father to Sam Weller.

TONY WELLER, THE YOUNGER, a very small boy; the son of Sam Weller.

MISTRESS ALICE, heroine of the tale told by Magog; the beautiful and only daughter of a wealthy London bowyer of the sixteenth century.

BELINDA, a distracted damsel, in distress over her faithless lover.

MISS BENTON, Master Humphrey's housekeeper.

CHAPTER I

THE reader must not expect to know where I live. At present, it is true, my abode may be a question of little or no import to anybody; but if I should carry my readers with me, as I hope to do, and there should spring up between them and me feelings of homely affection and regard attaching something of interest to matters ever so slightly connected with my fortunes or my speculations, even my place of residence might one day have a kind of charm for them. Bearing this possible contingency in mind, I wish them to understand, in the outset, that they must never expect to know it.

I am not a churlish old man. Friendless I can never be, for all mankind are my kindred, and I am on ill terms with no one member of my great family. But for many years I have led a lonely, solitary life;—what wound I sought to heal, what sorrow to forget, originally, matters not now; it is sufficient that retirement has become a habit with me, and that I am unwilling to break the spell which for so long a time has shed its quiet influence upon my home and heart.

I live in a venerable suburb of London, in an old house which in bygone days was a famous resort for merry roysterers and peerless ladies, long since departed. It is a silent, shady place, with a paved courtyard so full of echoes, that sometimes I am tempted to believe that faint responses to the noises of old times linger there yet, and that these ghosts of sound haunt my footsteps as I pace it up and down. I am the more confirmed in this belief, because, of late years, the echoes that attend my walks have been less loud and marked than they were wont to be; and it is pleasanter to imagine in them the rustling of silk brocade, and the light step of some lovely girl, than to recognise in their altered note the failing tread of an old man.

Those who like to read of brilliant rooms and gorgeous furniture would derive but little pleasure from a minute

description of my simple dwelling. It is dear to me for the
same reason that they would hold it in slight regard. Its
worm-eaten doors, and low ceilings crossed by clumsy beams;
its walls of wainscot, dark stairs, and gaping closets; its
small chambers, communicating with each other by winding
passages or narrow steps; its many nooks, scarce larger than
its corner-cupboards; its very dust and dulness, are all dear
to me. The moth and spider are my constant tenants: for
in my house the one basks in his long sleep, and the other
plies his busy loom secure and undisturbed. I have a
pleasure in thinking on a summer's day how many butter-
flies have sprung for the first time into light and sunshine
from some dark corner of these old walls.

When I first came to live here, which was many years ago,
the neighbours were curious to know who I was, and whence
I came, and why I lived so much alone. As time went on,
and they still remained unsatisfied on these points, I became
the centre of a popular ferment, extending for half a mile
round, and in one direction for a full mile. Various rumours
were circulated to my prejudice. I was a spy, an infidel, a
conjurer, a kidnapper of children, a refugee, a priest, a
monster. Mothers caught up their infants and ran into their
houses as I passed; men eyed me spitefully, and muttered
threats and curses. I was the object of suspicion and
distrust—ay, of downright hatred too.

But when in course of time they found I did no harm, but,
on the contrary, inclined towards them despite their unjust
usage, they began to relent. I found my footsteps no
longer dogged, as they had often been before, and observed
that the women and children no longer retreated, but would
stand and gaze at me as I passed their doors. I took this for
a good omen, and waited patiently for better times. By
degrees I began to make friends among these humble folks:
and though they were yet shy of speaking, would give them
'good day,' and so pass on. In a little time, those whom
I had thus accosted would make a point of coming to their
doors and windows at the usual hour, and nod or courtesy
to me; children, too, came timidly within my reach, and
ran away quite scared when I patted their heads and bade
them be good at school. These little people soon grew more
familiar. From exchanging mere words of course with my
older neighbours, I gradually became their friend and adviser, the depositary of their cares and sorrows, and some-

times, it may be, the reliever, in my small way, of their distresses. And now I never walk abroad but pleasant recognitions and smiling faces wait on Master Humphrey.

It was a whim of mine, perhaps as a whet to the curiosity of my neighbours, and a kind of retaliation upon them for their suspicions—it was, I say, a whim of mine, when I first took up my abode in this place, to acknowledge no other name than Humphrey. With my detractors, I was Ugly Humphrey. When I began to convert them into friends, I was Mr. Humphrey and Old Mr. Humphrey. At length I settled down into plain Master Humphrey, which was understood to be the title most pleasant to my ear; and so completely a matter of course has it become, that sometimes when I am taking my morning walk in my little courtyard, I overhear my barber—who has a profound respect for me, and would not, I am sure, abridge my honours for the world —holding forth on the other side of the wall, touching the state of 'Master Humphrey's' health, and communicating to some friend the substance of the conversation that he and Master Humphrey have had together in the course of the shaving which he has just concluded.

That I may not make acquaintance with my readers under false pretences, or give them cause to complain hereafter that I have withheld any matter which it was essential for them to have learnt at first, I wish them to know—and I smile sorrowfully to think that the time has been when the confession would have given me pain—that I am a misshapen, deformed old man.

I have never been made a misanthrope by this cause. I have never been stung by any insult, nor wounded by any jest upon my crooked figure. As a child I was melancholy and timid, but that was because the gentle consideration paid to my misfortune sunk deep into my spirit and made me sad, even in those early days. I was but a very young creature when my poor mother died, and yet I remember that often when I hung around her neck, and oftener still when I played about the room before her, she would catch me to her bosom, and bursting into tears, would soothe me with every term of fondness and affection. God knows I was a happy child at those times,—happy to nestle in her breast,—happy to weep when she did,—happy in not knowing why.

These occasions are so strongly impressed upon my

memory, that they seem to have occupied whole years. I had numbered very, very few when they ceased for ever, but before then their meaning had been revealed to me.

I do not know whether all children are imbued with a quick perception of childish grace and beauty, and a strong love for it, but I was. I had no thought that I remember, either that I possessed it myself or that I lacked it, but I admired it with an intensity that I cannot describe. A little knot of playmates—they must have been beautiful, for I see them now—were clustered one day round my mother's knee in eager admiration of some picture representing a group of

MASTER HUMPHREY WALKING ABROAD

infant angels, which she held in her hand. Whose the picture was, whether it was familiar to me or otherwise, or how all the children came to be there, I forget; I have some dim thought it was my birthday, but the beginning of my recollection is that we were all together in a garden, and it was summer weather,—I am sure of that, for one of the little girls had roses in her sash. There were many lovely angels in this picture, and I remember the fancy coming upon me to point out which of them represented each child there, and that when I had gone through my companions, I stopped and hesitated, wondering which was most like me. I

Master Humphrey's Room

remember the children looking at each other, and my turning red and hot, and their crowding round to kiss me, saying
that they loved me all the same; and then, and when the
old sorrow came into my dear mother's mild and tender
look, the truth broke upon me for the first time, and I knew,
while watching my awkward and ungainly sports, how
keenly she had felt for her poor crippled boy.

I used frequently to dream of it afterwards, and now my
heart aches for that child as if I had never been he, when
I think how often he awoke from some fairy change to his
own old form, and sobbed himself to sleep again.

Well, well,—all these sorrows are past. My glancing at
them may not be without its use, for it may help in some
measure to explain why I have all my life been attached
to the inanimate objects that people my chamber, and how
I have come to look upon them rather in the light of old
and constant friends, than as mere chairs and tables which
a little money could replace at will.

Chief and first among all these is my Clock,—my old,
cheerful, companionable Clock. How can I ever convey to
others an idea of the comfort and consolation that this old
Clock has been for years to me!

It is associated with my earliest recollections. It stood
upon the staircase at home (I call it home still mechanically),
nigh sixty years ago. I like it for that; but it is not on that
account, nor because it is a quaint old thing in a huge oaken
case curiously and richly carved, that I prize it as I do. I
incline to it as if it were alive, and could understand and
give me back the love I bear it.

And what other thing that has not life could cheer me as
it does? what other thing that has not life (I will not say how
few things that have) could have proved the same patient,
true, untiring friend? How often have I sat in the long
winter evenings feeling such society in its cricket-voice, that
raising my eyes from my book and looking gratefully
towards it, the face reddened by the glow of the shining fire
has seemed to relax from its staid expression and to regard
me kindly! how often in the summer twilight, when my
thoughts have wandered back to a melancholy past, have its
regular whisperings recalled them to the calm and peaceful
present! how often in the dead tranquillity of night has its
bell broken the oppressive silence, and seemed to give me
assurance that the old clock was still a faithful watcher at

my chamber-door! My easy-chair, my desk, my ancient furniture, my very books, I can scarcely bring myself to love even these last like my old clock.

It stands in a snug corner, midway between the fireside and a low arched door leading to my bedroom. Its fame is diffused so extensively throughout the neighbourhood, that I have often the satisfaction of hearing the publican, or the baker, and sometimes even the parish-clerk, petitioning my housekeeper (of whom I shall have much to say by and by) to inform him the exact time by Master Humphrey's clock. My barber, to whom I have referred, would sooner believe it than the sun. Nor are these its only distinctions. It has acquired, I am happy to say, another, inseparably connecting it not only with my enjoyments and reflections, but with those of other men; as I shall now relate.

I lived alone here for a long time without any friend or acquaintance. In the course of my wanderings by night and day, at all hours and seasons, in city streets and quiet country parts, I came to be familiar with certain faces, and to take it to heart as quite a heavy disappointment if they failed to present themselves each at its accustomed spot. But these were the only friends I knew, and beyond them I had none.

It happened, however, when I had gone on thus for a long time, that I formed an acquaintance with a deaf gentleman, which ripened into intimacy and close companionship. To this hour, I am ignorant of his name. It is his humour to conceal it, or he has a reason and purpose for so doing. In either case, I feel that he has a right to require a return of the trust he has reposed; and as he has never sought to discover my secret, I have never sought to penetrate his. There may have been something in this tacit confidence in each other flattering and pleasant to us both, and it may have imparted in the beginning an additional zest, perhaps, to our friendship. Be this as it may, we have grown to be like brothers, and still I only know him as the deaf gentleman.

I have said that retirement has become a habit with me. When I add, that the deaf gentleman and I have two friends, I communicate nothing which is inconsistent with that declaration. I spend many hours of every day in solitude and study, have no friends or change of friends but these, only see them at stated periods, and am supposed to be of a retired spirit by the very nature and object of our association.

We are men of secluded habits, with something of a cloud upon our early fortunes, whose enthusiasm, nevertheless, has not cooled with age, whose spirit of romance is not yet quenched, who are content to ramble through the world in a pleasant dream, rather than ever waken again to its harsh realities. We are alchemists who would extract the essence of perpetual youth from dust and ashes, tempt coy Truth in many light and airy forms from the bottom of her well, and discover one crumb of comfort or one grain of good in the commonest and least-regarded matter that passes through our crucible. Spirits of past times, creatures of imagination, and people of to-day are alike the objects of our seeking, and, unlike the objects of search with most philosophers, we can insure their coming at our command.

The deaf gentleman and I first began to beguile our days with these fancies, and our nights in communicating them to each other. We are now four. But in my room there are six old chairs, and we have decided that the two empty seats shall always be placed at our table when we meet, to remind us that we may yet increase our company by that number, if we should find two men to our mind. When one among us dies, his chair will always be set in its usual place, but never occupied again; and I have caused my will to be so drawn out, that when we are all dead the house shall be shut up, and the vacant chairs still left in their accustomed places. It is pleasant to think that even then our shades may, perhaps, assemble together as of yore we did, and join in ghostly converse.

One night in every week, as the clock strikes ten, we meet. At the second stroke of two, I am alone.

And now shall I tell how that my old servant, besides giving us note of time, and ticking cheerful encouragement of our proceedings, lends its name to our society, which for its punctuality and my love is christened 'Master Humphrey's Clock'? Now shall I tell how that in the bottom of the old dark closet, where the steady pendulum throbs and beats with healthy action, though the pulse of him who made it stood still long ago, and never moved again, there are piles of dusty papers constantly placed there by our hands, that we may link our enjoyments with my old friend, and draw means to beguile time from the heart of time itself?

Shall I, or can I, tell with what a secret pride I open this
repository when we meet at night, and still find new store
of pleasure in my dear old Clock?

Friend and companion of my solitude! mine is not a
selfish love; I would not keep your merits to myself, but
disperse something of pleasant association with your image
through the whole wide world; I would have men couple
with your name cheerful and healthy thoughts; I would
have them believe that you keep true and honest time; and
how it would gladden me to know that they recognised some
hearty English work in Master Humphrey's clock!

THE CLOCK-CASE

It is my intention constantly to address my readers from
the chimney-corner, and I would fain hope that such accounts as I shall give them of our histories and proceedings,
our quiet speculations or more busy adventures, will never
be unwelcome. Lest, however, I should grow prolix in the
outset by lingering too long upon our little association, con-
founding the enthusiasm with which I regard this chief
happiness of my life with that minor degree of interest which
those to whom I address myself may be supposed to feel for
it, I have deemed it expedient to break off as they have
seen.

But, still clinging to my old friend, and naturally desirous
that all its merits should be known, I am tempted to open
(somewhat irregularly and against our laws, I must admit)
the clock-case. The first roll of paper on which I lay my
hand is in the writing of the deaf gentleman. I shall have
to speak of him in my next paper; and how can I better
approach that welcome task than by prefacing it with a pro-
duction of his own pen, consigned to the safe keeping of my
honest Clock by his own hand?

The manuscript runs thus:

INTRODUCTION TO THE GIANT CHRONICLES

Once upon a time, that is to say, in this our time,—the
exact year, month, and day are of no matter,—there dwelt
in the city of London a substantial citizen, who united in
his single person the dignities of wholesale fruiterer, alderman, common-councilman, and member of the worshipful
Company of Patten-makers; who had superadded to these

The Giants

extraordinary distinctions the important post and title of
Sheriff, and who at length, and to crown all, stood next in
rotation for the high and honourable office of Lord Mayor.

He was a very substantial citizen indeed. His face was
like the full moon in a fog, with two little holes punched out
for his eyes, a very ripe pear stuck on for his nose, and a
wide gash to serve for a mouth. The girth of his waistcoat
was hung up and lettered in his tailor's shop as an extraordinary curiosity. He breathed like a heavy snorer, and
his voice in speaking came thickly forth, as if it were oppressed and stifled by feather-beds. He trod the ground like
an elephant, and eat and drank like—like nothing but an
alderman, as he was.

This worthy citizen had risen to his great eminence from
small beginnings. He had once been a very lean, weazen
little boy, never dreaming of carrying such a weight of flesh
upon his bones or of money in his pockets, and glad enough
to take his dinner at a baker's door, and his tea at a pump.
But he had long ago forgotten all this, as it was proper
that a wholesale fruiterer, alderman, common-councilman,
member of the worshipful Company of Patten-makers, past
sheriff, and, above all, a Lord Mayor that was to be, should;
and he never forgot it more completely in all his life than on
the eighth of November in the year of his election to the
great golden civic chair, which was the day before his grand
dinner at Guildhall.

It happened that as he sat that evening all alone in his
counting-house, looking over the bill of fare for next day,
and checking off the fat capons in fifties, and the turtle-
soup by the hundred quarts, for his private amusement,—
—it happened that as he sat alone occupied in these pleasant
calculations, a strange man came in and asked him how he
did, adding, 'If I am half as much changed as you, sir, you
have no recollection of me, I am sure.'

The strange man was not over and above well dressed,
and was very far from being fat or rich-looking in any sense
of the word, yet he spoke with a kind of modest confidence,
and assumed an easy, gentlemanly sort of an air, to which
nobody but a rich man can lawfully presume. Besides this,
he interrupted the good citizen just as he had reckoned three
hundred and seventy-two fat capons, and was carrying them
over to the next column; and as if that were not aggrava-
tion enough, the learned recorder for the city of London had

only ten minutes previously gone out at that very same door,
and had turned round and said, 'Good night, my lord.' Yes,
he had said, 'my lord;'—he, a man of birth and education,
of the Honourable Society of the Middle Temple, Barrister-
at-Law,—he who had an uncle in the House of Commons,
and an aunt almost but not quite in the House of Lords (for
she had married a feeble peer, and made him vote as she
liked),—he, this man, this learned recorder, had said, 'my
lord.' 'I'll not wait till to-morrow to give you your title,
my Lord Mayor,' says he, with a bow and a smile; 'you
are Lord Mayor *de facto*, if not *de jure*. Good night, my
lord.'

The Lord Mayor elect thought of this, and turning to the
stranger, and sternly bidding him 'go out of his private
counting-house,' brought forward the three hundred and
seventy-two fat capons, and went on with his account.

'Do you remember,' said the other, stepping forward,—
'*do* you remember little Joe Toddyhigh?'

The port wine fled for a moment from the fruiterer's nose
as he muttered, 'Joe Toddyhigh! What about Joe Toddyhigh?'

'*I* am Joe Toddyhigh,' cried the visitor. 'Look at me,
look hard at me,—harder, harder. You know me now?
You know little Joe again? What a happiness to us both,
to meet the very night before your grandeur! O! give me
your hand, Jack,—both hands,—both, for the sake of old
times.'

'You pinch me, sir. You're a-hurting of me,' said the
Lord Mayor elect pettishly. 'Don't,—suppose anybody
should come,—Mr. Toddyhigh, sir.'

'Mr. Toddyhigh!' repeated the other ruefully.

'O, don't bother,' said the Lord Mayor elect, scratching
his head. 'Dear me! Why, I thought you was dead. What
a fellow you are!'

Indeed, it was a pretty state of things, and worthy the
tone of vexation and disappointment in which the Lord
Mayor spoke. Joe Toddyhigh had been a poor boy with him
at Hull, and had oftentimes divided his last penny and
parted his last crust to relieve his wants; for though Joe was
a destitute child in those times, he was as faithful and
affectionate in his friendship as ever man of might could be.
They parted one day to seek their fortunes in different
directions. Joe went to sea, and the now wealthy citizen

begged his way to London. They separated with many tears, like foolish fellows as they were, and agreed to remain fast friends, and if they lived, soon to communicate again.

When he was an errand-boy, and even in the early days of his apprenticeship, the citizen had many a time trudged to the Post-office to ask if there were any letter from poor little Joe, and had gone home again with tears in his eyes, when he found no news of his only friend. The world is a wide place, and it was a long time before the letter came; when it did, the writer was forgotten. It turned from white to yellow from lying in the Post-office with nobody to claim it, and in course of time was torn up with five hundred others, and sold for waste-paper. And now at last, and when it might least have been expected, here was this Joe Toddyhigh turning up and claiming acquaintance with a great public character, who on the morrow would be cracking jokes with the Prime Minister of England, and who had only, at any time during the next twelve months, to say the word, and he could shut up Temple Bar, and make it no thoroughfare for the king himself!

'I am sure I don't know what to say, Mr. Toddyhigh,' said the Lord Mayor elect; 'I really don't. It's very inconvenient. I'd sooner have given twenty pound,—it's very inconvenient, really.'

A thought had come into his mind, that perhaps his old friend might say something passionate which would give him an excuse for being angry himself. No such thing. Joe looked at him steadily, but very mildly, and did not open his lips.

'Of course I shall pay you what I owe you,' said the Lord Mayor elect, fidgeting in his chair. 'You lent me—I think it was a shilling or some small coin—when we parted company, and that of course I shall pay with good interest. I can pay my way with any man, and always have done. If you look into the Mansion House the day after to-morrow,—some time after dusk,—and ask for my private clerk, you'll find he has a draft for you. I haven't got time to say anything more just now, unless,'—he hesitated, for, coupled with a strong desire to glitter for once in all his glory in the eyes of his former companion, was a distrust of his appearance, which might be more shabby than he could tell by that feeble light,—'unless you'd like to come to the dinner to-morrow. I don't mind your having this ticket, if you like

B

to take it. A great many people would give their ears for it,
I can tell you.'

His old friend took the card without speaking a word, and
instantly departed. His sunburnt face and grey hair were
present to the citizen's mind for a moment; but by the time
he reached three hundred and eighty-one fat capons, he had
quite forgotten him.

Joe Toddyhigh had never been in the capital of Europe
before, and he wandered up and down the streets that night
amazed at the number of churches and other public buildings, the splendour of the shops, the riches that were
heaped up on every side, the glare of light in which they
were displayed, and the concourse of people who hurried
to and fro, indifferent, apparently, to all the wonders that
surrounded them. But in all the long streets and broad
squares, there were none but strangers; it was quite a relief
to turn down a by-way and hear his own footsteps on the
pavement. He went home to his inn, thought that London
was a dreary, desolate place, and felt disposed to doubt the
existence of one true-hearted man in the whole worshipful
Company of Patten-makers. Finally, he went to bed, and
dreamed that he and the Lord Mayor elect were boys again.

He went next day to the dinner; and when in a burst of
light and music, and in the midst of splendid decorations
and surrounded by brilliant company, his former friend
appeared at the head of the Hall, and was hailed with shouts
and cheering, he cheered and shouted with the best, and for
the moment could have cried. The next moment he cursed
his weakness in behalf of a man so changed and selfish, and
quite hated a jolly-looking old gentleman opposite for declaring himself in the pride of his heart a Patten-maker.

As the banquet proceeded, he took more and more to
heart the rich citizen's unkindness; and that, not from any
envy, but because he felt that a man of his state and fortune could all the better afford to recognise an old friend,
even if he were poor and obscure. The more he thought of
this, the more lonely and sad he felt. When the company
dispersed and adjourned to the ball-room, he paced the hall
and passages alone, ruminating in a very melancholy condition upon the disappointment he had experienced.

It chanced, while he was lounging about in this moody
state, that he stumbled upon a flight of stairs, dark, steep,
and narrow, which he ascended without any thought about

the matter, and so came into a little music-gallery, empty
and deserted. From this elevated post, which commanded
the whole hall, he amused himself in looking down upon the
attendants who were clearing away the fragments of the
feast very lazily, and drinking out of all the bottles and
glasses with most commendable perseverance.

His attention gradually relaxed, and he fell fast asleep.

When he awoke, he thought there must be something the
matter with his eyes; but, rubbing them a little, he soon
found that the moonlight was really streaming through the
east window, that the lamps were all extinguished, and that
he was alone. He listened, but no distant murmur in the
echoing passages, not even the shutting of a door, broke the
deep silence; he groped his way down the stairs, and found
that the door at the bottom was locked on the other side.
He began now to comprehend that he must have slept a
long time, that he had been overlooked, and was shut up
there for the night.

His first sensation, perhaps, was not altogether a comfortable one, for it was a dark, chilly, earthy-smelling place,
and something too large, for a man so situated, to feel at
home in. However, when the momentary consternation of
his surprise was over, he made light of the accident, and
resolved to feel his way up the stairs again, and make himself as comfortable as he could in the gallery until morning.
As he turned to execute this purpose, he heard the clocks
strike three.

Any such invasion of a dead stillness as the striking of
distant clocks, causes it to appear the more intense and
insupportable when the sound has ceased. He listened with
strained attention in the hope that some clock, lagging
behind its fellows, had yet to strike,—looking all the time
into the profound darkness before him, until it seemed to
weave itself into a black tissue, patterned with a hundred
reflections of his own eyes. But the bells had all pealed out
their warning for that once, and the gust of wind that moaned
through the place seemed cold and heavy with their iron
breath.

The time and circumstances were favourable to reflection.
He tried to keep his thoughts to the current, unpleasant
though it was, in which they had moved all day, and to
think with what a romantic feeling he had looked forward
to shaking his old friend by the hand before he died, and

what a wide and cruel difference there was between the meeting they had had, and that which he had so often and so long anticipated. Still, he was disordered by waking to such sudden loneliness, and could not prevent his mind from running upon odd tales of people of undoubted courage, who, being shut up by night in vaults or churches, or other dismal places, had scaled great heights to get out, and fled from silence as they had never done from danger. This brought to his mind the moonlight through the window, and bethinking himself of it, he groped his way back up the crooked stairs,—but very stealthily, as though he were fearful of being overheard.

He was very much astonished when he approached the gallery again, to see a light in the building: still more so, on advancing hastily and looking round, to observe no visible source from which it could proceed. But how much greater yet was his astonishment at the spectacle which this light revealed.

The statues of the two giants, Gog and Magog, each above fourteen feet in height, those which succeeded to still older and more barbarous figures, after the Great Fire of London, and which stand in the Guildhall to this day, were endowed with life and motion. These guardian genii of the City had quitted their pedestals, and reclined in easy attitudes in the great stained glass window. Between them was an ancient cask, which seemed to be full of wine; for the younger Giant, clapping his huge hand upon it, and throwing up his mighty leg, burst into an exulting laugh, which reverberated through the hall like thunder.

Joe Toddyhigh instinctively stooped down, and, more dead than alive, felt his hair stand on end, his knees knock together, and a cold damp break out upon his forehead. But even at that minute curiosity prevailed over every other feeling, and somewhat reassured by the good-humour of the Giants and their apparent unconsciousness of his presence, he crouched in a corner of the gallery, in as small a space as he could, and, peeping between the rails, observed them closely.

FIRST NIGHT OF THE GIANT CHRONICLES

It was then that the elder Giant, who had a flowing grey beard, raised his thoughtful eyes to his companion's face, and in a grave and solemn voice addressed him thus:

'Magog, does boisterous mirth beseem the Giant Warder of this ancient city? Is this becoming demeanour for a watchful spirit over whose bodiless head so many years have rolled, so many changes swept like empty air—in whose impalpable nostrils the scent of blood and crime, pestilence, cruelty, and horror, has been familiar as breath to mortals —in whose sight Time has gathered in the harvest of centuries, and garnered so many crops of human pride, affections, hopes, and sorrows? Bethink you of our compact. The night wanes; feasting, revelry, and music have encroached upon our usual hours of solitude, and morning will be here apace. Ere we are stricken mute again, bethink you of our compact.'

Pronouncing these latter words with more of impatience than quite accorded with his apparent age and gravity, the Giant raised a long pole (which he still bears in his hand) and tapped his brother Giant rather smartly on the head; indeed, the blow was so smartly administered, that the latter quickly withdrew his lips from the cask, to which they had been applied, and, catching up his shield and halberd, assumed an attitude of defence. His irritation was but momentary, for he laid these weapons aside as hastily as he had assumed them, and said as he did so:

'You know, Gog, old friend, that when we animate these shapes which the Londoners of old assigned (and not unworthily) to the guardian genii of their city, we are susceptible of some of the sensations which belong to human kind. Thus when I taste wine, I feel blows; when I relish the one, I disrelish the other. Therefore, Gog, the more especially as your arm is none of the lightest, keep your good staff by your side, else we may chance to differ. Peace be between us!'

'Amen!' said the other, leaning his staff in the window-corner. 'Why did you laugh just now?'

'To think,' replied the Giant Magog, laying his hand upon the cask, 'of him who owned this wine, and kept it in a cellar hoarded from the light of day, for thirty years, —"till it should be fit to drink," quoth he. He was twoscore and ten years old when he buried it beneath his house, and yet never thought that he might be scarcely "fit to drink" when the wine became so. I wonder it never occurred to him to make himself unfit to be eaten. There is very little of him left by this time.'

'The night is waning,' said Gog mournfully.

'I know it,' replied his companion, 'and I see you are impatient. But look. Through the eastern window—placed opposite to us, that the first beams of the rising sun may every morning gild our giant faces—the moon-rays fall upon the pavement in a stream of light that to my fancy sinks through the cold stone and gushes into the old crypt below. The night is scarcely past its noon, and our great charge is sleeping heavily.'

They ceased to speak, and looked upward at the moon. The sight of their large, black, rolling eyes filled Joe Toddyhigh with such horror that he could scarcely draw his breath. Still they took no note of him, and appeared to believe themselves quite alone.

'Our compact,' said Magog after a pause, 'is, if I understand it, that, instead of watching here in silence through the dreary nights, we entertain each other with stories of our past experience; with tales of the past, the present, and the future; with legends of London and her sturdy citizens from the old simple times. That every night at midnight, when St. Paul's bell tolls out one, and we may move and speak, we thus discourse, nor leave such themes till the first gray gleam of day shall strike us dumb. Is that our bargain, brother?'

'Yes,' said the Giant Gog, 'that is the league between us who guard this city, by day in spirit, and by night in body also; and never on ancient holidays have its conduits run wine more merrily than we will pour forth our legendary lore. We are old chroniclers from this time hence. The crumbled walls encircle us once more, the postern-gates are closed, the drawbridge is up, and pent in its narrow den beneath, the water foams and struggles with the sunken starlings. Jerkins and quarter-staves are in the streets again, the nightly watch is set, the rebel, sad and lonely in his Tower dungeon, tries to sleep and weeps for home and children. Aloft upon the gates and walls are noble heads glaring fiercely down upon the dreaming city, and vexing the hungry dogs that scent them in the air, and tear the ground beneath with dismal howlings. The axe, the block, the rack, in their dark chambers give signs of recent use. The Thames, floating past long lines of cheerful windows whence come a burst of music and a stream of light, bears suddenly to the Palace wall the last red stain brought on the

The Cavalier

tide from Traitor's Gate. But your pardon, brother. The night wears, and I am talking idly.'

The other Giant appeared to be entirely of this opinion, for during the foregoing rhapsody of his fellow-sentinel he had been scratching his head with an air of comical uneasiness, or rather with an air that would have been very comical if he had been a dwarf or an ordinary-sized man. He winked too, and though it could not be doubted for a moment that he winked to himself, still he certainly cocked his enormous eye towards the gallery where the listener was concealed. Nor was this all, for he gaped; and when he gaped, Joe was horribly reminded of the popular prejudice on the subject of giants, and of their fabled power of smelling out Englishmen, however closely concealed.

His alarm was such that he nearly swooned, and it was some little time before his power of sight or hearing was restored. When he recovered he found that the elder Giant was pressing the younger to commence the Chronicles, and that the latter was endeavouring to excuse himself, on the ground that the night was far spent, and it would be better to wait until the next. Well assured by this that he was certainly about to begin directly, the listener collected his faculties by a great effort, and distinctly heard Magog express himself to the following effect:

In the sixteenth century and in the reign of Queen Elizabeth of glorious memory (albeit her golden days are sadly rusted with blood), there lived in the city of London a bold young 'prentice who loved his master's daughter. There were no doubt within the walls a great many 'prentices in this condition, but I speak of only one, and his name was Hugh Graham.

This Hugh was apprenticed to an honest Bowyer who dwelt in the ward of Cheype, and was rumoured to possess great wealth. Rumour was quite as infallible in those days as at the present time, but it happened then as now to be sometimes right by accident. It stumbled upon the truth when it gave the old Bowyer a mint of money. His trade had been a profitable one in the time of King Henry the Eighth, who encouraged English archery to the utmost, and he had been prudent and discreet. Thus it came to pass that Mistress Alice, his only daughter, was the richest heiress in all his wealthy ward. Young Hugh had often maintained with

staff and cudgel that she was the handsomest. To do him
justice, I believe she was.

If he could have gained the heart of pretty Mistress Alice
by knocking this conviction into stubborn people's heads,
Hugh would have had no cause to fear. But though the
Bowyer's daughter smiled in secret to hear of his doughty
deeds for her sake, and though her little waiting-woman
reported all her smiles (and many more) to Hugh, and
though he was at a vast expense in kisses and small coin
to recompense her fidelity, he made no progress in his love.
He durst not whisper it to Mistress Alice save on sure encouragement, and that she never gave him. A glance of her
dark eye as she sat at the door on a summer's evening after
prayer-time, while he and the neighbouring 'prentices exercised themselves in the street with blunted sword and buckler,
would fire Hugh's blood so that none could stand before
him; but then she glanced at others quite as kindly as on
him, and where was the use of cracking crowns if Mistress
Alice smiled upon the cracked as well as on the cracker ?

Still Hugh went on, and loved her more and more. He
thought of her all day, and dreamed of her all night long.
He treasured up her every word and gesture, and had a
palpitation of the heart whenever he heard her footstep on
the stairs or her voice in an adjoining room. To him, the
old Bowyer's house was haunted by an angel; there was
enchantment in the air and space in which she moved. It
would have been no miracle to Hugh if flowers had sprung
from the rush-strewn floors beneath the tread of lovely
Mistress Alice.

Never did 'prentice long to distinguish himself in the eyes
of his lady-love so ardently as Hugh. Sometimes he pictured
to himself the house taking fire by night, and he, when all
drew back in fear, rushing through flame and smoke, and
bearing her from the ruins in his arms. At other times he
thought of a rising of fierce rebels, an attack upon the city,
a strong assault upon the Bowyer's house in particular, and
he falling on the threshold pierced with numberless wounds
in defence of Mistress Alice. If he could only enact some
prodigy of valour, do some wonderful deed, and let her
know that she had inspired it, he thought he could die con-
tented.

Sometimes the Bowyer and his daughter would go out to
supper with a worthy citizen at the fashionable hour of six

o'clock, and on such occasions Hugh, wearing his blue 'prentice cloak as gallantly as 'prentice might, would attend with a lantern and his trusty club to escort them home. These were the brightest moments of his life. To hold the light while Mistress Alice picked her steps, to touch her hand as he helped her over broken ways, to have her leaning on his arm,—it sometimes even came to that,—this was happiness indeed!

When the nights were fair, Hugh followed in the rear, his eyes riveted on the graceful figure of the Bowyer's daughter as she and the old man moved on before him. So they threaded the narrow winding streets of the city, now passing beneath the overhanging gables of old wooden houses whence creaking signs projected into the street, and now emerging from some dark and frowning gateway into the clear moonlight. At such times, or when the shouts of straggling brawlers met her ear, the Bowyer's daughter would look timidly back at Hugh, beseeching him to draw nearer; and then how he grasped his club and longed to do battle with a dozen rufflers, for the love of Mistress Alice!

The old Bowyer was in the habit of lending money on interest to the gallants of the Court, and thus it happened that many a richly-dressed gentleman dismounted at his door. More waving plumes and gallant steeds, indeed, were seen at the Bowyer's house, and more embroidered silks and velvets sparkled in his dark shop and darker private closet, than at any merchant's in the city. In those times no less than in the present it would seem that the richest-looking cavaliers often wanted money the most.

Of these glittering clients there was one who always came alone. He was nobly mounted, and, having no attendant, gave his horse in charge to Hugh while he and the Bowyer were closeted within. Once as he sprung into the saddle Mistress Alice was seated at an upper window, and before she could withdraw he had doffed his jewelled cap and kissed his hand. Hugh watched him caracoling down the street, and burnt with indignation. But how much deeper was the glow that reddened in his cheeks when, raising his eyes to the casement, he saw that Alice watched the stranger too!

He came again and often, each time arrayed more gaily than before, and still the little casement showed him Mistress Alice. At length one heavy day, she fled from home. It had

cost her a hard struggle, for all her old father's gifts were
strewn about her chamber as if she had parted from them one
by one, and knew that the time must come when these tokens
of his love would wring her heart,—yet she was gone.

She left a letter commending her poor father to the care of
Hugh, and wishing he might be happier than ever he could
have been with her, for he deserved the love of a better and
a purer heart than she had to bestow. The old man's
forgiveness (she said) she had no power to ask, but she
prayed God to bless him,—and so ended with a blot upon
the paper where her tears had fallen.

At first the old man's wrath was kindled, and he carried
his wrong to the Queen's throne itself; but there was no
redress he learnt at Court, for his daughter had been conveyed abroad. This afterwards appeared to be the truth, as
there came from France, after an interval of several years, a
letter in her hand. It was written in trembling characters,
and almost illegible. Little could be made out save that she
often thought of home and her old dear pleasant room,—
and that she had dreamt her father was dead and had not
blessed her,—and that her heart was breaking.

The poor old Bowyer lingered on, never suffering Hugh
to quit his sight, for he knew now that he had loved his
daughter, and that was the only link that bound him to
earth. It broke at length and he died, bequeathing his
old 'prentice his trade and all his wealth, and solemnly
charging him with his last breath to revenge his child if ever
he who had worked her misery crossed his path in life again.

From the time of Alice's flight, the tilting-ground, the
fields, the fencing-school, the summer-evening sports, knew
Hugh no more. His spirit was dead within him. He rose
to great eminence and repute among the citizens, but was
seldom seen to smile, and never mingled in their revelries
or rejoicings. Brave, humane, and generous, he was beloved
by all. He was pitied too by those who knew his story, and
these were so many that when he walked along the streets
alone at dusk, even the rude common people doffed their
caps and mingled a rough air of sympathy with their respect.

One night in May—it was her birthnight, and twenty
years since she had left her home—Hugh Graham sat in
the room she had hallowed in his boyish days. He was now
a grey-haired man, though still in the prime of life. Old
thoughts had borne him company for many hours, and the

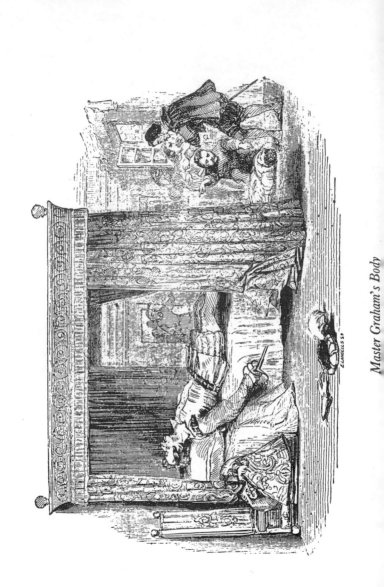

Master Graham's Body

chamber had gradually grown quite dark, when he was roused by a low knocking at the outer door.

He hastened down, and opening it saw by the light of a lamp which he had seized upon the way, a female figure crouching in the portal. It hurried swiftly past him and glided up the stairs. He looked for pursuers. There were none in sight. No, not one.

He was inclined to think it a vision of his own brain, when suddenly a vague suspicion of the truth flashed upon his mind. He barred the door, and hastened wildly back. Yes, there she was,—there, in the chamber he had quitted, —there in her old innocent happy home, so changed that none but he could trace one gleam of what she had been,— there upon her knees,—with her hands clasped in agony and shame before her burning face.

'My God, my God!' she cried, 'now strike me dead! Though I have brought death and shame and sorrow on this roof, O, let me die at home in mercy!'

There was no tear upon her face then, but she trembled and glanced round the chamber. Everything was in its old place. Her bed looked as if she had risen from it but that morning. The sight of these familiar objects, marking the dear remembrance in which she had been held, and the blight she had brought upon herself, was more than the woman's better nature that had carried her there could bear. She wept and fell upon the ground.

A rumour was spread about, in a few days' time, that the Bowyer's cruel daughter had come home, and that Master Graham had given her lodging in his house. It was rumoured too that he had resigned her fortune, in order that she might bestow it in acts of charity, and that he had vowed to guard her in her solitude, but that they were never to see each other more. These rumours greatly incensed all virtuous wives and daughters in the ward, especially when they appeared to receive some corroboration from the circumstance of Master Graham taking up his abode in another tenement hard by. The estimation in which he was held, however, forbade any questioning on the subject; and as the Bowyer's house was close shut up, and nobody came forth when public shows and festivities were in progress, or to flaunt in the public walks, or to buy new fashions at the mercers' booths, all the well-conducted females agreed among themselves that there could be no woman there.

These reports had scarcely died away when the wonder of every good citizen, male and female, was utterly absorbed and swallowed up by a Royal Proclamation, in which her Majesty, strongly censuring the practice of wearing long Spanish rapiers of preposterous length (as being a bullying and swaggering custom, tending to bloodshed and public disorder), commanded that on a particular day therein named, certain grave citizens should repair to the city gates, and there, in public, break all rapiers worn or carried by persons claiming admission, that exceeded, though it were only by a quarter of an inch, three standard feet in length.

Royal Proclamations usually take their course, let the public wonder never so much. On the appointed day two citizens of high repute took up their stations at each of the gates, attended by a party of the city guard, the main body to enforce the Queen's will, and take custody of all such rebels (if any) as might have the temerity to dispute it: and a few to bear the standard measures and instruments for reducing all unlawful sword-blades to the prescribed dimensions. In pursuance of these arrangements, Master Graham and another were posted at Lud Gate, on the hill before St. Paul's.

A pretty numerous company were gathered together at this spot; for, besides the officers in attendance to enforce the proclamation, there was a motley crowd of lookers-on of various degrees, who raised from time to time such shouts and cries as the circumstances called forth. A spruce young courtier was the first who approached: he unsheathed a weapon of burnished steel that shone and glistened in the sun, and handed it with the newest air to the officer, who, finding it exactly three feet long, returned it with a bow. Thereupon the gallant raised his hat and crying, 'God save the Queen!' passed on amidst the plaudits of the mob. Then came another—a better courtier still—who wore a blade but two feet long, whereat the people laughed, much to the disparagement of his honour's dignity. Then came a third, a sturdy old officer of the army, girded with a rapier at least a foot and a half beyond her Majesty's pleasure; at him they raised a great shout, and most of the spectators (but especially those who were armourers or cutlers) laughed very heartily at the breakage which would ensue. But they were disappointed; for the old campaigner, coolly unbuckling his sword and bidding his servant carry it home again, passed through unarmed, to the great indignation of all the beholders. They relieved themselves in some degree by hooting a tall blustering fellow with a prodigious weapon, who stopped short on coming in sight of the preparations, and after a little consideration turned back again. But all this time no rapier had been broken, although it was high noon, and all cavaliers of any quality or appearance were taking their way towards Saint Paul's churchyard.

During these proceedings, Master Graham had stood apart, strictly confining himself to the duty imposed upon him, and taking little heed of anything beyond. He stepped forward now as a richly-dressed gentleman on foot, followed by a single attendant, was seen advancing up the hill.

As this person drew nearer, the crowd stopped their clamour, and bent forward with eager looks. Master Graham standing alone in the gateway, and the stranger coming slowly towards him, they seemed, as it were, set face to face. The nobleman (for he looked one) had a haughty and disdainful air, which bespoke the slight estimation in which he held the citizen. The citizen, on the other hand, preserved the resolute bearing of one who was not to be frowned down or daunted, and who cared very little for any nobility but that of worth and manhood. It was perhaps some consciousness on the part of each, of these feelings in the other, that infused a more stern expression into their regards as they came closer together.

'Your rapier, worthy sir!'

At the instant that he pronounced these words Graham started, and falling back some paces, laid his hand upon the dagger in his belt.

'You are the man whose horse I used to hold before the Bowyer's door? You are that man? Speak!'

'Out, you 'prentice hound!' said the other.

'You are he! I know you well now!' cried Graham. 'Let no man step between us two, or I shall be his murderer.' With that he drew his dagger, and rushed in upon him.

The stranger had drawn his weapon from the scabbard ready for the scrutiny, before a word was spoken. He made a thrust at his assailant, but the dagger which Graham clutched in his left hand being the dirk in use at that time for parrying such blows, promptly turned the point aside. They closed. The dagger fell rattling on the ground, and Graham, wresting his adversary's sword from his grasp,

plunged it through his heart. As he drew it out it snapped
in two, leaving a fragment in the dead man's body.

All this passed so swiftly that the bystanders looked on
without an effort to interfere; but the man was no sooner
down than an uproar broke forth which rent the air. The
attendant rushing through the gate proclaimed that his
master, a nobleman, had been set upon and slain by a
citizen; the word quickly spread from mouth to mouth;
Saint Paul's Cathedral, and every book-shop, ordinary, and
smoking-house in the churchyard poured out its stream of
cavaliers and their followers, who mingling together in a
dense tumultuous body, struggled, sword in hand, towards
the spot.

With equal impetuosity, and stimulating each other by
loud cries and shouts, the citizens and common people took
up the quarrel on their side, and encircling Master Graham
a hundred deep, forced him from the gate. In vain he
waved the broken sword above his head, crying that he
would die on London's threshold for their sacred homes.
They bore him on, and ever keeping him in the midst, so
that no man could attack him, fought their way into the
city.

The clash of swords and roar of voices, the dust and heat
and pressure, the trampling under foot of men, the distracted
looks and shrieks of women at the windows above as they
recognised their relatives or lovers in the crowd, the rapid
tolling of alarm-bells, the furious rage and passion of the
scene, were fearful. Those who, being on the outskirts of
each crowd, could use their weapons with effect, fought
desperately, while those behind, maddened with baffled
rage, struck at each other over the heads of those before
them, and crushed their own fellows. Wherever the broken
sword was seen above the people's heads, towards that spot
the cavaliers made a new rush. Every one of these charges
was marked by sudden gaps in the throng where men were
trodden down, but as fast as they were made, the tide
swept over them, and still the multitude pressed on again,
a confused mass of swords, clubs, staves, broken plumes,
fragments of rich cloaks and doublets, and angry bleeding
faces, all mixed up together in inextricable disorder.

The design of the people was to force Master Graham to
take refuge in his dwelling, and to defend it until the authorities could interfere, or they could gain time for parley. But

either from ignorance or in the confusion of the moment they stopped at his old house, which was closely shut. Some time was lost in beating the doors open and passing him to the front. About a score of the boldest of the other party threw themselves into the torrent while this was being done, and reaching the door at the same moment with himself cut him off from his defenders.

'I never will turn in such a righteous cause, so help me Heaven!' cried Graham, in a voice that at last made itself heard, and confronting them as he spoke. 'Least of all will I turn upon this threshold which owes its desolation to such men as ye. I give no quarter, and I will have none! Strike!'

For a moment they stood at bay. At that moment a shot from an unseen hand, apparently fired by some person who had gained access to one of the opposite houses, struck Graham in the brain, and he fell dead. A low wail was heard in the air,—many people in the concourse cried that they had seen a spirit glide across the little casement window of the Bowyer's house

A dead silence succeeded. After a short time some of the flushed and heated throng laid down their arms and softly carried the body within doors. Others fell off or slunk away in knots of two or three, others whispered together in groups, and before a numerous guard which then rode up could muster in the street, it was nearly empty.

Those who carried Master Graham to the bed up-stairs were shocked to see a woman lying beneath the window with her hands clasped together. After trying to recover her in vain, they laid her near the citizen, who still retained, tightly grasped in his right hand, the first and last sword that was broken that day at Lud Gate.

The Giant uttered these concluding words with sudden precipitation; and on the instant the strange light which had filled the hall faded away. Joe Toddyhigh glanced involuntarily at the eastern window, and saw the first pale gleam of morning. He turned his head again towards the other window in which the Giants had been seated. It was empty. The cask of wine was gone, and he could dimly make out that the two great figures stood mute and motionless upon their pedestals.

After rubbing his eyes and wondering for full half an

hour, during which time he observed morning come creeping on apace, he yielded to the drowsiness which overpowered him and fell into a refreshing slumber. When he awoke it was broad day; the building was open, and workmen were busily engaged in removing the vestiges of last night's feast.

Stealing gently down the little stairs, and assuming the air of some early lounger who had dropped in from the street, he walked up to the foot of each pedestal in turn, and attentively examined the figure it supported. There could be no doubt about the features of either; he recollected the exact expression they had worn at different passages of their conversation, and recognised in every line and lineament the Giants of the night. Assured that it was no vision, but that he had heard and seen with his own proper senses, he walked forth, determining at all hazards to conceal himself in the Guildhall again that evening. He further resolved to sleep all day, so that he might be very wakeful and vigilant, and above all that he might take notice of the figures at the precise moment of their becoming animated and subsiding into their old state, which he greatly reproached himself for not having done already.

CORRESPONDENCE

TO MASTER HUMPHREY

Sir,—Before you proceed any further in your account of your friends and what you say and do when you meet together, excuse me if I proffer my claim to be elected to one of the vacant chairs in that old room of yours. Don't reject me without full consideration; for if you do, you will be sorry for it afterwards—you will, upon my life.

I enclose my card, sir, in this letter. I never was ashamed of my name, and I never shall be. I am considered a devilish gentlemanly fellow, and I act up to the character. If you want a reference, ask any of the men at our club. Ask any fellow who goes there to write his letters, what sort of conversation mine is. Ask him if he thinks I have the sort of voice that will suit your deaf friend and make him hear, if he can hear anything at all. Ask the servants what they think of me. There's not a rascal among 'em, sir, but will tremble to hear my name. That reminds me—don't you say too much about that housekeeper of yours; it's a low subject, damned low.

I tell you what, sir. If you vote me into one of those empty chairs, you'll have among you a man with a fund of gentlemanly information that'll rather astonish you. I can let you into a few anecdotes about some fine women of title, that are quite high life, sir—the tiptop sort of thing. I know

THE CORRESPONDENT

the name of every man who has been out on an affair of honour within the last five-and-twenty years; I know the private particulars of every cross and squabble that has taken place upon the turf, at the gaming-table, or elsewhere, during the whole of that time. I have been called the gentlemanly chronicle. You may consider yourself a lucky dog; upon my soul, you may congratulate yourself, though I say so.

It's an uncommon good notion that of yours, not letting anybody know where you live. I have tried it, but there has always been an anxiety respecting me, which has found me out. Your deaf friend is a cunning fellow to keep his name so close. I have tried that too, but have always failed. I shall be proud to make his acquaintance—tell him so, with my compliments.

You must have been a queer fellow when you were a child, confounded queer. It's odd, all that about the picture in your first paper—prosy, but told in a devilish gentlemanly sort of way. In places like that I could come in with great effect with a touch of life—don't you feel that?

I am anxiously waiting for your next paper to know whether your friends live upon the premises, and at your expense, which I take it for granted is the case. If I am right in this impression, I know a charming fellow (an excellent companion and most delightful company) who will be proud to join you. Some years ago he seconded a great many prize-fighters, and once fought an amateur match himself; since then he has driven several mails, broken at different periods all the lamps on the right-hand side of Oxford-street, and six times carried away every bell-handle in Bloomsbury-square, besides turning off the gas in various thoroughfares. In point of gentlemanliness he is unrivalled, and I should say that next to myself he is of all men the best suited to your purpose.

Expecting your reply,
I am,
&c. &c.

Master Humphrey informs this gentleman that his application, both as it concerns himself and his friend, is rejected.

CHAPTER II

My old companion tells me it is midnight. The fire glows brightly, crackling with a sharp and cheerful sound, as if it loved to burn. The merry cricket on the hearth (my constant visitor), this ruddy blaze, my clock, and I, seem to share the world among us, and to be the only things awake. The wind, high and boisterous but now, has died away and hoarsely mutters in its sleep. I love all times and seasons each in its turn, and am apt, perhaps, to think the present one the best; but past or coming I always love this peaceful time of night, when long-buried thoughts, favoured by the gloom and silence, steal from their graves, and haunt the scenes of faded happiness and hope.

The popular faith in ghosts has a remarkable affinity with the whole current of our thoughts at such an hour as this, and seems to be their necessary and natural consequence. For who can wonder that man should feel a vague belief in tales of disembodied spirits wandering through those places which they once dearly affected, when he himself, scarcely less separated from his old world than they, is for ever lingering upon past emotions and bygone times, and hovering, the ghost of his former self, about the places and people that warmed his heart of old ? It is thus that at this quiet hour I haunt the house where I was born, the rooms I used to tread, the scenes of my infancy, my boyhood, and my youth; it is thus that I prowl around my buried treasure (though not of gold or silver), and mourn my loss; it is thus that I revisit the ashes of extinguished fires, and take my silent stand at old bedsides. If my spirit should ever glide back to this chamber when my body is mingled with the dust, it will but follow the course it often took in the old man's lifetime, and add but one more change to the subjects of its contemplation.

In all my idle speculations I am greatly assisted by various legends connected with my venerable house, which are current in the neighbourhood, and are so numerous that there is scarce a cupboard or corner that has not some dismal story of its own. When I first entertained thoughts of becoming its tenant, I was assured that it was haunted from roof to cellar, and I believe that the bad opinion in which my neighbours once held me, had its rise in my not being torn to pieces, or at least distracted with terror, on the night I took possession; in either of which cases I should doubtless have arrived by a short cut at the very summit of popularity.

But traditions and rumours all taken into account, who so abets me in every fancy and chimes with my every thought, as my dear deaf friend? and how often have I cause to bless the day that brought us two together! Of all days in the year I rejoice to think that it should have been Christmas Day, with which from childhood we associate something friendly, hearty, and sincere.

I had walked out to cheer myself with the happiness of others, and, in the little tokens of festivity and rejoicing, of which the streets and houses present so many upon that day, had lost some hours. Now I stopped to look at a merry party hurrying through the snow on foot to their place of meeting, and now turned back to see a whole coachful of children safely deposited at the welcome house. At one time, I admired how carefully the working man carried the baby in its gaudy hat and feathers, and how his wife, trudging patiently on behind, forgot even her care of her gay clothes, in exchanging greetings with the child as it crowed and laughed over the father's shoulder; at another, I pleased myself with some passing scene of gallantry or courtship, and was glad to believe that for a season half the world of poverty was gay.

As the day closed in, I still rambled through the streets, feeling a companionship in the bright fires that cast their warm reflection on the windows as I passed, and losing all sense of my own loneliness in imagining the sociality and kind-fellowship that everywhere prevailed. At length I happened to stop before a Tavern, and, encountering a Bill of Fare in the window, it all at once brought it into my head to wonder what kind of people dined alone in Taverns upon Christmas Day.

Solitary men are accustomed, I suppose, unconsciously to look upon solitude as their own peculiar property. I had sat alone in my room on many, many anniversaries of this great holiday, and had never regarded it but as one of universal assemblage and rejoicing. I had excepted, and with an aching heart, a crowd of prisoners and beggars; but *these* were not the men for whom the Tavern doors were open. Had they any customers, or was it a mere form ?—a form, no doubt.

Trying to feel quite sure of this, I walked away; but before I had gone many paces, I stopped and looked back. There was a provoking air of business in the lamp above the door which I could not overcome. I began to be afraid there might be many customers—young men, perhaps, struggling with the world, utter strangers in this great place, whose friends lived at a long distance off, and whose means were too slender to enable them to make the journey. The supposition gave rise to so many distressing little pictures, that, in preference to carrying them home with me, I determined to encounter the realities. So I turned and walked in.

I was at once glad and sorry to find that there was only one person in the dining-room ; glad to know that there were not more, and sorry that he should be there by himself. He did not look so old as I, but like me he was advanced in life, and his hair was nearly white. Though I made more noise in entering and seating myself than was quite necessary, with the view of attracting his attention and saluting him in the good old form of that time of year, he did not raise his head, but sat with it resting on his hand, musing over his half-finished meal.

I called for something which would give me an excuse for remaining in the room (I had dined early, as my housekeeper was engaged at night to partake of some friend's good cheer), and sat where I could observe without intruding on him. After a time he looked up. He was aware that somebody had entered, but could see very little of me, as I sat in the shade and he in the light. He was sad and thoughtful, and I forbore to trouble him by speaking.

Let me believe it was something better than curiosity which riveted my attention and impelled me strongly towards this gentleman. I never saw so patient and kind a face. He should have been surrounded by friends, and yet here he sat dejected and alone when all men had their friends about them. As often as he roused himself from his reverie he would fall into it again, and it was plain that,

whatever were the subject of his thoughts, they were of a
melancholy kind, and would not be controlled.

He was not used to solitude. I was sure of that; for I
know by myself that if he had been, his manner would have
been different, and he would have taken some slight interest
in the arrival of another. I could not fail to mark that he had
no appetite; that he tried to eat in vain; that time after
time the plate was pushed away, and he relapsed into his
former posture.

His mind was wandering among old Christmas days, I
thought. Many of them sprung up together, not with a long
gap between each, but in unbroken succession like days of
the week. It was a great change to find himself for the first
time (I quite settled that it *was* the first) in an empty silent
room with no soul to care for. I could not help following him
in imagination through crowds of pleasant faces, and then
coming back to that dull place with its bough of mistletoe
sickening in the gas, and sprigs of holly parched up already
by a Simoom of roast and boiled. The very waiter had gone
home; and his representative, a poor, lean, hungry man,
was keeping Christmas in his jacket.

I grew still more interested in my friend. His dinner done,
a decanter of wine was placed before him. It remained un-
touched for a long time, but at length with a quivering hand
he filled a glass and raised it to his lips. Some tender wish
to which he had been accustomed to give utterance on that
day, or some beloved name that he had been used to pledge,
trembled upon them at the moment. He put it down very
hastily—took it up once more—again put it down—pressed
his hand upon his face—yes—and tears stole down his
cheeks, I am certain.

Without pausing to consider whether I did right or wrong,
I stepped across the room, and sitting down beside him
laid my hand gently on his arm.

'My friend,' I said, 'forgive me if I beseech you to take
comfort and consolation from the lips of an old man. I will
not preach to you what I have not practised, indeed. Whatever be your grief, be of a good heart—be of a good heart,
pray!'

'I see that you speak earnestly,' he replied, 'and kindly I
am very sure, but——'

I nodded my head to show that I understood what he
would say; for I had already gathered, from a certain fixed

expression in his face, and from the attention with which he watched me while I spoke, that his sense of hearing was destroyed. 'There should be a freemasonry between us,' said I, pointing from himself to me to explain my meaning; 'if not in our gray hairs, at least in our misfortunes. You see that I am but a poor cripple.'

I never felt so happy under my affliction since the trying moment of my first becoming conscious of it, as when he took my hand in his with a smile that has lighted my path in life from that day, and we sat down side by side.

This was the beginning of my friendship with the deaf gentleman; and when was ever the slight and easy service of a kind word in season repaid by such attachment and devotion as he has shown to me!

He produced a little set of tablets and a pencil to facilitate our conversation, on that our first acquaintance; and I well remember how awkward and constrained I was in writing down my share of the dialogue, and how easily he guessed my meaning before I had written half of what I had to say. He told me in a faltering voice that he had not been accustomed to be alone on that day—that it had always been a little festival with him; and seeing that I glanced at his dress in the expectation that he wore mourning, he added hastily that it was not that; if it had been he thought he could have borne it better. From that time to the present we have never touched upon this theme. Upon every return of the same day we have been together; and although we make it our annual custom to drink to each other hand in hand after dinner, and to recall with affectionate garrulity every circumstance of our first meeting, we always avoid this one as if by mutual consent.

Meantime we have gone on strengthening in our friendship and regard, and forming an attachment which, I trust and believe, will only be interrupted by death, to be renewed in another existence. I scarcely know how we communicate as we do; but he has long since ceased to be deaf to me. He is frequently my companion in my walks, and even in crowded streets replies to my slightest look or gesture, as though he could read my thoughts. From the vast number of objects which pass in rapid succession before our eyes, we frequently select the same for some particular notice or remark; and when one of these little coincidences occurs, I cannot describe the pleasure which animates my

friend, or the beaming countenance he will preserve for
half-an-hour afterwards at least.

He is a great thinker from living so much within himself,
and, having a lively imagination, has a facility of conceiving
and enlarging upon odd ideas, which renders him invaluable
to our little body, and greatly astonishes our two friends.
His powers in this respect are much assisted by a large pipe,
which he assures us once belonged to a German Student.
Be this as it may, it has undoubtedly a very ancient and
mysterious appearance, and is of such capacity that it takes
three hours and a half to smoke it out. I have reason to
believe that my barber, who is the chief authority of a knot
of gossips, who congregate every evening at a small tobacconist's hard by, has related anecdotes of this pipe and the
grim figures that are carved upon its bowl, at which all the
smokers in the neighbourhood have stood aghast; and
I know that my housekeeper, while she holds it in high
veneration, has a superstitious feeling connected with it
which would render her exceedingly unwilling to be left
alone in its company after dark.

Whatever sorrow my dear friend has known, and whatever grief may linger in some secret corner of his heart, he
is now a cheerful, placid, happy creature. Misfortune can
never have fallen upon such a man but for some good purpose; and when I see its traces in his gentle nature and his
earnest feeling, I am the less disposed to murmur at such
trials as I may have undergone myself. With regard to the
pipe, I have a theory of my own; I cannot help thinking that
it is in some manner connected with the event that brought
us together; for I remember that it was a long time before he
even talked about it; that when he did, he grew reserved
and melancholy; and that it was a long time yet before he
brought it forth. I have no curiosity, however, upon this
subject; for I know that it promotes his tranquillity and
comfort, and I need no other inducement to regard it with
my utmost favour.

Such is the deaf gentleman. I can call up his figure now,
clad in sober gray, and seated in the chimney-corner. As he
puffs out the smoke from his favourite pipe, he casts a look
on me brimful of cordiality and friendship, and says all
manner of kind and genial things in a cheerful smile; then
he raises his eyes to my clock, which is just about to strike,
and, glancing from it to me and back again, seems to divide

his heart between us. For myself, it is not too much to say that I would gladly part with one of my poor limbs, could he but hear the old clock's voice.

Of our two friends, the first has been all his life one of that easy, wayward, truant class whom the world is accustomed to designate as nobody's enemies but their own. Bred to a profession for which he never qualified himself, and reared in the expectation of a fortune he has never inherited, he has undergone every vicissitude of which such an existence is capable. He and his younger brother, both orphans from their childhood, were educated by a wealthy relative, who taught them to expect an equal division of his property; but too indolent to court, and too honest to flatter, the elder gradually lost ground in the affections of a capricious old man, and the younger, who did not fail to improve his opportunity, now triumphs in the possession of enormous wealth. His triumph is to hoard it in solitary wretchedness, and probably to feel with the expenditure of every shilling a greater pang than the loss of his whole inheritance ever cost his brother.

Jack Redburn—he was Jack Redburn at the first little school he went to, where every other child was mastered and surnamed, and he has been Jack Redburn all his life, or he would perhaps have been a richer man by this time—has been an inmate of my house these eight years past. He is my librarian, secretary, steward, and first minister; director of all my affairs, and inspector-general of my household. He is something of a musician, something of an author, something of an actor, something of a painter, very much of a carpenter, and an extraordinary gardener, having had all his life a wonderful aptitude for learning everything that was of no use to him. He is remarkably fond of children, and is the best and kindest nurse in sickness that ever drew the breath of life. He has mixed with every grade of society, and known the utmost distress; but there never was a less selfish, a more tender-hearted, a more enthusiastic, or a more guileless man; and I dare say, if few have done less good, fewer still have done less harm in the world than he. By what chance Nature forms such whimsical jumbles I don't know; but I do know that she sends them among us very often, and that the king of the whole race is Jack Redburn.

I should be puzzled to say how old he is. His health is

none of the best, and he wears a quantity of iron-gray hair,
which shades his face and gives it rather a worn appearance;
but we consider him quite a young fellow notwithstanding;
and if a youthful spirit, surviving the roughest contact with
the world, confers upon its possessor any title to be considered young, then he is a mere child. The only interruptions to his careless cheerfulness are on a wet Sunday, when
he is apt to be unusually religious and solemn, and sometimes of an evening, when he has been blowing a very slow
tune on the flute. On these last-named occasions he is apt
to incline towards the mysterious or the terrible. As a
specimen of his powers in this mood, I refer my readers to
the extract from the clock-case which follows this paper:
he brought it to me not long ago at midnight, and informed
me that the main incident had been suggested by a dream
of the night before.

His apartments are two cheerful rooms looking towards
the garden, and one of his great delights is to arrange and
rearrange the furniture in these chambers, and put it in every
possible variety of position. During the whole time he has
been here, I do not think he has slept for two nights running with the head of his bed in the same place; and every
time he moves it, is to be the last. My housekeeper was at
first well-nigh distracted by these frequent changes; but she
has become quite reconciled to them by degrees, and has so
fallen in with his humour, that they often consult together
with great gravity upon the next final alteration. Whatever
his arrangements are, however, they are always a pattern of
neatness; and every one of the manifold articles connected
with his manifold occupations is to be found in its own
particular place. Until within the last two or three years he
was subject to an occasional fit (which usually came upon
him in very fine weather), under the influence of which he
would dress himself with peculiar care, and, going out under
pretence of taking a walk, disappeared for several days together. At length, after the interval between each outbreak
of this disorder had gradually grown longer and longer, it
wholly disappeared; and now he seldom stirs abroad, except
to stroll out a little way on a summer's evening. Whether he
yet mistrusts his own constancy in this respect, and is
therefore afraid to wear a coat, I know not; but we seldom
see him in any other upper garment than an old spectral-
looking dressing-gown, with very disproportionate pockets,

full of a miscellaneous collection of odd matters, which he picks up wherever he can lay his hands upon them.

Everything that is a favourite with our friend is a favourite with us; and thus it happens that the fourth among us is Mr. Owen Miles, a most worthy gentleman, who had treated Jack with great kindness before my deaf friend and I encountered him by an accident, to which I may refer on some future occasion. Mr. Miles was once a very rich merchant; but receiving a severe shock in the death of his wife, he retired from business, and devoted himself to a quiet, unostentatious life. He is an excellent man, of thoroughly sterling character: not of quick apprehension, and not without some amusing prejudices, which I shall leave to their own development. He holds us all in profound veneration; but Jack Redburn he esteems as a kind of pleasant wonder, that he may venture to approach familiarly. He believes, not only that no man ever lived who could do so many things as Jack, but that no man ever lived who could do anything so well; and he never calls my attention to any of his ingenious proceedings, but he whispers in my ear, nudging me at the same time with his elbow: 'If he had only made it his trade, sir—if he had only made it his trade!'

They are inseparable companions; one would almost suppose that, although Mr. Miles never by any chance does anything in the way of assistance, Jack could do nothing without him. Whether he is reading, writing, painting, carpentering, gardening, flute-playing, or what not, there is Mr. Miles beside him, buttoned up to the chin in his blue coat, and looking on with a face of incredulous delight, as though he could not credit the testimony of his own senses, and had a misgiving that no man could be so clever but in a dream.

These are my friends; I have now introduced myself and them.

THE CLOCK-CASE

A CONFESSION FOUND IN A PRISON IN THE TIME OF CHARLES THE SECOND

I held a lieutenant's commission in his Majesty's army, and served abroad in the campaigns of 1677 and 1678. The treaty of Nimeguen being concluded, I returned home, and retiring from the service, withdrew to a small estate lying a few miles east of London, which I had recently acquired in right of my wife.

This is the last night I have to live, and I will set down the naked truth without disguise. I was never a brave man, and had always been from my childhood of a secret, sullen, distrustful nature. I speak of myself as if I had passed from the world; for while I write this, my grave is digging, and my name is written in the black-book of death.

Soon after my return to England, my only brother was seized with mortal illness. This circumstance gave me slight or no pain; for since we had been men, we had associated but very little together. He was open-hearted and generous, handsomer than I, more accomplished, and generally beloved. Those who sought my acquaintance abroad or at home, because they were friends of his, seldom attached themselves to me long, and would usually say, in our first conversation, that they were surprised to find two brothers so unlike in their manners and appearance. It was my habit to lead them on to this avowal; for I knew what comparisons they must draw between us; and having a rankling envy in my heart, I sought to justify it to myself.

We had married two sisters. This additional tie between us, as it may appear to some, only estranged us the more. His wife knew me well. I never struggled with any secret jealousy or gall when she was present but that woman knew it as well as I did. I never raised my eyes at such times but I found hers fixed upon me; I never bent them on the ground or looked another way but I felt that she overlooked me always. It was an inexpressible relief to me when we quarrelled, and a greater relief still when I heard abroad that she was dead. It seems to me now as if some strange and terrible foreshadowing of what has happened since must have hung over us then. I was afraid of her; she haunted me; her fixed and steady look comes back upon me now, like the memory of a dark dream, and makes my blood run cold.

She died shortly after giving birth to a child—a boy. When my brother knew that all hope of his own recovery was past, he called my wife to his bedside, and confided this orphan, a child of four years old, to her protection. He bequeathed to him all the property he had, and willed that, in case of his child's death, it should pass to my wife, as the only acknowledgment he could make her for her care and love. He exchanged a few brotherly words with me, deploring our long separation; and being exhausted, fell into a slumber, from which he never awoke.

We had no children; and as there had been a strong affection between the sisters, and my wife had almost supplied the place of a mother to this boy, she loved him as if he had been her own. The child was ardently attached to her; but he was his mother's image in face and spirit, and always mistrusted me.

I can scarcely fix the date when the feeling first came upon me; but I soon began to be uneasy when this child was by. I never roused myself from some moody train of thought but I marked him looking at me; not with mere childish wonder, but with something of the purpose and meaning that I had so often noted in his mother. It was no effort of my fancy, founded on close resemblance of feature and expression. I never could look the boy down. He feared me, but seemed by some instinct to despise me while he did so; and even when he drew back beneath my gaze—as he would when we were alone, to get nearer to the door—he would keep his bright eyes upon me still.

Perhaps I hide the truth from myself, but I do not think that, when this began, I meditated to do him any wrong. I may have thought how serviceable his inheritance would be to us, and may have wished him dead; but I believe I had no thought of compassing his death. Neither did the idea come upon me at once, but by very slow degrees, presenting itself at first in dim shapes at a very great distance, as men may think of an earthquake or the last day; then drawing nearer and nearer, and losing something of its horror and improbability; then coming to be part and parcel—nay nearly the whole sum and substance—of my daily thoughts, and resolving itself into a question of means and safety; not of doing or abstaining from the deed.

While this was going on within me, I never could bear that the child should see me looking at him, and yet I was under a fascination which made it a kind of business with me to contemplate his slight and fragile figure and think how easily it might be done. Sometimes I would steal upstairs and watch him as he slept; but usually I hovered in the garden near the window of the room in which he learnt his little tasks; and there, as he sat upon a low seat beside my wife, I would peer at him for hours together from behind a tree; starting, like the guilty wretch I was, at every rustling of a leaf, and still gliding back to look and start again.

Hard by our cottage, but quite out of sight, and (if there were any wind astir) of hearing too, was a deep sheet of water. I spent days in shaping with my pocket-knife a rough model of a boat, which I finished at last and dropped in the child's way. Then I withdrew to a secret place, which he must pass if he stole away alone to swim this bauble, and lurked there for his coming. He came neither that day nor the next, though I waited from noon till nightfall. I was sure that I had him in my net, for I had heard him prattling of the toy, and knew that in his infant pleasure he kept it by his side in bed. I felt no weariness or fatigue, but waited patiently, and on the third day he passed me, running joyously along, with his silken hair streaming in the wind, and he singing—God have mercy upon me!—singing a merry ballad,—who could hardly lisp the words.

I stole down after him, creeping under certain shrubs which grow in that place, and none but devils know with what terror I, a strong, full-grown man, tracked the footsteps of that baby as he approached the water's brink. I was close upon him, had sunk upon my knee and raised my hand to thrust him in, when he saw my shadow in the stream and turned him round.

His mother's ghost was looking from his eyes. The sun burst forth from behind a cloud; it shone in the bright sky, the glistening earth, the clear water, the sparkling drops of rain upon the leaves. There were eyes in everything. The whole great universe of light was there to see the murder done. I know not what he said; he came of bold and manly blood, and, child as he was, he did not crouch or fawn upon me. I heard him cry that he would try to love me,—not that he did,—and then I saw him running back towards the house. The next I saw was my own sword naked in my hand, and he lying at my feet stark dead,—dabbled here and there with blood, but otherwise no different from what I had seen him in his sleep—in the same attitude too, with his cheek resting upon his little hand.

I took him in my arms and laid him—very gently now that he was dead—in a thicket. My wife was from home that day, and would not return until the next. Our bedroom window, the only sleeping-room on that side of the house, was but a few feet from the ground, and I resolved to descend from it at night and bury him in the garden. I had no thought that I had failed in my design, no thought that the water would be dragged and nothing found, that the money must now lie waste, since I must encourage the idea that the child was lost or stolen. All my thoughts were bound up and knotted together in the one absorbing necessity of hiding what I had done.

How I felt when they came to tell me that the child was missing, when I ordered scouts in all directions, when I gasped and trembled at every one's approach, no tongue can tell or mind of man conceive. I buried him that night. When I parted the boughs and looked into the dark thicket, there was a glow-worm shining like the visible spirit of God upon the murdered child. I glanced down into his grave when I had placed him there, and still it gleamed upon his breast; an eye of fire looking up to Heaven in supplication to the stars that watched me at my work.

I had to meet my wife, and break the news, and give her hope that the child would soon be found. All this I did,—with some appearance, I suppose, of being sincere, for I was the object of no suspicion. This done, I sat at the bed-room window all day long, and watched the spot where the dreadful secret lay.

It was in a piece of ground which had been dug up to be newly turfed, and which I had chosen on that account, as the traces of my spade were less likely to attract attention. The men who laid down the grass must have thought me mad. I called to them continually to expedite their work, ran out and worked beside them, trod down the earth with my feet, and hurried them with frantic eagerness. They had finished their task before night, and then I thought myself comparatively safe.

I slept,—not as men do who awake refreshed and cheerful, but I did sleep, passing from vague and shadowy dreams of being hunted down, to visions of the plot of grass, through which now a hand, and now a foot, and now the head itself was starting out. At this point I always woke and stole to the window, to make sure that it was not really so. That done, I crept to bed again; and thus I spent the night in fits and starts, getting up and lying down full twenty times, and dreaming the same dream over and

over again,—which was far worse than lying awake, for
every dream had a whole night's suffering of its own. Once
I thought the child was alive, and that I had never tried
to kill him. To wake from that dream was the most dreadful agony of all.

The next day I sat at the window again, never once taking
my eyes from the place, which, although it was covered by
the grass, was as plain to me—its shape, its size, its depth,
its jagged sides, and all—as if it had been open to the light
of day. When a servant walked across it, I felt as if he must
sink in ; when he had passed, I looked to see that his feet had
not worn the edges. If a bird lighted there, I was in terror
lest by some tremendous interposition it should be instru-
mental in the discovery; if a breath of air sighed across it,
to me it whispered murder. There was not a sight or a
sound—how ordinary, mean, or unimportant soever—but
was fraught with fear. And in this state of ceaseless watching
I spent three days.

On the fourth there came to the gate one who had served
with me abroad, accompanied by a brother officer of his
whom I had never seen. I felt that I could not bear to be
out of sight of the place. It was a summer evening, and
I bade my people take a table and a flask of wine into the
garden. Then I sat down *with my chair upon the grave*, and
being assured that nobody could disturb it now without my
knowledge, tried to drink and talk.

They hoped that my wife was well,—that she was not
obliged to keep her chamber,—that they had not frightened
her away. What could I do but tell them with a faltering
tongue about the child ? The officer whom I did not know
was a down-looking man, and kept his eyes upon the ground
while I was speaking. Even that terrified me. I could not
divest myself of the idea that he saw something there which
caused him to suspect the truth. I asked him hurriedly if he
supposed that—and stopped. 'That the child has been
murdered ?' said he, looking mildly at me: 'O no! what could
a man gain by murdering a poor child ?' *I* could have told
him what a man gained by such a deed, no one better: but
I held my peace and shivered as with an ague.

Mistaking my emotion, they were endeavouring to cheer
me with the hope that the boy would certainly be found,—
great cheer that was for me!—when we heard a low deep
howl, and presently there sprung over the wall two great

The Arrest

dogs, who, bounding into the garden, repeated the baying sound we had heard before.

'Bloodhounds!' cried my visitors.

What need to tell me that! I had never seen one of that kind in all my life, but I knew what they were and for what purpose they had come. I grasped the elbows of my chair, and neither spoke nor moved.

'They are of the genuine breed,' said the man whom I had known abroad, 'and being out for exercise have no doubt escaped from their keeper.'

Both he and his friend turned to look at the dogs, who with their noses to the ground moved restlessly about, running to and fro, and up and down, and across, and round in circles, careering about like wild things, and all this time taking no notice of us, but ever and again repeating the yell we had heard already, then dropping their noses to the ground again and tracking earnestly here and there. They now began to snuff the earth more eagerly than they had done yet, and although they were still very restless, no longer beat about in such wide circuits, but kept near to one spot, and constantly diminished the distance between themselves and me.

At last they came up close to the great chair on which I sat, and raising their frightful howl once more, tried to tear away the wooden rails that kept them from the ground beneath. I saw how I looked, in the faces of the two who were with me.

'They scent some prey,' said they, both together.

'They scent no prey!' cried I.

'In Heaven's name, move!' said the one I knew, very earnestly, 'or you will be torn to pieces.'

'Let them tear me from limb to limb, I'll never leave this place!' cried I. 'Are dogs to hurry men to shameful deaths! Hew them down, cut them in pieces.'

'There is some foul mystery here!' said the officer whom I did not know, drawing his sword. 'In King Charles's name, assist me to secure this man.'

They both set upon me and forced me away, though I fought and bit and caught at them like a madman. After a struggle, they got me quietly between them; and then, my ·God! I saw the angry dogs tearing at the earth and throwing it up into the air like water.

What more have I to tell? That I fell upon my knees, and

with chattering teeth confessed the truth, and prayed to be forgiven. That I have since denied, and now confess to it again. That I have been tried for the crime, found guilty, and sentenced. That I have not the courage to anticipate my doom, or to bear up manfully against it. That I have no compassion, no consolation, no hope, no friend. That my wife has happily lost for the time those faculties which would enable her to know my misery or hers. That I am alone in this stone dungeon with my evil spirit, and that I die to-morrow.

[Old Curiosity Shop begins here.]

CORRESPONDENCE

Master Humphrey has been favoured with the following letter written on strongly-scented paper, and sealed in light-blue wax with the representation of two very plump doves interchanging beaks. It does not commence with any of the usual forms of address, but begins as is here set forth.

Bath, Wednesday night.

Heavens! into what an indiscretion do I suffer myself to be betrayed! To address these faltering lines to a total stranger, and that stranger one of a conflicting sex!—and yet I am precipitated into the abyss, and have no power of self-snatchation (forgive me if I coin that phrase) from the yawning gulf before me.

Yes, I am writing to a man; but let me not think of that, for madness is in the thought. You will understand my feelings? O yes, I am sure you will; and you will respect them too, and not despise them,—will you?

Let me be calm. That portrait,—smiling as once he smiled on me; that cane,—dangling as I have seen it dangle from his hand I know not how oft; those legs that have glided through my nightly dreams and never stopped to speak; the perfectly gentlemanly, though false original,—can I be mistaken? O no, no.

Let me be calmer yet; I would be calm as coffins. You have published a letter from one whose likeness is engraved, but whose name (and wherefore?) is suppressed. Shall *I* breathe that name! Is it—but why ask when my heart tells me too truly that it is!

I would not upbraid him with his treachery; I would not

remind him of those times when he plighted the most elo-
quent of vows, and procured from me a small pecuniary
accommodation; and yet I would see him—see him did I
say—*him*—alas! such is woman's nature. For as the poet
beautifully says—but you will already have anticipated the
sentiment. Is it not sweet ? O yes!

It was in this city (hallowed by the recollection) that I
met him first; and assuredly if mortal happiness be recorded anywhere, then those rubbers with their three-and-
sixpenny points are scored on tablets of celestial brass. He
always held an honour—generally two. On that eventful
night we stood at eight. He raised his eyes (luminous in
their seductive sweetness) to my agitated face. '*Can* you ?'
said he, with peculiar meaning. I felt the gentle pressure of
his foot on mine; our corns throbbed in unison. '*Can* you ?'
he said again; and every lineament of his expressive
countenance added the words 'resist me ?' I murmured
'No,' and fainted.

They said, when I recovered, it was the weather. *I* said
it was the nutmeg in the negus. How little did they suspect
the truth! How little did they guess the deep mysterious
meaning of that inquiry! He called next morning on his
knees; I do not mean to say that he actually came in that
position to the house-door, but that he went down upon
those joints directly the servant had retired. He brought
some verses in his hat, which he said were original, but
which I have since found were Milton's; likewise a little
bottle labelled laudanum; also a pistol and a sword-stick.
He drew the latter, uncorked the former, and clicked the
trigger of the pocket fire-arm. He had come, he said, to
conquer or to die. He did not die. He wrested from me an
avowal of my love, and let off the pistol out of a back
window previous to partaking of a slight repast.

Faithless, inconstant man! How many ages seem to have
elapsed since his unaccountable and perfidious disap-
pearance! Could I still forgive him both that and the bor-
rowed lucre that he promised to pay next week! Could I
spurn him from my feet if he approached in penitence, and
with a matrimonial object! Would the blandishing enchanter still weave his spells around me, or should I burst
them all and turn away in coldness! I dare not trust my
weakness with the thought.

My brain is in a whirl again. You know his address, his

occupations, his mode of life,—are acquainted, perhaps, with his inmost thoughts. You are a humane and philanthropic character; reveal all you know—all; but especially the street and number of his lodgings. The post is departing, the bellman rings,—pray Heaven it be not the knell of love and hope to

BELINDA.

P.S. Pardon the wanderings of a bad pen and a distracted mind. Address to the Post-office. The bellman, rendered impatient by delay, is ringing dreadfully in the passage.

P.P.S. I open this to say that the bellman is gone, and that you must not expect it till the next post; so don't be surprised when you don't get it.

Master Humphrey does not feel himself at liberty to furnish his fair correspondent with the address of the gentleman in question, but he publishes her letter as a public appeal to his faith and gallantry.

Master Humphrey meets Mr. Pickwick

CHAPTER III

MASTER HUMPHREY'S VISITOR

WHEN I am in a thoughtful mood, I often succeed in diverting the current of some mournful reflections, by conjuring up a number of fanciful associations with the objects that surround me, and dwelling upon the scenes and characters they suggest.

I have been led by this habit to assign to every room in my house and every old staring portrait on its walls a separate interest of its own. Thus, I am persuaded that a stately dame, terrible to behold in her rigid modesty, who hangs above the chimney-piece of my bedroom, is the former lady of the mansion. In the courtyard below is a stone face of surpassing ugliness, which I have somehow—in a kind of jealousy, I am afraid—associated with her husband. Above my study is a little room with ivy peeping through the lattice, from which I bring their daughter, a lovely girl of eighteen or nineteen years of age, and dutiful in all respects save one, that one being her devoted attachment to a young gentleman on the stairs, whose grandmother (degraded to a disused laundry in the garden) piques herself upon an old family quarrel, and is the implacable enemy of their love. With such materials as these I work out many a little drama, whose chief merit is, that I can bring it to a happy end at will. I have so many of them on hand, that if on my return home one of these evenings I were to find some bluff old wight of two centuries ago comfortably seated in my easy chair, and a lovelorn damsel vainly appealing to his heart, and leaning her white arm upon my clock itself, I verily believe I should only express my surprise that they had kept me waiting so long, and never honoured me with a call before.

I was in such a mood as this, sitting in my garden yesterday morning under the shade of a favourite tree, revelling in all the bloom and brightness about me, and feeling every sense of hope and enjoyment quickened by this most beautiful season of Spring, when my meditations were inter-

rupted by the unexpected appearance of my barber at the
end of the walk, who I immediately saw was coming towards
me with a hasty step that betokened something remarkable.

My barber is at all times a very brisk, bustling, active
little man,—for he is, as it were, chubby all over, without
being stout or unwieldy,—but yesterday his alacrity was so
very uncommon that it quite took me by surprise. For
could I fail to observe when he came up to me that his gray
eyes were twinkling in a most extraordinary manner, that
his little red nose was in an unusual glow, that every line in
his round bright face was twisted and curved into an expression of pleased surprise, and that his whole countenance was
radiant with glee? I was still more surprised to see my
housekeeper, who usually preserves a very staid air, and
stands somewhat upon her dignity, peeping round the hedge
at the bottom of the walk, and exchanging nods and smiles
with the barber, who twice or thrice looked over his shoulder
for that purpose. I could conceive no announcement to
which these appearances could be the prelude, unless it were
that they had married each other that morning.

I was, consequently, a little disappointed when it only
came out that there was a gentleman in the house who
wished to speak with me.

'And who is it?' said I.

The barber, with his face screwed up still tighter than
before, replied that the gentleman would not send his name,
but wished to see me. I pondered for a moment, wondering
who this visitor might be, and I remarked that he embraced
the opportunity of exchanging another nod with the housekeeper, who still lingered in the distance.

'Well!' said I, 'bid the gentleman come here.'

This seemed to be the consummation of the barber's
hopes, for he turned sharp round, and actually ran away.

Now, my sight is not very good at a distance, and therefore, when the gentleman first appeared in the walk, I was
not quite clear whether he was a stranger to me or otherwise.
He was an elderly gentleman, but came tripping along in the
pleasantest manner conceivable, avoiding the garden-roller
and the borders of the beds with inimitable dexterity,
picking his way among the flower-pots, and smiling with
unspeakable good humour. Before he was half-way up the
walk he began to salute me; then I thought I knew him;
but when he came towards me with his hat in his hand, the

sun shining on his bald head, his bland face, his bright spectacles, his fawn-coloured tights, and his black gaiters,— then my heart warmed towards him, and I felt quite certain that it was Mr. Pickwick.

'My dear sir,' said that gentleman as I rose to receive him, 'pray be seated. Pray sit down. Now, do not stand on my account. I must insist upon it, really.' With these words Mr. Pickwick gently pressed me down into my seat, and taking my hand in his, shook it again and again with a warmth of manner perfectly irresistible. I endeavoured to express in my welcome something of that heartiness and pleasure which the sight of him awakened, and made him sit down beside me. All this time he kept alternately releasing my hand and grasping it again, and surveying me through his spectacles with such a beaming countenance as I never till then beheld.

'You knew me directly!' said Mr. Pickwick. 'What a pleasure it is to think that you knew me directly!'

I remarked that I had read his adventures very often, and his features were quite familiar to me from the published portraits. As I thought it a good opportunity of adverting to the circumstance, I condoled with him upon the various libels on his character which had found their way into print. Mr. Pickwick shook his head, and for a moment looked very indignant, but smiling again directly, added that no doubt I was acquainted with Cervantes's introduction to the second part of Don Quixote, and that it fully expressed his sentiments on the subject.

'But now,' said Mr. Pickwick, 'don't you wonder how I found you out?'

'I shall never wonder, and, with your good leave, never know,' said I, smiling in my turn. 'It is enough for me that you give me this gratification. I have not the least desire that you should tell me by what means I have obtained it.'

'You are very kind,' returned Mr. Pickwick, shaking me by the hand again; 'you are so exactly what I expected! But for what particular purpose do you think I have sought you, my dear sir ? Now what *do* you think I have come for ?'

Mr. Pickwick put this question as though he were persuaded that it was morally impossible that I could by any means divine the deep purpose of his visit, and that it must be hidden from all human ken. Therefore, although I was rejoiced to think that I had anticipated his drift, I feigned to be quite ignorant of it, and after a brief consideration shook my head despairingly.

'What should you say,' said Mr. Pickwick, laying the forefinger of his left hand upon my coat-sleeve, and looking at me with his head thrown back, and a little on one side,—'what should you say if I confessed that after reading your account of yourself and your little society, I had come here, a humble candidate for one of those empty chairs ?'

'I should say,' I returned, 'that I know of only one circumstance which could still further endear that little society to me, and that would be the associating with it my old friend,—for you must let me call you so,—my old friend, Mr. Pickwick.'

As I made him this answer every feature of Mr. Pickwick's face fused itself into one all-pervading expression of delight. After shaking me heartily by both hands at once, he patted me gently on the back, and then—I well understood why—coloured up to the eyes, and hoped with great earnestness of manner that he had not hurt me.

If he had, I would have been content that he should have repeated the offence a hundred times rather than suppose so ; but as he had not, I had no difficulty in changing the subject by making an inquiry which had been upon my lips twenty times already.

'You have not told me,' said I, 'anything about Sam Weller.'

'O! Sam,' replied Mr. Pickwick, 'is the same as ever. The same true, faithful fellow that he ever was. What should I tell you about Sam, my dear sir, except that he is more indispensable to my happiness and comfort every day of my life ?'

'And Mr. Weller senior ?' said I.

'Old Mr. Weller,' returned Mr. Pickwick, 'is in no respect more altered than Sam, unless it be that he is a little more opinionated than he was formerly, and perhaps at times more talkative. He spends a good deal of his time now in our neighbourhood, and has so constituted himself a part of my bodyguard, that when I ask permission for Sam to have a seat in your kitchen on clock nights (supposing your three friends think me worthy to fill one of the chairs), I am afraid I must often include Mr. Weller too.'

I very readily pledged myself to give both Sam and his father a free admission to my house at all hours and seasons, and this point settled, we fell into a lengthy conversation which was carried on with as little reserve on both sides as if we had been intimate friends from our youth, and which conveyed to me the comfortable assurance that Mr. Pickwick's buoyancy of spirit, and indeed all his old cheerful characteristics, were wholly unimpaired. As he had spoken of the consent of my friends as being yet in abeyance, I repeatedly assured him that his proposal ,was certain to receive their most joyful sanction, and several times entreated that he would give me leave to introduce him to Jack Redburn and Mr. Miles (who were near at hand) without further ceremony.

To this proposal, however, Mr. Pickwick's delicacy would by no means allow him to accede, for he urged that his eligibility must be formally discussed, and that, until this had been done, he could not think of obtruding himself further. The utmost I could obtain from him was a promise that he would attend upon our next night of meeting, that I might have the pleasure of presenting him immediately on his election.

Mr. Pickwick, having with many blushes placed in my hands a small roll of paper, which he termed his 'qualification,' put a great many questions to me touching my friends, and particularly Jack Redburn, whom he repeatedly termed 'a fine fellow,' and in whose favour I could see he was strongly predisposed. When I had satisfied him on these points, I took him up into my room, that he might make acquaintance with the old chamber which is our place of meeting.

'And this,' said Mr. Pickwick, stopping short, 'is the clock! Dear me! And this is really the old clock!'

I thought he would never have come away from it. After advancing towards it softly, and laying his hand upon it with as much respect and as many smiling looks as if it were alive, he set himself to consider it in every possible direction, now mounting on a chair to look at the top, now going down upon his knees to examine the bottom, now surveying the sides with his spectacles almost touching the case, and now trying to peep between it and the wall to get a slight view of the back. Then he would retire a pace or two and look up at the dial to see it go, and then draw near again and stand with his head on one side to hear it tick: never failing to glance towards me at intervals of a few seconds each, and nod his head with such complacent gratification as I am quite unable to describe. His admiration was not confined to the clock either, but extended itself to every article in the room; and really, when he had gone through them every one, and at last sat himself down in all the six chairs, one after another, to try how they felt, I never saw such a picture of good-humour and happiness as he presented, from the top of his shining head down to the very last button of his gaiters.

I should have been well pleased, and should have had the utmost enjoyment of his company, if he had remained with me all day, but my favourite, striking the hour, reminded him that he must take his leave. I could not forbear telling him once more how glad he had made me, and we shook hands all the way down-stairs.

We had no sooner arrived in the Hall than my housekeeper, gliding out of her little room (she had changed her gown and cap, I observed), greeted Mr. Pickwick with her best smile and courtesy; and the barber, feigning to be accidentally passing on his way out, made him a vast number of bows. When the housekeeper courtesied, Mr. Pickwick bowed with the utmost politeness, and when he bowed, the housekeeper courtesied again; between the housekeeper and the barber, I should say that Mr. Pickwick faced about and bowed with undiminished affability fifty times at least.

I saw him to the door; an omnibus was at the moment passing the corner of the lane, which Mr. Pickwick hailed and ran after with extraordinary nimbleness. When he had got about half-way, he turned his head, and seeing that I was still looking after him, and that I waved my hand, stopped, evidently irresolute whether to come back and shake hands again, or to go on. The man behind the omnibus shouted, and Mr. Pickwick ran a little way towards him: then he looked round at me, and ran a little way back again. Then there was another shout, and he turned round once more and ran the other way. After several of these vibrations, the man settled the question by taking Mr. Pickwick by the arm and putting him into the carriage; but his last action was to let down the window and wave his hat to me as it drove off.

I lost no time in opening the parcel he had left with me. The following were its contents:—

MR. PICKWICK'S TALE

A good many years have passed away since old John Podgers lived in the town of Windsor, where he was born, and where, in course of time, he came to be comfortably and snugly buried. You may be sure that in the time of King James the First, Windsor was a very quaint queer old town, and you may take it upon my authority that John Podgers was a very quaint queer old fellow; consequently he and Windsor fitted each other to a nicety, and seldom parted company even for half a day.

John Podgers was broad, sturdy, Dutch-built, short, and a very hard eater, as men of his figure often are. Being a hard sleeper likewise, he divided his time pretty equally between these two recreations, always falling asleep when he had done eating, and always taking another turn at the trencher when he had done sleeping, by which means he grew more corpulent and more drowsy every day of his life. Indeed it used to be currently reported that when he sauntered up and down the sunny side of the street before dinner (as he never failed to do in fair weather), he enjoyed his soundest nap; but many people held this to be a fiction, as he had several times been seen to look after fat oxen on market-days, and had even been heard, by persons of good credit and reputation, to chuckle at the sight, and say to himself with great glee, 'Live beef, live beef!' It was upon this evidence that the wisest people in Windsor (beginning with the local authorities, of course) held that John Podgers was a man of strong, sound sense, not what is called smart, perhaps, and it might be of a rather lazy and apoplectic turn, but still a man of solid parts, and one who meant much more than he cared to show. This impression was confirmed by a very dignified way he had of shaking his head and imparting, at the same time, a pendulous motion to his double chin; in short, he passed for one of those people who, being plunged into the Thames, would make no vain efforts to set it afire, but would straightway flop down to the bottom with a deal of gravity, and be highly respected in consequence by all good men.

Being well to do in the world, and a peaceful widower,—having a great appetite, which, as he could afford to gratify it, was a luxury and no inconvenience, and a power of going to sleep, which, as he had no occasion to keep awake, was

a most enviable faculty,—you will readily suppose that John
Podgers was a happy man. But appearances are often
deceptive when they least seem so, and the truth is that,
notwithstanding his extreme sleekness, he was rendered
uneasy in his mind and exceedingly uncomfortable by a
constant apprehension that beset him night and day.

You know very well that in those times there flourished
divers evil old women who, under the name of Witches,
spread great disorder through the land, and inflicted various
dismal tortures upon Christian men; sticking pins and
needles into them when they least expected it, and causing
them to walk in the air with their feet upwards, to the great
terror of their wives and families, who were naturally very
much disconcerted when the master of the house unexpectedly came home, knocking at the door with his heels and
combing his hair on the scraper. These were their commonest pranks, but they every day played a hundred others,
of which none were less objectionable, and many were much
more so, being improper besides; the result was that vengeance was denounced against all old women, with whom
even the king himself had no sympathy (as he certainly
ought to have had), for with his own most Gracious hand he
penned a most Gracious consignment of them to everlasting
wrath, and devised most Gracious means for their confusion
and slaughter, in virtue whereof scarcely a day passed but
one witch at the least was most graciously hanged, drowned,
or roasted in some part of his dominions. Still the press
teemed with strange and terrible news from the North or
the South, or the East or the West, relative to witches and
their unhappy victims in some corner of the country, and the
Public's hair stood on end to that degree that it lifted its hat
off its head, and made its face pale with terror.

You may believe that the little town of Windsor did not
escape the general contagion. The inhabitants boiled a witch
on the king's birthday and sent a bottle of the broth to
court, with a dutiful address expressive of their loyalty.
The king, being rather frightened by the present, piously
bestowed it upon the Archbishop of Canterbury, and returned an answer to the address, wherein he gave them
golden rules for discovering witches, and laid great stress
upon certain protecting charms, and especially horseshoes.
Immediately the towns-people went to work nailing up
horseshoes over every door, and so many anxious parents

apprenticed their children to farriers to keep them out of harm's way, that it became quite a genteel trade, and flourished exceedingly.

In the midst of all this bustle John Podgers ate and slept as usual, but shook his head a great deal oftener than was his custom, and was observed to look at the oxen less, and at the old women more. He had a little shelf put up in his sitting-room, whereon was displayed, in a row which grew longer every week, all the witchcraft literature of the time; he grew learned in charms and exorcisms, hinted at certain questionable females on broomsticks whom he had seen from his chamber window, riding in the air at night, and was in constant terror of being bewitched. At length, from perpetually dwelling upon this one idea, which, being alone in his head, had all its own way, the fear of witches became the single passion of his life. He, who up to that time had never known what it was to dream, began to have visions of witches whenever he fell asleep; waking, they were incessantly present to his imagination likewise; and, sleeping or waking, he had not a moment's peace. He began to set witch-traps in the highway, and was often seen lying in wait round the corner for hours together, to watch their effect. These engines were of simple construction, usually consisting of two straws disposed in the form of a cross, or a piece of a Bible cover with a pinch of salt upon it; but they were infallible, and if an old woman chanced to stumble over them (as not unfrequently happened, the chosen spot being a broken and stony place), John started from a doze, pounced out upon her, and hung round her neck till assistance arrived, when she was immediately carried away and drowned. By dint of constantly inveigling old ladies and disposing of them in this summary manner, he acquired the reputation of a great public character; and as he received no harm in these pursuits beyond a scratched face or so, he came, in the course of time, to be considered witch-proof.

There was but one person who entertained the least doubt of John Podgers's gifts, and that person was his own nephew, a wild, roving young fellow of twenty who had been brought up in his uncle's house and lived there still,— that is to say, when he was at home, which was not as often as it might have been. As he was an apt scholar, it was he who read aloud every fresh piece of strange and terrible intelligence that John Podgers bought; and this he always did of an evening in the little porch in front of the house, round which the neighbours would flock in crowds to hear the direful news,—for people like to be frightened, and when they can be frightened for nothing and at another man's expense, they like it all the better.

One fine midsummer evening, a group of persons were gathered in this place, listening intently to Will Marks (that was the nephew's name), as with his cap very much on one side, his arm coiled slyly round the waist of a pretty girl who sat beside him, and his face screwed into a comical expression intended to represent extreme gravity, he read— with Heaven knows how many embellishments of his own— a dismal account of a gentleman down in Northamptonshire under the influence of witchcraft and taken forcible possession of by the Devil, who was playing his very self with him. John Podgers, in a high sugar-loaf hat and short cloak, filled the opposite seat, and surveyed the auditory with a look of mingled pride and horror very edifying to see ; while the hearers, with their heads thrust forward and their mouths open, listened and trembled, and hoped there was a great deal more to come. Sometimes Will stopped for an instant to look round upon his eager audience, and then, with a more comical expression of face than before and a settling of himself comfortably, which included a squeeze of the young lady before mentioned, he launched into some new wonder surpassing all the others.

The setting sun shed his last golden rays upon this little party, who, absorbed in their present occupation, took no heed of the approach of night, or the glory in which the day went down, when the sound of a horse, approaching at a good round trot, invading the silence of the hour, caused the reader to make a sudden stop, and the listeners to raise their heads in wonder. Nor was their wonder diminished when a horseman dashed up to the porch, and abruptly checking his steed, inquired where one John Podgers dwelt.

'Here!' cried a dozen voices, while a dozen hands pointed out sturdy John, still basking in the terrors of the pamphlet.

The rider, giving his bridle to one of those who surrounded him, dismounted, and approached John, hat in hand, but with great haste.

'Whence come ye?' said John.

'From Kingston, master.'

'And wherefore?'

Reading the Pamphlet

'On most pressing business.'

'Of what nature ?'

'Witchcraft.'

Witchcraft! Everybody looked aghast at the breathless messenger, and the breathless messenger looked equally aghast at everybody—except Will Marks, who, finding himself unobserved, not only squeezed the young lady again, but kissed her twice. Surely he must have been bewitched himself, or he never could have done it—and the young lady too, or she never would have let him.

'Witchcraft!' cried Will, drowning the sound of his last kiss, which was rather a loud one.

The messenger turned towards him, and with a frown repeated the word more solemnly than before ; then told his errand, which was, in brief, that the people of Kingston had been greatly terrified for some nights past by hideous revels, held by witches beneath the gibbet within a mile of the town, and related and deposed to by chance wayfarers who had passed within ear-shot of the spot ; that the sound of their voices in their wild orgies had been plainly heard by many persons ; that three old women laboured under strong suspicion, and that precedents had been consulted and solemn council had, and it was found that to identify the hags some single person must watch upon the spot alone ; that no single person had the courage to perform the task ; and that he had been despatched express to solicit John Podgers to undertake it that very night, as being a man of great renown, who bore a charmed life, and was proof against unholy spells.

John received this communication with much composure, and said in a few words, that it would have afforded him inexpressible pleasure to do the Kingston people so slight a service, if it were not for his unfortunate propensity to fall asleep, which no man regretted more than himself upon the present occasion, but which quite settled the question. Nevertheless, he said, there *was* a gentleman present (and here he looked very hard at a tall farrier), who, having been engaged all his life in the manufacture of horseshoes, must be quite invulnerable to the power of witches, and who, he had no doubt, from his own reputation for bravery and good-nature, would readily accept the commission. The farrier politely thanked him for his good opinion, which it would always be his study to deserve, but added that, with

regard to the present little matter, he couldn't think of it
on any account, as his departing on such an errand would
certainly occasion the instant death of his wife, to whom, as
they all knew, he was tenderly attached. Now, so far from
this circumstance being notorious, everybody had suspected
the reverse, as the farrier was in the habit of beating his
lady rather more than tender husbands usually do; all the
married men present, however, applauded his resolution
with great vehemence, and one and all declared that they
would stop at home and die if needful (which happily it was
not) in defence of their lawful partners.

This burst of enthusiasm over, they began to look, as by
one consent, toward Will Marks, who, with his cap more on
one side than ever, sat watching the proceedings with extraordinary unconcern. He had never been heard openly to
express his disbelief in witches, but had often cut such jokes
at their expense as left it to be inferred; publicly stating on
several occasions that he considered a broomstick an inconvenient charger, and one especially unsuited to the dignity
of the female character, and indulging in other free remarks
of the same tendency, to the great amusement of his wild
companions.

As they looked at Will they began to whisper and murmur
among themselves, and at length one man cried, 'Why don't
you ask Will Marks?'

As this was what everybody had been thinking of, they all
took up the word, and cried in concert, 'Ah! why don't you
ask Will?'

'*He* don't care,' said the farrier.

'Not he,' added another voice in the crowd.

'He don't believe in it, you know,' sneered a little man
with a yellow face and a taunting nose and chin, which he
thrust out from under the arm of a long man before him.

'Besides,' said a red-faced gentleman with a gruff voice,
'he's a single man.'

'That's the point!' said the farrier; and all the married
men murmured, ah! that was it, and they only wished they
were single themselves; they would show him what spirit
was, very soon.

The messenger looked towards Will Marks beseechingly.

'It will be a wet night, friend, and my grey nag is tired
after yesterday's work——'

Here there was a general titter.

'But,' resumed Will, looking about him with a smile, 'if nobody else puts in a better claim to go, for the credit of the town I am your man, and I would be, if I had to go afoot. In five minutes I shall be in the saddle, unless I am depriving any worthy gentleman here of the honour of the adventure, which I wouldn't do for the world.'

But here arose a double difficulty, for not only did John Podgers combat the resolution with all the words he had, which were not many, but the young lady combated it too with all the tears she had, which were very many indeed. Will, however, being inflexible, parried his uncle's objections with a joke, and coaxed the young lady into a smile in three short whispers. As it was plain that he set his mind upon it, and would go, John Podgers offered him a few first-rate charms out of his own pocket, which he dutifully declined to accept; and the young lady gave him a kiss, which he also returned.

'You see what a rare thing it is to be married,' said Will, 'and how careful and considerate all these husbands are. There's not a man among them but his heart is leaping to forestall me in this adventure, and yet a strong sense of duty keeps him back. The husbands in this one little town are a pattern to the world, and so must the wives be too, for that matter, or they could never boast half the influence they have!'

Waiting for no reply to this sarcasm, he snapped his fingers and withdrew into the house, and thence into the stable, while some busied themselves in refreshing the messenger, and others in baiting his steed. In less than the specified time he returned by another way, with a good cloak hanging over his arm, a good sword girded by his side, and leading his good horse caparisoned for the journey.

'Now,' said Will, leaping into the saddle at a bound, 'up and away. Upon your mettle, friend, and push on. Good night!'

He kissed his hand to the girl, nodded to his drowsy uncle, waved his cap to the rest—and off they flew pell-mell, as if all the witches in England were in their horses' legs. They were out of sight in a minute.

The men who were left behind shook their heads doubtfully, stroked their chins, and shook their heads again. The farrier said that certainly Will Marks was a good horseman, nobody should ever say he denied that: but he was rash, very rash, and there was no telling what the end of it might be; what did he go for, that was what he wanted to know? He wished the young fellow no harm, but why did he go? Everybody echoed these words, and shook their heads again, having done which they wished John Podgers good night, and straggled home to bed.

The Kingston people were in their first sleep when Will Marks and his conductor rode through the town and up to the door of a house where sundry grave functionaries were assembled, anxiously expecting the arrival of the renowned Podgers. They were a little disappointed to find a gay young man in his place; but they put the best face upon the matter, and gave him full instructions how he was to conceal himself behind the gibbet, and watch and listen to the witches, and how at a certain time he was to burst forth and cut and slash among them vigorously, so that the suspected parties might be found bleeding in their beds next day, and thoroughly confounded. They gave him a great quantity of wholesome advice besides, and—which was more to the purpose with Will—a good supper. All these things being done, and midnight nearly come, they sallied forth to show him the spot where he was to keep his dreary vigil.

The night was by this time dark and threatening. There was a rumbling of distant thunder, and a low sighing of wind among the trees, which was very dismal. The potentates of the town kept so uncommonly close to Will that they trod upon his toes, or stumbled against his ankles, or nearly tripped up his heels at every step he took, and, besides these annoyances, their teeth chattered so with fear, that he seemed to be accompanied by a dirge of castanets.

At last they made a halt at the opening of a lonely, desolate space, and, pointing to a black object at some distance, asked Will if he saw that, yonder.

'Yes,' he replied. 'What then?'

Informing him abruptly that it was the gibbet where he was to watch, they wished him good night in an extremely friendly manner, and ran back as fast as their feet would carry them.

Will walked boldly to the gibbet, and, glancing upwards when he came under it, saw—certainly with satisfaction—that it was empty, and that nothing dangled from the top but some iron chains, which swung mournfully to and fro as

they were moved by the breeze. After a careful survey of
every quarter he determined to take his station with his face
towards the town; both because that would place him with
his back to the wind, and because, if any trick or surprise
were attempted, it would probably come from that direction in the first instance. Having taken these precautions,
he wrapped his cloak about him so that it left the handle of

WILL AT THE GIBBET

his sword free, and ready to his hand, and leaning against
the gallows-tree with his cap not quite so much on one side
as it had been before, took up his position for the night.

SECOND CHAPTER OF MR. PICKWICK'S TALE

We left Will Marks leaning under the gibbet with his face
towards the town, scanning the distance with a keen eye,
which sought to pierce the darkness and catch the earliest
glimpse of any person or persons that might approach
towards him. But all was quiet, and, save the howling of the
wind as it swept across the heath in gusts, and the creaking
of the chains that dangled above his head, there was no
sound to break the sullen stillness of the night. After half an
hour or so this monotony became more disconcerting to Will
than the most furious uproar would have been, and he
heartily wished for some one antagonist with whom he

might have a fair stand-up fight, if it were only to warm himself.

Truth to tell, it was a bitter wind, and seemed to blow to the very heart of a man whose blood, heated but now with rapid riding, was the more sensitive to the chilling blast. Will was a daring fellow, and cared not a jot for hard knocks or sharp blades; but he could not persuade himself to move or walk about, having just that vague expectation of a sudden assault which made it a comfortable thing to have something at his back, even though that something were a gallows-tree. He had no great faith in the superstitions of the age, still such of them as occurred to him did not serve to lighten the time, or to render his situation the more endurable. He remembered how witches were said to repair at that ghostly hour to churchyards and gibbets, and such-like dismal spots, to pluck the bleeding mandrake or scrape the flesh from dead men's bones, as choice ingredients for their spells; how, stealing by night to lonely places, they dug graves with their finger-nails, or anointed themselves before riding in the air, with a delicate pomatum made of the fat of infants newly boiled. These, and many other fabled practices of a no less agreeable nature, and all having some reference to the circumstances in which he was placed, passed and repassed in quick succession through the mind of Will Marks, and adding a shadowy dread to that distrust and watchfulness which his situation inspired, rendered it, upon the whole, sufficiently uncomfortable. As he had foreseen, too, the rain began to descend heavily, and driving before the wind in a thick mist, obscured even those few objects which the darkness of the night had before imperfectly revealed.

'Look!' shrieked a voice. 'Great Heaven, it has fallen down, and stands erect as if it lived!'

The speaker was close behind him; the voice was almost at his ear. Will threw off his cloak, drew his sword, and darting swiftly round, seized a woman by the wrist, who, recoiling from him with a dreadful shriek, fell struggling upon her knees. Another woman, clad, like her whom he had grasped, in mourning garments, stood rooted to the spot on which they were, gazing upon his face with wild and glaring eyes that quite appalled him.

'Say,' cried Will, when they had confronted each other thus for some time, 'what are ye?'

The Burial in the Church

'Say what are *you*,' returned the woman, 'who trouble even this obscene resting-place of the dead, and strip the gibbet of its honoured burden ? Where is the body ?'

He looked in wonder and affright from the woman who questioned him to the other whose arm he clutched.

'Where is the body ?' repeated his questioner more firmly than before. 'You wear no livery which marks you for the hireling of the government. You are no friend to us, or I should recognise you, for the friends of such as we are few in number. What are you then, and wherefore are you here ?'

'I am no foe to the distressed and helpless,' said Will. 'Are ye among that number ? ye should be by your looks.'

'We are!' was the answer.

'Is it ye who have been wailing and weeping here under cover of the night ?' said Will.

'It is,' replied the woman sternly; and pointing, as she spoke, towards her companion, 'she mourns a husband, and I a brother. Even the bloody law that wreaks its vengeance on the dead does not make that a crime, and if it did 'twould be alike to us who are past its fear or favour.'

Will glanced at the two females, and could barely discern that the one whom he addressed was much the elder, and that the other was young and of a slight figure. Both were deadly pale, their garments wet and worn, their hair dishevelled and streaming in the wind, themselves bowed down with grief and misery; their whole appearance most dejected, wretched, and forlorn. A sight so different from any he had expected to encounter touched him to the quick, and all idea of anything but their pitiable condition vanished before it.

'I am a rough, blunt yeoman,' said Will. 'Why I came here is told in a word; you have been overheard at a distance in the silence of the night, and I have undertaken a watch for hags or spirits. I came here expecting an adventure, and prepared to go through with any. If there be aught that I can do to help or aid you, name it, and on the faith of a man who can be secret and trusty, I will stand by you to the death.'

'How comes this gibbet to be empty ?' asked the elder female.

'I swear to you,' replied Will, 'that I know as little as yourself. But this I know, that when I came here an hour ago or so, it was as it is now; and if, as I gather from your

question, it was not so last night, sure I am that it has
been secretly disturbed without the knowledge of the folks
in yonder town. Bethink you, therefore, whether you have
no friends in league with you or with him on whom the law
has done its worst, by whom these sad remains have been
removed for burial.'

The women spoke together, and Will retired a pace or two
while they conversed apart. He could hear them sob and
moan, and saw that they wrung their hands in fruitless
agony. He could make out little that they said, but
between whiles he gathered enough to assure him that his
suggestion was not very wide of the mark, and that they
not only suspected by whom the body had been removed,
but also whither it had been conveyed. When they had
been in conversation a long time, they turned towards him
once more. This time the younger female spoke.

'You have offered us your help ?'

'I have.'

'And given a pledge that you are still willing to redeem ?'

'Yes. So far as I may, keeping all plots and conspiracies
at arm's length.'

'Follow us, friend.'

Will, whose self-possession was now quite restored, needed
no second bidding, but with his drawn sword in his hand,
and his cloak so muffled over his left arm as to serve for
a kind of shield without offering any impediment to its free
action, suffered them to lead the way. Through mud and
mire, and wind and rain, they walked in silence a full mile.
At length they turned into a dark lane, where, suddenly
starting out from beneath some trees where he had taken
shelter, a man appeared, having in his charge three saddled
horses. One of these (his own apparently), in obedience to
a whisper from the women, he consigned to Will, who, seeing that they mounted, mounted also. Then, without a word
spoken, they rode on together, leaving the attendant behind.

They made no halt nor slackened their pace until they
arrived near Putney. At a large wooden house which stood
apart from any other they alighted, and giving their horses
to one who was already waiting, passed in by a side door,
and so up some narrow creaking stairs into a small panelled
chamber, where Will was left alone. He had not been here
very long, when the door was softly opened, and there

entered to him a cavalier whose face was concealed beneath a black mask.

Will stood upon his guard, and scrutinised this figure from head to foot. The form was that of a man pretty far advanced in life, but of a firm and stately carriage. His dress was of a rich and costly kind, but so soiled and disordered that it was scarcely to be recognised for one of those gorgeous suits which the expensive taste and fashion of the time prescribed for men of any rank or station. He was booted and spurred, and bore about him even as many tokens of the state of the roads as Will himself. All this he noted, while the eyes behind the mask regarded him with equal attention. This survey over, the cavalier broke silence.

'Thou'rt young and bold, and wouldst be richer than thou art ?'

'The two first I am,' returned Will. 'The last I have scarcely thought of. But be it so. Say that I would be richer than I am ; what then ?'

'The way lies before thee now,' replied the Mask.

'Show it me.'

'First let me inform thee, that thou wert brought here to-night lest thou shouldst too soon have told thy tale to those who placed thee on the watch.'

'I thought as much when I followed,' said Will. 'But I am no blab, not I.'

'Good,' returned the Mask. 'Now listen. He who was to have executed the enterprise of burying that body, which, as thou hast suspected, was taken down to-night, has left us in our need.'

Will nodded, and thought within himself that if the Mask were to attempt to play any tricks, the first eyelet-hole on the left-hand side of his doublet, counting from the buttons up the front, would be a very good place in which to pink him neatly.

'Thou art here, and the emergency is desperate. I propose his task to thee. Convey the body (now coffined in this house), by means that I shall show, to the Church of St. Dunstan in London to-morrow night, and thy service shall be richly paid. Thou'rt about to ask whose corpse it is. Seek not to know. I warn thee, seek not to know. Felons hang in chains on every moor and heath. Believe, as others do, that this was one, and ask no further. The murders of

state policy, its victims or avengers, had best remain
unknown to such as thee!'

'The mystery of this service,' said Will, 'bespeaks its
danger. What is the reward?'

'One hundred golden unities,' replied the cavalier. 'The
danger to one who cannot be recognised as the friend of a
fallen cause is not great, but there is some hazard to be run.
Decide between that and the reward.'

'What if I refuse?' said Will.

'Depart in peace, in God's name,' returned the Mask in a
melancholy tone, 'and keep our secret, remembering that
those who brought thee here were crushed and stricken
women, and that those who bade thee go free could have
had thy life with one word, and no man the wiser.'

Men were readier to undertake desperate adventures in
those times than they are now. In this case the temptation
was great, and the punishment, even in case of detection,
was not likely to be very severe, as Will came of a loyal
stock, and his uncle was in good repute, and a passable tale
to account for his possession of the body and his ignorance
of the identity might be easily devised.

The cavalier explained that a covered cart had been prepared for the purpose; that the time of departure could be
arranged so that he should reach London Bridge at dusk,
and proceed through the City after the day had closed in;
that people would be ready at his journey's end to place the
coffin in a vault without a minute's delay; that officious
inquirers in the streets would be easily repelled by the tale
that he was carrying for interment the corpse of one who
had died of the plague; and in short showed him every
reason why he should succeed, and none why he should fail.
After a time they were joined by another gentleman, masked
like the first, who added new arguments to those which had
been already urged; the wretched wife, too, added her tears
and prayers to their calmer representations; and in the end,
Will, moved by compassion and good-nature, by a love of
the marvellous, by a mischievous anticipation of the terrors
of the Kingston people when he should be missing next day,
and finally, by the prospect of gain, took upon himself the
task, and devoted all his energies to its successful execution.

The following night, when it was quite dark, the hollow
echoes of old London Bridge responded to the rumbling of
the cart which contained the ghastly load, the object of

Will Marks' care. Sufficiently disguised to attract no attention by his garb, Will walked at the horse's head, as uncon-
cerned as a man could be who was sensible that he had now
arrived at the most dangerous part of his undertaking, but
full of boldness and confidence.

It was now eight o'clock. After nine, none could walk the
streets without danger of their lives, and even at this hour,
robberies and murder were of no uncommon occurrence.
The shops upon the bridge were all closed; the low wooden
arches thrown across the way were like so many black pits,
in every one of which ill-favoured fellows lurked in knots of
three or four; some standing upright against the wall, lying
in wait; others skulking in gateways, and thrusting out
their uncombed heads and scowling eyes: others crossing
and recrossing, and constantly jostling both horse and man
to provoke a quarrel; others stealing away and summoning
their companions in a low whistle. Once, even in that short
passage, there was the noise of scuffling and the clash of
swords behind him, but Will, who knew the City and its
ways, kept straight on and scarcely turned his head.

The streets being unpaved, the rain of the night before
had converted them into a perfect quagmire, which the
splashing water-spouts from the gables, and the filth and
offal cast from the different houses, swelled in no small
degree. These odious matters being left to putrefy in the
close and heavy air, emitted an insupportable stench, to
which every court and passage poured forth a contribution
of its own. Many parts, even of the main streets, with their
projecting stories tottering overhead and nearly shutting
out the sky, were more like huge chimneys than open ways.
At the corners of some of these, great bonfires were burning
to prevent infection from the plague, of which it was
rumoured that some citizens had lately died; and few, who
availing themselves of the light thus afforded paused for a
moment to look around them, would have been disposed to
doubt the existence of the disease, or wonder at its dreadful
visitations.

But it was not in such scenes as these, or even in the
deep and miry road, that Will Marks found the chief
obstacles to his progress. There were kites and ravens feeding in the streets (the only scavengers the City kept), who,
scenting what he carried, followed the cart or fluttered
on its top, and croaked their knowledge of its burden and

their ravenous appetite for prey. There were distant fires, where the poor wood and plaster tenements wasted fiercely, and whither crowds made their way, clamouring eagerly for plunder, beating down all who came within their reach, and yelling like devils let loose. There were single-handed men flying from bands of ruffians, who pursued them with naked weapons, and hunted them savagely; there were drunken, desperate robbers issuing from their dens and staggering through the open streets where no man dared molest them; there were vagabond servitors returning from the Bear Garden, where had been good sport that day, dragging after them their torn and bleeding dogs, or leaving them to die and rot upon the road. Nothing was abroad but cruelty, violence, and disorder.

Many were the interruptions which Will Marks encountered from these stragglers, and many the narrow escapes he made. Now some stout bully would take his seat upon the cart, insisting to be driven to his own home, and now two or three men would come down upon him together, and demand that on peril of his life he showed them what he had inside. Then a party of the city watch, upon their rounds, would draw across the road, and not satisfied with his tale, question him closely, and revenge themselves by a little cuffing and hustling for maltreatment sustained at other hands that night. All these assailants had to be rebutted, some by fair words, some by foul, and some by blows. But Will Marks was not the man to be stopped or turned back now he had penetrated so far, and though he got on slowly, still he made his way down Fleet-street and reached the church at last.

As he had been forewarned, all was in readiness. Directly he stopped, the coffin was removed by four men, who appeared so suddenly that they seemed to have started from the earth. A fifth mounted the cart, and scarcely allowing Will time to snatch from it a little bundle containing such of his own clothes as he had thrown off on assuming his disguise, drove briskly away. Will never saw cart or man again.

He followed the body into the church, and it was well he lost no time in doing so, for the door was immediately closed. There was no light in the building save that which came from a couple of torches borne by two men in cloaks, who stood upon the brink of a vault. Each supported a female figure, and all observed a profound silence.

By this dim and solemn glare, which made Will feel as though light itself were dead, and its tomb the dreary arches that frowned above, they placed the coffin in the vault, with uncovered heads, and closed it up. One of the torch-bearers then turned to Will, and stretched forth his hand, in which was a purse of gold. Something told him directly that those were the same eyes which he had seen beneath the mask.

'Take it,' said the cavalier in a low voice, 'and be happy. Though these have been hasty obsequies, and no priest has blessed the work, there will not be the less peace with thee thereafter, for having laid his bones beside those of his little children. Keep thy own counsel, for thy sake no less than ours, and God be with thee!'

'The blessing of a widowed mother on thy head, good friend!' cried the younger lady through her tears; 'the blessing of one who has now no hope or rest but in this grave!'

Will stood with the purse in his hand, and involuntarily made a gesture as though he would return it, for though a thoughtless fellow, he was of a frank and generous nature. But the two gentlemen, extinguishing their torches, cautioned him to be gone, as their common safety would be endangered by a longer delay; and at the same time their retreating footsteps sounded through the church. He turned, therefore, towards the point at which he had entered, and seeing by a faint gleam in the distance that the door was again partially open, groped his way towards it and so passed into the street.

Meantime the local authorities of Kingston had kept watch and ward all the previous night, fancying every now and then that dismal shrieks were borne towards them on the wind, and frequently winking to each other, and drawing closer to the fire as they drank the health of the lonely sentinel, upon whom a clerical gentleman present was especially severe by reason of his levity and youthful folly. Two or three of the gravest in company, who were of a theological turn, propounded to him the question, whether such a character was not but poorly armed for single combat with the Devil, and whether he himself would not have been a stronger opponent; but the clerical gentleman, sharply reproving them for their presumption in discussing such questions, clearly showed that a fitter champion than Will

could scarcely have been selected, not only for that being a
child of Satan, he was the less likely to be alarmed by the
appearance of his own father, but because Satan himself
would be at his ease in such company, and would not scruple
to kick up his heels to an extent which it was quite certain
he would never venture before clerical eyes, under whose
influence (as was notorious) he became quite a tame and
milk-and-water character.

But when next morning arrived, and with it no Will Marks,
and when a strong party repairing to the spot, as a strong
party ventured to do in broad day, found Will gone and the
gibbet empty, matters grew serious indeed. The day passing
away and no news arriving, and the night going on also
without any intelligence, the thing grew more tremendous
still; in short, the neighbourhood worked itself up to such
a comfortable pitch of mystery and horror, that it is a great
question whether the general feeling was not one of excessive disappointment, when, on the second morning, Will
Marks returned.

However this may be, back Will came in a very cool and
collected state, and appearing not to trouble himself much
about anybody except old John Podgers, who, having been
sent for, was sitting in the Town Hall crying slowly, and
dozing between whiles. Having embraced his uncle and
assured him of his safety, Will mounted on a table and told
his story to the crowd.

And surely they would have been the most unreasonable
crowd that ever assembled together, if they had been in the
least respect disappointed with the tale he told them; for
besides describing the Witches' Dance to the minutest
motion of their legs, and performing it in character on the
table, with the assistance of a broomstick, he related how
they had carried off the body in a copper caldron, and so
bewitched him, that he lost his senses until he found himself
lying under a hedge at least ten miles off, whence he had
straightway returned as they then beheld. The story
gained such universal applause that it soon afterwards
brought down express from London the great witch-finder
of the age, the Heaven-born Hopkins, who having examined
Will closely on several points, pronounced it the most
extraordinary and the best accredited witch-story ever
known, under which title it was published at the Three
Bibles on London Bridge, in small quarto, with a view of the

caldron from an original drawing, and a portrait of the clerical gentleman as he sat by the fire.

On one point Will was particularly careful: and that was to describe for the witches he had seen, three impossible old females, whose likenesses never were or will be. Thus he saved the lives of the suspected parties, and of all other old women who were dragged before him to be identified.

This circumstance occasioned John Podgers much grief and sorrow, until happening one day to cast his eyes upon his housekeeper, and observing her to be plainly afflicted with rheumatism, he procured her to be burnt as an undoubted witch. For this service to the state he was immediately knighted, and became from that time Sir John Podgers.

Will Marks never gained any clue to the mystery in which he had been an actor, nor did any inscription in the church, which he often visited afterwards, nor any of the limited inquiries that he dared to make, yield him the least assistance. As he kept his own secret, he was compelled to spend the gold discreetly and sparingly. In the course of time he married the young lady of whom I have already told you, whose maiden name is not recorded, with whom he led a prosperous and happy life. Years and years after this adventure, it was his wont to tell her upon a stormy night that it was a great comfort to him to think those bones, to whomsoever they might have once belonged, were not bleaching in the troubled air, but were mouldering away with the dust of their own kith and kindred in a quiet grave.

FURTHER PARTICULARS OF MASTER HUMPHREY'S VISITOR

Being very full of Mr. Pickwick's application, and highly pleased with the compliment he had paid me, it will be readily supposed that long before our next night of meeting I communicated it to my three friends, who unanimously voted his admission into our body. We all looked forward with some impatience to the occasion which would enroll him among us, but I am greatly mistaken if Jack Redburn and myself were not by many degrees the most impatient of the party.

At length the night came, and a few minutes after ten Mr. Pickwick's knock was heard at the street-door. He was shown into a lower room, and I directly took my crooked stick and went to accompany him up-stairs, in order that he might be presented with all honour and formality.

'Mr. Pickwick,' said I, on entering the room, 'I am rejoiced to see you,—rejoiced to believe that this is but the opening of a long series of visits to this house, and but the beginning of a close and lasting friendship.'

That gentleman made a suitable reply with a cordiality and frankness peculiarly his own, and glanced with a smile towards two persons behind the door, whom I had not at first observed, and whom I immediately recognised as Mr. Samuel Weller and his father.

It was a warm evening, but the elder Mr. Weller was attired, notwithstanding, in a most capacious greatcoat, and his chin enveloped in a large speckled shawl, such as is usually worn by stage coachmen on active service. He looked very rosy and very stout, especially about the legs, which appeared to have been compressed into his top-boots with some difficulty. His broad-brimmed hat he held under his left arm, and with the forefinger of his right hand he touched his forehead a great many times in acknowledgment of my presence.

'I am very glad to see you in such good health, Mr. Weller,' said I.

'Why, thankee, sir,' returned Mr. Weller, 'the axle an't broke yet. We keeps up a steady pace,—not too sewere, but vith a moderate degree o' friction,—and the consekens is that ve're still a runnin' and comes in to the time reg'lar. —My son Samivel, sir, as you may have read on in history,' added Mr. Weller, introducing his first-born.

I received Sam very graciously, but before he could say a word his father struck in again.

'Samivel Veller, sir,' said the old gentleman, 'has conferred upon me the ancient title o' grandfather vich had long laid dormouse, and wos s'posed to be nearly hex-tinct in our family. Sammy, relate a anecdote o' vun o' them boys,— that 'ere little anecdote about young Tony sayin' as he *vould* smoke a pipe unbeknown to his mother.'

'Be quiet, can't you?' said Sam; 'I never see such a old magpie—never!'

'That 'ere Tony is the blessedest boy,' said Mr. Weller, heedless of this rebuff, 'the blessedest boy as ever *I* see in *my* days! of all the charmin'est infants as ever I heerd tell on, includin' them as was kivered over by the robin-red

Tony Weller and his Grandchild

breasts arter they'd committed sooicide with blackberries, there never wos any like that 'ere little Tony. He's alvays a playin' vith a quart pot, that boy is! To see him a settin' down on the doorstep pretending to drink out of it, and fetching a long breath artervards, and smoking a bit of fire-vood, and sayin', 'Now I'm grandfather,'—to see him a doin' that at two year old is better than any play as wos ever wrote. 'Now I'm grandfather!' He vouldn't take a pint pot if you wos to make him a present on it, but he gets his quart, and then he says, 'Now I'm grandfather!'"

Mr. Weller was so overpowered by this picture that he straightway fell into a most alarming fit of coughing, which must certainly have been attended with some fatal result but for the dexterity and promptitude of Sam, who, taking a firm grasp of the shawl just under his father's chin, shook him to and fro with great violence, at the same time administering some smart blows between his shoulders. By this curious mode of treatment Mr. Weller was finally recovered, but with a very crimson face, and in a state of great exhaustion.

'He'll do now, Sam,' said Mr. Pickwick, who had been in some alarm himself.

'He'll do, sir!' cried Sam, looking reproachfully at his parent. 'Yes, he *will* do one o' these days,—he'll do for his-self and then he'll wish he hadn't. Did anybody ever see sich a inconsiderate old file,—laughing into convulsions afore company, and stampin' on the floor as if he'd brought his own carpet vith him and wos under a wager to punch the pattern out in a given time? He'll begin again in a minute. There—he's a goin' off—I said he would!'

In fact, Mr. Weller, whose mind was still running upon his precocious grandson, was seen to shake his head from side to side, while a laugh, working like an earthquake, below the surface, produced various extraordinary appearances in his face, chest, and shoulders,—the more alarming because unaccompanied by any noise whatever. These emotions, however, gradually subsided, and after three or four short relapses he wiped his eyes with the cuff of his coat, and looked about him with tolerable composure.

'Afore the governor vith-draws,' said Mr. Weller, 'there is a pint, respecting vich Sammy has a qvestion to ask. Vile that qvestion is a perwadin' this here conwersation, p'raps the gen'lmen vill permit me to re-tire.'

'Wot are you goin' away for ?' demanded Sam, seizing his father by the coat-tail.

'I never see such a undootiful boy as you, Samivel,' returned Mr. Weller. 'Didn't you make a solemn promise, amountin' almost to a speeches o' wow, that you'd put that 'ere qvestion on my account ?'

'Well, I'm agreeable to do it,' said Sam, 'but not if you go cuttin' away like that, as the bull turned round and mildly observed to the drover ven they wos a goadin' him into the butcher's door. The fact is, sir,' said Sam, addressing me, 'that he wants to know somethin' respectin' that 'ere lady as is housekeeper here.'

'Ay. What is that ?'

'Vy, sir,' said Sam, grinning still more, 'he wishes to know vether she——'

'In short,' interposed old Mr. Weller decisively, a perspiration breaking out upon his forehead, 'vether that 'ere old creetur is or is not a widder.'

Mr. Pickwick laughed heartily, and so did I, as I replied decisively, that 'my housekeeper was a spinster.'

'There!' cried Sam, 'now you're satisfied. You hear she's a spinster.'

'A wot ?' said his father, with deep scorn.

'A spinster,' replied Sam.

Mr. Weller looked very hard at his son for a minute or two, and then said,

'Never mind vether she makes jokes or not, that's no matter. Wot I say is, is that 'ere female a widder, or is she not ?'

'Wot do you mean by her making jokes ?' demanded Sam, quite aghast at the obscurity of his parent's speech.

'Never you mind, Samivel,' returned Mr. Weller gravely ; 'puns may be wery good things or they may be wery bad 'uns, and a female may be none the better or she may be none the vurse for making of 'em ; that's got nothin' to do vith widders.'

'Vy now,' said Sam, looking round, 'would anybody believe as a man at his time o' life could be running his head agin spinsters and punsters being the same thing ?'

'There an't a straw's difference between 'em,' said Mr. Weller. 'Your father didn't drive a coach for so many years, not to be ekal to his own langvidge as far as *that* goes, Sammy.'

Avoiding the question of etymology, upon which the old gentleman's mind was quite made up, he was several times assured that the housekeeper had never been married. He expressed great satisfaction on hearing this, and apologised for the question, remarking that he had been greatly terrified by a widow not long before, and that his natural timidity was increased in consequence.

'It wos on the rail,' said Mr. Weller, with strong emphasis; 'I wos a goin' down to Birmingham by the rail, and I wos locked up in a close carriage vith a living widder. Alone ve wos; the widder and me wos alone; and I believe it wos only because ve *wos* alone and there wos no clergyman in the conwayance, that that 'ere widder didn't marry me afore ve reached the half-way station. Ven I think how she began a screaming as ve wos a goin' under them tunnels in the dark,—how she kept on a faintin' and ketchin' hold o' me,—and how I tried to bust open the door as was tight-locked and perwented all escape—Ah! It was a awful thing, most awful!'

Mr. Weller was so very much overcome by this retrospect that he was unable, until he had wiped his brow several times, to return any reply to the question whether he approved of railway communication, notwithstanding that it would appear from the answer which he ultimately gave, that he entertained strong opinions on the subject.

'I con-sider,' said Mr. Weller, 'that the rail is unconstitootional and an inwaser o' priwileges, and I should wery much like to know what that 'ere old Carter as once stood up for our liberties and wun 'em too,—I should like to know wot he vould say, if he wos alive now, to Englishmen being locked up vith widders, or vith anybody again their wills. Wot a old Carter vould have said, a old Coachman may say, and I as-sert that in that pint o' view alone, the rail is an inwaser. As to the comfort, vere's the comfort o' sittin' in a harm-cheer lookin' at brick walls or heaps o' mud, never comin' to a public-house, never seein' a glass o' ale, never goin' through a pike, never meetin' a change o' no kind (horses or othervise), but alvays comin' to a place, ven you come to one at all, the wery picter o' the last, vith the same p'leesemen standin' about, the same blessed old bell a ringin', the same unfort'nate people standin' behind the bars, a waitin' to be let in; and everythin' the same except the name, vich is wrote up in the same sized letters as the last name, and vith the same colours. As to the *h*onour and dignity o' travellin', vere can that be vithout a coachman; and wot's the rail to sich coachmen and guards as is sometimes forced to go by it, but a outrage and a insult ? As to the pace, wot sort o' pace do you think I, Tony Veller, could have kept a coach goin' at, for five hundred thousand pound a mile, paid in adwance afore the coach was on the road ? And as to the ingein,—a nasty, wheezin', creakin', gaspin', puffin', bustin' monster, alvays out o' breath, vith a shiny green-and-gold back, like a unpleasant beetle in that 'ere gas magnifier,—as to the ingein as is alvays a pourin' out red-hot coals at night, and black smoke in the day, the sensiblest thing it does, in my opinion, is, ven there's somethin' in the vay, and it sets up that 'ere frightful scream vich seems to say, "Now here's two hundred and forty passengers in the wery greatest extremity o' danger, and here's their two hundred and forty screams in vun!"'

By this time I began to fear that my friends would be rendered impatient by my protracted absence. I therefore begged Mr. Pickwick to accompany me up-stairs, and left the two Mr. Wellers in the care of the housekeeper, laying strict injunctions upon her to treat them with all possible hospitality.

CHAPTER IV

THE CLOCK

As we were going up-stairs, Mr. Pickwick put on his spec-tacles, which he had held in his hand hitherto; arranged his neckerchief, smoothed down his waistcoat, and made many other little preparations of that kind which men are accustomed to be mindful of, when they are going among strangers for the first time, and are anxious to impress them pleasantly. Seeing that I smiled, he smiled too, and said that if it had occurred to him before he left home, he would certainly have presented himself in pumps and silk stockings.

'I would, indeed, my dear sir,' he said very seriously; 'I would have shown my respect for the society, by laying aside my gaiters.'

'You may rest assured,' said I, 'that they would have regretted your doing so very much, for they are quite at-tached to them.'

'No, really!' cried Mr. Pickwick, with manifest pleasure. 'Do you think they care about my gaiters? Do you seriously think that they identify me at all with my gaiters?'

'I am sure they do,' I replied.

'Well, now,' said Mr. Pickwick, 'that is one of the most charming and agreeable circumstances that could possibly have occurred to me!'

I should not have written down this short conversation, but that it developed a slight point in Mr. Pickwick's character, with which I was not previously acquainted. He has a secret pride in his legs. The manner in which he spoke, and the accompanying glance he bestowed upon his tights, convince me that Mr. Pickwick regards his legs with much innocent vanity.

'But here are our friends,' said I, opening the door and taking his arm in mine; 'let them speak for themselves. —Gentlemen, I present to you Mr. Pickwick.'

Mr. Pickwick and I must have been a good contrast just then. I, leaning quietly on my crutch-stick, with something of a care-worn, patient air; he, having hold of my arm, and bowing in every direction with the most elastic politeness.

and an expression of face whose sprightly cheerfulness and good-humour knew no bounds. The difference between us must have been more striking yet, as we advanced towards the table, and the amiable gentleman, adapting his jocund step to my poor tread, had his attention divided between treating my infirmities with the utmost consideration, and affecting to be wholly unconscious that I required any.

I made him personally known to each of my friends in turn. First, to the deaf gentleman, whom he regarded with much interest, and accosted with great frankness and cordiality. He had evidently some vague idea, at the moment, that my friend being deaf must be dumb also; for when the latter opened his lips to express the pleasure it afforded him to know a gentleman of whom he had heard so much, Mr. Pickwick was so extremely disconcerted, that I was obliged to step in to his relief.

His meeting with Jack Redburn was quite a treat to see. Mr. Pickwick smiled, and shook hands, and looked at him through his spectacles, and under them, and over them, and nodded his head approvingly, and then nodded to me, as much as to say, 'This is just the man; you were quite right;' and then turned to Jack and said a few hearty words, and then did and said everything over again with unimpaired vivacity. As to Jack himself, he was quite as much delighted with Mr. Pickwick as Mr. Pickwick could possibly be with him. Two people never can have met together since the world began, who exchanged a warmer or more enthusiastic greeting.

It was amusing to observe the difference between this encounter and that which succeeded, between Mr. Pickwick and Mr. Miles. It was clear that the latter gentleman viewed our new member as a kind of rival in the affections of Jack Redburn, and besides this, he had more than once hinted to me, in secret, that although he had no doubt Mr. Pickwick was a very worthy man, still he did consider that some of his exploits were unbecoming a gentleman of his years and gravity. Over and above these grounds of distrust, it is one of his fixed opinions, that the law never can by possibility do anything wrong; he therefore looks upon Mr. Pickwick as one who has justly suffered in purse and peace for a breach of his plighted faith to an unprotected female, and holds that he is called upon to regard him with some suspicion on that account. These causes led to a rather cold and formal reception; which Mr. Pickwick acknowledged with the same stateliness and intense politeness as was displayed on the other side. Indeed, he assumed an air of such majestic defiance, that I was fearful he might break out into some solemn protest or declaration, and therefore inducted him into his chair without a moment's delay.

This piece of generalship was perfectly successful. The instant he took his seat, Mr. Pickwick surveyed us all with a most benevolent aspect, and was taken with a fit of smiling full five minutes long. His interest in our ceremonies was immense. They are not very numerous or complicated, and a description of them may be comprised in very few words. As our transactions have already been, and must necessarily continue to be, more or less anticipated by being presented in these pages at different times, and under various forms, they do not require a detailed account.

Our first proceeding when we are assembled is to shake hands all round, and greet each other with cheerful and pleasant looks. Remembering that we assemble not only for the promotion of our happiness, but with the view of adding something to the common stock, an air of languor or indifference in any member of our body would be regarded by the others as a kind of treason. We have never had an offender in this respect; but if we had, there is no doubt that he would be taken to task pretty severely.

Our salutation over, the venerable piece of antiquity from which we take our name is wound up in silence. The ceremony is always performed by Master Humphrey himself (in treating of the club, I may be permitted to assume the historical style, and speak of myself in the third person), who mounts upon a chair for the purpose, armed with a large key. While it is in progress, Jack Redburn is required to keep at the farther end of the room under the guardianship of Mr. Miles, for he is known to entertain certain aspiring and unhallowed thoughts connected with the clock, and has even gone so far as to state that if he might take the works out for a day or two, he thinks he could improve them. We pardon him his presumption in consideration of his good intentions, and his keeping this respectful distance, which last penalty is insisted on, lest by secretly wounding the object of our regard in some tender part, in the ardour of his zeal for its improvement, he should fill us with dismay and consternation.

This regulation afforded Mr. Pickwick the highest delight, and seemed, if possible, to exalt Jack in his good opinion.

The next ceremony is the opening of the clock-case (of which Master Humphrey has likewise the key), the taking from it as many papers as will furnish forth our evening's entertainment, and arranging in the recess such new contributions as have been provided since our last meeting. This is always done with peculiar solemnity. The deaf gentleman then fills and lights his pipe, and we once more take our seats round the table before mentioned, Master Humphrey acting as president,—if we can be said to have any president, where all are on the same social footing,— and our friend Jack as secretary. Our preliminaries being now concluded, we fall into any train of conversation that happens to suggest itself, or proceed immediately to one of our readings. In the latter case, the paper selected is consigned to Master Humphrey, who flattens it carefully on the table and makes dog's ears in the corner of every page, ready for turning over easily; Jack Redburn trims the lamp with a small machine of his own invention which usually puts it out; Mr. Miles looks on with great approval notwithstanding; the deaf gentleman draws in his chair, so that he can follow the words on the paper or on Master Humphrey's lips as he pleases; and Master Humphrey himself, looking round with mighty gratification, and glancing up at his old clock, begins to read aloud.

Mr. Pickwick's face, while his tale was being read, would have attracted the attention of the dullest man alive. The complacent motion of his head and forefinger as he gently beat time, and corrected the air with imaginary punctuation, the smile that mantled on his features at every jocose passage, and the sly look he stole around to observe its effect, the calm manner in which he shut his eyes and listened when there was some little piece of description, the changing expression with which he acted the dialogue to himself, his agony that the deaf gentleman should know what it was all about, and his extraordinary anxiety to correct the reader when he hesitated at a word in the manuscript, or substituted a wrong one, were alike worthy of remark. And when at last, endeavouring to communicate with the deaf gentleman by means of the finger alphabet, with which he constructed such words as are unknown in any civilised or savage language, he took up a slate and wrote in large text,

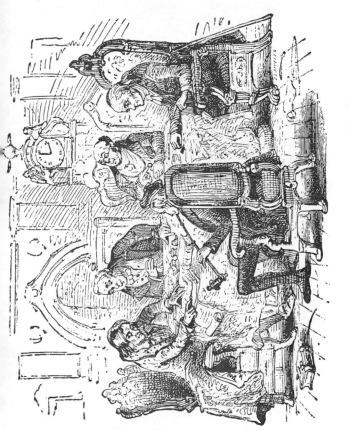

Mr. Pickwick and Master Humphrey's Friends

one word in a line, the question, 'How—do—you—like—it?'—when he did this, and handing it over the table awaited the reply, with a countenance only brightened and improved by his great excitement, even Mr. Miles relaxed, and could not forbear looking at him for the moment with interest and favour.

'It has occurred to me,' said the deaf gentleman, who had watched Mr. Pickwick and everybody else with silent satisfaction—'it has occurred to me,' said the deaf gentleman, taking his pipe from his lips, 'that now is our time for filling our only empty chair.'

As our conversation had naturally turned upon the vacant seat, we lent a willing ear to this remark, and looked at our friend inquiringly.

'I feel sure,' said he, 'that Mr. Pickwick must be acquainted with somebody who would be an acquisition to us; that he must know the man we want. Pray let us not lose any time, but set this question at rest. Is it so, Mr. Pickwick?'

The gentleman addressed was about to return a verbal reply, but remembering our friend's infirmity, he substituted for this kind of answer some fifty nods. Then taking up the slate and printing on it a gigantic 'Yes,' he handed it across the table, and rubbing his hands as he looked round upon our faces, protested that he and the deaf gentleman quite understood each other, already.

'The person I have in my mind,' said Mr. Pickwick, 'and whom I should not have presumed to mention to you until some time hence, but for the opportunity you have given me, is a very strange old man. His name is Bamber.'

'Bamber!' said Jack. 'I have certainly heard the name before.'

'I have no doubt, then,' returned Mr. Pickwick, 'that you remember him in those adventures of mine (the Posthumous Papers of our old club, I mean), although he is only incidentally mentioned; and, if I remember right, appears but once.'

'That's it,' said Jack. 'Let me see. He is the person who has a grave interest in old mouldy chambers and the Inns of Court, and who relates some anecdotes having reference to his favourite theme,—and an odd ghost story,—is that the man?'

'The very same. Now,' said Mr. Pickwick, lowering his voice to a mysterious and confidential tone, 'he is a very extraordinary and remarkable person; living, and talking, and looking, like some strange spirit, whose delight is to haunt old buildings; and absorbed in that one subject which you have just mentioned, to an extent which is quite wonderful. When I retired into private life, I sought him out, and I do assure you that the more I see of him, the more strongly I am impressed with the strange and dreamy character of his mind.'

'Where does he live?' I inquired.

'He lives,' said Mr. Pickwick, 'in one of those dull, lonely old places with which his thoughts and stories are all connected; quite alone, and often shut up close for several weeks together. In this dusty solitude he broods upon the fancies he has so long indulged, and when he goes into the world, or anybody from the world without goes to see him, they are still present to his mind and still his favourite topic. I may say, I believe, that he has brought himself to entertain a regard for me, and an interest in my visits; feelings which I am certain he would extend to Master Humphrey's Clock if he were once tempted to join us. All I wish you to understand is, that he is a strange secluded visionary, in the world but not of it; and as unlike anybody here as he is unlike anybody elsewhere that I have ever met or known.'

Mr. Miles received this account of our proposed companion with rather a wry face, and after murmuring that perhaps he was a little mad, inquired if he were rich.

'I never asked him,' said Mr. Pickwick.

'You might know, sir, for all that,' retorted Mr. Miles, sharply.

'Perhaps so, sir,' said Mr. Pickwick, no less sharply than the other, 'but I do not. Indeed,' he added, relapsing into his usual mildness, 'I have no means of judging. He lives poorly, but that would seem to be in keeping with his character. I never heard him allude to his circumstances, and never fell into the society of any man who had the slightest acquaintance with them. I have really told you all I know about him, and it rests with you to say whether you wish to know more, or know quite enough already.'

We were unanimously of opinion that we would seek to know more; and as a sort of compromise with Mr. Miles (who, although he said 'Yes—O certainly—he should like to know more about the gentleman—he had no right to put himself in opposition to the general wish,' and so forth, shook his head doubtfully and hemmed several times with peculiar gravity), it was arranged that Mr. Pickwick should carry me with him on an evening visit to the subject of our discussion, for which purpose an early appointment between that gentleman and myself was immediately agreed upon; it being understood that I was to act upon my own responsibility, and to invite him to join us or not, as I might think proper. This solemn question determined, we returned to the clock-case (where we have been forestalled by the reader), and between its contents, and the conversation they occasioned, the remainder of our time passed very quickly.

When we broke up, Mr. Pickwick took me aside to tell me that he had spent a most charming and delightful evening. Having made this communication with an air of the strictest secrecy, he took Jack Redburn into another corner to tell him the same, and then retired into another corner with the deaf gentleman and the slate, to repeat the assurance. It was amusing to observe the contest in his mind whether he should extend his confidence to Mr. Miles, or treat him with dignified reserve. Half a dozen times he stepped up behind him with a friendly air, and as often stepped back again without saying a word; at last, when he was close at that gentleman's ear and upon the very point of whispering something conciliating and agreeable, Mr. Miles happened suddenly to turn his head, upon which Mr. Pickwick skipped away, and said with some fierceness, 'Good night, sir—I was about to say good night, sir,—nothing more;' and so made a bow and left him.

'Now, Sam,' said Mr. Pickwick, when he had got downstairs.

'All right, sir,' replied Mr. Weller. 'Hold hard, sir. Right arm fust—now the left—now one strong conwulsion, and the great-coat's on, sir.'

Mr. Pickwick acted upon these directions, and being further assisted by Sam, who pulled at one side of the collar, and Mr. Weller, who pulled hard at the other, was speedily enrobed. Mr. Weller, senior, then produced a full-sized stable lantern, which he had carefully deposited in a remote corner, on his arrival, and inquired whether Mr. Pickwick would have 'the lamps alight.'

'I think not to-night,' said Mr. Pickwick.

'Then if this here lady vill per-mit,' rejoined Mr. Weller, 'we'll leave it here, ready for next journey. This here lantern, mum,' said Mr. Weller, handing it to the house-keeper, 'vunce belonged to the celebrated Bill Blinder as is now at grass, as all on us vill be in our turns. Bill, mum, wos the hostler as had charge o' them two vell-known pie-bald leaders that run in the Bristol fast coach, and vould never go to no other tune but a sutherly vind and a cloudy

BLINDER'S WILL

sky, which wos consekvently played incessant, by the guard, wenever they wos on duty. He wos took wery bad one arternoon, arter having been off his feed, and wery shaky on his legs for some veeks; and he says to his mate, "Matey," he says, "I think I'm a-goin' the wrong side o' the post, and that my foot's wery near the bucket. Don't say I an't," he says, "for I know I am, and don't let me be interrupted," he says, "for I've saved a little money, and I'm a-goin' into the stable to make my last vill and testymint." "I'll take care as nobody interrupts," says his mate, "but you on'y hold up your head, and shake your ears a bit, and you're good for twenty years to come." Bill Blinder makes him no answer, but he goes avay into the stable, and there he soon artervards lays himself down a'tween the two piebalds, and dies,—previously a writin' outside the corn-chest, "This is the last vill and testymint of Villiam Blinder." They wos nat'rally wery much amazed at this, and arter looking among the litter, and up in the loft, and vere not, they opens the corn-chest, and finds that he'd been and chalked his vill inside the lid; so the lid was obligated to be took off the hinges, and sent up to Doctor Commons to be proved, and under that 'ere wery instrument this here lantern was passed to Tony Veller; vich circumstarnce, mum, gives it a wally in my eyes, and makes me rekvest, if you vill be so kind, as to take partickler care on it.'

The housekeeper graciously promised to keep the object of Mr. Weller's regard in the safest possible custody, and Mr. Pickwick, with a laughing face, took his leave. The body-guard followed, side by side; old Mr. Weller buttoned and wrapped up from his boots to his chin; and Sam with his hands in his pockets and his hat half off his head, remonstrating with his father, as he went, on his extreme loquacity.

I was not a little surprised, on turning to go up-stairs, to encounter the barber in the passage at that late hour; for his attendance is usually confined to some half-hour in the morning. But Jack Redburn, who finds out (by instinct, I think) everything that happens in the house, informed me with great glee, that a society in imitation of our own had been that night formed in the kitchen, under the title of 'Mr. Weller's Watch,' of which the barber was a member; and that he could pledge himself to find means of making me acquainted with the whole of its future proceedings, which I begged him, both on my own account and that of my readers, by no means to neglect doing.

[Old Curiosity Shop is continued here, completing No. IV.]

CHAPTER V

MR. WELLER'S WATCH

IT seems that the housekeeper and the two Mr. Wellers were no sooner left together on the occasion of their first becoming acquainted, than the housekeeper called to her assistance Mr. Slithers the barber, who had been lurking in the kitchen in expectation of her summons; and with many smiles and much sweetness introduced him as one who would assist her in the responsible office of entertaining her distinguished visitors.

'Indeed,' said she, 'without Mr. Slithers I should have been placed in quite an awkward situation.'

'There is no call for any hock'erdness, mum,' said Mr. Weller with the utmost politeness; 'no call wotsumever. A lady,' added the old gentleman, looking about him with the air of one who establishes an incontrovertible position,— 'a lady can't be hock'erd. Natur' has otherwise purwided.'

The housekeeper inclined her head and smiled yet more sweetly. The barber, who had been fluttering about Mr. Weller and Sam in a state of great anxiety to improve their acquaintance, rubbed his hands and cried, 'Hear, hear! Very true, sir;' whereupon Sam turned about and steadily regarded him for some seconds in silence.

'I never knew,' said Sam, fixing his eyes in a ruminative manner upon the blushing barber,—'I never knew but vun o' your trade, but *he* wos worth a dozen, and wos indeed dewoted to his callin'!'

'Was he in the easy shaving way, sir,' inquired Mr. Slithers, 'or in the cutting and curling line?'

'Both,' replied Sam; 'easy shavin' was his natur', and cuttin' and curlin' was his pride and glory. His whole delight wos in his trade. He spent all his money in bears, and run in debt for 'em besides, and there they wos a growling avay down in the front cellar all day long, and ineffectooally gnashing their teeth, vile the grease o' their relations and friends wos being re-tailed in gallipots in the shop above, and the first-floor winder wos ornamented vith their heads;

not to speak o' the dreadful aggrawation it must have been to 'em to see a man alvays a walkin' up and down the pavement outside, vith the portrait of a bear in his last agonies, and underneath in large letters, "Another fine animal wos slaughtered yesterday at Jinkinson's!" Hows'ever, there they wos, and there Jinkinson wos, till he wos took wery ill with some inn'ard disorder, lost the use of his legs, and wos confined to his bed, vere he laid a wery long time, but sich wos his pride in his profession, even then, that wenever he wos worse than usual the doctor used to go down-stairs and say, "Jinkinson's wery low this mornin'; we must give the bears a stir;" and as sure as ever they stirred 'em up a bit and made 'em roar, Jinkinson opens his eyes if he wos ever so bad, calls out, "There's the bears!" and rewives agin.'

'Astonishing!' cried the barber.

'Not a bit,' said Sam, 'human natur' neat as imported. Vun day the doctor happenin' to say, "I shall look in as usual to-morrow mornin'," Jinkinson catches hold of his hand and says, "Doctor," he says, "will you grant me one favour?" "I will, Jinkinson," says the doctor. "Then, doctor," says Jinkinson, "vill you come unshaved, and let me shave you?" "I will," says the doctor. "God bless you," says Jinkinson. Next day the doctor came, and arter he'd been shaved all skilful and reg'lar, he says, "Jinkinson," he says, "it's wery plain this does you good. Now," he says, "I've got a coachman as has got a beard that it 'ud warm your heart to work on, and though the footman," he says, "hasn't got much of a beard, still he's a trying it on vith a pair o' viskers to that extent that razors is Christian charity. If they take it in turns to mind the carriage when it's a waitin' below," he says, "wot's to hinder you from operatin' on both of 'em ev'ry day as well as upon me? you've got six children," he says, "wot's to hinder you from shavin' all their heads and keepin' 'em shaved? you've got two assistants in the shop down-stairs, wot's to hinder you from cuttin' and curlin' them as often as you like? Do this," he says, "and you're a man agin." Jinkinson squeedged the doctor's hand and begun that wery day; he kept his tools upon the bed, and wenever he felt his-self gettin' worse, he turned to at vun o' the children who wos a runnin' about the house vith heads like clean Dutch cheeses, and shaved him agin. Vun day the lawyer come to make his vill; all the time

he wos a takin' it down, Jinkinson was secretly a clippin'
avay at his hair vith a large pair of scissors. "Wot's that
'ere snippin' noise?" says the lawyer every now and then; "it's
like a man havin' his hair cut." "It *is* wery like a man havin'
his hair cut," says poor Jinkinson, hidin' the scissors, and
lookin' quite innocent. By the time the lawyer found it out,
he was wery nearly bald. Jinkinson wos kept alive in this
vay for a long time, but at last vun day he has in all the
children vun arter another, shaves each on 'em wery clean,
and gives him vun kiss on the crown o' his head; then he
has in the two assistants, and arter cuttin' and curlin' of
'em in the first style of elegance, says he should like to hear
the woice o' the greasiest bear, vich rekvest is immediately
complied with; then he says that he feels wery happy in his
mind and vishes to be left alone; and then he dies, previously cuttin' his own hair and makin' one flat curl in the
wery middle of his forehead.'

This anecdote produced an extraordinary effect, not only
upon Mr. Slithers, but upon the housekeeper also, who
evinced so much anxiety to please and be pleased, that
Mr. Weller, with a manner betokening some alarm, conveyed
a whispered inquiry to his son whether he had gone 'too
fur.'

'Wot do you mean by too fur?' demanded Sam.

'In that 'ere little compliment respectin' the want of
hock'erdness in ladies, Sammy,' replied his father.

'You don't think she's fallen in love with you in consekens o' that, do you?' said Sam.

'More unlikelier things have come to pass, my boy,' replied Mr. Weller in a hoarse whisper; 'I'm always afeerd
of inadwertent captiwation, Sammy. If I know'd how to
make myself ugly or unpleasant, I'd do it, Samivel, rayther
than live in this here state of perpetival terror!'

Mr. Weller had, at that time, no further opportunity of
dwelling upon the apprehensions which beset his mind, for
the immediate occasion of his fears proceeded to lead the
way down-stairs, apologising as they went for conducting
him into the kitchen, which apartment, however, she was
induced to proffer for his accommodation in preference to
her own little room, the rather as it afforded greater facili-
ties for smoking, and was immediately adjoining the ale-
cellar. The preparations which were already made sufficiently proved that these were not mere words of course, for

on the deal table were a sturdy ale-jug and glasses, flanked
with clean pipes and a plentiful supply of tobacco for the
old gentleman and his son, while on a dresser hard by was
goodly store of cold meat and other eatables. At sight of
these arrangements Mr. Weller was at first distracted
between his love of joviality and his doubts whether they
were not to be considered as so many evidences of captivation having already taken place; but he soon yielded to his
natural impulse, and took his seat at the table with a very
jolly countenance.

'As to imbibin' any o' this here flagrant veed, mum, in
the presence of a lady,' said Mr. Weller, taking up a pipe
and laying it down again, 'it couldn't be. Samivel, total
abstinence, if *you* please.'

'But I like it of all things,' said the housekeeper.

'No,' rejoined Mr. Weller, shaking his head,—'no.'

'Upon my word I do,' said the housekeeper. 'Mr.
Slithers knows I do.'

Mr. Weller coughed, and notwithstanding the barber's
confirmation of the statement, said 'No' again, but more
feebly than before. The housekeeper lighted a piece of
paper, and insisted on applying it to the bowl of the pipe
with her own fair hands; Mr. Weller resisted; the housekeeper cried that her fingers would be burnt; Mr. Weller
gave way. The pipe was ignited, Mr. Weller drew a long
puff of smoke, and detecting himself in the very act of
smiling on the housekeeper, put a sudden constraint upon
his countenance and looked sternly at the candle, with a
determination not to captivate, himself, or encourage
thoughts of captivation in others. From this iron frame
of mind he was roused by the voice of his son.

'I don't think,' said Sam, who was smoking with great
composure and enjoyment, 'that if the lady wos agreeable it
'ud be wery far out o' the vay for us four to make up a club
of our own like the governors does up-stairs, and let him,'
Sam pointed with the stem of his pipe towards his parent,
'be the president.'

The housekeeper affably declared that it was the very
thing she had been thinking of. The barber said the same.
Mr. Weller said nothing, but he laid down his pipe as if in a
fit of inspiration, and performed the following manœuvres.

Unbuttoning the three lower buttons of his waistcoat and
pausing for a moment to enjoy the easy flow of breath con-

E

sequent upon this process, he laid violent hands upon his watch-chain, and slowly and with extreme difficulty drew from his fob an immense double-cased silver watch, which brought the lining of the pocket with it, and was not to be disentangled but by great exertions and an amazing redness of face. Having fairly got it out at last, he detached the outer case and wound it up with a key of corresponding magnitude; then put the case on again, and having applied the watch to his ear to ascertain that it was still going, gave it some half-dozen hard knocks on the table to improve its performance.

'That,' said Mr. Weller, laying it on the table with its face upwards, 'is the title and emblem o' this here society. Sammy, reach them two stools this vay for the wacant cheers. Ladies and gen'lmen, Mr. Weller's Watch is vound up and now a-goin'. Order!'

By way of enforcing this proclamation, Mr. Weller, using the watch after the manner of a president's hammer, and remarking with great pride that nothing hurt it, and that falls and concussions of all kinds materially enhanced the excellence of the works and assisted the regulator, knocked the table a great many times, and declared the association formally constituted.

'And don't let's have no grinnin' at the cheer, Samivel,' said Mr. Weller to his son, 'or I shall be committin' you to the cellar, and then p'r'aps we may get into what the 'Merrikins call a fix, and the English a qvestion o' privileges.'

Having uttered this friendly caution, the President settled himself in his chair with great dignity, and requested that Mr. Samuel would relate an anecdote.

'I've told one,' said Sam.

'Wery good, sir; tell another,' returned the chair.

'We wos a talking jist now, sir,' said Sam, turning to Slithers, 'about barbers. Pursuing that 'ere fruitful theme, sir, I'll tell you in a wery few words a romantic little story about another barber as p'r'aps you may never have heerd.'

'Samivel!' said Mr. Weller, again bringing his watch and the table into smart collision, 'address your obserwations to the cheer, sir, and not to priwate indiwiduals!'

'And if I might rise to order,' said the barber in a soft voice, and looking round him with a conciliatory smile as he leant over the table, with the knuckles of his left hand resting upon it,—'if I *might* rise to order, I would suggest that

Tony and Sam Weller in the Kitchen

"barbers" is not exactly the kind of language which is
agreeable and soothing to our feelings. You, sir, will correct
me if I'm wrong, but I believe there *is* such a word in the
dictionary as hairdressers.'

'Well, but suppose he wasn't a hairdresser,' suggested
Sam.

'Wy then, sir, be parliamentary and call him vun all the
more,' returned his father. 'In the same vay as ev'ry
gen'lman in another place is a *h*onourable, ev'ry barber in
this place is a hairdresser. Ven you read the speeches in the
papers, and see as vun gen'lman says of another, "the
*h*onourable member, if he vill allow me to call him so," you
vill understand, sir, that that means, "if he vill allow me
to keep up that 'ere pleasant and uniwersal fiction."''

It is a common remark, confirmed by history and experience, that great men rise with the circumstances in which
they are placed. Mr. Weller came out so strong in his
capacity of chairman, that Sam was for some time prevented from speaking by a grin of surprise, which held his
faculties enchained, and at last subsided in a long whistle of
a single note. Nay, the old gentleman appeared even to
have astonished himself, and that to no small extent, as was
demonstrated by the vast amount of chuckling in which he
indulged, after the utterance of these lucid remarks.

'Here's the story,' said Sam. 'Vunce upon a time there
wos a young hairdresser as opened a wery smart little shop
vith four wax dummies in the winder, two gen'lmen and two
ladies—the gen'lmen vith blue dots for their beards, wery
large viskers, oudacious heads of hair, uncommon clear eyes,
and nostrils of amazin' pinkness; the ladies vith their heads
o' one side, their right forefingers on their lips, and their
forms deweloped beautiful, in vich last respect they had the
adwantage over the gen'lmen, as wasn't allowed but wery
little shoulder, and terminated rayther abrupt in fancy
drapery. He had also a many hair-brushes and tooth-
brushes bottled up in the winder, neat glass-cases on the
counter, a floor-clothed cuttin'-room up-stairs, and a
weighin'-macheen in the shop, right opposite the door. But
the great attraction and ornament wos the dummies, which
this here young hairdresser wos constantly a runnin' out in
the road to look at, and constantly a runnin' in again to
touch up and polish; in short, he wos so proud on 'em, that
ven Sunday come, he wos always wretched and mis'rable

to think they wos behind the shutters, and looked anxiously for Monday on that account. Vun o' these dummies wos a fav'rite vith him beyond the others; and ven any of his acquaintance asked him wy he didn't get married—as the young ladies he know'd, in partickler, often did—he used to say, "Never! I never vill enter into the bonds of vedlock," he says, "until I meet vith a young 'ooman as realises my idea o' that 'ere fairest dummy vith the light hair. Then, and not till then", he says, "I vill approach the altar." All the young ladies he know'd as had got dark hair told him this wos wery sinful, and that he wos wurshippin' a idle; but them as wos at all near the same shade as the dummy coloured up wery much, and wos observed to think him a wery nice young man.'

'Samivel,' said Mr. Weller, gravely, 'a member o' this associashun bein' one o' that 'ere tender sex which is now immedetly referred to, I have to rekvest that you vill make no reflections.'

'I ain't a makin' any, am I?' inquired Sam.

'Order, sir!' rejoined Mr. Weller, with severe dignity. Then, sinking the chairman in the father, he added, in his usual tone of voice: 'Samivel, drive on!'

Sam interchanged a smile with the housekeeper, and proceeded:

'The young hairdresser hadn't been in the habit o' makin' this avowal above six months, ven he en-countered a young lady as wos the wery picter o' the fairest dummy. "Now," he says, "it's all up. I am a slave!" The young lady wos not only the picter o' the fairest dummy, but she was wery romantic, as the young hairdresser was, too, and he says, "O!" he says, "here's a community o' feelin', here's a flow o' soul!" he says, "here's a interchange o' sentiment!" The young lady didn't say much, o' course, but she expressed herself agreeable, and shortly artervards vent to see him vith a mutual friend. The hairdresser rushes out to meet her, but d'rectly she sees the dummies she changes colour and falls a tremblin' wiolently. "Look up, my love," says the hairdresser, "behold your imige in my winder, but not correcter than in my art!" "My imige!" she says. "Yourn!" replies the hairdresser. "But whose imige is *that?*" she says, a pinting at vun o' the gen'lmen. "No vun's, my love," he says, "it is but a idea." "A idea!" she cries: "it is a portrait, I feel it is a portrait, and that 'ere noble face must be in the millingtary!" "Wot do I hear!" says he, a crumplin' his curls. "Villiam Gibbs," she says, quite firm, "never renoo the subject. I respect you as a friend," she says, "but my affections is set upon that manly brow." "This," says the hairdresser, "is a reg'lar blight, and in it I perceive the hand of Fate. Farevell!" Vith these vords he rushes into the shop, breaks the dummy's nose vith a blow of his curlin'-irons, melts him down at the parlour fire, and never smiles artervards.'

'The young lady, Mr. Weller?' said the housekeeper.

'Why, ma'am,' said Sam, 'findin' that Fate had a spite agin her, and everybody she come into contact vith, she never smiled neither, but read a deal o' poetry and pined avay,—by rayther slow degrees, for she ain't dead yet. It took a deal o' poetry to kill the hairdresscr, and some people say arter all that it wos more the gin and water as caused him to be run over; p'r'aps it was a little o' both, and came o' mixing the two.'

The barber declared that Mr. Weller had related one of the most interesting stories that had ever come within his knowledge, in which opinion the housekeeper entirely concurred.

'Are you a married man, sir?' inquired Sam.

The barber replied that he had not that honour.

'I s'pose you mean to be?' said Sam.

'Well,' replied the barber, rubbing his hands smirkingly, 'I don't know, I don't think it's very likely.'

'That's a bad sign,' said Sam; 'if you'd said you meant to be vun o' these days, I should ha' looked upon you as bein' safe. You're in a wery precarious state.'

'I am not conscious of any danger, at all events,' returned the barber.

'No more wos I, sir,' said the elder Mr. Weller, interposing; 'those vere my symptoms, exactly. I've been took that vay twice. Keep your vether eye open, my friend, or you're gone.'

There was something so very solemn about this admonition, both in its matter and manner, and also in the way in which Mr. Weller still kept his eye fixed upon the unsuspecting victim, that nobody cared to speak for some little time, and might not have cared to do so for some time longer, if the housekeeper had not happened to sigh, which called off the old gentleman's attention and gave rise to a gallant inquiry whether 'there wos anythin' wery piercin in that 'ere little heart ?'

'Dear me, Mr. Weller!' said the housekeeper, laughing.

'No, but is there anythin' as agitates it ?' pursued the old gentleman. 'Has it always been obderrate, always opposed to the happiness o' human creeturs ? Eh ? Has it ?'

At this critical juncture for her blushes and confusion, the housekeeper discovered that more ale was wanted, and hastily withdrew into the cellar to draw the same, followed by the barber, who insisted on carrying the candle. Having looked after her with a very complacent expression of face, and after him with some disdain, Mr. Weller caused his glance to travel slowly round the kitchen, until at length it rested on his son.

'Sammy,' said Mr. Weller, 'I mistrust that barber.'

'Wot for ?' returned Sam ; 'wot's he got to do with you ? You're a nice man, you are, arter pretendin' all kinds o' terror, to go a payin' compliments and talkin' about hearts and piercers.'

The imputation of gallantry appeared to afford Mr. Weller the utmost delight, for he replied in a voice choked by suppressed laughter, and with the tears in his eyes.

'Wos I a talkin' about hearts and piercers,—wos I though, Sammy, eh ?'

'Wos you ? of course you wos.'

'She don't know no better, Sammy, there ain't no harm in it,—no danger, Sammy ; she's only a punster. She seemed pleased, though, didn't she ? O' course, she wos pleased, it's nat'ral she should be, wery nat'ral.'

'He's wain of it!' exclaimed Sam, joining in his father's mirth. 'He's actually wain!'

'Hush!' replied Mr. Weller, composing his features, 'they're a comin' back,—the little heart's a comin' back. But mark these wurds o' mine once more, and remember 'em ven your father says he said 'em. Samivel, I mistrust that 'ere deceitful barber.'

[Old Curiosity Shop is continued to the end of the number.]

CHAPTER VI

MASTER HUMPHREY, FROM HIS CLOCK-SIDE
IN THE CHIMNEY-CORNER

Two or three evenings after the institution of Mr. Weller's Watch, I thought I heard, as I walked in the garden, the voice of Mr. Weller himself at no great distance; and stopping once or twice to listen more attentively, I found that the sounds proceeded from my housekeeper's little sitting-room, which is at the back of the house. I took no further notice of the circumstance at that time, but it formed the subject of a conversation between me and my friend Jack Redburn next morning, when I found that I had not been deceived in my impression. Jack furnished me with the following particulars; and as he appeared to take extraordinary pleasure in relating them, I have begged him in future to jot down any such domestic scenes or occurrences that may please his humour, in order that they may be told in his own way. I must confess that, as Mr. Pickwick and he are constantly together, I have been influenced, in making this request, by a secret desire to know something of their proceedings.

On the evening in question, the housekeeper's room was arranged with particular care, and the housekeeper herself was very smartly dressed. The preparations, however, were not confined to mere showy demonstrations, as tea was prepared for three persons, with a small display of preserves and jams and sweet cakes, which heralded some uncommon occasion. Miss Benton (my housekeeper bears that name) was in a state of great expectation, too, frequently going to the front door and looking anxiously down the lane, and more than once observing to the servant-girl that she expected company, and hoped no accident had happened to delay them.

A modest ring at the bell at length allayed her fears, and Miss Benton, hurrying into her own room and shutting herself up, in order that she might preserve that appearance of being taken by surprise which is so essential to the polite

reception of visitors, awaited their coming with a smiling
countenance.

'Good ev'nin', mum,' said the older Mr. Weller, looking
in at the door after a prefatory tap. 'I'm afeerd we've come
in rayther arter the time, mum, but the young colt being full
o' wice, has been a boltin' and shyin' and gettin' his leg over
the traces to sich a extent that if he an't wery soon broke in,
he'll wex me into a broken heart, and then he'll never be
brought out no more except to learn his letters from the
writin' on his grandfather's tombstone.'

With these pathetic words, which were addressed to
something outside the door about two feet six from the
ground, Mr. Weller introduced a very small boy firmly set
upon a couple of very sturdy legs, who looked as if nothing
could ever knock him down. Besides having a very round
face strongly resembling Mr. Weller's, and a stout little
body of exactly his build, this young gentleman, standing
with his little legs very wide apart, as if the top-boots were
familiar to them, actually winked upon the housekeeper
with his infant eye, in imitation of his grandfather.

'There's a naughty boy, mum,' said Mr. Weller, bursting
with delight, 'there's a immoral Tony. Wos there ever
a little chap o' four year and eight months old as vinked his
eye at a strange lady afore?'

As little affected by this observation as by the former
appeal to his feelings, Master Weller elevated in the air
a small model of a coach whip which he carried in his hand,
and addressing the housekeeper with a shrill 'ya—hip!'
inquired if she was 'going down the road;' at which happy
adaptation of a lesson he had been taught from infancy,
Mr. Weller could restrain his feelings no longer, but gave
him twopence on the spot.

'It's in wain to deny it, mum,' said Mr. Weller, 'this
here is a boy arter his grandfather's own heart, and beats
out all the boys as ever wos or will be. Though at the same
time, mum,' added Mr. Weller, trying to look gravely down
upon his favourite, 'it was wery wrong on him to want to—
over all the posts as we come along, and wery cruel on him
to force poor grandfather to lift him cross-legged over every
vun of 'em. He vouldn't pass vun single blessed post, mum,
and at the top o' the lane there's seven-and-forty on 'em all
in a row, and wery close together.'

Here Mr. Weller, whose feelings were in a perpetual con-

Tony Weller and his Grandson at the Housekeeper's

flict between pride in his grandson's achievements and a
sense of his own responsibility, and the importance of im-
pressing him with moral truths, burst into a fit of laughter,
and suddenly checking himself, remarked in a severe tone
that little boys as made their grandfathers put 'em over
posts never went to heaven at any price.

By this time the housekeeper had made tea, and little
Tony, placed on a chair beside her, with his eyes nearly on a
level with the top of the table, was provided with various
delicacies which yielded him extreme contentment. The
housekeeper (who seemed rather afraid of the child, notwithstanding her caresses) then patted him on the head, and
declared that he was the finest boy she had ever seen.

'Wy, mum,' said Mr. Weller, 'I don't think you'll see
a many sich, and that's the truth. But if my son Samivel
vould give me my vay, mum, and only dis-pense vith his—
might I wenter to say the vurd?'

'What word, Mr. Weller?' said the housekeeper, blushing
slightly.

'Petticuts, mum,' returned that gentleman, laying his
hand upon the garments of his grandson. 'If my son
Samivel, mum, vould only dis-pense vith these here, you'd
see sich a alteration in his appearance, as the imagination
can't depicter.'

'But what would you have the child wear instead, Mr.
Weller?' said the housekeeper.

'I've offered my son Samivel, mum, agen and agen,'
returned the old gentleman, 'to purwide him at my own
cost vith a suit o' clothes as 'ud be the makin' on him, and
form his mind in infancy for those pursuits as I hope the
family o' the Vellers vill alvays dewote themselves to. Tony,
my boy, tell the lady wot them clothes are, as grandfather
says, father ought to let you vear.'

'A little white hat and a little sprig weskut and little
knee cords and little top-boots and a little green coat with
little bright buttons and a little welwet collar,' replied Tony,
with great readiness and no stops.

'That's the cos-toom, mum,' said Mr. Weller, looking
proudly at the housekeeper. 'Once make sich a model on
him as that, and you'd say he *wos* a angel!'

Perhaps the housekeeper thought that in such a guise
young Tony would look more like the angel at Islington than
anything else of that name, or perhaps she was disconcerted

to find her previously-conceived ideas disturbed, as angels are not commonly represented in top-boots and sprig waist-coats. She coughed doubtfully, but said nothing.

'How many brothers and sisters have you, my dear?' she asked, after a short silence.

'One brother and no sister at all,' replied Tony, 'Sam his name is, and so's my father's. Do you know my father?'

'O yes, I know him,' said the housekeeper, graciously.

'Is my father fond of you?' pursued Tony.

'I hope so,' rejoined the smiling housekeeper.

Tony considered a moment, and then said, 'Is my grand-father fond of you?'

This would seem a very easy question to answer, but in-stead of replying to it, the housekeeper smiled in great confusion, and said that really children did ask such extra-ordinary questions that it was the most difficult thing in the world to talk to them. Mr. Weller took upon himself to reply that he was very fond of the lady; but the housekeeper entreating that he would not put such things into the child's head, Mr. Weller shook his own while she looked another way, and seemed to be troubled with a misgiving that cap-tivation was in progress. It was, perhaps, on this account that he changed the subject precipitately.

'It's wery wrong in little boys to make game o' their grandfathers, an't it, mum?' said Mr. Weller, shaking his head waggishly, until Tony looked at him, when he counter-fcitcd the deepest dejection and sorrow.

'O, very sad!' assented the housekeeper. 'But I hope no little boys do that?'

'There is vun young Turk, mum,' said Mr. Weller, 'as havin' seen his grandfather a little overcome vith drink on the occasion of a friend's birthday, goes a reelin' and stag-gerin' about the house, and makin' believe that he's the old gen'lm'n.'

'O, quite shocking!' cried the housekeeper.

'Yes, mum,' said Mr. Weller; 'and previously to so doin', this 'ere young traitor that I'm a speakin' of, pinches his little nose to make it red, and then he gives a hiccup and says,"I'm all right," he says; "give us another song!" Ha, ha! "Give us another song," he says. Ha, ha, ha!'

In his excessive delight, Mr. Weller was quite unmindful of his moral responsibility, until little Tony kicked up his legs, and laughing immoderately, cried, 'That was me, that was;' whereupon the grandfather, by a great effort, became extremely solemn.

'No, Tony, not you,' said Mr. Weller. 'I hope it warn't you, Tony. It must ha' been that 'ere naughty little chap as comes sometimes out o' the empty watch-box round the corner,—that same little chap as wos found standin' on the table afore the lookin'-glass, pretending to shave himself vith a oyster-knife.'

'He didn't hurt himself, I hope?' observed the house-keeper.

'Not he, mum,' said Mr. Weller proudly; 'bless your heart, you might trust that 'ere boy vith a steam-engine a'most, he's sich a knowin' young'—but suddenly recollecting himself and observing that Tony perfectly understood and appreciated the compliment, the old gentleman groaned and observed that 'it wos all wery shockin''—wery.'

'O, he's a bad 'un,' said Mr. Weller, 'is that 'ere watch-box boy, makin' sich a noise and litter in the back yard, he does, watcrin' wooden horses and feedin' of 'em vith grass, and perpetivally spillin' his little brother out of a veelbarrow and frightenin' his mother out of her vits, at the wery moment wen she's expectin' to increase his stock of happiness vith another play-feller,—O, he's a bad 'un! He's even gone so far as to put on a pair of paper spectacles as he got his father to make for him, and walk up and down the garden vith his hands behind him in imitation of Mr. Pickwick,—but Tony don't do sich things, O no!'

'O no!' echoed Tony.

'He knows better, he does,' said Mr. Weller. 'He knows that if he wos to come sich games as these nobody vouldn't love him, and that his grandfather in partickler couldn't abear the sight on him; for vich reasons Tony's alvays good.'

'Always good,' echoed Tony; and his grandfather immediately took him on his knee and kissed him, at the same time, with many nods and winks, slyly pointing at the child's head with his thumb, in order that the housekeeper, otherwise deceived by the admirable manner in which he (Mr. Weller) had sustained his character, might not suppose that any other young gentleman was referred to, and might clearly understand that the boy of the watch-box was but an imaginary creation, and a fetch of Tony himself, invented for his improvement and reformation.

Not confining himself to a mere verbal description of his

grandson's abilities, Mr. Weller, when tea was finished, invited him by various gifts of pence and halfpence to smoke imaginary pipes, drink visionary beer from real pots, imitate his grandfather without reserve, and in particular to go through the drunken scene, which threw the old gentleman into ecstasies and filled the housekeeper with wonder. Nor was Mr. Weller's pride satisfied with even this display, for when he took his leave he carried the child, like some rare and astonishing curiosity, first to the barber's house and afterwards to the tobacconist's, at each of which places he repeated his performances with the utmost effect to applauding and delighted audiences. It was half-past nine o'clock when Mr. Weller was last seen carrying him home upon his shoulder, and it has been whispered abroad that at that time the infant Tony was rather intoxicated.

[Old Curiosity Shop is continued from here to the end without further break.]

_____

[Master Humphrey is revived thus at the close of the Old Curiosity Shop, merely to introduce Barnaby Rudge.]

I was musing the other evening upon the characters and incidents with which I had been so long engaged; wondering how I could ever have looked forward with pleasure to the completion of my tale, and reproaching myself for having done so, as if it were a kind of cruelty to those companions of my solitude whom I had now dismissed, and could never again recall; when my clock struck ten. Punctual to the hour, my friends appeared.

On our last night of meeting, we had finished the story which the reader has just concluded. Our conversation took the same current as the meditations which the entrance of my friends had interrupted, and The Old Curiosity Shop was the staple of our discourse.

I may confide to the reader now, that in connection with this little history I had something upon my mind; something to communicate which I had all along with difficulty repressed; something I had deemed it, during the progress of the story, necessary to its interest to disguise, and which, now that it was over, I wished, and was yet reluctant, to disclose.

To conceal anything from those to whom I am attached, is not in my nature. I can never close my lips where I have opened my heart. This temper, and the consciousness of having done some violence to it in my narrative, laid me under a restraint which I should have had great difficulty in overcoming, but for a timely remark from Mr. Miles, who, as I hinted in a former paper, is a gentleman of business habits, and of great exactness and propriety in all his transactions.

'I could have wished,' my friend objected, 'that we had been made acquainted with the single gentleman's name. I don't like his withholding his name. It made me look upon him at first with suspicion, and caused me to doubt his moral character, I assure you. I am fully satisfied by this time of his being a worthy creature; but in this respect he certainly would not appear to have acted at all like a man of business.'

'My friends,' said I, drawing to the table, at which they were by this time seated in their usual chairs, 'do you remember that this story bore another title besides that one we have so often heard of late ?'

Mr. Miles had his pocket-book out in an instant, and referring to an entry therein, rejoined, 'Certainly. Personal Adventures of Master Humphrey. Here it is. I made a note of it at the time.'

I was about to resume what I had to tell them, when the same Mr. Miles again interrupted me, observing that the narrative originated in a personal adventure of my own, and that was no doubt the reason for its being thus designated.

This led me to the point at once.

'You will one and all forgive me,' I returned, 'if for the greater convenience of the story, and for its better introduction, that adventure was fictitious. I had my share, indeed, —no light or trivial one,—in the pages we have read, but it was not the share I feigned to have at first. The younger brother, the single gentleman, the nameless actor in this little drama, stands before you now.'

It was easy to see they had not expected this disclosure.

'Yes,' I pursued. 'I can look back upon my part in it with a calm, half-smiling pity for myself as for some other man. But I am he, indeed; and now the chief sorrows of my life are yours.'

I need not say what true gratification I derived from the sympathy and kindness with which this acknowledgment was received; nor how often it had risen to my lips before;

nor how difficult I had found it—how impossible, when I came to those passages which touched me most, and most nearly concerned me—to sustain the character I had assumed. It is enough to say that I replaced in the clock-case the record of so many trials,—sorrowfully, it is true, but with a softened sorrow which was almost pleasure; and felt that in living through the past again, and communicating to others the lesson it had helped to teach me, I had been a happier man.

We lingered so long over the leaves from which I had read, that as I consigned them to their former resting-place, the hand of my trusty clock pointed to twelve, and there came towards us upon the wind the voice of the deep and distant bell of St. Paul's as it struck the hour of midnight.

'This,' said I, returning with a manuscript I had taken at the moment from the same repository, 'to be opened to such music, should be a tale where London's face by night is darkly seen, and where some deed of such a time as this is dimly shadowed out. Which of us here has seen the working of that great machine whose voice has just now ceased?'

Mr. Pickwick had, of course, and so had Mr. Miles. Jack and my deaf friend were in the minority.

I had seen it but a few days before, and could not help telling them of the fancy I had about it.

I paid my fee of twopence upon entering, to one of the money-changers who sit within the Temple; and falling, after a few turns up and down, into the quiet train of thought which such a place awakens, paced the echoing stones like some old monk whose present world lay all within its walls. As I looked afar up into the lofty dome, I could not help wondering what were his reflections whose genius reared that mighty pile, when, the last small wedge of timber fixed, the last nail driven into its home for many centuries, the clang of hammers, and the hum of busy voices gone, and the Great Silence whole years of noise had helped to make, reigning undisturbed around, he mused, as I did now, upon his work, and lost himself amid its vast extent. I could not quite determine whether the contemplation of it would impress him with a sense of greatness or of insignificance; but when I remembered how long a time it had taken to erect, in how short a space it might be traversed even to its remotest parts, for how brief a term he, or any of

Barnaby Rudge in *Master Humphrey's*
Imagination

those who cared to bear his name, would live to see it, or know of its existence, I imagined him far more melancholy than proud, and looking with regret upon his labour done. With these thoughts in my mind, I began to ascend, almost unconsciously, the flight of steps leading to the several wonders of the building, and found myself before a barrier where another money-taker sat, who demanded which among them I would choose to see. There were the stone gallery, he said, and the whispering gallery, the geometrical staircase, the room of models, the clock—the clock being quite in my way, I stopped him there, and chose that sight from all the rest.

I groped my way into the Turret which it occupies, and saw before me, in a kind of loft, what seemed to be a great, old oaken press with folding doors. These being thrown back by the attendant (who was sleeping when I came upon him, and looked a drowsy fellow, as though his close companionship with Time had made him quite indifferent to it), disclosed a complicated crowd of wheels and chains in iron and brass,—great, sturdy, rattling engines,—suggestive of breaking a finger put in here or there, and grinding the bone to powder,—and these were the Clock! Its very pulse, if I may use the word, was like no other clock. It did not mark the flight of every moment with a gentle second stroke, as though it would check old Time, and have him stay his pace in pity, but measured it with one sledge-hammer beat, as if its business were to crush the seconds as they came trooping on, and remorselessly to clear a path before the Day of Judgment.

I sat down opposite to it, and hearing its regular and never-changing voice, that one deep constant note, uppermost amongst all the noise and clatter in the streets below,— marking that, let that tumult rise or fall, go on or stop,—let it be night or noon, to-morrow or to-day, this year or next, —it still performed its functions with the same dull constancy, and regulated the progress of the life around, the fancy came upon me that this was London's Heart, and that when it should cease to beat, the City would be no more.

It is night. Calm and unmoved amidst the scenes that darkness favours, the great heart of London throbs in its Giant breast. Wealth and beggary, vice and virtue, guilt and innocence, repletion and the direst hunger, all treading on each other and crowding together, are gathered round it. Draw but a little circle above the clustering housetops, and you shall have within its space everything, with its opposite extreme and contradiction, close beside. Where yonder feeble light is shining, a man is but this moment dead. The taper at a few yards' distance is seen by eyes that have this instant opened on the world. There are two houses separated by but an inch or two of wall. In one, there are quiet minds at rest; in the other, a waking conscience that one might think would trouble the very air. In that close corner where the roofs shrink down and cower together as if to hide their secrets from the handsome street hard by, there are such dark crimes, such miseries and horrors, as could be hardly told in whispers. In the handsome street, there are folks asleep who have dwelt there all their lives, and have no more knowledge of these things than if they had never been, or were transacted at the remotest limits of the world,—who, if they were hinted at, would shake their heads, look wise, and frown, and say they were impossible, and out of Nature,—as if all great towns were not. Does not this Heart of London, that nothing moves, nor stops, nor quickens,—that goes on the same let what will be done,—does it not express the City's character well?

The day begins to break, and soon there is the hum and noise of life. Those who have spent the night on doorsteps and cold stones crawl off to beg; they who have slept in beds come forth to their occupation, too, and business is astir. The fog of sleep rolls slowly off, and London shines awake. The streets are filled with carriages, and people gaily clad. The jails are full, too, to the throat, nor have the workhouses or hospitals much room to spare. The courts of law are crowded. Taverns have their regular frequenters by this time, and every mart of traffic has its throng. Each of these places is a world, and has its own inhabitants; each is distinct from, and almost unconscious of the existence of any other. There are some few people well to do, who remember to have heard it said, that numbers of men and women—thousands, they think it was—get up in London every day, unknowing where to lay their heads at night; and that there are quarters of the town where misery and famine always are. They don't believe it quite,—there may be some truth in it, but it is exaggerated, of course. So, each of these thousand worlds goes on, intent upon itself, until night comes again,—first with its lights and pleasures, and its cheerful streets; then with its guilt and darkness.

Heart of London, there is a moral in thy every stroke! as I look on at thy indomitable working, which neither death, nor press of life, nor grief, nor gladness out of doors will influence one jot, I seem to hear a voice within thee which sinks into my heart, bidding me, as I elbow my way among the crowd, have some thought for the meanest wretch that passes, and, being a man, to turn away with scorn and pride from none that bear the human shape.

I am by no means sure that I might not have been tempted to enlarge upon the subject, had not the papers that lay before me on the table been a silent reproach for even this digression. I took them up again when I had got thus far, and seriously prepared to read.

The handwriting was strange to me, for the manuscript had been fairly copied. As it is against our rules, in such a case, to inquire into the authorship until the reading is concluded, I could only glance at the different faces round me, in search of some expression which should betray the writer. Whoever he might be, he was prepared for this, and gave no sign for my enlightenment.

I had the papers in my hand, when my deaf friend interposed with a suggestion.

'It has occurred to me,' he said, 'bearing in mind your sequel to the tale we have finished, that if such of us as have anything to relate of our own lives could interweave it with our contribution to the Clock, it would be well to do so. This need be no restraint upon us, either as to time, or place, or incident, since any real passage of this kind may be surrounded by fictitious circumstances, and represented by fictitious characters. What if we make this an article of agreement among ourselves?'

The proposition was cordially received, but the difficulty appeared to be that here was a long story written before we had thought of it.

'Unless,' said I, 'it should have happened that the writer of this tale—which is not impossible, for men are apt to do so when they write—has actually mingled with it something of his own endurance and experience.'

Nobody spoke, but I thought I detected in one quarter that this was really the case.

'If I have no assurance to the contrary,' I added, there-fore, 'I shall take it for granted that he has done so, and that even these papers come within our new agreement. Everybody being mute, we hold that understanding, if you please.'

And here I was about to begin again, when Jack informed us softly, that during the progress of our last narrative, Mr. Weller's Watch had adjourned its sittings from the kitchen, and regularly met outside our door, where he had no doubt that august body would be found at the present moment. As this was for the convenience of listening to our stories, he submitted that they might be suffered to come in, and hear them more pleasantly.

To this we one and all yielded a ready assent, and the party being discovered, as Jack had supposed, and invited to walk in, entered (though not without great confusion at having been detected), and were accommodated with chairs at a little distance.

Then, the lamp being trimmed, the fire well stirred and burning brightly, the hearth clean swept, the curtains closely drawn, the clock wound up, we entered on our new story.

[This was Barnaby Rudge.]

[This is, as indicated, the final appearance of Master Humphrey's Clock. It forms the conclusion of Barnaby Rudge.]

It is again midnight. My fire burns cheerfully; the room is filled with my old friend's sober voice; and I am left to muse upon the story we have just now finished.

It makes me smile, at such a time as this, to think if there were any one to see me sitting in my easy-chair, my gray head hanging down, my eyes bent thoughtfully upon the glowing embers, and my crutch—emblem of my helplessness—lying upon the hearth at my feet, how solitary I should seem. Yet though I am the sole tenant of this chimney-corner, though I am childless and old, I have no sense of loneliness at this hour; but am the centre of a silent group whose company I love.

Thus, even age and weakness have their consolations. If I were a younger man, if I were more active, more strongly bound and tied to life, these visionary friends would shun me, or I should desire to fly from them. Being what I am, I can court their society, and delight in it; and pass whole hours in picturing to myself the shadows that perchance flock every night into this chamber, and in imagining with pleasure what kind of interest they have in the frail, feeble mortal who is its sole inhabitant.

All the friends I have ever lost I find again among these visitors. I love to fancy their spirits hovering about me, feeling still some earthly kindness for their old companion, and watching his decay. 'He is weaker, he declines apace, he draws nearer and nearer to us, and will soon be conscious of our existence.' What is there to alarm me in this? It is encouragement and hope.

These thoughts have never crowded on me half so fast as they have done to-night. Faces I had long forgotten have become familiar to me once again; traits I had endeavoured to recall for years have come before me in an instant; nothing is changed but me; and even I can be my former self at will.

Raising my eyes but now to the face of my old clock, I remember, quite involuntarily, the veneration, not un-mixed with a sort of childish awe, with which I used to sit and watch it as it ticked, unheeded in a dark staircase corner. I recollect looking more grave and steady when I met its dusty face, as if, having that strange kind of life within it, and being free from all excess of vulgar appetite, and warning all the house by night and day, it were a sage. How often have I listened to it as it told the beads of time and wondered at its constancy! How often watched it slowly pointing round the dial, and, while I panted for the eagerly expected hour to come, admired, despite myself, its steadiness of purpose and lofty freedom from all human strife, impatience, and desire!

I thought it cruel once. It was very hard of heart, to my mind, I remember. It was an old servant even then; and I felt as though it ought to show some sorrow; as though it wanted sympathy with us in our distress, and were a dull, heartless, mercenary creature. Ah! how soon I learnt to know that in its ceaseless going on, and in its being checked or stayed by nothing, lay its greatest kind-ness, and the only balm for grief and wounded peace of mind.

To-night, to-night, when this tranquillity and calm are on my spirits, and memory presents so many shifting scenes before me, I take my quiet stand at will by many a fire that has been long extinguished, and mingle with the cheerful group that cluster round it. If I could be sorrowful in such a mood, I should grow sad to think what a poor blot I was upon their youth and beauty once, and now how few remain to put me to the blush; I should grow sad to think that such among them as I sometimes meet with in my daily walks are scarcely less infirm than I; that time has brought us to a level; and that all distinctions fade and vanish as we take our trembling steps towards the grave.

But memory was given us for better purposes than this, and mine is not a torment, but a source of pleasure. To muse upon the gaiety and youth I have known suggests to me glad scenes of harmless mirth that may be passing now. From contemplating them apart, I soon become an actor in these little dramas, and humouring my fancy, lose myself among the beings it invokes.

When my fire is bright and high, and a warm blush mantles in the walls and ceiling of this ancient room; when my clock makes cheerful music, like one of those chirping insects who delight in the warm hearth, and are sometimes, by a good superstition, looked upon as the harbingers of fortune and plenty to that household in whose mercies they put their humble trust; when everything is in a ruddy genial glow, and there are voices in the crackling flame, and smiles in its flashing light, other smiles and other voices congregate around me, invading, with their pleasant harmony, the silence of the time.

For then a knot of youthful creatures gather round my fireside, and the room re-echoes to their merry voices. My solitary chair no longer holds its ample place before the fire, but is wheeled into a smaller corner, to leave more room for the broad circle formed about the cheerful hearth. I have sons, and daughters, and grandchildren, and we are assembled on some occasion of rejoicing common to us all. It is a birthday, perhaps, or perhaps it may be Christmas time; but be it what it may, there is rare holiday among us; we are full of glee.

In the chimney-corner, opposite myself, sits one who has grown old beside me. She is changed, of course; much changed; and yet I recognise the girl even in that gray hair and wrinkled brow. Glancing from the laughing child who half hides in her ample skirts, and half peeps out,—and from her to the little matron of twelve years old, who sits so womanly and so demure at no great distance from me,—

and from her again, to a fair girl in the full bloom of early
womanhood, the centre of the group, who has glanced more
than once towards the opening door, and by whom the
children, whispering and tittering among themselves, *will*
leave a vacant chair, although she bids them not,—I see
her image thrice repeated, and feel how long it is before one
form and set of features wholly pass away, if ever, from
among the living. While I am dwelling upon this, and
tracing out the gradual change from infancy to youth, from
youth to perfect growth, from that to age, and thinking,
with an old man's pride, that she is comely yet, I feel a
slight thin hand upon my arm, and, looking down, see seated
at my feet a crippled boy,—a gentle, patient child,—
whose aspect I know well. He rests upon a little crutch,
—I know it too,—and leaning on it as he climbs my footstool, whispers in my ear, 'I am hardly one of these, dear
grandfather, although I love them dearly. They are very
kind to me, but you will be kinder still, I know.'

I have my hand upon his neck, and stoop to kiss him,
when my clock strikes, my chair is in its old spot, and I am
alone.

What if I be ? What if this fireside be tenantless, save
for the presence of one weak old man ? From my house-top
I can look upon a hundred homes, in every one of which
these social companions are matters of reality. In my daily
walks I pass a thousand men whose cares are all forgotten,
whose labours are made light, whose dull routine of work
from day to day is cheered and brightened by their glimpses
of domestic joy at home. Amid the struggles of this
struggling town what cheerful sacrifices are made; what toil
endured with readiness; what patience shown and fortitude
displayed for the mere sake of home and its affections! Let
me thank Heaven that I can people my fireside with shadows
such as these; with shadows of bright objects that exist in
crowds about me; and let me say, 'I am alone no more.'

I never was less so—I write it with a grateful heart—than
I am to-night. Recollections of the past and visions of the
present come to bear me company; the meanest man to
whom I have ever given alms appears, to add his mite of
peace and comfort to my stock; and whenever the fire
within me shall grow cold, to light my path upon this earth
no more, I pray that it may be at such an hour as this, and
when I love the world as well as I do now.

THE DEAF GENTLEMAN FROM HIS OWN APARTMENT

Our dear friend laid down his pen at the end of the foregoing paragraph, to take it up no more. I little thought
ever to employ mine upon so sorrowful a task as that which
he has left me, and to which I now devote it.

As he did not appear among us at his usual hour next
morning, we knocked gently at his door. No answer being
given, it was softly opened; and then, to our surprise, we
saw him seated before the ashes of his fire, with a little table
I was accustomed to set at his elbow when I left him for the
night at a short distance from him, as though he had pushed
it away with the idea of rising and retiring to his bed. His
crutch and footstool lay at his feet as usual, and he was
dressed in his chamber-gown, which he had put on before I
left him. He was reclining in his chair, in his accustomed
posture, with his face towards the fire, and seemed absorbed
in meditation,—indeed, at first, we almost hoped he was.

Going up to him, we found him dead. I have often, very
often, seen him sleeping, and always peacefully, but I never
saw him look so calm and tranquil. His face wore a serene,
benign expression, which had impressed me very strongly
when we last shook hands; not that he had ever had any
other look, God knows; but there was something in this so
very spiritual, so strangely and indefinably allied to youth,
although his head was gray and venerable, that it was new
even in him. It came upon me all at once when on some
slight pretence he called me back upon the previous night
to take me by the hand again, and once more say, 'God
bless you.'

A bell-rope hung within his reach, but he had not moved
towards it; nor had he stirred, we all agreed, except, as I
have said, to push away his table, which he could have done,
and no doubt did, with a very slight motion of his hand.
He had relapsed for a moment into his late train of meditation, and, with a thoughtful smile upon his face, had died.

I had long known it to be his wish that whenever this
event should come to pass we might be all assembled in the
house. I therefore lost no time in sending for Mr. Pickwick
and for Mr. Miles, both of whom arrived before the
messenger's return.

It is not my purpose to dilate upon the sorrow and affectionate emotions of which I was at once the witness and
the sharer. But I may say, of the humbler mourners, that

his faithful housekeeper was fairly heart-broken; that the poor barber would not be comforted; and that I shall respect the homely truth and warmth of heart of Mr. Weller and his son to the last moment of my life.

'And the sweet old creetur, sir,' said the elder Mr. Weller to me in the afternoon, 'has bolted. Him as had no wice, and was so free from temper that a infant might ha' drove him, has been took at last with that 'ere unawoidable fit of staggers as we all must come to, and gone off his feed for ever! I see him,' said the old gentleman, with a moisture in his eye, which could not be mistaken,—'I see him gettin', every journey, more and more groggy; I says to Samivel, "My boy! the Grey's a-goin' at the knees;" and now my predilictions is fatally werified, and him as I could never do enough to serve or show my likin' for, is up the great uniwersal spout o' natur'.'

I was not the less sensible of the old man's attachment because he expressed it in his peculiar manner. Indeed, I can truly assert of both him and his son, that notwithstanding the extraordinary dialogues they held together, and the strange commentaries and corrections with which each of them illustrated the other's speech, I do not think it possible to exceed the sincerity of their regret; and that I am sure their thoughtfulness and anxiety in anticipating the discharge of many little offices of sympathy would have done honour to the most delicate-minded persons.

Our friend had frequently told us that his will would be found in a box in the Clock-case, the key of which was in his writing-desk. As he had told us also that he desired it to be opened immediately after his death, whenever that should happen, we met together that night for the fulfilment of his request.

We found it where he had told us, wrapped in a sealed paper, and with it a codicil of recent date, in which he named Mr. Miles and Mr. Pickwick his executors,—as having no need of any greater benefit from his estate than a generous token (which he bequeathed to them) of his friendship and remembrance.

After pointing out the spot in which he wished his ashes to repose, he gave to 'his dear old friends,' Jack Redburn and myself, his house, his books, his furniture,—in short, all that his house contained; and with this legacy more ample means of maintaining it in its present state than we, with our habits and at our terms of life, can ever exhaust. Besides these gifts, he left to us, in trust, an annual sum of no insignificant amount, to be distributed in charity among his accustomed pensioners—they are a long list—and such other claimants on his bounty as might, from time to time, present themselves. And as true charity not only covers a multitude of sins, but includes a multitude of virtues, such as forgiveness, liberal construction, gentleness and mercy to the faults of others, and the remembrance of our own imperfections and advantages, he bade us not inquire too closely into the venial errors of the poor, but finding that they *were* poor, first to relieve and then endeavour—at an advantage— to reclaim them.

To the housekeeper he left an annuity, sufficient for her comfortable maintenance and support through life. For the barber, who had attended him many years, he made a similar provision. And I may make two remarks in this place: first, that I think this pair are very likely to club their means together and make a match of it; and secondly, that I think my friend had this result in his mind, for I have heard him say, more than once, that he could not concur with the generality of mankind in censuring equal marriages made in later life, since there were many cases in which such unions could not fail to be a wise and rational source of happiness to both parties.

The elder Mr. Weller is so far from viewing this prospect with any feelings of jealousy, that he appears to be very much relieved by its contemplation; and his son, if I am not mistaken, participates in this feeling. We are all of opinion, however, that the old gentleman's danger, even at its crisis, was very slight, and that he merely laboured under one of those transitory weaknesses to which persons of his temperament are now and then liable, and which become less and less alarming at every return, until they wholly subside. I have no doubt he will remain a jolly old widower for the rest of his life, as he has already inquired of me, with much gravity, whether a writ of habeas corpus would enable him to settle his property upon Tony beyond the possibility of recall; and has, in my presence, conjured his son, with tears in his eyes, that in the event of his ever becoming amorous again, he will put him in a strait-waistcoat until the fit is past, and distinctly inform the lady that his property is 'made over.'

Although I have very little doubt that Sam would dutifully comply with these injunctions in a case of extreme necessity, and that he would do so with perfect composure and coolness, I do not apprehend things will ever come to that pass, as the old gentleman seems perfectly happy in the society of his son, his pretty daughter-in-law, and his grandchildren, and has solemnly announced his determination to 'take arter the old 'un in all respects'; from which I infer that it is his intention to regulate his conduct by the model of Mr. Pickwick, who will certainly set him the example of a single life.

I have diverged for a moment from the subject with which I set out, for I know that my friend was interested in these little matters, and I have a natural tendency to linger upon any topic that occupied his thoughts or gave him pleasure and amusement. His remaining wishes are very briefly told. He desired that we would make him the frequent subject of our conversation; at the same time, that we would never speak of him with an air of gloom or restraint, but frankly, and as one whom we still loved and hoped to meet again. He trusted that the old house would wear no aspect of mourning, but that it would be lively and cheerful; and that we would not remove or cover up his picture, which hangs in our dining-room, but make it our companion as he had been. His own room, our place of meeting, remains, at his desire, in its accustomed state; our seats are placed about the table as of old; his easy-chair, his desk, his crutch, his footstool, hold their accustomed places, and the clock stands in its familiar corner. We go into the chamber at stated times to see that all is as it should be, and to take care that the light and air are not shut out, for on that point he expressed a strong solicitude. But it was his fancy that the apartment should not be inhabited; that it should be religiously preserved in this condition, and that the voice of his old companion should be heard no more.

My own history may be summed up in very few words; and even those I should have spared the reader but for my friend's allusion to me some time since. I have no deeper sorrow than the loss of a child,—an only daughter, who is living, and who fled from her father's house but a few weeks before our friend and I first met. I had never spoken of this even to him, because I have always loved her, and I could not bear to tell him of her error until I could tell him

also of her sorrow and regret. Happily I was enabled to do
so some time ago. And it will not be long, with Heaven's
leave, before she is restored to me; before I find in her and
her husband the support of my declining years.

For my pipe, it is an old relic of home, a thing of no
great worth, a poor trifle, but sacred to me for her sake.

Thus, since the death of our venerable friend, Jack Redburn and I have been the sole tenants of the old house; and,
day by day, have lounged together in his favourite walks.
Mindful of his injunctions, we have long been able to speak
of him with ease and cheerfulness, and to remember him as he
would be remembered. From certain allusions which Jack
has dropped, to his having been deserted and cast off in early
life, I am inclined to believe that some passages of his youth
may possibly be shadowed out in the history of Mr. Chester
and his son, but seeing that he avoids the subject, I have not
pursued it.

My task is done. The chamber in which we have whiled
away so many hours, not, I hope, without some pleasure and
some profit, is deserted; our happy hour of meeting strikes
no more; the chimney-corner has grown cold; and MASTER
HUMPHREY'S CLOCK has stopped for ever.

THE END

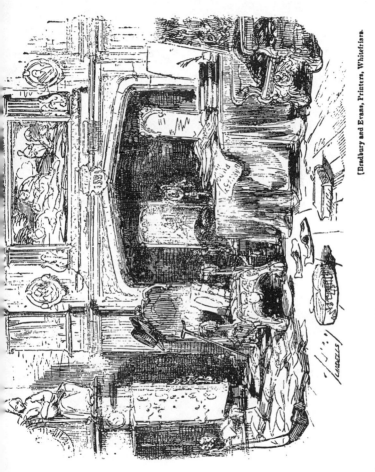

CHARLES

Master Humphrey's Room Deserted

[Bradbury and Evans, Printers, Whitefriars.

A CHILD'S HISTORY
OF ENGLAND

*The Frontispiece to Volume I of the first edition in
book form, 1852*

TABLE OF THE REIGNS

BEGINNING WITH KING ALFRED THE GREAT

THE SAXONS

	BEGAN	ENDED	LASTED
The Reign of Alfred the Great	871	901	30 years
The Reign of Edward the Elder	901	925	24 years
The Reign of Athelstan	925	941	16 years
The Reigns of the Six Boy-Kings	941	1016	75 years

THE DANES, AND THE RESTORED SAXONS

The Reign of Canute	1016	1035	19 years
The Reign of Harold Harefoot	1035	1040	5 years
The Reign of Hardicanute	1040	1042	2 years
The Reign of Edward the Confessor	1042	1066	24 years

The Reign of Harold the Second, and the Norman Conquest,
were also within the year 1066

THE NORMANS

The Reign of William the First, called the Conqueror	1066	1087	21 years
The Reign of William the Second, called Rufus	1087	1100	13 years
The Reign of Henry the First, called Fine-Scholar	1100	1135	35 years
The Reigns of Matilda and Stephen	1135	1154	19 years

THE PLANTAGENETS

The Reign of Henry the Second	1154	1189	35 years
The Reign of Richard the First, called the Lion-Heart	1189	1199	10 years
The Reign of John, called Lackland	1199	1216	17 years
The Reign of Henry the Third	1216	1272	56 years
The Reign of Edward the First, called Longshanks	1272	1307	35 years
The Reign of Edward the Second	1307	1327	20 years
The Reign of Edward the Third	1327	1377	50 years
The Reign of Richard the Second	1377	1399	22 years
The Reign of Henry the Fourth, called Bolingbroke	1399	1413	14 years
The Reign of Henry the Fifth	1413	1422	9 years
The Reign of Henry the Sixth	1422	1461	39 years
The Reign of Edward the Fourth	1461	1483	22 years
The Reign of Edward the Fifth	1483	1483	a few weeks
The Reign of Richard the Third	1483	1485	2 years

THE TUDORS

	BEGAN	ENDED	LASTED
The Reign of Henry the Seventh	1485	1509	24 years
The Reign of Henry the Eighth	1509	1547	38 years
The Reign of Edward the Sixth	1547	1553	6 years
The Reign of Mary	1553	1558	5 years
The Reign of Elizabeth	1558	1603	45 years

THE STUARTS

The Reign of James the First	1603	1625	22 years
The Reign of Charles the First	1625	1649	24 years

THE COMMONWEALTH

The Council of State and Government by Parliament	1649	1653	4 years
The Protectorate of Oliver Cromwell	1653	1658	5 years
The Protectorate of Richard Cromwell	1658	1659	7 months
The Council of State and Government by Parliament, resumed in	1659	1660	13 months

THE STUARTS RESTORED

The Reign of Charles the Second	1660	1685	25 years
The Reign of James the Second	1685	1688	3 years

THE REVOLUTION—1688
(Comprised in the concluding chapter)

The Reign of William III and Mary II	1689	1695	6 years
The Reign of William the Third		1702	13 years
The Reign of Anne	1702	1714	12 years
The Reign of George the First	1714	1727	13 years
The Reign of George the Second	1727	1760	33 years
The Reign of George the Third	1760	1820	60 years
The Reign of George the Fourth	1820	1830	10 years
The Reign of William the Fourth	1830	1837	7 years
The Reign of Victoria	1837		

CHRONOLOGICAL TABLE, AND TABLE OF CONTENTS

LIST OF ILLUSTRATIONS

By F. W. TOPHAM

By MARCUS STONE

CHAPTER I

ANCIENT ENGLAND AND THE ROMANS

If you look at a Map of the World, you will see, in the left-hand upper corner of the Eastern Hemisphere, two Islands lying in the sea. They are England and Scotland, and Ireland. England and Scotland form the greater part of these Islands. Ireland is the next in size. The little neighbouring islands, which are so small upon the Map as to be mere dots, are chiefly little bits of Scotland,— broken off, I dare say, in the course of a great length of time, by the power of the restless water.

In the old days, a long, long while ago, before Our Saviour was born on earth and lay asleep in a manger, these Islands were in the same place, and the stormy sea roared round them, just as it roars now. But the sea was not alive, then, with great ships and brave sailors, sailing to and from all parts of the world. It was very lonely. The Islands lay solitary, in the great expanse of water. The foaming waves dashed against their cliffs, and the bleak winds blew over their forests; but the winds and waves brought no adventurers to land upon the Islands, and the savage Islanders knew nothing of the rest of the world, and the rest of the world knew nothing of them.

It is supposed that the Phœnicians, who were an ancient people, famous for carrying on trade, came in ships to these Islands, and found that they produced tin and lead; both very useful things, as you know, and both produced to this very hour upon the sea-coast. The most celebrated tin mines in Cornwall are, still, close to the sea. One of them, which I have seen, is so close to it that it is hollowed out underneath the ocean ; and the miners say, that in stormy weather, when they are at work down in that deep place, they can hear the noise ot the waves thundering above their heads. So, the Phœnicians, coasting about the Islands, would come, without much difficulty, to where the tin and lead were.

The Phœnicians traded with the Islanders for these metals, and gave the Islanders some other useful things in exchange. The Islanders were, at first, poor savages, going almost naked, or only dressed in the rough skins of beasts, and staining their bodies, as other savages do, with coloured earths and the juices of plants. But the Phœnicians, sailing over to the opposite coasts of France and Belgium, and saying to the people there, "We have been to those white cliffs across the water, which you can see in fine weather, and from that country, which is called BRITAIN, we bring this tin and lead," tempted some of the French and Belgians to come over also. These people settled themselves on the south coast of England, which is now called Kent; and, although they were a rough people too, they taught the savage Britons some useful arts, and improved that part of the Islands. It is probable that other people came over from Spain to Ireland, and settled there.

Thus, by little and little, strangers became mixed with the Islanders, and the savage Britons grew into a wild bold people; almost savage, still, especially in the interior of the country away from the sea where the foreign settlers seldom went ; but hardy, brave, and strong.

The whole country was covered with forests, and swamps. The greater part of it was very misty and cold. There were no roads, no bridges, no streets, no houses that you would think deserving of the name. A town was nothing but a collection of straw-covered huts, hidden in a thick wood, with a ditch all round, and a low wall, made of mud, or the trunks of trees placed one upon another. The people planted little or no corn, but lived upon the flesh of their flocks and cattle. They made no coins, but used metal rings for money. They were clever in basket-work, as savage people often are ; and they could make a coarse kind of cloth, and some very bad earthenware. But in building fortresses they were much more clever.

They made boats of basket-work, covered with the skins

of animals, but seldom, if ever, ventured far from the shore.
They made swords, of copper mixed with tin; but, these
swords were of an awkward shape, and so soft that a heavy
blow would bend one. They made light shields, short
pointed daggers, and spears—which they jerked back after
they had thrown them at an enemy, by a long strip of
leather fastened to the stem. The butt-end was a rattle,
to frighten an enemy's horse. The ancient Britons, being
divided into as many as thirty or forty tribes, each commanded
by its own little king, were constantly fighting with one
another, as savage people usually do; and they always
fought with these weapons.

They were very fond of horses. The standard of Kent
was the picture of a white horse. They could break them
in and manage them wonderfully well. Indeed, the horses
(of which they had an abundance, though they were rather
small) were so well taught in those days, that they can
scarcely be said to have improved since; though the men
are so much wiser. They understood, and obeyed, every
word of command; and would stand still by themselves,
in all the din and noise of battle, while their masters went
to fight on foot. The Britons could not have succeeded
in their most remarkable art, without the aid of these
sensible and trusty animals. The art I mean, is the construction and management of war-chariots or cars, for which
they have ever been celebrated in history. Each of the best
sort of these chariots, not quite breast high in front, and
open at the back, contained one man to drive, and two
or three others to fight—all standing up. The horses who
drew them were so well trained, that they would tear, at full
gallop, over the most stony ways, and even through the
woods; dashing down their masters' enemies beneath their
hoofs, and cutting them to pieces with the blades of swords,
or scythes, which were fastened to the wheels, and stretched
out beyond the car on each side, for that cruel purpose. In
a moment, while at full speed, the horses would stop, at the
driver's command. The men within would leap out, deal
blows about them with their swords like hail, leap on the
horses, on the pole, spring back into the chariots any-
how; and, as soon as they were safe, the horses tore away
again.

The Britons had a strange and terrible religion, called the
Religion of the Druids. It seems to have been brought

over, in very early times indeed, from the opposite country of France, anciently called Gaul, and to have mixed up the worship of the Serpent, and of the Sun and Moon, with the worship of some of the Heathen Gods and Goddesses. Most of its ceremonies were kept secret by the priests, the Druids, who pretended to be enchanters, and who carried magicians' wands, and wore, each of them, about his neck, what he told the ignorant people was a Serpent's egg in a golden case. But it is certain that the Druidical ceremonies included the sacrifice of human victims, the torture of some suspected criminals, and, on particular occasions, even the burning alive, in immense wicker cages, of a number of men and animals together. The Druid Priests had some kind of veneration for the Oak, and for the mistletoe—the same plant that we hang up in houses at Christmas Time now—when its white berries grew upon the Oak. They met together in dark woods, which they called Sacred Groves ; and there they instructed, in their mysterious arts, young men who came to them as pupils, and who sometimes stayed with them as long as twenty years.

These Druids built great Temples and altars, open to the sky, fragments of some of which are yet remaining. Stonehenge, on Salisbury Plain, in Wiltshire, is the most extraordinary of these. Three curious stones, called Kits Coty House, on Bluebell Hill, near Maidstone, in Kent, form another. We know, from examination of the great blocks of which such buildings are made, that they could not have been raised without the aid of some ingenious machines, which are common now, but which the ancient Britons certainly did not use in making their own uncomfortable houses. I should not wonder if the Druids, and their pupils who stayed with them twenty years, knowing more than the rest of the Britons, kept the people out of sight while they made these buildings, and then pretended that they built them by magic. Perhaps they had a hand in the fortresses too ; at all events, as they were very powerful, and very much believed in, and as they made and executed the laws, and paid no taxes, I don't wonder that they liked their trade. And, as they persuaded the people the more Druids there were, the better off the people would be, I don't wonder that there were a good many of them. But it is pleasant to think that there are no Druids, *now*, who go on in that way, and pretend to carry Enchanters' Wands and Serpents'

Eggs—and of course there is nothing of the kind, any-where.

Such was the improved condition of the ancient Britons, fifty-five years before the birth of Our Saviour, when the Romans, under their great General, Julius Cæsar, were masters of all the rest of the known world. Julius Cæsar had then just conquered Gaul; and hearing, in Gaul, a good deal about the opposite Island with the white cliffs, and about the bravery of the Britons who inhabited it—some of whom had been fetched over to help the Gauls in the war against him—he resolved, as he was so near, to come and conquer Britain next.

So, Julius Cæsar came sailing over to this Island of ours, with eighty vessels and twelve thousand men. And he came from the French coast between Calais and Boulogne, "because thence was the shortest passage into Britain;" just for the same reason as our steam-boats now take the same track, every day. He expected to conquer Britain easily: but it was not such easy work as he supposed—for the bold Britons fought most bravely; and, what with not having his horse-soldiers with him (for they had been driven back by a storm), and what with having some of his vessels dashed to pieces by a high tide after they were drawn ashore, he ran great risk of being totally defeated. However, for once that the bold Britons beat him, he beat them twice; though not so soundly but that he was very glad to accept their proposals of peace, and go away.

But, in the spring of the next year, he came back; this time, with eight hundred vessels and thirty thousand men. The British tribes chose, as their general-in-chief, a Briton, whom the Romans in their Latin language called CASSIVEL-LAUNUS, but whose British name is supposed to have been CASWALLON. A brave general he was, and well he and his soldiers fought the Roman army! So well, that whenever in that war the Roman soldiers saw a great cloud of dust, and heard the rattle of the rapid British chariots, they trembled in their hearts. Besides a number of smaller battles, there was a battle fought near Canterbury, in Kent; there was a battle fought near Chertsey, in Surrey; there was a battle fought near a marshy little town in a wood, the capital of that part of Britain which belonged to CASSIVELLAUNUS, and which was probably near what is now Saint Albans, in Hertfordshire. However, brave

CASSIVELLAUNUS had the worst of it, on the whole; though he and his men always fought like lions. As the other British chiefs were jealous of him, and were always quarrelling with him, and with one another, he gave up, and proposed peace. Julius Cæsar was very glad to grant peace easily, and to go away again with all his remaining ships and men. He had expected to find pearls in Britain, and he may have found a few for anything I know; but, at all events, he found delicious oysters, and I am sure he found tough Britons —of whom, I dare say, he made the same complaint as Napoleon Bonaparte the great French General did, eighteen hundred years afterwards, when he said they were such unreasonable fellows that they never knew when they were beaten. They never *did* know, I believe, and never will.

Nearly a hundred years passed on, and all that time, there was peace in Britain. The Britons improved their towns and mode of life: became more civilised, travelled, and learnt a great deal from the Gauls and Romans. At last, the Roman Emperor, Claudius, sent AULUS PLAUTIUS, a skilful general, with a mighty force, to subdue the Island, and shortly afterwards arrived himself. They did little; and OSTORIUS SCAPULA, another general, came. Some of the British Chiefs of Tribes submitted. Others resolved to fight to the death. Of these brave men, the bravest was CARACTACUS, or CARADOC, who gave battle to the Romans, with his army, among the mountains of North Wales. "This day," said he to his soldiers, "decides the fate of Britain! Your liberty, or your eternal slavery, dates from this hour. Remember your brave ancestors, who drove the great Cæsar himself across the sea!" On hearing these words, his men, with a great shout, rushed upon the Romans. But the strong Roman swords and armour were too much for the weaker British weapons in close conflict. The Britons lost the day. The wife and daughter of the brave CARACTACUS were taken prisoners; his brothers delivered themselves up; he himself was betrayed into the hands of the Romans by his false and base step-mother: and they carried him, and all his family, in triumph to Rome.

But a great man will be great in misfortune, great in prison, great in chains. His noble air, and dignified endurance of distress, so touched the Roman people who thronged the streets to see him, that he and his family were restored to freedom. No one knows whether his great heart broke, and he died in Rome, or whether he ever returned to his own dear country. English oaks have grown up from acorns, and withered away, when they were hundreds of years old—and other oaks have sprung up in their places, and died too, very aged—since the rest of the history of the brave CARACTACUS was forgotten.

Still, the Britons *would not* yield. They rose again and again, and died by thousands, sword in hand. They rose, on every possible occasion. SUETONIUS, another Roman general, came, and stormed the Island of Anglesey (then called MONA), which was supposed to be sacred, and he burnt the Druids in their own wicker cages, by their own fires. But, even while he was in Britain, with his victorious troops, the BRITONS rose. Because BOADICEA, a British queen, the widow of the King of the Norfolk and Suffolk people, resisted the plundering of her property by the Romans who were settled in England, she was scourged, by order of CATUS a Roman officer; and her two daughters were shamefully insulted in her presence, and her husband's relations were made slaves. To avenge this injury, the Britons rose, with all their might and rage. They drove CATUS into Gaul; they laid the Roman possessions waste; they forced the Romans out of London, then a poor little town, but a trading place; they hanged, burnt, crucified, and slew by the sword, seventy thousand Romans in a few days. SUETONIUS strengthened his army, and advanced to give them battle. They strengthened their army, and desperately attacked his, on the field where it was strongly posted. Before the first charge of the Britons was made, BOADICEA, in a war-chariot, with her fair hair streaming in the wind, and her injured daughters lying at her feet, drove among the troops, and cried to them for vengeance on their oppressors, the licentious Romans. The Britons fought to the last; but they were vanquished with great slaughter, and the unhappy queen took poison.

Still, the spirit of the Britons was not broken. When SUETONIUS left the country, they fell upon his troops, and retook the Island of Anglesey. AGRICOLA came, fifteen or twenty years afterwards, and retook it once more, and devoted seven years to subduing the country, especially that part of it which is now called SCOTLAND; but, its people, the Caledonians, resisted him at every inch of ground. They fought the bloodiest battles with him ; they killed their very wives and children, to prevent his making prisoners of them; they fell, fighting, in such great numbers that certain hills in Scotland are yet supposed to be vast heaps of stones piled up above their graves. HADRIAN came, thirty years afterwards, and still they resisted him. SEVERUS came, nearly a hundred years afterwards, and they worried his great army like dogs, and rejoiced to see them die, by thousands, in the bogs and swamps. CARACALLA, the son and successor of SEVERUS, did the most to conquer them, for a time ; but not by force of arms. He knew how little that would do. He yielded up a quantity of land to the Caledonians, and gave the Britons the same privileges as the Romans possessed. There was peace, after this, for seventy years.

Then new enemies arose. They were the SAXONS, a fierce, seafaring people from the countries to the North of the Rhine, the great river of Germany on the banks of which the best grapes grow to make the German wine. They began to come, in pirate ships, to the sea-coast of Gaul and Britain, and to plunder them. They were repulsed by CARAUSIUS, a native either of Belgium or of Britain, who was appointed by the Romans to the command, and under whom the Britons first began to fight upon the sea. But, after this time, they renewed their ravages. A few years more, and the Scots (which was then the name for the people of Ireland), and the Picts, a northern people, began to make frequent plundering incursions into the South of Britain. All these attacks were repeated, at intervals, during two hundred years, and through a long succession of Roman Emperors and chiefs ; during all which length of time, the Britons rose against the Romans, over and over again. At last, in the days of the Roman HONORIUS, when the Roman power all over the world was fast declining, and when Rome wanted all her soldiers at home, the Romans abandoned all hope of conquering Britain, and went away. And still, at last, as at first, the Britons rose against them, in their old brave manner ; for, a very little while before, they had turned away the Roman magistrates, and declared themselves an independent people.

Five hundred years had passed, since Julius Cæsar's first invasion of the Island, when the Romans departed from it for ever. In the course of that time, although they had been the cause of terrible fighting and bloodshed, they had done much to improve the condition of the Britons. They had made great military roads; they had built forts; they had taught them how to dress, and arm themselves, much better than they had ever known how to do before; they had refined the whole British way of living. AGRICOLA had built a great wall of earth, more than seventy miles long, extending from Newcastle to beyond Carlisle, for the purpose of keeping out the Picts and Scots; HADRIAN had strengthened it; SEVERUS, finding it much in want of repair, had built it afresh of stone. Above all, it was in the Roman time, and by means of Roman ships, that the Christian Religion was first brought into Britain, and its people first taught the great lesson that, to be good in the sight of GOD, they must love their neighbours as themselves, and do unto others as they would be done by. The Druids declared that it was very wicked to believe in any such thing, and cursed all the people who did believe it, very heartily. But, when the people found that they were none the better for the blessings of the Druids, and none the worse for the curses of the Druids, but, that the sun shone and the rain fell without consulting the Druids at all, they just began to think that the Druids were mere men, and that it signified very little whether they cursed or blessed. After which, the pupils of the Druids fell off greatly in numbers, and the Druids took to other trades.

Thus I have come to the end of the Roman time in England. It is but little that is known of those five hundred years; but some remains of them are still found. Often, when labourers are digging up the ground, to make foundations for houses or churches, they light on rusty money that once belonged to the Romans. Fragments of plates from which they ate, of goblets from which they drank, and of pavement on which they trod, are discovered among the earth that is broken by the plough, or the dust that is crumbled by the gardener's spade. Wells that the Romans sunk, still yield water; roads that the Romans made, form part of our highways. In some old battle-fields, British spear-heads and Roman armour have been found, mingled together in decay, as they fell in the thick pressure of the fight. Traces of Roman camps overgrown with grass, and of mounds that are the burial-places of heaps of Britons, are to be seen in almost all parts of the country. Across the bleak moors of Northumberland, the wall of SEVERUS, overrun with moss and weeds, still stretches, a strong ruin; and the shepherds and their dogs lie sleeping on it in the summer weather. On Salisbury Plain, Stonehenge yet stands: a monument of the earlier time when the Roman name was unknown in Britain, and when the Druids, with their best magic wands, could not have written it in the sands of the wild sea-shore.

CHAPTER II

ANCIENT ENGLAND UNDER THE EARLY SAXONS

THE Romans had scarcely gone away from Britain, when the Britons began to wish they had never left it. For, the Romans being gone, and the Britons being much reduced in numbers by their long wars, the Picts and Scots came pouring in, over the broken and unguarded wall of SEVERUS, in swarms. They plundered the richest towns, and killed the people; and came back so often for more booty and more slaughter, that the unfortunate Britons lived a life of terror. As if the Picts and Scots were not bad enough on land, the Saxons attacked the islanders by sea; and, as if something more were still wanting to make them miserable, they quarrelled bitterly among themselves as to what prayers they ought to say, and how they ought to say them. The priests, being very angry with one another on these questions, cursed one another in the heartiest manner; and (uncommonly like the old Druids) cursed all the people whom they could not persuade. So, altogether, the Britons were very badly off, you may believe.

They were in such distress, in short, that they sent a letter to Rome entreating help—which they called the Groans of the Britons; and in which they said, "The barbarians chase us into the sea, the s a throws us back upon the barbarians, and we have only the hard choice left us of perishing by the sword, or perishing by the waves." But, the Romans could not help them, even if they were so inclined; for they had enough to do to defend themselves against their own enemies, who were then very fierce and strong. At last, the Britons, unable to bear their hard condition any longer, resolved to make peace with the Saxons, and to invite the Saxons to come into their country, and help them to keep out the Picts and Scots.

It was a British Prince named VORTIGERN who took this

resolution, and who made a treaty of friendship with HENGIST
and HORSA, two Saxon chiefs. Both of these names, in the
old Saxon language, signify Horse; for the Saxons, like
many other nations in a rough state, were fond of giving
men the names of animals, as Horse, Wolf, Bear, Hound.
The Indians of North America,—a very inferior people to
the Saxons, though—do the same to this day.

HENGIST and HORSA drove out the Picts and Scots; and
VORTIGERN, being grateful to them for that service, made
no opposition to their settling themselves in that part of
England which is called the Isle of Thanet, or to their inviting over more of their countrymen to join them. But
HENGIST had a beautiful daughter named ROWENA; and
when, at a feast, she filled a golden goblet to the brim with
wine, and gave it to VORTIGERN, saying in a sweet voice,
"Dear King, thy health!" the King fell in love with her.
My opinion is, that the cunning HENGIST meant him to do
so, in order that the Saxons might have greater influence
with him; and that the fair ROWENA came to that feast,
golden goblet and all, on purpose.

At any rate, they were married; and, long afterwards,
whenever the King was angry with the Saxons, or jealous
of their encroachments, ROWENA would put her beautiful
arms round his neck, and softly say, "Dear King, they are
my people! Be favourable to them, as you loved that
Saxon girl who gave you the golden goblet of wine at the
feast!" And, really, I don't see how the King could help
himself.

Ah! We must all die! In the course of years, VORTIGERN
died—he was dethroned, and put in prison, first, I am
afraid; and ROWENA died; and generations of Saxons and
Britons died; and events that happened during a long, long
time, would have been quite forgotten but for the tales
and songs of the old Bards, who used to go about from feast
to feast, with their white beards, recounting the deeds of
their forefathers. Among the histories of which they sang
and talked, there was a famous one, concerning the bravery
and virtues of KING ARTHUR, supposed to have been a British
Prince in those old times. But, whether such a person
really lived, or whether there were several persons whose
histories came to be confused together under that one name,
or whether all about him was invention, no one knows.

I will tell you, shortly, what is most interesting in the

early Saxon times, as they are described in these songs and stories of the Bards.

In, and long after, the days of VORTIGERN, fresh bodies of Saxons, under various chiefs, came pouring into Britain. One body, conquering the Britons in the East, and settling there, called their kingdom Essex; another body settled in the West, and called their kingdom Wessex; the Northfolk, or Norfolk people, established themselves in one place; the Southfolk, or Suffolk people, established themselves in another; and gradually seven kingdoms or states arose in England, which were called the Saxon Heptarchy. The poor Britons, falling back before these crowds of fighting men whom they had innocently invited over as friends, retired into Wales and the adjacent country; into Devonshire, and into Cornwall. Those parts of England long remained unconquered. And in Cornwall now—where the sea-coast is very gloomy, steep, and rugged—where, in the dark winter-time, ships have often been wrecked close to the land, and every soul on board has perished—where the winds and waves howl drearily, and split the solid rocks into arches and caverns—there are very ancient ruins, which the people call the ruins of KING ARTHUR's Castle.

Kent is the most famous of the seven Saxon kingdoms, because the Christian religion was preached to the Saxons there (who domineered over the Britons too much, to care for what *they* said about their religion, or anything else) by AUGUSTINE, a monk from Rome. KING ETHELBERT, of Kent, was soon converted; and the moment he said he was a Christian, his courtiers all said *they* were Christians; after which, ten thousand of his subjects said they were Christians too. AUGUSTINE built a little church. close to this King's palace, on the ground now occupied by the beautiful cathedral of Canterbury. SEBERT, the King's nephew, built on a muddy marshy place near London, where there had been a temple to Apollo, a church dedicated to Saint Peter, which is now Westminster Abbey. And, in London itself, on the foundation of a temple to Diana, he built another little church which has risen up, since that old time, to be Saint Paul's.

After the death of ETHELBERT, EDWIN, King of Northumbria, who was such a good king that it was said a woman or child might openly carry a purse of gold, in his reign, without fear, allowed his child to be baptised, and held a great council to consider whether he and his people should all be Christians or not. It was decided that they should be. COIFI, the chief priest of the old religion, made a great speech on the occasion. In this discourse, he told the people that he had found out the old gods to be impostors. " I am quite satisfied of it," he said. "Look at me! I have been serving them all my life, and they have done nothing for me; whereas, if they had been really powerful, they could not have decently done less, in return for all I have done for them, than make my fortune. As they have never made my fortune, I am quite convinced they are impostors!" When this singular priest had finished speaking, he hastily armed himself with sword and lance, mounted a war-horse, rode at a furious gallop in sight of all the people to the temple, and flung his lance against it as an insult. From that time, the Christian religion spread itself among the Saxons, and became their faith.

The next very famous prince was EGBERT. He lived about a hundred and fifty years afterwards, and claimed to have a better right to the throne of Wessex than BEORTRIC, another Saxon prince who was at the head of that kingdom, and who married EDBURGA, the daughter of OFFA, king of another of the seven kingdoms. This QUEEN EDBURGA was a handsome murderess, who poisoned people when they offended her. One day, she mixed a cup of poison for a certain noble belonging to the court; but her husband drank of it too, by mistake, and died. Upon this, the people revolted, in great crowds; and running to the palace, and thundering at the gates, cried, "Down with the wicked queen, who poisons men!" They drove her out of the country, and abolished the title she had disgraced. When years had passed away, some travellers came home from Italy, and said that in the town of Pavia they had seen a ragged beggar-woman, who had once been handsome, but was then shrivelled, bent, and yellow, wandering about the streets, crying for bread; and that this beggar-woman was the poisoning English queen. It was, indeed, EDBURGA; and so she died, without a shelter for her wretched head.

EGBERT, not considering himself safe in England, in consequence of his having claimed the crown of Wessex (for he thought his rival might take him prisoner and put him to death), sought refuge at the court of CHARLEMAGNE, King of France. On the death of BEORTRIC, so unhappily poisoned

by mistake, EGBERT came back to Britain ; succeeded to the
throne of Wessex ; conquered some of the other monarchs
of the seven kingdoms ; added their territories to his own ;
and, for the first time, called the. country over which he
ruled, ENGLAND.

And now, new enemies arose, who, for a long time, troubled
England sorely. These were the Northmen, the people of
Denmark and Norway, whom the English called the Danes.
They were a warlike people, quite at home upon the sea ;
not Christians ; very daring and cruel. They came over in
ships, and plundered and burned wheresoever they landed.
Once, they beat EGBERT in battle. Once, EGBERT beat them.
But, they cared no more for being beaten than the English
themselves. In the four following short reigns, of ETHEL-
WULF, and his sons, ETHELBALD, ETHELBERT, and ETHELRED,
they came back, over and over again, burning and plundering, and laying England waste. In the last-mentioned reign,
they seized EDMUND, King of East England, and bound him
to a tree. Then, they proposed to him that he should change
his religion ; but he, being a good Christian, steadily refused.
Upon that, they beat him, made cowardly jests upon him.
all defenceless as he was, shot arrows at him, and, finally,
struck off his head. It is impossible to say whose head
they might have struck off next, but for the death of KING
ETHELRED from a wound he had received in fighting against
them, and the succession to his throne of the best and
wisest king that ever lived in England.

CHAPTER III

ENGLAND UNDER THE GOOD SAXON, ALFRED

ALFRED THE GREAT was a young man, three-and-twenty years of age, when he became king. Twice in his childhood, he had been taken to Rome, where the Saxon nobles were in the habit of going on journeys which they supposed to be religious; and, once, he had stayed for some time in Paris. Learning, however, was so little cared for, then, that at twelve years old he had not been taught to read; although, of the sons of KING ETHELWULF, he, the youngest, was the favourite. But he had—as most men who grow up to be great and good are generally found to have had—an excellent mother; and, one day, this lady, whose name was OSBURGA, happened, as she was sitting among her sons, to read a book of Saxon poetry. The art of printing was not known until long and long after that period, and the book, which was written, was what is called "illuminated," with beautiful bright letters, richly painted. The brothers admiring it very much, their mother said, " I will give it to that one of you four princes who first learns to read." ALFRED sought out a tutor that very day, applied himself to learn with great diligence, and soon won the book. He was proud of it, all his life.

This great king, in the first year of his reign, fought nine battles with the Danes. He made some treaties with them too, by which the false Danes swore they would quit the country. They pretended to consider that they had taken a very solemn oath, in swearing this upon the holy bracelets that they wore, and which were always buried with them when they died; but they cared little for it, for they thought nothing of breaking oaths and treaties too, as soon as it suited their purpose. and coming back again to fight, plunder, and burn, as usual. One fatal winter, in the fourth year of KING ALFRED's reign, they spread themselves in great numbers over the whole of England; and so dispersed and

Alfred in the Cowherd's Cottage

routed the King's soldiers that the King was left alone, and was obliged to disguise himself as a common peasant, and to take refuge in the cottage of one of his cowherds who did not know his face.

Here, KING ALFRED, while the Danes sought him far and near, was left alone one day, by the cowherd's wife, to watch some cakes which she put to bake upon the hearth. But, being at work upon his bow and arrows, with which he hoped to punish the false Danes when a brighter time should come, and thinking deeply of his poor unhappy subjects whom the Danes chased through the land, his noble mind forgot the cakes, and they were burnt. "What!" said the cowherd's wife, who scolded him well when she came back, and little thought she was scolding the King, "you will be ready enough to eat them by-and-by, and yet you cannot watch them, idle dog?"

At length, the Devonshire men made head against a new host of Danes who landed on their coast; killed their chief, and captured their flag; on which was represented the like-ness of a Raven—a very fit bird for a thievish army like that, I think. The loss of their standard troubled the Danes greatly, for they believed it to be enchanted—woven by the three daughters of one father in a single afternoon—and they had a story among themselves that when they were victorious in battle, the Raven stretched his wings and seemed to fly; and that when they were defeated, he would droop. He had good reason to droop, now, if he could have done anything half so sensible; for, KING ALFRED joined the Devonshire men; made a camp with them on a piece of firm ground in the midst of a bog in Somersetshire; and prepared for a great attempt for vengeance on the Danes, and the deliverance of his oppressed people.

But, first, as it was important to know how numerous those pestilent Danes were, and how they were fortified, KING ALFRED, being a good musician, disguised himself as a glee-man or minstrel, and went, with his harp, to the Danish camp. He played and sang in the very tent of GUTHRUM the Danish leader, and entertained the Danes as they caroused. While he seemed to think of nothing but his music, he was watchful of their tents, their arms, their discipline, everything that he desired to know. And right soon did this great king entertain them to a different tune; for, summoning all his true followers to meet him at an

appointed place, where they received him with joyful shouts
and tears, as the monarch whom many of them had given
up for lost or dead, he put himself at their head, marched
on the Danish camp, defeated the Danes with great slaughter,
and besieged them for fourteen days to prevent their escape.
But, being as merciful as he was good and brave, he then,
instead of killing them, proposed peace : on condition that
they should altogether depart from that Western part of
England, and settle in the East ; and that GUTHRUM should
become a Christian, in remembrance of the Divine religion
which now taught his conqueror, the noble ALFRED, to
forgive the enemy who had so often injured him. This,
GUTHRUM did. At his baptism, KING ALFRED was his godfather.   And GUTHRUM was an honourable chief who well
deserved that clemency ; for, ever afterwards he was loyal
and faithful to the king.   The Danes under him were faithful
too.   They plundered and burned no more, but worked like
honest men.   They ploughed, and sowed, and reaped, and
led good honest English lives.   And I hope the children of
those Danes played, many a time, with Saxon children in
the sunny fields ; and that Danish young men fell in love
with Saxon girls, and married them ; and that English
travellers, benighted at the doors of Danish cottages, often
went in for shelter until morning ; and that Danes and
Saxons sat by the red fire, friends, talking of KING ALFRED
THE GREAT.

All the Danes were not like these under GUTHRUM ; for,
after some years, more of them came over, in the old
plundering and burning way—among them a fierce pirate
of the name of HASTINGS, who had the boldness to sail up
the Thames to Gravesend, with eighty ships.   For three
years, there was a war with these Danes ; and there was
a famine in the country, too, and a plague, both upon
human creatures and beasts.   But KING ALFRED, whose
mighty heart never failed him, built large ships nevertheless,
with which to pursue the pirates on the sea ; and he
encouraged his soldiers, by his brave example, to fight
valiantly against them on the shore.   At last, he drove
them all away ; and then there was repose in England.

As great and good in peace, as he was great and good in
war, KING ALFRED never rested from his labours to improve
his people.   He loved to talk with clever men, and with
travellers from foreign countries, and to write down what

they told him, for his people to read. He had studied Latin after learning to read English, and now another of his labours was, to translate Latin books into the English-Saxon tongue, that his people might be interested, and improved by their contents. He made just laws, that they might live more happily and freely; he turned away all partial judges, that no wrong might be done them; he was so careful of their property, and punished robbers so severely, that it was a common thing to say that under the great KING ALFRED. garlands of golden chains and jewels might have hung across the streets, and no man would have touched one. He founded schools; he patiently heard causes himself in his Court of Justice; the great desires of his heart were, to do right to all his subjects, and to leave England better, wiser, happier in all ways, than he found it. His industry in these efforts was quite astonishing. Every day he divided into certain portions, and in each portion devoted himself to a certain pursuit. That he might divide his time exactly, he had wax torches or candles made, which were all of the same size, were notched across at regular distances, and were always kept burning. Thus, as the candles burnt down, he divided the day into notches, almost as accurately as we now divide it into hours upon the clock. But when the candles were first invented, it was found that the wind and draughts of air, blowing into the palace through the doors and windows, and through the chinks in the walls, caused them to gutter and burn unequally. To prevent this, the King had them put into cases formed of wood and white horn. And these were the first lanthorns ever made in England.

All this time, he was afflicted with a terrible unknown disease, which caused him violent and frequent pain that nothing could relieve. He bore it, as he had borne all the troubles of his life, like a brave good man, until he was fifty-three years old; and then, having reigned thirty years, he died. He died in the year nine hundred and one; but, long ago as that is, his fame, and the love and gratitude with which his subjects regarded him, are freshly remembered to the present hour.

In the next reign, which was the reign of EDWARD, sur-named THE ELDER, who was chosen in council to succeed, a nephew of KING ALFRED troubled the country by trying to obtain the throne. The Danes in the East of England took part with this usurper (perhaps because they had honoured his uncle so much, and honoured him for his uncle's sake), and there was hard fighting; but, the King, with the assistance of his sister. gained the day, and reigned in peace for four and twenty years. He gradually extended his power over the whole of England, and so the Seven Kingdoms were united into one.

When England thus became one kingdom, ruled over by one Saxon king, the Saxons had been settled in the country more than four hundred and fifty years. Great changes had taken place in its customs during that time. The Saxons were still greedy eaters and great drinkers, and their feasts were often of a noisy and drunken kind; but many new comforts and even elegances had become known, and were fast increasing. Hangings for the walls of rooms, where, in these modern days, we paste up paper, are known to have been sometimes made of silk, ornamented with birds and flowers in needlework. Tables and chairs were curiously carved in different woods; were sometimes decorated with gold or silver; sometimes even made of those precious metals. Knives and spoons were used at table; golden ornaments were worn—with silk and cloth, and golden tissues and embroideries; dishes were made of gold and silver, brass and bone. There were varieties of drinking-horns, bedsteads, musical instruments. A harp was passed round, at a feast, like the drinking-bowl, from guest to guest; and each one usually sang or played when his turn came. The weapons of the Saxons were stoutly made, and among them was a terrible iron hammer that gave deadly blows, and was long remembered. The Saxons themselves were a handsome people. The men were proud of their long fair hair, parted on the forehead; their ample beards, their fresh complexions, and clear eyes. The beauty of the Saxon women filled all England with a new delight and grace.

I have more to tell of the Saxons yet, but I stop to say this now, because under the GREAT ALFRED, all the best points of the English-Saxon character were first encouraged, and in him first shown. It has been the greatest character among the nations of the earth. Wherever the descendants of the Saxon race have gone, have sailed, or otherwise made their way, even to the remotest regions of the world, they have been patient, persevering, never to be broken in spirit, never to be turned aside from enterprises on which they have resolved. In Europe, Asia, Africa, America, the whole world over; in the desert, in the forest, on the sea; scorched by a burning sun, or frozen by ice that never melts; the Saxon blood remains unchanged. Wheresoever that race goes, there, law, and industry, and safety for life and property, and all the great results of steady perseverance, are certain to arise.

I pause to think with admiration, of the noble king who, in his single person, possessed all the Saxon virtues. Whom misfortune could not subdue, whom prosperity could not spoil, whose perseverance nothing could shake. Who was hopeful in defeat, and generous in success. Who loved justice, freedom, truth, and knowledge. Who, in his care to instruct his people, probably did more to preserve the beautiful old Saxon language, than I can imagine. Without whom, the English tongue in which I tell this story might have wanted half its meaning. As it is said that his spirit still inspires some of our best English laws, so, let you and I pray that it may animate our English hearts, at least to this—to resolve, when we see any of our fellow-creatures left in ignorance, that we will do our best, while life is in us, to have them taught; and to tell those rulers whose duty it is to teach them, and who neglect their duty, that they have profited very little by all the years that have rolled away since the year nine hundred and one, and that they are far behind the bright example of KING ALFRED THE GREAT.

CHAPTER IV

ATHELSTAN, the son of Edward the Elder, succeeded that king. He reigned only fifteen years; but he remembered the glory of his grandfather, the great Alfred, and governed England well. He reduced the turbulent people of Wales, and obliged them to pay him a tribute in money, and in cattle, and to send him their best hawks and hounds. He was victorious over the Cornish men, who were not yet quite under the Saxon government. He restored such of the old laws as were good, and had fallen into disuse; made some wise new laws, and took care of the poor and weak. A strong alliance, made against him by ANLAF a Danish prince, CONSTANTINE King of the Scots, and the people of North Wales, he broke and defeated in one great battle, long famous for the vast numbers slain in it. After that, he had a quiet reign; the lords and ladies about him had leisure to become polite and agreeable; and foreign princes were glad (as they have sometimes been since) to come to England on visits to the English court.

When Athelstan died, at forty-seven years old, his brother EDMUND, who was only eighteen, became king. He was the first of six boy-kings, as you will presently know.

They called him the Magnificent, because he showed a taste for improvement and refinement. But he was beset by the Danes, and had a short and troubled reign, which came to a troubled end. One night, when he was feasting in his hall, and had eaten much and drunk deep, he saw, among the company, a noted robber named LEOF, who had been banished from England. Made very angry by the boldness of this man, the King turned to his cup-bearer, and said, "There is a robber sitting at the table yonder, who, for his crimes, is an outlaw in the land—a hunted wolf, whose life any man may take, at any time. Command that robber to depart!" "I will not depart!" said Leof.

"No?" cried the King. "No, by the Lord!" said Leof.
Upon that the King rose from his seat, and, making
passionately at the robber, and seizing him by his long
hair, tried to throw him down. But the robber had a
dagger underneath his cloak, and, in the scuffle, stabbed
the King to death. That done, he set his back against the
wall, and fought so desperately, that although he was soon
cut to pieces by the King's armed men, and the wall and
pavement were splashed with his blood, yet it was not
before he had killed and wounded many of them. You
may imagine what rough lives the kings of those times led,
when one of them could struggle, half drunk, with a public
robber in his own dining-hall, and be stabbed in presence of
the company who ate and drank with him.

Then succeeded the boy-king EDRED, who was weak and
sickly in body, but of a strong mind. And his armies fought
the Northmen, the Danes, and Norwegians, or the Sea-
Kings, as they were called, and beat them for the time.
And, in nine years, Edred died, and passed away.

Then came the boy-king EDWY, fifteen years of age; but
the real king, who had the real power, was a monk named
DUNSTAN—a clever priest, a little mad, and not a little proud
and cruel.

Dunstan was then Abbot of Glastonbury Abbey, whither
the body of King Edmund the Magnificent was carried, to
be buried. While yet a boy, he had got out of his bed one
night (being then in a fever), and walked about Glastonbury
Church when it was under repair; and, because he did not
tumble off some scaffolds that were there, and break his
neck, it was reported that he had been shown over the
building by an angel. He had also made a harp that was
said to play of itself—which it very likely did, as Æolian
Harps, which are played by the wind, and are understood
now, always do. For these wonders he had been once
denounced by his enemies, who were jealous of his favour
with the late King Athelstan, as a magician; and he had
been waylaid, bound hand and foot, and thrown into a
marsh. But he got out again, somehow, to cause a great
deal of trouble yet.

The priests of those days were, generally, the only scholars.
They were learned in many things. Having to make their
own convents and monasteries on uncultivated grounds that
were granted to them by the Crown, it was necessary that

they should be good farmers and good gardeners, or their lands would have been too poor to support them. For the decoration of the chapels where they prayed, and for the comfort of the refectories where they ate and drank, it was necessary that there should be good carpenters, good smiths, good painters, among them. For their greater safety in sickness and accident, living alone by themselves in solitary places, it was necessary that they should study the virtues of plants and herbs, and should know how to dress cuts, burns, scalds, and bruises, and how to set broken limbs. Accordingly, they taught themselves, and one another, a great variety of useful arts; and became skilful in agriculture, medicine, surgery, and handicraft. And when they wanted the aid of any little piece of machinery, which would be simple enough now, but was marvellous then, to impose a trick upon the poor peasants, they knew very well how to make it; and *did* make it many a time and often, I have no doubt.

Dunstan, Abbot of Glastonbury Abbey, was one of the most sagacious of these monks. He was an ingenious smith, and worked at a forge in a little cell. This cell was made too short to admit of his lying at full length when he went to sleep—as if *that* did any good to anybody!—and he used to tell the most extraordinary lies about demons and spirits, who, he said, came there to persecute him. For instance, he related that one day when he was at work, the devil looked in at the little window, and tried to tempt him to lead a life of idle pleasure; whereupon, having his pincers in the fire, red hot, he seized the devil by the nose, and put him to such pain, that his bellowings were heard for miles and miles. Some people are inclined to think this nonsense a part of Dunstan's madness (for his head never quite recovered the fever), but I think not. I observe that it induced the ignorant people to consider him a holy man, and that it made him very powerful. Which was exactly what he always wanted.

On the day of the coronation of the handsome boy-king Edwy, it was remarked by ODO, Archbishop of Canterbury (who was a Dane by birth), that the King quietly left the coronation feast, while all the company were there. Odo, much displeased, sent his friend Dunstan to seek him. Dunstan finding him in the company of his beautiful young wife ELGIVA, and her mother ETHELGIVA, a good and virtuous lady, not only grossly abused them, but dragged the young King back into the feasting-hall by force. Some, again, think Dunstan did this because the young King's fair wife was his own cousin, and the monks objected to people marrying their own cousins; but I believe he did it, because he was an imperious, audacious, ill-conditioned priest, who, having loved a young lady himself before he became a sour monk, hated all love now, and everything belonging to it.

The young King was quite old enough to feel this insult. Dunstan had been Treasurer in the last reign, and he soon charged Dunstan with having taken some of the last king's money. The Glastonbury Abbot fled to Belgium (very narrowly escaping some pursuers who were sent to put out his eyes, as you will wish they had, when you read what follows), and his abbey was given to priests who were married; whom he always, both before and afterwards, opposed. But he quickly conspired with his friend, Odo the Dane, to set up the King's young brother, EDGAR, as his rival for the throne; and, not content with this revenge, he caused the beautiful queen Elgiva, though a lovely girl of only seventeen or eighteen, to be stolen from one of the Royal Palaces, branded in the cheek with a red-hot iron, and sold into slavery in Ireland. But the Irish people pitied and befriended her; and they said, "Let us restore the girl-queen to the boy-king, and make the young lovers happy!" and they cured her of her cruel wound, and sent her home as beautiful as before. But the villain Dunstan, and that other villain, Odo, caused her to be waylaid at Gloucester as she was joyfully hurrying to join her husband, and to be hacked and hewn with swords, and to be barbarously maimed and lamed, and left to die. When Edwy the Fair (his people called him so, because he was so young and handsome) heard of her dreadful fate, he died of a broken heart; and so the pitiful story of the poor young wife and husband ends! Ah! Better to be two cottagers in these better times, than king and queen of England in those bad days, though never so fair!

Then came the boy-king, EDGAR, called the Peaceful, fifteen years old. Dunstan, being still the real king, drove all married priests out of the monasteries and abbeys, and replaced them by solitary monks like himself, of the rigid order called the Benedictines. He made himself Archbishop of Canterbury, for his greater glory; and exercised such

power over the neighbouring British princes, and so collected
them about the King, that once, when the King held his
court at Chester, and went on the river Dee to visit the
monastery of St. John, the eight oars of his boat were
pulled (as the people used to delight in relating in stories
and songs) by eight crowned kings, and steered by the King
of England.   As Edgar was very obedient to Dunstan and
the monks, they took great pains to represent him as the
best of kings.   But he was really profligate, debauched, and
vicious.   He once forcibly carried off a young lady from the
convent at Wilton ; and Dunstan, pretending to be very
much shocked, condemned him not to wear his crown
upon his head for seven years—no great punishment, I dare
say, as it can hardly have been a more comfortable ornament to wear, than a stewpan without a handle.   His
marriage with his second wife, ELFRIDA, is one of the
worst events of his reign.   Hearing of the beauty of this
lady, he despatched his favourite courtier. ATHELWOLD, to
her father's castle in Devonshire, to see if she were really
as charming as fame reported.   Now, she was so exceedingly
beautiful that Athelwold fell in love with her himself, and
married her ; but he told the King that she was only rich—
not handsome.   The King, suspecting the truth when they
came home, resolved to pay the newly-married couple a visit ;
and, suddenly, told Athelwold to prepare for his immediate
coming.   Athelwold, terrified, confessed to his young wife
what he had said and done, and implored her to disguise her
beauty by some ugly dress or silly manner, that he might
be safe from the King's anger.   She promised that she
would ; but she was a proud woman, who would far rather
have been a queen than the wife of a courtier.   She dressed
herself in her best dress, and adorned herself with her richest
jewels ; and when the King came, presently, he discovered
the cheat.   So, he caused his false friend, Athelwold, to be
murdered in a wood, and married his widow, this bad
Elfrida.   Six or seven years afterwards, he died ; and was
buried, as if he had been all that the monks said he was,
in the abbey of Glastonbury, which he—or Dunstan for
him—had much enriched.

England, in one part of this reign, was so troubled by
wolves, which, driven out of the open country, hid themselves in the mountains of Wales when they were not
attacking travellers and animals, that the tribute payable

by the Welsh people was forgiven them, on condition of their producing. every year, three hundred wolves' heads. And the Welshmen were so sharp upon the wolves, to save their money, that in four years there was not a wolf left.

Then came the boy-king, EDWARD, called the Martyr, from the manner of his death. Elfrida had a son, named ETHELRED, for whom she claimed the throne ; but Dunstan did not choose to favour him, and he made Edward king. The boy was hunting, one day, down in Dorsetshire, when he rode near to Corfe Castle, where Elfrida and Ethelred lived. Wishing to see them kindly, he rode away from his attendants and galloped to the castle gate, where he arrived at twilight. and blew his hunting-horn. " You are welcome, dear King." said Elfrida, coming out, with her brightest smiles. " Pray you dismount and enter." " Not so, dear madam," said the King. " My company will miss me, and fear that I have met with some harm. Please you to give me a cup of wine, that I may drink here, in the saddle, to you and to my little brother, and so ride away with the good speed I have made in riding here." Elfrida, going in to bring the wine, whispered to an armed servant, one of her attendants, who stole out of the darkening gateway, and crept round behind the King's horse. As the King raised the cup to his lips, saying, " Health ! " to the wicked woman who was smiling on him, and to his innocent brother whose hand she held in hers, and who was only ten years old, this armed man made a spring and stabbed him in the back. He dropped the cup and spurred his horse away ; but, soon fainting with loss of blood, drooped from the saddle, and, in his fall, en- tangled one of his feet in the stirrup. The frightened horse dashed on ; trailing his rider's curls upon the ground ; dragging his smooth young face through ruts, and stones, and briers, and fallen leaves, and mud ; until the hunters, tracking the animal's course by the King's blood, caught his bridle, and released the disfigured body.

Then came the sixth and last of the boy-kings, ETHELRED, whom Elfrida, when he cried out at the sight of his murdered brother riding away from the castle gate, unmercifully beat with a torch which she snatched from one of the attendants. The people so disliked this boy, on account of his cruel mother and the murder she had done to promote him, that Dunstan would not have had him for king, but would have made EDGITHA, the daughter of the dead King Edgar, and of the lady whom he stole out of the convent at Wilton, Queen of England, if she would have consented. But she knew the stories of the youthful kings too well, and would not be persuaded from the convent where she lived in peace ; so, Dunstan put Ethelred on the throne, having no one else to put there and gave him the nickname of THE UNREADY—knowing that he wanted resolution and firmness.

At first, Elfrida possessed great influence over the young King, but, as he grew older and came of age, her influence declined. The infamous woman, not having it in her power to do any more evil, then retired from court, and, according to the fashion of the time, built churches and monasteries, to expiate her guilt. As if a church, with a steeple reaching to the very stars, would have been any sign of true repentance for the blood of the poor boy, whose murdered form was trailed at his horse's heels ! As if she could have buried her wickedness beneath the senseless stones of the whole world, piled up one upon another, for the monks to live in !

About the ninth or tenth year of this reign, Dunstan died. He was growing old then, but was as stern and artful as ever. Two circumstances that happened in connexion with him, in this reign of Ethelred, made a great noise. Once, he was present at a meeting of the Church, when the question was discussed whether priests should have permission to marry ; and, as he sat with his head hung down, apparently thinking about it, a voice seemed to come out of a crucifix in the room. and warn the meeting to be of his opinion. This was some juggling of Dunstan's, and was probably his own voice disguised. But he played off a worse juggle than that, soon afterwards ; for, another meeting being held on the same subject, and he and his supporters being seated on one side of a great room, and their opponents on the other, he rose and said, " To Christ himself, as Judge, do I commit this cause ! " Immediately on these words being spoken, the floor where the opposite party sat gave way, and some were killed and many wounded. You may be pretty sure that it had been weakened under Dunstan's direction, and that it fell at Dunstan's signal. *His* part of the floor did not go down. No, no. He was too good a workman for that.

When he died, the monks settled that he was a Saint, and called him Saint Dunstan ever afterwards. They might just as well have settled that he was a coach-horse, and could just as easily have called him one.

Ethelred the Unready was glad enough, I dare say, to be rid of this holy saint; but, left to himself, he was a poor weak king, and his reign was a reign of defeat and shame. The restless Danes, led by SWEYN, a son of the King of Denmark who had quarrelled with his father and had been banished from home, again came into England, and, year after year, attacked and despoiled large towns. To coax these sea-kings away, the weak Ethelred paid them money; but, the more money he paid, the more money the Danes wanted. At first, he gave them ten thousand pounds; on their next invasion, sixteen thousand pounds; on their next invasion, four and twenty thousand pounds: to pay which large sums, the unfortunate English people were heavily taxed. But, as the Danes still came back and wanted more, he thought it would be a good plan to marry into some powerful foreign family that would help him with soldiers. So, in the year one thousand and two, he courted and married Emma, the sister of Richard Duke of Normandy; a lady who was called the Flower of Normandy.

And now, a terrible deed was done in England, the like of which was never done on English ground before or since. On the thirteenth of November, in pursuance of secret in-structions sent by the King over the whole country, the inhabitants of every town and city armed, and murdered all the Danes who were their neighbours. Young and old, babies and soldiers, men and women, every Dane was killed. No doubt there were among them many ferocious men who had done the English great wrong, and whose pride and insolence, in swaggering in the houses of the English and insulting their wives and daughters, had become unbearable; but no doubt there were also among them many peaceful Christian Danes who had married English women and become like English men. They were all slain, even to GUNHILDA, the sister of the King of Denmark, married to an English lord; who was first obliged to see the murder of her husband and her child, and then was killed herself.

When the King of the sea-kings heard of this deed of blood, he swore that he would have a great revenge. He raised an army, and a mightier fleet of ships than ever yet had sailed to England; and in all his army there was not a slave or an old man, but every soldier was a free man, and the son of a free man, and in the prime of life, and sworn to

be revenged upon the English nation, for the massacre of
that dread thirteenth of November, when his countrymen
and countrywomen, and the little children whom they loved,
were killed with fire and sword. And so, the sea-kings came
to England in many great ships, each bearing the flag of its
own commander   Golden eagles, ravens, dragons, dolphins,
beasts of prey, threatened England from the prows of those
ships, as they came onward through the water ; and were
reflected in the shining shields that hung upon their sides.
The ship that bore the standard of the King of the sea-kings
was carved and painted like a mighty serpent ; and the King
in his anger prayed that the Gods in whom he trusted might
all desert him, if his serpent did not strike its fangs into
England's heart.

And indeed it did.   For, the great army landing from the
great fleet, near Exeter, went forward, laying England waste,
and striking their lances in the earth as they advanced, or
throwing them into rivers, in token of their making all
the island theirs.   In remembrance of the black November
night when the Danes were murdered, wheresoever the
invaders came, they made the Saxons prepare and spread for
them great feasts ; and when they had eaten those feasts,
and had drunk a curse to England with wild rejoicings,
they drew their swords, and killed their Saxon entertainers,
and marched on.   For six long years they carried on this
war : burning the crops, farmhouses, barns, mills, granaries ;
killing the labourers in the fields ; preventing the seed from
being sown in the ground ; causing famine and starvation ;
leaving only heaps of ruin and smoking ashes, where they
had found rich towns.   To crown this misery, English officers
and men deserted, and even the favourites of Ethelred the
Unready, becoming traitors, seized many of the English
ships, turned pirates against their own country, and aided
by a storm occasioned the loss of nearly the whole English
navy.

There was but one man of note, at this miserable pass,
who was true to his country and the feeble King.   He was
a priest, and a brave one.   For twenty days, the Archbishop
of Canterbury defended that city against its Danish besiegers ; and when a traitor in the town threw the gates
open and admitted them, he said, in chains, " I will not
buy my life with money that must be extorted from the
suffering people.   Do with me what you please ! "   Again

and again, he steadily refused to purchase his release with
gold wrung from the poor.

At last, the Danes being tired of this, and being assembled
at a drunken merry-making, had him brought into the
feasting-hall.

"Now, bishop," they said, "we want gold!"

He looked round on the crowd of angry faces; from the
shaggy beards close to him, to the shaggy beards against
the walls, where men were mounted on tables and forms to
see him over the heads of others: and he knew that his
time was come.

"I have no gold," he said.

"Get it, bishop!" they all thundered.

"That, I have often told you I will not," said he.

They gathered closer round him, threatening, but he stood
unmoved. Then, one man struck him; then, another; then
a cursing soldier picked up from a heap in a corner of the
hall, where fragments had been rudely thrown at dinner,
a great ox-bone, and cast it at his face, from which the blood
came spurting forth; then, others ran to the same heap, and
knocked him down with other bones, and bruised and
battered him; until one soldier whom he had baptised
(willing, as I hope for the sake of that soldier's soul, to
shorten the sufferings of the good man) struck him dead with
his battle-axe.

If Ethelred had had the heart to emulate the courage of
this noble archbishop, he might have done something yet.
But he paid the Danes forty-eight thousand pounds, instead,
and gained so little by the cowardly act, that Sweyn soon
afterwards came over to subdue all England. So broken
was the attachment of the English people, by this time, to
their incapable King and their forlorn country which could
not protect them, that they welcomed Sweyn on all sides, as
a deliverer. London faithfully stood out, as long as the
King was within its walls; but, when he sneaked away, it
also welcomed the Dane. Then, all was over; and the King
took refuge abroad with the Duke of Normandy, who had
already given shelter to the King's wife, once the Flower of
that country, and to her children.

Still, the English people, in spite of their sad sufferings.
could not quite forget the great King Alfred and the Saxon
race. When Sweyn died suddenly, in little more than
a month after he had been proclaimed King of England, they

generously sent to Ethelred, to say that they would have him for their King again, "if he would only govern them better than he had governed them before." The Unready, instead of coming himself, sent Edward, one of his sons, to make promises for him. At last, he followed, and the English declared him King. The Danes declared CANUTE, the son of Sweyn, King. Thus, direful war began again, and lasted for three years, when the Unready died. And I know of nothing better that he did, in all his reign of eight and thirty years.

Was Canute to be King now? Not over the Saxons, they said ; they must have EDMUND, one of the sons of the Unready, who was surnamed IRONSIDE, because of his strength and stature. Edmund and Canute thereupon fell to, and fought five battles—O unhappy England, what a fighting-ground it was!—and then Ironside, who was a big man, proposed to Canute, who was a little man, that they two should fight it out in single combat. If Canute had been the big man, he would probably have said yes, but, being the little man, he decidedly said no. However, he declared that he was willing to divide the kingdom—to take all that lay north of Watling Street, as the old Roman military road from Dover to Chester was called, and to give Ironside all that lay south of it. Most men being weary of so much bloodshed, this was done. But Canute soon became sole King of England ; for Ironside died suddenly within two months. Some think that he was killed, and killed by Canute's orders. No one knows.

CHAPTER V

ENGLAND UNDER CANUTE THE DANE

CANUTE reigned eighteen years. He was a merciless King at first. After he had clasped the hands of the Saxon chiefs, in token of the sincerity with which he swore to be just and good to them in return for their acknowledging him, he denounced and slew many of them, as well as many relations of the late King. "He who brings me the head of one of my enemies," he used to say, "shall be dearer to me than a brother." And he was so severe in hunting down his enemies, that he must have got together a pretty large family of these dear brothers. He was strongly inclined to kill EDMUND and EDWARD, two children, sons of poor Ironside; but, being afraid to do so in England, he sent them over to the King of Sweden, with a request that the King would be so good as "dispose of them." If the King of Sweden had been like many, many other men of that day, he would have had their innocent throats cut; but he was a kind man, and brought them up tenderly.

Normandy ran much in Canute's mind. In Normandy were the two children of the late king— EDWARD and ALFRED by name ; and their uncle the Duke might one day claim the crown for them. But the Duke showed so little inclination to do so now, that he proposed to Canute to marry his sister, the widow of The Unready ; who, being but a showy flower, and caring for nothing so much as becoming a queen again, left her children and was wedded to him.

Successful and triumphant, assisted by the valour of the English in his foreign wars, and with little strife to trouble him at home, Canute had a prosperous reign, and made many improvements. He was a poet and a musician. He grew sorry, as he grew older, for the blood he had shed at first ; and went to Rome in a Pilgrim's dress, by way of washing it out. He gave a great deal of money to foreigners on his journey ; but he took it from the English before he started.

On the whole, however, he certainly became a far better man when he had no opposition to contend with, and was as great a King as England had known for some time.

The old writers of history relate how that Canute was one day disgusted with his courtiers for their flattery, and how he caused his chair to be set on the sea-shore, and feigned to command the tide as it came up not to wet the edge of his robe, for the land was his; how the tide came up, of course, without regarding him; and how he then turned to his flatterers, and rebuked them, saying, what was the might of any earthly king, to the might of the Creator, who could say unto the sea, "Thus far shalt thou go, and no farther!" We may learn from this, I think, that a little sense will go a long way in a king; and that courtiers are not easily cured of flattery, nor kings of a liking for it. If the courtiers of Canute had not known, long before, that the King was fond of flattery, they would have known better than to offer it in such large doses. And if they had not known that he was vain of this speech (anything but a wonderful speech it seems to me, if a good child had made it), they would not have been at such great pains to repeat it. I fancy I see them all on the sea-shore together; the King's chair sinking in the sand; the King in a mighty good humour with his own wisdom; and the courtiers pretending to be quite stunned by it!

It is not the sea alone that is bidden to go "thus far, and no farther." The great command goes forth to all the kings upon the earth, and went to Canute in the year one thousand and thirty-five, and stretched him dead upon his bed. Beside it, stood his Norman wife. Perhaps, as the King looked his last upon her, he, who had so often thought distrustfully of Normandy, long ago, thought once more of the two exiled Princes in their uncle's court, and of the little favour they could feel for either Danes or Saxons, and of a rising cloud in Normandy that slowly moved towards England.

CHAPTER VI

ENGLAND UNDER HAROLD HAREFOOT, HARDICANUTE, AND EDWARD THE CONFESSOR

CANUTE left three sons, by name SWEYN, HAROLD, and HARDI-CANUTE; but his Queen, Emma, once the Flower of Normandy, was the mother of only Hardicanute. Canute had wished his dominions to be divided between the three, and had wished Harold to have England; but the Saxon people in the South of England, headed by a nobleman with great possessions, called the powerful EARL GODWIN (who is said to have been originally a poor cow-boy), opposed this, and desired to have, instead, either Hardicanute, or one of the two exiled Princes who were over in Normandy. It seemed so certain that there would be more bloodshed to settle this dispute, that many people left their homes, and took refuge in the woods and swamps. Happily, however, it was agreed to refer the whole question to a great meeting at Oxford, which decided that Harold should have all the country north of the Thames, with London for his capital city, and that Hardicanute should have all the south. The quarrel was so arranged ; and, as Hardicanute was in Denmark troubling himself very little about anything but eating and getting drunk, his mother and Earl Godwin governed the south for him.

They had hardly begun to do so, and the trembling people who had hidden themselves were scarcely at home again, when Edward, the elder of the two exiled Princes, came over from Normandy with a few followers, to claim the English Crown. His mother Emma, however, who only cared for her last son Hardicanute, instead of assisting him, as he expected, opposed him so strongly with all her influence that he was very soon glad to get safely back. His brother Alfred was not so fortunate. Believing in an affectionate letter, written some time afterwards to him and his brother,

in his mother's name (but whether really with or without
his mother's knowledge is now uncertain), he allowed himself
to be tempted over to England, with a good force of soldiers,
and landing on the Kentish coast, and being met and
welcomed by Earl Godwin, proceeded into Surrey, as far
as the town of Guildford. Here, he and his men halted
in the evening to rest, having still the Earl in their company;
who had ordered lodgings and good cheer for them.   But,
in the dead of the night, when they were off their guard,
being divided into small parties sleeping soundly after
a long march and a plentiful supper in different houses,
they were set upon by the King's troops, and taken prisoners.
Next morning they were drawn out in a line, to the number
of six hundred men, and were barbarously tortured and
killed; with the exception of every tenth man, who was
sold into slavery.   As to the wretched Prince Alfred, he
was stripped naked, tied to a horse and sent away into the
Isle of Ely, where his eyes were torn out of his head, and
where in a few days he miserably died.   I am not sure
that the Earl had wilfully entrapped him, but I suspect it
strongly.

Harold was now King all over England, though it is
doubtful whether the Archbishop of Canterbury (the greater
part of the priests were Saxons, and not friendly to the
Danes) ever consented to crown him.   Crowned or un-
crowned, with the Archbishop's leave or without it, he
was King for four years: after which short reign he died,
and was buried; having never done much in life but go
a hunting.   He was such a fast runner at this, his favourite
sport, that the people called him Harold Harefoot.

Hardicanute was then at Bruges, in Flanders, plotting,
with his mother (who had gone over there after the cruel
murder of Prince Alfred), for the invasion of England.   The
Danes and Saxons, finding themselves without a King, and
dreading new disputes, made common cause, and joined in
inviting him to occupy the Throne.   He consented, and soon
troubled them enough; for he brought over numbers of
Danes, and taxed the people so insupportably to enrich
those greedy favourites that there were many insurrections,
especially one at Worcester, where the citizens rose and
killed his tax-collectors; in revenge for which he burned
their city.   He was a brutal King, whose first public act
was to order the dead body of poor Harold Harefoot to be

dug up, beheaded, and thrown into the river. His end was
worthy of such a beginning. He fell down drunk, with
a goblet of wine in his hand, at a wedding-feast at Lambeth,
given in honour of the marriage of his standard-bearer,
a Dane named TOWED THE PROUD. And he never spoke
again.

EDWARD, afterwards called by the monks THE CONFESSOR,
succeeded ; and his first act was to oblige his mother Emma,
who had favoured him so little, to retire into the country ;
where she died some ten years afterwards. He was the
exiled prince whose brother Alfred had been so foully killed.
He had been invited over from Normandy by Hardicanute,
in the course of his short reign of two years, and had been
handsomely treated at court. His cause was now favoured
by the powerful Earl Godwin, and he was soon made King.
This Earl had been suspected by the people, ever since
Prince Alfred's cruel death ; he had even been tried in the
last reign for the Prince's murder, but had been pronounced
not guilty ; chiefly. as it was supposed, because of a present
he had made to the swinish King, of a gilded ship with
a figure-head of solid gold, and a crew of eighty splendidly
armed men. It was his interest to help the new King with
his power, if the new King would help him against the
popular distrust and hatred. So they made a bargain.
Edward the Confessor got the Throne. The Earl got more
power and more land, and his daughter Editha was made
queen ; for it was a part of their compact that the King
should take her for his wife.

But, although she was a gentle lady, in all things worthy
to be beloved—good, beautiful, sensible, and kind—the King
from the first neglected her. Her father and her six proud
brothers, resenting this cold treatment. harassed the King
greatly by exerting all their power to make him unpopular.
Having lived so long in Normandy, he preferred the
Normans to the English. He made a Norman Archbishop,
and Norman Bishops ; his great officers and favourites were
all Normans ; he introduced the Norman fashions and the
Norman language ; in imitation of the state custom of
Normandy, he attached a great seal to his state documents,
instead of merely marking them, as the Saxon Kings had
done, with the sign of the cross—just as poor people who
have never been taught to write, now make the same mark
for their names. All this, the powerful Earl Godwin and

his six proud sons represented to the people as disfavour shown towards the English; and thus they daily increased their own power, and daily diminished the power of the King.

They were greatly helped by an event that occurred when he had reigned eight years. Eustace, Earl of Boulogne, who had married the King's sister, came to England on a visit. After staying at the court some time, he set forth, with his numerous train of attendants, to return home. They were to embark at Dover. Entering that peaceful town in armour, they took possession of the best houses, and noisily demanded to be lodged and entertained without payment. One of the bold men of Dover, who would not endure to have these domineering strangers jingling their heavy swords and iron corselets up and down his house, eating his meat and drinking his strong liquor, stood in his doorway and refused admission to the first armed man who came there. The armed man drew, and wounded him. The man of Dover struck the armed man dead. Intelligence of what he had done, spreading through the streets to where the Count Eustace and his men were standing by their horses, bridle in hand, they passionately mounted, galloped to the house, surrounded it, forced their way in (the doors and windows being closed when they came up), and killed the man of Dover at his own fireside. They then clattered through the streets, cutting down and riding over men, women, and children. This did not last long, you may believe. The men of Dover set upon them with great fury, killed nineteen of the foreigners, wounded many more, and, blockading the road to the port so that they should not embark, beat them out of the town by the way they had come. Hereupon, Count Eustace rides as hard as man can ride to Gloucester, where Edward is, surrounded by Norman monks and Norman lords. "Justice!" cries the Count, "upon the men of Dover, who have set upon and slain my people!" The King sends immediately for the powerful Earl Godwin, who happens to be near; reminds him that Dover is under his government; and orders him to repair to Dover and do military execution on the inhabitants. "It does not become you," says the proud Earl in reply, "to condemn without a hearing those whom you have sworn to protect. I will not do it."

The King, therefore, summoned the Earl, on pain of banishment and loss of his titles and property, to appear before the court to answer this disobedience. The Earl refused to appear. He, his eldest son Harold, and his second son Sweyn, hastily raised as many fighting men as their utmost power could collect, and demanded to have Count Eustace and his followers surrendered to the justice of the country. The King, in his turn, refused to give them up, and raised a strong force. After some treaty and delay, the troops of the great Earl and his sons began to fall off. The Earl, with a part of his family and abundance of treasure, sailed to Flanders; Harold escaped to Ireland; and the power of the great family was for that time gone in England. But, the people did not forget them.

Then, Edward the Confessor, with the true meanness of a mean spirit, visited his dislike of the once powerful father and sons upon the helpless daughter and sister, his unoffend-ing wife, whom all who saw her (her husband and his monks excepted) loved. He seized rapaciously upon her fortune and her jewels, and allowing her only one attendant, con-fined her in a gloomy convent, of which a sister of his—no doubt an unpleasant lady after his own heart—was abbess or jailer.

Having got Earl Godwin and his six sons well out of his way, the King favoured the Normans more than ever. He invited over WILLIAM, DUKE OF NORMANDY, the son of that Duke who had received him and his murdered brother long ago, and of a peasant girl, a tanner's daughter, with whom that Duke had fallen in love for her beauty as he saw her washing clothes in a brook. William, who was a great warrior, with a passion for fine horses, dogs, and arms, accepted the invitation; and the Normans in England, finding themselves more numerous than ever when he arrived with his retinue, and held in still greater honour at court than before, became more and more haughty towards the people, and were more and more disliked by them.

The old Earl Godwin, though he was abroad, knew well how the people felt; for, with part of the treasure he had carried away with him, he kept spies and agents in his pay all over England. Accordingly, he thought the time was come for fitting out a great expedition against the Norman-loving King. With it, he sailed to the Isle of Wight, where he was joined by his son Harold, the most gallant and brave of all his family. And so the father and son came sailing

up the Thames to Southwark ; great numbers of the people
declaring for them, and shouting for the English Earl and
the English Harold, against the Norman favourites!

The King was at first as blind and stubborn as kings
usually have been whensoever they have been in the hands
of monks. But the people rallied so thickly round the old
Earl and his son, and the old Earl was so steady in demanding without bloodshed the restoration of himself and his
family to their rights, that at last the court took the alarm.
The Norman Archbishop of Canterbury, and the Norman
Bishop of London, surrounded by their retainers, fought
their way out of London, and escaped from Essex to France
in a fishing-boat. The other Norman favourites dispersed
in all directions. The old Earl and his sons (except Sweyn,
who had committed crimes against the law) were restored
to their possessions and dignities. Editha, the virtuous and
lovely Queen of the insensible King, was triumphantly
released from her prison, the convent, and once more sat in
her chair of state, arrayed in the jewels of which, when she
had no champion to support her rights, her cold-blooded
husband had deprived her.

The old Earl Godwin did not long enjoy his restored
fortune. He fell down in a fit at the King's table, and died
upon the third day afterwards. Harold succeeded to his
power, and to a far higher place in the attachment of the
people than his father had ever held. By his valour he
subdued the King's enemies in many bloody fights. He
was vigorous against rebels in Scotland—this was the time
when Macbeth slew Duncan, upon which event our English
Shakespeare, hundreds of years afterwards, wrote his great
tragedy ; and he killed the restless Welsh King GRIFFITH,
and brought his head to England.

What Harold was doing at sea, when he was driven on
the French coast by a tempest, is not at all certain ; nor
does it at all matter. That his ship was forced by a storm
on that shore, and that he was taken prisoner, there is no
doubt. In those barbarous days, all shipwrecked strangers
were taken prisoners, and obliged to pay ransom. So,
a certain Count Guy, who was the Lord of Ponthieu where
Harold's disaster happened, seized him, instead of relieving
him like a hospitable and Christian lord as he ought to have
done, and expected to make a very good thing of it.

But Harold sent off immediately to Duke William of

Normandy, complaining of this treatment; and the Duke no sooner heard of it than he ordered Harold to be escorted to the ancient town of Rouen, where he then was, and where he received him as an honoured guest. Now, some writers tell us that Edward the Confessor, who was by this time old and had no children, had made a will, appointing Duke William of Normandy his successor, and had informed the Duke of his having done so. There is no doubt that he was anxious about his successor; because he had even invited over, from abroad, EDWARD THE OUTLAW, a son of Ironside, who had come to England with his wife and three children, but whom the King had strangely refused to see when he did come, and who had died in London suddenly (princes were terribly liable to sudden death in those days), and had been buried in St. Paul's Cathedral. The King might possibly have made such a will; or, having always been fond of the Normans, he might have encouraged Norman William to aspire to the English crown, by something that he said to him when he was staying at the English court. But, certainly William did now aspire to it; and knowing that Harold would be a powerful rival, he called together a great assembly of his nobles, offered Harold his daughter ADELE in marriage, informed him that he meant on King Edward's death to claim the English crown as his own inheritance, and required Harold then and there to swear to aid him. Harold, being in the Duke's power, took this oath upon the Missal, or Prayer-book. It is a good example of the superstitions of the monks, that this Missal, instead of being placed upon a table, was placed upon a tub; which, when Harold had sworn, was uncovered, and shown to be full of dead men's bones—bones, as the monks pretended, of saints. This was supposed to make Harold's oath a great deal more impressive and binding. As if the great name of the Creator of Heaven and earth could be made more solemn by a knuckle-bone, or a double-tooth, or a finger-nail, of Dunstan!

Within a week or two after Harold's return to England, the dreary old Confessor was found to be dying. After wandering in his mind like a very weak old man, he died. As he had put himself entirely in the hands of the monks when he was alive, they praised him lustily when he was dead. They had gone so far, already, as to persuade him that he could work miracles; and had brought people afflicted with a bad disorder of the skin, to him, to be touched and cured. This was called "touching for the King's Evil," which afterwards became a royal custom. You know, however, Who really touched the sick, and healed them ; and you know His sacred name is not among the dusty line of human kings.

CHAPTER VII

ENGLAND UNDER HAROLD THE SECOND, AND CONQUERED BY THE NORMANS

HAROLD was crowned King of England on the very day of the maudlin Confessor's funeral. He had good need to be quick about it. When the news reached Norman William, hunting in his park at Rouen, he dropped his bow, returned to his palace, called his nobles to council, and presently sent ambassadors to Harold, calling on him to keep his oath and resign the Crown. Harold would do no such thing. The barons of France leagued together round Duke William for the invasion of England. Duke William promised freely to distribute English wealth and English lands among them. The Pope sent to Normandy a consecrated banner, and a ring containing a hair which he warranted to have grown on the head of Saint Peter. He blessed the enterprise ; and cursed Harold ; and requested that the Normans would pay " Peter's Pence "—or a tax to himself of a penny a year on every house—a little more regularly in future, if they could make it convenient.

King Harold had a rebel brother in Flanders, who was a vassal of HAROLD HARDRADA, King of Norway. This brother, and this Norwegian King, joining their forces against England, with Duke William's help, won a fight in which the English were commanded by two nobles ; and then besieged York. Harold, who was waiting for the Normans on the coast at Hastings, with his army, marched to Stamford Bridge upon the river Derwent to give them instant battle.

He found them drawn up in a hollow circle, marked out by their shining spears. Riding round this circle at a distance, to survey it, he saw a brave figure on horseback, in a blue mantle and a bright helmet, whose horse suddenly stumbled and threw him.

" Who is that man who has fallen ? " Harold asked of one of his captains.

"The King of Norway," he replied.

"He is a tall and stately king," said Harold, "but his end is near."

He added, in a little while, "Go yonder to my brother, and tell him, if he withdraw his troops, he shall be Earl of Northumberland, and rich and powerful in England."

The captain rode away and gave the message.

"What will he give to my friend the King of Norway?" asked the brother.

"Seven feet of earth for a grave," replied the captain.

"No more?" returned the brother, with a smile.

"The King of Norway being a tall man, perhaps a little more," replied the captain.

"Ride back!" said the brother, "and tell King Harold to make ready for the fight!"

He did so, very soon. And such a fight King Harold led against that force, that his brother, and the Norwegian King, and every chief of note in all their host, except the Norwegian King's son, Olave, to whom he gave honourable dismissal, were left dead upon the field. The victorious army marched to York. As King Harold sat there at the feast, in the midst of all his company, a stir was heard at the doors; and messengers all covered with mire from riding far and fast through broken ground came hurrying in, to report that the Normans had landed in England.

The intelligence was true. They had been tossed about by contrary winds, and some of their ships had been wrecked. A part of their own shore, to which they had been driven back, was strewn with Norman bodies. But they had once more made sail, led by the Duke's own galley, a present from his wife, upon the prow whereof the figure of a golden boy stood pointing towards England. By day, the banner of the three Lions of Normandy, the diverse coloured sails, the gilded vans, the many decorations of this gorgeous ship, had glittered in the sun and sunny water; by night, a light had sparkled like a star at her mast-head. And now, encamped near Hastings, with their leader lying in the old Roman castle of Pevensey, the English retiring in all directions, the land for miles around scorched and smoking, fired and pillaged, was the whole Norman power, hopeful and strong on English ground.

Harold broke up the feast and hurried to London. Within a week, his army was ready. He sent out spies to ascertain the Norman strength. William took them, caused them to be led through his whole camp, and then dismissed. "The Normans," said these spies to Harold, "are not bearded on the upper lip as we English are, but are shorn. They are priests." "My men," replied Harold, with a laugh, "will find those priests good soldiers!"

"The Saxons," reported Duke William's outposts of Norman soldiers, who were instructed to retire as King Harold's army advanced, "rush on us through their pillaged country with the fury of madmen."

"Let them come, and come soon!" said Duke William.

Some proposals for a reconciliation were made, but were soon abandoned. In the middle of the month of October, in the year one thousand and sixty-six, the Normans and the English came front to front. All night the armies lay encamped before each other, in a part of the country then called Senlac, now called (in remembrance of them) Battle. With the first dawn of day, they arose. There, in the faint light, were the English on a hill; a wood behind them; in their midst, the Royal banner, representing a fighting warrior, woven in gold thread, adorned with precious stones; beneath the banner, as it rustled in the wind, stood King Harold on foot, with two of his remaining brothers by his side; around them, still and silent as the dead, clustered the whole English army—every soldier covered by his shield, and bearing in his hand his dreaded English battle-axe.

On an opposite hill, in three lines, archers, foot-soldiers, horsemen, was the Norman force. Of a sudden, a great battle-cry, "God help us!" burst from the Norman lines. The English answered with their own battle-cry, "God's Rood! Holy Rood!" The Normans then came sweeping down the hill to attack the English.

There was one tall Norman Knight who rode before the Norman army on a prancing horse, throwing up his heavy sword and catching it, and singing of the bravery of his countrymen. An English Knight, who rode out from the English force to meet him, fell by this Knight's hand. Another English Knight rode out, and he fell too. But then a third rode out, and killed the Norman. This was in the first beginning of the fight. It soon raged everywhere.

The English, keeping side by side in a great mass, cared no more for the showers of Norman arrows than if they had been showers of Norman rain. When the Norman horsemen rode against them, with their battle-axes they cut men and horses down. The Normans gave way. The English pressed forward. A cry went forth among the Norman troops that Duke William was killed. Duke William took off his helmet, in order that his face might be distinctly seen, and rode along the line before his men. This gave them courage. As they turned again to face the English, some of their Norman horse divided the pursuing body of the English from the rest, and thus all that foremost portion of the English army fell, fighting bravely. The main body still remaining firm, heedless of the Norman arrows, and with their battle-axes cutting down the crowds of horsemen when they rode up, like forests of young trees, Duke William pretended to retreat. The eager English followed. The Norman army closed again, and fell upon them with great slaughter.

"Still," said Duke William, "there are thousands of the English, firm as rocks around their King. Shoot upward Norman archers, that your arrows may fall down upon their faces!"

The sun rose high, and sank, and the battle still raged. Through all the wild October day, the clash and din resounded in the air. In the red sunset, and in the white moonlight, heaps upon heaps of dead men lay strewn, a dreadful spectacle, all over the ground. King Harold, wounded with an arrow in the eye, was nearly blind. His brothers were already killed. Twenty Norman Knights, whose battered armour had flashed fiery and golden in the sunshine all day long, and now looked silvery in the moonlight, dashed forward to seize the Royal banner from the English Knights and soldiers, still faithfully collected round their blinded King. The King received a mortal wound, and dropped. The English broke and fled. The Normans rallied, and the day was lost.

O what a sight beneath the moon and stars, when lights were shining in the tent of the victorious Duke William, which was pitched near the spot where Harold fell—and he and his knights were carousing, within—and soldiers with torches, going slowly to and fro, without, sought for the corpse of Harold among piles of dead—and the Warrior, worked in golden thread and precious stones, lay low, all torn and soiled with blood—and the three Norman Lions kept watch over the field!

CHAPTER VIII

ENGLAND UNDER WILLIAM THE FIRST, THE NORMAN CONQUEROR

Upon the ground where the brave Harold fell, William the Norman afterwards founded an abbey, which, under the name of Battle Abbey, was a rich and splendid place through many a troubled year, though now it is a grey ruin overgrown with ivy. But the first work he had to do, was to conquer the English thoroughly; and that, as you know by this time, was hard work for any man.

He ravaged several counties; he burned and plundered many towns; he laid waste scores upon scores of miles of pleasant country; he destroyed innumerable lives. At length STIGAND, Archbishop of Canterbury, with other representatives of the clergy and the people, went to his camp and submitted to him. EDGAR, the insignificant son of Edmund Ironside, was proclaimed King by others, but nothing came of it. He fled to Scotland afterwards, where his sister, who was young and beautiful, married the Scottish King. Edgar himself was not important enough for anybody to care much about him.

On Christmas Day, William was crowned in Westminster Abbey, under the title of WILLIAM THE FIRST; but he is best known as WILLIAM THE CONQUEROR. It was a strange coronation. One of the bishops who performed the ceremony asked the Normans in French, if they would have Duke William for their king? They answered Yes. Another of the bishops put the same question to the Saxons, in English. They too answered Yes, with a loud shout. The noise being heard by a guard of Norman horse-soldiers outside, was mistaken for resistance on the part of the English. The guard instantly set fire to the neighbouring houses, and a tumult ensued; in the midst of which the King, being left alone in the Abbey, with a few priests (and they all being in a terrible fright together), was hurriedly crowned. When the crown was placed upon his head, he swore to govern the English as well as the best of their own monarchs. I dare say you think, as I do, that if we except the Great Alfred, he might pretty easily have done that.

Numbers of the English nobles had been killed in the last disastrous battle. Their estates, and the estates of all the nobles who had fought against him there, King William seized upon, and gave to his own Norman knights and nobles. Many great English families of the present time acquired their English lands in this way, and are very proud of it.

But what is got by force must be maintained by force. These nobles were obliged to build castles all over England, to defend their new property; and, do what he would, the King could neither soothe nor quell the nation as he wished. He gradually introduced the Norman language and the Norman customs; yet, for a long time the great body of the English remained sullen and revengeful. On his going over to Normandy, to visit his subjects there, the oppressions of his half-brother ODO, whom he left in charge of his English kingdom, drove the people mad. The men of Kent even invited over, to take possession of Dover, their old enemy Count Eustace of Boulogne, who had led the fray when the Dover man was slain at his own fireside. The men of Hereford, aided by the Welsh, and commanded by a chief named EDRIC THE WILD, drove the Normans out of their country. Some of those who had been dispossessed of their lands, banded together in the North of England; some, in Scotland; some, in the thick woods and marshes; and whensoever they could fall upon the Normans, or upon the English who had submitted to the Normans, they fought, despoiled, and murdered, like the desperate outlaws that they were. Conspiracies were set on foot for a general massacre of the Normans, like the old massacre of the Danes. In short, the English were in a murderous mood all through the kingdom.

King William, fearing he might lose his conquest, came back, and tried to pacify the London people by soft words. He then set forth to repress the country people by stern deeds. Among the towns which he besieged, and where he killed and maimed the inhabitants without any distinction, sparing none, young or old, armed or unarmed, were Oxford, Warwick, Leicester, Nottingham, Derby, Lincoln, York. In all these places, and in many others, fire and sword worked their utmost horrors, and made the land dreadful to behold. The streams and rivers were discoloured with blood ; the sky was blackened with smoke ; the fields were wastes of ashes ; the waysides were heaped up with dead. Such are the fatal results of conquest and ambition ! Although William was a harsh and angry man, I do not suppose that he deliberately meant to work this shocking ruin, when he invaded England. But what he had got by the strong hand, he could only keep by the strong hand, and in so doing he made England a great grave.

Two sons of Harold, by name EDMUND and GODWIN, came over from Ireland, with some ships, against the Normans, but were defeated. This was scarcely done, when the outlaws in the woods so harassed York, that the Governor sent to the King for help. The King despatched a general and a large force to occupy the town of Durham. The Bishop of that place met the general outside the town, and warned him not to enter, as he would be in danger there. The general cared nothing for the warning, and went in with all his men. That night, on every hill within sight of Durham, signal fires were seen to blaze. When the morning dawned, the English, who had assembled in great strength, forced the gates, rushed into the town, and slew the Normans every one. The English afterwards besought the Danes to come and help them. The Danes came, with two hundred and forty ships. The outlawed nobles joined them ; they captured York, and drove the Normans out of that city. Then, William bribed the Danes to go away ; and took such vengeance on the English, that all the former fire and sword, smoke and ashes, death and ruin, were nothing compared with it. In melancholy songs, and doleful stories, it was still sung and told by cottage fires on winter evenings, a hundred years afterwards, how, in those dreadful days of the Normans, there was not, from the River Humber to the River Tyne, one inhabited village left, nor one cultivated field—how there was nothing but a dismal ruin, where the human creatures and the beasts lay dead together.

The outlaws had, at this time, what they called a Camp of Refuge, in the midst of the fens of Cambridgeshire. Protected by those marshy grounds which were difficult of approach, they lay among the reeds and rushes, and were hidden by the mists that rose up from the watery earth. Now, there also was, at that time, over the sea in Flanders,

H

an Englishman named HEREWARD, whose father had died in his absence, and whose property had been given to a Norman. When he heard of this wrong that had been done him (from such of the exiled English as chanced to wander into that country), he longed for revenge; and joining the outlaws in their camp of refuge, became their commander. He was so good a soldier, that the Normans supposed him to be aided by enchantment. William, even after he had made a road three miles in length across the Cambridgeshire marshes, on purpose to attack this supposed enchanter, thought it necessary to engage an old lady, who pretended to be a sorceress, to come and do a little enchantment in the royal cause. For this purpose she was pushed on before the troops in a wooden tower; but Hereward very soon disposed of this unfortunate sorceress, by burning her, tower and all. The monks of the convent of Ely near at hand, however, who were fond of good living, and who found it very uncomfortable to have the country blockaded and their supplies of meat and drink cut off. showed the King a secret way of surprising the camp. So Hereward was soon defeated. Whether he afterwards died quietly, or whether he was killed after killing sixteen of the men who attacked him (as some old rhymes relate that he did), I cannot say. His defeat put an end to the Camp of Refuge; and, very soon afterwards, the King, victorious both in Scotland and in England, quelled the last rebellious English noble. He then surrounded himself with Norman lords, enriched by the property of English nobles; had a great survey made of all the land in England, which was entered as the property of its new owners, on a roll called Dooms-day Book; obliged the people to put out their fires and candles at a certain hour every night, on the ringing of a bell which was called The Curfew; introduced the Norman dresses and manners; made the Normans masters every-where, and the English, servants; turned out the English bishops, and put Normans in their places; and showed himself to be the Conqueror indeed.

But, even with his own Normans, he had a restless life. They were always hungering and thirsting for the riches of the English; and the more he gave, the more they wanted. His priests were as greedy as his soldiers. We know of only one Norman who plainly told his master, the King, that he had come with him to England to do his duty as a faithful servant, and that property taken by force from other men had no charms for him. His name was GUILBERT. We should not forget his name, for it is good to remember and to honour honest men.

Besides all these troubles, William the Conqueror was troubled by quarrels among his sons. He had three living. ROBERT, called CURTHOSE, because of his short legs; WILLIAM, called RUFUS or the Red, from the colour of his hair; and HENRY, fond of learning, and called, in the Norman language. BEAUCLERC, or Fine-Scholar. When Robert grew up, he asked of his father the government of Normandy, which he had nominally possessed, as a child, under his mother, MATILDA. The King refusing to grant it, Robert became jealous and discontented; and happening one day, while in this temper, to be ridiculed by his brothers, who threw water on him from a balcony as he was walking before the door, he drew his sword, rushed up-stairs, and was only prevented by the King himself from putting them to death. That same night, he hotly departed with some followers from his father's court, and endeavoured to take the Castle of Rouen by surprise. Failing in this, he shut himself up in another Castle in Normandy, which the King besieged, and where Robert one day unhorsed and nearly killed him without knowing who he was. His submission when he discovered his father, and the intercession of the queen and others, reconciled them; but not soundly; for Robert soon strayed abroad, and went from court to court with his complaints. He was a gay, careless, thoughtless fellow, spending all he got on musicians and dancers; but his mother loved him, and often, against the King's command, supplied him with money through a messenger named SAMSON. At length the incensed King swore he would tear out Samson's eyes; and Samson, thinking that his only hope of safety was in becoming a monk, became one, went on such errands no more, and kept his eyes in his head.

All this time, from the turbulent day of his strange coronation, the Conqueror had been struggling, you see, at any cost of cruelty and bloodshed, to maintain what he had seized. All his reign, he struggled still, with the same object ever before him. He was a stern bold man, and he succeeded in it.

He loved money, and was particular in his eating, but he had only leisure to indulge one other passion, and that was his love of hunting. He carried it to such a height that he ordered whole villages and towns to be swept away to make forests for the deer. Not satisfied with sixty-eight Royal Forests, he laid waste an immense district, to form another in Hampshire, called the New Forest. The many thousands of miserable peasants who saw their little houses pulled down, and themselves and children turned into the open country without a shelter, detested him for his merciless addition to their many sufferings ; and when, in the twenty-first year of his reign (which proved to be the last), he went over to Rouen, England was as full of hatred against him, as if every leaf on every tree in all his Royal Forests had been a curse upon his head. In the New Forest, his son Richard (for he had four sons) had been gored to death by a Stag ; and the people said that this so cruelly-made Forest would yet be fatal to others of the Conqueror's race.

He was engaged in a dispute with the King of France about some territory. While he stayed at Rouen, negotiating with that King, he kept his bed and took medicines : being advised by his physicians to do so, on account of having grown to an unwieldy size. Word being brought to him that the King of France made light of this, and joked about it, he swore in a great rage that he should rue his jests. He assembled his army, marched into the disputed territory, burnt—his old way !—the vines, the crops, and fruit, and set the town of Mantes on fire. But, in an evil hour ; for, as he rode over the hot ruins, his horse, setting his hoofs upon some burning embers, started, threw him forward against the pommel of the saddle, and gave him a mortal hurt. For six weeks he lay dying in a monastery near Rouen, and then made his will, giving England to William, Normandy to Robert, and five thousand pounds to Henry. And now, his violent deeds lay heavy on his mind. He ordered money to be given to many English churches and monasteries, and—which was much better repentance—released his prisoners of state, some of whom had been confined in his dungeons twenty years.

It was a September morning, and the sun was rising, when the King was awakened from slumber by the sound of a church bell. "What bell is that ?" he faintly asked. They told him it was the bell of the chapel of Saint Mary. "I commend my soul," said he, "to Mary ! " and died.

Think of his name, The Conqueror, and then consider how

he lay in death! The moment he was dead, his physicians, priest, and nobles, not knowing what contest for the throne might now take place, or what might happen in it, hastened away, each man for himself and his own property; the mercenary servants of the court began to rob and plunder; the body of the King, in the indecent strife, was rolled from the bed, and lay alone, for hours, upon the ground. O Conqueror, of whom so many great names are proud now, of whom so many great names thought nothing then, it were better to have conquered one true heart, than England!

By-and-by, the priests came creeping in with prayers and candles ; and a good knight, named HERLUIN, undertook (which no one else would do) to convey the body to Caen, in Normandy, in order that it might be buried in St. Stephen's church there, which the Conqueror had founded. But fire, of which he had made such bad use in his life, seemed to follow him of itself in death. A great conflagration broke out in the town when the body was placed in the church ; and those present running out to extinguish the flames, it was once again left alone.

It was not even buried in peace. It was about to be let down, in its Royal robes, into a tomb near the high altar, in presence of a great concourse of people, when a loud voice in the crowd cried out, "This ground is mine! Upon it, stood my father's house. This King despoiled me of both ground and house to build this church. In the great name of GOD, I here forbid his body to be covered with the earth that is my right !" The priests and bishops present, knowing the speaker's right, and knowing that the King had often denied him justice, paid him down sixty shillings for the grave. Even then, the corpse was not at rest. The tomb was too small, and they tried to force it in. It broke, a dreadful smell arose, the people hurried out into the air, and, for the third time, it was left alone.

Where were the Conqueror's three sons, that they were not at their father's burial? Robert was lounging among minstrels, dancers, and gamesters, in France or Germany. Henry was carrying his five thousand pounds safely away in a convenient chest he had got made. William the Red was hurrying to England, to lay hands upon the Royal treasure and the crown.

CHAPTER IX

ENGLAND UNDER WILLIAM THE SECOND, CALLED RUFUS

WILLIAM THE RED, in breathless haste, secured the three great forts of Dover, Pevensey, and Hastings, and made with hot speed for Winchester, where the Royal treasure was kept. The treasurer delivering him the keys, he found that it amounted to sixty thousand pounds in silver, besides gold and jewels. Possessed of this wealth, he soon persuaded the Archbishop of Canterbury to crown him, and became William the Second, King of England.

Rufus was no sooner on the throne, than he ordered into prison again the unhappy state captives whom his father had set free, and directed a goldsmith to ornament his father's tomb profusely with gold and silver. It would have been more dutiful in him to have attended the sick Conqueror when he was dying; but England, itself, like this Red King, who once governed it, has sometimes made expensive tombs for dead men whom it treated shabbily when they were alive.

The King's brother, Robert of Normandy, seeming quite content to be only Duke of that country; and the King's other brother, Fine-Scholar, being quiet enough with his five thousand pounds in a chest; the King flattered himself, we may suppose, with the hope of an easy reign. But easy reigns were difficult to have in those days. The turbulent Bishop Odo (who had blessed the Norman army at the Battle of Hastings, and who, I dare say, took all the credit of the victory to himself) soon began, in concert with some powerful Norman nobles, to trouble the Red King.

The truth seems to be that this bishop and his friends, who had lands in England and lands in Normandy, wished to hold both under one Sovereign; and greatly preferred a thoughtless good-natured person, such as Robert was, to Rufus; who, though far from being an amiable man in any respect, was keen, and not to be imposed upon. They declared in

Robert's favour, and retired to their castles (those castles were very troublesome to kings) in a sullen humour. The Red King, seeing the Normans thus falling from him, revenged himself upon them by appealing to the English; to whom he made a variety of promises, which he never meant to perform—in particular, promises to soften the cruelty of the Forest Laws; and who, in return, so aided him with their valour, that Odo was besieged in the Castle of Rochester, and forced to abandon it, and to depart from England for ever: whereupon the other rebellious Norman nobles were soon reduced and scattered.

Then, the Red King went over to Normandy, where the people suffered greatly under the loose rule of Duke Robert. The King's object was to seize upon the Duke's dominions. This, the Duke, of course, prepared to resist; and miserable war between the two brothers seemed inevitable, when the powerful nobles on both sides, who had seen so much of war, interfered to prevent it. A treaty was made. Each of the two brothers agreed to give up something of his claims, and that the longer-liver of the two should inherit all the dominions of the other. When they had come to this loving understanding, they embraced and joined their forces against Fine-Scholar; who had bought some territory of Robert with a part of his five thousand pounds, and was considered a dangerous individual in consequence.

St. Michael's Mount, in Normandy (there is another St. Michael's Mount, in Cornwall, wonderfully like it), was then, as it is now, a strong place perched upon the top of a high rock, around which, when the tide is in, the sea flows, leaving no road to the mainland. In this place, Fine-Scholar shut himself up with his soldiers, and here he was closely besieged by his two brothers. At one time, when he was reduced to great distress for want of water, the generous Robert not only permitted his men to get water, but sent Fine-Scholar wine from his own table; and, on being remonstrated with by the Red King, said " What! shall we let our own brother die of thirst? Where shall we get another, when he is gone ? " At another time, the Red King riding alone on the shore of the bay, looking up at the Castle, was taken by two of Fine-Scholar's men, one of whom was about to kill him, when he cried out, " Hold, knave ! I am the King of England ! " The story says that the soldier raised him from the ground respectfully and humbly, and that the King took him into his service. The story may or may not be true; but at any rate it is true that Fine-Scholar could not hold out against his united brothers, and that he abandoned Mount St. Michael, and wandered about—as poor and forlorn as other scholars have been sometimes known to be.

The Scotch became unquiet in the Red King's time, and were twice defeated—the second time, with the loss of their King, Malcolm, and his son. The Welsh became unquiet too. Against them, Rufus was less successful; for they fought among their native mountains, and did great execution on the King's troops. Robert of Normandy became unquiet too; and, complaining that his brother the King did not faithfully perform his part of their agreement, took up arms, and obtained assistance from the King of France, whom Rufus, in the end, bought off with vast sums of money. England became unquiet too. Lord Mowbray, the powerful Earl of Northumberland, headed a great conspiracy to depose the King, and to place upon the throne, STEPHEN, the Conqueror's near relative. The plot was discovered; all the chief conspirators were seized; some were fined, some were put in prison, some were put to death. The Earl of Northumberland himself was shut up in a dungeon beneath Windsor Castle, where he died, an old man, thirty long years afterwards. The Priests in England were more unquiet than any other class, or power; for the Red King treated them with such small ceremony that he refused to appoint new bishops or archbishops when the old ones died, but kept all the wealth belonging to those offices in his own hands. In return for this, the Priests wrote his life when he was dead, and abused him well. I am inclined to think, myself, that there was little to choose between the Priests and the Red King; that both sides were greedy and designing; and that they were fairly matched.

The Red King was false of heart, selfish, covetous, and mean. He had a worthy minister in his favourite, Ralph, nicknamed—for almost every famous person had a nickname in those rough days—Flambard, or the Firebrand. Once, the King being ill, became penitent, and made ANSELM, a foreign priest and a good man, Archbishop of Canterbury. But he no sooner got well again than he repented of his repentance, and persisted in wrongfully keeping to himself some of the wealth belonging to the archbishopric. This led to violent disputes, which were aggravated by there being

in Rome at that time two rival Popes; each of whom declared he was the only real original infallible Pope, who
couldn't make a mistake. At last, Anselm, knowing the
Red King's character, and not feeling himself safe in England, asked leave to return abroad. The Red King gladly
gave it; for he knew that as soon as Anselm was gone, he
could begin to store up all the Canterbury money again, for
his own use.

By such means, and by taxing and oppressing the English
people in every possible way, the Red King became very rich.
When he wanted money for any purpose, he raised it by
some means or other, and cared nothing for the injustice
he did, or the misery he caused. Having the opportunity
of buying from Robert the whole duchy of Normandy for five
years, he taxed the English people more than ever, and made
the very convents sell their plate and valuables to supply
him with the means to make the purchase. But he was as
quick and eager in putting down revolt as he was in raising
money; for, a part of the Norman people objecting—very
naturally, I think—to being sold in this way, he headed an
army against them with all the speed and energy of his
father. He was so impatient, that he embarked for Normandy in a great gale of wind. And when the sailors told
him it was dangerous to go to sea in such angry weather, he
replied, "Hoist sail and away! Did you ever hear of a
king who was drowned?"

You will wonder how it was that even the careless Robert
came to sell his dominions. It happened thus. It had long
been the custom for many English people to make journeys
to Jerusalem, which were called pilgrimages, in order that
they might pray beside the tomb of Our Saviour there.
Jerusalem belonging to the Turks, and the Turks hating
Christianity, these Christian travellers were often insulted
and ill used. The Pilgrims bore it patiently for some time,
but at length a remarkable man, of great earnestness and
eloquence, called PETER THE HERMIT, began to preach in
various places against the Turks, and to declare that it was
the duty of good Christians to drive away those unbelievers
from the tomb of Our Saviour, and to take possession of it,
and protect it. An excitement such as the world had never
known before was created. Thousands and thousands of
men of all ranks and conditions departed for Jerusalem to
make war against the Turks. The war is called in history

the first Crusade, and every Crusader wore a cross marked on his right shoulder.

All the Crusaders were not zealous Christians. Among them were vast numbers of the restless, idle, profligate, and adventurous spirits of the time. Some became Crusaders for the love of change; some, in the hope of plunder; some, because they had nothing to do at home; some, because they did what the priests told them; some, because they liked to see foreign countries; some, because they were fond of knocking men about, and would as soon knock a Turk about as a Christian. Robert of Normandy may have been influenced by all these motives; and by a kind desire, besides, to save the Christian Pilgrims from bad treatment in future. He wanted to raise a number of armed men, and to go to the Crusade. He could not do so without money. He had no money; and he sold his dominions to his brother, the Red King, for five years. With the large sum he thus obtained, he fitted out his Crusaders gallantly, and went away to Jerusalem in martial state. The Red King, who made money out of everything, stayed at home, busily squeezing more money out of Normans and English.

After three years of great hardship and suffering—from shipwreck at sea; from travel in strange lands; from hunger, thirst, and fever, upon the burning sands of the desert; and from the fury of the Turks—the valiant Crusaders got possession of Our Saviour's tomb. The Turks were still resisting and fighting bravely, but this success increased the general desire in Europe to join the Crusade. Another great French Duke was proposing to sell his dominions for a term to the rich Red King, when the Red King's reign came to a sudden and violent end.

You have not forgotten the New Forest which the Conqueror made, and which the miserable people whose homes he had laid waste, so hated. The cruelty of the Forest Laws, and the torture and death they brought upon the peasantry, increased this hatred. The poor persecuted country people believed that the New Forest was enchanted. They said that in thunder-storms, and on dark nights, demons appeared, moving beneath the branches of the gloomy trees. They said that a terrible spectre had foretold to Norman hunters that the Red King should be punished there. And now, in the pleasant season of May, when the Red King had reigned almost thirteen years; and a second

Prince of the Conqueror's blood—another Richard, the son of Duke Robert—was killed by an arrow in this dreaded Forest; the people said that the second time was not the last, and that there was another death to come.

It was a lonely forest, accursed in the people's hearts for the wicked deeds that had been done to make it; and no man save the King and his Courtiers and Huntsmen, liked to stray there. But, in reality, it was like any other forest. In the spring, the green leaves broke out of the buds; in the summer, flourished heartily, and made deep shades; in the winter, shrivelled and blew down, and lay in brown heaps on the moss. Some trees were stately, and grew high and strong; some had fallen of themselves; some were felled by the forester's axe; some were hollow, and the rabbits burrowed at their roots; some few were struck by lightning, and stood white and bare. There were hill-sides covered with rich fern, on which the morning dew so beautifully sparkled; there were brooks, where the deer went down to drink, or over which the whole herd bounded, flying from the arrows of the huntsmen; there were sunny glades, and solemn places where but little light came through the rustling leaves. The songs of the birds in the New Forest were pleasanter to hear than the shouts of fighting men outside; and even when the Red King and his Court came hunting through its solitudes, cursing loud and riding hard, with a jingling of stirrups and bridles and knives and daggers, they did much less harm there than among the English or Normans, and the stags died (as they lived) far easier than the people.

Upon a day in August, the Red King, now reconciled to his brother, Fine-Scholar, came with a great train to hunt in the New Forest. Fine-Scholar was of the party. They were a merry party, and had lain all night at Malwood-Keep, a hunting-lodge in the forest, where they had made good cheer, both at supper and breakfast, and had drunk a deal of wine. The party dispersed in various directions, as the custom of hunters then was. The King took with him only Sir Walter Tyrrel, who was a famous sportsman, and to whom he had given, before they mounted horse that morning, two fine arrows.

The last time the King was ever seen alive, he was riding with Sir Walter Tyrrel, and their dogs were hunting together.

It was almost night, when a poor charcoal-burner, passing through the forest with his cart, came upon the solitary body of a dead man, shot with an arrow in the breast, and still bleeding. He got it into his cart. It was the body of the King. Shaken and tumbled, with its red beard all whitened with lime and clotted with blood, it was driven in the cart by the charcoal-burner next day to Winchester Cathedral, where it was received and buried.

Sir Walter Tyrrel, who escaped to Normandy, and claimed the protection of the King of France, swore in France that the Red King was suddenly shot dead by an arrow from an unseen hand, while they were hunting together; that he was fearful of being suspected as the King's murderer; and that he instantly set spurs to his horse, and fled to the sea-shore. Others declared that the King and Sir Walter Tyrrel were hunting in company, a little before sunset, standing in bushes opposite one another, when a stag came between them. That the King drew his bow and took aim, but the string broke. That the King then cried, "Shoot, Walter, in the Devil's name!" That Sir Walter shot. That the arrow glanced against a tree, was turned aside from the stag, and struck the King from his horse, dead.

By whose hand the Red King really fell, and whether that hand despatched the arrow to his breast by accident or by design, is only known to God. Some think his brother may have caused him to be killed; but the Red King had made so many enemies, both among priests and people, that suspicion may reasonably rest upon a less unnatural murderer. Men know no more than that he was found dead in the New Forest, which the suffering people had regarded as a doomed ground for his race.

The Finding of the Body of Rufus

CHAPTER X

FINE-SCHOLAR, on hearing of the Red King's death, hurried to Winchester with as much speed as Rufus himself had made, to seize the Royal treasure. But the keeper of the treasure, who had been one of the hunting-party in the Forest, made haste to Winchester too, and, arriving there at about the same time, refused to yield it up. Upon this, Fine-Scholar drew his sword, and threatened to kill the treasurer; who might have paid for his fidelity with his life, but that he knew longer resistance to be useless when he found the Prince supported by a company of powerful barons, who declared they were determined to make him King. The treasurer, therefore, gave up the money and jewels of the Crown: and on the third day after the death of the Red King, being a Sunday, Fine-Scholar stood before the high altar in Westminster Abbey, and made a solemn declaration that he would resign the Church property which his brother had seized ; that he would do no wrong to the nobles ; and that he would restore to the people the laws of Edward the Confessor, with all the improvements of William the Conqueror. So began the reign of KING HENRY THE FIRST.

The people were attached to their new King, both because he had known distresses, and because he was an Englishman by birth and not a Norman. To strengthen this last hold upon them, the King wished to marry an English lady; and could think of no other wife than MAUD THE GOOD, the daughter of the King of Scotland. Although this good Princess did not love the King, she was so affected by the representations the nobles made to her of the great charity it would be in her to unite the Norman and Saxon races, and prevent hatred and bloodshed between them for the future, that she consented to become his wife. After some disputing among the priests, who said that as she had been in a convent in her youth, and had worn the veil of a nun, she could not lawfully be married—against which the Princess stated that her aunt, with whom she had lived in her youth, had indeed sometimes thrown a piece of black stuff over her, but for no other reason than because the nun's veil was the only dress the conquering Normans respected in girl or woman, and not because she had taken the vows of a nun, which she never had—she was declared free to marry, and was made King Henry's Queen. A good Queen she was; beautiful, kind-hearted, and worthy of a better husband than the King.

For he was a cunning and unscrupulous man, though firm and clever. He cared very little for his word, and took any means to gain his ends. All this is shown in his treatment of his brother Robert—Robert, who had suffered him to be refreshed with water, and who had sent him the wine from his own table, when he was shut up, with the crows flying below him, parched with thirst, in the castle on the top of St. Michael's Mount, where his Red brother would have let him die.

Before the King began to deal with Robert, he removed and disgraced all the favourites of the late King; who were for the most part base characters, much detested by the people. Flambard, or Firebrand, whom the late King had made Bishop of Durham, of all things in the world, Henry imprisoned in the Tower; but Firebrand was a great joker and a jolly companion, and made himself so popular with his guards that they pretended to know nothing about a long rope that was sent into his prison at the bottom of a deep flagon of wine. The guards took the wine, and Firebrand took the rope; with which, when they were fast asleep, he let himself down from a window in the night, and so got cleverly aboard ship and away to Normandy.

Now Robert, when his brother Fine-Scholar came to the throne, was still absent in the Holy Land. Henry pretended that Robert had been made Sovereign of that country; and he had been away so long, that the ignorant people believed it. But, behold, when Henry had been some time King of England, Robert came home to Normandy; having leisurely returned from Jerusalem through Italy, in which beautiful country he had enjoyed himself very much, and had married a lady as beautiful as itself! In Normandy, he found Firebrand waiting to urge him to assert his claim to the English crown, and declare war against King Henry. This, after great loss of time in feasting and dancing with his beautiful Italian wife among his Norman friends, he at last did.

The English in general were on King Henry's side, though many of the Normans were on Robert's. But the English sailors deserted the King, and took a great part of the English fleet over to Normandy; so that Robert came to invade this country in no foreign vessels, but in English ships. The virtuous Anselm, however, whom Henry had invited back from abroad, and made Archbishop of Canterbury, was steadfast in the King's cause; and it was so well supported that the two armies, instead of fighting, made a peace. Poor Robert, who trusted anybody and everybody, readily trusted his brother, the King; and agreed to go home and receive a pension from England, on condition that all his followers were fully pardoned. This the King very faithfully promised, but Robert was no sooner gone than he began to punish them.

Among them was the Earl of Shrewsbury, who, on being summoned by the King to answer to five-and-forty accusations, rode away to one of his strong castles, shut himself up therein, called around him his tenants and vassals, and fought for his liberty, but was defeated and banished. Robert, with all his faults, was so true to his word, that when he first heard of this nobleman having risen against his brother, he laid waste the Earl of Shrewsbury's estates in Normandy, to show the King that he would favour no breach of their treaty. Finding, on better information, afterwards, that the Earl's only crime was having been his friend, he came over to England, in his old thoughtless warm-hearted way, to intercede with the King, and remind him of the solemn promise to pardon all his followers.

This confidence might have put the false King to the blush, but it did not. Pretending to be very friendly, he so surrounded his brother with spies and traps, that Robert, who was quite in his power, had nothing for it but to renounce his pension and escape while he could. Getting home to Normandy, and understanding the King better now, he naturally allied himself with his old friend the Earl of Shrewsbury, who had still thirty castles in that country. This was exactly what Henry wanted. He immediately declared that Robert had broken the treaty, and next year invaded Normandy.

He pretended that he came to deliver the Normans, at their own request, from his brother's misrule. There is reason to fear that his misrule was bad enough; for his beautiful wife had died, leaving him with an infant son, and his court was again so careless, dissipated, and ill-regulated, that it was said he sometimes lay in bed of a day for want of clothes to put on—his attendants having stolen all his dresses. But he headed his army like a brave prince and a gallant soldier, though he had the misfortune to be taken prisoner by King Henry, with four hundred of his Knights. Among them was poor harmless Edgar Atheling, who loved Robert well. Edgar was not important enough to be severe with. The King afterwards gave him a small pension, which he lived upon and died upon, in peace, among the quiet woods and fields of England.

And Robert—poor, kind, generous, wasteful, heedless Robert, with so many faults, and yet with virtues that might have made a better and a happier man—what was the end of him? If the King had had the magnanimity to say with a kind air, "Brother, tell me, before these noblemen, that from this time you will be my faithful follower and friend, and never raise your hand against me or my forces more!" he might have trusted Robert to the death. But the King was not a magnanimous man. He sentenced his brother to be confined for life in one of the Royal Castles. In the beginning of his imprisonment, he was allowed to ride out, guarded; but he one day broke away from his guard and galloped off. He had the evil fortune to ride into a swamp, where his horse stuck fast and he was taken. When the King heard of it he ordered him to be blinded, which was done by putting a red-hot metal basin on his eyes.

And so, in darkness and in prison, many years, he thought of all his past life, of the time he had wasted, of the treasure he had squandered, of the opportunities he had lost, of the youth he had thrown away, of the talents he had neglected. Sometimes, on fine autumn mornings, he would sit and think of the old hunting parties in the free Forest, where he had been the foremost and the gayest. Sometimes, in the still nights, he would wake, and mourn for the many nights that had stolen past him at the gaming-table; sometimes, would seem to hear, upon the melancholy wind, the old songs of the minstrels; sometimes, would dream, in

his blindness, of the light and glitter of the Norman Court.
Many and many a time, he groped back, in his fancy, to
Jerusalem, where he had fought so well; or, at the head
of his brave companions, bowed his feathered helmet to
the shouts of welcome greeting him in Italy, and seemed
again to walk among the sunny vineyards, or on the shore
of the blue sea, with his lovely wife. And then, thinking
of her grave, and of his fatherless boy, he would stretch out
his solitary arms and weep.

At length, one day, there lay in prison, dead, with cruel
and disfiguring scars upon his eyelids, bandaged from his
jailer's sight, but on which the eternal Heavens looked
down, a worn old man of eighty. He had once been
Robert of Normandy. Pity him!

At the time when Robert of Normandy was taken prisoner
by his brother, Robert's little son was only five years old.
This child was taken, too, and carried before the King,
sobbing and crying; for, young as he was, he knew he had
good reason to be afraid of his Royal uncle. The King was
not much accustomed to pity those who were in his power,
but his cold heart seemed for the moment to soften towards
the boy. He was observed to make a great effort, as if to
prevent himself from being cruel, and ordered the child to
be taken away; whereupon a certain Baron, who had married
a daughter of Duke Robert's (by name, Helie of Saint Saen),
took charge of him, tenderly. The King's gentleness did not
last long. Before two years were over, he sent messengers
to this lord's Castle to seize the child and bring him away.
The Baron was not there at the time, but his servants were
faithful, and carried the boy off in his sleep and hid him.
When the Baron came home, and was told what the King
had done, he took the child abroad, and, leading him by
the hand, went from King to King and from Court to Court,
relating how the child had a claim to the throne of England,
and how his uncle the King, knowing that he had that claim,
would have murdered him, perhaps, but for his escape.

The youth and innocence of the pretty little WILLIAM
FITZ-ROBERT (for that was his name) made him many friends
at that time. When he became a young man, the King of
France, uniting with the French Counts of Anjou and
Flanders, supported his cause against the King of England,
and took many of the King's towns and castles in Normandy.
But, King Henry, artful and cunning always, bribed some

of William's friends with money, some with promises, some with power. He bought off the Count of Anjou, by promising to marry his eldest son, also named WILLIAM, to the Count's daughter ; and indeed the whole trust of this King's life was in such bargains, and he believed (as many another King has done since, and as one King did in France a very little time ago) that every man's truth and honour can be bought at some price. For all this, he was so afraid of William Fitz-Robert and his friends, that, for a long time, he believed his life to be in danger ; and never lay down to sleep, even in his palace surrounded by his guards, without having a sword and buckler at his bedside.

To strengthen his power, the King with great ceremony betrothed his eldest daughter MATILDA, then a child only eight years old, to be the wife of Henry the Fifth, the Emperor of Germany. To raise her marriage-portion, he taxed the English people in a most oppressive manner ; then treated them to a great procession, to restore their good humour ; and sent Matilda away, in fine state, with the German ambassadors, to be educated in the country of her future husband.

And now his Queen, Maud the Good, unhappily died. It was a sad thought for that gentle lady, that the only hope with which she had married a man whom she had never loved—the hope of reconciling the Norman and English races —had failed. At the very time of her death, Normandy and all France was in arms against England ; for, so soon as his last danger was over, King Henry had been false to all the French powers he had promised, bribed, and bought, and they had naturally united against him. After some fighting, however, in which few suffered but the unhappy common people (who always suffered, whatsoever was the matter), he began to promise, bribe, and buy again ; and by those means, and by the help of the Pope, who exerted himself to save more bloodshed, and by solemnly declaring, over and over again, that he really was in earnest this time, and would keep his word, the King made peace.

One of the first consequences of this peace was, that the King went over to Normandy with his son Prince William and a great retinue, to have the Prince acknowledged as his successor by the Norman Nobles, and to contract the promised marriage (this was one of the many promises the King had broken) between him and the daughter of the Count of Anjou.

Both these things were triumphantly done, with great show and rejoicing; and on the twenty-fifth of November, in the year one thousand one hundred and twenty, the whole retinue prepared to embark at the Port of Barfleur, for the voyage home.

On that day, and at that place, there came to the King, Fitz-Stephen, a sea-captain, and said :

"My liege, my father served your father all his life, upon the sea. He steered the ship with the golden boy upon the prow, in which your father sailed to conquer England. I beseech you to grant me the same office. I have a fair vessel in the harbour here, called The White Ship, manned by fifty sailors of renown. I pray you, Sire, to let your servant have the honour of steering you in The White Ship to England ! "

"I am sorry, friend," replied the King, "that my vessel is already chosen, and that I cannot (therefore) sail with the son of the man who served my father. But the Prince and all his company shall go along with you, in the fair White Ship, manned by the fifty sailors of renown."

An hour or two afterwards, the King set sail in the vessel he had chosen, accompanied by other vessels, and, sailing all night with a fair and gentle wind, arrived upon the coast of England in the morning. While it was yet night, the people in some of those ships heard a faint wild cry come over the sea, and wondered what it was.

Now, the Prince was a dissolute, debauched young man of eighteen, who bore no love to the English, and had declared that when he came to the throne he would yoke them to the plough like oxen. He went aboard The White Ship, with one hundred and forty youthful Nobles like him-self, among whom were eighteen noble ladies of the highest rank. All this gay company, with their servants and the fifty sailors, made three hundred souls aboard the fair White Ship.

"Give three casks of wine, Fitz-Stephen," said the Prince, "to the fifty sailors of renown ! My father the King has sailed out of the harbour. What time is there to make merry here, and yet reach England with the rest ? "

"Prince," said Fitz-Stephen, " before morning, my fifty and The White Ship shall overtake the swiftest vessel in atten-dance on your father the King, if we sail at midnight ! "

Then, the Prince commanded to make merry; and the

sailors drank out the three casks of wine ; and the Prince and all the noble company danced in the moonlight on the deck of The White Ship.

When, at last, she shot out of the harbour of Barfleur. there was not a sober seaman on board. But the sails were all set, and the oars all going merrily. Fitz-Stephen had the helm. The gay young nobles and the beautiful ladies, wrapped in mantles of various bright colours to protect them from the cold, talked, laughed, and sang. The Prince encouraged the fifty sailors to row harder yet, for the honour of The White Ship.

Crash! A terrific cry broke from three hundred hearts. It was the cry the people in the distant vessels of the King heard faintly on the water. The White Ship had struck upon a rock—was filling—going down!

Fitz-Stephen hurried the Prince into a boat, with some few Nobles. "Push off," he whispered ; "and row to land. It is not far, and the sea is smooth. The rest of us must die."

But, as they rowed away, fast, from the sinking ship, the Prince heard the voice of his sister MARIE, the Countess of Perche, calling for help. He never in his life had been so good as he was then. He cried in an agony, "Row back at any risk! I cannot bear to leave her!"

They rowed back. As the Prince held out his arms to catch his sister, such numbers leaped in, that the boat was overset. And in the same instant The White Ship went down.

Only two men floated. They both clung to the main yard of the ship, which had broken from the mast, and now supported them. One asked the other who he was? He said, "I am a nobleman, GODFREY by name, the son of GILBERT DE L'AIGLE. And you?" said he. "I am BEROLD, a poor butcher of Rouen," was the answer. Then, they said together, "Lord be merciful to us both!" and tried to encourage one another, as they drifted in the cold benumbing sea on that unfortunate November night.

By-and-by, another man came swimming towards them, whom they knew, when he pushed aside his long wet hair, to be Fitz-Stephen. "Where is the Prince?" said he. "Gone! Gone!" the two cried together. "Neither he, nor his brother, nor his sister, nor the King's niece, nor her brother, nor any one of all the brave three hundred, noble or commoner, except we three, has risen above the water!" Fitz-Stephen, with a ghastly face, cried, "Woe! woe, to me!" and sunk to the bottom.

The other two clung to the yard for some hours. At length the young noble said faintly, "I am exhausted, and chilled with the cold, and can hold no longer. Farewell, good friend! God preserve you!" So, he dropped and sunk; and of all the brilliant crowd, the poor Butcher of Rouen alone was saved. In the morning, some fishermen saw him floating in his sheep-skin coat, and got him into their boat—the sole relater of the dismal tale.

For three days, no one dared to carry the intelligence to the King. At length, they sent into his presence a little boy, who, weeping bitterly, and kneeling at his feet, told him that The White Ship was lost with all on board. The King fell to the ground like a dead man, and never, never afterwards, was seen to smile.

But he plotted again, and promised again, and bribed and bought again, in his old deceitful way. Having no son to succeed him, after all his pains ("The Prince will never yoke us to the plough, now!" said the English people), he took a second wife—ADELAIS or ALICE, a duke's daughter, and the Pope's niece. Having no more children, however, he proposed to the Barons to swear that they would recognise as his successor, his daughter Matilda, whom, as she was now a widow, he married to the eldest son of the Count of Anjou, GEOFFREY, surnamed PLANTAGENET, from a custom he had of wearing a sprig of flowering broom (called Genêt in French) in his cap for a feather. As one false man usually makes many, and as a false King, in particular, is pretty certain to make a false Court, the Barons took the oath about the succession of Matilda (and her children after her), twice over, without in the least intending to keep it. The King was now relieved from any remaining fears of William Fitz-Robert, by his death in the Monastery of St. Omer, in France, at twenty-six years old, of a pike-wound in the hand. And as Matilda gave birth to three sons, he thought the succession to the throne secure.

He spent most of the latter part of his life, which was troubled by family quarrels, in Normandy, to be near Matilda. When he had reigned upwards of thirty-five years, and was sixty-seven years old, he died of an indigestion and fever, brought on by eating, when he was far from well, of a fish called Lamprey, against which he had often been cautioned

by his physicians.   His remains were brought over to Reading
Abbey to be buried.

You may perhaps hear the cunning and promise-breaking
of King Henry the First, called "policy" by some people,
and "diplomacy" by others.   Neither of these fine words will
in the least mean that it was true ; and nothing that is not
true can possibly be good.

His greatest merit, that I know of, was his love of learning.
I should have given him greater credit even for that, if it
had been strong enough to induce him to spare the eyes of a
certain poet he once took prisoner, who was a knight besides.
But he ordered the poet's eyes to be torn from his head,
because he had laughed at him in his verses ; and the poet,
in the pain of that torture, dashed out his own brains against
his prison wall.   King Henry the First was avaricious, revengeful, and so false, that I suppose a man never lived
whose word was less to be relied upon.

CHAPTER XI

ENGLAND UNDER MATILDA AND STEPHEN

THE King was no sooner dead than all the plans and schemes he had laboured at so long, and lied so much for, crumbled away like a hollow heap of sand. STEPHEN, whom he had never mistrusted or suspected, started up to claim the throne.

Stephen was the son of ADELA, the Conqueror's daughter, married to the Count of Blois. To Stephen, and to his brother HENRY, the late King had been liberal; making Henry Bishop of Winchester, and finding a good marriage for Stephen, and much enriching him. This did not prevent Stephen from hastily producing a false witness, a servant of the late King, to swear that the King had named him for his heir upon his death-bed. On this evidence the Archbishop of Canterbury crowned him. The new King, so suddenly made, lost not a moment in seizing the Royal treasure, and hiring foreign soldiers with some of it to protect his throne.

If the dead King had even done as the false witness said, he would have had small right to will away the English people, like so many sheep or oxen, without their consent. But he had, in fact, bequeathed all his territory to Matilda; who, supported by ROBERT, Earl of Gloucester, soon began to dispute the crown. Some of the powerful barons and priests took her side; some took Stephen's; all fortified their castles; and again the miserable English people were involved in war, from which they could never derive advantage whosoever was victorious, and in which all parties plundered, tortured, starved, and ruined them.

Five years had passed since the death of Henry the First —and during those five years there had been two terrible invasions by the people of Scotland under their King, David, who was at last defeated with all his army—when Matilda, attended by her brother Robert and a large force, appeared in England to maintain her claim. A battle was fought between her troops and King Stephen's at Lincoln ; in which the King himself was taken prisoner, after bravely fighting until his battle-axe and sword were broken, and was carried into strict confinement at Gloucester. Matilda then submitted herself to the Priests, and the Priests crowned her Queen of England.

She did not long enjoy this dignity. The people of London had a great affection for Stephen ; many of the Barons considered it degrading to be ruled by a woman ; and the Queen's temper was so haughty that she made innumerable enemies. The people of London revolted ; and, in alliance with the troops of Stephen, besieged her at Winchester, where they took her brother Robert prisoner, whom, as her best soldier and chief general, she was glad to exchange for Stephen himself, who thus regained his liberty. Then, the long war went on afresh. Once, she was pressed so hard in the Castle of Oxford, in the winter weather when the snow lay thick upon the ground, that her only chance of escape was to dress herself all in white, and, accompanied by no more than three faithful Knights, dressed in like manner that their figures might not be seen from Stephen's camp as they passed over the snow, to steal away on foot, cross the frozen Thames, walk a long distance, and at last gallop away on horseback. All this she did, but to no great purpose then ; for her brother dying while the struggle was yet going on, she at last withdrew to Normandy.

In two or three years after her withdrawal her cause appeared in England, afresh. in the person of her son Henry, young Plantagenet, who at only eighteen years of age, was very powerful: not only on account of his mother having resigned all Normandy to him, but also from his having married ELEANOR, the divorced wife of the French King, a bad woman, who had great possessions in France. Louis, the French King, not relishing this arrangement, helped EUSTACE, King Stephen's son, to invade Normandy: but Henry drove their united forces out of that country, and then returned here, to assist his partisans, whom the King was then besieging at Wallingford upon the Thames. Here, for two days, divided only by the river, the two armies lay encamped opposite to one another—on the eve, as it seemed to all men, of another desperate fight, when the EARL OF ARUNDEL took heart and said "that it was not reasonable to prolong the unspeakable miseries of two kingdoms to minister to the ambition of two princes."

Many other noblemen repeating and supporting this when it was once uttered, Stephen and young Plantagenet went down, each to his own bank of the river, and held a con-versation across it, in which they arranged a truce; very much to the dissatisfaction of Eustace, who swaggered away with some followers, and laid violent hands on the Abbey of St. Edmund's-Bury, where he presently died mad. The truce led to a solemn council at Winchester, in which it was agreed that Stephen should retain the crown, on condition of his declaring Henry his successor ; that WILLIAM, another son of the King's, should inherit his father's right-ful possessions ; and that all the Crown lands which Stephen had given away should be recalled, and all the Castles he had permitted to be built demolished. Thus terminated the bitter war, which had now lasted fifteen years, and had again laid England waste. In the next year STEPHEN died, after a troubled reign of nineteen years.

Although King Stephen was, for the time in which he lived, a humane and moderate man, with many excellent qualities ; and although nothing worse is known of him than his usurpation of the Crown, which he probably ex-cused to himself by the consideration that King Henry the First was an usurper too—which was no excuse at all ; the people of England suffered more in these dread nineteen years, than at any former period even of their suffering history. In the division of the nobility between the two rival claimants of the Crown, and in the growth of what is called the Feudal System (which made the peasants the born vassals and mere slaves of the Barons), every Noble had his strong Castle, where he reigned the cruel king of all the neighbouring people. Accordingly, he perpetrated whatever cruelties he chose. And never were worse cruel-ties committed upon earth than in wretched England in those nineteen years.

The writers who were living then describe them fearfully. They say that the castles were filled with devils rather than with men ; that the peasants, men and women, were put into dungeons for their gold and silver, were tortured with fire and smoke, were hung up by the thumbs, were hung up by the heels with great weights to their heads, were torn with jagged irons, killed with hunger, broken to death in narrow chests filled with sharp-pointed stones, murdered in countless fiendish ways. In England there was no corn, no meat, no cheese, no butter, there were no tilled lands, no harvests. Ashes of burnt towns, and dreary wastes, were all that the traveller, fearful of the robbers who prowled abroad at all hours, would see in a long day's journey; and from sunrise until night, he would not come upon a home.

The clergy sometimes suffered, and heavily too, from pillage, but many of them had castles of their own, and fought in helmet and armour like the barons, and drew lots with other fighting men for their share of booty. The Pope (or Bishop of Rome), on King Stephen's resisting his ambition, laid England under an Interdict at one period of this reign; which means that he allowed no service to be performed in the churches, no couples to be married, no bells to be rung, no dead bodies to be buried. Any man having the power to refuse these things, no matter whether he were called a Pope or a Poulterer, would, of course, have the power of afflicting numbers of innocent people. That nothing might be wanting to the miseries of King Stephen's time, the Pope threw in this contribution to the public store—not very like the widow's contribution, as I think, when Our Saviour sat in Jerusalem over against the Treasury, "and she threw in two mites, which make a farthing."

CHAPTER XII

ENGLAND UNDER HENRY THE SECOND

PART THE FIRST.

HENRY PLANTAGENET, when he was but twenty-one years old, quietly succeeded to the throne of England, according to his agreement made with the late King at Winchester. Six weeks after Stephen's death, he and his Queen, Eleanor, were crowned in that city ; into which they rode on horse-back in great state, side by side, amidst much shouting and rejoicing, and clashing of music, and strewing of flowers.

The reign of King Henry the Second began well. The King had great possessions, and (what with his own rights, and what with those of his wife) was lord of one-third part of France. He was a young man of vigour, ability, and resolution, and immediately applied himself to remove some of the evils which had arisen in the last unhappy reign. He revoked all the grants of land that had been hastily made, on either side, during the late struggles ; he obliged numbers of disorderly soldiers to depart from England ; he reclaimed all the castles belonging to the Crown ; and he forced the wicked nobles to pull down their own castles, to the number of eleven hundred, in which such dismal cruelties had been inflicted on the people. The King's brother, GEOFFREY, rose against him in France, while he was so well employed, and rendered it necessary for him to repair to that country ; where. after he had subdued and made a friendly arrangement with his brother (who did not live long), his ambition to increase his possessions involved him in a war with the French King, Louis, with whom he had been on such friendly terms just before, that to the French King's infant daughter, then a baby in the cradle, he had promised one of his little sons in marriage, who was a child of five years old. However, the war came to nothing at last, and the Pope made the two Kings friends again.

Now, the clergy, in the troubles of the last reign, had
gone on very ill indeed.   There were all kinds of criminals
among them—murderers, thieves, and vagabonds; and the
worst of the matter was, that the good priests would not
give up the bad priests to justice, when they committed
crimes, but persisted in sheltering and defending them.
The King, well knowing that there could be no peace or
rest in England while such things lasted, resolved to reduce
the power of the clergy; and, when he had reigned seven
years, found (as he considered) a good opportunity for doing
so, in the death of the Archbishop of Canterbury.   " I will
have for the new Archbishop," thought the King, "a friend
in whom I can trust, who will help me to humble these
rebellious priests, and to have them dealt with, when they
do wrong, as other men who do wrong are dealt with."   So,
he resolved to make his favourite, the new Archbishop;
and this favourite was so extraordinary a man, and his
story is so curious, that I must tell you all about him.

Once upon a time, a worthy merchant of London, named
GILBERT À BECKET, made a pilgrimage to the Holy Land,
and was taken prisoner by a Saracen lord.   This lord, who
treated him kindly and not like a slave, had one fair daughter,
who fell in love with the merchant; and who told him that
she wanted to become a Christian, and was willing to marry
him if they could fly to a Christian country.   The merchant
returned her love, until he found an opportunity to escape,
when he did not trouble himself about the Saracen lady,
but escaped with his servant Richard, who had been taken
prisoner along with him, and arrived in England and forgot
her.   The Saracen lady, who was more loving than the
merchant, left her father's house in disguise to follow him,
and made her way, under many hardships, to the sea-shore.
The merchant had taught her only two English words (for
I suppose he must have learnt the Saracen tongue himself,
and made love in that language), of which LONDON was one,
and his own name, GILBERT, the other.   She went among
the ships, saying, "London! London!" over and over
again, until the sailors understood that she wanted to find
an English vessel that would carry her there; so they showed
her such a ship, and she paid for her passage with some of
her jewels, and sailed away.   Well!   The merchant was
sitting in his counting-house in London one day, when he
heard a great noise in the street; and presently Richard

came running in from the warehouse, with his eyes wide
open and his breath almost gone, saying, "Master, master,
here is the Saracen lady!" The merchant thought Richard
was mad; but Richard said, "No, master! As I live, the
Saracen lady is going up and down the city, calling Gilbert!
Gilbert!" Then, he took the merchant by the sleeve, and
pointed out at window; and there they saw her among the
gables and water-spouts of the dark dirty street, in her
foreign dress, so forlorn, surrounded by a wondering crowd,
and passing slowly along, calling Gilbert, Gilbert! When
the merchant saw her, and thought of the tenderness she
had shown him in his captivity, and of her constancy, his
heart was moved, and he ran down into the street; and she
saw him coming, and with a great cry fainted in his arms.
They were married without loss of time, and Richard (who
was an excellent man) danced with joy the whole day of the
wedding; and they all lived happy ever afterwards.

This merchant and this Saracen lady had one son, THOMAS
À BECKET. He it was who became the Favourite of King
Henry the Second.

He had become Chancellor, when the King thought of
making him Archbishop. He was clever, gay, well educated,
brave; had fought in several battles in France; had defeated
a French knight in single combat, and brought his horse
away as a token of the victory. He lived in a noble palace,
he was the tutor of the young Prince Henry, he was served
by one hundred and forty knights, his riches were immense.
The King once sent him as his ambassador to France; and
the French people, beholding in what state he travelled,
cried out in the streets, "How splendid must the King of
England be, when this is only the Chancellor!" They had
good reason to wonder at the magnificence of Thomas à
Becket, for, when he entered a French town, his procession
was headed by two hundred and fifty singing boys; then,
came his hounds in couples; then, eight waggons, each drawn
by five horses driven by five drivers: two of the waggons
filled with strong ale to be given away to the people; four,
with his gold and silver plate and stately clothes; two, with
the dresses of his numerous servants. Then, came twelve
horses, each with a monkey on his back; then, a train of
people bearing shields and leading fine war-horses splendidly
equipped; then, falconers with hawks upon their wrists;
then, a host of knights, and gentlemen and priests; then,

the Chancellor with his brilliant garments flashing in the sun, and all the people capering and shouting with delight.

The King was well pleased with all this, thinking that it only made himself the more magnificent to have so magnificent a favourite; but he sometimes jested with the Chancellor upon his splendour too. Once, when they were riding together through the streets of London in hard winter weather, they saw a shivering old man in rags. "Look at the poor object!" said the King. "Would it not be a charitable act to give that aged man a comfortable warm cloak?" "Undoubtedly it would," said Thomas à Becket, "and you do well, Sir, to think of such Christian duties." "Come!" cried the King, "then give him your cloak!" It was made of rich crimson trimmed with ermine. The King tried to pull it off, the Chancellor tried to keep it on, both were near rolling from their saddles in the mud, when the Chancellor submitted, and the King gave the cloak to the old beggar: much to the beggar's astonishment, and much to the merriment of all the courtiers in attendance. For, courtiers are not only eager to laugh when the King laughs, but they really do enjoy a laugh against a Favourite.

"I will make," thought King Henry the Second, "this Chancellor of mine, Thomas à Becket, Archbishop of Canterbury. He will then be the head of the Church, and, being devoted to me, will help me to correct the Church. He has always upheld my power against the power of the clergy, and once publicly told some bishops (I remember), that men of the Church were equally bound to me with men of the sword. Thomas à Becket is the man, of all other men in England, to help me in my great design." So the King, regardless of all objection, either that he was a fighting man, or a lavish man, or a courtly man, or a man of pleasure, or anything but a likely man for the office, made him Archbishop accordingly.

Now, Thomas à Becket was proud and loved to be famous. He was already famous for the pomp of his life, for his riches, his gold and silver plate, his waggons, horses, and attendants. He could do no more in that way than he had done; and being tired of that kind of fame (which is a very poor one), he longed to have his name celebrated for something else. Nothing, he knew, would render him so famous in the world, as the setting of his utmost power and ability against the utmost power and ability of the King. He resolved with the whole strength of his mind to do it.

He may have had some secret grudge against the King besides. The King may have offended his proud humour at some time or other, for anything I know. I think it likely, because it is a common thing for Kings, Princes, and other great people, to try the tempers of their favourites rather severely. Even the little affair of the crimson cloak must have been anything but a pleasant one to a haughty man. Thomas à Becket knew better than any one in England what the King expected of him. In all his sumptuous life, he had never yet been in a position to disappoint the King. He could take up that proud stand now, as head of the Church; and he determined that it should be written in history, either that he subdued the King, or that the King subdued him.

So, of a sudden, he completely altered the whole manner of his life. He turned off all his brilliant followers, ate coarse food, drank bitter water, wore next his skin sack-cloth covered with dirt and vermin (for it was then thought very religious to be very dirty), flogged his back to punish himself, lived chiefly in a little cell, washed the feet of thirteen poor people every day, and looked as miserable as he possibly could. If he had put twelve hundred monkeys on horseback instead of twelve, and had gone in procession with eight thousand waggons instead of eight, he could not have half astonished the people so much as by this great change. It soon caused him to be more talked about as an Archbishop than he had been as a Chancellor.

The King was very angry; and was made still more so, when the new Archbishop, claiming various estates from the nobles as being rightfully Church property, required the King him-self, for the same reason, to give up Rochester Castle, and Rochester City too. Not satisfied with this, he declared that no power but himself should appoint a priest to any Church in the part of England over which he was Archbishop; and when a certain gentleman of Kent made such an appoint-ment, as he claimed to have the right to do, Thomas à Becket excommunicated him.

Excommunication was, next to the Interdict I told you of at the close of the last chapter, the great weapon of the clergy. It consisted in declaring the person who was excom-municated, an outcast from the Church and from all religious

I

offices; and in cursing him all over, from the top of his head to the sole of his foot, whether he was standing up, lying down, sitting, kneeling, walking, running, hopping, jumping, gaping, coughing, sneezing, or whatever else he was doing. This unchristian nonsense would of course have made no sort of difference to the person cursed—who could say his prayers at home if he were shut out of church, and whom none but GOD could judge—but for the fears and superstitions of the people, who avoided excommunicated persons, and made their lives unhappy. So, the King said to the new Archbishop, "Take off this Excommunication from this gentleman of Kent." To which the Archbishop replied, "I shall do no such thing."

The quarrel went on. A priest in Worcestershire committed a most dreadful murder, that aroused the horror of the whole nation. The King demanded to have this wretch delivered up, to be tried in the same court and in the same way as any other murderer. The Archbishop refused, and kept him in the Bishop's prison. The King, holding a solemn assembly in Westminster Hall, demanded that in future all priests found guilty before their Bishops of crimes against the law of the land should be considered priests no longer, and should be delivered over to the law of the land for punishment. The Archbishop again refused. The King required to know whether the clergy would obey the ancient customs of the country? Every priest there, but one, said, after Thomas à Becket, "Saving my order." This really meant that they would only obey those customs when they did not interfere with their own claims; and the King went out of the Hall in great wrath.

Some of the clergy began to be afraid, now, that they were going too far. Though Thomas à Becket was otherwise as unmoved as Westminster Hall, they prevailed upon him, for the sake of their fears, to go to the King at Woodstock, and promise to observe the ancient customs of the country, without saying anything about his order. The King received this submission favourably, and summoned a great council of the clergy to meet at the Castle of Clarendon, by Salisbury. But when the council met, the Archbishop again insisted on the words "saving my order;" and he still insisted, though lords entreated him, and priests wept before him and knelt to him, and an adjoining room was thrown open, filled with armed soldiers of the King, to threaten him.

At length he gave way, for that time, and the ancient customs (which included what the King had demanded in vain) were stated in writing, and were signed and sealed by the chief of the clergy, and were called the Constitutions of Clarendon.

The quarrel went on, for all that. The Archbishop tried to see the King. The King would not see him. The Archbishop tried to escape from England. The sailors on the coast would launch no boat to take him away. Then, he again resolved to do his worst in opposition to the King, and began openly to set the ancient customs at defiance.

The King summoned him before a great council at Northampton, where he accused him of high treason, and made a claim against him, which was not a just one, for an enormous sum of money. Thomas à Becket was alone against the whole assembly, and the very Bishops advised him to resign his office and abandon his contest with the King. His great anxiety and agitation stretched him on a sick-bed for two days, but he was still undaunted. He went to the adjourned council, carrying a great cross in his right hand, and sat down holding it erect before him. The King angrily retired into an inner room. The whole assembly angrily retired and left him there. But there he sat. The Bishops came out again in a body, and renounced him as a traitor. He only said, "I hear!" and sat there still. They retired again into the inner room, and his trial proceeded without him. By-and-by, the Earl of Leicester, heading the barons, came out to read his sentence. He refused to hear it, denied the power of the court, and said he would refer his cause to the Pope. As he walked out of the hall, with the cross in his hand, some of those present picked up rushes—rushes were strewn upon the floors in those days by way of carpet—and threw them at him. He proudly turned his head, and said that were he not Archbishop, he would chastise those cowards with the sword he had known how to use in bygone days. He then mounted his horse, and rode away, cheered and surrounded by the common people, to whom he threw open his house that night and gave a supper, supping with them himself. That same night he secretly departed from the town; and so, travelling by night and hiding by day, and calling himself "Brother Dearman," got away, not without difficulty, to Flanders.

The struggle still went on. The angry King took posses-

sion of the revenues of the archbishopric, and banished all
the relations and servants of Thomas à Becket, to the number
of four hundred. The Pope and the French King both protected him, and an abbey was assigned for his residence.
Stimulated by this support, Thomas à Becket, on a great
festival day, formally proceeded to a great church crowded
with people, and going up into the pulpit publicly cursed
and excommunicated all who had supported the Constitutions
of Clarendon : mentioning many English noblemen by name,
and not distantly hinting at the King of England himself.

When intelligence of this new affront was carried to the
King in his chamber, his passion was so furious that he tore
his clothes, and rolled like a madman on his bed of straw
and rushes. But he was soon up and doing. He ordered
all the ports and coasts of England to be narrowly watched,
that no letters of Interdict might be brought into the kingdom ; and sent messengers and bribes to the Pope's palace
at Rome. Meanwhile, Thomas à Becket, for his part, was
not idle at Rome, but constantly employed his utmost arts
in his own behalf. Thus the contest stood, until there was
peace between France and England (which had been for
some time at war), and until the two children of the two
Kings were married in celebration of it. Then, the French
King brought about a meeting between Henry and his old
favourite, so long his enemy.

Even then, though Thomas à Becket knelt before the King,
he was obstinate and immovable as to those words about his
order. King Louis of France was weak enough in his
veneration for Thomas à Becket and such men, but this was
a little too much for him. He said that à Becket "wanted
to be greater than the saints and better than St. Peter,"
and rode away from him with the King of England. His
poor French Majesty asked à Becket's pardon for so doing,
however, soon afterwards, and cut a very pitiful figure.

At last, and after a world of trouble, it came to this.
There was another meeting on French ground between King
Henry and Thomas à Becket, and it was agreed that Thomas
à Becket should be Archbishop of Canterbury, according to
the customs of former Archbishops, and that the King should
put him in possession of the revenues of that post. And
now, indeed, you might suppose the struggle at an end, and
Thomas à Becket at rest. No, not even yet. For Thomas
à Becket hearing, by some means, that King Henry, when

he was in dread of his kingdom being placed under an interdict, had had his eldest son Prince Henry secretly crowned,
not only persuaded the Pope to suspend the Archbishop of
York who had performed that ceremony, and to excommuni-
cate the Bishops who had assisted at it, but sent a messenger
of his own into England, in spite of all the King's precautions
along the coast, who delivered the letters of excommunication
into the Bishops' own hands. Thomas à Becket then came
over to England himself, after an absence of seven years.
He was privately warned that it was dangerous to come, and
that an ireful knight, named RANULF DE BROC, had threatened
that he should not live to eat a loaf of bread in England ;
but he came.

The common people received him well, and marched about
with him in a soldierly way, armed with such rustic weapons
as they could get. He tried to see the young prince who
had once been his pupil, but was prevented. He hoped for
some little support among the nobles and priests, but found
none. He made the most of the peasants who attended him,
and feasted them, and went from Canterbury to Harrow-on-
the-Hill, and from Harrow-on-the-Hill back to Canterbury,
and on Christmas Day preached in the Cathedral there, and
told the people in his sermon that he had come to die among
them, and that it was likely he would be murdered. He
had no fear, however—or, if he had any, he had much more
obstinacy—for he, then and there, excommunicated three of
his enemies, of whom Ranulf de Broc the ireful knight was
one.

As men in general had no fancy for being cursed, in their
sitting and walking, and gaping and sneezing, and all the
rest of it, it was very natural in the persons so freely
excommunicated to complain to the King. It was equally
natural in the King, who had hoped that this troublesome
opponent was at last quieted, to fall into a mighty rage when
he heard of these new affronts ; and, on the Archbishop of
York telling him that he never could hope for rest while
Thomas à Becket lived, to cry out hastily before his court,
" Have I no one here who will deliver me from this man ? "
There were four knights present, who, hearing the King's
words, looked at one another, and went out.

The names of these knights were REGINALD FITZURSE,
WILLIAM TRACY, HUGH DE MORVILLE, and RICHARD BRITO ;
three of whom had been in the train of Thomas à Becket in

the old days of his splendour. They rode away on horse-back, in a very secret manner, and on the third day after Christmas Day arrived at Saltwood House, not far from Canterbury, which belonged to the family of Ranulf de Broc. They quietly collected some followers here, in case they should need any; and proceeding to Canterbury, suddenly appeared (the four knights and twelve men) before the Arch-bishop, in his own house, at two o'clock in the afternoon. They neither bowed nor spoke, but sat down on the floor in silence, staring at the Archbishop.

Thomas à Becket said, at length, "What do you want?"

"We want," said Reginald Fitzurse, "the excommunication taken from the Bishops, and you to answer for your offences to the King."

Thomas à Becket defiantly replied, that the power of the clergy was above the power of the King. That it was not for such men as they were, to threaten him. That if he were threatened by all the swords in England, he would never yield.

"Then we will do more than threaten!" said the knights. And they went out with the twelve men, and put on their armour, and drew their shining swords, and came back.

His servants, in the meantime, had shut up and barred the great gate of the palace. At first, the knights tried to shatter it with their battle-axes; but, being shown a window by which they could enter, they let the gate alone, and climbed in that way. While they were battering at the door, the attendants of Thomas à Becket had implored him to take refuge in the Cathedral; in which, as a sanctuary or sacred place, they thought the knights would dare to do no violent deed. He told them, again and again, that he would not stir. Hearing the distant voices of the monks singing the evening service, however, he said it was now his duty to attend, and therefore, and for no other reason, he would go.

There was a near way between his Palace and the Cathedral, by some beautiful old cloisters which you may yet see. He went into the Cathedral, without any hurry, and having the Cross carried before him as usual. When he was safely there, his servants would have fastened the door, but he said No! it was the house of God and not a fortress.

As he spoke, the shadow of Reginald Fitzurse appeared in the Cathedral doorway, darkening the little light there was outside, on the dark winter evening. This knight said, in a strong voice, "Follow me, loyal servants of the King!" The rattle of the armour of the other knights echoed through the Cathedral, as they came clashing in.

It was so dark, in the lofty aisles and among the stately pillars of the church, and there were so many hiding-places in the crypt below and in the narrow passages above, that Thomas à Becket might even at that pass have saved himself if he would. But he would not. He told the monks resolutely that he would not. And though they all dispersed and left him there with no other follower than EDWARD GRYME, his faithful cross-bearer, he was as firm then, as ever he had been in his life.

The knights came on, through the darkness, making a terrible noise with their armed tread upon the stone pavement of the church. "Where is the traitor?" they cried out. He made no answer. But when they cried, "Where is the Archbishop?" he said proudly, "I am here!" and came out of the shade and stood before them.

The knights had no desire to kill him, if they could rid the King and themselves of him by any other means. They told him he must either fly or go with them. He said he would do neither; and he threw William Tracy off with such force when he took hold of his sleeve, that Tracy reeled again. By his reproaches and his steadiness, he so incensed them, and exasperated their fierce humour, that Reginald Fitzurse, whom he called by an ill name, said, "Then die!" and struck at his head. But the faithful Edward Gryme put out his arm, and there received the main force of the blow, so that it only made his master bleed. Another voice from among the knights again called to Thomas à Becket to fly; but, with his blood running down his face, and his hands clasped, and his head bent, he commended himself to God, and stood firm. Then they cruelly killed him close to the altar of St. Bennet; and his body fell upon the pavement, which was dirtied with his blood and brains.

It is an awful thing to think of the murdered mortal, who had so showered his curses about, lying, all disfigured, in the church, where a few lamps here and there were but red specks on a pall of darkness; and to think of the guilty knights riding away on horseback, looking over their shoulders at the dim Cathedral, and remembering what they had left inside.

PART THE SECOND.

WHEN the King heard how Thomas à Becket had lost his
life in Canterbury Cathedral, through the ferocity of the
four Knights, he was filled with dismay. Some have supposed that when the King spoke those hasty words, " Have
I no one here who will deliver me from this man?" he
wished, and meant à Becket to be slain. But few things are
more unlikely ; for, besides that the King was not naturally
cruel (though very passionate), he was wise, and must have
known full well what any stupid man in his dominions must
have known, namely, that such a murder would rouse the
Pope and the whole Church against him.

He sent respectful messengers to the Pope, to represent
his innocence (except in having uttered the hasty words);
and he swore solemnly and publicly to his innocence, and
contrived in time to make his peace. As to the four guilty
Knights, who fled into Yorkshire, and never again dared to
show themselves at Court, the Pope excommunicated them ;
and they lived miserably for some time, shunned by all
their countrymen. At last, they went humbly to Jerusalem
as a penance, and there died and were buried.

It happened, fortunately for the pacifying of the Pope, that
an opportunity arose very soon after the murder of à Becket,
for the King to declare his power in Ireland –which was an
acceptable undertaking to the Pope, as the Irish, who had
been converted to Christianity by one Patricius (otherwise
Saint Patrick) long ago, before any Pope existed, considered
that the Pope had nothing at all to do with them, or they
with the Pope, and accordingly refused to pay him Peter's
Pence, or that tax of a penny a house which I have elsewhere
mentioned. The King's opportunity arose in this way.

The Irish were, at that time, as barbarous a people as you
can well imagine. They were continually quarrelling and
fighting, cutting one another's throats, slicing one another's
noses, burning one another's houses, carrying away one
another's wives, and committing all sorts of violence. The
country was divided into five kingdoms—DESMOND, THOMOND,
CONNAUGHT, ULSTER, and LEINSTER—each governed by a
separate King, of whom one claimed to be the chief of
the rest. Now, one of these Kings, named DERMOND MAC
MURROUGH (a wild kind of name, spelt in more than one wild
kind of way), had carried off the wife of a friend of his,

and concealed her on an island in a bog. The friend resent-ing this (though it was quite the custom of the country), complained to the chief King, and, with the chief King's help, drove Dermond Mac Murrough out of his dominions. Dermond came over to England for revenge; and offered to hold his realm as a vassal of King Henry, if King Henry would help him to regain it. The King consented to these terms; but only assisted him, then, with what were called Letters Patent, authorising any English subjects who were so disposed, to enter into his service, and aid his cause.

There was, at Bristol, a certain EARL RICHARD DE CLARE, called STRONGBOW; of no very good character; needy and desperate, and ready for anything that offered him a chance of improving his fortunes. There were, in South Wales, two other broken knights of the same good-for-nothing sort, called ROBERT FITZ-STEPHEN, and MAURICE FITZ-GERALD. These three, each with a small band of followers, took up Dermond's cause ; and it was agreed that if it proved suc-cessful, Strongbow should marry Dermond's daughter EVA, and be declared his heir.

The trained English followers of these knights were so superior in all the discipline of battle to the Irish, that they beat them against immense superiority of numbers. In one fight, early in the war, they cut off three hundred heads, and laid them before Mac Murrough ; who turned them every one up with his hands, rejoicing, and, coming to one which was the head of a man whom he had much disliked, grasped it by the hair and ears, and tore off the nose and lips with his teeth. You may judge from this, what kind of a gentle-man an Irish King in those times was. The captives, all through this war, were horribly treated ; the victorious party making nothing of breaking their limbs, and casting them into the sea from the tops of high rocks. It was in the midst of the miseries and cruelties attendant on the taking of Waterford, where the dead lay piled in the streets, and the filthy gutters ran with blood, that Strongbow married Eva. An odious marriage-company those mounds of corpses must have made, I think, and one quite worthy of the young lady's father.

He died, after Waterford and Dublin had been taken, and various successes achieved ; and Strongbow became King of Leinster. Now came King Henry's opportunity. To restrain the growing power of Strongbow, he himself repaired to

Dublin, as Strongbow's Royal Master, and deprived him of
his kingdom, but confirmed him in the enjoyment of great
possessions.   The King, then, holding state in Dublin, received the homage of nearly all the Irish Kings and Chiefs,
and so came home again with a great addition to his reputation as Lord of Ireland, and with a new claim on the favour
of the Pope.   And now, their reconciliation was completed
—more easily and mildly by the Pope, than the King might
have expected, I think.

At this period of his reign, when his troubles seemed so
few and his prospects so bright, those domestic miseries began
which gradually made the King the most unhappy of men,
reduced his great spirit, wore away his health, and broke
his heart.

He had four sons.   HENRY, now aged eighteen—his secret
crowning of whom had given such offence to Thomas à
Becket; RICHARD, aged sixteen; GEOFFREY, fifteen; and
JOHN, his favourite, a young boy whom the courtiers named
LACKLAND, because he had no inheritance, but to whom the
King meant to give the Lordship of Ireland.   All these mis-
guided boys, in their turn, were unnatural sons to him, and
unnatural brothers to each other.   Prince Henry, stimulated
by the French King, and by his bad mother, Queen Eleanor,
began the undutiful history.

First, he demanded that his young wife, MARGARET, the
French King's daughter, should be crowned as well as he.
His father, the King, consented, and it was done.   It was no
sooner done, than he demanded to have a part of his father's
dominions, during his father's life.   This being refused, he
made off from his father in the night, with his bad heart
full of bitterness, and took refuge at the French King's
Court.   Within a day or two, his brothers Richard and
Geoffrey followed.   Their mother tried to join them—escaping
in man's clothes—but she was seized by King Henry's men,
and immured in prison, where she lay, deservedly, for sixteen
years.   Every day, however, some grasping English noblemen,
to whom the King's protection of his people from their
avarice and oppression had given offence, deserted him and
joined the Princes.   Every day he heard some fresh intelligence of the Princes levying armies against him ; of Prince
Henry's wearing a crown before his own ambassadors at the
French Court, and being called the Junior King of England ;
of all the Princes swearing never to make peace with him,

their father, without the consent and approval of the Barons of France. But, with his fortitude and energy unshaken, King Henry met the shock of these disasters with a resolved and cheerful face. He called upon all Royal fathers who had sons, to help him, for his cause was theirs; he hired, out of his riches, twenty thousand men to fight the false French King, who stirred his own blood against him; and he carried on the war with such vigour, that Louis soon proposed a conference to treat for peace.

The conference was held beneath an old wide-spreading green elm-tree, upon a plain in France. It led to nothing. The war recommenced. Prince Richard began his fighting career, by leading an army against his father; but his father beat him and his army back; and thousands of his men would have rued the day in which they fought in such a wicked cause, had not the King received news of an invasion of England by the Scots, and promptly come home through a great storm to repress it. And whether he really began to fear that he suffered these troubles because à Becket had been murdered; or whether he wished to rise in the favour of the Pope, who had now declared à Becket to be a saint, or in the favour of his own people, of whom many believed that even à Becket's senseless tomb could work miracles, I don't know: but the King no sooner landed in England than he went straight to Canterbury; and when he came within sight of the distant Cathedral, he dismounted from his horse, took off his shoes, and walked with bare and bleeding feet to à Becket's grave. There, he lay down on the ground, lamenting, in the presence of many people; and by-and-by he went into the Chapter House, and, removing his clothes from his back and shoulders, submitted himself to be beaten with knotted cords (not beaten very hard, I dare say though) by eighty Priests, one after another. It chanced that on the very day when the King made this curious exhibition of himself, a complete victory was obtained over the Scots; which very much delighted the Priests, who said that it was won because of his great example of repentance. For the Priests in general had found out, since à Becket's death, that they admired him of all things—though they had hated him very cordially when he was alive.

The Earl of Flanders, who was at the head of the base conspiracy of the King's undutiful sons and their foreign friends, took the opportunity of the King being thus employed at home, to lay siege to Rouen, the capital of Normandy. But the King, who was extraordinarily quick and active in all his movements, was at Rouen, too, before it was supposed possible that he could have left England; and there he so defeated the said Earl of Flanders, that the conspirators proposed peace, and his bad sons Henry and Geoffrey submitted. Richard resisted for six weeks; but, being beaten out of castle after castle, he at last submitted too, and his father forgave him.

To forgive these unworthy princes was only to afford them breathing-time for new faithlessness. They were so false, disloyal, and dishonourable, that they were no more to be trusted than common thieves. In the very next year, Prince Henry rebelled again, and was again forgiven. In eight years more, Prince Richard rebelled against his elder brother; and Prince Geoffrey infamously said that the brothers could never agree well together, unless they were united against their father. In the very next year after their reconciliation by the King, Prince Henry again rebelled against his father; and again submitted, swearing to be true; and was again forgiven; and again rebelled with Geoffrey.

But the end of this perfidious Prince was come. He fell sick at a French town; and his conscience terribly reproaching him with his baseness, he sent messengers to the King his father, imploring him to come and see him, and to forgive him for the last time on his bed of death. The generous King, who had a royal and forgiving mind towards his children always, would have gone; but this Prince had been so unnatural, that the noblemen about the King suspected treachery, and represented to him that he could not safely trust his life with such a traitor, though his own eldest son. Therefore the King sent him a ring from off his finger as a token of forgiveness; and when the Prince had kissed it, with much grief and many tears, and had confessed to those around him how bad, and wicked, and undutiful a son he had been; he said to the attendant Priests: "O, tie a rope about my body, and draw me out of bed, and lay me down upon a bed of ashes, that I may die with prayers to God in a repentant manner!" And so he died, at twenty-seven years old.

Three years afterwards, Prince Geoffrey, being unhorsed at a tournament, had his brains trampled out by a crowd of horses passing over him. So, there only remained Prince Richard, and Prince John—who had grown to be a young man now, and had solemnly sworn to be faithful to his father. Richard soon rebelled again, encouraged by his friend the French King, PHILIP THE SECOND (son of Louis, who was dead); and soon submitted and was again forgiven, swearing on the New Testament never to rebel again; and in another year or so, rebelled again; and, in the presence of his father, knelt down on his knee before the King of France; and did the French King homage: and declared that with his aid he would possess himself, by force, of all his father's French dominions.

And yet this Richard called himself a soldier of Our Saviour! And yet this Richard wore the Cross, which the Kings of France and England had both taken, in the previous year, at a brotherly meeting underneath the old wide-spreading elm-tree on the plain, when they had sworn (like him) to devote themselves to a new Crusade, for the love and honour of the Truth!

Sick at heart, wearied out by the falsehood of his sons, and almost ready to lie down and die, the unhappy King who had so long stood firm, began to fail. But the Pope, to his honour, supported him; and obliged the French King and Richard, though successful in fight, to treat for peace. Richard wanted to be crowned King of England, and pretended that he wanted to be married (which he really did not) to the French King's sister, his promised wife, whom King Henry detained in England. King Henry wanted, on the other hand, that the French King's sister should be married to his favourite son, John: the only one of his sons (he said) who had never rebelled against him. At last King Henry, deserted by his nobles one by one, distressed, exhausted, broken-hearted, consented to establish peace.

One final heavy sorrow was reserved for him, even yet. When they brought him the proposed treaty of peace, in writing, as he lay very ill in bed, they brought him also the list of the deserters from their allegiance, whom he was required to pardon. The first name upon this list was John, his favourite son, in whom he had trusted to the last.

"O John! child of my heart!" exclaimed the King, in a great agony of mind. "O John, whom I have loved the best! O John, for whom I have contended through these many troubles! Have you betrayed me too!" And then he lay down with a heavy groan, and said, "Now let the world go as it will. I care for nothing more!"

After a time, he told his attendants to take him to the French town of Chinon—a town he had been fond of, during many years. But he was fond of no place now; it was too true that he could care for nothing more upon this earth. He wildly cursed the hour when he was born, and cursed the children whom he left behind him; and expired.

As, one hundred years before, the servile followers of the Court had abandoned the Conqueror in the hour of his death, so they now abandoned his descendant. The very body was stripped, in the plunder of the Royal chamber; and it was not easy to find the means of carrying it for burial to the abbey church of Fontevraud.

Richard was said in after years, by way of flattery, to have the heart of a Lion. It would have been far better, I think, to have had the heart of a Man. His heart, whatever it was, had cause to beat remorsefully within his breast, when he came—as he did—into the solemn abbey, and looked on his dead father's uncovered face. His heart, whatever it was, had been a black and perjured heart, in all its dealings with the deceased King, and more deficient in a single touch of tenderness than any wild beast's in the forest.

There is a pretty story told of this reign, called the story of FAIR ROSAMOND. It relates how the King doted on Fair Rosamond, who was the loveliest girl in all the world; and how he had a beautiful Bower built for her in a Park at Woodstock; and how it was erected in a labyrinth, and could only be found by a clue of silk. How the bad Queen Eleanor, becoming jealous of Fair Rosamond, found out the secret of the clue, and one day, appeared before her, with a dagger and cup of poison, and left her to the choice between those deaths. How Fair Rosamond, after shedding many piteous tears and offering many useless prayers to the cruel Queen, took the poison, and fell dead in the midst of the beautiful bower, while the unconscious birds sang gaily all around her.

Now, there *was* a fair Rosamond, and she was (I dare say) the loveliest girl in all the world, and the King was certainly very fond of her, and the bad Queen Eleanor was certainly made jealous. But I am afraid—I say afraid, because I like the story so much—that there was no bower, no labyrinth, no silken clue, no dagger, no poison. I am afraid fair Rosamond retired to a nunnery near Oxford, and died there, peaceably; her sister-nuns hanging a silken drapery over her tomb, and often dressing it with flowers, in remembrance of the youth and beauty that had enchanted the King when he too was young, and when his life lay fair before him.

It was dark and ended now; faded and gone. Henry Plantagenet lay quiet in the abbey church of Fontevraud, in the fifty-seventh year of his age—never to be completed—after governing England well, for nearly thirty-five years.

CHAPTER XIII

ENGLAND UNDER RICHARD THE FIRST, CALLED THE LION-HEART

In the year of our Lord one thousand one hundred and eighty-nine, Richard of the Lion Heart succeeded to the throne of King Henry the Second, whose paternal heart he had done so much to break.   He had been, as we have seen, a rebel from his boyhood ; but, the moment he became a king against whom others might rebel, he found out that rebellion was a great wickedness.   In the heat of this pious discovery, he punished all the leading people who had befriended him against his father.   He could scarcely have done anything that would have been a better instance of his real nature, or a better warning to fawners and parasites not to trust in lion-hearted princes.

He likewise put his late father's treasurer in chains, and locked him up in a dungeon from which he was not set free until he had relinquished, not only all the Crown treasure, but all his own money too.   So, Richard certainly got the Lion's share of the wealth of this wretched treasurer, whether he had a Lion's heart or not.

He was crowned King of England, with great pomp, at Westminster : walking to the Cathedral under a silken canopy stretched on the tops of four lances, each carried by a great lord.   On the day of his coronation, a dreadful murdering of the Jews took place, which seems to have given great delight to numbers of savage persons calling themselves Christians. The King had issued a proclamation forbidding the Jews (who were generally hated, though they were the most useful merchants in England) to appear at the ceremony ; but as they had assembled in London from all parts, bringing presents to show their respect for the new Sovereign, some of them ventured down to Westminster Hall with their gifts; which were very readily accepted.   It is supposed, now, that some noisy fellow in the crowd, pretending to be a very delicate Christian, set up a howl at this, and struck a Jew who was trying to get in at the Hall door with his present. A riot arose. The Jews who had got into the Hall, were driven forth ; and some of the rabble cried out that the new King had commanded the unbelieving race to be put to death. Thereupon the crowd rushed through the narrow streets of the city, slaughtering all the Jews they met ; and when they could find no more out of doors (on account of their having fled to their houses, and fastened themselves in), they ran madly about, breaking open all the houses where the Jews lived, rushing in and stabbing or spearing them, sometimes even flinging old people and children out of window into blazing fires they had lighted up below. This great cruelty lasted four-and-twenty hours, and only three men were punished for it. Even they forfeited their lives not for murdering and robbing the Jews, but for burning the houses of some Christians.

King Richard, who was a strong restless burly man, with one idea always in his head, and that the very troublesome idea of breaking the heads of other men, was mightily impatient to go on a Crusade to the Holy Land, with a great army. As great armies could not be raised to go, even to the Holy Land, without a great deal of money, he sold the Crown domains, and even the high offices of State ; recklessly appointing noblemen to rule over his English subjects, not because they were fit to govern, but because they could pay high for the privilege. In this way, and by selling pardons at a dear rate, and by varieties of avarice and oppression, he scraped together a large treasure. He then appointed two Bishops to take care of his kingdom in his absence, and gave great powers and possessions to his brother John, to secure his friendship. John would rather have been made Regent of England ; but he was a sly man, and friendly to the expedition ; saying to himself, no doubt, " The more fighting, the more chance of my brother being killed ; and when he is killed, then I become King John ! "

Before the newly levied army departed from England, the recruits and the general populace distinguished themselves by astonishing cruelties on the unfortunate Jews: whom, in many large towns, they murdered by hundreds in the most horrible manner.

At York, a large body of Jews took refuge in the Castle, in the absence of its Governor, after the wives and children of many of them had been slain before their eyes. Presently came the Governor, and demanded admission. "How can we give it thee, O Governor!" said the Jews upon the walls, "when, if we open the gate by so much as the width of a foot, the roaring crowd behind thee will press in and kill us?"

Upon this, the unjust Governor became angry, and told the people that he approved of their killing those Jews; and a mischievous maniac of a friar, dressed all in white, put himself at the head of the assault, and they assaulted the Castle for three days.

Then said JOCEN, the head-Jew (who was a Rabbi or Priest), to the rest, "Brethren, there is no hope for us with the Christians who are hammering at the gates and walls, and who must soon break in. As we and our wives and children must die, either by Christian hands. or by our own, let it be by our own. Let us destroy by fire what jewels and other treasure we have here, then fire the castle, and then perish!"

A few could not resolve to do this, but the greater part complied. They made a blazing heap of all their valuables, and, when those were consumed, set the castle in flames. While the flames roared and crackled around them, and shooting up into the sky, turned it blood-red, Jocen cut the throat of his beloved wife, and stabbed himself. All the others who had wives or children, did the like dreadful deed. When the populace broke in, they found (except the trembling few, cowering in corners, whom they soon killed) only heaps of greasy cinders, with here and there something like part of the blackened trunk of a burnt tree, but which had lately been a human creature, formed by the beneficent hand of the Creator as they were.

After this bad beginning, Richard and his troops went on, in no very good manner, with the Holy Crusade. It was undertaken jointly by the King of England and his old friend Philip of France. They commenced the business by reviewing their forces, to the number of one hundred thousand men. Afterwards, they severally embarked their troops for Messina, in Sicily, which was appointed as the next place of meeting.

King Richard's sister had married the King of this place, but he was dead: and his uncle TANCRED had usurped the crown, cast the Royal Widow into prison, and possessed himself of her estates. Richard fiercely demanded his sister's release, the restoration of her lands, and (according to the Royal custom of the Island) that she should have a golden chair, a golden table, four-and-twenty silver cups, and four-and-twenty silver dishes. As he was too powerful to be successfully resisted, Tancred yielded to his demands; and then the French King grew jealous, and complained that the English King wanted to be absolute in the Island of Messina and everywhere else. Richard, however, cared little or nothing for this complaint; and in consideration of a present of twenty thousand pieces of gold, promised his pretty little nephew ARTHUR, then a child of two year's old, in marriage to Tancred's daughter. We shall hear again of pretty little Arthur by-and-by.

This Sicilian affair arranged without anybody's brains being knocked out (which must have rather disappointed him), King Richard took his sister away, and also a fair lady named BERENGARIA, with whom he had fallen in love in France, and whom his mother, Queen Eleanor (so long in prison, you remember, but released by Richard on his coming to the Throne), had brought out there to be his wife; and sailed with them for Cyprus.

He soon had the pleasure of fighting the King of the Island of Cyprus, for allowing his subjects to pillage some of the English troops who were shipwrecked on the shore; and easily conquering this poor monarch, he seized his only daughter, to be a companion to the lady Berengaria, and put the King himself into silver fetters. He then sailed away again with his mother, sister, wife, and the captive princess; and soon arrived before the town of Acre, which the French King with his fleet was besieging from the sea. But the French King was in no triumphant condition, for his army had been thinned by the swords of the Saracens, and wasted by the plague; and SALADIN, the brave Sultan of the Turks, at the head of a numerous army, was at that time gallantly defending the place from the hills that rise above it.

Wherever the united army of Crusaders went, they agreed in few points except in gaming, drinking, and quarrelling, in a most unholy manner; in debauching the people among whom they tarried, whether they were friends or foes; and in carrying disturbance and ruin into quiet places. The French King was jealous of the English King, and the

English King was jealous of the French King, and the disorderly and violent soldiers of the two nations were jealous of one another; consequently, the two Kings could not at first agree, even upon a joint assault on Acre; but when they did make up their quarrel for that purpose, the Saracens promised to yield the town, to give up to the Christians the wood of the Holy Cross, to set at liberty all their Christian captives, and to pay two hundred thousand pieces of gold. All this was to be done within forty days; but, not being done, King Richard ordered some three thousand Saracen prisoners to be brought out in the front of his camp, and there, in full view of their own countrymen, to be butchered.

The French King had no part in this crime; for he was by that time travelling homeward with the greater part of his men; being offended by the overbearing conduct of the English King; being anxious to look after his own dominions; and being ill, besides, from the unwholesome air of that hot and sandy country. King Richard carried on the war without him; and remained in the East, meeting with a variety of adventures, nearly a year and a half. Every night when his army was on the march, and came to a halt, the heralds cried out three times, to remind all the soldiers of the cause in which they were engaged, "Save the Holy Sepulchre!" and then all the soldiers knelt and said "Amen!" Marching or encamping, the army had continually to strive with the hot air of the glaring desert, or with the Saracen soldiers animated and directed by the brave Saladin, or with both together. Sickness and death, battle and wounds, were always among them; but through every difficulty King Richard fought like a giant, and worked like a common labourer. Long and long after he was quiet in his grave, his terrible battle-axe, with twenty English pounds of English steel in its mighty head, was a legend among the Saracens; and when all the Saracen and Christian hosts had been dust for many a year, if a Saracen horse started at any object by the wayside, his rider would exclaim, "What dost thou fear, Fool? Dost thou think King Richard is behind it?"

No one admired this King's renown for bravery more than Saladin himself, who was a generous and gallant enemy. When Richard lay ill of a fever, Saladin sent him fresh fruits from Damascus, and snow from the mountain-tops. Courtly messages and compliments were frequently exchanged between them—and then King Richard would mount his horse and kill as many Saracens as he could; and Saladin would mount his, and kill as many Christians as he could. In this way King Richard fought to his heart's content at Arsoof and at Jaffa; and finding himself with nothing exciting to do at Ascalon, except to rebuild, for his own defence, some fortifications there which the Saracens had destroyed, he kicked his ally the Duke of Austria, for being too proud to work at them.

The army at last came within sight of the Holy City of Jerusalem; but, being then a mere nest of jealousy, and quarrelling and fighting, soon retired, and agreed with the Saracens upon a truce for three years, three months, three days, and three hours. Then, the English Christians, protected by the noble Saladin from Saracen revenge, visited Our Saviour's tomb; and then King Richard embarked with a small force at Acre to return home.

But he was shipwrecked in the Adriatic Sea, and was fain to pass through Germany, under an assumed name. Now, there were many people in Germany who had served in the Holy Land under that proud Duke of Austria who had been kicked; and some of them, easily recognising a man so remarkable as King Richard, carried their intelligence to the kicked Duke, who straightway took him prisoner at a little inn near Vienna.

The Duke's master the Emperor of Germany, and the King of France, were equally delighted to have so troublesome a monarch in safe keeping. Friendships which are founded on a partnership in doing wrong, are never true; and the King of France was now quite as heartily King Richard's foe, as he had ever been his friend in his unnatural conduct to his father. He monstrously pretended that King Richard had designed to poison him in the East; he charged him with having murdered, there, a man whom he had in truth befriended; he bribed the Emperor of Germany to keep him close prisoner; and, finally, through the plotting of these two princes, Richard was brought before the German legislature, charged with the foregoing crimes, and many others. But he defended himself so well, that many of the assembly were moved to tears by his eloquence and earnestness. It was decided that he should be treated, during the rest of his captivity, in a manner more becoming his dignity than he had been, and that he should be set free on the payment of a heavy ransom. This ransom the English people willingly raised. When Queen Eleanor took it over to Germany, it was at first evaded and refused. But she appealed to the honour of all the princes of the German Empire in behalf of her son, and appealed so well that it was accepted, and the King released. Thereupon, the King of France wrote to Prince John—"Take care of thyself. The devil is unchained!"

Prince John had reason to fear his brother, for he had been a traitor to him in his captivity. He had secretly joined the French King; had vowed to the English nobles and people that his brother was dead; and had vainly tried to seize the crown. He was now in France, at a place called Evreux. Being the meanest and basest of men, he contrived a mean and base expedient for making himself acceptable to his brother. He invited the French officers of the garrison in that town to dinner, murdered them all, and then took the fortress. With this recommendation to the good will of a lion-hearted monarch, he hastened to King Richard, fell on his knees before him, and obtained the intercession of Queen Eleanor. "I forgive him," said the King, "and I hope I may forget the injury he has done me, as easily as I know he will forget my pardon."

While King Richard was in Sicily, there had been trouble in his dominions at home: one of the bishops whom he had left in charge thereof, arresting the other; and making, in his pride and ambition, as great a show as if he were King himself. But the King hearing of it at Messina, and appointing a new Regency, this LONGCHAMP (for that was his name) had fled to France in a woman's dress, and had there been encouraged and supported by the French King. With all these causes of offence against Philip in his mind, King Richard had no sooner been welcomed home by his enthusiastic subjects with great display and splendour, and had no sooner been crowned afresh at Winchester, than he resolved to show the French King that the Devil was unchained indeed, and made war against him with great fury.

There was fresh trouble at home about this time, arising out of the discontents of the poor people, who complained that they were far more heavily taxed than the rich, and who found a spirited champion in WILLIAM FITZ-OSBERT, called LONGBEARD. He became the leader of a secret society, comprising fifty thousand men ; he was seized by surprise ; he stabbed the citizen who first laid hands upon him ; and retreated, bravely fighting, to a church, which he maintained four days, until he was dislodged by fire, and run through the body as he came out. He was not killed, though ; for he was dragged, half dead, at the tail of a horse to Smith-field, and there hanged. Death was long a favourite remedy for silencing the people's advocates ; but as we go on with this history, I fancy we shall find them difficult to make an end of, for all that.

The French war, delayed occasionally by a truce, was still in progress when a certain Lord named VIDOMAR, Viscount of Limoges, chanced to find in his ground a treasure of ancient coins. As the King's vassal, he sent the King half of it ; but the King claimed the whole. The lord refused to yield the whole. The King besieged the lord in his castle, swore that he would take the castle by storm, and hang every man of its defenders on the battlements.

There was a strange old song in that part of the country, to the effect that in Limoges an arrow would be made by which King Richard would die. It may be that BERTRAND DE GOURDON, a young man who was one of the defenders of the castle, had often sung it or heard it sung of a winter night, and remembered it when he saw, from his post upon the ramparts, the King attended only by his chief officer riding below the walls surveying the place. He drew an arrow to the head, took steady aim, said between his teeth, " Now I pray God speed thee well, arrow ! " discharged it, and struck the King in the left shoulder.

Although the wound was not at first considered dangerous, it was severe enough to cause the King to retire to his tent, and direct the assault to be made without him. The castle was taken ; and every man of its defenders was hanged, as the King had sworn all should be, except Bertrand de Gourdon, who was reserved until the royal pleasure respect-ing him should be known.

By that time unskilful treatment had made the wound mortal, and the King knew that he was dying. He directed Bertrand to be brought into his tent. The young man was brought there, heavily chained. King Richard looked at him steadily. He looked, as steadily, at the King.

" Knave ! " said King Richard. " What have I done to thee that thou shouldest take my life ? "

"What hast thou done to me?" replied the young man. "With thine own hands thou hast killed my father and my two brothers. Myself thou wouldest have hanged. Let me die now, by any torture that thou wilt. My comfort is, that no torture can save thee. Thou too must die; and through me, the world is quit of thee!"

Again the King looked at the young man steadily. Again the young man looked steadily at him. Perhaps some remembrance of his generous enemy Saladin, who was not a Christian, came into the mind of the dying King.

"Youth!" he said, "I forgive thee. Go unhurt!"

Then, turning to the chief officer who had been riding in his company when he received the wound, King Richard said:

"Take off his chains, give him a hundred shillings, and let him depart."

He sunk down on his couch, and a dark mist seemed in his weakened eyes to fill the tent wherein he had so often rested, and he died. His age was forty-two; he had reigned ten years. His last command was not obeyed; for the chief officer flayed Bertrand de Gourdon alive, and hanged him.

There is an old tune yet known—a sorrowful air will sometimes outlive many generations of strong men, and even last longer than battle-axes with twenty pounds of steel in the head—by which this King is said to have been discovered in his captivity. BLONDEL, a favourite Minstrel of King Richard, as the story relates, faithfully seeking his Royal master, went singing it outside the gloomy walls of many foreign fortresses and prisons; until at last he heard it echoed from within a dungeon, and knew the voice, and cried out in ecstasy, "O Richard, O my King!" You may believe it, if you like; it would be easy to believe worse things. Richard was himself a Minstrel and a Poet. If he had not been a Prince too, he might have been a better man perhaps, and might have gone out of the world with less bloodshed and waste of life to answer for.

CHAPTER XIV

AT two-and-thirty years of age, JOHN became King of
England. His pretty little nephew ARTHUR had the best
claim to the throne; but John seized the treasure, and
made fine promises to the nobility, and got himself crowned
at Westminster within a few weeks after his brother
Richard's death. I doubt whether the crown could possibly have been put upon the head of a meaner coward, or
a more detestable villain, if England had been searched
from end to end to find him out.

The French King, Philip, refused to acknowledge the
right of John to his new dignity, and declared in favour
of Arthur. You must not suppose that he had any gener-
osity of feeling for the fatherless boy; it merely suited his
ambitious schemes to oppose the King of England. So John
and the French King went to war about Arthur.

He was a handsome boy, at that time only twelve years
old. He was not born when his father, Geoffrey, had his
brains trampled out at the tournament; and, besides the
misfortune of never having known a father's guidance and
protection, he had the additional misfortune to have a
foolish mother (CONSTANCE by name), lately married to
her third husband. She took Arthur, upon John's accession, to the French King, who pretended to be very much
his friend, and who made him a Knight, and promised him
his daughter in marriage; but, who cared so little about
him in reality, that finding it his interest to make peace
with King John for a time, he did so without the least consideration for the poor little Prince, and heartlessly sacrificed
all his interests.

Young Arthur, for two years afterwards, lived quietly;
and in the course of that time his mother died. But, the
French King then finding it his interest to quarrel with King

John again, again made Arthur his pretence, and invited the orphan boy to court. " You know your rights, Prince," said the French King, " and you would like to be a King. Is it not so ? " "Truly," said Prince Arthur, "I should greatly like to be a King ! " " Then," said Philip, " you shall have two hundred gentlemen who are Knights of mine, and with them you shall go to win back the provinces belonging to you, of which your uncle, the usurping King of England, has taken possession. I myself, meanwhile, will head a force against him in Normandy." Poor Arthur was so flattered and so grateful that he signed a treaty with the crafty French King, agreeing to consider him his superior Lord, and that the French King should keep for himself whatever he could take from King John.

Now, King John was so bad in all ways, and King Philip was so perfidious, that Arthur, between the two, might as well have been a lamb between a fox and a wolf. But, being so young, he was ardent and flushed with hope ; and, when the people of Brittany (which was his inheritance) sent him five hundred more knights and five thousand foot soldiers, he believed his fortune was made. The people of Brittany had been fond of him from his birth, and had requested that he might be called Arthur, in remembrance of that dimly-famous English Arthur, of whom I told you early in this book, whom they believed to have been the brave friend and companion of an old King of their own. They had tales among them about a prophet called MERLIN (of the same old time), who had foretold that their own King should be restored to them after hundreds of years ; and they believed that the prophecy would be fulfilled in Arthur ; that the time would come when he would rule them with a crown of Brittany upon his head ; and when neither King of France nor King of England would have any power over them. When Arthur found himself riding in a glittering suit of armour on a richly caparisoned horse, at the head of his train of knights and soldiers, he began to believe this too, and to consider old Merlin a very superior prophet.

He did not know—how could he, being so innocent and inexperienced ?—that his little army was a mere nothing against the power of the King of England. The French King knew it ; but the poor boy's fate was little to him, so that the King of England was worried and distressed. Therefore, King Philip went his way into Normandy, and Prince

Arthur and Hubert

Arthur went his way towards Mirebeau, a French town near Poictiers, both very well pleased.

Prince Arthur went to attack the town of Mirebeau, because his grandmother Eleanor, who has so often made her appearance in this history (and who had always been his mother's enemy), was living there, and because his Knights said, "Prince, if you can take her prisoner, you will be able to bring the King your uncle to terms!" But she was not to be easily taken. She was old enough by this time—eighty—but she was as full of stratagem as she was full of years and wickedness. Receiving intelligence of young Arthur's approach, she shut herself up in a high tower, and encouraged her soldiers to defend it like men. Prince Arthur with his little army besieged the high tower. King John, hearing how matters stood, came up to the rescue, with *his* army. So here was a strange family-party! The boy-Prince besieging his grandmother, and his uncle besieging him!

This position of affairs did not last long. One summer night King John, by treachery, got his men into the town, surprised Prince Arthur's force, took two hundred of his knights, and seized the Prince himself in his bed. The Knights were put in heavy irons, and driven away in open carts drawn by bullocks, to various dungeons where they were most inhumanly treated, and where some of them were starved to death. Prince Arthur was sent to the castle of Falaise.

One day, while he was in prison at that castle, mournfully thinking it strange that one so young should be in so much trouble, and looking out of the small window in the deep dark wall, at the summer sky and the birds, the door was softly opened, and he saw his uncle the King standing in the shadow of the archway, looking very grim.

"Arthur," said the King, with his wicked eyes more on the stone floor than on his nephew, "will you not trust to the gentleness, the friendship, and the truthfulness of your loving uncle?"

"I will tell my loving uncle that," replied the boy, "when he does me right. Let him restore to me my kingdom of England, and then come to me and ask the question."

The King looked at him and went out. "Keep that boy close prisoner," said he to the warden of the castle.

Then, the King took secret counsel with the worst of his nobles how the Prince was to be got rid of. Some said,

"Put out his eyes and keep him in prison, as Robert of Normandy was kept." Others said, "Have him stabbed." Others, "Have him hanged." Others, "Have him poisoned."

King John, feeling that in any case, whatever was done afterwards. it would be a satisfaction to his mind to have those handsome eyes burnt out that had looked at him so proudly while his own royal eyes were blinking at the stone floor, sent certain ruffians to Falaise to blind the boy with red-hot irons. But Arthur so pathetically entreated them, and shed such piteous tears, and so appealed to HUBERT DE BOURG (or BURGH), the warden of the castle, who had a love for him. and was an honourable tender man, that Hubert could not bear it. To his eternal honour he prevented the torture from being performed, and, at his own risk, sent the savages away.

The chafed and disappointed King bethought himself of the stabbing suggestion next, and, with his shuffling manner and his cruel face, proposed it to one William de Bray. "I am a gentleman and not an executioner," said William de Bray, and left the presence with disdain.

But it was not difficult for a King to hire a murderer in those days. King John found one for his money, and sent him down to the castle of Falaise. "On what errand dost thou come?" said Hubert to this fellow. "To despatch young Arthur," he returned. "Go back to him who sent thee," answered Hubert, "and say that I will do it!"

King John very well knowing that Hubert would never do it, but that he courageously sent this reply to save the Prince or gain time, despatched messengers to convey the young prisoner to the castle of Rouen.

Arthur was soon forced from the good Hubert—of whom he had never stood in greater need than then—carried away by night, and lodged in his new prison: where, through his grated window, he could hear the deep waters of the river Seine, rippling against the stone wall below.

One dark night, as he lay sleeping, dreaming perhaps of rescue by those unfortunate gentlemen who were obscurely suffering and dying in his cause, he was roused, and bidden by his jailer to come down the staircase to the foot of the tower. He hurriedly dressed himself and obeyed. When they came to the bottom of the winding stairs, and the night air from the river blew upon their faces, the jailer trod upon his torch and put it out. Then, Arthur, in the darkness, was hurriedly drawn into a solitary boat. And in that boat, he found his uncle and one other man.

He knelt to them, and prayed them not to murder him. Deaf to his entreaties, they stabbed him and sunk his body in the river with heavy stones. When the spring-morning broke, the tower-door was closed, the boat was gone, the river sparkled on its way, and never more was any trace of the poor boy beheld by mortal eyes.

The news of this atrocious murder being spread in England, awakened a hatred of the King (already odious for his many vices, and for his having stolen away and married a noble lady while his own wife was living) that never slept again through his whole reign. In Brittany, the indignation was intense. Arthur's own sister ELEANOR was in the power of John and shut up in a convent at Bristol, but his half-sister ALICE was in Brittany. The people chose her, and the murdered prince's father-in-law, the last husband of Constance, to represent them; and carried their fiery complaints to King Philip. King Philip summoned King John (as the holder of territory in France) to come before him and defend himself. King John refusing to appear, King Philip declared him false, perjured, and guilty ; and again made war. In a little time, by conquering the greater part of his French territory, King Philip deprived him of one-third of his dominions. And, through all the fighting that took place, King John was always found, either to be eating and drinking, like a gluttonous fool, when the danger was at a distance, or to be running away, like a beaten cur, when it was near.

You might suppose that when he was losing his dominions at this rate, and when his own nobles cared so little for him or his cause that they plainly refused to follow his banner out of England, he had enemies enough. But he made another enemy of the Pope, which he did in this way.

The Archbishop of Canterbury dying, and the junior monks of that place wishing to get the start of the senior monks in the appointment of his successor, met together at midnight, secretly elected a certain REGINALD, and sent him off to Rome to get the Pope's approval. The senior monks and the King soon finding this out, and being very angry about it, the junior monks gave way, and all the monks together elected the Bishop of Norwich, who was the King's favourite. The Pope, hearing the whole story, declared that neither election would do for him, and that *he* elected STEPHEN

LANGTON. The monks submitting to the Pope, the King turned them all out bodily, and banished them as traitors. The Pope sent three bishops to the King, to threaten him with an Interdict. The King told the bishops that if any Interdict were laid upon his kingdom, he would tear out the eyes and cut off the noses of all the monks he could lay hold of, and send them over to Rome in that undecorated state as a present for their master. The bishops, nevertheless, soon published the Interdict, and fled.

After it had lasted a year, the Pope proceeded to his next step ; which was Excommunication. King John was declared excommunicated, with all the usual ceremonies. The King was so incensed at this, and was made so desperate by the disaffection of his Barons and the hatred of his people, that it is said he even privately sent ambassadors to the Turks in Spain, offering to renounce his religion and hold his kingdom of them if they would help him. It is related that the ambassadors were admitted to the presence of the Turkish Emir through long lines of Moorish guards, and that they found the Emir with his eyes seriously fixed on the pages of a large book, from which he never once looked up. That they gave him a letter from the King containing his proposals, and were gravely dismissed. That presently the Emir sent for one of them, and conjured him, by his faith in his religion, to say what kind of man the King of England truly was ? That the ambassador, thus pressed, replied that the King of England was a false tyrant, against whom his own subjects would soon rise. And that this was quite enough for the Emir.

Money being, in his position, the next best thing to men, King John spared no means of getting it. He set on foot another oppressing and torturing of the unhappy Jews (which was quite in his way), and invented a new punishment for one wealthy Jew of Bristol. Until such time as that Jew should produce a certain large sum of money, the King sentenced him to be imprisoned, and, every day, to have one tooth violently wrenched out of his head—beginning with the double teeth. For seven days, the oppressed man bore the daily pain and lost the daily tooth ; but, on the eighth, he paid the money. With the treasure raised in such ways, the King made an expedition into Ireland, where some English nobles had revolted. It was one of the very few places from which he did not run away; because no resistance was shown.

He made another expedition into Wales—whence he *did* run away in the end: but not before he had got from the Welsh people, as hostages, twenty-seven young men of the best families; every one of whom he caused to be slain in the following year.

To Interdict and Excommunication, the Pope now added his last sentence; Deposition. He proclaimed John no longer King, absolved all his subjects from their allegiance, and sent Stephen Langton and others to the King of France to tell him that, if he would invade England, he should be forgiven all his sins—at least, should be forgiven them by the Pope, if that would do.

As there was nothing that King Philip desired more than to invade England, he collected a great army at Rouen, and a fleet of seventeen hundred ships to bring them over. But the English people, however bitterly they hated the King, were not a people to suffer invasion quietly. They flocked to Dover, where the English standard was, in such great numbers to enrol themselves as defenders of their native land, that there were not provisions for them, and the King could only select and retain sixty thousand. But, at this crisis, the Pope, who had his own reasons for objecting to either King John or King Philip being too powerful, interfered. He entrusted a legate, whose name was PANDOLF, with the easy task of frightening King John. He sent him to the English Camp, from France, to terrify him with exaggerations of King Philip's power, and his own weakness in the dis-content of the English Barons and people. Pandolf discharged his commission so well, that King John, in a wretched panic, consented to acknowledge Stephen Langton; to resign his kingdom "to God, Saint Peter, and Saint Paul"—which meant the Pope; and to hold it, ever afterwards, by the Pope's leave, on payment of an annual sum of money. To this shameful contract he publicly bound himself in the church of the Knights Templars at Dover: where he laid at the legate's feet a part of the tribute, which the legate haughtily trampled upon. But they *do* say, that this was merely a genteel flourish, and that he was afterwards seen to pick it up and pocket it.

There was an unfortunate prophet, of the name of Peter, who had greatly increased King John's terrors by predicting that he would be unknighted (which the King supposed to signify that he would die) before the Feast of the Ascension

K

should be past. That was the day after this humiliation.
When the next morning came, and the King, who had been
trembling all night, found himself alive and safe, he ordered
the prophet—and his son too—to be dragged through the
streets at the tails of horses, and then hanged, for having
frightened him.

As King John had now submitted, the Pope, to King
Philip's great astonishment, took him under his protection,
and informed King Philip that he found he could not give
him leave to invade England. The angry Philip resolved to
do it without his leave; but he gained nothing and lost
much ; for, the English, commanded by the Earl of Salisbury,
went over, in five hundred ships, to the French coast, before
the French fleet had sailed away from it, and utterly defeated
the whole.

The Pope then took off his three sentences, one after
another, and empowered Stephen Langton publicly to receive
King John into the favour of the Church again, and to ask him
to dinner. The King, who hated Langton with all his might
and main—and with reason too, for he was a great and
a good man, with whom such a King could have no sympathy
—pretended to cry and to be very grateful. There was
a little difficulty about settling how much the King should
pay as a recompense to the clergy for the losses he had
caused them ; but, the end of it was, that the superior
clergy got a good deal, and the inferior clergy got little or
nothing—which has also happened since King John's time,
I believe.

When all these matters were arranged, the King in his
triumph became more fierce, and false, and insolent to all
around him than he had ever been.   An alliance of
sovereigns against King Philip, gave him an opportunity
of landing an army in France ; with which he even took
a town !   But, on the French King's gaining a great
victory, he ran away, of course, and made a truce for five
years.

And now the time approached when he was to be still
further humbled, and made to feel, if he could feel anything,
what a wretched creature he was.   Of all men in the world,
Stephen Langton seemed raised up by Heaven to oppose
and subdue him.   When he ruthlessly burnt and destroyed
the property of his own subjects, because their Lords, the
Barons, would not serve him abroad, Stephen Langton

fearlessly reproved and threatened him. When he swore to restore the laws of King Edward, or the laws of King Henry the First, Stephen Langton knew his falsehood, and pursued him through all his evasions. When the Barons met at the abbey of Saint Edmund's-Bury, to consider their wrongs and the King's oppressions, Stephen Langton roused them by his fervid words to demand a solemn charter of rights and liberties from their perjured master, and to swear, one by one, on the High Altar, that they would have it, or would wage war against him to the death. When the King hid himself in London from the Barons, and was at last obliged to receive them, they told him roundly they would not believe him unless Stephen Langton became a surety that he would keep his word. When he took the Cross to invest himself with some interest, and belong to something that was received with favour, Stephen Langton was still immovable. When he appealed to the Pope, and the Pope wrote to Stephen Langton in behalf of his new favourite, Stephen Langton was deaf, even to the Pope himself, and saw before him nothing but the welfare of England and the crimes of the English King.

At Easter-time, the Barons assembled at Stamford, in Lincolnshire, in proud array, and, marching near to Oxford where the King was, delivered into the hands of Stephen Langton and two others, a list of grievances. "And these," they said, "he must redress, or we will do it for ourselves!" When Stephen Langton told the King as much, and read the list to him, he went half mad with rage. But that did him no more good than his afterwards trying to pacify the Barons with lies. They called themselves and their followers, "The army of God and the Holy Church." Marching through the country, with the people thronging to them everywhere (except at Northampton, where they failed in an attack upon the castle), they at last triumphantly set up their banner in London itself, whither the whole land, tired of the tyrant, seemed to flock to join them. Seven knights alone, of all the knights in England, remained with the King; who, reduced to this strait, at last sent the Earl of Pembroke to the Barons to say that he approved of everything, and would meet them to sign their charter when they would. "Then," said the Barons, "let the day be the fifteenth of June, and the place, Runny-Mead."

On Monday, the fifteenth of June, one thousand two

hundred and fourteen, the King came from Windsor Castle, and the Barons came from the town of Staines, and they met on Runny-Mead, which is still a pleasant meadow by the Thames, where rushes grow in the clear water of the winding river, and its banks are green with grass and trees. On the side of the Barons, came the General of their army, ROBERT FITZ-WALTER. and a great concourse of the nobility of England. With the King, came in all, some four-and-twenty persons of any note, most of whom despised him, and were merely his advisers in form. On that great day, and in that great company, the King signed MAGNA CHARTA—the great charter of England—by which he pledged himself to maintain the Church in its rights; to relieve the Barons of oppressive obligations as vassals of the Crown—of which the Barons, in their turn, pledged themselves to relieve *their* vassals, the people ; to respect the liberties of London and all other cities and boroughs ; to protect foreign merchants who came to England ; to imprison no man without a fair trial; and to sell, delay, or deny justice to none. As the Barons knew his falsehood well, they further required, as their securities, that he should send out of his kingdom all his foreign troops ; that for two months they should hold possession of the city of London, and Stephen Langton of the Tower; and that five-and-twenty of their body, chosen by themselves, should be a lawful committee to watch the keeping of the charter, and to make war upon him if he broke it.

All this he was obliged to yield. He signed the charter with a smile, and, if he could have looked agreeable, would have done so, as he departed from the splendid assembly. When he got home to Windsor Castle, he was quite a madman in his helpless fury. And he broke the charter immediately afterwards.

He sent abroad for foreign soldiers, and sent to the Pope for help, and plotted to take London by surprise, while the Barons should be holding a great tournament at Stamford, which they had agreed to hold there as a celebration of the charter. The Barons, however, found him out and put it off. Then, when the Barons desired to see him and tax him with his treachery, he made numbers of appointments with them, and kept none, and shifted from place to place, and was constantly sneaking and skulking about. At last he appeared at Dover, to join his foreign soldiers, of whom numbers came into his pay ; and with them he besieged and took Rochester

Castle, which was occupied by knights and soldiers of the
Barons. He would have hanged them every one; but the
leader of the foreign soldiers, fearful of what the English
people might afterwards do to him, interfered to save the
knights; therefore the King was fain to satisfy his vengeance
with the death of all the common men. Then, he sent the
Earl of Salisbury, with one portion of his army, to ravage
the eastern part of his own dominions, while he carried fire
and slaughter into the northern part; torturing, plundering,
killing, and inflicting every possible cruelty upon the people;
and, every morning, setting a worthy example to his men by
setting fire, with his own monster-hands, to the house where
he had slept last night. Nor was this all; for the Pope,
coming to the aid of his precious friend, laid the kingdom
under an Interdict again, because the people took part with
the Barons. It did not much matter, for the people had
grown so used to it now, that they had begun to think
nothing about it. It occurred to them—perhaps to Stephen
Langton too—that they could keep their churches open, and
ring their bells, without the Pope's permission as well as
with it. So, they tried the experiment— and found that it
succeeded perfectly.

It being now impossible to bear the country, as a wilderness
of cruelty, or longer to hold any terms with such a forsworn
outlaw of a King, the Barons sent to Louis, son of the
French monarch, to offer him the English crown. Caring as
little for the Pope's excommunication of him if he accepted
the offer, as it is possible his father may have cared for
the Pope's forgiveness of his sins, he landed at Sandwich
(King John immediately running away from Dover, where
he happened to be), and went on to London. The Scottish
King, with whom many of the Northern English Lords had
taken refuge; numbers of the foreign soldiers, numbers of
the Barons, and numbers of the people went over to him every
day;—King John, the while, continually running away in all
directions. The career of Louis was checked, however, by
the suspicions of the Barons, founded on the dying declaration of a French Lord, that when the kingdom was conquered
he was sworn to banish them as traitors, and to give their
estates to some of his own Nobles. Rather than suffer this,
some of the Barons hesitated: others even went over to
King John.

It seemed to be the turning-point of King John's fortunes,

for, in his savage and murderous course, he had now taken
some towns and met with some successes. But, happily for
England and humanity, his death was near.   Crossing a
dangerous quicksand, called the Wash, not very far from
Wisbeach, the tide came up and nearly drowned his army.
He and his soldiers escaped ; but, looking back from the
shore when he was safe, he saw the roaring water sweep
down in a torrent, overturn the waggons, horses, and men,
that carried his treasure, and engulph them in a raging
whirlpool from which nothing could be delivered.

Cursing, and swearing, and gnawing his fingers, he went
on to Swinestead Abbey, where the monks set before him
quantities of pears, and peaches, and new cider—some say
poison too, but there is very little reason to suppose so—of
which he ate and drank in an immoderate and beastly way.
All night he lay ill of a burning fever, and haunted with
horrible fears. Next day, they put him in a horse-litter, and
carried him to Sleaford Castle, where he passed another night
of pain and horror.   Next day, they carried him, with greater
difficulty than on the day before, to the castle of Newark
upon Trent ; and there, on the eighteenth of October, in the
forty-ninth year of his age, and the seventeenth of his vile
reign, was an end of this miserable brute.

CHAPTER XV

IF any of the English Barons remembered the murdered
Arthur's sister, Eleanor the fair maid of Brittany, shut up
in her convent at Bristol, none among them spoke of her now,
or maintained her right to the Crown. The dead Usurper's
eldest boy, HENRY by name, was taken by the Earl of
Pembroke, the Marshal of England, to the city of Gloucester,
and there crowned in great haste when he was only ten
years old. As the Crown itself had been lost with the
King's treasure, in the raging water, and, as there was no
time to make another, they put a circle of plain gold upon
his head instead. "We have been the enemies of this
child's father," said Lord Pembroke, a good and true gentleman, to the few Lords who were present, "and he merited
our ill-will; but the child himself is innocent, and his youth
demands our friendship and protection." Those Lords felt
tenderly towards the little boy, remembering their own
young children; and they bowed their heads, and said,
"Long live King Henry the Third!"

Next, a great council met at Bristol, revised Magna Charta,
and made Lord Pembroke Regent or Protector of England,
as the King was too young to reign alone. The next thing
to be done, was to get rid of Prince Louis of France, and to
win over those English Barons who were still ranged under
his banner. He was strong in many parts of England, and
in London itself; and he held, among other places, a certain
Castle called the Castle of Mount Sorel, in Leicestershire.
To this fortress, after some skirmishing and truce-making,
Lord Pembroke laid siege. Louis despatched an army of six
hundred knights and twenty thousand soldiers to relieve it.
Lord Pembroke, who was not strong enough for such a force,
retired with all his men. The army of the French Prince,
which had marched there with fire and plunder, marched

away with fire and plunder, and came, in a boastful swaggering manner, to Lincoln. The town submitted ; but the
Castle in the town, held by a brave widow lady, named
NICHOLA DE CAMVILLE (whose property it was), made such
a sturdy resistance, that the French Count in command of
the army of the French Prince found it necessary to besiege
this Castle. While he was thus engaged, word was brought
to him that Lord Pembroke, with four hundred knights, two
hundred and fifty men with cross-bows, and a stout force
both of horse and foot, was marching towards him. "What
care I ?" said the French Count. "The Englishman is not
so mad as to attack me and my great army in a walled town !"
But the Englishman did it for all that, and did it—not so
madly but so wisely, that he decoyed the great army into
the narrow, ill-paved lanes and byways of Lincoln, where
its horse-soldiers could not ride in any strong body ; and
there he made such havoc with them, that the whole force
surrendered themselves prisoners, except the Count; who
said that he would never yield to any English traitor alive,
and accordingly got killed. The end of this victory, which the
English called, for a joke, the Fair of Lincoln, was the usual
one in those times—the common men were slain without
any mercy, and the knights and gentlemen paid ransom and
went home.

The wife of Louis, the fair BLANCHE OF CASTILE, dutifully
equipped a fleet of eighty good ships, and sent it over from
France to her husband's aid. An English fleet of forty ships,
some good and some bad, gallantly met them near the mouth
of the Thames, and took or sunk sixty-five in one fight.
This great loss put an end to the French Prince's hopes.
A treaty was made at Lambeth, in virtue of which the
English Barons who had remained attached to his cause
returned to their allegiance, and it was engaged on both
sides that the Prince and all his troops should retire peacefully to France. It was time to go ; for war had made him
so poor that he was obliged to borrow money from the
citizens of London to pay his expenses home.

Lord Pembroke afterwards applied himself to governing
the country justly, and to healing the quarrels and disturbances that had arisen among men in the days of the bad
King John. He caused Magna Charta to be still more
improved, and so amended the Forest Laws that a Peasant
was no longer put to death for killing a stag in a Royal

Forest, but was only imprisoned. It would have been well for England if it could have had so good a Protector many years longer, but that was not to be. Within three years after the young King's Coronation, Lord Pembroke died; and you may see his tomb, at this day, in the old Temple Church in London.

The Protectorship was now divided. PETER DE ROCHES, whom King John had made Bishop of Winchester, was entrusted with the care of the person of the young sovereign; and the exercise of the Royal authority was confided to EARL HUBERT DE BURGH. These two personages had from the first no liking for each other, and soon became enemies. When the young King was declared of age, Peter de Roches, finding that Hubert increased in power and favour, retired discontentedly, and went abroad. For nearly ten years afterwards Hubert had full sway alone.

But ten years is a long time to hold the favour of a King. This King, too, as he grew up, showed a strong resemblance to his father, in feebleness, inconsistency, and irresolution. The best that can be said of him is that he was not cruel. De Roches coming home again, after ten years, and being a novelty, the King began to favour him and to look coldly on Hubert. Wanting money besides, and having made Hubert rich, he began to dislike Hubert. At last he was made to believe, or pretended to believe, that Hubert had misappropriated some of the Royal treasure; and ordered him to furnish an account of all he had done in his administration. Besides which, the foolish charge was brought against Hubert that he had made himself the King's favourite by magic. Hubert very well knowing that he could never defend himself against such nonsense, and that his old enemy must be determined on his ruin, instead of answering the charges fled to Merton Abbey. Then the King, in a violent passion, sent for the Mayor of London, and said to the Mayor, "Take twenty thousand citizens, and drag me Hubert de Burgh out of that abbey, and bring him here." The Mayor posted off to do it, but the Archbishop of Dublin (who was a friend of Hubert's) warning the King that an abbey was a sacred place, and that if he committed any violence there, he must answer for it to the Church, the King changed his mind and called the Mayor back, and declared that Hubert should have four months to prepare his defence, and should be safe and free during that time.

Hubert, who relied upon the King's word, though I think he was old enough to have known better, came out of Merton Abbey upon these conditions, and journeyed away to see his wife : a Scottish Princess who was then at St. Edmund's-Bury.

Almost as soon as he had departed from the Sanctuary, his enemies persuaded the weak King to send out one Sir Godfrey de Crancumb, who commanded three hundred vagabonds called the Black Band, with orders to seize him. They came up with him at a little town in Essex, called Brentwood, when he was in bed. He leaped out of bed, got out of the house, fled to the church, ran up to the altar, and laid his hand upon the cross. Sir Godfrey and the Black Band, caring neither for church, altar, nor cross, dragged him forth to the church door, with their drawn swords flashing round his head, and sent for a Smith to rivet a set of chains upon him. When the Smith (I wish I knew his name !) was brought, all dark and swarthy with the smoke of his forge, and panting with the speed he had made; and the Black Band, falling aside to show him the Prisoner, cried with a loud uproar, "Make the fetters heavy ! make them strong ! " the Smith dropped upon his knee—but not to the Black Band—and said, "This is the brave Earl Hubert de Burgh, who fought at Dover Castle, and destroyed the French fleet, and has done his country much good service. You may kill me, if you like, but I will never make a chain for Earl Hubert de Burgh ! "

The Black Band never blushed, or they might have blushed at this. They knocked the Smith about from one to another, and swore at him, and tied the Earl on horseback, undressed as he was, and carried him off to the Tower of London. The Bishops, however, were so indignant at the violation of the Sanctuary of the Church, that the frightened King soon ordered the Black Band to take him back again ; at the same time commanding the Sheriff of Essex to prevent his escaping out of Brentwood Church. Well ! the Sheriff dug a deep trench all round the church, and erected a high fence, and watched the church night and day ; the Black Band and their Captain watched it too, like three hundred and one black wolves. For thirty-nine days, Hubert de Burgh remained within. At length, upon the fortieth day, cold and hunger were too much for him, and he gave himself up to the Black Band, who carried him off, for the second time, to the Tower. When his trial came on, he refused to plead ; but at last it was arranged that he should give up all the royal lands which had been bestowed upon him, and should be kept at the Castle of Devizes, in what was called " free prison," in charge of four knights appointed by four lords. There, he remained almost a year, until, learning that a follower of his old enemy the Bishop was made Keeper of the Castle, and fearing that he might be killed by treachery, he climbed the ramparts one dark night, dropped from the top of the high Castle wall into the moat, and coming safely to the ground, took refuge in another church. From this place he was delivered by a party of horse despatched to his help by some nobles, who were by this time in revolt against the King, and assembled in Wales. He was finally pardoned and restored to his estates, but he lived privately, and never more aspired to a high post in the realm, or to a high place in the King's favour. And thus end--more happily than the stories of many favourites of Kings—the adventures of Earl Hubert de Burgh.

The nobles, who had risen in revolt, were stirred up to rebellion by the overbearing conduct of the Bishop of Win-chester, who, finding that the King secretly hated the Great Charter which had been forced from his father, did his utmost to confirm him in that dislike, and in the preference he showed to foreigners over the English. Of this, and of his even publicly declaring that the Barons of England were inferior to those of France, the English Lords complained with such bitterness, that the King, finding them well sup-ported by the clergy, became frightened for his throne, and sent away the Bishop and all his foreign associates. On his marriage, however, with ELEANOR, a French lady, the daugh-ter of the Count of Provence, he openly favoured the foreigners again ; and so many of his wife's relations came over, and made such an immense family-party at court, and got so many good things, and pocketed so much money, and were so high with the English whose money they pocketed, that the bolder English Barons murmured openly about a clause there was in the Great Charter, which provided for the banishment of unreasonable favourites. But, the foreigners only laughed disdainfully, and said, "What are your English laws to us?"

King Philip of France had died, and had been succeeded by Prince Louis, who had also died after a short reign of three years, and had been succeeded by his son of the same name—so moderate and just a man that he was not the least in the world like a King, as Kings went. ISABELLA, King Henry's mother, wished very much (for a certain spite she had) that England should make war against this King; and, as King Henry was a mere puppet in anybody's hands who knew how to manage his feebleness, she easily carried her point with him. But, the Parliament were determined to give him no money for such a war. So, to defy the Parliament, he packed up thirty large casks of silver—I don't know how he got so much; I dare say he screwed it out of the miserable Jews—and put them aboard ship, and went away himself to carry war into France: accompanied by his mother and his brother Richard, Earl of Cornwall, who was rich and clever. But he only got well beaten, and came home.

The good-humour of the Parliament was not restored by this. They reproached the King with wasting the public money to make greedy foreigners rich, and were so stern with him, and so determined not to let him have more of it to waste if they could help it, that he was at his wit's end for some, and tried so shamelessly to get all he could from his subjects, by excuses or by force, that the people used to say the King was the sturdiest beggar in England. He took the Cross, thinking to get some money by that means; but, as it was very well known that he never meant to go on a crusade, he got none. In all this contention, the Londoners were particularly keen against the King, and the King hated them warmly in return. Hating or loving, however, made no difference; he continued in the same condition for nine or ten years, when at last the Barons said that if he would solemnly confirm their liberties afresh, the Parliament would vote him a large sum.

As he readily consented, there was a great meeting held in Westminster Hall, one pleasant day in May, when all the clergy, dressed in their robes and holding every one of them a burning candle in his hand, stood up (the Barons being also there) while the Archbishop of Canterbury read the sentence of excommunication against any man, and all men, who should henceforth, in any way, infringe the Great Charter of the Kingdom. When he had done, they all put out their burning candles with a curse upon the soul of any one, and every one, who should merit that sentence. The

King concluded with an oath to keep the Charter, "As I am a man, as I am a Christian, as I am a Knight, as I am a King!"

It was easy to make oaths, and easy to break them; and the King did both, as his father had done before him. He took to his old courses again when he was supplied with money, and soon cured of their weakness the few who had ever really trusted him. When his money was gone, and he was once more borrowing and begging everywhere with a meanness worthy of his nature, he got into a difficulty with the Pope respecting the Crown of Sicily, which the Pope said he had a right to give away, and which he offered to King Henry for his second son, PRINCE EDMUND. But, if you or I give away what we have not got, and what belongs to somebody else, it is likely that the person to whom we give it, will have some trouble in taking it. It was exactly so in this case. It was necessary to conquer the Sicilian Crown before it could be put upon young Edmund's head. It could not be conquered without money. The Pope ordered the clergy to raise money. The clergy, however, were not so obedient to him as usual; they had been disputing with him for some time about his unjust preference of Italian Priests in England; and they had begun to doubt whether the King's chaplain, whom he allowed to be paid for preaching in seven hundred churches, could possibly be, even by the Pope's favour, in seven hundred places at once. "The Pope and the King together," said the Bishop of London, "may take the mitre off my head; but, if they do, they will find that I shall put on a soldier's helmet. I pay nothing." The Bishop of Worcester was as bold as the Bishop of London, and would pay nothing either. Such sums as the more timid or more helpless of the clergy did raise were squandered away, without doing any good to the King, or bringing the Sicilian Crown an inch nearer to Prince Edmund's head. The end of the business was, that the Pope gave the Crown to the brother of the King of France (who conquered it for himself), and sent the King of England in, a bill of one hundred thousand pounds for the expenses of not having won it.

The King was now so much distressed that we might almost pity him, if it were possible to pity a King so shabby and ridiculous. His clever brother, Richard, had bought the title of King of the Romans from the German people, and was no longer near him, to help him with advice. The clergy, resisting the very Pope, were in alliance with the Barons. The Barons were headed by SIMON DE MONTFORT, Earl of Leicester, married to King Henry's sister, and, though a foreigner himself, the most popular man in England against the foreign favourites. When the King next met his Parliament, the Barons, led by this Earl, came before him, armed from head to foot, and cased in armour. When the Parliament again assembled, in a month's time, at Oxford, this Earl was at their head, and the King was obliged to consent, on oath, to what was called a Committee of Government: consisting of twenty-four members: twelve chosen by the Barons, and twelve chosen by himself.

But, at a good time for him, his brother Richard came back. Richard's first act (the Barons would not admit him into England on other terms) was to swear to be faithful to the Committee of Government—which he immediately began to oppose with all his might. Then, the Barons began to quarrel among themselves; especially the proud Earl of Gloucester with the Earl of Leicester, who went abroad in disgust. Then, the people began to be dissatisfied with the Barons, because they did not do enough for them. The King's chances seemed so good again at length, that he took heart enough—or caught it from his brother—to tell the Committee of Government that he abolished them—as to his oath, never mind that, the Pope said !—and to seize all the money in the Mint, and to shut himself up in the Tower of London. Here he was joined by his eldest son, Prince Edward ; and, from the Tower, he made public a letter of the Pope's to the world in general, informing all men that he had been an excellent and just King for five-and-forty years.

As everybody knew he had been nothing of the sort, nobody cared much for this document. It so chanced that the proud Earl of Gloucester dying, was succeeded by his son ; and that his son, instead of being the enemy of the Earl of Leicester, was (for the time) his friend. It fell out, therefore, that these two Earls joined their forces, took several of the Royal Castles in the country, and advanced as hard as they could on London. The London people, always opposed to the King, declared for them with great joy. The King himself remained shut up, not at all gloriously, in the Tower. Prince Edward made the best of his way to

Windsor Castle. His mother, the Queen, attempted to follow him by water ; but, the people seeing her barge rowing up the river, and hating her with all their hearts, ran to London Bridge, got together a quantity of stones and mud, and pelted the barge as it came through, crying furiously, "Drown the Witch ! Drown her ! " They were so near doing it, that the Mayor took the old lady under his protection, and shut her up in St. Paul's until the danger was past.

It would require a great deal of writing on my part, and a great deal of reading on yours, to follow the King through his disputes with the Barons, and to follow the Barons through their disputes with one another—so I will make short work of it for both of us, and only relate the chief events that arose out of these quarrels. The good King of France was asked to decide between them. He gave it as his opinion that the King must maintain the Great Charter, and that the Barons must give up the Committee of Government, and all the rest that had been done by the Parliament at Oxford : which the Royalists, or King's party, scornfully called the Mad Parliament. The Barons declared that these were not fair terms, and they would not accept them. Then they caused the great bell of St. Paul's to be tolled, for the purpose of rousing up the London people, who armed themselves at the dismal sound and formed quite an army in the streets. I am sorry to say, however, that instead of falling upon the King's party with whom their quarrel was, they fell upon the miserable Jews, and killed at least five hundred of them. They pretended that some of these Jews were on the King's side, and that they kept hidden in their houses, for the destruction of the people, a certain terrible composition called Greek Fire, which could not be put out with water, but only burnt the fiercer for it. What they really did keep in their houses was money ; and this their cruel enemies wanted, and this their cruel enemies took, like robbers and murderers.

The Earl of Leicester put himself at the head of these Londoners and other forces, and followed the King to Lewes in Sussex, where he lay encamped with his army. Before giving the King's forces battle here, the Earl addressed his soldiers, and said that King Henry the Third had broken so many oaths, that he had become the enemy of God, and therefore they would wear white crosses on their breasts, as if they were arrayed, not against a fellow-Christian, but against a Turk. White-crossed accordingly, they rushed into the fight. They would have lost the day—the King having on his side all the foreigners in England: and, from Scotland, JOHN COMYN, JOHN BALIOL, and ROBERT BRUCE, with all their men—but for the impatience of PRINCE EDWARD, who, in his hot desire to have vengeance on the people of London, threw the whole of his father's army into confusion. He was taken Prisonèr; so was the King; so was the King's brother the King of the Romans; and five thousand Englishmen were left dead upon the bloody grass.

For this success, the Pope excommunicated the Earl of Leicester: which neither the Earl nor the people cared at all about. The people loved him and supported him, and he became the real King; having all the power of the government in his own hands, though he was outwardly respectful to King Henry the Third, whom he took with him wherever he went, like a poor old limp court-card. He summoned a Parliament (in the year one thousand two hundred and sixty-five) which was the first Parliament in England that the people had any real share in electing; and he grew more and more in favour with the people every day, and they stood by him in whatever he did.

Many of the other Barons, and particularly the Earl of Gloucester, who had become by this time as proud as his father, grew jealous of this powerful and popular Earl, who was proud too, and began to conspire against him. Since the battle of Lewes, Prince Edward had been kept as a hostage, and, though he was otherwise treated like a Prince, had never been allowed to go out without attendants appointed by the Earl of Leicester, who watched him. The conspiring Lords found means to propose to him, in secret, that they should assist him to escape, and should make him their leader; to which he very heartily consented.

So, on a day that was agreed upon, he said to his attendants after dinner (being then at Hereford), "I should like to ride on horseback, this fine afternoon, a little way into the country." As they, too, thought it would be very pleasant to have a canter in the sunshine, they all rode out of the town together in a gay little troop. When they came to a fine level piece of turf, the Prince fell to comparing their horses one with another, and offering bets that one was faster than another; and the attendants, suspecting no harm, rode galloping matches until their horses were quite tired. The Prince rode no matches himself, but looked on from his saddle, and staked his money. Thus they passed the whole merry afternoon. Now, the sun was setting, and they were all going slowly up a hill, the Prince's horse very fresh and all the other horses very weary, when a strange rider mounted on a grey steed appeared at the top of the hill, and waved his hat. "What does the fellow mean?" said the attendants one to another. The Prince answered on the instant by setting spurs to his horse, dashing away at his utmost speed, joining the man, riding into the midst of a little crowd of horsemen who were then seen waiting under some trees, and who closed around him; and so he departed in a cloud of dust, leaving the road empty of all but the baffled attendants, who sat looking at one another, while their horses drooped their ears and panted.

The Prince joined the Earl of Gloucester at Ludlow. The Earl of Leicester, with a part of the army and the stupid old King, was at Hereford. One of the Earl of Leicester's sons, Simon de Montfort, with another part of the army, was in Sussex. To prevent these two parts from uniting was the Prince's first object. He attacked Simon de Montfort by night, defeated him, seized his banners and treasure, and forced him into Kenilworth Castle in Warwickshire, which belonged to his family.

His father, the Earl of Leicester, in the meanwhile, not knowing what had happened, marched out of Hereford, with his part of the army and the King, to meet him. He came, on a bright morning in August, to Evesham, which is watered by the pleasant river Avon. Looking rather anxiously across the prospect towards Kenilworth, he saw his own banners advancing; and his face brightened with joy. But, it clouded darkly when he presently perceived that the banners were captured, and in the enemy's hands; and he said, "It is over. The Lord have mercy on our souls, for our bodies are Prince Edward's!"

He fought like a true Knight, nevertheless. When his horse was killed under him, he fought on foot. It was a fierce battle, and the dead lay in heaps everywhere. The old King, stuck up in a suit of armour on a big war-horse, which didn't mind him at all, and which carried him into all sorts of places where he didn't want to go, got into every-body's way, and very nearly got knocked on the head by one

of his son's men.   But he managed to pipe out, "I am
Harry of Winchester!" and the Prince, who heard him,
seized his bridle, and took him out of peril.   The Earl of
Leicester still fought bravely, until his best son Henry was
killed, and the bodies of his best friends choked his path;
and then he fell, still fighting, sword in hand.   They
mangled his body, and sent it as a present to a noble lady—
but a very unpleasant lady, I should think—who was the
wife of his worst enemy.   They could not mangle his
memory in the minds of the faithful people, though.   Many
years afterwards, they loved him more than ever, and
regarded him as a Saint, and always spoke of him as "Sir
Simon the Righteous."

And even though he was dead, the cause for which he had
fought still lived, and was strong, and forced itself upon the
King in the very hour of victory.   Henry found himself
obliged to respect the Great Charter, however much he hated
it, and to make laws similar to the laws of the Great Earl
of Leicester, and to be moderate and forgiving towards the
people at last—even towards the people of London, who had
so long opposed him.   There were more risings before all
this was done, but they were set at rest by these means, and
Prince Edward did his best in all things to restore peace.
One Sir Adam de Gourdon was the last dissatisfied knight
in arms; but, the Prince vanquished him in single combat,
in a wood, and nobly gave him his life, and became his
friend, instead of slaying him.   Sir Adam was not ungrateful.   He ever afterwards remained devoted to his
generous conqueror.

When the troubles of the Kingdom were thus calmed,
Prince Edward and his cousin Henry took the Cross, and
went away to the Holy Land, with many English Lords and
Knights.   Four years afterwards the King of the Romans
died, and, next year (one thousand two hundred and seventy-
two), his brother the weak King of England died.   He was
sixty-eight years old then, and had reigned fifty-six years.
He was as much of a King in death, as he had ever been in
life.   He was the mere pale shadow of a King at all times.

CHAPTER XVI

ENGLAND UNDER EDWARD THE FIRST, CALLED LONGSHANKS

It was now the year of our Lord one thousand two hundred and seventy-two ; and Prince Edward, the heir to the throne, being away in the Holy Land, knew nothing of his father's death. The Barons, however, proclaimed him King, immediately after the Royal funeral ; and the people very willingly consented, since most men knew too well by this time what the horrors of a contest for the crown were. So King Edward the First, called, in a not very complimentary manner, Longshanks, because of the slenderness of his legs, was peacefully accepted by the English Nation.

His legs had need to be strong, however long and thin they were ; for they had to support him through many difficulties on the fiery sands of Asia, where his small force of soldiers fainted, died, deserted, and seemed to melt away. But his prowess made light of it, and he said, "I will go on, if I go on with no other follower than my groom ! "

A Prince of this spirit gave the Turks a deal of trouble. He stormed Nazareth, at which place, of all places on earth, I am sorry to relate, he made a frightful slaughter of innocent people ; and then he went to Acre, where he got a truce of ten years from the Sultan. He had very nearly lost his life in Acre, through the treachery of a Saracen Noble, called the Emir of Jaffa, who, making the pretence that he had some idea of turning Christian and wanted to know all about that religion, sent a trusty messenger to Edward very often—with a dagger in his sleeve. At last, one Friday in Whitsun week, when it was very hot, and all the sandy prospect lay beneath the blazing sun, burnt up like a great overdone biscuit, and Edward was lying on a couch, dressed for coolness in only a loose robe, the messenger, with his chocolate-coloured face and his bright dark eyes and white teeth, came creeping in with a letter, and kneeled down like a tame tiger. But, the moment Edward stretched out his hand to take the letter, the tiger made a spring at his heart. He was quick, but Edward was quick too. He seized the traitor by his chocolate throat, threw him to the ground, and slew him with the very dagger he had drawn. The weapon had struck Edward in the arm, and although the wound itself was slight, it threatened to be mortal, for the blade of the dagger had been smeared with poison. Thanks, however, to a better surgeon than was often to be found in those times, and to some wholesome herbs, and above all, to his faithful wife, ELEANOR, who devotedly nursed him, and is said by some to have sucked the poison from the wound with her own red lips (which I am very willing to believe), Edward soon recovered and was sound again.

As the King his father had sent entreaties to him to return home, he now began the journey. He had got as far as Italy, when he met messengers who brought him intelligence of the King's death. Hearing that all was quiet at home, he made no haste to return to his own dominions, but paid a visit to the Pope, and went in state through various Italian Towns, where he was welcomed with acclamations as a mighty champion of the Cross from the Holy Land, and where he received presents of purple mantles and prancing horses, and went along in great triumph. The shouting people little knew that he was the last English monarch who would ever embark in a crusade, or that within twenty years every conquest which the Christians had made in the Holy Land at the cost of so much blood, would be won back by the Turks. But all this came to pass.

There was, and there is, an old town standing in a plain in France, called Châlons. When the King was coming towards this place on his way to England, a wily French Lord, called the Count of Châlons, sent him a polite challenge to come with his knights and hold a fair tournament with the Count and *his* knights, and make a day of it with sword and lance. It was represented to the King that the Count of Châlons was not to be trusted, and that, instead of a holiday fight for mere show and in good humour, he secretly meant a real battle, in which the English should be defeated by superior force.

The King, however, nothing afraid, went to the appointed

place on the appointed day with a thousand followers. When the Count came with two thousand and attacked the English in earnest, the English rushed at them with such valour that the Count's men and the Count's horses soon began to be tumbled down all over the field. The Count himself seized the King round the neck, but the King tumbled *him* out of his saddle in return for the compliment, and, jumping from his own horse, and standing over him, beat away at his iron armour like a blacksmith hammering on his anvil. Even when the Count owned himself defeated and offered his sword, the King would not do him the honour to take it, but made him yield it up to a common soldier. There had been such fury shown in this fight, that it was afterwards called the little Battle of Châlons.

The English were very well disposed to be proud of their King after these adventures ; so, when he landed at Dover in the year one thousand two hundred and seventy-four (being then thirty-six years old), and went on to Westminster where he and his good Queen were crowned with great magnificence, splendid rejoicings took place. For the coronation-feast there were provided, among other eatables, four hundred oxen, four hundred sheep, four hundred and fifty pigs, eighteen wild boars, three hundred flitches of bacon, and twenty thousand fowls. The fountains and conduits in the street flowed with red and white wine instead of water ; the rich citizens hung silks and cloths of the brightest colours out of their windows to increase the beauty of the show, and threw out gold and silver by whole handfuls to make scrambles for the crowd. In short, there was such eating and drinking, such music and capering, such a ringing of bells and tossing of caps, such a shouting, and singing, and revelling, as the narrow overhanging streets of old London City had not witnessed for many a long day. All the people were merry—except the poor Jews, who, trembling within their houses, and scarcely daring to peep out, began to foresee that they would have to find the money for this joviality sooner or later.

To dismiss this sad subject of the Jews for the present, I am sorry to add that in this reign they were most unmercifully pillaged. They were hanged in great numbers, on accusations of having clipped the King's coin—which all kinds of people had done. They were heavily taxed ; they were disgracefully badged ; they were, on one day, thirteen years after the coronation, taken up with their wives and children and thrown into beastly prisons, until they purchased their release by paying to the King twelve thousand pounds. Finally, every kind of property belonging to them was seized by the King, except so little as would defray the charge of their taking themselves away into foreign countries. Many years elapsed before the hope of gain induced any of their race to return to England, where they had been treated so heartlessly and had suffered so much.

If King Edward the First had been as bad a king to Christians as he was to Jews, he would have been bad indeed. But he was, in general, a wise and great monarch, under whom the country much improved. He had no love for the Great Charter—few Kings had, through many many years—but he had high qualities. The first bold object which he conceived when he came home, was, to unite under one Sovereign England, Scotland, and Wales; the two last of which countries had each a little king of its own, about whom the people were always quarrelling and fighting, and making a prodigious disturbance—a great deal more than he was worth. In the course of King Edward's reign he was engaged, besides, in a war with France. To make these quarrels clearer, we will separate their histories and take them thus. Wales, first. France, second. Scotland, third.

LLEWELLYN was the Prince of Wales. He had been on the side of the Barons in the reign of the stupid old King, but had afterwards sworn allegiance to him. When King Edward came to the throne, Llewellyn was required to swear allegiance to him also; which he refused to do. The King, being crowned and in his own dominions, three times more required Llewellyn to come and do homage; and three times more Llewellyn said he would rather not. He was going to be married to ELEANOR DE MONTFORT, a young lady of the family mentioned in the last reign; and it chanced that this young lady, coming from France with her youngest brother, EMERIC, was taken by an English ship, and was ordered by the English King to be detained. Upon this, the quarrel came to a head. The King went, with his fleet, to the coast of Wales, where, so encompassing Llewellyn, that he could only take refuge in the bleak mountain region of Snowdon in which no provisions could reach him, he was soon starved into an apology, and into a treaty of peace, and into paying the expenses of the war. The King, however, forgave him some of the hardest conditions of the treaty, and consented to his marriage. And he now thought he had reduced Wales to obedience.

But, the Welsh, although they were naturally a gentle, quiet, pleasant people, who liked to receive strangers in their cottages among the mountains, and to set before them with free hospitality whatever they had to eat and drink, and to play to them on their harps, and sing their native ballads to them, were a people of great spirit when their blood was up. Englishmen, after this affair, began to be insolent in Wales, and to assume the air of masters ; and the Welsh pride could not bear it. Moreover, they believed in that unlucky old Merlin, some of whose unlucky old prophecies somebody always seemed doomed to remember when there was a chance of its doing harm ; and just at this time some blind old gentleman with a harp and a long white beard, who was an excellent person, but had become of an unknown age and tedious, burst out with a declaration that Merlin had predicted that when English money had become round, a Prince of Wales would be crowned in London. Now, King Edward had recently forbidden the English penny to be cut into halves and quarters for halfpence and farthings, and had actually introduced a round coin; therefore, the Welsh people said this was the time Merlin meant, and rose accordingly.

King Edward had bought over PRINCE DAVID, Llewellyn's brother, by heaping favours upon him ; but he was the first to revolt, being perhaps troubled in his conscience. One stormy night, he surprised the Castle of Hawarden, in possession of which an English nobleman had been left; killed the whole garrison, and carried off the nobleman a prisoner to Snowdon. Upon this, the Welsh people rose like one man. King Edward, with his army, marching from Worcester to the Menai Strait, crossed it—near to where the wonderful tubular iron bridge now, in days so different, makes a passage for railway trains—by a bridge of boats that enabled forty men to march abreast. He subdued the Island of Anglesea, and sent his men forward to observe the enemy. The sudden appearance of the Welsh created a panic among them, and they fell back to the bridge. The tide had in the mean-time risen and separated the boats; the Welsh pursuing them, they were driven into the sea, and there they sunk, in their heavy iron armour, by thousands. After this victory

Llewellyn, helped by the severe winter-weather of Wales, gained another battle ; but the King ordering a portion of his English army to advance through South Wales, and catch him between two foes, and Llewellyn bravely turning to meet this new enemy, he was surprised and killed—very meanly, for he was unarmed and defenceless. His head was struck off and sent to London, where it was fixed upon the Tower, encircled with a wreath, some say of ivy, some say of willow, some say of silver, to make it look like a ghastly coin in ridicule of the prediction.

David, however, still held out for six months, though eagerly sought after by the King, and hunted by his own countrymen. One of them finally betrayed him with his wife and children. He was sentenced to be hanged, drawn, and quartered ; and from that time this became the established punishment of Traitors in England—a punishment wholly without excuse, as being revolting, vile, and cruel, after its object is dead ; and which has no sense in it, as its only real degradation (and that nothing can blot out) is to the country that permits on any consideration such abominable bar-barity.

Wales was now subdued. The Queen giving birth to a young prince in the Castle of Carnarvon, the King showed him to the Welsh people as their countryman, and called him Prince of Wales ; a title that has ever since been borne by the heir-apparent to the English throne—which that little Prince soon became, by the death of his elder brother. The King did better things for the Welsh than that, by improving their laws and encouraging their trade. Disturbances still took place, chiefly occasioned by the avarice and pride of the English Lords, on whom Welsh lands and castles had been bestowed ; but they were subdued, and the country never rose again. There is a legend that to prevent the people from being incited to rebellion by the songs of their bards and harpers, Edward had them all put to death. Some of them may have fallen among other men who held out against the King ; but this general slaughter is, I think, a fancy of the harpers themselves, who, I dare say, made a song about it many years afterwards, and sang it by the Welsh firesides until it came to be believed.

The foreign war of the reign of Edward the First arose in this way. The crews of two vessels, one a Norman ship, and the other an English ship, happened to go to the same place in their boats to fill their casks with fresh water. Being rough angry fellows, they began to quarrel, and then to fight—the English with their fists; the Normans with their knives—and, in the fight, a Norman was killed. The Norman crew, instead of revenging themselves upon those English sailors with whom they had quarrelled (who were too strong for them. I suspect). took to their ship again in a great rage, attacked the first English ship they met, laid hold of an unoffending merchant who happened to be on board, and brutally hanged him in the rigging of their own vessel with a dog at his feet. This so enraged the English sailors that there was no restraining them ; and whenever, and wherever, English sailors met Norman sailors, they fell upon each other tooth and nail. The Irish and Dutch sailors took part with the English ; the French and Genoese sailors helped the Normans ; and thus the greater part of the mariners sailing over the sea became, in their way, as violent and raging as the sea itself when it is disturbed.

King Edward's fame had been so high abroad that he had been chosen to decide a difference between France and another foreign power, and had lived upon the Continent three years. At first, neither he nor the French King PHILIP (the good Louis had been dead some time) interfered in these quarrels ; but when a fleet of eighty English ships engaged and utterly defeated a Norman fleet of two hundred, in a pitched battle fought round a ship at anchor, in which no quarter was given, the matter became too serious to be passed over. King Edward. as Duke of Guienne. was summoned to present himself before the King of France, at Paris, and answer for the damage done by his sailor subjects. At first, he sent the Bishop of London as his representative. and then his brother EDMUND. who was married to the French Queen's mother. I am afraid Edmund was an easy man, and allowed himself to be talked over by his charming relations, the French court ladies ; at all events, he was induced to give up his brother's dukedom for forty days—as a mere form, the French King said, to satisfy his honour—and he was so very much astonished, when the time was out, to find that the French King had no idea of giving it up again, that I should not wonder if it hastened his death : which soon took place.

King Edward was a King to win his foreign dukedom back again, if it could be won by energy and valour. He raised a large army, renounced his allegiance as Duke of Guienne, and crossed the sea to carry war into France. Before any important battle was fought, however, a truce was agreed upon for two years; and in the course of that time, the Pope effected a reconciliation. King Edward, who was now a widower, having lost his affectionate and good wife, Eleanor, married the French King's sister, MARGARET; and the Prince of Wales was contracted to the French King's daughter ISABELLA.

Out of bad things, good things sometimes arise. Out of this hanging of the innocent merchant, and the bloodshed and strife it caused, there came to be established one of the greatest powers that the English people now possess. The preparations for the war being very expensive, and King Edward greatly wanting money, and being very arbitrary in his ways of raising it, some of the Barons began firmly to oppose him. Two of them, in particular, HUMPHREY BOHUN, Earl of Hereford, and ROGER BIGOD, Earl of Norfolk, were so stout against him, that they maintained he had no right to command them to head his forces in Guienne, and flatly refused to go there. "By Heaven, Sir Earl," said the King to the Earl of Hereford, in a great passion, "you shall either go or be hanged!" "By Heaven, Sir King," replied the Earl, "I will neither go nor yet will I be hanged!" and both he and the other Earl sturdily left the court, attended by many Lords. The King tried every means of raising money. He taxed the clergy, in spite of all the Pope said to the contrary; and when they refused to pay, reduced them to submission, by saying Very well, then they had no claim upon the government for protection, and any man might plunder them who would—which a good many men were very ready to do, and very readily did, and which the clergy found too losing a game to be played at long. He seized all the wool and leather in the hands of the merchants, promising to pay for it some fine day; and he set a tax upon the exportation of wool, which was so unpopular among the traders that it was called "The evil toll." But all would not do. The Barons, led by those two great Earls, declared any taxes imposed without the consent of Parliament, unlawful; and the Parliament refused to impose taxes, until the King should confirm afresh the two Great Charters, and should solemnly declare in writing, that there was no power in the country to raise money from the people, evermore,

but the power of Parliament representing all ranks of the
people. The King was very unwilling to diminish his own
power by allowing this great privilege in the Parliament;
but there was no help for it, and he at last complied. We
shall come to another King by-and-by, who might have
saved his head from rolling off, if he had profited by this
example.

The people gained other benefits in Parliament from the
good sense and wisdom of this King. Many of the laws
were much improved; provision was made for the greater
safety of travellers, and the apprehension of thieves and
murderers; the priests were prevented from holding too
much land, and so becoming too powerful; and Justices of
the Peace were first appointed (though not at first under that
name) in various parts of the country.

And now we come to Scotland, which was the great and
lasting trouble of the reign of King Edward the First.

About thirteen years after King Edward's coronation,
Alexander the Third, the King of Scotland, died of a fall
from his horse. He had been married to Margaret, King
Edward's sister. All their children being dead, the Scottish
crown became the right of a young Princess only eight years
old, the daughter of ERIC, King of Norway, who had married
a daughter of the deceased sovereign. King Edward proposed, that the Maiden of Norway, as this Princess was
called, should be engaged to be married to his eldest son;
but, unfortunately, as she was coming over to England she
fell sick, and landing on one of the Orkney Islands, died
there. A great commotion immediately began in Scotland,
where as many as thirteen noisy claimants to the vacant
throne started up and made a general confusion.

King Edward being much renowned for his sagacity and
justice, it seems to have been agreed to refer the dispute to
him. He accepted the trust, and went, with an army, to
the Border-land where England and Scotland joined. There,
he called upon the Scottish gentlemen to meet him at the
Castle of Norham, on the English side of the river Tweed;
and to that Castle they came. But, before he would take
any step in the business, he required those Scottish gentlemen, one and all, to do homage to him as their superior
Lord; and when they hesitated, he said, "By holy Edward,
whose crown I wear, I will have my rights, or I will die in

maintaining them !" The Scottish gentlemen, who had not expected this, were disconcerted, and asked for three weeks to think about it.

At the end of the three weeks, another meeting took place, on a green plain on the Scottish side of the river. Of all the competitors for the Scottish throne, there were only two who had any real claim, in right of their near kindred to the Royal Family. These were JOHN BALIOL and ROBERT BRUCE: and the right was, I have no doubt, on the side of John Baliol. At this particular meeting John Baliol was not present, but Robert Bruce was; and on Robert Bruce being formally asked whether he acknowledged the King of England for his superior lord, he answered, plainly and distinctly, Yes, he did. Next day, John Baliol appeared, and said the same. This point settled, some arrangements were made for inquiring into their titles.

The inquiry occupied a pretty long time—more than a year. While it was going on, King Edward took the opportunity of making a journey through Scotland, and calling upon the Scottish people of all degrees to acknowledge themselves his vassals, or be imprisoned until they did. In the meanwhile, Commissioners were appointed to conduct the inquiry, a Parliament was held at Berwick about it, the two claimants were heard at full length, and there was a vast amount of talking. At last, in the great hall of the Castle of Berwick, the King gave judgment in favour of John Baliol: who, consenting to receive his crown by the King of England's favour and permission, was crowned at Scone, in an old stone chair which had been used for ages in the abbey there, at the coronations of Scottish Kings. Then, King Edward caused the great seal of Scotland, used since the late King's death, to be broken in four pieces, and placed in the English Treasury; and considered that he now had Scotland (according to the common saying) under his thumb.

Scotland had a strong will of its own yet, however. King Edward, determined that the Scottish King should not forget he was his vassal, summoned him repeatedly to come and defend himself and his Judges before the English Parliament when appeals from the decisions of Scottish courts of justice were being heard. At length, John Baliol, who had no great heart of his own, had so much heart put into him by the brave spirit of the Scottish people, who took this as a national insult, that he refused to come any more. Thereupon, the King further required him to help him in his war abroad (which was then in progress), and to give up, as security for his good behaviour in future, the three strong Scottish Castles of Jedburgh, Roxburgh, and Berwick. Nothing of this being done; on the contrary, the Scottish people concealing their King among their mountains in the Highlands and showing a determination to resist; Edward marched to Berwick with an army of thirty thousand foot, and four thousand horse ; took the Castle and slew its whole garrison, and the inhabitants of the town as well—men, women, and children. LORD WARRENNE, Earl of Surrey, then went on to the Castle of Dunbar, before which a battle was fought, and the whole Scottish army defeated with great slaughter. The victory being complete, the Earl of Surrey was left as guardian of Scotland ; the principal offices in that kingdom were given to Englishmen ; the more powerful Scottish Nobles were obliged to come and live in England ; the Scottish crown and sceptre were brought away ; and even the old stone chair was carried off and placed in Westminster Abbey, where you may see it now. Baliol had the Tower of London lent him for a residence, with permission to range about within a circle of twenty miles. Three years afterwards he was allowed to go to Normandy, where he had estates, and where he passed the remaining six years of his life : far more happily, I dare say, than he had lived for a long while in angry Scotland.

Now, there was, in the West of Scotland, a gentleman of small fortune, named WILLIAM WALLACE, the second son of a Scottish knight. He was a man of great size and great strength ; he was very brave and daring ; when he spoke to a body of his countrymen, he could rouse them in a wonderful manner by the power of his burning words; he loved Scotland dearly, and he hated England with his utmost might. The domineering conduct of the English, who now held the places of trust in Scotland made them as intolerable to the proud Scottish people as they had been, under similar circumstances, to the Welsh ; and no man in all Scotland regarded them with so much smothered rage as William Wallace. One day, an Englishman in office, little knowing what he was, affronted *him*. Wallace instantly struck him dead, and taking refuge among the rocks and hills, and there joining with his countryman, SIR WILLIAM DOUGLAS, who was also in arms against King Edward, became the most resolute and undaunted champion of a people struggling for their independence that ever lived upon the earth.

The English Guardian of the Kingdom fled before him, and, thus encouraged, the Scottish people revolted everywhere, and fell upon the English without mercy. The Earl of Surrey, by the King's commands, raised all the power of the Border-counties, and two English armies poured into Scotland. Only one Chief, in the face of those armies, stood by Wallace, who, with a force of forty thousand men, awaited the invaders at a place on the river Forth, within two miles of Stirling. Across the river there was only one poor wooden bridge, called the bridge of Kildean—so narrow, that but two men could cross it abreast. With his eyes upon this bridge, Wallace posted the greater part of his men among some rising grounds, and waited calmly. When the English army came up on the opposite bank of the river, messengers were sent forward to offer terms. Wallace sent them back with a defiance, in the name of the freedom of Scotland. Some of the officers of the Earl of Surrey in command of the English, with *their* eyes also on the bridge, advised him to be discreet and not hasty. He, however, urged to immediate battle by some other officers, and particularly by CRESSINGHAM, King Edward's treasurer, and a rash man, gave the word of command to advance. One thousand English crossed the bridge, two abreast; the Scottish troops were as motionless as stone images. Two thousand English crossed; three thousand, four thousand, five. Not a feather, all this time, had been seen to stir among the Scottish bonnets. Now, they all fluttered. "Forward, one party, to the foot of the Bridge!" cried Wallace, "and let no more English cross! The rest, down with me on the five thousand who have come over, and cut them all to pieces." It was done, in the sight of the whole remainder of the English army, who could give no help. Cressingham himself was killed, and the Scotch made whips for their horses of his skin.

King Edward was abroad at this time, and during the successes on the Scottish side which followed, and which enabled bold Wallace to win the whole country back again, and even to ravage the English borders. But, after a few winter months, the King returned, and took the field with more than his usual energy. One night, when a kick from his horse as they both lay on the ground together broke two of his ribs, and a cry arose that he was killed, he leaped into his saddle, regardless of the pain he suffered, and rode through the camp. Day then appearing, he gave the word (still, of course, in that bruised and aching state) Forward! and led his army on to near Falkirk, where the Scottish forces were seen drawn up on some stony ground, behind a morass. Here, he defeated Wallace, and killed fifteen thousand of his men. With the shattered remainder, Wallace drew back to Stirling; but, being pursued, set fire to the town that it might give no help to the English, and escaped. The inhabitants of Perth afterwards set fire to their houses for the same reason, and the King, unable to find provisions, was forced to withdraw his army.

Another ROBERT BRUCE, the grandson of him who had disputed the Scottish crown with Baliol, was now in arms against the King (that elder Bruce being dead), and also JOHN COMYN, Baliol's nephew. These two young men might agree in opposing Edward, but could agree in nothing else, as they were rivals for the throne of Scotland. Probably it was because they knew this, and knew what troubles must arise even if they could hope to get the better of the great English King, that the principal Scottish people applied to the Pope for his interference. The Pope, on the principle of losing nothing for want of trying to get it, very coolly claimed that Scotland belonged to him; but this was a little too much, and the Parliament in a friendly manner told him so.

In the spring time of the year one thousand three hundred and three, the King sent SIR JOHN SEGRAVE, whom he made Governor of Scotland, with twenty thousand men, to reduce the rebels. Sir John was not as careful as he should have been, but encamped at Rosslyn, near Edinburgh, with his army divided into three parts. The Scottish forces saw their advantage; fell on each part separately; defeated each; and killed all the prisoners. Then, came the King himself once more, as soon as a great army could be raised; he passed through the whole north of Scotland, laying waste whatsoever came in his way; and he took up his winter quarters at Dunfermline. The Scottish cause now looked so hopeless, that Comyn and the other nobles made submission and received their pardons. Wallace alone stood out. He was invited to surrender, though on no distinct pledge that his life should be spared; but he still defied the ireful King, and lived among the steep crags of the Highland glens, where the eagles made their nests, and where the mountain torrents roared, and the white snow was deep, and the bitter winds blew round his unsheltered head, as he lay through many a pitch-dark night wrapped up in his plaid. Nothing could break his spirit; nothing could lower his courage; nothing could induce him to forget or to forgive his country's wrongs. Even when the Castle of Stirling, which had long held out, was besieged by the King with every kind of military engine then in use; even when the lead upon cathedral roofs was taken down to help to make them; even when the King, though an old man, commanded in the siege as if he were a youth, being so resolved to conquer; even when the brave garrison (then found with amazement to be not two hundred people, including several ladies) were starved and beaten out and were made to submit on their knees, and with every form of disgrace that could aggravate their sufferings; even then, when there was not a ray of hope in Scotland, William Wallace was as proud and firm as if he had beheld the powerful and relentless Edward lying dead at his feet.

Who betrayed William Wallace in the end, is not quite certain. That he was betrayed—probably by an attendant —is too true. He was taken to the Castle of Dumbarton, under SIR JOHN MENTEITH, and thence to London, where the great fame of his bravery and resolution attracted immense concourses of people to behold him. He was tried in Westminster Hall, with a crown of laurel on his head—it is supposed because he was reported to have said that he ought to wear, or that he would wear, a crown there—and was found guilty as a robber, a murderer, and a traitor. What they called a robber (he said to those who tried him) he was, because he had taken spoil from the King's men. What they called a murderer, he was, because he had slain an insolent Englishman. What they called a traitor, he was not, for he had never sworn allegiance to the King, and had ever scorned to do it. He was dragged at the tails of horses to West Smithfield, and there hanged on a high gallows, torn open before he was dead, beheaded, and quartered. His head was set upon a pole on London Bridge, his right arm was sent to Newcastle, his left arm to Berwick, his legs to Perth and Aberdeen. But, if King Edward had had his body cut into inches, and had sent every separate inch into a separate town, he could not have dispersed it half so far and wide as his fame. Wallace will be remembered in songs and stories, while there are songs and stories in the English tongue, and Scotland will hold him dear while her lakes and mountains last.

Released from this dreaded enemy, the King made a fairer plan of Government for Scotland, divided the offices of honour among Scottish gentlemen and English gentlemen, forgave past offences, and thought, in his old age, that his work was done.

But he deceived himself. Comyn and Bruce conspired, and made an appointment to meet at Dumfries, in the church of the Minorites. There is a story that Comyn was false to Bruce, and had informed against him to the King; that Bruce was warned of his danger and the necessity of flight, by receiving, one night as he sat at supper, from his friend the Earl of Gloucester, twelve pennies and a pair of spurs ; that as he was riding angrily to keep his appoint-ment (through a snow-storm, with his horse's shoes reversed that he might not be tracked), he met an evil-looking serv-ing man, a messenger of Comyn, whom he killed, and con-cealed in whose dress he found letters that proved Comyn's treachery. However this may be, they were likely enough to quarrel in any case, being hot-headed rivals ; and, what-ever they quarrelled about, they certainly did quarrel in the church where they met, and Bruce drew his dagger and stabbed Comyn, who fell upon the pavement. When Bruce came out, pale and disturbed, the friends who were waiting for him asked what was the matter? "I think I have killed Comyn," said he. "You only think so?" returned one of them ; "I will make sure!" and going into the church, and finding him alive, stabbed him again and again. Knowing that the King would never forgive this new deed of violence, the party then declared Bruce King of Scotland : got him crowned at Scone—without the chair ; and set up the rebellious standard once again.

When the King heard of it he kindled with fiercer anger than he had ever shown yet. He caused the Prince of Wales and two hundred and seventy of the young nobility to be knighted—the trees in the Temple Gardens were cut down to make room for their tents, and they watched their armour all night, according to the old usage : some in the

L

Temple Church : some in Westminster Abbey—and at the public Feast which then took place, he swore, by Heaven and by two swans covered with gold network which his minstrels placed upon the table, that he would avenge the death of Comyn, and would punish the false Bruce. And before all the company, he charged the Prince his son, in case that he should die before accomplishing his vow, not to bury him until it was fulfilled. Next morning the Prince and the rest of the young Knights rode away to the Border-country to join the English army ; and the King, now weak and sick, followed in a horse-litter.

Bruce, after losing a battle and undergoing many dangers and much misery, fled to Ireland, where he lay concealed through the winter. That winter, Edward passed in hunting down and executing Bruce's relations and adherents, sparing neither youth nor age, and showing no touch of pity or sign of mercy. In the following spring, Bruce reappeared and gained some victories. In these frays, both sides were grievously cruel. For instance—Bruce's two brothers, being taken captives desperately wounded, were ordered by the King to instant execution. Bruce's friend Sir John Douglas, taking his own Castle of Douglas out of the hands of an English Lord, roasted the dead bodies of the slaughtered garrison in a great fire made of every movable within it ; which dreadful cookery his men called the Douglas Larder. Bruce, still successful, however, drove the Earl of Pembroke and the Earl of Gloucester into the Castle of Ayr and laid siege to it.

The King, who had been laid up all the winter, but had directed the army from his sick-bed, now advanced to Carlisle, and there, causing the litter in which he had travelled to be placed in the Cathedral as an offering to Heaven, mounted his horse once more, and for the last time. He was now sixty-nine years old, and had reigned thirty-five years. He was so ill, that in four days he could go no more than six miles ; still, even at that pace, he went on and resolutely kept his face towards the Border. At length, he lay down at the village of Burgh-upon-Sands ; and there, telling those around him to impress upon the Prince that he was to remember his father's vow, and was never to rest until he had thoroughly subdued Scotland, he yielded up his last breath.

CHAPTER XVII

ENGLAND UNDER EDWARD THE SECOND

KING Edward the Second, the first Prince of Wales, was twenty-three years old when his father died. There was a certain favourite of his, a young man from Gascony, named PIERS GAVESTON, of whom his father had so much disapproved that he had ordered him out of England, and had made his son swear by the side of his sick-bed, never to bring him back. But, the Prince no sooner found himself King, than he broke his oath, as so many other Princes and Kings did (they were far too ready to take oaths), and sent for his dear friend immediately.

Now, this same Gaveston was handsome enough, but was a reckless, insolent, audacious fellow. He was detested by the proud English Lords: not only because he had such power over the King, and made the Court such a dissipated place, but, also, because he could ride better than they at tournaments, and was used, in his impudence, to cut very bad jokes on them; calling one, the old hog; another, the stage-player; another, the Jew; another, the black dog of Ardenne. This was as poor wit as need be, but it made those Lords very wroth; and the surly Earl of Warwick, who was the black dog, swore that the time should come when Piers Gaveston should feel the black dog's teeth.

It was not come yet, however, nor did it seem to be coming. The King made him Earl of Cornwall, and gave him vast riches; and, when the King went over to France to marry the French Princess, ISABELLA, daughter of PHILIP LE BEL: who was said to be the most beautiful woman in the world: he made Gaveston, Regent of the Kingdom. His splendid marriage-ceremony in the Church of Our Lady at Boulogne, where there were four Kings and three Queens present (quite a pack of Court Cards, for I dare say the Knaves were not wanting), being over, he seemed to care little or nothing for his beautiful wife; but was wild with impatience to meet Gaveston again.

When he landed at home, he paid no attention to anybody else, but ran into the favourite's arms before a great concourse of people, and hugged him, and kissed him, and called him his brother. At the coronation which soon followed, Gaveston was the richest and brightest of all the glittering company there, and had the honour of carrying the crown. This made the proud Lords fiercer than ever; the people, too, despised the favourite, and would never call him Earl of Cornwall, however much he complained to the King and asked him to punish them for not doing so, but persisted in styling him plain Piers Gaveston.

The Barons were so unceremonious with the King in giving him to understand that they would not bear this favourite, that the King was obliged to send him out of the country. The favourite himself was made to take an oath (more oaths!) that he would never come back, and the Barons supposed him to be banished in disgrace, until they heard that he was appointed Governor of Ireland. Even this was not enough for the besotted King, who brought him home again in a year's time, and not only disgusted the Court and the people by his doting folly, but offended his beautiful wife too, who never liked him afterwards.

He had now the old Royal want—of money—and the Barons had the new power of positively refusing to let him raise any. He summoned a Parliament at York; the Barons refused to make one, while the favourite was near him. He summoned another Parliament at Westminster, and sent Gaveston away. Then, the Barons came, completely armed, and appointed a committee of themselves to correct abuses in the state and in the King's household. He got some money on these conditions, and directly set off with Gaveston to the Border-country, where they spent it in idling away the time, and feasting, while Bruce made ready to drive the English out of Scotland. For, though the old King had even made this poor weak son of his swear (as some say) that he would not bury his bones, but would have them boiled clean in a caldron, and carried before the English army until Scotland was entirely subdued, the second Edward was so unlike the first that Bruce gained strength and power every day.

The committee of Nobles, after some months of deliberation, ordained that the King should henceforth call a Parliament together, once every year, and even twice if necessary, instead of summoning it only when he chose. Further, that Gaveston should once more be banished, and, this time, on pain of death if he ever came back. The King's tears were of no avail; he was obliged to send his favourite to Flanders. As soon as he had done so, however, he dissolved the Parliament, with the low cunning of a mere fool, and set off to the North of England, thinking to get an army about him to oppose the Nobles. And once again he brought Gaveston home, and heaped upon him all the riches and titles of which the Barons had deprived him.

The Lords saw, now, that there was nothing for it but to put the favourite to death. They could have done so, legally, according to the terms of his banishment; but they did so, I am sorry to say, in a shabby manner. Led by the Earl of Lancaster, the King's cousin, they first of all attacked the King and Gaveston at Newcastle. They had time to escape by sea, and the mean King, having his precious Gaveston with him, was quite content to leave his lovely wife behind. When they were comparatively safe, they separated; the King went to York to collect a force of soldiers; and the favourite shut himself up, in the meantime, in Scarborough Castle overlooking the sea. This was what the Barons wanted. They knew that the Castle could not hold out; they attacked it, and made Gaveston surrender. He delivered himself up to the Earl of Pembroke—that Lord whom he had called the Jew—on the Earl's pledging his faith and knightly word, that no harm should happen to him and no violence be done him.

Now, it was agreed with Gaveston that he should be taken to the Castle of Wallingford, and there kept in honourable custody. They travelled as far as Deddington. near Banbury, where, in the Castle of that place, they stopped for a night to rest. Whether the Earl of Pembroke left his prisoner there, knowing what would happen, or really left him thinking no harm, and only going (as he pretended) to visit his wife, the Countess, who was in the neighbourhood, is no great matter now; in any case, he was bound as an honourable gentleman to protect his prisoner, and he did not do it. In the morning, while the favourite was yet in bed, he was required to dress himself and come down into the court-yard. He did so without any mistrust, but started and turned pale when he found it full of strange armed men. "I think you know me?" said their leader, also armed from head to foot. "I am the black dog of Ardenne!"

The time was come when Piers Gaveston was to feel the black dog's teeth indeed. They set him on a mule, and carried him, in mock state and with military music, to the black dog's kennel—Warwick Castle—where a hasty council, composed of some great noblemen, considered what should be done with him. Some were for sparing him, but one loud voice—it was the black dog's bark, I dare say—sounded through the Castle Hall, uttering these words: "You have the fox in your power. Let him go now, and you must hunt him again."

They sentenced him to death. He threw himself at the feet of the Earl of Lancaster—the old hog—but the old hog was as savage as the dog. He was taken out upon the pleasant road, leading from Warwick to Coventry, where the beautiful river Avon, by which, long afterwards, WILLIAM SHAKESPEARE was born and now lies buried, sparkled in the bright landscape of the beautiful May-day; and there they struck off his wretched head, and stained the dust with his blood.

When the King heard of this black deed, in his grief and rage he denounced relentless war against his Barons, and both sides were in arms for half a year. But, it then became necessary for them to join their forces against Bruce, who had used the time well while they were divided, and had now a great power in Scotland.

Intelligence was brought that Bruce was then besieging Stirling Castle, and that the Governor had been obliged to pledge himself to surrender it, unless he should be relieved before a certain day. Hereupon, the King ordered the nobles and their fighting-men to meet him at Berwick; but, the nobles cared so little for the King, and so neglected the summons, and lost time, that only on the day before that appointed for the surrender, did the King find himself at Stirling, and even then with a smaller force than he had expected. However, he had, altogether, a hundred thousand men, and Bruce had not more than forty thousand; but, Bruce's army was strongly posted in three square columns, on the ground lying between the Burn or Brook of Bannock and the walls of Stirling Castle.

On the very evening, when the King came up, Bruce did

a brave act that encouraged his men. He was seen by a certain HENRY DE BOHUN, an English Knight, riding about before his army on a little horse, with a light battle-axe in his hand, and a crown of gold on his head. This English Knight, who was mounted on a strong war-horse, cased in steel, strongly armed, and able (as he thought) to overthrow Bruce by crushing him with his mere weight, set spurs to his great charger, rode on him, and made a thrust at him. with his heavy spear. Bruce parried the thrust, and with one blow of his battle-axe split his skull.

The Scottish men did not forget this, next day when the battle raged. RANDOLPH, Bruce's valiant Nephew, rode, with the small body of men he commanded, into such a host of the English, all shining in polished armour in the sunlight, that they seemed to be swallowed up and lost, as if they had plunged into the sea. But, they fought so well, and did such dreadful execution, that the English staggered. Then came Bruce himself upon them, with all the rest of his army. While they were thus hard pressed and amazed, there appeared upon the hills what they supposed to be a new Scottish army, but what were really only the camp followers, in number fifteen thousand: whom Bruce had taught to show themselves at that place and time. The Earl of Gloucester, commanding the English horse, made a last rush to change the fortune of the day; but Bruce (like Jack the Giant-killer in the story) had had pits dug in the ground, and covered over with turfs and stakes. Into these, as they gave way beneath the weight of the horses, riders and horses rolled by hundreds. The English were completely routed; all their treasure, stores, and engines, were taken by the Scottish men; so many waggons and other wheeled vehicles were seized, that it is related that they would have reached, if they had been drawn out in a line, one hundred and eighty miles. The fortunes of Scotland were, for the time, completely changed; and never was a battle won, more famous upon Scottish ground, than this great battle of BANNOCKBURN.

Plague and famine succeeded in England; and still the powerless King and his disdainful Lords were always in contention. Some of the turbulent chiefs of Ireland made proposals to Bruce, to accept the rule of that country. He sent his brother Edward to them, who was crowned King of Ireland. He afterwards went himself to help his brother in his Irish wars, but his brother was defeated in the end and killed. Robert Bruce, returning to Scotland, still increased his strength there.

As the King's ruin had begun in a favourite, so it seemed likely to end in one. He was too poor a creature to rely at all upon himself; and his new favourite was one HUGH LE DESPENSER, the son of a gentleman of ancient family. Hugh was handsome and brave, but he was the favourite of a weak King, whom no man cared a rush for, and that was a dangerous place to hold. The Nobles leagued against him, because the King liked him; and they lay in wait, both for his ruin and his father's. Now, the King had married him to the daughter of the late Earl of Gloucester, and had given both him and his father great possessions in Wales. In their endeavours to extend these, they gave violent offence to an angry Welsh gentleman, named JOHN DE MOWBRAY, and to divers other angry Welsh gentlemen, who resorted to arms, took their castles, and seized their estates. The Earl of Lancaster had first placed the favourite (who was a poor relation of his own) at Court, and he considered his own dignity offended by the preference he received and the honours he acquired ; so he, and the Barons who were his friends, joined the Welshmen, marched on London, and sent a message to the King demanding to have the favourite and his father banished. At first, the King unaccountably took it into his head to be spirited, and to send them a bold reply ; but when they quartered themselves around Holborn and Clerkenwell, and went down, armed, to the Parliament at Westminster, he gave way, and complied with their demands.

His turn of triumph came sooner than he expected. It arose out of an accidental circumstance. The beautiful Queen happening to be travelling, came one night to one of the royal castles, and demanded to be lodged and entertained there until morning. The governor of this castle, who was one of the enraged lords, was away, and in his absence, his wife refused admission to the Queen ; a scuffle took place among the common men on either side, and some of the royal attendants were killed. The people, who cared nothing for the King, were very angry that their beautiful Queen should be thus rudely treated in her own dominions ; and the King, taking advantage of this feeling, besieged the castle, took it, and then called the two Despensers home.

Upon this, the confederate lords and the Welshmen went over to Bruce. The King encountered them at Borough-bridge, gained the victory, and took a number of distinguished prisoners; among them, the Earl of Lancaster, now an old man, upon whose destruction he was resolved. This Earl was taken to his own castle of Pontefract, and there tried and found guilty by an unfair court appointed for the purpose; he was not even allowed to speak in his own defence. He was insulted, pelted, mounted on a starved pony without saddle or bridle, carried out, and beheaded. Eight-and-twenty knights were hanged, drawn, and quartered. When the King had despatched this bloody work, and had made a fresh and a long truce with Bruce, he took the Despensers into greater favour than ever, and made the father Earl of Winchester.

One prisoner, and an important one, who was taken at Boroughbridge, made his escape, however, and turned the tide against the King. This was ROGER MORTIMER, always resolutely opposed to him, who was sentenced to death, and placed for safe custody in the Tower of London. He treated his guards to a quantity of wine into which he had put a sleeping potion; and, when they were insensible, broke out of his dungeon, got into a kitchen, climbed up the chimney, let himself down from the roof of the building with a rope-ladder, passed the sentries, got down to the river, and made away in a boat to where servants and horses were waiting for him. He finally escaped to France, where CHARLES LE BEL, the brother of the beautiful Queen, was King. Charles sought to quarrel with the King of England, on pretence of his not having come to do him homage at his coronation. It was proposed that the beautiful Queen should go over to arrange the dispute; she went, and wrote home to the King, that as he was sick and could not come to France himself, perhaps it would be better to send over the young Prince, their son, who was only twelve years old, who could do homage to her brother in his stead, and in whose company she would immediately return. The King sent him: but, both he and the Queen remained at the French Court, and Roger Mortimer became the Queen's lover.

When the King wrote, again and again, to the Queen to come home, she did not reply that she despised him too much to live with him any more (which was the truth), but said she was afraid of the two Despensers. In short, her design was to overthrow the favourites' power, and the King's power, such as it was, and invade England. Having obtained a French force of two thousand men, and being joined by all the English exiles then in France, she landed, within a year, at Orewell, in Suffolk, where she was immediately joined by the Earls of Kent and Norfolk, the King's two brothers; by other powerful noblemen; and lastly, by the first English general who was despatched to check her: who went over to her with all his men. The people of London, receiving these tidings, would do nothing for the King, but broke open the Tower, let out all his prisoners, and threw up their caps and hurrahed for the beautiful Queen.

The King, with his two favourites, fled to Bristol, where he left old Despenser in charge of the town and castle, while he went on with the son to Wales. The Bristol men being opposed to the King, and it being impossible to hold the town with enemies everywhere within the walls, Despenser yielded it up on the third day, and was instantly brought to trial for having traitorously influenced what was called "the King's mind"—though I doubt if the King ever had any. He was a venerable old man, upwards of ninety years of age, but his age gained no respect or mercy. He was hanged, torn open while he was yet alive, cut up into pieces, and thrown to the dogs. His son was soon taken, tried at Hereford before the same judge on a long series of foolish charges, found guilty, and hanged upon a gallows fifty feet high, with a chaplet of nettles round his head. His poor old father and he were innocent enough of any worse crimes than the crime of having been friends of a King, on whom, as a mere man, they would never have deigned to cast a favourable look. It is a bad crime, I know, and leads to worse; but, many lords and gentlemen—I even think some ladies, too, if I recollect right—have committed it in England, who have neither been given to the dogs, nor hanged up fifty feet high.

The wretched King was running here and there, all this time, and never getting anywhere in particular, until he gave himself up, and was taken off to Kenilworth Castle. When he was safely lodged there, the Queen went to London and met the Parliament. And the Bishop of Hereford, who was the most skilful of her friends, said, What was to be done now? Here was an imbecile, indolent, miserable King upon the throne; wouldn't it be better to take him off, and put his son there instead? I don't know whether the Queen really pitied him at this pass,.but she began to cry; so, the Bishop said, Well, my Lords and Gentlemen, what do you think, upon the whole, of sending down to Kenilworth, and seeing if His Majesty (God bless him, and forbid we should depose him!) won't resign?

My Lords and Gentlemen thought it a good notion, so a deputation of them went down to Kenilworth; and there the King came into the great hall of the Castle, commonly dressed in a poor black gown; and when he saw a certain bishop among them, fell down, poor feeble-headed man, and made a wretched spectacle of himself. Somebody lifted him up, and then Sir William Trussel, the Speaker of the House of Commons, almost frightened him to death by making him a tremendous speech to the effect that he was no longer a King, and that everybody renounced allegiance to him. After which, Sir Thomas Blount, the Steward of the Household, nearly finished him, by coming forward and breaking his white wand—which was a ceremony only performed at a King's death. Being asked in this pressing manner what he thought of resigning, the King said he thought it was the best thing he could do. So, he did it, and they proclaimed his son next day.

I wish I could close his history by saying that he lived a harmless life in the Castle and the Castle gardens at Kenilworth, many years—that he had a favourite, and plenty to eat and drink—and, having that, wanted nothing. But he was shamefully humiliated. He was outraged, and slighted, and had dirty water from ditches given him to shave with, and wept and said he would have clean warm water, and was altogether very miserable. He was moved from this castle to that castle, and from that castle to the other castle, because this lord or that lord, or the other lord, was too kind to him: until at last he came to Berkeley Castle, near the River Severn, where (the Lord Berkeley being then ill and absent) he fell into the hands of two black ruffians, called Thomas Gournay and William Ogle.

One night—it was the night of September the twenty-first, one thousand three hundred and twenty-seven—dreadful screams were heard, by the startled people in the neighbouring town, ringing through the thick walls of the Castle, and the dark deep night; and they said, as they were thus horribly awakened from their sleep, "May Heaven be merciful to the King; for those cries forbode that no good is being done to him in his dismal prison!" Next morning he was dead—not bruised, or stabbed, or marked upon the body, but much distorted in the face; and it was whispered afterwards, that those two villains, Gournay and Ogle, had burnt up his inside with a red-hot iron.

If you ever come near Gloucester, and see the centre tower of its beautiful Cathedral, with its four rich pinnacles, rising lightly in the air; you may remember that the wretched Edward the Second was buried in the old abbey of that ancient city, at forty-three years old, after being for nineteen years and a half a perfectly incapable King.

CHAPTER XVIII

ENGLAND UNDER EDWARD THE THIRD

ROGER MORTIMER, the Queen's lover (who escaped to France in the last chapter), was far from profiting by the examples he had had of the fate of favourites. Having, through the Queen's influence, come into possession of the estates of the two Despensers, he became extremely proud and ambitious, and sought to be the real ruler of England. The young King, who was crowned at fourteen years of age with all the usual solemnities, resolved not to bear this, and soon pursued Mortimer to his ruin.

The people themselves were not fond of Mortimer—first, because he was a Royal favourite; secondly, because he was supposed to have helped to make a peace with Scotland which now took place, and in virtue of which the young King's sister Joan, only seven years old, was promised in marriage to David, the son and heir of Robert Bruce, who was only five years old. The nobles hated Mortimer because of his pride, riches, and power. They went so far as to take up arms against him; but were obliged to submit. The Earl of Kent, one of those who did so, but who afterwards went over to Mortimer and the Queen, was made an example of in the following cruel manner:

He seems to have been anything but a wise old earl; and he was persuaded by the agents of the favourite and the Queen, that poor King Edward the Second was not really dead; and thus was betrayed into writing letters favouring his rightful claim to the throne. This was made out to be high treason, and he was tried, found guilty, and sentenced to be executed. They took the poor old lord outside the town of Winchester, and there kept him waiting some three or four hours until they could find somebody to cut off his head. At last, a convict said he would do it, if the government would pardon him in return; and they gave him the pardon ; and at one blow he put the Earl of Kent out of his last suspense.

While the Queen was in France, she had found a lovely and good young lady, named Philippa, who she thought would make an excellent wife for her son. The young King married this lady, soon after he came to the throne ; and her first child, Edward, Prince of Wales, afterwards became celebrated, as we shall presently see, under the famous title of EDWARD THE BLACK PRINCE.

The young King, thinking the time ripe for the downfall of Mortimer, took counsel with Lord Montacute how he should proceed. A Parliament was going to be held at Nottingham, and that lord recommended that the favourite should be seized by night in Nottingham Castle, where he was sure to be. Now, this, like many other things, was more easily said than done ; because, to guard against treachery, the great gates of the Castle were locked every night, and the great keys were carried up-stairs to the Queen, who laid them under her own pillow. But the Castle had a governor, and the governor being Lord Monta-cute's friend, confided to him how he knew of a secret passage underground, hidden from observation by the weeds and brambles with which it was overgrown ; and how, through that passage, the conspirators might enter in the dead of the night, and go straight to Mortimer's room. Accordingly, upon a certain dark night, at midnight, they made their way through this dismal place : startling the rats, and frightening the owls and bats : and came safely to the bottom of the main tower of the Castle, where the King met them, and took them up a profoundly-dark staircase in a deep silence. They soon heard the voice of Mortimer in council with some friends ; and bursting into the room with a sudden noise, took him prisoner. The Queen cried out from her bed-chamber, "Oh, my sweet son, my dear son, spare my gentle Mortimer!" They carried him off, however ; and, before the next Parliament, accused him of having made differences between the young King and his mother, and of having brought about the death of the Earl of Kent, and even of the late King ; for, as you know by this time, when they wanted to get rid of a man in those old days, they were not very particular of what they accused him. Mortimer was found guilty of all this, and was sentenced to be hanged at Tyburn. The King shut his mother up in genteel confinement, where she passed the rest of her life ; and now he became King in earnest.

The first effort he made was to conquer Scotland. The English lords who had lands in Scotland, finding that their rights were not respected under the late peace, made war on their own account : choosing for their general, Edward, the son of John Baliol, who made such a vigorous fight, that in less than two months he won the whole Scottish Kingdom. He was joined, when thus triumphant, by the King and Parliament ; and he and the King in person besieged the Scottish forces in Berwick. The whole Scottish army coming to the assistance of their countrymen, such a furious battle ensued, that thirty thousand men are said to have been killed in it. Baliol was then crowned King of Scotland, doing homage to the King of England ; but little came of his successes after all, for the Scottish men rose against him, within no very long time, and David Bruce came back within ten years and took his kingdom.

France was a far richer country than Scotland, and the King had a much greater mind to conquer it. So, he let Scotland alone, and pretended that he had a claim to the French throne in right of his mother. He had, in reality, no claim at all ; but that mattered little in those times. He brought over to his cause many little princes and sovereigns, and even courted the alliance of the people of Flanders—a busy, working community, who had very small respect for kings, and whose head man was a brewer. With such forces as he raised by these means, Edward invaded France ; but he did little by that, except run into debt in carrying on the war to the extent of three hundred thousand pounds. The next year he did better ; gaining a great sea-fight in the harbour of Sluys. This success, however, was very short-lived, for the Flemings took fright at the siege of Saint Omer and ran away, leaving their weapons and baggage behind them. Philip, the French King, coming up with his army, and Edward being very anxious to decide the war, proposed to settle the difference by single combat with him, or by a fight of one hundred knights on each side. The French King said, he thanked him ; but being very well as he was, he would rather not. So, after some skirmishing and talking, a short peace was made.

It was soon broken by King Edward's favouring the cause of John, Earl of Montford ; a French nobleman, who asserted a claim of his own against the French King, and offered to do homage to England for the Crown of France, if he could obtain it through England's help. This French lord, himself, was soon defeated by the French King's son, and shut up in a tower in Paris; but his wife, a courageous and beautiful woman, who is said to have had the courage of a man, and the heart of a lion, assembled the people of Brittany, where she then was; and, showing them her infant son, made many pathetic entreaties to them not to desert her and their young Lord. They took fire at this appeal, and rallied round her in the strong castle of Hennebon. Here she was not only besieged without by the French under Charles de Blois, but was endangered within by a dreary old bishop, who was always representing to the people what horrors they must undergo if they were faithful—first from famine, and afterwards from fire and sword. But this noble lady, whose heart never failed her, encouraged her soldiers by her own example; went from post to post like a great general; even mounted on horseback fully armed, and, issuing from the castle by a by-path, fell upon the French camp, set fire to the tents, and threw the whole force into disorder. This done, she got safely back to Hennebon again, and was received with loud shouts of joy by the defenders of the castle, who had given her up for lost. As they were now very short of provisions, however, and as they could not dine off enthusiasm, and as the old bishop was always saying, "I told you what it would come to!" they began to lose heart, and to talk of yielding the castle up. The brave Countess retiring to an upper room and looking with great grief out to sea, where she expected relief from England, saw, at this very time, the English ships in the distance, and was relieved and rescued! Sir Walter Manning, the English commander, so admired her courage, that, being come into the castle with the English knights, and having made a feast there, he assaulted the French by way of dessert, and beat them off triumphantly. Then he and the knights came back to the castle with great joy; and the Countess who had watched them from a high tower, thanked them with all her heart, and kissed them every one.

This noble lady distinguished herself afterwards in a sea-fight with the French off Guernsey, when she was on her way to England to ask for more troops. Her great spirit roused another lady, the wife of another French lord (whom the French King very barbarously murdered), to distinguish herself scarcely less. The time was fast coming, however, when Edward, Prince of Wales, was to be the great star of this French and English war.

It was in the month of July, in the year one thousand three hundred and forty-six, when the King embarked at Southampton for France, with an army of about thirty thousand men in all, attended by the Prince of Wales and by several of the chief nobles. He landed at La Hogue in Normandy; and, burning and destroying as he went, according to custom, advanced up the left bank of the River Seine, and fired the small towns even close to Paris; but, being watched from the right bank of the river by the French King and all his army, it came to this at last, that Edward found himself, on Saturday the twenty-sixth of August, one thousand three hundred and forty-six, on a rising ground behind the little French village of Crecy, face to face with the French King's force. And, although the French King had an enormous army—in number more than eight times his—he there resolved to beat him or be beaten.

The young Prince, assisted by the Earl of Oxford and the Earl of Warwick, led the first division of the English army; two other great Earls led the second; and the King, the third. When the morning dawned, the King received the sacrament, and heard prayers, and then, mounted on horseback with a white wand in his hand, rode from company to company, and rank to rank, cheering and encouraging both officers and men. Then the whole army breakfasted, each man sitting on the ground where he had stood; and then they remained quietly on the ground with their weapons ready.

Up came the French King with all his great force. It was dark and angry weather; there was an eclipse of the sun; there was a thunder-storm, accompanied with tremendous rain; the frightened birds flew screaming above the soldiers' heads. A certain captain in the French army advised the French King, who was by no means cheerful, not to begin the battle until the morrow. The King, taking this advice, gave the word to halt. But, those behind not understanding it, or desiring to be foremost with the rest, came pressing on. The roads for a great distance were covered with this immense army, and with the common people from the villages, who were flourishing their rude weapons, and making a great noise. Owing to these circumstances, the French army advanced in the greatest confusion; every French lord doing what he liked with his own men, and putting out the men of every other French lord.

Now, their King relied strongly upon a great body of cross-bowmen from Genoa; and these he ordered to the front to begin the battle, on finding that he could not stop it. They shouted once, they shouted twice, they shouted three times, to alarm the English archers; but, the English would have heard them shout three thousand times and would have never moved. At last the cross-bowmen went forward a little, and began to discharge their bolts; upon which, the English let fly such a hail of arrows, that the Genoese speedily made off—for their cross-bows, besides being heavy to carry, required to be wound up with a handle, and consequently took time to re-load; the English, on the other hand, could discharge their arrows almost as fast as the arrows could fly.

When the French King saw the Genoese turning, he cried out to his men to kill those scoundrels, who were doing harm instead of service. This increased the confusion. Meanwhile the English archers, continuing to shoot as fast as ever, shot down great numbers of the French soldiers and knights; whom certain sly Cornish-men and Welsh-men, from the English army, creeping along the ground, despatched with great knives.

The Prince and his division were at this time so hard-pressed, that the Earl of Warwick sent a message to the King, who was overlooking the battle from a windmill, beseeching him to send more aid.

"Is my son killed?" said the King.

"No, sire, please God," returned the messenger.

"Is he wounded?" said the King.

"No, sire."

"Is he thrown to the ground?" said the King.

"No, sire, not so; but, he is very hard-pressed."

"Then," said the King, "go back to those who sent you, and tell them I shall send no aid; because I set my heart upon my son proving himself this day a brave knight, and because I am resolved, please God, that the honour of a great victory shall be his!"

These bold words, being reported to the Prince and his

division, so raised their spirits, that they fought better than ever. The King of France charged gallantly with his men many times; but it was of no use. Night closing in, his horse was killed under him by an English arrow, and the knights and nobles who had clustered thick about him early in the day, were now completely scattered. At last, some of his few remaining followers led him off the field by force, since he would not retire of himself, and they journeyed away to Amiens. The victorious English, lighting their watch-fires, made merry on the field, and the King, riding to meet his gallant son, took him in his arms, kissed him. and told him that he had acted nobly, and proved himself worthy of the day and of the crown. While it was yet night, King Edward was hardly aware of the great victory he had gained ; but, next day, it was discovered that eleven princes, twelve hundred knights, and thirty thousand common men lay dead upon the French side. Among these was the King of Bohemia, an old blind man ; who, having been told that his son was wounded in the battle, and that no force could stand against the Black Prince, called to him two knights, put himself on horseback between them, fastened the three bridles together, and dashed in among the English, where he was presently slain. He bore as his crest three white ostrich feathers, with the motto *Ich dien*, signifying in English "I serve." This crest and motto were taken by the Prince of Wales in remembrance of that famous day, and have been borne by the Prince of Wales ever since.

Five days after this great battle, the King laid siege to Calais. This siege—ever afterwards memorable—lasted nearly a year. In order to starve the inhabitants out, King Edward built so many wooden houses for the lodgings of his troops, that it is said their quarters looked like a second Calais suddenly sprung around the first. Early in the siege, the governor of the town drove out what he called the useless mouths, to the number of seventeen hundred persons, men and women, young and old. King Edward allowed them to pass through his lines, and even fed them, and dismissed them with money ; but, later in the siege, he was not so merciful—five hundred more, who were afterwards driven out, dying of starvation and misery. The garrison were so hard-pressed at last, that they sent a letter to King Philip, telling him that they had eaten all the horses, all the dogs, and all the rats and mice that could be found in the place ;

and, that if he did not relieve them, they must either surrender to the English, or eat one another. Philip made one effort to give them relief; but they were so hemmed in by the English power, that he could not succeed, and was fain to leave the place. Upon this they hoisted the English flag, and surrendered to King Edward. " Tell your general," said he to the humble messengers who came out of the town, " that I require to have sent here, six of the most distinguished citizens, bare-legged, and in their shirts, with ropes about their necks; and let those six men bring with them the keys of the castle and the town."

When the Governor of Calais related this to the people in the Market-place, there was great weeping and distress; in the midst of which, one worthy citizen, named Eustace de Saint Pierre, rose up and said, that if the six men required were not sacrificed, the whole population would be; therefore, he offered himself as the first. Encouraged by this bright example, five other worthy citizens rose up one after another, and offered themselves to save the rest. The Governor, who was too badly wounded to be able to walk, mounted a poor old horse that had not been eaten, and conducted these good men to the gate, while all the people cried and mourned.

Edward received them wrathfully, and ordered the heads of the whole six to be struck off. However, the good Queen fell upon her knees, and besought the King to give them up to her. The King replied, " I wish you had been somewhere else; but I cannot refuse you." So she had them properly dressed, made a feast for them, and sent them back with a handsome present, to the great rejoicing of the whole camp. I hope the people of Calais loved the daughter to whom she gave birth soon afterwards, for her gentle mother's sake.

Now came that terrible disease, the Plague, into Europe, hurrying from the heart of China; and killed the wretched people—especially the poor—in such enormous numbers, that one-half of the inhabitants of England are related to have died of it. It killed the cattle, in great numbers, too; and so few working men remained alive, that there were not enough left to till the ground.

After eight years of differing and quarrelling, the Prince of Wales again invaded France with an army of sixty thousand men. He went through the south of the country,

The Intercession of Queen Philippa for the Citizens
of Calais

burning and plundering wheresoever he went; while his father, who had still the Scottish war upon his hands, did the like in Scotland, but was harassed and worried in his retreat from that country by the Scottish men, who repaid his cruelties with interest.

The French King, Philip, was now dead, and was succeeded by his son John. The Black Prince, called by that name from the colour of the armour he wore to set off his fair complexion, continuing to burn and destroy in France, roused John into determined opposition; and so cruel had the Black Prince been in his campaign, and so severely had the French peasants suffered, that he could not find one who, for love, or money, or the fear of death, would tell him what the French King was doing, or where he was. Thus it happened that he came upon the French King's forces, all of a sudden, near the town of Poitiers, and found that the whole neighbouring country was occupied by a vast French army. "God help us!" said the Black Prince, "we must make the best of it."

So, on a Sunday morning, the eighteenth of September, the Prince—whose army was now reduced to ten thousand men in all—prepared to give battle to the French King, who had sixty thousand horse alone. While he was so engaged, there came riding from the French camp, a Cardinal, who had persuaded John to let him offer terms, and try to save the shedding of Christian blood. "Save my honour," said the Prince to this good priest, "and save the honour of my army, and I will make any reasonable terms." He offered to give up all the towns, castles, and prisoners, he had taken, and to swear to make no war in France for seven years; but, as John would hear of nothing but his surrender, with a hundred of his chief knights, the treaty was broken off, and the Prince said quietly—"God defend the right; we shall fight to-morrow."

Therefore, on the Monday morning, at break of day, the two armies prepared for battle. The English were posted in a strong place, which could only be approached by one narrow lane, skirted by hedges on both sides. The French attacked them by this lane; but were so galled and slain by English arrows from behind the hedges, that they were forced to retreat. Then went six hundred English bowmen round about, and, coming upon the rear of the French army, rained arrows on them thick and fast. The French knights, thrown into confusion, quitted their banners and dispersed in all directions. Said Sir John Chandos to the Prince, "Ride forward, noble Prince, and the day is yours. The King of France is so valiant a gentleman, that I know he will never fly, and may be taken prisoner." Said the Prince to this, "Advance, English banners, in the name of God and St. George!" and on they pressed until they came up with the French King, fighting fiercely with his battle-axe, and, when all his nobles had forsaken him, attended faithfully to the last by his youngest son Philip, only sixteen years of age. Father and son fought well, and the King had already two wounds in his face, and had been beaten down, when he at last delivered himself to a banished French knight, and gave him his right-hand glove in token that he had done so.

The Black Prince was generous as well as brave, and he invited his royal prisoner to supper in his tent, and waited upon him at table, and, when they afterwards rode into London in a gorgeous procession, mounted the French King on a fine cream-coloured horse, and rode at his side on a little pony. This was all very kind, but I think it was, perhaps, a little theatrical too, and has been made more meritorious than it deserved to be; especially as I am inclined to think that the greatest kindness to the King of France would have been not to have shown him to the people at all. However, it must be said, for these acts of politeness, that, in course of time, they did much to soften the horrors of war and the passions of conquerors. It was a long, long time before the common soldiers began to have the benefit of such courtly deeds; but they did at last; and thus it is possible that a poor soldier who asked for quarter at the battle of Waterloo, or any other such great fight, may have owed his life indirectly to Edward the Black Prince.

At this time there stood in the Strand, in London, a palace called the Savoy, which was given up to the captive King of France and his son for their residence. As the King of Scotland had now been King Edward's captive for eleven years too, his success was, at this time, tolerably complete. The Scottish business was settled by the prisoner being released under the title of Sir David, King of Scotland, and by his engaging to pay a large ransom. The state of France encouraged England to propose harder terms to that country, where the people

rose against the unspeakable cruelty and barbarity of its
nobles; where the nobles rose in turn against the people;
where the most frightful outrages were committed on all
sides; and where the insurrection of the peasants, called
the insurrection of the Jacquerie, from Jacques, a common
Christian name among the country people of France,
awakened terrors and hatreds that have scarcely yet passed
away. A treaty called the Great Peace, was at last signed,
under which King Edward agreed to give up the greater
part of his conquests, and King John to pay, within six
years, a ransom of three million crowns of gold. He was
so beset by his own nobles and courtiers for having yielded
to these conditions—though they could help him to no
better—that he came back of his own will to his old palace-
prison of the Savoy, and there died.

There was a Sovereign of Castile at that time, called
PEDRO THE CRUEL, who deserved the name remarkably
well: having committed, among other cruelties, a variety
of murders. This amiable monarch being driven from his
throne for his crimes, went to the province of Bordeaux,
where the Black Prince—now married to his cousin JOAN,
a pretty widow—was residing, and besought his help. The
Prince, who took to him much more kindly than a prince
of such fame ought to have taken to such a ruffian, readily
listened to his fair promises, and agreeing to help him, sent
secret orders to some troublesome disbanded soldiers of his
and his father's, who called themselves the Free Companions, and who had been a pest to the French people,
for some time, to aid this Pedro. The Prince, himself,
going into Spain to head the army of relief, soon set Pedro
on his throne again—where he no sooner found himself,
than, of course, he behaved like the villain he was, broke
his word without the least shame, and abandoned all the
promises he had made to the Black Prince.

Now, it had cost the Prince a good deal of money to pay
soldiers to support this murderous King; and finding himself, when he came back disgusted to Bordeaux, not only in
bad health, but deeply in debt, he began to tax his French
subjects to pay his creditors. They appealed to the French
King, CHARLES; war again broke out; and the French town
of Limoges, which the Prince had greatly benefited, went
over to the French King. Upon this he ravaged the province
of which it was the capital; burnt, and plundered, and

killed in the old sickening way ; and refused mercy to the
prisoners, men, women, and children taken in the offending
town, though he was so ill and so much in need of pity
himself from Heaven, that he was carried in a litter. He
lived to come home and make himself popular with the
people and Parliament, and he died on Trinity Sunday,
the eighth of June, one thousand three hundred and
seventy-six, at forty-six years old.

The whole nation mourned for him as one of the most
renowned and beloved princes it had ever had ; and he was
buried with great lamentations in Canterbury Cathedral.
Near to the tomb of Edward the Confessor, his monument,
with his figure, carved in stone, and represented in the old
black armour, lying on its back, may be seen at this day,
with an ancient coat of mail, a helmet, and a pair of
gauntlets hanging from a beam above it, which most people
like to believe were once worn by the Black Prince.

King Edward did not outlive his renowned son, long.
He was old, and one Alice Perrers, a beautiful lady, had
contrived to make him so fond of her in his old age, that
he could refuse her nothing, and made himself ridiculous.
She little deserved his love, or—what I dare say she valued
a great deal more—the jewels of the late Queen, which he
gave her among other rich presents. She took the very
ring from his finger on the morning of the day when he
died, and left him to be pillaged by his faithless servants.
Only one good priest was true to him, and attended him to
the last.

Besides being famous for the great victories I have
related, the reign of King Edward the Third was rendered
memorable in better ways, by the growth of architecture
and the erection of Windsor Castle. In better ways still,
by the rising up of WICKLIFFE, originally a poor parish
priest: who devoted himself to exposing, with wonderful
power and success, the ambition and corruption of the Pope,
and of the whole church of which he was the head.

Some of those Flemings were induced to come to England
in this reign too, and to settle in Norfolk, where they made
better woollen cloths than the English had ever had before.
The Order of the Garter (a very fine thing in its way, but
hardly so important as good clothes for the nation) also
dates from this period. The King is said to have picked
up a lady's garter at a ball, and to have said, *Honi soit qui*

mal y pense—in English, "Evil be to him who evil thinks of it." The courtiers were usually glad to imitate what the King said or did, and hence from a slight incident the Order of the Garter was instituted, and became a great dignity. So the story goes.

CHAPTER XIX

ENGLAND UNDER RICHARD THE SECOND

RICHARD, son of the Black Prince, a boy eleven years of age, succeeded to the Crown under the title of King Richard the Second. The whole English nation were ready to admire him for the sake of his brave father. As to the lords and ladies about the Court, they declared him to be the most beautiful, the wisest, and the best—even of princes—whom the lords and ladies about the Court, generally declare to be the most beautiful, the wisest, and the best of mankind. To flatter a poor boy in this base manner was not a very likely way to develop whatever good was in him; and it brought him to anything but a good or happy end.

The Duke of Lancaster, the young King's uncle—commonly called John of Gaunt, from having been born at Ghent, which the common people so pronounced—was supposed to have some thoughts of the throne himself; but, as he was not popular, and the memory of the Black Prince was, he submitted to his nephew.

The war with France being still unsettled, the Government of England wanted money to provide for the expenses that might arise out of it; accordingly a certain tax, called the Poll-tax, which had originated in the last reign, was ordered to be levied on the people. This was a tax on every person in the kingdom, male and female, above the age of fourteen, of three groats (or three fourpenny pieces) a year; clergymen were charged more, and only beggars were exempt.

I have no need to repeat that the common people of England had long been suffering under great oppression. They were still the mere slaves of the lords of the land on which they lived, and were on most occasions harshly and unjustly treated. But, they had begun by this time to think very seriously of not bearing quite so much; and, probably, were emboldened by that French insurrection I mentioned in the last chapter.

The people of Essex rose against the Poll-tax, and being severely handled by the government officers, killed some of them. At this very time one of the tax-collectors, going his rounds from house to house, at Dartford in Kent came to the cottage of one WAT, a tiler by trade, and claimed the tax upon his daughter. Her mother, who was at home, declared that she was under the age of fourteen; upon that, the collector (as other collectors had already done in different parts of England) behaved in a savage way, and brutally insulted Wat Tyler's daughter. The daughter screamed, the mother screamed. Wat the Tiler, who was at work not far off, ran to the spot, and did what any honest father under such provocation might have done—struck the collector dead at a blow.

Instantly the people of that town uprose as one man. They made Wat Tyler their leader; they joined with the people of Essex, who were in arms under a priest called JACK STRAW; they took out of prison another priest named JOHN BALL; and gathering in numbers as they went along, advanced, in a great confused army of poor men, to Black-heath. It is said that they wanted to abolish all property, and to declare all men equal. I do not think this very likely; because they stopped the travellers on the roads and made them swear to be true to King Richard and the people. Nor were they at all disposed to injure those who had done them no harm, merely because they were of high station; for, the King's mother, who had to pass through their camp at Blackheath, on her way to her young son, lying for safety in the Tower of London, had merely to kiss a few dirty-faced rough-bearded men who were noisily fond of royalty, and so got away in perfect safety. Next day the whole mass marched on to London Bridge.

There was a drawbridge in the middle, which WILLIAM WALWORTH the Mayor caused to be raised to prevent their coming into the city; but they soon terrified the citizens into lowering it again, and spread themselves, with great uproar, over the streets. They broke open the prisons; they burned the papers in Lambeth Palace; they destroyed the DUKE OF LANCASTER'S Palace, the Savoy, in the Strand, said to be the most beautiful and splendid in England; they set fire to the books and documents in the Temple;

and made a great riot. Many of these outrages were committed in drunkenness; since those citizens, who had well-filled cellars, were only too glad to throw them open to save the rest of their property; but even the drunken rioters were very careful to steal nothing. They were so angry with one man, who was seen to take a silver cup at the Savoy Palace, and put it in his breast, that they drowned him in the river, cup and all.

The young King had been taken out to treat with them before they committed these excesses; but, he and the people about him were so frightened by the riotous shouts, that they got back to the Tower in the best way they could. This made the insurgents bolder; so they went on rioting away, striking off the heads of those who did not, at a moment's notice, declare for King Richard and the people; and killing as many of the unpopular persons whom they supposed to be their enemies as they could by any means lay hold of. In this manner they passed one very violent day, and then proclamation was made that the King would meet them at Mile-end, and grant their requests.

The rioters went to Mile-end to the number of sixty thousand, and the King met them there, and to the King the rioters peaceably proposed four conditions. First, that neither they, nor their children, nor any coming after them, should be made slaves any more. Secondly, that the rent of land should be fixed at a certain price in money, instead of being paid in service. Thirdly, that they should have liberty to buy and sell in all markets and public places, like other free men. Fourthly, that they should be pardoned for past offences. Heaven knows, there was nothing very unreasonable in these proposals! The young King deceitfully pretended to think so, and kept thirty clerks up, all night, writing out a charter accordingly.

Now, Wat Tyler himself wanted more than this. He wanted the entire abolition of the forest laws. He was not at Mile-end with the rest, but, while that meeting was being held, broke into the Tower of London and slew the archbishop and the treasurer, for whose heads the people had cried out loudly the day before. He and his men even thrust their swords into the bed of the Princess of Wales while the Princess was in it, to make certain that none of their enemies were concealed there.

So, Wat and his men still continued armed, and rode

about the city. Next morning, the King with a small train
of some sixty gentlemen—among whom was WALWORTH
the Mayor—rode into Smithfield, and saw Wat and his
people at a little distance. Says Wat to his men, "There
is the King. I will go speak with him, and tell him what
we want."

Straightway Wat rode up to him, and began to talk.
"King," says Wat, "dost thou see all my men there?"

"Ah," says the King. "Why?"

"Because," says Wat, "they are all at my command, and
have sworn to do whatever I bid them."

Some declared afterwards that as Wat said this, he laid
his hand on the King's bridle. Others declared that he was
seen to play with his own dagger. I think, myself, that he
just spoke to the King like a rough, angry man as he was,
and did nothing more. At any rate he was expecting no
attack, and preparing for no resistance, when Walworth
the Mayor did the not very valiant deed of drawing a short
sword and stabbing him in the throat. He dropped from
his horse, and one of the King's people speedily finished
him. So fell Wat Tyler. Fawners and flatterers made
a mighty triumph of it, and set up a cry which will
occasionally find an echo to this day. But Wat was a
hard-working man, who had suffered much, and had been
foully outraged; and it is probable that he was a man of
a much higher nature and a much braver spirit than any
of the parasites who exulted then, or have exulted since,
over his defeat.

Seeing Wat down, his men immediately bent their bows
to avenge his fall. If the young King had not had presence
of mind at that dangerous moment, both he and the Mayor
to boot, might have followed Tyler pretty fast. But the
King riding up to the crowd, cried out that Tyler was
a traitor, and that he would be their leader. They were
so taken by surprise, that they set up a great shouting, and
followed the boy until he was met at Islington by a large
body of soldiers.

The end of this rising was the then usual end. As soon
as the King found himself safe, he unsaid all he had said,
and undid all he had done; some fifteen hundred of the
rioters were tried (mostly in Essex) with great rigour, and
executed with great cruelty. Many of them were hanged
on gibbets, and left there as a terror to the country people;

and, because their miserable friends took some of the bodies down to bury, the King ordered the rest to be chained up—which was the beginning of the barbarous custom of hanging in chains. The King's falsehood in this business makes such a pitiful figure, that I think Wat Tyler appears in history as beyond comparison the truer and more respectable man of the two.

Richard was now sixteen years of age, and married Anne of Bohemia, an excellent princess, who was called " the good Queen Anne." She deserved a better husband ; for the King had been fawned and flattered into a treacherous, wasteful, dissolute, bad young man.

There were two Popes at this time (as if one were not enough !), and their quarrels involved Europe in a great deal of trouble. Scotland was still troublesome too ; and at home there was much jealousy and distrust, and plotting and counter-plotting, because the King feared the ambition of his relations, and particularly of his uncle, the Duke of Lancaster, and the duke had his party against the King, and the King had his party against the duke. Nor were these home troubles lessened when the duke went to Castile to urge his claim to the crown of that kingdom ; for then the Duke of Gloucester, another of Richard's uncles, opposed him, and influenced the Parliament to demand the dismissal of the King's favourite ministers. The King said in reply, that he would not for such men dismiss the meanest servant in his kitchen. But, it had begun to signify little what a King said when a Parliament was determined ; so Richard was at last obliged to give way, and to agree to another Government of the kingdom, under a commission of fourteen nobles, for a year. His uncle of Gloucester was at the head of this commission, and, in fact, appointed everybody com-posing it.

Having done all this, the King declared as soon as he saw an opportunity that he had never meant to do it, and that it was all illegal; and he got the judges secretly to sign a declaration to that effect. The secret oozed out directly, and was carried to the Duke of Gloucester. The Duke of Gloucester, at the head of forty thousand men, met the King on his entering into London to enforce his authority ; the King was helpless against him ; his favourites and ministers were impeached and were mercilessly executed. Among them were two men whom the people regarded with very different feelings; one, Robert Tresilian, Chief Justice, who was hated for having made what was called "the bloody circuit" to try the rioters; the other, Sir Simon Burley, an honourable knight, who had been the dear friend of the Black Prince, and the governor and guardian of the King. For this gentleman's life the good Queen even begged of Gloucester on her knees; but Gloucester (with or without reason) feared and hated him, and replied, that if she valued her husband's crown, she had better beg no more. All this was done under what was called by some the wonderful—and by others, with better reason, the merciless—Parliament.

But Gloucester's power was not to last for ever. He held it for only a year longer; in which year the famous battle of Otterbourne, sung in the old ballad of Chevy Chase, was fought. When the year was out, the King, turning suddenly to Gloucester, in the midst of a great council said, "Uncle, how old am I?" "Your highness," returned the Duke, "is in your twenty-second year." "Am I so much?" said the King; "then I will manage my own affairs! I am much obliged to you, my good lords, for your past services, but I need them no more." He followed this up, by appointing a new Chancellor and a new Treasurer, and announced to the people that he had resumed the Government. He held it for eight years without opposition. Through all that time, he kept his determination to revenge himself some day upon his uncle Gloucester, in his own breast.

At last the good Queen died, and then the King, desiring to take a second wife, proposed to his council that he should marry Isabella, of France, the daughter of Charles the Sixth: who, the French courtiers said (as the English courtiers had said of Richard), was a marvel of beauty and wit, and quite a phenomenon—of seven years old. The council were divided about this marriage, but it took place. It secured peace between England and France for a quarter of a century; but it was strongly opposed to the prejudices of the English people. The Duke of Gloucester, who was anxious to take the occasion of making himself popular, declaimed against it loudly, and this at length decided the King to execute the vengeance he had been nursing so long.

He went with a gay company to the Duke of Gloucester's house, Pleshey Castle, in Essex, where the Duke, suspecting nothing, came out into the court-yard to receive his royal visitor. While the King conversed in a friendly manner

M

with the Duchess, the Duke was quietly seized, hurried away, shipped for Calais, and lodged in the castle there. His friends, the Earls of Arundel and Warwick, were taken in the same treacherous manner, and confined to their castles. A few days after, at Nottingham, they were impeached of high treason. The Earl of Arundel was condemned and beheaded, and the Earl of Warwick was banished. Then, a writ was sent by a messenger to the Governor of Calais, requiring him to send the Duke of Gloucester over to be tried. In three days he returned an answer that he could not do that, because the Duke of Gloucester had died in prison. The Duke was declared a traitor, his property was confiscated to the King, a real or pretended confession he had made in prison to one of the Justices of the Common Pleas was produced against him, and there was an end of the matter. How the unfortunate duke died, very few cared to know. Whether he really died naturally; whether he killed himself; whether, by the King's order, he was strangled, or smothered between two beds (as a serving-man of the Governor's named Hall, did afterwards declare), cannot be discovered. There is not much doubt that he was killed, somehow or other, by his nephew's orders. Among the most active nobles in these proceedings were the King's cousin, Henry Bolingbroke, whom the King had made Duke of Hereford to smooth down the old family quarrels, and some others: who had in the family-plotting times done just such acts themselves as they now condemned in the duke. They seem to have been a corrupt set of men; but such men were easily found about the court in such days.

The people murmured at all this, and were still very sore about the French marriage. The nobles saw how little the King cared for law, and how crafty he was, and began to be somewhat afraid of themselves. The King's life was a life of continued feasting and excess; his retinue, down to the meanest servants, were dressed in the most costly manner, and caroused at his tables, it is related, to the number of ten thousand persons every day. He himself, surrounded by a body of ten thousand archers, and enriched by a duty on wool which the Commons had granted him for life, saw no danger of ever being otherwise than powerful and absolute, and was as fierce and haughty as a King could be.

He had two of his old enemies left, in the persons of the Dukes of Hereford and Norfolk. Sparing these no more than the others, he tampered with the Duke of Hereford until he got him to declare before the Council that the Duke of Norfolk had lately held some treasonable talk with him, as he was riding near Brentford; and that he had told him, among other things, that he could not believe the King's oath—which nobody could, I should think. For this treachery he obtained a pardon, and the Duke of Norfolk was summoned to appear and defend himself. As he denied the charge and said his accuser was a liar and a traitor, both noblemen, according to the manner of those times, were held in custody, and the truth was ordered to be decided by wager of battle at Coventry. This wager of battle meant that whosoever won the combat was to be considered in the right; which nonsense meant in effect, that no strong man could ever be wrong. A great holiday was made; a great crowd assembled, with much parade and show; and the two combatants were about to rush at each other with their lances, when the King, sitting in a pavilion to see fair, threw down the truncheon he carried in his hand, and forbade the battle. The Duke of Hereford was to be banished for ten years, and the Duke of Norfolk was to be banished for life. So said the King. The Duke of Hereford went to France, and went no farther. The Duke of Norfolk made a pilgrimage to the Holy Land, and afterwards died at Venice of a broken heart.

Faster and fiercer, after this, the King went on in his career. The Duke of Lancaster, who was the father of the Duke of Hereford, died soon after the departure of his son; and, the King, although he had solemnly granted to that son leave to inherit his father's property, if it should come to him during his banishment, immediately seized it all, like a robber. The judges were so afraid of him, that they disgraced themselves by declaring this theft to be just and lawful. His avarice knew no bounds. He outlawed seventeen counties at once, on a frivolous pretence, merely to raise money by way of fines for misconduct. In short, he did as many dishonest things as he could; and cared so little for the discontent of his subjects—though even the spaniel favourites began to whisper to him that there was such a thing as discontent afloat—that he took that time, of all others, for leaving England and making an expedition against the Irish.

He was scarcely gone, leaving the DUKE OF YORK Regent

in his absence, when his cousin, Henry of Hereford, came over from France to claim the rights of which he had been so monstrously deprived. He was immediately joined by the two great Earls of Northumberland and Westmoreland ; and his uncle, the Regent, finding the King's cause unpopular, and the disinclination of the army to act against Henry, very strong, withdrew with the Royal forces towards Bristol. Henry, at the head of an army, came from Yorkshire (where he had landed) to London and followed him. They joined their forces—how they brought that about, is not distinctly understood—and proceeded to Bristol Castle, whither three noblemen had taken the young Queen. The castle surrendering, they presently put those three noblemen to death. The Regent then remained there, and Henry went on to Chester.

All this time, the boisterous weather had prevented the King from receiving intelligence of what had occurred. At length it was conveyed to him in Ireland, and he sent over the EARL OF SALISBURY, who, landing at Conway, rallied the Welshmen, and waited for the King a whole fortnight ; at the end of that time the Welshmen, who were perhaps not very warm for him in the beginning, quite cooled down and went home. When the King did land on the coast at last, he came with a pretty good power, but his men cared nothing for him, and quickly deserted. Supposing the Welshmen to be still at Conway, he disguised himself as a priest, and made for that place in company with his two brothers and some few of their adherents. But, there were no Welshmen left—only Salisbury and a hundred soldiers. In this distress, the King's two brothers, Exeter and Surrey, offered to go to Henry to learn what his intentions were. Surrey, who was true to Richard, was put into prison. Exeter, who was false, took the royal badge, which was a hart, off his shield, and assumed the rose, the badge of Henry. After this, it was pretty plain to the King what Henry's intentions were, without sending any more messengers to ask.

The fallen King, thus deserted—hemmed in on all sides, and pressed with hunger—rode here and rode there, and went to this castle, and went to that castle, endeavouring to obtain some provisions, but could find none. He rode wretchedly back to Conway, and there surrendered himself to the Earl of Northumberland, who came from Henry, in reality to take him prisoner, but in appearance to offer terms ; and whose men were hidden not far off. By this earl he was conducted to the castle of Flint, where his cousin Henry met him, and dropped on his knee as if he were still respectful to his sovereign.

"Fair cousin of Lancaster," said the King, "you are very welcome" (very welcome, no doubt; but he would have been more so, in chains or without a head).

"My lord," replied Henry, "I am come a little before my time; but, with your good pleasure, I will show you the reason. Your people complain with some bitterness, that you have ruled them rigorously for two-and-twenty years. Now, if it please God, I will help you to govern them better in future."

"Fair cousin," replied the abject King, "since it pleaseth you, it pleaseth me mightily."

After this, the trumpets sounded, and the King was stuck on a wretched horse, and carried prisoner to Chester, where he was made to issue a proclamation, calling a Parliament. From Chester he was taken on towards London. At Lichfield he tried to escape by getting out of a window and letting himself down into a garden; it was all in vain, however, and he was carried on and shut up in the Tower, where no one pitied him, and where the whole people, whose patience he had quite tired out, reproached him without mercy. Before he got there, it is related, that his very dog left him and departed from his side to lick the hand of Henry.

The day before the Parliament met, a deputation went to this wrecked King, and told him that he had promised the Earl of Northumberland at Conway Castle to resign the crown. He said he was quite ready to do it, and signed a paper in which he renounced his authority and absolved his people from their allegiance to him. He had so little spirit left that he gave his royal ring to his triumphant cousin Henry with his own hand, and said, that if he could have had leave to appoint a successor, that same Henry was the man of all others whom he would have named. Next day, the Parliament assembled in Westminster Hall, where Henry sat at the side of the throne, which was empty and covered with a cloth of gold. The paper just signed by the King was read to the multitude amid shouts of joy, which were echoed through all the streets; when some of the noise had died away, the King was formally deposed. Then Henry arose, and, making the sign of the cross on his forehead and breast, challenged the realm of England as his right ; the archbishops of Canterbury and York seated him on the throne.

The multitude shouted again, and the shouts re-echoed throughout all the streets. No one remembered, now, that Richard the Second had ever been the most beautiful, the wisest, and the best of princes ; and he now made living (to my thinking) a far more sorry spectacle in the Tower of London, than Wat Tyler had made, lying dead, among the hoofs of the royal horses in Smithfield.

The Poll-tax died with Wat. The Smiths to the King and Royal Family, could make no chains in which the King could hang the people's recollection of him ; so the Poll-tax was never collected.

CHAPTER XX

DURING the last reign, the preaching of Wickliffe against the
pride and cunning of the Pope and all his men, had made
a great noise in England. Whether the new King wished
to be in favour with the priests, or whether he hoped, by
pretending to be very religious, to cheat Heaven itself into
the belief that he was not an usurper, I don't know. Both
suppositions are likely enough. It is certain that he began
his reign by making a strong show against the followers of
Wickliffe, who were called Lollards, or heretics—although
his father, John of Gaunt, had been of that way of thinking,
as he himself had been more than suspected of being. It is
no less certain that he first established in England the
detestable and atrocious custom, brought from abroad, of
burning those people as a punishment for their opinions.
It was the importation into England of one of the practices
of what was called the Holy Inquisition: which was the
most *un*holy and the most infamous tribunal that ever
disgraced mankind, and made men more like demons than
followers of Our Saviour.

No real right to the crown, as you know, was in this King.
Edward Mortimer, the young Earl of March—who was only
eight or nine years old, and who was descended from the
Duke of Clarence, the elder brother of Henry's father—was,
by succession, the real heir to the throne. However, the
King got his son declared Prince of Wales ; and, obtaining
possession of the young Earl of March and his little brother,
kept them in confinement (but not severely) in Windsor
Castle. He then required the Parliament to decide what
was to be done with the deposed King, who was quiet
enough, and who only said that he hoped his cousin Henry
would be "a good lord" to him. The Parliament replied
that they would recommend his being kept in some secret

place where the people could not resort, and where his friends could not be admitted to see him. Henry accordingly passed this sentence upon him, and it now began to be pretty clear to the nation that Richard the Second would not live very long.

It was a noisy Parliament, as it was an unprincipled one, and the Lords quarrelled so violently among themselves as to which of them had been loyal and which disloyal, and which consistent and which inconsistent, that forty gauntlets are said to have been thrown upon the floor at one time as challenges to as many battles: the truth being that they were all false and base together, and had been, at one time with the old King, and at another time with the new one, and seldom true for any length of time to any one. They soon began to plot again. A conspiracy was formed to invite the King to a tournament at Oxford, and then to take him by surprise and kill him. This murderous enterprise, which was agreed upon at secret meetings in the house of the Abbot of Westminster, was betrayed by the Earl of Rutland — one of the conspirators. The King, instead of going to the tournament or staying at Windsor (where the conspirators suddenly went, on finding themselves discovered, with the hope of seizing him), retired to London, proclaimed them all traitors, and advanced upon them with a great force. They retired into the west of England, proclaiming Richard King; but, the people rose against them, and they were all slain. Their treason hastened the death of the deposed monarch. Whether he was killed by hired assassins, or whether he was starved to death, or whether he refused food on hearing of his brothers being killed (who were in that plot), is very doubtful. He met his death somehow; and his body was publicly shown at St. Paul's Cathedral with only the lower part of the face uncovered. I can scarcely doubt that he was killed by the King's orders.

The French wife of the miserable Richard was now only ten years old; and, when her father, Charles of France, heard of her misfortunes and of her lonely condition in England, he went mad: as he had several times done before, during the last five or six years. The French Dukes of Burgundy and Bourbon took up the poor girl's cause, without caring much about it, but on the chance of getting something out of England. The people of Bordeaux, who had a sort of superstitious attachment to the memory of Richard, because he was born there, swore by the Lord that he had been the best man in all his kingdom—which was going rather far—and promised to do great things against the English. Nevertheless, when they came to consider that they, and the whole people of France were ruined by their own nobles, and that the English rule was much the better of the two, they cooled down again ; and the two dukes, although they were very great men, could do nothing without them. Then, began negotiations between France and England for the sending home to Paris of the poor little Queen with all her jewels and her fortune of two hundred thousand francs in gold. The King was quite willing to restore the young lady, and even the jewels ; but he said he really could not part with the money. So, at last she was safely deposited at Paris without her fortune, and then the Duke of Burgundy (who was cousin to the French King) began to quarrel with the Duke of Orleans (who was brother to the French King) about the whole matter ; and those two dukes made France even more wretched than ever.

As the idea of conquering Scotland was still popular at home, the King marched to the river Tyne and demanded homage of the King of that country. This being refused, he advanced to Edinburgh, but did little there ; for, his army being in want of provisions, and the Scotch being very careful to hold him in check without giving battle, he was obliged to retire. It is to his immortal honour that in this sally he burnt no villages and slaughtered no people, but was particularly careful that his army should be merciful and harmless. It was a great example in those ruthless times.

A war among the border people of England and Scotland went on for twelve months, and then the Earl of Northumberland, the nobleman who had helped Henry to the crown, began to rebel against him—probably because nothing that Henry could do for him would satisfy his extravagant expectations. There was a certain Welsh gentleman, named OWEN GLENDOWER, who had been a student in one of the Inns of Court, and had afterwards been in the service of the late King, whose Welsh property was taken from him by a powerful lord related to the present King, who was his neighbour. Appealing for redress, and getting none, he took up arms, was made an outlaw, and declared himself sovereign of Wales. He pretended to be a magician; and not only were the Welsh people stupid enough to believe him, but, even Henry believed him too; for, making three expeditions into Wales, and being three times driven back by the wildness of the country, the bad weather, and the skill of Glendower, he thought he was defeated by the Welshman's magic arts. However, he took Lord Grey and Sir Edmund Mortimer, prisoners, and allowed the relatives of Lord Grey to ransom him, but would not extend such favour to Sir Edmund Mortimer. Now, Henry Percy, called HOTSPUR, son of the Earl of Northumberland, who was married to Mortimer's sister, is supposed to have taken offence at this; and, therefore, in conjunction with his father and some others, to have joined Owen Glendower, and risen against Henry. It is by no means clear that this was the real cause of the conspiracy; but perhaps it was made the pretext. It was formed, and was very powerful; including SCROOP, Archbishop of York, and the EARL OF DOUGLAS, a powerful and brave Scottish nobleman. The King was prompt and active, and the two armies met at Shrewsbury.

There were about fourteen thousand men in each. The old Earl of Northumberland being sick, the rebel forces were led by his son. The King wore plain armour to deceive the enemy; and four noblemen, with the same object, wore the royal arms. The rebel charge was so furious, that every one of those gentlemen was killed, the royal standard was beaten down, and the young Prince of Wales was severely wounded in the face. But he was one of the bravest and best soldiers that ever lived, and he fought so well, and the King's troops were so encouraged by his bold example, that they rallied immediately, and cut the enemy's forces all to pieces. Hotspur was killed by an arrow in the brain, and the rout was so complete that the whole rebellion was struck down by this one blow. The Earl of Northumberland surrendered himself soon after hearing of the death of his son, and received a pardon for all his offences.

There were some lingerings of rebellion yet: Owen Glendower being retired to Wales, and a preposterous story being spread among the ignorant people that King Richard was still alive. How they could have believed such nonsense it is difficult to imagine; but they certainly did suppose that the Court fool of the late King, who was something like

him, was he, himself; so that it seemed as if, after giving
so much trouble to the country in his life, he was still to
trouble it after his death. This was not the worst. The
young Earl of March and his brother were stolen out of
Windsor Castle. Being retaken, and being found to have
been spirited away by one Lady Spencer, she accused her
own brother, that Earl of Rutland who was in the former
conspiracy and was now Duke of York, of being in the plot.
For this he was ruined in fortune, though not put to death ;
and then another plot arose among the old Earl of Northumberland, some other lords, and that same Scroop, Archbishop
of York, who was with the rebels before. These conspiratois
caused a writing to be posted on the church doors, accusing
the King of a variety of crimes ; but, the King being eager
and vigilant to oppose them, they were all taken, and the
Archbishop was executed. This was the first time that
a great churchman had been slain by the law in England ;
but the King was resolved that it should be done, and done
it was.

The next most remarkable event of this time was the
seizure, by Henry, of the heir to the Scottish throne—
James, a boy of nine years old. He had been put aboard-
ship by his father, the Scottish King Robert, to save him
from the designs of his uncle, when, on his way to France,
he was accidentally taken by some English cruisers. He
remained a prisoner in England for nineteen years, and
became in his prison a student and a famous poet.

With the exception of occasional troubles with the Welsh
and with the French, the rest of King Henry's reign was
quiet enough. But, the King was far from happy, and
probably was troubled in his conscience by knowing that he
had usurped the crown, and had occasioned the death of his
miserable cousin. The Prince of Wales, though brave and
generous, is said to have been wild and dissipated, and even
to have drawn his sword on GASCOIGNE, the Chief Justice
of the King's Bench, because he was firm in dealing im-
partially with one of his dissolute companions. Upon this
the Chief Justice is said to have ordered him immediately
to prison ; the Prince of Wales is said to have submitted
with a good grace; and the King is said to have exclaimed,
"Happy is the monarch who has so just a judge, and a son
so willing to obey the laws." This is all very doubtful, and
so is another story (of which Shakespeare has made beautiful

use), that the Prince once took the crown out of his father's chamber as he was sleeping, and tried it on his own head.

The King's health sank more and more, and he became subject to violent eruptions on the face and to bad epileptic fits, and his spirits sank every day. At last, as he was praying before the shrine of St. Edward at Westminster Abbey, he was seized with a terrible fit, and was carried into the Abbot's chamber, where he presently died. It had been foretold that he would die at Jerusalem, which certainly is not, and never was, Westminster. But, as the Abbot's room had long been called the Jerusalem chamber, people said it was all the same thing, and were quite satisfied with the prediction.

The King died on the 20th of March, 1413, in the forty-seventh year of his age, and the fourteenth of his reign. He was buried in Canterbury Cathedral. He had been twice married, and had, by his first wife, a family of four sons and two daughters. Considering his duplicity before he came to the throne, his unjust seizure of it, and above all, his making that monstrous law for the burning of what the priests called heretics, he was a reasonably good king, as kings went.

CHAPTER XXI

FIRST PART.

THE Prince of Wales began his reign like a generous and honest man. He set the young Earl of March free; he restored their estates and their honours to the Percy family, who had lost them by their rebellion against his father; he ordered the imbecile and unfortunate Richard to be honourably buried among the Kings of England; and he dismissed all his wild companions, with assurances that they should not want, if they would resolve to be steady, faithful, and true.

It is much easier to burn men than to burn their opinions; and those of the Lollards were spreading every day. The Lollards were represented by the priests—probably falsely for the most part—to entertain treasonable designs against the new King; and Henry, suffering himself to be worked upon by these representations, sacrificed his friend Sir John Oldcastle, the Lord Cobham, to them, after trying in vain to convert him by arguments. He was declared guilty, as the head of the sect, and sentenced to the flames; but he escaped from the Tower before the day of execution (postponed for fifty days by the King himself), and summoned the Lollards to meet him near London on a certain day. So the priests told the King, at least. I doubt whether there was any conspiracy beyond such as was got up by their agents. On the day appointed, instead of five-and-twenty thousand men, under the command of Sir John Oldcastle, in the meadows of St. Giles, the King found only eighty men, and no Sir John at all. There was, in another place, an addle-headed brewer, who had gold trappings to his horses, and a pair of gilt spurs in his breast—expecting to be made a knight next day by Sir John, and so to gain the right to wear them—but there was no Sir John, nor did anybody give information respecting him, though the King offered

great rewards for such intelligence. Thirty of these unfortunate Lollards were hanged and drawn immediately, and
were then burnt, gallows and all ; and the various prisons
in and around London were crammed full of others.   Some
of these unfortunate men made various confessions of treasonable designs ; but, such confessions were easily got, under
torture and the fear of fire, and are very little to be trusted.
To finish the sad story of Sir John Oldcastle at once, I may
mention that he escaped into Wales, and remained there
safely, for four years.   When discovered by Lord Powis, it
is very doubtful if he would have been taken alive—so great
was the old soldier's bravery—if a miserable old woman had
not come behind him and broken his legs with a stool.   He
was carried to London in a horse-litter, was fastened by an
iron chain to a gibbet, and so roasted to death.

To make the state of France as plain as I can in a few
words, I should tell you that the Duke of Orleans, and the
Duke of Burgundy, commonly called "John without fear,"
had had a grand reconciliation of their quarrel in the last
reign, and had appeared to be quite in a heavenly state of
mind.   Immediately after which, on a Sunday, in the public
streets of Paris, the Duke of Orleans was murdered by
a party of twenty men, set on by the Duke of Burgundy—
according to his own deliberate confession.   The widow of
King Richard had been married in France to the eldest son
of the Duke of Orleans.   The poor mad King was quite
powerless to help her, and the Duke of Burgundy became
the real master of France.   Isabella dying, her husband
(Duke of Orleans since the death of his father) married the
daughter of the Count of Armagnac, who, being a much
abler man than his young son-in-law, headed his party ;
thence called after him Armagnacs.   Thus. France was now
in this terrible condition, that it had in it the party of the
King's son, the Dauphin Louis ; the party of the Duke of
Burgundy, who was the father of the Dauphin's ill-used
wife ; and the party of the Armagnacs ; all hating each
other ; all fighting together ; all composed of the most de-
praved nobles that the earth has ever known ; and all
tearing unhappy France to pieces.

The late King had watched these dissensions from England,
sensible (like the French people) that no enemy of France
could injure her more than her own nobility.   The present
King now advanced a claim to the French throne.   His

demand being, of course, refused, he reduced his proposal to a certain large amount of French territory, and to demanding the French princess, Catherine, in marriage, with a fortune of two millions of golden crowns. He was offered less territory and fewer crowns, and no princess; but he called his ambassadors home and prepared for war. Then, he proposed to take the princess with one million of crowns. The French Court replied that he should have the princess with two hundred thousand crowns less; he said this would not do (he had never seen the princess in his life), and assembled his army at Southampton. There was a short plot at home just at that time, for deposing him, and making the Earl of March king; but the conspirators were all speedily condemned and executed, and the King embarked for France.

It is dreadful to observe how long a bad example will be followed; but, it is encouraging to know that a good example is never thrown away. The King's first act on disembarking at the mouth of the river Seine, three miles from Harfleur, was to imitate his father, and to proclaim his solemn orders that the lives and property of the peaceable inhabitants should be respected on pain of death. It is agreed by French writers, to his lasting renown, that even while his soldiers were suffering the greatest distress from want of food, these commands were rigidly obeyed.

With an army in all of thirty thousand men, he besieged the town of Harfleur both by sea and land for five weeks; at the end of which time the town surrendered, and the inhabitants were allowed to depart with only fivepence each, and a part of their clothes. All the rest of their possessions was divided amongst the English army. But, that army suffered so much, in spite of its successes, from disease and privation, that it was already reduced one half. Still, the King was determined not to retire until he had struck a greater blow. Therefore, against the advice of all his counsellors, he moved on with his little force towards Calais. When he came up to the river Somme he was unable to cross, in consequence of the fort being fortified; and, as the English moved up the left bank of the river looking for a crossing, the French, who had broken all the bridges, moved up the right bank, watching them, and waiting to attack them when they should try to pass it. At last the English found a crossing and got safely over.

The French held a council of war at Rouen, resolved to give the English battle, and sent heralds to King Henry to know by which road he was going. "By the road that will take me straight to Calais!" said the King, and sent them away with a present of a hundred crowns.

The English moved on, until they beheld the French, and then the King gave orders to form in line of battle. The French not coming on, the army broke up after remaining in battle array till night, and got good rest and refreshment at a neighbouring village. The French were now all lying in another village, through which they knew the English must pass. They were resolved that the English should begin the battle. The English had no means of retreat, if their King had any such intention; and so the two armies passed the night, close together.

To understand these armies well, you must bear in mind that the immense French army had, among its notable persons, almost the whole of that wicked nobility, whose debauchery had made France a desert; and so besotted were they by pride, and by contempt for the common people, that they had scarcely any bowmen (if indeed they had any at all) in their whole enormous number: which, compared with the English army, was at least as six to one. For these proud fools had said that the bow was not a fit weapon for knightly hands, and that France must be defended by gentlemen only. We shall see, presently, what hand the gentlemen made of it.

Now, on the English side, among the little force, there was a good proportion of men who were not gentlemen by any means, but who were good stout archers for all that. Among them, in the morning—having slept little at night, while the French were carousing and making sure of victory —the King rode, on a grey horse; wearing on his head a helmet of shining steel, surmounted by a crown of gold, sparkling with precious stones; and bearing over his armour, embroidered together, the arms of England and the arms of France. The archers looked at the shining helmet and the crown of gold and the sparkling jewels, and admired them all; but, what they admired most was the King's cheerful face, and his bright blue eye, as he told them that, for himself, he had made up his mind to conquer there or to die there, and that England should never have a ransom to pay for *him*. There was one brave knight who

chanced to say that he wished some of the many gallant
gentlemen and good soldiers, who were then idle at home
in England, were there to increase their numbers. But
the King told him that, for his part, he did not wish for
one more man. "The fewer we have," said he, "the
greater will be the honour we shall win!" His men, being
now all in good heart, were refreshed with bread and wine,
and heard prayers, and waited quietly for the French. The
King waited for the French, because they were drawn up
thirty deep (the little English force was only three deep),
on very difficult and heavy ground; and he knew that when
they moved, there must be confusion among them.

As they did not move, he sent off two parties:—one to
lie concealed in a wood on the left of the French: the other,
to set fire to some houses behind the French after the battle
should be begun. This was scarcely done, when three of
the proud French gentlemen, who were to defend their
country without any help from the base peasants, came
riding out, calling upon the English to surrender. The
King warned those gentlemen himself to retire with all
speed if they cared for their lives, and ordered the English
banners to advance. Upon that, Sir Thomas Erpingham,
a great English general, who commanded the archers, threw
his truncheon into the air, joyfully, and all the English
men, kneeling down upon the ground and biting it as if
they took possession of the country, rose up with a great
shout and fell upon the French.

Every archer was furnished with a great stake tipped
with iron; and his orders were, to thrust this stake into
the ground, to discharge his arrow, and then to fall back,
when the French horsemen came on. As the haughty
French gentlemen, who were to break the English archers
and utterly destroy them with their knightly lances, came
riding up, they were received with such a blinding storm of
arrows, that they broke and turned. Horses and men rolled
over one another, and the confusion was terrific. Those
who rallied and charged the archers got among the stakes
on slippery and boggy ground, and were so bewildered that
the English archers—who wore no armour, and even took
off their leathern coats to be more active—cut them to
pieces, root and branch. Only three French horsemen got
within the stakes, and those were instantly despatched.
All this time the dense French army, being in armour, were

sinking knee-deep into the mire; while the light English archers, half-naked, were as fresh and active as if they were fighting on a marble floor.

But now, the second division of the French coming to the relief of the first, closed up in a firm mass; the English, headed by the King, attacked them; and the deadliest part of the battle began. The King's brother, the Duke of Clarence, was struck down, and numbers of the French surrounded him; but, King Henry, standing over the body, fought like a lion until they were beaten off.

Presently, came up a band of eighteen French knights, bearing the banner of a certain French lord, who had sworn to kill or take the English King. One of them struck him such a blow with a battle-axe that he reeled and fell upon his knees; but, his faithful men, immediately closing round him, killed every one of those eighteen knights, and so that French lord never kept his oath.

The French Duke of Alençon, seeing this, made a desperate charge, and cut his way close up to the Royal Standard of England. He beat down the Duke of York, who was standing near it; and, when the King came to his rescue, struck off a piece of the crown he wore. But, he never struck another blow in this world; for, even as he was in the act of saying who he was, and that he surrendered to the King; and even as the King stretched out his hand to give him a safe and honourable acceptance of the offer; he fell dead, pierced by innumerable wounds.

The death of this nobleman decided the battle. The third division of the French army, which had never struck a blow yet, and which was, in itself, more than double the whole English power, broke and fled. At this time of the fight, the English, who as yet had made no prisoners, began to take them in immense numbers, and were still occupied in doing so, or in killing those who would not surrender, when a great noise arose in the rear of the French—their flying banners were seen to stop—and King Henry, supposing a great reinforcement to have arrived, gave orders that all the prisoners should be put to death. As soon, however, as it was found that the noise was only occasioned by a body of plundering peasants, the terrible massacre was stopped.

Then King Henry called to him the French herald, and asked him to whom the victory belonged.

The herald replied, "To the King of England."

"We have not made this havoc and slaughter," said the King. "It is the wrath of Heaven on the sins of France. What is the name of that castle yonder?"

The herald answered him, "My lord, it is the castle of Azincourt."

Said the King, "From henceforth this battle shall be known to posterity, by the name of the battle of Azincourt."

Our English historians have made it Agincourt; but, under that name, it will ever be famous in English annals.

The loss upon the French side was enormous. Three Dukes were killed, two more were taken prisoners, seven Counts were killed, three more were taken prisoners, and ten thousand knights and gentlemen were slain upon the field. The English loss amounted to sixteen hundred men, among whom were the Duke of York and the Earl of Suffolk.

War is a dreadful thing; and it is appalling to know how the English were obliged, next morning, to kill those prisoners mortally wounded, who yet writhed in agony upon the ground; how the dead upon the French side were stripped by their own countrymen and countrywomen, and afterwards buried in great pits; how the dead upon the English side were piled up in a great barn, and how their bodies and the barn were all burned together. It is in such things, and in many more much too horrible to relate, that the real desolation and wickedness of war consist. Nothing can make war otherwise than horrible. But the dark side of it was little thought of and soon forgotten; and it cast no shade of trouble on the English people, except on those who had lost friends or relations in the fight. They welcomed their King home with shouts of rejoicing, and plunged into the water to bear him ashore on their shoulders, and flocked out in crowds to welcome him in every town through which he passed, and hung rich carpets and tapestries out of the windows, and strewed the streets with flowers, and made the fountains run.with wine, as the great field of Agincourt had run with blood.

SECOND PART.

THAT proud and wicked French nobility who dragged their country to destruction, and who were every day and every year regarded with deeper hatred and detestation in the hearts of the French people, learnt nothing, even from the defeat of Agincourt. So far from uniting against the common enemy, they became, among themselves, more violent, more bloody, and more false—if that were possible —than they had been before. The Count of Armagnac persuaded the French king to plunder of her treasures Queen Isabella of Bavaria, and to make her a prisoner. She, who had hitherto been the bitter enemy of the Duke of Burgundy, proposed to join him, in revenge. He carried her off to Troyes, where she proclaimed herself Regent of France, and made him her lieutenant. The Armagnac party were at that time possessed of Paris; but, one of the gates of the city being secretly opened on a certain night to a party of the duke's men, they got into Paris, threw into the prisons all the Armagnacs upon whom they could lay their hands, and, a few nights afterwards, with the aid of a furious mob of sixty thousand people, broke the prisons open, and killed them all. The former Dauphin was now dead, and the King's third son bore the title. Him, in the height of this murderous scene, a French knight hurried out of bed, wrapped in a sheet, and bore away to Poitiers. So, when the revengeful Isabella and the Duke of Burgundy entered Paris in triumph after the slaughter of their enemies, the Dauphin was proclaimed at Poitiers as the real Regent.

King Henry had not been idle since his victory of Agincourt, but had repulsed a brave attempt of the French to recover Harfleur; had gradually conquered a great part of Normandy; and, at this crisis of affairs, took the important town of Rouen, after a siege of half a year. This great loss so alarmed the French, that the Duke of Burgundy proposed that a meeting to treat of peace should be held between the French and the English kings in a plain by the river Seine. On the appointed day, King Henry appeared there, with his two brothers, Clarence and Gloucester, and a thousand men. The unfortunate French King, being more mad than usual that day, could not come; but the Queen came, and with her the Princess Catherine: who was a very lovely creature, and who made a real impression on King Henry, now that he saw her for the first time. This was the most important circumstance that arose out of the meeting.

As if it were impossible for a French nobleman of that time to be true to his word of honour in anything, Henry discovered that the Duke of Burgundy was, at that very moment, in secret treaty with the Dauphin; and he therefore abandoned the negotiation.

The Duke of Burgundy and the Dauphin, each of whom with the best reason distrusted the other as a noble ruffian surrounded by a party of noble ruffians, were rather at a loss how to proceed after this; but, at length they agreed to meet, on a bridge over the river Yonne, where it was arranged that there should be two strong gates put up, with an empty space between them; and that the Duke of Burgundy should come into that space by one gate, with ten men only; and that the Dauphin should come into that space by the other gate, also with ten men, and no more.

So far the Dauphin kept his word, but no farther. When the Duke of Burgundy was on his knee before him in the act of speaking, one of the Dauphin's noble ruffians cut the said duke down with a small axe, and others speedily finished him.

It was in vain for the Dauphin to pretend that this base murder was not done with his consent; it was too bad, even for France, and caused a general horror. The duke's heir hastened to make a treaty with King Henry, and the French Queen engaged that her husband should consent to it, whatever it was. Henry made peace, on condition of receiving the Princess Catherine in marriage, and being made Regent of France during the rest of the King's lifetime, and succeeding to the French crown at his death. He was soon married to the beautiful Princess, and took her proudly home to England, where she was crowned with great honour and glory.

This peace was called the Perpetual Peace; we shall soon see how long it lasted. It gave great satisfaction to the French people, although they were so poor and miserable, that, at the time of the celebration of the Royal marriage, numbers of them were dying with starvation, on the dunghills in the streets of Paris. There was some resistance on the part of the Dauphin in some few parts of France, but King Henry beat it all down.

And now, with his great possessions in France secured, and his beautiful wife to cheer him, and a son born to give him greater happiness, all appeared bright before him. But, in the fulness of his triumph and the height of his power, Death came upon him, and his day was done. When he fell ill at Vincennes, and found that he could not recover, he was very calm and quiet, and spoke serenely to those who wept around his bed.   His wife and child, he said, he left to the loving care of his brother the Duke of Bedford, and his other faithful nobles.   He gave them his advice that England should establish a friendship with the new Duke of Burgundy, and offer him the regency of France; that it should not set free the royal princes who had been taken at Agincourt; and that, whatever quarrel might arise with France, England should never make peace without holding Normandy.   Then, he laid down his head, and asked the attendant priests to chant the penitential psalms.   Amid which solemn sounds, on the thirty-first of August, one thousand four hundred and twenty-two, in only the thirty-fourth year of his age and the tenth of his reign, King Henry the Fifth passed away.

Slowly and mournfully they carried his embalmed body in a procession of great state to Paris, and thence to Rouen where his Queen was: from whom the sad intelligence of his death was concealed until he had been dead some days. Thence, lying on a bed of crimson and gold, with a golden crown upon the head, and a golden ball and sceptre lying in the nerveless hands, they carried it to Calais, with such a great retinue as seemed to dye the road black.   The King of Scotland acted as chief mourner, all the Royal Household followed, the knights wore black armour and black plumes of feathers, crowds of men bore torches, making the night as light as day; and the widowed Princess followed last of all.   At Calais there was a fleet of ships to bring the funeral host to Dover.   And so, by way of London Bridge, where the service for the dead was chanted as it passed along, they brought the body to Westminster Abbey, and there buried it with great respect.

CHAPTER XXII

ENGLAND UNDER HENRY THE SIXTH

Part the First.

It had been the wish of the late King, that while his infant son King Henry the Sixth, at this time only nine months old, was under age, the Duke of Gloucester should be appointed Regent. The English Parliament, however, preferred to appoint a Council of Regency, with the Duke of Bedford at its head: to be represented, in his absence only, by the Duke of Gloucester. The Parliament would seem to have been wise in this, for Gloucester soon showed himself to be ambitious and troublesome, and, in the gratification of his own personal schemes, gave dangerous offence to the Duke of Burgundy, which was with difficulty adjusted.

As that duke declined the Regency of France, it was bestowed by the poor French King upon the Duke of Bedford. But, the French King dying within two months, the Dauphin instantly asserted his claim to the French throne, and was actually crowned under the title of Charles the Seventh. The Duke of Bedford, to be a match for him, entered into a friendly league with the Dukes of Burgundy and Brittany, and gave them his two sisters in marriage. War with France was immediately renewed, and the Perpetual Peace came to an untimely end.

In the first campaign, the English, aided by this alliance, were speedily successful. As Scotland, however, had sent the French five thousand men, and might send more, or attack the North of England while England was busy with France, it was considered that it would be a good thing to offer the Scottish King, James, who had been so long imprisoned, his liberty, on his paying forty thousand pounds for his board and lodging during nineteen years, and engaging to forbid his subjects from serving under the flag of France. It is pleasant to know, not only that the amiable captive at last regained his freedom upon these terms, but, that he married a noble English lady, with whom he had been long in love, and became an excellent King. I am afraid we have met with some Kings in this history, and shall meet with some more, who would have been very much the better, and would have left the world much happier, if they had been imprisoned nineteen years too.

In the second campaign, the English gained a considerable victory at Verneuil, in a battle which was chiefly remark-able, otherwise, for their resorting to the odd expedient of tying their baggage-horses together by the heads and tails, and jumbling them up with the baggage, so as to convert them into a sort of live fortification—which was found useful to the troops, but which I should think was not agreeable to the horses. For three years afterwards very little was done, owing to both sides being too poor for war, which is a very expensive entertainment; but, a council was then held in Paris, in which it was decided to lay siege to the town of Orleans, which was a place of great importance to the Dauphin's cause. An English army of ten thousand men was despatched on this service, under the command of the Earl of Salisbury, a general of fame. He being unfortunately killed early in the siege, the Earl of Suffolk took his place; under whom (reinforced by SIR JOHN FALSTAFF, who brought up four hundred waggons laden with salt herrings and other provisions for the troops, and, beating off the French who tried to intercept him, came victorious out of a hot skirmish, which was afterwards called in jest the Battle of the Herrings) the town of Orleans was so completely hemmed in, that the besieged proposed to yield it up to their countryman the Duke of Burgundy. The English general, however, replied that his English men had won it, so far, by their blood and valour, and that his English men must have it. There seemed to be no hope for the town, or for the Dauphin, who was so dismayed that he even thought of flying to Scotland or to Spain—when a peasant girl rose up and changed the whole state of affairs.

The story of this peasant girl I have now to tell.

Joan of Arc tending her Flock

Part the Second.

THE STORY OF JOAN OF ARC.

In a remote village among some wild hills in the province of Lorraine, there lived a countryman whose name was JACQUES D'ARC. He had a daughter, JOAN OF ARC, who was at this time in her twentieth year. She had been a solitary girl from her childhood ; she had often tended sheep and cattle for whole days where no human figure was seen or human voice heard ; and she had often knelt, for hours together, in the gloomy empty little village chapel, looking up at the altar and at the dim lamp burning before it, until she fancied that she saw shadowy figures standing there, and even that she heard them speak to her. The people in that part of France were very ignorant and super-stitious, and they had many ghostly tales to tell about what they had dreamed, and what they saw among the lonely hills when the clouds and the mists were resting on them. So, they easily believed that Joan saw strange sights, and they whispered among themselves that angels and spirits talked to her.

At last, Joan told her father that she had one day been surprised by a great unearthly light, and had afterwards heard a solemn voice, which said it was Saint Michael's voice, telling her that she was to go and help the Dauphin. Soon after this (she said), Saint Catherine and Saint Margaret had appeared to her with sparkling crowns upon their heads, and had encouraged her to be virtuous and resolute. These visions had returned sometimes ; but the Voices very often ; and the voices always said, " Joan, thou art appointed by Heaven to go and help the Dauphin ! " She almost always heard them while the chapel bells were ringing.

There is no doubt, now, that Joan believed she saw and heard these things. It is very well known that such delu-sions are a disease which is not by any means uncommon. It is probable enough that there were figures of Saint Michael, and Saint Catherine, and Saint Margaret, in the little chapel (where they would be very likely to have shining crowns upon their heads), and that they first gave Joan the idea of those three personages. She had long been a moping, fanciful girl, and, though she was a very good girl, I dare say she was a little vain, and wishful for notoriety.

Her father, something wiser than his neighbours, said, "I tell thee, Joan, it is thy fancy. Thou hadst better have a kind husband to take care of thee, girl, and work to employ thy mind!" But Joan told him in reply, that she had taken a vow never to have a husband, and that she must go as Heaven directed her, to help the Dauphin.

It happened, unfortunately for her father's persuasions, and most unfortunately for the poor girl, too, that a party of the Dauphin's enemies found their way into the village while Joan's disorder was at this point, and burnt the chapel, and drove out the inhabitants. The cruelties she saw committed, touched Joan's heart and made her worse. She said that the voices and the figures were now continually with her; that they told her she was the girl who, according to an old prophecy, was to deliver France; and she must go and help the Dauphin, and must remain with him until he should be crowned at Rheims: and that she must travel a long way to a certain lord named BAUDRICOURT, who could and would, bring her into the Dauphin's presence.

As her father still said, "I tell thee, Joan, it is thy fancy," she set off to find out this lord, accompanied by an uncle, a poor village wheelwright and cart-maker, who believed in the reality of her visions. They travelled a long way and went on and on, over a rough country, full of the Duke of Burgundy's men, and of all kinds of robbers and marauders, until they came to where this lord was.

When his servants told him that there was a poor peasant girl named Joan of Arc, accompanied by nobody but an old village wheelwright and cart-maker, who wished to see him because she was commanded to help the Dauphin and save France, Baudricourt burst out a-laughing, and bade them send the girl away. But, he soon heard so much about her lingering in the town, and praying in the churches, and seeing visions, and doing harm to no one, that he sent for her, and questioned her. As she said the same things after she had been well sprinkled with holy water as she had said before the sprinkling, Baudricourt began to think there might be something in it. At all events, he thought it worth while to send her on to the town of Chinon, where the Dauphin was. So, he bought her a horse, and a sword, and gave her two squires to conduct her. As the Voices had told Joan that she was to wear a man's dress, now, she put one on, and girded her sword to her side, and bound spurs to her heels, and mounted her horse and rode away with her two squires. As to her uncle the wheelwright, he stood staring at his niece in wonder until she was out of sight—as well he might—and then went home again. The best place, too.

Joan and her two squires rode on and on, until they came to Chinon, where she was, after some doubt, admitted into the Dauphin's presence. Picking him out immediately from all his court, she told him that she came commanded by Heaven to subdue his enemies and conduct him to his coronation at Rheims. She also told him (or he pretended so afterwards, to make the greater impression upon his soldiers) a number of his secrets known only to himself, and, furthermore, she said there was an old, old sword in the cathedral of Saint Catherine at Fierbois, marked with five old crosses on the blade, which Saint Catherine had ordered her to wear.

Now, nobody knew anything about this old, old sword, but when the cathedral came to be examined— which was immediately done — there, sure enough, the sword was found! The Dauphin then required a number of grave priests and bishops to give him their opinion whether the girl derived her power from good spirits or from evil spirits, which they held prodigiously long debates about, in the course of which several learned men fell fast asleep and snored loudly. At last, when one gruff old gentleman had said to Joan, "What language do your Voices speak?" and when Joan had replied to the gruff old gentleman, "A pleasanter language than yours," they agreed that it was all correct, and that Joan of Arc was inspired from Heaven. This wonderful circumstance put new heart into the Dauphin's soldiers when they heard of it, and dispirited the English army, who took Joan for a witch.

So Joan mounted horse again, and again rode on and on, until she came to Orleans. But she rode now, as never peasant girl had ridden yet. She rode upon a white war-horse, in a suit of glittering armour; with the old, old sword from the cathedral, newly burnished, in her belt; with a white flag carried before her, upon which were a picture of God, and the words JESUS MARIA. In this splendid state, at the head of a great body of troops escorting provisions of all kinds for the starving inhabitants of Orleans, she appeared before that beleaguered city.

When the people on the walls beheld her, they cried out "The Maid is come! The Maid of the Prophecy is come to deliver us!" And this, and the sight of the Maid fighting at the head of their men, made the French so bold, and made the English so fearful, that the English line of forts was soon broken, the troops and provisions were got into the town, and Orleans was saved.

Joan, henceforth called THE MAID OF ORLEANS, remained within the walls for a few days, and caused letters to be thrown over, ordering Lord Suffolk and his Englishmen to depart from before the town according to the will of Heaven. As the English general very positively declined to believe that Joan knew anything about the will of Heaven (which did not mend the matter with his soldiers, for they stupidly said if she were not inspired she was a witch, and it was of no use to fight against a witch), she mounted her white war-horse again, and ordered her white banner to advance.

The besiegers held the bridge, and some strong towers upon the bridge; and here the Maid of Orleans attacked them. The fight was fourteen hours long. She planted a scaling ladder with her own hands, and mounted a tower wall, but was struck by an English arrow in the neck, and fell into the trench. She was carried away and the arrow was taken out, during which operation she screamed and cried with the pain, as any other girl might have done; but presently she said that the Voices were speaking to her and soothing her to rest. After a while, she got up, and was again foremost in the fight. When the English who had seen her fall and supposed her dead, saw this, they were troubled with the strangest fears, and some of them cried out that they beheld Saint Michael on a white horse (probably Joan herself) fighting for the French. They lost the bridge, and lost the towers, and next day set their chain of forts on fire, and left the place.

But as Lord Suffolk himself retired no farther than the town of Jargeau, which was only a few miles off, the Maid of Orleans besieged him there, and he was taken prisoner. As the white banner scaled the wall, she was struck upon the head with a stone, and was again tumbled down into the ditch; but, she only cried all the more, as she lay there, "On, on, my countrymen! And fear nothing, for the Lord hath delivered them into our hands!" After this new

success of the Maid's, several other fortresses and places
which had previously held out against the Dauphin were
delivered up without a battle ; and at Patay she defeated
the remainder of the English army, and set up her victorious
white banner on a field where twelve hundred Englishmen
lay dead.

She now urged the Dauphin (who always kept out of the
way when there was any fighting) to proceed to Rheims,
as the first part of her mission was accomplished ; and to
complete the whole by being crowned there.   The Dauphin
was in no particular hurry to do this, as Rheims was a long
way off, and the English and the Duke of Burgundy were
still strong in the country through which the road lay.
However, they set forth, with ten thousand men, and again
the Maid of Orleans rode on and on, upon her white war-
horse, and in her shining armour.   Whenever they came to
a town which yielded readily, the soldiers believed in her;
but, whenever they came to a town which gave them any
trouble, they began to murmur that she was an impostor.
The latter was particularly the case at Troyes, which finally
yielded, however, through the persuasion of one Richard,
a friar of the place.   Friar Richard was in the old doubt
about the Maid of Orleans, until he had sprinkled her well
with holy water, and had also well sprinkled the threshold
of the gate by which she came into the city.   Finding that
it made no change in her or the gate, he said, as the other
grave old gentlemen had said, that it was all right, and
became her great ally.

So, at last, by dint of riding on and on, the Maid of
Orleans, and the Dauphin, and the ten thousand sometimes
believing and sometimes unbelieving men, came to Rheims.
And in the great cathedral of Rheims, the Dauphin actually
was crowned Charles the Seventh in a great assembly of the
people.   Then, the Maid, who with her white banner stood
beside the King in that hour of his triumph, kneeled down
upon the pavement at his feet, and said, with tears, that
what she had been inspired to do, was done, and that the
only recompense she asked for, was, that she should now
have leave to go back to her distant home, and her sturdily
incredulous father, and her first simple escort the village
wheelwright and cart-maker.   But the King said "No!"
and made her and her family as noble as a King could, and
settled upon her the income of a Count.

Ah! happy had it been for the Maid of Orleans, if she had resumed her rustic dress that day, and had gone home to the little chapel and the wild hills, and had forgotten all these things, and had been a good man's wife, and had heard no stranger voices than the voices of little children!

It was not to be, and she continued helping the King (she did a world for him, in alliance with Friar Richard), and trying to improve the lives of the coarse soldiers, and leading a religious, an unselfish, and a modest life, herself, beyond any doubt. Still, many times she prayed the King to let her go home; and once she even took off her bright armour and hung it up in a church, meaning never to wear it more. But, the King always won her back again—while she was of any use to him—and so she went on and on and on, to her doom.

When the Duke of Bedford, who was a very able man, began to be active for England, and, by bringing the war back into France and by holding the Duke of Burgundy to his faith, to distress and disturb Charles very much, Charles sometimes asked the Maid of Orleans what the Voices said about it? But, the Voices had become (very like ordinary voices in perplexed times) contradictory and confused, so that now they said one thing, and now said another, and the Maid lost credit every day. Charles marched on Paris, which was opposed to him, and attacked the suburb of Saint Honoré. In this fight, being again struck down into the ditch, she was abandoned by the whole army. She lay unaided among a heap of dead, and crawled out how she could. Then, some of her believers went over to an opposition Maid, Catherine of La Rochelle, who said she was inspired to tell where there were treasures of buried money—though she never did—and then Joan accidentally broke the old, old sword, and others said that her power was broken with it. Finally, at the siege of Compiègne, held by the Duke of Burgundy, where she did valiant service, she was basely left alone in a retreat, though facing about and fighting to the last; and an archer pulled her off her horse.

O the uproar that was made, and the thanksgivings that were sung, about the capture of this one poor country-girl! O the way in which she was demanded to be tried for sorcery and heresy, and anything else you like, by the Inquisitor-General of France, and by this great man, and

by that great man, until it is wearisome to think of! She
was bought at last by the Bishop of Beauvais for ten
thousand francs, and was shut up in her narrow prison:
plain Joan of Arc again, and Maid of Orleans no more.

I should never have done if I were to tell you how they
had Joan out to examine her, and cross-examine her, and
re-examine her, and worry her into saying anything and
everything; and how all sorts of scholars and doctors
bestowed their utmost tediousness upon her. Sixteen times
she was brought out and shut up again, and worried, and
entrapped, and argued with, until she was heart-sick of the
dreary business. On the last occasion of this kind she was
brought into a burial-place at Rouen, dismally decorated
with a scaffold, and a stake and faggots, and the executioner,
and a pulpit with a friar therein, and an awful sermon ready.
It is very affecting to know that even at that pass the poor
girl honoured the mean vermin of a King, who had so used
her for his purposes and so abandoned her; and, that while
she had been regardless of reproaches heaped upon herself,
she spoke out courageously for him.

It was natural in one so young to hold to life. To save
her life, she signed a declaration prepared for her—signed it
with a cross, for she couldn't write—that all her visions and
Voices had come from the Devil. Upon her recanting the
past, and protesting that she would never wear a man's
dress in future, she was condemned to imprisonment for
life, " on the bread of sorrow and the water of affliction."

But, on the bread of sorrow and the water of affliction,
the visions and the Voices soon returned. It was quite
natural that they should do so, for that kind of disease is
much aggravated by fasting, loneliness, and anxiety of mind.
It was not only got out of Joan that she considered herself
inspired again, but, she was taken in a man's dress, which
had been left—to entrap her—in her prison, and which she
put on, in her solitude; perhaps, in remembrance of her
past glories, perhaps, because the imaginary Voices told her.
For this relapse into the sorcery and heresy and anything
else you like, she was sentenced to be burnt to death. And,
in the market-place of Rouen, in the hideous dress which the
monks had invented for such spectacles; with priests and
bishops sitting in a gallery looking on, though some had the
Christian grace to go away, unable to endure the infamous
scene; this shrieking girl—last seen amidst the smoke and

fire, holding a crucifix between her hands; last heard, calling upon Christ—was burnt to ashes. They threw her ashes into the river Seine; but they will rise against her murderers on the last day.

From the moment of her capture, neither the French King nor one single man in all his court raised a finger to save her. It is no defence of them that they may have never really believed in her, or that they may have won her victories by their skill and bravery. The more they pretended to believe in her, the more they had caused her to believe in herself; and she had ever been true to them, ever brave, ever nobly devoted. But, it is no wonder, that they, who were in all things false to themselves, false to one another, false to their country, false to Heaven, false to Earth, should be monsters of ingratitude and treachery to a helpless peasant girl.

In the picturesque old town of Rouen, where weeds and grass grow high on the cathedral towers, and the venerable Norman streets are still warm in the blessed sunlight though the monkish fires that once gleamed horribly upon them have long grown cold, there is a statue of Joan of Arc, in the scene of her last agony, the square to which she has given its present name. I know some statues of modern times—even in the World's metropolis, I think—which commemorate less constancy, less earnestness, smaller claims upon the world's attention, and much greater impostors.

PART THE THIRD.

BAD deeds seldom prosper, happily for mankind; and the English cause gained no advantage from the cruel death of Joan of Arc. For a long time, the war went heavily on. The Duke of Bedford died; the alliance with the Duke of Burgundy was broken; and Lord Talbot became a great general on the English side in France. But, two of the consequences of wars are, Famine—because the people cannot peacefully cultivate the ground—and Pestilence, which comes of want, misery, and suffering. Both these horrors broke out in both countries, and lasted for two wretched years. Then, the war went on again, and came by slow degrees to be so badly conducted by the English government, that, within twenty years from the execution of the Maid of Orleans, of all the great French conquests, the town of Calais alone remained in English hands.

While these victories and defeats were taking place in the course of time, many strange things happened at home. The young King, as he grew up, proved to be very unlike his great father, and showed himself a miserable puny creature. There was no harm in him—he had a great aversion to shedding blood : which was something—but, he was a weak, silly, helpless young man, and a mere shuttlecock to the great lordly battledores about the Court.

Of these battledores, Cardinal Beaufort, a relation of the King, and the Duke of Gloucester, were at first the most powerful. The Duke of Gloucester had a wife, who was nonsensically accused of practising witchcraft to cause the King's death and lead to her husband's coming to the throne, he being the next heir. She was charged with having, by the help of a ridiculous old woman named Margery (who was called a witch), made a little waxen doll in the King's likeness, and put it before a slow fire that it might gradually melt away. It was supposed, in such cases, that the death of the person whom the doll was made to represent, was sure to happen. Whether the duchess was as ignorant as the rest of them, and really did make such a doll with such an intention, I don't know ; but, you and I know very well that she might have made a thousand dolls, if she had been stupid enough, and might have melted them all, without hurting the King or anybody else. However, she was tried for it, and so was old Margery, and so was one of the duke's chaplains, who was charged with having assisted them. Both he and Margery were put to death, and the duchess, after being taken on foot and bearing a lighted candle, three times round the City, as a penance, was imprisoned for life. The duke, himself, took all this pretty quietly, and made as little stir about the matter as if he were rather glad to be rid of the duchess.

But, he was not destined to keep himself out of trouble long. The royal shuttlecock being three-and-twenty, the battledores were very anxious to get him married. The Duke of Gloucester wanted him to marry a daughter of the Count of Armagnac ; but, the Cardinal and the Earl of Suffolk were all for MARGARET, the daughter of the King of Sicily, who they knew was a resolute ambitious woman and would govern the King as she chose. To make friends with this lady, the Earl of Suffolk, who went over to arrange the match, consented to accept her for the King's wife without any fortune, and even to give up the two most valuable possessions England then had in France. So, the marriage was arranged, on terms very advantageous to the lady; and Lord Suffolk brought her to England, and she was married at Westminster. On what pretence this queen and her party charged the Duke of Gloucester with high treason within a couple of years, it is impossible to make out, the matter is so confused; but, they pretended that the King's life was in danger, and they took the duke prisoner. A fortnight afterwards, he was found dead in bed (they said), and his body was shown to the people, and Lord Suffolk came in for the best part of his estates. You know by this time how strangely liable state prisoners were to sudden death.

If Cardinal Beaufort had any hand in this matter, it did him no good, for he died within six weeks; thinking it very hard and curious—at eighty years old!—that he could not live to be Pope.

This was the time when England had completed her loss of all her great French conquests. The people charged the loss principally upon the Earl of Suffolk, now a duke, who had made those easy terms about the Royal Marriage, and who, they believed, had even been bought by France. So he was impeached as a traitor, on a great number of charges, but chiefly on accusations of having aided the French King, and of designing to make his own son King of England. The Commons and the people being violent against him, the King was made (by his friends) to interpose to save him, by banishing him for five years, and proroguing the Parliament. The duke had much ado to escape from a London mob, two thousand strong, who lay in wait for him in St. Giles's fields; but, he got down to his own estates in Suffolk, and sailed away from Ipswich. Sailing across the Channel, he sent into Calais to know if he might land there; but, they kept his boat and men in the harbour, until an English ship, carrying a hundred and fifty men and called the Nicholas of the Tower, came alongside his little vessel, and ordered him on board. "Welcome, traitor, as men say," was the captain's grim and not very respectful salutation. He was kept on board, a prisoner, for eight-and-forty hours, and then a small boat appeared rowing toward the ship. As this boat came nearer, it was seen to have in it a block, a rusty sword, and an executioner in a black mask. The duke was handed down into it, and there his head was cut off with six strokes of the rusty sword. Then, the little boat rowed away to Dover beach, where the body was cast out, and left until the duchess claimed it. By whom, high in authority, this murder was committed, has never appeared. No one was ever punished for it.

There now arose in Kent an Irishman, who gave himself the name of Mortimer, but whose real name was JACK CADE. Jack, in imitation of Wat Tyler, though he was a very different and inferior sort of man, addressed the Kentish men upon their wrongs, occasioned by the bad government of England, among so many battledores and such a poor shuttlecock; and the Kentish men rose up to the number of twenty thousand. Their place of assembly was Blackheath, where, headed by Jack, they put forth two papers, which they called "The Complaint of the Commons of Kent," and "The Requests of the Captain of the Great Assembly in Kent." They then retired to Sevenoaks. The royal army coming up with them here, they beat it and killed their general. Then, Jack dressed himself in the dead general's armour, and led his men to London.

Jack passed into the City from Southwark, over the bridge, and entered it in triumph, giving the strictest orders to his men not to plunder. Having made a show of his forces there, while the citizens looked on quietly, he went back into Southwark in good order, and passed the night. Next day, he came back again, having got hold in the meantime of Lord Say, an unpopular nobleman. Says Jack to the Lord Mayor and judges: "Will you be so good as to make a tribunal in Guildhall, and try me this noble-man?" The court being hastily made, he was found guilty, and Jack and his men cut his head off on Cornhill. They also cut off the head of his son-in-law, and then went back in good order to Southwark again.

But, although the citizens could bear the beheading of an unpopular lord, they could not bear to have their houses pillaged. And it did so happen that Jack, after dinner— perhaps he had drunk a little too much—began to plunder the house where he lodged; upon which, of course, his men began to imitate him. Wherefore, the Londoners took counsel with Lord Scales, who had a thousand soldiers in the Tower; and defended London Bridge, and kept Jack and his people out. This advantage gained, it was resolved by divers great men to divide Jack's army in the old way, by making a great many promises on behalf of the state, that were never intended to be performed. This *did* divide them; some of Jack's men saying that they ought to take the conditions which were offered, and others saying that they ought not, for they were only a snare; some going home at once; others staying where they were; and all doubting and quarrelling among themselves.

Jack, who was in two minds about fighting or accepting a pardon, and who indeed did both, saw at last that there was nothing to expect from his men, and that it was very likely some of them would deliver him up and get a reward of a thousand marks, which was offered for his apprehension. So, after they had travelled and quarrelled all the way from Southwark to Blackheath, and from Blackheath to Rochester, he mounted a good horse and galloped away into Sussex. But, there galloped after him, on a better horse, one Alexander Iden, who came up with him, had a hard fight with him, and killed him. Jack's head was set aloft on London Bridge, with the face looking towards Blackheath, where he had raised his flag; and Alexander Iden got the thousand marks.

It is supposed by some, that the Duke of York, who had been removed from a high post abroad through the Queen's influence, and sent out of the way, to govern Ireland, was at the bottom of this rising of Jack and his men, because he wanted to trouble the government. He claimed (though not yet publicly) to have a better right to the throne than Henry of Lancaster, as one of the family of the Earl of March, whom Henry the Fourth had set aside. Touching this claim, which, being through female relationship, was not according to the usual descent, it is enough to say that Henry the Fourth was the free choice of the people and the Parliament, and that his family had now reigned undisputed for sixty years. The memory of Henry the Fifth was so famous, and the English people loved it so much, that the Duke of York's claim would, perhaps, never have been thought of (it would have been so hopeless) but for the unfortunate circumstance of the present King's being by this time quite an idiot, and the country very ill governed.

These two circumstances gave the Duke of York a power he could not otherwise have had.

Whether the Duke knew anything of Jack Cade, or not, he came over from Ireland while Jack's head was on London Bridge; being secretly advised that the Queen was setting up his enemy, the Duke of Somerset, against him. He went to Westminster, at the head of four thousand men, and on his knees before the King, represented to him the bad state of the country, and petitioned him to summon a Parliament to consider it. This the King promised. When the Parliament was summoned, the Duke of York accused the Duke of Somerset, and the Duke of Somerset accused the Duke of York; and, both in and out of Parliament, the followers of each party were full of violence and hatred towards the other. At length the Duke of York put himself at the head of a large force of his tenants, and, in arms, demanded the reformation of the Government. Being shut out of London, he encamped at Dartford, and the royal army encamped at Blackheath. According as either side triumphed, the Duke of York was arrested, or the Duke of Somerset was arrested. The trouble ended, for the moment, in the Duke of York renewing his oath of allegiance, and going in peace to one of his own castles.

Half a year afterwards the Queen gave birth to a son, who was very ill received by the people, and not believed to be the son of the King. It shows the Duke of York to have been a moderate man, unwilling to involve England in new troubles, that he did not take advantage of the general discontent at this time, but really acted for the public good. He was made a member of the cabinet, and the King being now so much worse that he could not be carried about and shown to the people with any decency, the duke was made Lord Protector of the kingdom, until the King should recover, or the Prince should come of age. At the same time the Duke of Somerset was committed to the Tower. So, now the Duke of Somerset was down, and the Duke of York was up. By the end of the year, however, the King recovered his memory and some spark of sense; upon which the Queen used her power—which recovered with him—to get the Protector disgraced, and her favourite released. So now the Duke of York was down, and the Duke of Somerset was up.

These ducal ups and downs gradually separated the whole

nation into the two parties of York and Lancaster, and led
to those terrible civil wars long known as the Wars of the
Red and White Roses, because the red rose was the badge
of the House of Lancaster, and the white rose was the
badge of the House of York.

The Duke of York, joined by some other powerful noblemen of the White Rose party, and leading a small army,
met the King with another small army at St. Alban's, and
demanded that the Duke of Somerset should be given up.
The poor King, being made to say in answer that he would
sooner die, was instantly attacked. The Duke of Somerset
was killed, and the King himself was wounded in the neck,
and took refuge in the house of a poor tanner. Whereupon,
the Duke of York went to him, led him with great submission to the Abbey, and said he was very sorry for what
had happened. Having now the King in his possession, he
got a Parliament summoned and himself once more made
Protector, but, only for a few months; for, on the King
getting a little better again, the Queen and her party got
him into their possession, and disgraced the Duke once
more. So, now the Duke of York was down again.

Some of the best men in power, seeing the danger of these
constant changes, tried even then to prevent the Red and
the White Rose Wars. They brought about a great council
in London between the two parties. The White Roses
assembled in Blackfriars, the Red Roses in Whitefriars;
and some good priests communicated between them, and
made the proceedings known at evening to the King and
the judges. They ended in a peaceful agreement that there
should be no more quarrelling; and there was a great royal
procession to St. Paul's, in which the Queen walked arm-in-
arm with her old enemy, the Duke of York, to show the
people how comfortable they all were. This state of peace
lasted half a year, when a dispute between the Earl of
Warwick (one of the Duke's powerful friends) and some
of the King's servants at Court, led to an attack upon that
Earl—who was a White Rose—and to a sudden breaking
out of all old animosities. So, here were greater ups and
downs than ever.

There were even greater ups and downs than these, soon
after. After various battles, the Duke of York fled to
Ireland, and his son the Earl of March to Calais, with
their friends the Earls of Salisbury and Warwick; and

a Parliament was held declaring them all traitors. Little the worse for this, the Earl of Warwick presently came back, landed in Kent, was joined by the Archbishop of Canterbury and other powerful noblemen and gentlemen, engaged the King's forces at Northampton, signally defeated them, and took the King himself prisoner, who was found in his tent. Warwick would have been glad, I dare say, to have taken the Queen and Prince too, but they escaped into Wales and thence into Scotland.

The King was carried by the victorious force straight to London, and made to call a new Parliament, which immediately declared that the Duke of York and those other noblemen were not traitors, but excellent subjects. Then, back comes the Duke from Ireland at the head of five hundred horsemen, rides from London to Westminster, and enters the House of Lords. There, he laid his hand upon the cloth of gold which covered the empty throne, as if he had half a mind to sit down in it—but he did not. On the Archbishop of Canterbury asking him if he would visit the King, who was in his palace close by, he replied, "I know no one in this country, my lord, who ought not to visit *me*." None of the lords present, spoke a single word; so, the duke went out as he had come in, established himself royally in the King's palace, and, six days afterwards, sent in to the Lords a formal statement of his claim to the throne. The lords went to the King on this momentous subject, and after a great deal of discussion, in which the judges and the other law officers were afraid to give an opinion on either side, the question was compromised. It was agreed that the present King should retain the crown for his life, and that it should then pass to the Duke of York and his heirs.

But, the resolute Queen, determined on asserting her son's right, would hear of no such thing. She came from Scotland to the north of England, where several powerful lords armed in her cause. The Duke of York, for his part, set off with some five thousand men, a little time before Christmas Day, one thousand four hundred and sixty, to give her battle. He lodged at Sandal Castle, near Wakefield, and the Red Roses defied him to come out on Wakefield Green, and fight them then and there. His generals said, he had best wait until his gallant son, the Earl of March, came up with his power; but, he was determined to accept the challenge. He did so, in an evil hour. He was hotly pressed on all sides, two thousand of his men lay dead on Wakefield Green, and he himself was taken prisoner. They set him down in mock state on an ant-hill, and twisted grass about his head, and pretended to pay court to him on their knees, saying, " O King, without a kingdom, and Prince without a people, we hope your gracious Majesty is very well and happy ! " They did worse than this ; they cut his head off, and handed it on a pole to the Queen, who laughed with delight when she saw it (you recollect their walking so religiously and comfortably to St. Paul's !), and had it fixed, with a paper crown upon its head, on the walls of York. The Earl of Salisbury lost his head, too ; and the Duke of York's second son, a handsome boy who was flying with his tutor over Wakefield Bridge, was stabbed in the heart by a murderous lord—Lord Clifford by name—whose father had been killed by the White Roses in the fight at St. Alban's. There was awful sacrifice of life in this battle, for no quarter was given, and the Queen was wild for revenge. When men unnaturally fight against their own countrymen, they are always observed to be more unnaturally cruel and filled with rage than they are against any other enemy.

But, Lord Clifford had stabbed the second son of the Duke of York—not the first. The eldest son, Edward Earl of March, was at Gloucester ; and, vowing vengeance for the death of his father, his brother, and their faithful friends, he began to march against the Queen. He had to turn and fight a great body of Welsh and Irish first, who worried his advance. These he defeated in a great fight at Mortimer's Cross, near Hereford, where he beheaded a number of the Red Roses taken in battle, in retaliation for the beheading of the White Roses at Wakefield. The Queen had the next turn of beheading. Having moved towards London, and falling in, between St. Alban's and Barnet, with the Earl of Warwick and the Duke of Norfolk, White Roses both, who were there with an army to oppose her, and had got the King with them ; she defeated them with great loss, and struck off the heads of two prisoners of note, who were in the King's tent with him, and to whom the King had promised his protection. Her triumph, however, was very short. She had no treasure, and her army subsisted by plunder. This caused them to be hated and dreaded by the people, and particularly by the London people, who were

wealthy. As soon as the Londoners heard that Edward,
Earl of March, united with the Earl of Warwick, was advancing towards the city, they refused to send the Queen
supplies, and made a great rejoicing.

The Queen and her men retreated with all speed, and
Edward and Warwick came on, greeted with loud acclamations on every side. The courage, beauty, and virtues of
young Edward could not be sufficiently praised by the whole
people. He rode into London like a conqueror, and met
with an enthusiastic welcome. A few days afterwards, Lord
Falconbridge and the Bishop of Exeter assembled the citizens
in St. John's Field, Clerkenwell, and asked them if they
would have Henry of Lancaster for their King? To this
they all roared, " No, no, no ! " and " King Edward ! King
Edward ! " Then, said those noblemen, would they love
and serve young Edward ? To this they all cried, " Yes,
yes ! " and threw up their caps and clapped their hands,
and cheered tremendously.

Therefore, it was declared that by joining the Queen and
not protecting those two prisoners of note, Henry of Lancaster had forfeited the crown ; and Edward of York was
proclaimed King. He made a great speech to the applauding
people at Westminster, and sat down as sovereign of England
on that throne, on the golden covering of which his father
—worthy of a better fate than the bloody axe which cut
the thread of so many lives in England, through so many
years—had laid his hand.

CHAPTER XXIII

ENGLAND UNDER EDWARD THE FOURTH

KING EDWARD THE FOURTH was not quite twenty-one years of age when he took that unquiet seat upon the throne of England. The Lancaster party, the Red Roses, were then assembling in great numbers near York, and it was necessary to give them battle instantly. But, the stout Earl of Warwick leading for the young King, and the young King himself closely following him, and the English people crowding round the Royal standard, the White and the Red Roses met, on a wild March day when the snow was falling heavily, at Towton; and there such a furious battle raged between them, that the total loss amounted to forty thousand men—all Englishmen, fighting, upon English ground, against one another. The young King gained the day, took down the heads of his father and brother from the walls of York, and put up the heads of some of the most famous noblemen engaged in the battle on the other side. Then, he went to London and was crowned with great splendour.

A new Parliament met. No fewer than one hundred and fifty of the principal noblemen and gentlemen on the Lancaster side were declared traitors, and the King—who had very little humanity, though he was handsome in person and agreeable in manners—resolved to do all he could, to pluck up the Red Rose root and branch.

Queen Margaret, however, was still active for her young son. She obtained help from Scotland and from Normandy, and took several important English castles. But, Warwick soon retook them; the Queen lost all her treasure on board ship in a great storm; and both she and her son suffered great misfortunes. Once, in the winter weather, as they were riding through a forest, they were attacked and plundered by a party of robbers; and, when they had escaped from these men and were passing alone and on foot through

Queen Margaret and the Robbers

a thick dark part of the wood, they came, all at once, upon
another robber. So the Queen, with a stout heart, took the
little Prince by the hand, and going straight up to that
robber, said to him, "My friend, this is the young son of
your lawful King! I confide him to your care." The robber
was surprised, but took the boy in his arms, and faithfully
restored him and his mother to their friends. In the end,
the Queen's soldiers being beaten and dispersed, she went
abroad again, and kept quiet for the present.

Now, all this time, the deposed King Henry was concealed
by a Welsh knight, who kept him close in his castle. But,
next year, the Lancaster party recovering their spirits, raised
a large body of men, and called him out of his retirement,
to put him at their head. They were joined by some powerful noblemen who had sworn fidelity to the new King, but
who were ready, as usual, to break their oaths, whenever
they thought there was anything to be got by it. One of
the worst things in the history of the war of the Red and
White Roses, is the ease with which these noblemen, who
should have set an example of honour to the people, left
either side as they took slight offence, or were disappointed
in their greedy expectations, and joined the other. Well!
Warwick's brother soon beat the Lancastrians, and the false
noblemen, being taken, were beheaded without a moment's
loss of time. The deposed King had a narrow escape;
three of his servants were taken, and one of them bore his
cap of estate, which was set with pearls and embroidered
with two golden crowns. However, the head to which the
cap belonged, got safely into Lancashire, and lay pretty
quietly there (the people in the secret being very true) for
more than a year. At length, an old monk gave such intelligence as led to Henry's being taken while he was sitting
at dinner in a place called Waddington Hall. He was immediately sent to London, and met at Islington by the Earl
of Warwick, by whose directions he was put upon a horse,
with his legs tied under it, and paraded three times round
the pillory. Then, he was carried off to the Tower, where
they treated him well enough.

The White Rose being so triumphant, the young King
abandoned himself entirely to pleasure, and led a jovial life.
But, thorns were springing up under his bed of roses, as he
soon found out. For, having been privately married to
ELIZABETH WOODVILLE, a young widow lady, very beautiful

and very captivating; and at last resolving to make his secret known, and to declare her his Queen; he gave some offence to the Earl of Warwick, who was usually called the King-Maker, because of his power and influence, and because of his having lent such great help to placing Edward on the throne. This offence was not lessened by the jealousy with which the Nevil family (the Earl of Warwick's) regarded the promotion of the Woodville family. For, the young Queen was so bent on providing for her relations, that she made her father an earl and a great officer of state; married her five sisters to young noblemen of the highest rank; and provided for her younger brother, a young man of twenty, by marrying him to an immensely rich old duchess of eighty. The Earl of Warwick took all this pretty graciously for a man of his proud temper, until the question arose to whom the King's sister, MARGARET, should be married. The Earl of Warwick said, "To one of the French King's sons," and was allowed to go over to the French King to make friendly proposals for that purpose, and to hold all manner of friendly interviews with him. But, while he was so engaged, the Woodville party married the young lady to the Duke of Burgundy! Upon this he came back in great rage and scorn, and shut himself up discontented, in his Castle of Middleham.

A reconciliation, though not a very sincere one, was patched up between the Earl of Warwick and the King, and lasted until the Earl married his daughter, against the King's wishes, to the Duke of Clarence. While the marriage was being celebrated at Calais, the people in the north of England where the influence of the Nevil family was strongest, broke out into rebellion; their complaint was, that England was oppressed and plundered by the Woodville family, whom they demanded to have removed from power. As they were joined by great numbers of people, and as they openly declared that they were supported by the Earl of Warwick, the King did not know what to do. At last, as he wrote to the Earl beseeching his aid, he and his new son-in-law came over to England, and began to arrange the business by shutting the King up in Middleham Castle in the safe keeping of the Archbishop of York; so England was not only in the strange position of having two kings at once, but they were both prisoners at the same time.

Even as yet, however, the King-Maker was so far true to the King, that he dispersed a new rising of the Lancastrians, took their leader prisoner, and brought him to the King, who ordered him to be immediately executed. He presently allowed the King to return to London, and there innumerable pledges of forgiveness and friendship were exchanged between them, and between the Nevils and the Woodvilles ; the King's eldest daughter was promised in marriage to the heir of the Nevil family ; and more friendly oaths were sworn, and more friendly promises made, than this book would hold.

They lasted about three months. At the end of that time, the Archbishop of York made a feast for the King, the Earl of Warwick, and the Duke of Clarence, at his house, the Moor, in Hertfordshire. The King was washing his hands before supper, when some one whispered him that a body of a hundred men were lying in ambush outside the house. Whether this were true or untrue, the King took fright, mounted his horse, and rode through the dark night to Windsor Castle. Another reconciliation was patched up between him and the King-Maker, but it was a short one, and it was the last. A new rising took place in Lincolnshire, and the King marched to repress it. Having done so, he proclaimed that both the Earl of Warwick and the Duke of Clarence were traitors, who had secretly assisted it, and who had been prepared publicly to join it on the following day. In these dangerous circumstances they both took ship and sailed away to the French court.

And here a meeting took place between the Earl of Warwick and his old enemy, the Dowager Queen Margaret, through whom his father had had his head struck off, and to whom he had been a bitter foe. But, now, when he said that he had done with the ungrateful and perfidious Edward of York, and that henceforth he devoted himself to the restoration of the House of Lancaster, either in the person of her husband or of her little son, she embraced him as if he had ever been her dearest friend. She did more than that ; she married her son to his second daughter, the Lady Anne. However agreeable this marriage was to the new friends, it was very disagreeable to the Duke of Clarence, who perceived that his father-in-law, the King-Maker, would never make *him* King, now. So, being but a weak-minded young traitor, possessed of very little worth or sense, he readily listened to an artful court lady sent over for the purpose, and promised to turn traitor once more, and go over to his brother, King Edward, when a fitting opportunity should come.

The Earl of Warwick, knowing nothing of this, soon redeemed his promise to the Dowager Queen Margaret, by invading England and landing at Plymouth, where he instantly proclaimed King Henry, and summoned all Englishmen between the ages of sixteen and sixty, to join his banner. Then, with his army increasing as he marched along, he went northward, and came so near King Edward, who was in that part of the country, that Edward had to ride hard for it to the coast of Norfolk, and thence to get away in such ships as he could find, to Holland. Thereupon, the triumphant King-Maker and his false son-in-law, the Duke of Clarence, went to London, took the old King out of the Tower, and walked him in a great procession to Saint Paul's Cathedral with the crown upon his head. This did not improve the temper of the Duke of Clarence, who saw himself farther off from being King than ever ; but he kept his secret, and said nothing. The Nevil family were restored to all their honours and glories, and the Woodvilles and the rest were disgraced. The King-Maker, less sanguinary than the King, shed no blood except that of the Earl of Worcester, who had been so cruel to the people as to have gained the title of the Butcher. Him they caught hidden in a tree, and him they tried and executed. No other death stained the King-Maker's triumph.

To dispute this triumph, back came King Edward again, next year, landing at Ravenspur, coming on to York, causing all his men to cry "Long live King Henry!" and swearing on the altar, without a blush, that he came to lay no claim to the crown. Now was the time for the Duke of Clarence, who ordered his men to assume the White Rose, and declare for his brother. The Marquis of Montague, though the Earl of Warwick's brother, also declining to fight against King Edward, he went on successfully to London, where the Archbishop of York let him into the City, and where the people made great demonstrations in his favour. For this they had four reasons. Firstly, there were great numbers of the King's adherents hiding in the City and ready to break out ; secondly, the King owed them a great deal of money, which they could never hope to get if he were unsuccessful ; thirdly, there was a young prince to inherit the crown ; and fourthly, the King was gay and handsome, and more popular than a better man might have been with the City ladies. After a stay of only two days with these worthy supporters, the King marched out to Barnet Common, to give the Earl of Warwick battle. And now it was to be seen, for the last time, whether the King or the King-Maker was to carry the day.

While the battle was yet pending, the faint-hearted Duke of Clarence began to repent, and sent over secret messages to his father-in-law, offering his services in mediation with the King. But, the Earl of Warwick disdainfully rejected them, and replied that Clarence was false and perjured, and that he would settle the quarrel by the sword. The battle began at four o'clock in the morning and lasted until ten, and during the greater part of the time it was fought in a thick mist—absurdly supposed to be raised by a magician. The loss of life was very great, for the hatred was strong on both sides. The King-Maker was defeated, and the King triumphed. Both the Earl of Warwick and his brother were slain, and their bodies lay in St. Paul's, for some days, as a spectacle to the people.

Margaret's spirit was not broken even by this great blow. Within five days she was in arms again, and raised her standard in Bath, whence she set off with her army, to try and join Lord Pembroke, who had a force in Wales. But, the King, coming up with her outside the town of Tewkesbury, and ordering his brother, the DUKE OF GLOUCESTER, who was a brave soldier, to attack her men, she sustained an entire defeat, and was taken prisoner, together with her son, now only eighteen years of age. The conduct of the King to this poor youth was worthy of his cruel character. He ordered him to be led into his tent. "And what," said he, "brought you to England?" "I came to England," replied the prisoner, with a spirit which a man of spirit might have admired in a captive, "to recover my father's kingdom, which descended to him as his right, and from him descends to me, as mine." The King, drawing off his iron gauntlet, struck him with it in the face ; and the Duke of Clarence and some other lords, who were there, drew their noble swords, and killed him.

His mother survived him, a prisoner, for five years ; after her ransom by the King of France, she survived for six years more. Within three weeks of this murder, Henry died one of those convenient sudden deaths which were so common in the Tower; in plainer words, he was murdered by the King's order.

Having no particular excitement on his hands after this great defeat of the Lancaster party, and being perhaps desirous to get rid of some of his fat (for he was now getting too corpulent to be handsome), the King thought of making war on France. As he wanted more money for this purpose than the Parliament could give him, though they were usually ready enough for war, he invented a new way of raising it, by sending for the principal citizens of London, and telling them, with a grave face, that he was very much in want of cash, and would take it very kind in them if they would lend him some. It being impossible for them safely to refuse, they complied, and the moneys thus forced from them were called—no doubt to the great amusement of the King and the Court—as if they were free gifts, "Benevolences." What with grants from Parliament, and what with Benevolences, the King raised an army and passed over to Calais. As nobody wanted war, however, the French King made proposals of peace, which were accepted, and a truce was concluded for seven long years. The proceedings between the Kings of France and England on this occasion, were very friendly, very splendid, and very distrustful. They finished with a meeting between the two Kings, on a temporary bridge over the river Somme, where they embraced through two holes in a strong wooden grating like a lion's cage, and made several bows and fine speeches to one another.

It was time, now, that the Duke of Clarence should be punished for his treacheries; and Fate had his punishment in store. He was, probably, not trusted by the King—for who could trust him who knew him!—and he had certainly a powerful opponent in his brother Richard, Duke of Gloucester, who, being avaricious and ambitious, wanted to marry that widowed daughter of the Earl of Warwick's who had been espoused to the deceased young Prince, at Calais. Clarence, who wanted all the family wealth for himself, secreted this lady, whom Richard found disguised as a servant in the City of London, and whom he married; arbitrators appointed by the King, then divided the property between the brothers. This led to ill-will and mistrust between them. Clarence's wife dying, and he wishing to make another marriage, which was obnoxious to the King, his ruin was hurried by that means, too. At first, the Court struck at his retainers and dependents, and accused some of them of magic and witchcraft, and similar nonsense. Successful against this small game, it then mounted to the Duke himself, who was impeached by his brother the King, in person, on a variety of such charges. He was found guilty, and sentenced to be publicly executed. He never was publicly executed, but he met his death somehow, in the Tower, and, no doubt, through some agency of the King or his brother Gloucester, or both. It was supposed at the time that he was told to choose the manner of his death, and that he chose to be drowned in a butt of Malmsey wine. I hope the story may be true, for it would have been a becoming death for such a miserable creature.

The King survived him some five years. He died in the forty-second year of his life, and the twenty-third of his reign. He had a very good capacity and some good points, but he was selfish, careless, sensual, and cruel. He was a favourite with the people for his showy manners; and the people were a good example to him in the constancy of their attachment. He was penitent on his death-bed for his " Benevolences," and other extortions, and ordered restitution to be made to the people who had suffered from them. He also called about his bed the enriched members of the Woodville family, and the proud lords whose honours were of older date, and endeavoured to reconcile them, for the sake of the peaceful succession of his son and the tranquillity of England.

CHAPTER XXIV

ENGLAND UNDER EDWARD THE FIFTH

THE late King's eldest son, the Prince of Wales, called EDWARD after him, was only thirteen years of age at his father's death. He was at Ludlow Castle with his uncle, the Earl of Rivers. The prince's brother, the Duke of York, only eleven years of age, was in London with his mother. The boldest, most crafty, and most dreaded nobleman in England at that time was their uncle RICHARD, Duke of Gloucester, and everybody wondered how the two poor boys would fare with such an uncle for a friend or a foe.

The Queen, their mother, being exceedingly uneasy about this, was anxious that instructions should be sent to Lord Rivers to raise an army to escort the young King safely to London. But, Lord Hastings, who was of the Court party opposed to the Woodvilles, and who disliked the thought of giving them that power, argued against the proposal, and obliged the Queen to be satisfied with an escort of two thousand horse. The Duke of Gloucester did nothing, at first, to justify suspicion. He came from Scotland (where he was commanding an army) to York, and was there the first to swear allegiance to his nephew. He then wrote a condoling letter to the Queen-Mother, and set off to be present at the coronation in London.

Now, the young King, journeying towards London too, with Lord Rivers and Lord Gray, came to Stony Stratford, as his uncle came to Northampton, about ten miles distant; and when those two lords heard that the Duke of Gloucester was so near, they proposed to the young King that they should go back and greet him in his name. The boy being very willing that they should do so, they rode off and were received with great friendliness, and asked by the Duke of Gloucester to stay and dine with him. In the evening, while they were merry together, up came the Duke of Buckingham with three hundred horsemen; and next morning the two lords and the two dukes, and the three hundred horsemen, rode away together to rejoin the King. Just as they were entering Stony Stratford, the Duke of Gloucester, checking his horse, turned suddenly on the two lords, charged them with alienating from him the affections of his sweet nephew, and caused them to be arrested by the three hundred horsemen and taken back. Then, he and the Duke of Buckingham went straight to the King (whom they had now in their power), to whom they made a show of kneeling down, and offering great love and submission; and then they ordered his attendants to disperse, and took him, alone with them, to Northampton.

A few days afterwards they conducted him to London, and lodged him in the Bishop's Palace. But, he did not remain there long; for, the Duke of Buckingham with a tender face made a speech expressing how anxious he was for the Royal boy's safety, and how much safer he would be in the Tower until his coronation, than he could be any-where else. So, to the Tower he was taken, very carefully, and the Duke of Gloucester was named Protector of the State.

Although Gloucester had proceeded thus far with a very smooth countenance—and although he was a clever man, fair of speech, and not ill-looking, in spite of one of his shoulders being something higher than the other—and although he had come into the City riding bare-headed at the King's side, and looking very fond of him—he had made the King's mother more uneasy yet; and when the Royal boy was taken to the Tower, she became so alarmed that she took sanctuary in Westminster with her five daughters.

Nor did she do this without reason, for, the Duke of Gloucester, finding that the lords who were opposed to the Woodville family were faithful to the young King never-theless, quickly resolved to strike a blow for himself. Accordingly, while those lords met in council at the Tower, he and those who were in his interest met in separate council at his own residence, Crosby Palace, in Bishopsgate Street. Being at last quite prepared, he one day appeared unexpectedly at the council in the Tower, and appeared to be very jocular and merry. He was particularly gay with the Bishop of Ely: praising the strawberries that grew in his garden on Holborn Hill, and asking him to have some gathered that he might eat them at dinner. The Bishop, quite proud of the honour, sent one of his men to fetch some ; and the Duke, still very jocular and gay, went out ; and the council all said what a very agreeable duke he was ! In a little time, however, he came back quite altered—not at all jocular—frowning and fierce—and suddenly said,—

" What do those persons deserve who have compassed my destruction ; I being the King's lawful, as well as natural, protector ? "

To this strange question, Lord Hastings replied, that they deserved death, whosoever they were.

" Then," said the Duke, " I tell you that they are that sorceress my brother's wife ; " meaning the Queen : " and that other sorceress, Jane Shore. Who, by witchcraft, have withered my body, and caused my arm to shrink as I now show you."

He then pulled up his sleeve and showed them his arm, which was shrunken, it is true, but which had been so, as they all very well knew, from the hour of his birth.

Jane Shore, being then the lover of Lord Hastings, as she had formerly been of the late King, that lord knew that he himself was attacked. So, he said, in some confusion, " Certainly, my Lord, if they have done this, they be worthy of punishment."

" If ? " said the Duke of Gloucester ; " do you talk to me of ifs ? I tell you that they *have* so done, and I will make it good upon thy body, thou traitor ! "

With that, he struck the table a great blow with his fist. This was a signal to some of his people outside to cry " Treason ! " They immediately did so, and there was a rush into the chamber of so many armed men that it was filled in a moment.

" First," said the Duke of Gloucester to Lord Hastings, " I arrest thee, traitor ! And let him," he added to the armed men who took him, " have a priest at once, for by St. Paul I will not dine until I have seen his head off ! "

Lord Hastings was hurried to the green by the Tower chapel, and there beheaded on a log of wood that happened to be lying on the ground. Then, the Duke dined with a good appetite, and after dinner summoning the principal citizens to attend him, told them that Lord Hastings and the rest had designed to murder both himself and the Duke of Buckingham, who stood by his side, if he had not providentially discovered their design. He requested them to be so obliging as to inform their fellow-citizens of the truth of what he said, and issued a proclamation (prepared and neatly copied out beforehand) to the same effect.

On the same day that the Duke did these things in the Tower, Sir Richard Ratcliffe, the boldest and most undaunted of his men, went down to Pontefract; arrested Lord Rivers, Lord Gray, and two other gentlemen; and publicly executed them on the scaffold, without any trial, for having intended the Duke's death. Three days afterwards the Duke, not to lose time, went down the river to Westminster in his barge, attended by divers bishops, lords, and soldiers, and demanded that the Queen should deliver her second son, the Duke of York, into his safe keeping. The Queen, being obliged to comply, resigned the child after she had wept over him; and Richard of Gloucester placed him with his brother in the Tower. Then, he seized Jane Shore, and, because she had been the lover of the late King, confiscated her property, and got her sentenced to do public penance in the streets by walking in a scanty dress, with bare feet, and carrying a lighted candle, to St. Paul's Cathedral, through the most crowded part of the City.

Having now all things ready for his own advancement, he caused a friar to preach a sermon at the cross which stood in front of St. Paul's Cathedral, in which he dwelt upon the profligate manners of the late King, and upon the late shame of Jane Shore, and hinted that the princes were not his children. "Whereas, good people," said the friar, whose name was SHAW, "my Lord the Protector, the noble Duke of Gloucester, that sweet prince, the pattern of all the noblest virtues, is the perfect image and express likeness of his father." There had been a little plot between the Duke and the friar, that the Duke should appear in the crowd at this moment, when it was expected that the people would cry "Long live King Richard!" But, either through the friar saying the words too soon, or through the Duke's coming too late, the Duke and the words did not come together, and the people only laughed, and the friar sneaked off ashamed.

The Duke of Buckingham was a better hand at such business than the friar, so he went to the Guildhall the next day, and addressed the citizens in the Lord Protector's behalf. A few dirty men, who had been hired and stationed there for the purpose, crying when he had done, "God save King Richard!" he made them a great bow, and thanked them with all his heart. Next day, to make an end of it, he went with the mayor and some lords and citizens to Bayard Castle, by the river, where Richard then was, and read an address, humbly entreating him to accept the Crown of England. Richard, who looked down upon them out of a window and pretended to be in great uneasiness and alarm, assured them there was nothing he desired less, and that his deep affection for his nephews forbade him to think of it. To this the Duke of Buckingham replied, with pretended warmth, that the free people of England would never submit to his nephew's rule, and that if Richard, who was the lawful heir, refused the Crown, why then they must find some one else to wear it. The Duke of Gloucester returned, that since he used that strong language, it became his painful duty to think no more of himself, and to accept the Crown.

Upon that, the people cheered and dispersed; and the Duke of Gloucester and the Duke of Buckingham passed a pleasant evening, talking over the play they had just acted with so much success, and every word of which they had prepared together.

CHAPTER XXV

ENGLAND UNDER RICHARD THE THIRD

KING RICHARD THE THIRD was up betimes in the morning, and went to Westminster Hall. In the Hall was a marble seat, upon which he sat himself down between two great noblemen, and told the people that he began the new reign in that place, because the first duty of a sovereign was to administer the laws equally to all, and to maintain justice. He then mounted his horse and rode back to the City, where he was received by the clergy and the crowd as if he really had a right to the throne, and really were a just man. The clergy and the crowd must have been rather ashamed of themselves in secret, I think, for being such poor-spirited knaves.

The new King and his Queen were soon crowned with a great deal of show and noise, which the people liked very much; and then the King set forth on a royal progress through his dominions. He was crowned a second time at York, in order that the people might have show and noise enough; and wherever he went was received with shouts of rejoicing—from a good many people of strong lungs, who were paid to strain their throats in crying, "God save King Richard!" The plan was so successful that I am told it has been imitated since, by other usurpers, in other progresses through other dominions.

While he was on this journey, King Richard stayed a week at Warwick. And from Warwick he sent instructions home for one of the wickedest murders that ever was done—the murder of the two young princes, his nephews, who were shut up in the Tower of London.

Sir Robert Brackenbury was at that time Governor of the Tower. To him, by the hands of a messenger named JOHN GREEN, did King Richard send a letter, ordering him by some means to put the two young princes to death. But Sir Robert—I hope because he had children of his own, and loved them—sent John Green back again, riding and spurring along the dusty roads, with the answer that he could not do so horrible a piece of work. The King, having frowningly considered a little, called to him SIR JAMES TYRREL, his master of the horse, and to him gave authority to take command of the Tower, whenever he would, for twenty-four hours, and to keep all the keys of the Tower during that space of time. Tyrrel, well knowing what was wanted, looked about him for two hardened ruffians, and chose JOHN DIGHTON, one of his own grooms, and MILES FOREST, who was a murderer by trade. Having secured these two assistants, he went, upon a day in August, to the Tower, showed his authority from the King, took the command for four-and-twenty hours, and obtained possession of the keys. And when the black night came, he went creeping, creeping, like a guilty villain as he was, up the dark stone winding stairs, and along the dark stone passages, until he came to the door of the room where the two young princes, having said their prayers, lay fast asleep, clasped in each other's arms. And while he watched and listened at the door, he sent in those evil demons, John Dighton and Miles Forest, who smothered the two princes with the bed and pillows, and carried their bodies down the stairs, and buried them under a great heap of stones at the staircase foot. And when the day came, he gave up the command of the Tower, and restored the keys, and hurried away without once looking behind him ; and Sir Robert Brackenbury went with fear and sadness to the princes' room, and found the princes gone for ever.

You know, through all this history, how true it is that traitors are never true, and you will not be surprised to learn that the Duke of Buckingham soon turned against King Richard, and joined a great conspiracy that was formed to dethrone him, and to place the crown upon its rightful owner's head. Richard had meant to keep the murder secret ; but when he heard through his spies that this conspiracy existed, and that many lords and gentlemen drank in secret to the healths of the two young princes in the Tower, he made it known that they were dead. The conspirators, though thwarted for a moment, soon resolved to set up for the crown against the murderous Richard, HENRY Earl of Richmond, grandson of Catherine : that widow of Henry the Fifth who married Owen Tudor. And as Henry was of the house of Lancaster, they proposed that he should marry the Princess Elizabeth, the eldest daughter of the late King, now the heiress of the house of York, and thus by uniting the rival families put an end to the fatal wars of the Red and White Roses. All being settled, a time was appointed for Henry to come over from Brittany, and for a great rising against Richard to take place in several parts of England at the same hour. On a certain day, therefore, in October, the revolt took place ; but unsuccessfully. Richard was prepared, Henry was driven back at sea by a storm, his followers in England were dispersed, and the Duke of Buckingham was taken, and at once beheaded in the market-place at Salisbury.

The time of his success was a good time, Richard thought, for summoning a Parliament and getting some money. So, a Parliament was called, and it flattered and fawned upon him as much as he could possibly desire, and declared him to be the rightful King of England, and his only son Edward, then eleven years of age, the next heir to the throne.

Richard knew full well that, let the Parliament say what it would, the Princess Elizabeth was remembered by people as the heiress of the house of York ; and having accurate information besides, of its being designed by the conspirators to marry her to Henry of Richmond, he felt that it would much strengthen him and weaken them, to be beforehand with them, and marry her to his son. With this view he went to the Sanctuary at Westminster, where the late King's widow and her daughter still were, and besought them to come to Court ; where (he swore by anything and everything) they should be safely and honourably entertained. They came, accordingly, but had scarcely been at Court a month when his son died suddenly—or was poisoned—and his plan was crushed to pieces.

In this extremity, King Richard, always active, thought, " I must make another plan." And he made the plan of marrying the Princess Elizabeth himself, although she was his niece. There was one difficulty in the way : his wife, the Queen Anne, was alive. But, he knew (remembering his nephews) how to remove that obstacle, and he made love to the Princess Elizabeth, telling her he felt perfectly confident that the Queen would die in February. The Princess was not a very scrupulous young lady, for, instead

of rejecting the murderer of her brothers with scorn and
hatred, she openly declared she loved him dearly; and,
when February came and the Queen did not die, she expressed her impatient opinion that she was too long about
it. However, King Richard was not so far out in his prediction, but that she died in March—he took good care of
that—and then this precious pair hoped to be married. But
they were disappointed, for the idea of such a marriage was
so unpopular in the country, that the King's chief counsellors, RATCLIFFE and CATESBY, would by no means undertake to propose it, and the King was even obliged to declare
in public that he had never thought of such a thing.

He was, by this time, dreaded and hated by all classes of
his subjects. His nobles deserted every day to Henry's
side; he dared not call another Parliament, lest his
crimes should be denounced there; and for want of money,
he was obliged to get Benevolences from the citizens, which
exasperated them all against him. It was said too, that,
being stricken by his conscience, he dreamed frightful
dreams, and started up in the night-time, wild with terror
and remorse. Active to the last, through all this, he issued
vigorous proclamations against Henry of Richmond and all
his followers, when he heard that they were coming against
him with a Fleet from France; and took the field as fierce
and savage as a wild boar—the animal represented on his
shield.

Henry of Richmond landed with six thousand men at
Milford Haven, and came on against King Richard, then
encamped at Leicester with an army twice as great, through
North Wales. On Bosworth Field the two armies met;
and Richard, looking along Henry's ranks, and seeing them
crowded with the English nobles who had abandoned him,
turned pale when he beheld the powerful Lord Stanley and
his son (whom he had tried hard to retain) among them.
But, he was as brave as he was wicked, and plunged into
the thickest of the fight. He was riding hither and thither,
laying about him in all directions, when he observed the
Earl of Northumberland—one of his few great allies—to
stand inactive, and the main body of his troops to hesitate.
At the same moment, his desperate glance caught Henry of
Richmond among a little group of his knights. Riding
hard at him, and crying "Treason!" he killed his standard-
bearer, fiercely unhorsed another gentleman, and aimed a

powerful stroke at Henry himself, to cut him down. But, Sir William Stanley parried it as it fell, and before Richard could raise his arm again, he was borne down in a press of numbers, unhorsed, and killed. Lord Stanley picked up the crown, all bruised and trampled, and stained with blood, and put it upon Richmond's head, amid loud and rejoicing cries of " Long live King Henry ! "

That night, a horse was led up to the church of the Grey Friars at Leicester ; across whose back was tied, like some worthless sack, a naked body brought there for burial. It was the body of the last of the Plantagenet line, King Richard the Third, usurper and murderer, slain at the battle of Bosworth Field in the thirty-second year of his age, after a reign of two years.

CHAPTER XXVI

ENGLAND UNDER HENRY THE SEVENTH

KING HENRY THE SEVENTH did not turn out to be as fine a fellow as the nobility and people hoped, in the first joy of their deliverance from Richard the Third. He was very cold, crafty, and calculating, and would do almost anything for money. He possessed considerable ability, but his chief merit appears to have been that he was not cruel when there was nothing to be got by it.

The new King had promised the nobles who had espoused his cause that he would marry the Princess Elizabeth. The first thing he did, was, to direct her to be removed from the castle of Sheriff Hutton in Yorkshire, where Richard had placed her, and restored to the care of her mother in London. The young Earl of Warwick, Edward Plantagenet, son and heir of the late Duke of Clarence, had been kept a prisoner in the same old Yorkshire Castle with her. This boy, who was now fifteen, the new King placed in the Tower for safety. Then he came to London in great state, and gratified the people with a fine procession ; on which kind of show he often very much relied for keeping them in good humour. The sports and feasts which took place were followed by a terrible fever, called the Sweating Sickness ; of which great numbers of people died. Lord Mayors and Aldermen are thought to have suffered most from it ; whether, because they were in the habit of over-eating themselves, or because they were very jealous of preserving filth and nuisances in the City (as they have been since), I don't know.

The King's coronation was postponed on account of the general ill-health, and he afterwards deferred his marriage, as if he were not very anxious that it should take place : and, even after that, deferred the Queen's coronation so long that he gave offence to the York party. However, he set these things right in the end, by hanging some men and

seizing on the rich possessions of others ; by granting more
popular pardons to the followers of the late King than
could, at first, be got from him ; and, by employing about
his Court, some not very scrupulous persons who had been
employed in the previous reign.

As this reign was principally remarkable for two very
curious impostures which have become famous in history,
we will make those two stories its principal feature.

There was a priest at Oxford of the name of Simons, who
had for a pupil a handsome boy named Lambert Simnel,
the son of a baker. Partly to gratify his own ambitious
ends, and partly to carry out the designs of a secret party
formed against the King, this priest declared that his pupil,
the boy, was no other than the young Earl of Warwick ;
who (as everybody might have known) was safely locked up
in the Tower of London. The priest and the boy went
over to Ireland ; and, at Dublin, enlisted in their cause all
ranks of the people : who seem to have been generous
enough, but exceedingly irrational. The Earl of Kildare,
the governor of Ireland, declared that he believed the boy
to be what the priest represented ; and the boy, who had
been well tutored by the priest, told them such things of
his childhood, and gave them so many descriptions of the
Royal Family, that they were perpetually shouting and
hurrahing, and drinking his health, and making all kinds
of noisy and thirsty demonstrations, to express their belief
in him. Nor was this feeling confined to Ireland alone,
for the Earl of Lincoln—whom the late usurper had named
as his successor—went over to the young Pretender ; and,
after holding a secret correspondence with the Dowager
Duchess of Burgundy—the sister of Edward the Fourth,
who detested the present King and all his race—sailed to
Dublin with two thousand German soldiers of her providing. In this promising state of the boy's fortunes, he
was crowned there, with a crown taken off the head of a
statue of the Virgin Mary ; and was then, according to the
Irish custom of those days, carried home on the shoulders
of a big chieftain possessing a great deal more strength than
sense. Father Simons, you may be sure, was mighty busy
at the coronation.

Ten days afterwards, the Germans, and the Irish, and the
priest, and the boy, and the Earl of Lincoln, all landed in
Lancashire to invade England. The King, who had good

intelligence of their movements, set up his standard at Nottingham, where vast numbers resorted to him every day; while the Earl of Lincoln could gain but very few. With his small force he tried to make for the town of Newark; but the King's army getting between him and that place, he had no choice but to risk a battle at Stoke. It soon ended in the complete destruction of the Pretender's forces, one half of whom were killed; among them, the Earl himself. The priest and the baker's boy were taken prisoners. The priest, after confessing the trick, was shut up in prison, where he afterwards died—suddenly perhaps. The boy was taken into the King's kitchen and made a turnspit. He was afterwards raised to the station of one of the King's falconers; and so ended this strange imposition.

There seems reason to suspect that the Dowager Queen—always a restless and busy woman—had had some share in tutoring the baker's son. The King was very angry with her, whether or no. He seized upon her property, and shut her up in a convent at Bermondsey.

One might suppose that the end of this story would have put the Irish people on their guard; but they were quite ready to receive a second impostor, as they had received the first, and that same troublesome Duchess of Burgundy soon gave them the opportunity. All of a sudden there appeared at Cork, in a vessel arriving from Portugal, a young man of excellent abilities, of very handsome appearance and most winning manners, who declared himself to be Richard, Duke of York, the second son of King Edward the Fourth. "O," said some, even of those ready Irish believers, "but surely that young Prince was murdered by his uncle in the Tower!"—"It *is* supposed so," said the engaging young man; "and my brother *was* killed in that gloomy prison; but I escaped—it don't matter how, at present—and have been wandering about the world for seven long years." This explanation being quite satisfactory to numbers of the Irish people, they began again to shout and to hurrah, and to drink his health, and to make the noisy and thirsty demonstrations all over again. And the big chieftain in Dublin began to look out for another coronation, and another young King to be carried home on his back.

Now, King Henry being then on bad terms with France, the French King, Charles the Eighth, saw that, by pretending to believe in the handsome young man, he could trouble his enemy sorely. So, he invited him over to the French Court, and appointed him a body-guard, and treated him in all respects as if he really were the Duke of York. Peace, however, being soon concluded between the two Kings, the pretended Duke was turned adrift, and wandered for protection to the Duchess of Burgundy. She, after feigning to inquire into the reality of his claims, declared him to be the very picture of her dear departed brother; gave him a body-guard at her Court, of thirty halberdiers; and called him by the sounding name of the White Rose of England.

The leading members of the White Rose party in England sent over an agent, named Sir Robert Clifford, to ascertain whether the White Rose's claims were good: the King also sent over his agents to inquire into the Rose's history. The White Roses declared the young man to be really the Duke of York; the King declared him to be PERKIN WARBECK, the son of a merchant of the city of Tournay, who had acquired his knowledge of England, its language and manners, from the English merchants who traded in Flanders; it was also stated by the Royal agents that he had been in the service of Lady Brompton, the wife of an exiled English nobleman, and that the Duchess of Burgundy had caused him to be trained and taught, expressly for this deception. The King then required the Archduke Philip—who was the sovereign of Burgundy— to banish this new Pretender, or to deliver him up; but, as the Archduke replied that he could not control the Duchess in her own land, the King, in revenge, took the market of English cloth away from Antwerp, and prevented all commercial intercourse between the two countries.

He also, by arts and bribes, prevailed on Sir Robert Clifford to betray his employers; and he denouncing several famous English noblemen as being secretly the friends of Perkin Warbeck, the King had three of the foremost executed at once. Whether he pardoned the remainder because they were poor, I do not know; but it is only too probable that he refused to pardon one famous nobleman against whom the same Clifford soon afterwards informed separately, because he was rich. This was no other than Sir William Stanley, who had saved the King's life at the battle of Bosworth Field. It is very doubtful whether his treason amounted to much more than his having said, that if he were sure the young man was the Duke of York, he would not take arms against him. Whatever he had done he admitted, like an honourable spirit; and he lost his head for it, and the covetous King gained all his wealth.

Perkin Warbeck kept quiet for three years; but. as the Flemings began to complain heavily of the loss of their trade by the stoppage of the Antwerp market on his account, and as it was not unlikely that they might even go so far as to take his life, or give him up, he found it necessary to do something. Accordingly he made a desperate sally, and landed, with only a few hundred men, on the coast of Deal. But he was soon glad to get back to the place from whence he came; for the country people rose against his followers, killed a great many, and took a hundred and fifty prisoners: who were all driven to London, tied together with ropes, like a team of cattle. Every one of them was hanged on some part or other of the sea-shore; in order, that if any more men should come over with Perkin Warbeck, they might see the bodies as a warning before they landed.

Then the wary King, by making a treaty of commerce with the Flemings, drove Perkin Warbeck out of that country; and, by completely gaining over the Irish to his side, deprived him of that asylum too. He wandered away to Scotland, and told his story at that Court. King James the Fourth of Scotland, who was no friend to King Henry and had no reason to be (for King Henry had bribed his Scotch lords to betray him more than once; but had never succeeded in his plots), gave him a great reception, called him his cousin, and gave him in marriage the Lady Catherine Gordon, a beautiful and charming creature related to the royal house of Stuart.

Alarmed by this successful reappearance of the Pretender, the King still undermined, and bought, and bribed, and kept his doings and Perkin Warbeck's story in the dark, when he might, one would imagine, have rendered the matter clear to all England. But, for all this bribing of the Scotch lords at the Scotch King's Court, he could not procure the Pretender to be delivered up to him. James, though not very particular in many respects, would not betray him; and the ever-busy Duchess of Burgundy so provided him with arms, and good soldiers, and with money besides, that he had soon a little army of fifteen hundred

men of various nations. With these, and aided by the
Scottish King in person, he crossed the border into England,
and made a proclamation to the people, in which he called
the King "Henry Tudor;" offered large rewards to any
who should take or distress him; and announced himself
as King Richard the Fourth come to receive the homage of
his faithful subjects. His faithful subjects, however, cared
nothing for him, and hated his faithful troops: who, being
of different nations, quarrelled also among themselves.
Worse than this, if worse were possible, they began to
plunder the country; upon which the White Rose said,
that he would rather lose his rights, than gain them through
the miseries of the English people. The Scottish King made
a jest of his scruples; but they and their whole force went
back again without fighting a battle.

The worst consequence of this attempt was, that a rising
took place among the people of Cornwall, who considered
themselves too heavily taxed to meet the charges of the expected war. Stimulated by Flammock, a lawyer, and Joseph,
a blacksmith, and joined by Lord Audley and some other
country gentlemen, they marched on all the way to Deptford
Bridge, where they fought a battle with the King's army.
They were defeated—though the Cornish men fought with
great bravery—and the lord was beheaded, and the lawyer
and the blacksmith were hanged, drawn, and quartered. The
rest were pardoned. The King, who believed every man to
be as avaricious as himself, and thought that money could
settle anything, allowed them to make bargains for their
liberty with the soldiers who had taken them.

Perkin Warbeck, doomed to wander up and down, and
never to find rest anywhere—a sad fate: almost a sufficient
punishment for an imposture, which he seems in time to
have half believed himself – lost his Scottish refuge through
a truce being made between the two Kings; and found
himself, once more, without a country before him in which
he could lay his head. But James (always honourable and
true to him, alike when he melted down his plate, and even
the great gold chain he had been used to wear, to pay soldiers
in his cause; and now, when that cause was lost and
hopeless) did not conclude the treaty, until he had safely
departed out of the Scottish dominions. He, and his
beautiful wife, who was faithful to him under all reverses,
and left her state and home to follow his poor fortunes,

were put aboard ship with everything necessary for their comfort and protection, and sailed for Ireland.

But, the Irish people had had enough of counterfeit Earls of Warwick and Dukes of York, for one while; and would give the White Rose no aid. So, the White Rose—encircled by thorns indeed—resolved to go with his beautiful wife to Cornwall as a forlorn resource, and see what might be made of the Cornish men, who had risen so valiantly a little while before, and who had fought so bravely at Deptford Bridge.

To Whitsand Bay, in Cornwall, accordingly, came Perkin Warbeck and his wife; and the lovely lady he shut up for safety in the Castle of St. Michael's Mount, and then marched into Devonshire at the head of three thousand Cornish men. These were increased to six thousand by the time of his arrival in Exeter; but, there the people made a stout resistance, and he went on to Taunton, where he came in sight of the King's army. The stout Cornish men, although they were few in number, and badly armed, were so bold, that they never thought of retreating; but bravely looked forward to a battle on the morrow. Unhappily for them, the man who was possessed of so many engaging qualities, and who attracted so many people to his side when he had nothing else with which to tempt them, was not as brave as they. In the night, when the two armies lay opposite to each other, he mounted a swift horse and fled. When morning dawned, the poor confiding Cornish men, discovering that they had no leader, surrendered to the King's power. Some of them were hanged, and the rest were pardoned and went miserably home.

Before the King pursued Perkin Warbeck to the sanctuary of Beaulieu in the New Forest, where it was soon known that he had taken refuge, he sent a body of horsemen to St. Michael's Mount, to seize his wife. She was soon taken and brought as a captive before the King. But she was so beautiful, and so good, and so devoted to the man in whom she believed, that the King regarded her with compassion, treated her with great respect, and placed her at Court, near the Queen's person. And many years after Perkin Warbeck was no more, and when his strange story had become like a nursery tale, *she* was called the White Rose, by the people, in remembrance of her beauty.

The sanctuary at Beaulieu was soon surrounded by the

King's men; and the King, pursuing his usual dark artful ways, sent pretended friends to Perkin Warbeck to persuade him to come out and surrender himself. This he soon did; the King having taken a good look at the man of whom he had heard so much—from behind a screen—directed him to be well mounted, and to ride behind him at a little distance, guarded, but not bound in any way. So they entered London with the King's favourite show—a procession; and some of the people hooted as the Pretender rode slowly through the streets to the Tower; but the greater part were quiet, and very curious to see him. From the Tower, he was taken to the Palace at Westminster, and there lodged like a gentleman. though closely watched. He was examined every now and then as to his imposture; but the King was so secret in all he did, that even then he gave it a consequence, which it cannot be supposed to have in itself deserved.

At last Perkin Warbeck ran away, and took refuge in another sanctuary near Richmond in Surrey. From this he was again persuaded to deliver himself up; and, being conveyed to London, he stood in the stocks for a whole day, outside Westminster Hall, and there read a paper purporting to be his full confession, and relating his history as the King's agents had originally described it. He was then shut up in the Tower again, in the company of the Earl of Warwick, who had now been there for fourteen years: ever since his removal out of Yorkshire, except when the King had had him at Court, and had shown him to the people, to prove the imposture of the Baker's boy. It is but too probable, when we consider the crafty character of Henry the Seventh, that these two were brought together for a cruel purpose. A plot was soon discovered between them and the keepers, to murder the Governor, get possession of the keys, and proclaim Perkin Warbeck as King Richard the Fourth. That there was some such plot, is likely; that they were tempted into it, is at least as likely; that the unfortunate Earl of Warwick—last male of the Plantagenet line—was too unused to the world, and too ignorant and simple to know much about it, whatever it was, is perfectly certain; and that it was the King's interest to get rid of him, is no less so. He was beheaded on Tower Hill, and Perkin Warbeck was hanged at Tyburn.

Such was the end of the pretended Duke of York, whose shadowy history was made more shadowy—and ever will be—by the mystery and craft of the King. If he had turned his great natural advantages to a more honest account, he might have lived a happy and respected life, even in those days. But he died upon a gallows at Tyburn, leaving the Scottish lady, who had loved him so well, kindly protected at the Queen's Court. After some time she forgot her old loves and troubles, as many people do with Time's merciful assistance, and married a Welsh gentleman. Her second husband, SIR MATTHEW CRADOC, more honest and more happy than her first, lies beside her in a tomb in the old church of Swansea.

The ill-blood between France and England in this reign, arose out of the continued plotting of the Duchess of Burgundy, and disputes respecting the affairs of Brittany. The King feigned to be very patriotic, indignant, and war-like ; but he always contrived so as never to make war in reality, and always to make money. His taxation of the people, on pretence of war with France, involved, at one time, a very dangerous insurrection, headed by Sir John Egremont, and a common man called John à Chambre. But it was subdued by the royal forces, under the command of the Earl of Surrey. The knighted John escaped to the Duchess of Burgundy, who was ever ready to receive any one who gave the King trouble; and the plain John was hanged at York, in the midst of a number of his men, but on a much higher gibbet, as being a greater traitor. Hung high or hung low, however, hanging is much the same to to the person hung.

Within a year after her marriage, the Queen had given birth to a son, who was called Prince Arthur in remembrance of the old British prince of romance and story; and who, when all these events had happened, being then in his fifteenth year, was married to CATHERINE, the daughter of the Spanish monarch, with great rejoicings and bright prospects; but in a very few months he sickened and died. As soon as the King had recovered from his grief, he thought it a pity that the fortune of the Spanish Princess, amounting to two hundred thousand crowns, should go out of the family; and therefore arranged that the young widow should marry his second son HENRY, then twelve years of age, when he too should be fifteen. There were objections to this marriage on the part of the clergy ; but, as the infallible Pope was gained over, and, as he *must* be right, that settled the business for the time. The King's eldest daughter was provided for, and a long course of disturbance was considered to be set at rest, by her being married to the Scottish King.

And now the Queen died. When the King had got over that grief too, his mind once more reverted to his darling money for consolation, and he thought of marrying the Dowager Queen of Naples, who was immensely rich : but, as it turned out not to be practicable to gain the money however practicable it might have been to gain the lady, he gave up the idea. He was not so fond of her but that he soon proposed to marry the Dowager Duchess of Savoy; and, soon afterwards, the widow of the King of Castile, who was raving mad. But he made a money-bargain instead, and married neither.

The Duchess of Burgundy, among the other discontented people to whom she had given refuge, had sheltered EDMUND DE LA POLE (younger brother of that Earl of Lincoln who was killed at Stoke), now Earl of Suffolk. The King had prevailed upon him to return to the marriage of Prince Arthur; but, he soon afterwards went away again; and then the King, suspecting a conspiracy, resorted to his favourite plan of sending him some treacherous friends, and buying of those scoundrels the secrets they disclosed or invented. Some arrests and executions took place in con· sequence. In the end, the King, on a promise of not taking his life, obtained possession of the person of Edmund de la Pole, and shut him up in the Tower.

This was his last enemy. If he had lived much longer he would have made many more among the people, by the grinding exaction to which he constantly exposed them, and by the tyrannical acts of his two prime favourites in all money-raising matters, EDMUND DUDLEY and RICHARD EMPSON. But Death—the enemy who is not to be bought off or deceived, and on whom no money, and no treachery, has any effect—presented himself at this juncture, and ended the King's reign. He died of the gout, on the twenty-second of April, one thousand five hundred and nine, and in the fifty-third year of his age, after reigning twenty-four years; he was buried in the beautiful Chapel of Westminster Abbey, which he had himself founded, and which still bears his name.

It was in this reign that the great CHRISTOPHER COLUMBUS,

on behalf of Spain, discovered what was then called The New World. Great wonder, interest, and hope of wealth being awakened in England thereby, the King and the merchants of London and Bristol fitted out an English expedition for further discoveries in the New World, and entrusted it to SEBASTIAN CABOT, of Bristol, the son of a Venetian pilot there He was very successful in his voyage, and gained high reputation, both for himself and England.

CHAPTER XXVII

ENGLAND UNDER HENRY THE EIGHTH, CALLED BLUFF KING HAL AND BURLY KING HARRY

PART THE FIRST.

WE now come to King Henry the Eighth, whom it has been too much the fashion to call "Bluff King Hal," and "Burly King Harry," and other fine names; but whom I shall take the liberty to call, plainly, one of the most detestable villains that ever drew breath. You will be able to judge, long before we come to the end of his life, whether he deserves the character.

He was just eighteen years of age when he came to the throne. People said he was handsome then; but I don't believe it. He was a big, burly, noisy, small-eyed, large-faced, double-chinned, swinish-looking fellow in later life (as we know from the likenesses of him, painted by the famous HANS HOLBEIN), and it is not easy to believe that so bad a character can ever have been veiled under a prepossessing appearance.

He was anxious to make himself popular; and the people, who had long disliked the late King, were very willing to believe that he deserved to be so. He was extremely fond of show and display, and so were they. Therefore there was great rejoicing when he married the Princess Catherine, and when they were both crowned. And the King fought at tournaments and always came off victorious—for the courtiers took care of that—and there was a general outcry that he was a wonderful man. Empson, Dudley, and their supporters were accused of a variety of crimes they had never committed, instead of the offences of which they really had been guilty; and they were pilloried, and set upon horses with their faces to the tails, and knocked about and beheaded, to the satisfaction of the people, and the enrichment of the King.

The Pope, so indefatigable in getting the world into

trouble, had mixed himself up in a war on the continent of
Europe, occasioned by the reigning Princes of little quarrelling states in Italy having at various times married into
other Royal families, and so led to *their* claiming a share
in those petty Governments. The King, who discovered
that he was very fond of the Pope, sent a herald to the
King of France, to say that he must not make war upon
that holy personage, because he was the father of all
Christians. As the French King did not mind this relationship in the least, and also refused to admit a claim King
Henry made to certain lands in France, war was declared
between the two countries. Not to perplex this story with
an account of the tricks and designs of all the sovereigns
who were engaged in it, it is enough to say that England
made a blundering alliance with Spain, and got stupidly
taken in by that country ; which made its own terms with
France when it could, and left England in the lurch. SIR
EDWARD HOWARD, a bold admiral, son of the Earl of Surrey,
distinguished himself by his bravery against the French in
this business; but, unfortunately, he was more brave than
wise, for, skimming into the French harbour of Brest with
only a few row-boats, he attempted (in revenge for the
defeat and death of SIR THOMAS KNYVETT, another bold
English admiral) to take some strong French ships, well
defended with batteries of cannon. The upshot was, that
he was left on board of one of them (in consequence of its
shooting away from his own boat), with not more than about
a dozen men, and was thrown into the sea and drowned :
though not until he had taken from his breast his gold
chain and gold whistle, which were the signs of his office,
and had cast them into the sea to prevent their being made
a boast of by the enemy. After this defeat—which was a
great one, for Sir Edward Howard was a man of valour and
fame—the King took it into his head to invade France in
person; first executing that dangerous Earl of Suffolk whom
his father had left in the Tower, and appointing Queen
Catherine to the charge of his kingdom in his absence. He
sailed to Calais, where he was joined by MAXIMILIAN,
Emperor of Germany, who pretended to be his soldier, and
who took pay in his service : with a good deal of nonsense
of that sort, flattering enough to the vanity of a vain
blusterer. The King might be successful enough in sham
fights; but his idea of real battles chiefly consisted in

pitching silken tents of bright colours that were igno-
miniously blown down by the wind, and in making a vast
display of gaudy flags and golden curtains. Fortune, however, favoured him better than he deserved; for, after much
waste of time in tent pitching, flag flying, gold curtaining,
and other such masquerading, he gave the French battle
at a place called Guinegate: where they took such an
unaccountable panic, and fled with such swiftness, that it
was ever afterwards called by the English the Battle of
Spurs. Instead of following up his advantage, the King,
finding that he had had enough of real fighting, came home
again.

The Scottish King, though nearly related to Henry by
marriage, had taken part against him in this war. The Earl
of Surrey, as the English general, advanced to meet him
when he came out of his own dominions and crossed the
river Tweed. The two armies came up with one another
when the Scottish King had also crossed the river Till, and
was encamped upon the last of the Cheviot Hills, called the
Hill of Flodden. Along the plain below it, the English,
when the hour of battle came, advanced. The Scottish
army, which had been drawn up in five great bodies, then
came steadily down in perfect silence. So they, in their
turn, advanced to meet the English army, which came on
in one long line; and they attacked it with a body of
spearmen, under Lord Home. At first they had the best
of it; but the English recovered themselves so bravely, and
fought with such valour, that, when the Scottish King
had almost made his way up to the Royal standard, he
was slain, and the whole Scottish power routed. Ten
thousand Scottish men lay dead that day on Flodden Field;
and among them, numbers of the nobility and gentry. For
a long time afterwards, the Scottish peasantry used to
believe that their King had not been really killed in this
battle, because no Englishman had found an iron belt he
wore about his body as a penance for having been an
unnatural and undutiful son. But, whatever became of
his belt, the English had his sword and dagger, and the
ring from his finger, and his body too, covered with wounds.
There is no doubt of it; for it was seen and recognised
by English gentlemen who had known the Scottish King
well.

When King Henry was making ready to renew the war

in France, the French King was contemplating peace. His queen, dying at this time, he proposed, though he was upwards of fifty years old, to marry King Henry's sister, the Princess Mary, who, besides being only sixteen, was betrothed to the Duke of Suffolk. As the inclinations of young Princesses were not much considered in such matters, the marriage was concluded, and the poor girl was escorted to France, where she was immediately left as the French King's bride, with only one of all her English attendants. That one was a pretty young girl named ANNE BOLEYN, niece of the Earl of Surrey, who had been made Duke of Norfolk, after the victory of Flodden Field. Anne Boleyn's is a name to be remembered, as you will presently find.

And now the French King, who was very proud of his young wife, was preparing for many years of happiness, and she was looking forward, I dare say, to many years of misery, when he died within three months, and left her a young widow. The new French monarch, FRANCIS THE FIRST, seeing how important it was to his interests that she should take for her second husband no one but an Englishman, advised her first lover, the Duke of Suffolk, when King Henry sent him over to France to fetch her home, to marry her. The Princess being herself so fond of that Duke, as to tell him that he must either do so then, or for ever lose her, they were wedded; and Henry afterwards forgave them. In making interest with the King, the Duke of Suffolk had addressed his most powerful favourite and adviser, THOMAS WOLSEY—a name very famous in history for its rise and downfall.

Wolsey was the son of a respectable butcher at Ipswich, in Suffolk, and received so excellent an education that he became a tutor to the family of the Marquis of Dorset, who afterwards got him appointed one of the late King's chaplains. On the accession of Henry the Eighth, he was promoted and taken into great favour. He was now Archbishop of York; the Pope had made him a Cardinal besides; and whoever wanted influence in England or favour with the King—whether he were a foreign monarch or an English nobleman — was obliged to make a friend of the great Cardinal Wolsey.

He was a gay man, who could dance and jest, and sing and drink; and those were the roads to so much, or rather so little, of a heart as King Henry had. He was wonderfully

fond of pomp and glitter, and so was the King. He knew
a good deal of the Church learning of that time ; much of
which consisted in finding artful excuses and pretences for
almost any wrong thing, and in arguing that black was
white, or any other colour. This kind of learning pleased
the King too. For many such reasons, the Cardinal was
high in estimation with the King ; and, being a man of far
greater ability, knew as well how to manage him, as a clever
keeper may know how to manage a wolf or a tiger, or any
other cruel and uncertain beast, that may turn upon him
and tear him any day. Never had there been seen in
England such state as my Lord Cardinal kept. His wealth
was enormous ; equal, it was reckoned, to the riches of the
Crown. His palaces were as splendid as the King's, and
his retinue was eight hundred strong. He held his Court,
dressed out from top to toe in flaming scarlet ; and his very
shoes were golden, set with precious stones. His followers
rode on blood horses ; while he, with a wonderful affectation
of humility in the midst of his great splendour, ambled on
a mule with a red velvet saddle and bridle and golden
stirrups.

Through the influence of this stately priest, a grand
meeting was arranged to take place between the French and
English Kings in France ; but on ground belonging to
England. A prodigious show of friendship and rejoicing
was to be made on the occasion ; and heralds were sent to
proclaim with brazen trumpets through all the principal
cities of Europe, that, on a certain day, the Kings of France
and England, as companions and brothers in arms, each
attended by eighteen followers, would hold a tournament
against all knights who might choose to come.

CHARLES, the new Emperor of Germany (the old one being
dead), wanted to prevent too cordial an alliance between
these sovereigns, and came over to England before the King
could repair to the place of meeting ; and, besides making
an agreeable impression upon him, secured Wolsey's interest
by promising that his influence should make him Pope
when the next vacancy occurred. On the day when the
Emperor left England, the King and all the Court went
over to Calais, and thence to the place of meeting, between
Ardres and Guisnes, commonly called the Field of the Cloth
of Gold. Here, all manner of expense and prodigality was
lavished on the decorations of the show ; many of the

knights and gentlemen being so superbly dressed that it was said they carried their whole estates upon their shoulders.

There were sham castles, temporary chapels, fountains running wine, great cellars full of wine free as water to all comers, silk tents, gold lace and foil, gilt lions, and such things without end ; and, in the midst of all, the rich Cardinal out-shone and out-glittered all the noblemen and gentlemen assembled. After a treaty made between the two Kings with as much solemnity as if they had intended to keep it, the lists—nine hundred feet long, and three hundred and twenty broad—were opened for the tournament; the Queens of France and England looking on with great array of lords and ladies. Then, for ten days, the two sovereigns fought five combats every day, and always beat their polite adversaries ; though they *do* write that the King of England, being thrown in a wrestle one day by the King of France, lost his kingly temper with his brother in arms, and wanted to make a quarrel of it. Then, there is a great story belonging to this Field of the Cloth of Gold, showing how the English were distrustful of the French, and the French of the English, until Francis rode alone one morning to Henry's tent; and, going in before he was out of bed, told him in joke that he was his prisoner ; and how Henry jumped out of bed and embraced Francis ; and how Francis helped Henry to dress, and warmed his linen for him ; and how Henry gave Francis a splendid jewelled collar, and how Francis gave Henry, in return, a costly bracelet. All this and a great deal more was so written about, and sung about, and talked about at that time (and, indeed, since that time too), that the world has had good cause to be sick of it, for ever.

Of course, nothing came of all these fine doings but a speedy renewal of the war between England and France, in which the two Royal companions and brothers in arms longed very earnestly to damage one another. But, before it broke out again, the Duke of Buckingham was shamefully executed on Tower Hill, on the evidence of a discharged servant — really for nothing, except the folly of having believed in a friar of the name of HOPKINS, who had pretended to be a prophet, and who had mumbled and jumbled out some nonsense about the Duke's son being destined to be very great in the land. It was believed that the un-

fortunate Duke had given offence to the great Cardinal by
expressing his mind freely about the expense and absurdity
of the whole business of the Field of the Cloth of Gold.
At any rate, he was beheaded, as I have said, for nothing.
And the people who saw it done were very angry, and cried
out that it was the work of "the butcher's son!"

The new war was a short one, though the Earl of Surrey
invaded France again, and did some injury to that country.
It ended in another treaty of peace between the two kingdoms,
and in the discovery that the Emperor of Germany was not
such a good friend to England in reality, as he pretended
to be. Neither did he keep his promise to Wolsey to make
him Pope, though the King urged him. Two Popes died
in pretty quick succession; but the foreign priests were too
much for the Cardinal, and kept him out of the post. So the
Cardinal and King together found out that the Emperor of
Germany was not a man to keep faith with; broke off a projected marriage between the King's daughter MARY, Princess
of Wales, and that sovereign; and began to consider whether
it might not be well to marry the young lady, either to
Francis himself, or to his eldest son.

There now arose at Wittemberg, in Germany, the great
leader of the mighty change in England which is called The
Reformation, and which set the people free from their slavery
to the priests. This was a learned Doctor, named MARTIN
LUTHER, who knew all about them, for he had been a priest,
and even a monk, himself. The preaching and writing of
Wickliffe had set a number of men thinking on this subject;
and Luther, finding one day to his great surprise, that there
really was a book called the New Testament which the priests
did not allow to be read, and which contained truths that
they suppressed, began to be very vigorous against the whole
body, from the Pope downward. It happened, while he was
yet only beginning his vast work of awakening the nation,
that an impudent fellow named TETZEL, a friar of very bad
character, came into his neighbourhood selling what were
called Indulgences, by wholesale, to raise money for beautify-
ing the great Cathedral of St. Peter's, at Rome. Whoever
bought an Indulgence of the Pope was supposed to buy
himself off from the punishment of Heaven for his offences.
Luther told the people that these Indulgences were worthless
bits of paper, before God, and that Tetzel and his masters
were a crew of impostors in selling them.

The King and the Cardinal were mightily indignant at this presumption ; and the King (with the help of SIR THOMAS MORE. a wise man, whom he afterwards repaid by striking off his head) even wrote a book about it, with which the Pope was so well pleased that he gave the King the title of Defender of the Faith. The King and the Cardinal also issued flaming warnings to the people not to read Luther's books, on pain of excommunication. But they did read them for all that : and the rumour of what was in them spread far and wide.

When this great change was thus going on, the King began to show himself in his truest and worst colours. Anne Boleyn, the pretty little girl who had gone abroad to France with his sister, was by this time grown up to be very beautiful, and was one of the ladies in attendance on Queen Catherine. Now, Queen Catherine was no longer young or handsome, and it is likely that she was not particularly good-tempered ; having been always rather melancholy, and having been made more so by the deaths of four of her children when they were very young. So, the King fell in love with the fair Anne Boleyn, and said to himself, "How can I be best rid of my own troublesome wife whom I am tired of, and marry Anne ? "

You recollect that Queen Catherine had been the wife of Henry's brother. What does the King do, after thinking it over, but calls his favourite priests about him, and says, O ! his mind is in such a dreadful state, and he is so frightfully uneasy, because he is afraid it was not lawful for him to marry the Queen ! Not one of those priests had the courage to hint that it was rather curious he had never thought of that before, and that his mind seemed to have been in a tolerably jolly condition during a great many years, in which he certainly had not fretted himself thin ; but, they all said, Ah ! that was very true, and it was a serious business ; and perhaps the best way to make it right, would be for his Majesty to be divorced ! The King replied, Yes, he thought that would be the best way, certainly ; so they all went to work.

If I were to relate to you the intrigues and plots that took place in the endeavour to get this divorce, you would think the History of England the most tiresome book in the world. So I shall say no more, than that after a vast deal of negotia- tion and evasion, the Pope issued a commission to Cardinal

Wolsey and CARDINAL CAMPEGGIO (whom he sent over from Italy for the purpose), to try the whole case in England. It is supposed—and I think with reason—that Wolsey was the Queen's enemy, because she had reproved him for his proud and gorgeous manner of life. But, he did not at first know that the King wanted to marry Anne Boleyn; and when he did know it, he even went down on his knees, in the endeavour to dissuade him.

The Cardinals opened their court in the Convent of the Black Friars, near to where the bridge of that name in London now stands; and the King and Queen, that they might be near it, took up their lodgings at the adjoining palace of Bridewell, of which nothing now remains but a bad prison. On the opening of the court, when the King and Queen were called on to appear, that poor ill-used lady, with a dignity and firmness and yet with a womanly affection worthy to be always admired, went and kneeled at the King's feet, and said that she had come, a stranger, to his dominions; that she had been a good and true wife to him for twenty years; and that she could acknowledge no power in those Cardinals to try whether she should be considered his wife after all that time, or should be put away. With that, she got up and left the court, and would never afterwards come back to it.

The King pretended to be very much overcome, and said, O! my lords and gentlemen, what a good woman she was to be sure, and how delighted he would be to live with her unto death, but for that terrible uneasiness in his mind which was quite wearing him away! So, the case went on, and there was nothing but talk for two months. Then Cardinal Campeggio, who, on behalf of the Pope, wanted nothing so much as delay, adjourned it for two more months; and before that time was elapsed, the Pope himself adjourned it indefinitely, by requiring the King and Queen to come to Rome and have it tried there. But by good luck for the King, word was brought to him by some of his people, that they had happened to meet at supper, THOMAS CRANMER, a learned Doctor of Cambridge, who had proposed to urge the Pope on, by referring the case to all the learned doctors and bishops, here and there and everywhere, and getting their opinions that the King's marriage was unlawful. The King, who was now in a hurry to marry Anne Boleyn, thought this such a good idea, that he sent for Cranmer, post haste, and said to LORD ROCHFORT, Anne Boleyn's father, "Take this learned Doctor down to your country-house, and there let him have a good room for a study, and no end of books out of which to prove that I may marry your daughter." Lord Rochfort, not at all reluctant, made the learned Doctor as comfortable as he could; and the learned Doctor went to work to prove his case. All this time, the King and Anne Boleyn were writing letters to one another almost daily, full of impatience to have the case settled; and Anne Boleyn was showing herself (as I think) very worthy of the fate which afterwards befel her.

It was bad for Cardinal Wolsey that he had left Cranmer to render this help. It was worse for him that he had tried to dissuade the King from marrying Anne Boleyn. Such a servant as he, to such a master as Henry, would probably have fallen in any case; but, between the hatred of the party of the Queen that was, and the hatred of the party of the Queen that was to be, he fell suddenly and heavily. Going down one day to the Court of Chancery, where he now presided, he was waited upon by the Dukes of Norfolk and Suffolk, who told him that they brought an order to him to resign that office, and to withdraw quietly to a house he had at Esher, in Surrey. The Cardinal refusing, they rode off to the King; and next day came back with a letter from him, on reading which, the Cardinal submitted. An inventory was made out of all the riches in his palace at York Place (now Whitehall), and he went sorrowfully up the river, in his barge, to Putney. An abject man he was, in spite of his pride; for being overtaken, riding out of that place towards Esher, by one of the King's chamberlains who brought him a kind message and a ring, he alighted from his mule, took off his cap, and kneeled down in the dirt. His poor Fool, whom in his prosperous days he had always kept in his palace to entertain him, cut a far better figure than he; for, when the Cardinal said to the chamberlain that he had nothing to send to his lord the King as a present, but that jester who was a most excellent one, it took six strong yeomen to remove the faithful fool from his master.

The once proud Cardinal was soon further disgraced, and wrote the most abject letters to his vile sovereign; who humbled him one day and encouraged him the next, according to his humour, until he was at last ordered to go and

reside in his diocese of York. He said he was too poor ;
but I don't know how he made that out, for he took a hundred and sixty servants with him, and seventy-two cart-
loads of furniture, food, and wine. He remained in that
part of the country for the best part of a year, and showed
himself so improved by his misfortunes, and was so mild
and so conciliating, that he won all hearts. And indeed,
even in his proud days, he had done some magnificent
things for learning and education. At last, he was arrested
for high treason ; and, coming slowly on his journey towards
London, got as far as Leicester. Arriving at Leicester
Abbey after dark, and very ill, he said—when the monks
came out at the gate with lighted torches to receive him—
that he had come to lay his bones among them. He had
indeed ; for he was taken to a bed, from which he never
rose again. His last words were, "Had I but served God as
diligently as I have served the King, He would not have
given me over, in my grey hairs. Howbeit, this is my just
reward for my pains and diligence, not regarding my service
to God, but only my duty to my prince." The news of his
death was quickly carried to the King, who was amusing
himself with archery in the garden of the magnificent
Palace at Hampton Court, which that very Wolsey had
presented to him. The greatest emotion his royal mind
displayed at the loss of a servant so faithful and so ruined,
was a particular desire to lay hold of fifteen hundred pounds
which the Cardinal was reported to have hidden somewhere.

The opinions concerning the divorce, of the learned doctors
and bishops and others, being at last collected, and being
generally in the King's favour, were forwarded to the Pope,
with an entreaty that he would now grant it. The unfortunate Pope, who was a timid man, was half distracted
between his fear of his authority being set aside in England
if he did not do as he was asked, and his dread of offending
the Emperor of Germany, who was Queen Catherine's
nephew. In this state of mind he still evaded and did
nothing. Then, THOMAS CROMWELL, who had been one of
Wolsey's faithful attendants, and had remained so even in
his decline, advised the King to take the matter into his
own hands, and make himself the head of the whole Church.
This, the King by various artful means, began to do ; but
he recompensed the clergy by allowing them to burn as
many people as they pleased, for holding Luther's opinions.

You must understand that Sir Thomas More, the wise man who had helped the King with his book, had been made Chancellor in Wolsey's place. But, as he was truly attached to the Church as it was even in its abuses, he, in this state of things, resigned.

Being now quite resolved to get rid of Queen Catherine, and to marry Anne Boleyn without more ado, the King made Cranmer Archbishop of Canterbury, and directed Queen Catherine to leave the Court. She obeyed; but replied that wherever she went, she was Queen of England still, and would remain so, to the last. The King then married Anne Boleyn privately; and the new Archbishop of Canterbury, within half a year, declared his marriage with Queen Catherine void, and crowned Anne Boleyn Queen.

She might have known that no good could ever come from such wrong, and that the corpulent brute who had been so faithless and so cruel to his first wife, could be more faithless and more cruel to his second. She might have known that, even when he was in love with her, he had been a mean and selfish coward, running away, like a frightened cur, from her society and her house, when a dangerous sickness broke out in it, and when she might easily have taken it and died, as several of the household did. But, Anne Boleyn arrived at all this knowledge too late, and bought it at a dear price. Her bad marriage with a worse man came to its natural end. Its natural end was not, as we shall too soon see, a natural death for her.

CHAPTER XXVIII

ENGLAND UNDER HENRY THE EIGHTH

Part the Second.

The Pope was thrown into a very angry state of mind when he heard of the King's marriage, and fumed exceedingly. Many of the English monks and friars, seeing that their order was in danger, did the same; some even declaimed against the King in church before his face, and were not to be stopped until he himself roared out "Silence!" The King, not much the worse for this, took it pretty quietly; and was very glad when his Queen gave birth to a daughter, who was christened ELIZABETH, and declared Princess of Wales as her sister Mary had already been.

One of the most atrocious features of this reign was that Henry the Eighth was always trimming between the reformed religion and the unreformed one; so that the more he quarrelled with the Pope, the more of his own subjects he roasted alive for not holding the Pope's opinions. Thus, an unfortunate student named John Frith, and a poor simple tailor named Andrew Hewet who loved him very much, and said that whatever John Frith believed *he* believed, were burnt in Smithfield—to show what a capital Christian the King was.

But, these were speedily followed by two much greater victims, Sir Thomas More, and John Fisher, the Bishop of Rochester. The latter, who was a good and amiable old man, had committed no greater offence than believing in Elizabeth Barton, called the Maid of Kent—another of those ridiculous women who pretended to be inspired, and to make all sorts of heavenly revelations, though they indeed uttered nothing but evil nonsense. For this offence —as it was pretended, but really for denying the King to be the supreme Head of the Church—he got into trouble, and was put in prison; but, even then, he might have been suffered to die naturally (short work having been made of executing the Kentish Maid and her principal followers), but that the Pope, to spite the King, resolved to make him a cardinal. Upon that the King made a ferocious joke to the effect that the Pope might send Fisher a red hat—which is the way they make a cardinal—but he should have no head on which to wear it; and he was tried with all unfairness and injustice, and sentenced to death. He died like a noble and virtuous old man, and left a worthy name behind him. The King supposed, I dare say, that Sir Thomas More would be frightened by this example; but, as he was not to be easily terrified, and, thoroughly believing in the Pope, had made up his mind that the King was not the rightful Head of the Church, he positively refused to say that he was. For this crime he too was tried and sentenced, after having been in prison a whole year. When he was doomed to death, and came away from his trial with the edge of the executioner's axe turned towards him—as was always done in those times when a state prisoner came to that hopeless pass—he bore it quite serenely, and gave his blessing to his son, who pressed through the crowd in Westminster Hall and kneeled down to receive it. But, when he got to the Tower Wharf on his way back to his prison, and his favourite daughter, MARGARET ROPER, a very good woman, rushed through the guards again and again, to kiss him and to weep upon his neck, he was overcome at last. He soon recovered, and never more showed any feeling but cheerfulness and courage. When he was going up the steps of the scaffold to his death, he said jokingly to the Lieutenant of the Tower, observing that they were weak and shook beneath his tread, "I pray you, master Lieutenant, see me safe up; and, for my coming down, I can shift for myself." Also he said to the executioner, after he had laid his head upon the block, "Let me put my beard out of the way; for that, at least, has never committed any treason." Then his head was struck off at a blow. These two executions were worthy of King Henry the Eighth. Sir Thomas More was one of the most virtuous men in his dominions, and the Bishop was one of his oldest and truest friends. But to be a friend of that fellow was almost as dangerous as to be his wife.

When the news of these two murders got to Rome, the Pope raged against the murderer more than ever Pope raged since the world began, and prepared a Bull, ordering his subjects to take arms against him and dethrone him. The King took all possible precautions to keep that document out of his dominions, and set to work in return to suppress a great number of the English monasteries and abbeys.

This destruction was begun by a body of commissioners, of whom Cromwell (whom the King had taken into great favour) was the head ; and was carried on through some few years to its entire completion. There is no doubt that many of these religious establishments were religious in nothing but in name, and were crammed with lazy, indolent, and sensual monks. There is no doubt that they imposed upon the people in every possible way ; that they had images moved by wires, which they pretended were miraculously moved by Heaven ; that they had among them a whole tun measure full of teeth, all purporting to have come out of the head of one saint, who must indeed have been a very extra-ordinary person with that enormous allowance of grinders : that they had bits of coal which they said had fried Saint Lawrence, and bits of toe-nails which they said belonged to other famous saints ; penknives, and boots, and girdles, which they said belonged to others ; and that all these bits of rubbish were called Relics, and adored by the ignorant people. But, on the other hand, there is no doubt either, that the King's officers and men punished the good monks with the bad ; did great injustice ; demolished many beauti-ful things and many valuable libraries ; destroyed numbers of paintings, stained glass windows, fine pavements, and carvings ; and that the whole court were ravenously greedy and rapacious for the division of this great spoil among them. The King seems to have grown almost mad in the ardour of this pursuit ; for he declared Thomas à Becket a traitor, though he had been dead so many years, and had his body dug up out of his grave. He must have been as miraculous as the monks pretended, if they had told the truth, for he was found with one head on his shoulders, and they had shown another as his undoubted and genuine head ever since his death ; it had brought them vast sums of money, too. The gold and jewels on his shrine filled two great chests, and eight men tottered as they carried them away. How rich the monasteries were you may infer from the fact that, when they were all suppressed, one hundred and thirty thousand pounds a year—in those days an immense sum—came to the Crown.

These things were not done without causing great discontent among the people. The monks had been good landlords and hospitable entertainers of all travellers, and had been accustomed to give away a great deal of corn, and fruit, and meat, and other things. In those days it was difficult to change goods into money, in consequence of the roads being very few and very bad, and the carts and waggons of the worst description; and they must either have given away some of the good things they possessed in enormous quantities, or have suffered them to spoil and moulder. So, many of the people missed what it was more agreeable to get idly than to work for; and the monks who were driven out of their homes and wandered about encouraged their discontent; and there were, consequently, great risings in Lincolnshire and Yorkshire. These were put down by terrific executions, from which the monks themselves did not escape, and the King went on grunting and growling in his own fat way, like a Royal pig.

I have told all this story of the religious houses at one time, to make it plainer, and to get back to the King's domestic affairs.

The unfortunate Queen Catherine was by this time dead; and the King was by this time as tired of his second Queen as he had been of his first. As he had fallen in love with Anne when she was in the service of Catherine, so he now fell in love with another lady in the service of Anne. See how wicked deeds are punished, and how bitterly and self-reproachfully the Queen must now have thought of her own rise to the throne! The new fancy was a LADY JANE SEYMOUR; and the King no sooner set his mind on her, than he resolved to have Anne Boleyn's head. So, he brought a number of charges against Anne, accusing her of dreadful crimes which she had never committed, and implicating in them her own brother and certain gentlemen in her service: among whom one Norris, and Mark Smeaton a musician, are best remembered. As the lords and councillors were as afraid of the King and as subservient to him as the meanest peasant in England was, they brought in Anne Boleyn guilty, and the other unfortunate persons accused with her, guilty too. Those gentlemen died like men, with the exception of Smeaton, who had been tempted by the King into telling lies, which he called confessions, and who had expected to be pardoned ; but who, I am very glad to say, was not. There was then only the Queen to dispose of. She had been surrounded in the Tower with women spies ; had been monstrously persecuted and foully slandered ; and had received no justice. But her spirit rose with her afflictions ; and, after having in vain tried to soften the King by writing an affecting letter to him which still exists, "from her doleful prison in the Tower," she resigned herself to death. She said to those about her, very cheerfully, that she had heard say the executioner was a good one, and that she had a little neck (she laughed and clasped it with her hands as she said that), and would soon be out of her pain. And she *was* soon out of her pain, poor creature, on the Green inside the Tower, and her body was flung into an old box and put away in the ground under the chapel.

There is a story that the King sat in his palace listening very anxiously for the sound of the cannon which was to announce this new murder ; and that, when he heard it come booming on the air, he rose up in great spirits and ordered out his dogs to go a-hunting. He was bad enough to do it ; but whether he did it or not, it is certain that he married Jane Seymour the very next day.

I have not much pleasure in recording that she lived just long enough to give birth to a son who was christened EDWARD, and then to die of a fever : for, I cannot but think that any woman who married such a ruffian, and knew what innocent blood was on his hands, deserved the axe that would assuredly have fallen on the neck of Jane Seymour, if she had lived much longer.

Cranmer had done what he could to save some of the Church property for purposes of religion and education ; but, the great families had been so hungry to get hold of it, that very little could be rescued for such objects. Even MILES COVERDALE, who did the people the inestimable service of translating the Bible into English (which the unreformed religion never permitted to be done), was left in poverty while the great families clutched the Church lands and money. The people had been told that when the Crown came into possession of these funds, it would not be necessary to tax them ; but they were taxed afresh directly afterwards. It was fortunate for them, indeed, that so many nobles were so greedy for this wealth ; since, if it had remained with the Crown, there might have been no end to tyranny for hundreds of years. One of the most active writers on the Church's side against the King was a member of his own family—a sort of distant cousin, REGINALD POLE by name— who attacked him in the most violent manner (though he received a pension from him all the time), and fought for the Church with his pen, day and night. As he was beyond the King's reach—being in Italy—the King politely invited him over to discuss the subject; but he, knowing better than to come, and wisely staying where he was, the King's rage fell upon his brother Lord Montague, the Marquis of Exeter, and some other gentlemen: who were tried for high treason in corresponding with him and aiding him—which they probably did—and were all executed. The Pope made Reginald Pole a cardinal; but, so much against his will, that it is thought he even aspired in his own mind to the vacant throne of England, and had hopes of marrying the Princess Mary. His being made a high priest, however, put an end to all that. His mother, the venerable Countess of Salisbury—who was, unfortunately for herself, within the tyrant's reach—was the last of his relatives on whom his wrath fell. When she was told to lay her grey head upon the block, she answered the executioner, "No! My head never committed treason, and if you want it, you shall seize it." So, she ran round and round the scaffold with the executioner striking at her, and her grey hair bedabbled with blood; and even when they held her down upon the block she moved her head about to the last, resolved to be no party to her own barbarous murder. All this the people bore, as they had borne everything else.

Indeed they bore much more; for the slow fires of Smith-field were continually burning, and people were constantly being roasted to death—still to show what a good Christian the King was. He defied the Pope and his Bull, which was now issued, and had come into England; but he burned innumerable people whose only offence was that they differed from the Pope's religious opinions. There was a wretched man named LAMBERT, among others, who was tried for this before the King, and with whom six bishops argued one after another. When he was quite exhausted (as well he might be, after six bishops), he threw himself on the King's mercy; but the King blustered out that he had no mercy for heretics. So, *he* too fed the fire.

All this the people bore, and more than all this yet. The national spirit seems to have been banished from the kingdom at this time. The very people who were executed for treason, the very wives and friends of the "bluff" King, spoke of him on the scaffold as a good prince, and a gentle prince—just as serfs in similar circumstances have been known to do, under the Sultan and Bashaws of the East, or under the fierce old tyrants of Russia, who poured boiling and freezing water on them alternately, until they died. The Parliament were as bad as the rest, and gave the King whatever he wanted ; among other vile accommodations, they gave him new powers of murdering, at his will and pleasure, any one whom he might choose to call a traitor. But the worst measure they passed was an Act of Six Articles, commonly called at the time "the whip with six strings ; " which punished offences against the Pope's opinions, without mercy, and enforced the very worst parts of the monkish religion. Cranmer would have modified it, if he could ; but, being overborne by the Romish party, had not the power. As one of the articles declared that priests should not marry, and as he was married himself, he sent his wife and children into Germany, and began to tremble at his danger ; none the less because he was, and had long been, the King's friend. This whip of six strings was made under the King's own eye. It should never be forgotten of him how cruelly he supported the worst of the Popish doctrines when there was nothing to be got by opposing them.

This amiable monarch now thought of taking another wife. He proposed to the French King to have some of the ladies of the French Court exhibited before him, that he might make his Royal choice; but the French King answered that he would rather not have his ladies trotted out to be shown like horses at a fair. He proposed to the Dowager Duchess of Milan, who replied that she might have thought of such a match if she had had two heads ; but, that only owning one, she must beg to keep it safe. At last Cromwell represented that there was a Protestant Princess in Germany —those who held the reformed religion were called Protestants, because their leaders had Protested against the abuses and impositions of the unreformed Church—named ANNE OF CLEVES, who was beautiful, and would answer the purpose admirably. The King said was she a large woman, because he must have a fat wife? "O yes," said Cromwell; "she was very large, just the thing." On hearing this the King sent over his famous painter, Hans Holbein, to take her portrait. Hans made her out to be so good-looking that the King was satisfied, and the marriage was arranged. But, whether anybody had paid Hans to touch up the picture; or whether Hans, like one or two other painters, flattered a princess in the ordinary way of business, I cannot say: all I know is, that when Anne came over and the King went to Rochester to meet her, and first saw her without her seeing him, he swore she was " a great Flanders mare," and said he would never marry her. Being obliged to do it now matters had gone so far, he would not give her the presents he had prepared, and would never notice her. He never forgave Cromwell his part in the affair. His downfall dates from that time.

It was quickened by his enemies, in the interests of the unreformed religion, putting in the King's way, at a state dinner, a niece of the Duke of Norfolk, CATHERINE HOWARD, a young lady of fascinating manners, though small in stature and not particularly beautiful. Falling in love with her on the spot, the King soon divorced Anne of Cleves after making her the subject of much brutal talk, on pretence that she had been previously betrothed to some one else— which would never do for one of his dignity—and married Catherine. It is probable that on his wedding day, of all days in the year, he sent his faithful Cromwell to the scaffold, and had his head struck off. He further celebrated the occasion by burning at one time, and causing to be drawn to the fire on the same hurdles, some Protestant prisoners for denying the Pope's doctrines, and some Roman Catholic prisoners for denying his own supremacy. Still the people bore it, and not a gentleman in England raised his hand.

But, by a just retribution, it soon came out that Catherine Howard, before her marriage, had been really guilty of such crimes as the King had falsely attributed to his second wife Anne Boleyn; so, again the dreadful axe made the King a widower, and this Queen passed away as so many in that reign had passed away before her. As an appropriate pursuit under the circumstances, Henry then applied himself to superintending the composition of a religious book called " A necessary doctrine for any Christian Man." He must have been a little confused in his mind, I think, at about this period ; for he was so false to himself as to be true to some one: that some one being Cranmer, whom the Duke of Norfolk and others of his enemies tried to ruin ; but to whom the King was steadfast, and to whom he one night gave his ring, charging him when he should find himself, next day, accused of treason, to show it to the council board. This Cranmer did to the confusion of his enemies. I suppose the King thought he might want him a little longer.

He married yet once more. Yes, strange to say, he found in England another woman who would become his wife, and she was CATHERINE PARR, widow of Lord Latimer. She leaned towards the reformed religion ; and it is some comfort to know, that she tormented the King considerably by arguing a variety of doctrinal points with him on all possible occasions. She had very nearly done this to her own destruction. After one of these conversations the King in a very black mood actually instructed GARDINER, one of his Bishops who favoured the Popish opinions, to draw a bill of accusation against her, which would have inevitably brought her to the scaffold where her predecessors had died, but that one of her friends picked up the paper of instruc-tions which had been dropped in the palace, and gave her timely notice. She fell ill with terror ; but managed the King so well when he came to entrap her into further state-ments—by saying that she had only spoken on such points to divert his mind and to get some information from his extraordinary wisdom—that he gave her a kiss and called her his sweetheart. And, when the Chancellor came next day actually to take her to the Tower, the King sent him about his business, and honoured him with the epithets of a beast, a knave, and a fool. So near was Catherine Parr to the block, and so narrow was her escape !

There was war with Scotland in this reign, and a short clumsy war with France for favouring Scotland ; but, the events at home were so dreadful, and leave such an enduring stain on the country, that I need say no more of what happened abroad.

A few more horrors, and this reign is over. There was a lady, ANNE ASKEW, in Lincolnshire, who inclined to the Protestant opinions, and whose husband being a fierce Catholic, turned her out of his house. She came to London, and was considered as offending against the six articles, and

was taken to the Tower, and put upon the rack—probably
because it was hoped that she might, in her agony, criminate
some obnoxious persons ; if falsely, so much the better. She
was tortured without uttering a cry, until the Lieutenant of
the Tower would suffer his men to torture her no more ;
and then two priests who were present actually pulled off
their robes, and turned the wheels of the rack with their
own hands, so rending and twisting and breaking her that
she was afterwards carried to the fire in a chair. She was
burned with three others, a gentleman, a clergyman, and
a tailor ; and so the world went on.

Either the King became afraid of the power of the Duke
of Norfolk, and his son the Earl of Surrey, or they gave him
some offence, but he resolved to pull *them* down, to follow
all the rest who were gone. The son was tried first—of
course for nothing—and defended himself bravely ; but
of course he was found guilty, and of course he was
executed. Then his father was laid hold of, and left for
death too.

But the King himself was left for death by a Greater
King, and the earth was to be rid of him at last. He was
now a swollen, hideous spectacle, with a great hole in his
leg, and so odious to every sense that it was dreadful to
approach him. When he was found to be dying, Cranmer
was sent for from his palace at Croydon, and came with all
speed, but found him speechless. Happily, in that hour he
perished. He was in the fifty-sixth year of his age, and the
thirty-eighth of his reign.

Henry the Eighth has been favoured by some Protestant
writers, because the Reformation was achieved in his time.
But the mighty merit of it lies with other men and not
with him ; and it can be rendered none the worse by this
monster's crimes, and none the better by any defence of
them. The plain truth is, that he was a most intolerable
ruffian, a disgrace to human nature, and a blot of blood and
grease upon the History of England.

CHAPTER XXIX

ENGLAND UNDER EDWARD THE SIXTH

HENRY THE EIGHTH had made a will, appointing a council
of sixteen to govern the kingdom for his son while he was
under age (he was now only ten years old), and another
council of twelve to help them. The most powerful of the
first council was the EARL OF HERTFORD, the young King's
uncle, who lost no time in bringing his nephew with great
state up to Enfield, and thence to the Tower. It was considered at the time a striking proof of virtue in the young
King that he was sorry for his father's death; but, as
common subjects have that virtue too, sometimes, we will
say no more about it.

There was a curious part of the late King's will, requiring
his executors to fulfil whatever promises he had made.
Some of the court wondering what these might be, the Earl
of Hertford and the other noblemen interested, said that
they were promises to advance and enrich *them*. So, the
Earl of Hertford made himself DUKE OF SOMERSET, and
made his brother EDWARD SEYMOUR a baron; and there
were various similar promotions, all very agreeable to the
parties concerned, and very dutiful, no doubt, to the late
King's memory. To be more dutiful still, they made themselves rich out of the Church lands, and were very comfortable. The new Duke of Somerset caused himself to be
declared PROTECTOR of the kingdom, and was, indeed, the
King.

As young Edward the Sixth had been brought up in the
principles of the Protestant religion, everybody knew that
they would be maintained. But Cranmer, to whom they
were chiefly entrusted, advanced them steadily and tem-
perately. Many superstitious and ridiculous practices were
stopped; but practices which were harmless were not interfered with.

P

The Duke of Somerset, the Protector, was anxious to have the young King engaged in marriage to the young Queen of Scotland, in order to prevent that princess from making an alliance with any foreign power; but, as a large party in Scotland were unfavourable to this plan, he invaded that country. His excuse for doing so was, that the Border men —that is, the Scotch who lived in that part of the country where England and Scotland joined—troubled the English very much. But there were two sides to this question; for the English Border men troubled the Scotch too; and, through many long years, there were perpetual border quarrels which gave rise to numbers of old tales and songs. However, the Protector invaded Scotland; and ARRAN, the Scottish Regent, with an army twice as large as his, advanced to meet him. They encountered on the banks of the river Esk, within a few miles of Edinburgh; and there, after a little skirmish, the Protector made such moderate proposals, in offering to retire if the Scotch would only engage not to marry their princess to any foreign prince, that the Regent thought the English were afraid. But in this he made a horrible mistake; for the English soldiers on land, and the English sailors on the water, so set upon the Scotch, that they broke and fled, and more than ten thousand of them were killed. It was a dreadful battle, for the fugitives were slain without mercy. The ground for four miles, all the way to Edinburgh, was strewn with dead men, and with arms, and legs, and heads. Some hid themselves in streams and were drowned; some threw away their armour and were killed running, almost naked; but in this battle of Pinkey the English lost only two or three hundred men. They were much better clothed than the Scotch; at the poverty of whose appearance and country they were exceedingly astonished.

A Parliament was called when Somerset came back, and it repealed the whip with six strings, and did one or two other good things; though it unhappily retained the punishment of burning for those people who did not make believe to believe, in all religious matters, what the Government had declared that they must and should believe. It also made a foolish law (meant to put down beggars), that any man who lived idly and loitered about for three days together, should be burned with a hot iron, made a slave, and wear an iron fetter. But this savage absurdity soon came to an end, and went the way of a great many other foolish laws.

The Protector was now so proud that he sat in Parliament before all the nobles, on the right hand of the throne. Many other noblemen, who only wanted to be as proud if they could get a chance, became his enemies of course ; and it is supposed that he came back suddenly from Scotland because he had received news that his brother, LORD SEYMOUR, was becoming dangerous to him. This lord was now High Admiral of England ; a very handsome man, and a great favourite with the Court ladies—even with the young Princess Elizabeth, who romped with him a little more than young princesses in these times do with any one. He had married Catherine Parr, the late King's widow, who was now dead ; and, to strengthen his power, he secretly supplied the young King with money. He may even have engaged with some of his brother's enemies in a plot to carry the boy off. On these and other accusations, at any rate, he was confined in the Tower, impeached, and found guilty; his own brother's name being—unnatural and sad to tell—the first signed to the warrant for his execution. He was executed on Tower Hill, and died denying his treason. One of his last proceedings in this world was to write two letters, one to the Princess Elizabeth, and one to the Princess Mary, which a servant of his took charge of, and concealed in his shoe. These letters are supposed to have urged them against his brother, and to revenge his death. What they truly contained is not known; but there is no doubt that he had, at one time, obtained great influence over the Princess Elizabeth.

All this while, the Protestant religion was making progress. The images which the people had gradually come to worship, were removed from the churches ; the people were informed that they need not confess themselves to priests unless they chose ; a common prayer-book was drawn up in the English language, which all could understand ; and many other improvements were made ; still moderately. For Cranmer was a very moderate man, and even restrained the Protestant clergy from violently abusing the unreformed religion—as they very often did, and which was not a good example. But the people were at this time in great distress. The rapacious nobility who had come into possession of the Church lands, were very bad landlords. They enclosed great quantities of ground for the feeding of sheep, which was then more profitable than the growing of crops; and this increased the general distress. So the people, who still understood little of what was going on about them, and still readily believed what the homeless monks told them—many of whom had been their good friends in their better days—took it into their heads that all this was owing to the reformed religion, and therefore rose in many parts of the country.

The most powerful risings were in Devonshire and Norfolk. In Devonshire, the rebellion was so strong that ten thousand men united within a few days, and even laid siege to Exeter. But LORD RUSSELL, coming to the assistance of the citizens who defended that town, defeated the rebels; and, not only hanged the Mayor of one place, but hanged the vicar of another from his own church steeple. What with hanging and killing by the sword, four thousand of the rebels are supposed to have fallen in that one county. In Norfolk (where the rising was more against the enclosure of open lands than against the reformed religion), the popular leader was a man named ROBERT KET, a tanner of Wymondham. The mob were, in the first instance, excited against the tanner by one JOHN FLOWERDEW, a gentleman who owed him a grudge: but the tanner was more than a match for the gentleman, since he soon got the people on his side, and established himself near Norwich with quite an army. There was a large oak-tree in that place, on a spot called Moushold Hill, which Ket named the Tree of Reformation; and under its green boughs, he and his men sat, in the midsummer weather, holding courts of justice, and debating affairs of state. They were even impartial enough to allow some rather tiresome public speakers to get up into this Tree of Reformation, and point out their errors to them, in long discourses, while they lay listening (not always without some grumbling and growling) in the shade below. At last, one sunny July day, a herald appeared below the tree, and proclaimed Ket and all his men traitors, unless from that moment they dispersed and went home: in which case they were to receive a pardon. But, Ket and his men made light of the herald and became stronger than ever, until the Earl of Warwick went after them with a sufficient force, and cut them all to pieces. A few were hanged, drawn, and quartered, as traitors, and their limbs were sent into various country places to be a terror to the people. Nine of them were hanged upon nine green branches of the Oak of Reformation ; and so, for the time, that tree may be said to have withered away.

The Protector, though a haughty man, had compassion for the real distresses of the common people, and a sincere desire to help them. But he was too proud and too high in degree to hold even their favour steadily ; and many of the nobles always envied and hated him, because they were as proud and not as high as he. He was at this time building a great Palace in the Strand: to get the stone for which he blew up church steeples with gunpowder, and pulled down bishops' houses: thus making himself still more disliked. At length, his principal enemy, the Earl of Warwick—Dudley by name, and the son of that Dudley who had made himself so odious with Empson, in the reign of Henry the Seventh—joined with seven other members of the Council against him, formed a separate Council ; and, becoming stronger in a few days, sent him to the Tower under twenty-nine articles of accusation. After being sentenced by the Council to the forfeiture of all his offices and lands, he was liberated and pardoned, on making a very humble submission. He was even taken back into the Council again, after having suffered this fall, and married his daughter, LADY ANNE SEYMOUR, to Warwick's eldest son. But such a reconciliation was little likely to last, and did not outlive a year. Warwick, having got himself made Duke of Northumberland, and having advanced the more important of his friends, then finished the history by causing the Duke of Somerset and his friend LORD GREY, and others, to be arrested for treason, in having conspired to seize and dethrone the King. They were also accused of having intended to seize the new Duke of Northumberland, with his friends LORD NORTHAMPTON and LORD PEMBROKE ; to murder them if they found need ; and to raise the City to revolt. All this the fallen Protector positively denied : except that he confessed to having spoken of the murder of those three noblemen, but having never designed it. He was acquitted of the charge of treason, and found guilty of the other charges ; so when the people—who remembered his having been their friend, now that he was disgraced and in danger, saw him come out from his trial with the axe turned from him—they thought he was altogether acquitted, and set up a loud shout of joy.

But the Duke of Somerset was ordered to be beheaded on Tower Hill, at eight o'clock in the morning, and proclamations were issued bidding the citizens keep at home until after ten. They filled the streets, however, and crowded the place of execution as soon as it was light; and, with sad faces and sad hearts, saw the once powerful Protector ascend the scaffold to lay his head upon the dreadful block. While he was yet saying his last words to them with manly courage, and telling them, in particular, how it comforted him, at that pass, to have assisted in reforming the national religion, a member of the Council was seen riding up on horseback. They again thought that the Duke was saved by his bringing a reprieve, and again shouted for joy. But the Duke himself told them they were mistaken, and laid down his head and had it struck off at a blow.

Many of the bystanders rushed forward and steeped their handkerchiefs in his blood, as a mark of their affection. He had, indeed, been capable of many good acts, and one of them was discovered after he was no more. The Bishop of Durham, a very good man, had been informed against to the Council, when the Duke was in power, as having answered a treacherous letter proposing a rebellion against the reformed religion. As the answer could not be found, he could not be declared guilty; but it was now discovered, hidden by the Duke himself among some private papers, in his regard for that good man. The Bishop lost his office, and was deprived of his possessions.

It is not very pleasant to know that while his uncle lay in prison under sentence of death, the young King was being vastly entertained by plays, and dances, and sham fights: but there is no doubt of it, for he kept a journal himself. It is pleasanter to know that not a single Roman Catholic was burnt in this reign for holding that religion; though two wretched victims suffered for heresy. One, a woman named JOAN BOCHER, for professing some opinions that even she could only explain in unintelligible jargon. The other, a Dutchman, named VON PARIS, who practised as a surgeon in London. Edward was, to his credit, exceedingly unwilling to sign the warrant for the woman's execution: shedding tears before he did so, and telling

Cranmer, who urged him to do it (though Cranmer really would have spared the woman at first, but for her own determined obstinacy), that the guilt was not his, but that of the man who so strongly urged the dreadful act. We shall see, too soon, whether the time ever came when Cranmer is likely to have remembered this with sorrow and remorse.

Cranmer and RIDLEY (at first Bishop of Rochester, and afterwards Bishop of London) were the most powerful of the clergy of this reign. Others were imprisoned and deprived of their property for still adhering to the unreformed religion ; the most important among whom were GARDINER Bishop of Winchester, HEATH Bishop of Worcester, DAY Bishop of Chichester, and BONNER that Bishop of London who was superseded by Ridley. The Princess Mary, who inherited her mother's gloomy temper, and hated the reformed religion as connected with her mother's wrongs and sorrows—she knew nothing else about it, always refusing to read a single book in which it was truly described—held by the unreformed religion too, and was the only person in the kingdom for whom the old Mass was allowed to be performed ; nor would the young King have made that exception even in her favour, but for the strong persuasions of Cranmer and Ridley. He always viewed it with horror ; and when he fell into a sickly condition, after having been very ill, first of the measles and then of the small-pox, he was greatly troubled in mind to think that if he died, and she, the next heir to the throne, succeeded, the Roman Catholic religion would be set up again.

This uneasiness, the Duke of Northumberland was not slow to encourage: for, if the Princess Mary came to the throne, he, who had taken part with the Protestants, was sure to be disgraced. Now, the Duchess of Suffolk was descended from King Henry the Seventh ; and, if she resigned what little or no right she had, in favour of her daughter LADY JANE GREY, that would be the succession to promote the Duke's greatness ; because LORD GUILFORD DUDLEY, one of his sons, was, at this very time, newly married to her. So, he worked upon the King's fears, and persuaded him to set aside both the Princess Mary and the Princess Elizabeth, and assert his right to appoint his successor. Accordingly the young King handed to the Crown lawyers a writing signed half a dozen times over by himself appointing Lady Jane Grey to succeed to the Crown, and requiring them to have his will made out according to law. They were much against it at first, and told the King so; but the Duke of Northumberland—being so violent about it that the lawyers even expected him to beat them, and hotly declaring that, stripped to his shirt, he would fight any man in such a quarrel—they yielded. Cranmer, also, at first hesitated; pleading that he had sworn to maintain the succession of the Crown to the Princess Mary; but, he was a weak man in his resolutions, and afterwards signed the document with the rest of the council.

It was completed none too soon; for Edward was now sinking in a rapid decline; and, by way of making him better, they handed him over to a woman-doctor who pretended to be able to cure it. He speedily got worse. On the sixth of July, in the year one thousand five hundred and fifty-three, he died, very peaceably and piously, praying God, with his last breath, to protect the reformed religion.

This King died in the sixteenth year of his age, and in the seventh of his reign. It is difficult to judge what the character of one so young might afterwards have become among so many bad, ambitious, quarrelling nobles. But, he was an amiable boy, of very good abilities, and had nothing coarse or cruel or brutal in his disposition—which in the son of such a father is rather surprising.

CHAPTER XXX

ENGLAND UNDER MARY

THE Duke of Northumberland was very anxious to keep the young King's death a secret, in order that he might get the two Princesses into his power. But, the Princess Mary, being informed of that event as she was on her way to London to see her sick brother, turned her horse's head, and rode away into Norfolk. The Earl of Arundel was her friend, and it was he who sent her warning of what had happened.

As the secret could not be kept, the Duke of Northumberland and the council sent for the Lord Mayor of London and some of the aldermen, and made a merit of telling it to them. Then, they made it known to the people, and set off to inform Lady Jane Grey that she was to be Queen.

She was a pretty girl of only sixteen, and was amiable, learned, and clever. When the lords who came to her, fell on their knees before her, and told her what tidings they brought, she was so astonished that she fainted. On recovering, she expressed her sorrow for the young King's death, and said that she knew she was unfit to govern the kingdom; but that if she must be Queen, she prayed God to direct her. She was then at Sion House, near Brentford; and the lords took her down the river in state to the Tower, that she might remain there (as the custom was) until she was crowned. But the people were not at all favourable to Lady Jane, considering that the right to be Queen was Mary's, and greatly disliking the Duke of Northumberland. They were not put into a better humour by the Duke's causing a vintner's servant, one Gabriel Pot, to be taken up for expressing his dissatisfaction among the crowd, and to have his ears nailed to the pillory, and cut off. Some powerful men among the nobility declared on Mary's side. They raised troops to support her cause, had her proclaimed Queen at Norwich, and gathered around her at the castle of Framlingham, which belonged to the Duke of Norfolk. For, she was not considered so safe as yet, but that it was best to keep her in a castle on the sea-coast, from whence she might be sent abroad, if necessary.

The Council would have despatched Lady Jane's father, the Duke of Suffolk, as the general of the army against this force; but, as Lady Jane implored that her father might remain with her, and as he was known to be but a weak man, they told the Duke of Northumberland that he must take the command himself. He was not very ready to do so, as he mistrusted the Council much; but there was no help for it, and he set forth with a heavy heart, observing to a lord who rode beside him through Shoreditch at the head of the troops, that, although the people pressed in great numbers to look at them, they were terribly silent.

And his fears for himself turned out to be well founded. While he was waiting at Cambridge for further help from the Council, the Council took it into their heads to turn their backs on Lady Jane's cause, and to take up the Princess Mary's. This was chiefly owing to the before-mentioned Earl of Arundel, who represented to the Lord Mayor and aldermen, in a second interview with those sagacious persons, that, as for himself, he did not perceive the Reformed religion to be in much danger—which Lord Pembroke backed by flourishing his sword as another kind of persuasion. The Lord Mayor and aldermen, thus enlightened, said there could be no doubt that the Princess Mary ought to be Queen. So, she was proclaimed at the Cross by St. Paul's, and barrels of wine were given to the people, and they got very drunk, and danced round blazing bonfires—little thinking, poor wretches, what other bonfires would soon be blazing in Queen Mary's name.

After a ten days' dream of royalty, Lady Jane Grey resigned the Crown with great willingness, saying that she had only accepted it in obedience to her father and mother; and went gladly back to her pleasant house by the river, and her books. Mary then came on towards London; and at Wanstead in Essex, was joined by her half-sister, the Princess Elizabeth. They passed through the streets of London to the Tower, and there the new Queen met some eminent prisoners then confined in it, kissed them, and gave them their liberty. Among these was that Gardiner, Bishop of Winchester, who had been imprisoned in the last reign for holding to the unreformed religion. Him she soon made chancellor.

The Duke of Northumberland had been taken prisoner, and, together with his son and five others, was quickly brought before the Council. He, not unnaturally, asked that Council, in his defence, whether it was treason to obey orders that had been issued under the great seal; and, if it were, whether they, who had obeyed them too, ought to be his judges? But they made light of these points; and, being resolved to have him out of the way, soon sentenced him to death. He had risen into power upon the death of another man, and made but a poor show (as might be expected) when he himself lay low. He entreated Gardiner to let him live. if it were only in a mouse's hole; and, when he ascended the scaffold to be beheaded on Tower Hill, addressed the people in a miserable way, saying that he had been incited by others, and exhorting them to return to the unreformed religion, which he told them was his faith. There seems reason to suppose that he expected a pardon even then, in return for this confession; but it matters little whether he did or not. His head was struck off.

Mary was now crowned Queen. She was thirty-seven years of age, short and thin, wrinkled in the face, and very unhealthy. But she had a great liking for show and for bright colours, and all the ladies of her Court were magnificently dressed. She had a great liking too for old customs. without much sense in them; and she was oiled in the oldest way, and blessed in the oldest way, and done all manner of things to in the oldest way, at her coronation. I hope they did her good.

She soon began to show her desire to put down the Reformed religion, and put up the unreformed one: though it was dangerous work as yet, the people being something wiser than they used to be. They even cast a shower of stones—and among them a dagger—at one of the royal chaplains who attacked the Reformed religion in a public sermon. But the Queen and her priests went steadily on. Ridley, the powerful bishop of the last reign, was seized and sent to the Tower. LATIMER, also celebrated among the Clergy of the last reign, was likewise sent to the Tower, and Cranmer speedily followed. Latimer was an aged man: and, as his guards took him through Smithfield, he looked round it, and said, "This is a place that hath long groaned

for me." For he knew well, what kind of bonfires would
soon be burning. Nor was the knowledge confined to him.
The prisons were fast filled with the chief Protestants, who
were there left rotting in darkness, hunger, dirt, and separation
from their friends ; many, who had time left them for escape,
fled from the kingdom ; and the dullest of the people began,
now, to see what was coming.

It came on fast. A Parliament was got together ; not
without strong suspicion of unfairness ; and they annulled
the divorce, formerly pronounced by Cranmer between the
Queen's mother and King Henry the Eighth, and unmade
all the laws on the subject of religion that had been made in
the last King Edward's reign. They began their proceedings,
in violation of the law, by having the old mass said before
them in Latin, and by turning out a bishop who would not
kneel down. They also declared guilty of treason, Lady
Jane Grey for aspiring to the Crown ; her husband, for being
her husband ; and Cranmer, for not believing in the mass
aforesaid. They then prayed the Queen graciously to choose
a husband for herself, as soon as might be.

Now, the question who should be the Queen's husband
had given rise to a great deal of discussion, and to several
contending parties. Some said Cardinal Pole was the man—
but the Queen was of opinion that he was *not* the man, he
being too old and too much of a student. Others said that
the gallant young COURTENAY, whom the Queen had made
Earl of Devonshire, was the man—and the Queen thought
so too, for a while ; but she changed her mind. At last it
appeared that PHILIP, PRINCE OF SPAIN, was certainly the
man—though certainly not the people's man ; for they
detested the idea of such a marriage from the beginning
to the end, and murmured that the Spaniard would establish
in England, by the aid of foreign soldiers, the worst abuses
of the Popish religion, and even the terrible Inquisition
itself.

These discontents gave rise to a conspiracy for marrying
young Courtenay to the Princess Elizabeth, and setting
them up, with popular tumults all over the kingdom,
against the Queen. This was discovered in time by Gardiner ;
but in Kent, the old bold county, the people rose in their
old bold way. SIR THOMAS WYAT, a man of great daring,
was their leader. He raised his standard at Maidstone,
marched on to Rochester, established himself in the old

castle there, and prepared to hold out against the Duke of Norfolk, who came against him with a party of the Queen's guards, and a body of five hundred London men. The London men, however, were all for Elizabeth, and not at all for Mary. They declared, under the castle walls, for Wyat; the Duke retreated; and Wyat came on to Deptford, at the head of fifteen thousand men.

But these, in their turn, fell away. When he came to Southwark, there were only two thousand left. Not dismayed by finding the London citizens in arms, and the guns at the Tower ready to oppose his crossing the river there, Wyat led them off to Kingston-upon-Thames, intending to cross the bridge that he knew to be in that place, and so to work his way round to Ludgate, one of the old gates of the City. He found the bridge broken down, but mended it, came across, and bravely fought his way up Fleet Street to Ludgate Hill. Finding the gate closed against him, he fought his way back again, sword in hand, to Temple Bar. Here, being overpowered, he surrendered himself, and three or four hundred of his men were taken, besides a hundred killed. Wyat, in a moment of weakness (and perhaps of torture) was afterwards made to accuse the Princess Elizabeth as his accomplice to some very small extent. But his manhood soon returned to him, and he refused to save his life by making any more false confessions. He was quartered and distributed in the usual brutal way, and from fifty to a hundred of his followers were hanged. The rest were led out, with halters round their necks, to be pardoned, and to make a parade of crying out, " God save Queen Mary ! "

In the danger of this rebellion, the Queen showed herself to be a woman of courage and spirit. She disdained to retreat to any place of safety, and went down to the Guildhall, sceptre in hand, and made a gallant speech to the Lord Mayor and citizens. But on the day after Wyat's defeat, she did the most cruel act, even of her cruel reign, in signing the warrant for the execution of Lady Jane Grey.

They tried to persuade Lady Jane to accept the unreformed religion; but she steadily refused. On the morning when she was to die, she saw from her window the bleeding and headless body of her husband brought back in a cart from the scaffold on Tower Hill where he had laid 'down his life. But, as she had declined to see him before his execution, lest she should be overpowered and not make a good end,

so, she even now showed a constancy and calmness that will
never be forgotten. She came up to the scaffold with a firm
step and a quiet face, and addressed the bystanders in a
steady voice. They were not numerous; for she was too
young, too innocent and fair, to be murdered before the
people on Tower Hill, as her husband had just been; so,
the place of her execution was within the Tower itself.
She said that she had done an unlawful act in taking
what was Queen Mary's right; but that she had done so
with no bad intent, and that she died a humble Christian.
She begged the executioner to despatch her quickly, and she
asked him, "Will you take my head off before I lay me
down?" He answered, "No, Madam," and then she was
very quiet while they bandaged her eyes. Being blinded,
and unable to see the block on which she was to lay her
young head, she was seen to feel about for it with her hands,
and was heard to say, confused, "O what shall I do! Where
is it?" Then they guided her to the right place, and the
executioner struck off her head. You know too well, now,
what dreadful deeds the executioner did in England, through
many many years, and how his axe descended on the hateful
block through the necks of some of the bravest, wisest, and
best in the land. But it never struck so cruel and so vile
a blow as this.

The father of Lady Jane soon followed, but was little
pitied. Queen Mary's next object was to lay hold of
Elizabeth, and this was pursued with great eagerness. Five
hundred men were sent to her retired house at Ashridge,
by Berkhampstead, with orders to bring her up, alive or dead.
They got there at ten at night, when she was sick in bed.
But, their leaders followed her lady into her bedchamber,
whence she was brought out betimes next morning, and put
into a litter to be conveyed to London. She was so weak
and ill, that she was five days on the road; still, she was
so resolved to be seen by the people that she had the curtains
of the litter opened; and so, very pale and sickly, passed
through the streets. She wrote to her sister, saying she was
innocent of any crime, and asking why she was made
a prisoner; but she got no answer, and was ordered to the
Tower. They took her in by the Traitor's Gate, to which
she objected, but in vain. One of the lords who conveyed
her offered to cover her with his cloak, as it was raining,
but she put it away from her, proudly and scornfully, and

Jane Grey seeing from the Window the Body of her Husband

passed into the Tower, and sat down in a court-yard on a stone. They besought her to come in out of the wet; but she answered that it was better sitting there, than in a worse place. At length she went to her apartment, where she was kept a prisoner, though not so close a prisoner as at Woodstock, whither she was afterwards removed, and where she is said to have one day envied a milkmaid whom she heard singing in the sunshine as she went through the green fields. Gardiner, than whom there were not many worse men among the fierce and sullen priests, cared little to keep secret his stern desire for her death : being used to say that it was of little service to shake off the leaves, and lop the branches of the tree of heresy, if its root, the hope of heretics, were left. He failed, however, in his benevolent design. Elizabeth was, at length. released ; and Hatfield House was assigned to her as a residence, under the care of one SIR THOMAS POPE.

It would seem that Philip, the Prince of Spain, was a main cause of this change in Elizabeth's fortunes. He was not an amiable man, being, on the contrary, proud, over-bearing, and gloomy ; but he and the Spanish lords who came over with him, assuredly did discountenance the idea of doing any violence to the Princess. It may have been mere prudence, but we will hope it was manhood and honour. The Queen had been expecting her husband with great impatience, and at length he came, to her great joy, though he never cared much for her. They were married by Gardiner, at Winchester, and there was more holiday-making among the people ; but they had their old distrust of this Spanish marriage, in which even the Parliament shared. Though the members of that Parliament were far from honest, and were strongly suspected to have been bought with Spanish money, they would pass no bill to enable the Queen to set aside the Princess Elizabeth and appoint her own successor.

Although Gardiner failed in this object, as well as in the darker one of bringing the Princess to the scaffold, he went on at a great pace in the revival of the unreformed religion. A new Parliament was packed, in which there were no Protestants. Preparations were made to receive Cardinal Pole in England as the Pope's messenger, bringing his holy declaration that all the nobility who had acquired Church property, should keep it—which was done to enlist their

selfish interest on the Pope's side. Then a great scene
was enacted, which was the triumph of the Queen's plans.
Cardinal Pole arrived in great splendour and dignity, and
was received with great pomp. The Parliament joined in
a petition expressive of their sorrow at the change in the
national religion, and praying him to receive the country
again into the Popish Church. With the Queen sitting
on her throne, and the King on one side of her, and the
Cardinal on the other, and the Parliament present, Gardiner
read the petition aloud. The Cardinal then made a great
speech, and was so obliging as to say that all was forgotten
and forgiven, and that the kingdom was solemnly made
Roman Catholic again.

Everything was now ready for the lighting of the terrible
bonfires. The Queen having declared to the Council, in
writing, that she would wish none of her subjects to be
burnt without some of the Council being present, and that
she would particularly wish there to be good sermons at all
burnings, the Council knew pretty well what was to be done
next. So, after the Cardinal had blessed all the bishops as
a preface to the burnings, the Chancellor Gardiner opened a
High Court at Saint Mary Overy, on the Southwark side of
London Bridge, for the trial of heretics. Here, two of the
late Protestant clergymen, HOOPER, Bishop of Gloucester,
and ROGERS, a Prebendary of St. Paul's, were brought to be
tried. Hooper was tried first for being married, though
a priest, and for not believing in the mass. He admitted
both of these accusations, and said that the mass was
a wicked imposition. Then they tried Rogers, who said
the same. Next morning the two were brought up to be
sentenced; and then Rogers said that his poor wife, being
a German woman and a stranger in the land, he hoped
might be allowed to come to speak to him before he died.
To this the inhuman Gardiner replied, that she was not his
wife. "Yea, but she is, my lord," said Rogers, "and she
hath been my wife these eighteen years." His request was
still refused, and they were both sent to Newgate; all those
who stood in the streets to sell things, being ordered to put
out their lights that the people might not see them. But,
the people stood at their doors with candles in their hands,
and prayed for them as they went by. Soon afterwards,
Rogers was taken out of jail to be burnt in Smithfield;
and, in the crowd as he went along, he saw his poor wife

and his ten children, of whom the youngest was a little baby. And so he was burnt to death.

The next day, Hooper, who was to be burnt at Gloucester, was brought out to take his last journey, and was made to wear a hood over his face that he might not be known by the people. But, they did know him for all that, down in his own part of the country; and, when he came near Gloucester, they lined the road, making prayers and lamenta- tions. His guards took him to a lodging, where he slept soundly all night. At nine o'clock next morning, he was brought forth leaning on a staff; for he had taken cold in prison, and was infirm. The iron stake, and the iron chain which was to bind him to it, were fixed up near a great elm-tree in a pleasant open place before the cathedral, where, on peaceful Sundays, he had been accustomed to preach and to pray, when he was bishop of Gloucester. This tree, which had no leaves then, it being February, was filled with people; and the priests of Gloucester College were looking complacently on from a window, and there was a great concourse of spectators in every spot from which a glimpse of the dreadful sight could be beheld. When the old man kneeled down on the small platform at the foot of the stake, and prayed aloud, the nearest people were observed to be so attentive to his prayers that they were ordered to stand farther back; for it did not suit the Romish Church to have those Protestant words heard. His prayers concluded, he went up to the stake and was stripped to his shirt, and chained ready for the fire. One of his guards had such compassion on him that, to shorten his agonies, he tied some packets of gunpowder about him. Then they heaped up wood and straw and reeds, and set them all alight. But, unhappily, the wood was green and damp, and there was a wind blowing that blew what flame there was, away. Thus, through three-quarters of an hour, the good old man was scorched and roasted and smoked, as the fire rose and sank; and all that time they saw him, as he burned, moving his lips in prayer, and beating his breast with one hand, even after the other was burnt away and had fallen off.

Cranmer, Ridley, and Latimer, were taken to Oxford to dispute with a commission of priests and doctors about the mass. They were shamefully treated; and it is recorded that the Oxford scholars hissed and howled and groaned,

and misconducted themselves in an anything but a scholarly
way.   The prisoners were taken back to jail, and afterwards
tried in St. Mary's Church.   They were all found guilty.   On
the sixteenth of the month of October, Ridley and Latimer
were brought out, to make another of the dreadful bonfires.

The scene of the suffering of these two good Protestant
men was in the City ditch, near Baliol College.   On coming
to the dreadful spot, they kissed the stakes, and then embraced each other.   And then a learned doctor got up into
a pulpit which was placed there, and preached a sermon
from the text, "Though I give my body to be burned, and
have not charity, it profiteth me nothing."   When you
think of the charity of burning men alive, you may imagine
that this learned doctor had a rather brazen face.   Ridley
would have answered his sermon when it came to an end,
but was not allowed.   When Latimer was stripped, it
appeared that he had dressed himself under his other
clothes, in a new shroud ; and, as he stood in it before all
the people, it was noted of him, and long remembered, that,
whereas he had been stooping and feeble but a few minutes
before, he now stood upright and handsome, in the knowledge that he was dying for a just and a great cause.
Ridley's brother-in-law was there with bags of gunpowder ;
and when they were both chained up, he tied them round
their bodies.   Then, a light was thrown upon the pile to
fire it.   "Be of good comfort, Master Ridley," said Latimer,
at that awful moment, "and play the man !   We shall this
day light such a candle, by God's grace, in England, as
I trust shall never be put out."   And then he was seen to
make motions with his hands as if he were washing them
in the flames, and to stroke his aged face with them, and
was heard to cry, "Father of Heaven, receive my soul !"
He died quickly, but the fire, after having burned the legs
of Ridley, sunk.   There he lingered, chained to the iron
post, and crying, "O ! I cannot burn !   O ! for Christ's sake
let the fire come unto me !"   And still, when his brother-
in-law had heaped on more wood, he was heard through the
blinding smoke, still dismally crying, "O ! I cannot burn,
I cannot burn !"   At last, the gunpowder caught fire, and
ended his miseries.

Five days after this fearful scene, Gardiner went to his
tremendous account before God, for the cruelties he had so
much assisted in committing.

Cranmer remained still alive and in prison. He was brought out again in February, for more examining and trying, by Bonner, Bishop of London: another man of blood, who had succeeded to Gardiner's work, even in his lifetime, when Gardiner was tired of it. Cranmer was now degraded as a priest, and left for death ; but, if the Queen hated any one on earth, she hated him, and it was resolved that he should be ruined and disgraced to the utmost. There is no doubt that the Queen and her husband personally urged on these deeds, because they wrote to the Council, urging them to be active in the kindling of the fearful fires. As Cranmer was known not to be a firm man, a plan was laid for surrounding him with artful people, and inducing him to recant to the unreformed religion. Deans and friars visited him, played at bowls with him, showed him various attentions, talked persuasively with him, gave him money for his prison comforts, and induced him to sign, I fear, as many as six recantations. But when, after all, he was taken out to be burnt, he was nobly true to his better self, and made a glorious end.

After prayers and a sermon, Dr. Cole, the preacher of the day (who had been one of the artful priests about Cranmer in prison), required him to make a public confession of his faith before the people. This, Cole did, expecting that he would declare himself a Roman Catholic. "I *will* make a profession of my faith," said Cranmer, "and with a good will too."

Then, he arose before them all, and took from the sleeve of his robe a written prayer and read it aloud. That done, he kneeled and said the Lord's Prayer, all the people joining ; and then he arose again and told them that he believed in the Bible, and that in what he had lately written, he had written what was not the truth, and that, because his right hand had signed those papers, he would burn his right hand first when he came to the fire. As for the Pope, he did refuse him and denounce him as the enemy of Heaven. Hereupon the pious Dr. Cole cried out to the guards to stop that heretic's mouth and take him away.

So they took him away, and chained him to the stake, where he hastily took off his own clothes to make ready for the flames. And he stood before the people with a bald head and a white and flowing beard. He was so firm now when the worst was come, that he again declared against his recantation, and was so impressive and so undismayed, that a certain lord, who was one of the directors of the execution, called out to the men to make haste! When the fire was lighted, Cranmer, true to his latest word, stretched out his right hand, and crying out, "This hand hath offended!" held it among the flames, until it blazed and burned away. His heart was found entire among his ashes, and he left at last a memorable name in English history. Cardinal Pole celebrated the day by saying his first mass, and next day he was made Archbishop of Canterbury in Cranmer's place.

The Queen's husband, who was now mostly abroad in his own dominions, and generally made a coarse jest of her to his more familiar courtiers, was at war with France, and came over to seek the assistance of England. England was very unwilling to engage in a French war for his sake; but it happened that the King of France, at this very time, aided a descent upon the English coast. Hence, war was declared, greatly to Philip's satisfaction; and the Queen raised a sum of money with which to carry it on, by every unjustifiable means in her power. It met with no profitable return, for the French Duke of Guise surprised Calais, and the English sustained a complete defeat. The losses they met with in France greatly mortified the national pride, and the Queen never recovered the blow.

There was a bad fever raging in England at this time, and I am glad to write that the Queen took it, and the hour of her death came. "When I am dead and my body is opened," she said to those around her, "ye shall find CALAIS written on my heart." I should have thought, if anything were written on it, they would have found the words—JANE GREY, HOOPER, ROGERS, RIDLEY, LATIMER, CRANMER, AND THREE HUNDRED PEOPLE BURNT ALIVE WITHIN FOUR YEARS OF MY WICKED REIGN, INCLUDING SIXTY WOMEN AND FORTY LITTLE CHILDREN. But it is enough that their deaths were written in Heaven.

The Queen died on the seventeenth of November, fifteen hundred and fifty-eight, after reigning not quite five years and a half, and in the forty-fourth year of her age. Cardinal Pole died of the same fever next day.

As BLOODY QUEEN MARY, this woman has become famous, and as BLOODY QUEEN MARY, she will ever be justly remembered with horror and detestation in Great Britain. Her memory has been held in such abhorrence that some writers have arisen in later years to take her part, and to show that she was, upon the whole, quite an amiable and cheerful sovereign! "By their fruits ye shall know them," said OUR SAVIOUR. The stake and the fire were the fruits of this reign, and you will judge this Queen by nothing else.

CHAPTER XXXI

ENGLAND UNDER ELIZABETH

THERE was great rejoicing all over the land when the Lords of the Council went down to Hatfield, to hail the Princess Elizabeth as the new Queen of England. Weary of the barbarities of Mary's reign, the people looked with hope and gladness to the new Sovereign. The nation seemed to wake from a horrible dream ; and Heaven, so long hidden by the smoke of the fires that roasted men and women to death, appeared to brighten once more.

Queen Elizabeth was five-and-twenty years of age when she rode through the streets of London, from the Tower to Westminster Abbey, to be crowned. Her countenance was strongly marked, but on the whole, commanding and dignified ; her hair was red, and her nose something too long and sharp for a woman's. She was not the beautiful creature her courtiers made out ; but she was well enough, and no doubt looked all the better for coming after the dark and gloomy Mary. She was well educated, but a round-about writer, and rather a hard swearer and coarse talker. She was clever, but cunning and deceitful, and inherited much of her father's violent temper. I mention this now, because she has been so over-praised by one party, and so over-abused by another, that it is hardly possible to under-stand the greater part of her reign without first understand-ing what kind of woman she really was.

She began her reign with the great advantage of having a very wise and careful Minister, SIR WILLIAM CECIL, whom she afterwards made LORD BURLEIGH. Altogether, the people had greater reason for rejoicing than they usually had, when there were processions in the streets ; and they were happy with some reason. All kinds of shows and images were set up ; GOG and MAGOG were hoisted to the top of Temple Bar ; and (which was more to the purpose) the Corporation dutifully presented the young Queen with the sum of a thousand marks in gold—so heavy a present, that she was obliged to take it into her carriage with both hands. The coronation was a great success ; and, on the next day, one of the courtiers presented a petition to the new Queen, praying that as it was the custom to release some prisoners on such occasions, she would have the goodness to release the four Evangelists, Matthew, Mark, Luke, and John, and also the Apostle Saint Paul, who had been for some time shut up in a strange language so that the people could not get at them.

To this, the Queen replied that it would be better first to inquire of themselves whether they desired to be released or not ; and, as a means of finding out, a great public discussion—a sort of religious tournament—was appointed to take place between certain champions of the two religions, in Westminster Abbey. You may suppose that it was soon made pretty clear to common sense, that for people to benefit by what they repeat or read, it is rather necessary they should understand something about it. Accordingly, a Church Service in plain English was settled, and other laws and regulations were made, completely establishing the great work of the Reformation. The Romish bishops and champions were not harshly dealt with, all things considered ; and the Queen's ministers were both prudent and merciful.

The one great trouble of this reign, and the unfortunate cause of the greater part of such turmoil and bloodshed as occurred in it, was MARY STUART, QUEEN OF SCOTS. We will try to understand, in as few words as possible, who Mary was, what she was, and how she came to be a thorn in the royal pillow of Elizabeth.

She was the daughter of the Queen Regent of Scotland, MARY OF GUISE. She had been married, when a mere child, to the Dauphin, the son and heir of the King of France. The Pope, who pretended that no one could rightfully wear the crown of England without his gracious permission, was strongly opposed to Elizabeth, who had not asked for the said gracious permission. And as Mary Queen of Scots would have inherited the English crown in right of her birth, supposing the English Parliament not to have altered the succession, the Pope himself, and most of the discontented who were followers of his, maintained that Mary was the rightful Queen of England, and Elizabeth the wrongful Queen. Mary being so closely connected with France, and France being jealous of England, there was far greater danger in this than there would have been if she had had no alliance with that great power. And when her young husband, on the death of his father, became FRANCIS THE SECOND, King of France, the matter grew very serious. For, the young couple styled themselves King and Queen of England, and the Pope was disposed to help them by doing all the mischief he could.

Now, the reformed religion, under the guidance of a stern and powerful preacher, named JOHN KNOX, and other such men, had been making fierce progress in Scotland. It was still a half savage country, where there was a great deal of murdering and rioting continually going on; and the Reformers, instead of reforming those evils as they should have done, went to work in the ferocious old Scottish spirit, laying churches and chapels waste, pulling down pictures and altars, and knocking about the Grey Friars, and the Black Friars, and the White Friars, and the friars of all sorts of colours, in all directions. This obdurate and harsh spirit of the Scottish reformers (the Scotch have always been rather a sullen and frowning people in religious matters) put up the blood of the Romish French court, and caused France to send troops over to Scotland, with the hope of setting the friars of all sorts of colours on their legs again; of conquering that country first, and England afterwards; and so crushing the Reformation all to pieces. The Scottish Reformers, who had formed a great league which they called The Congregation of the Lord, secretly represented to Eliza-beth that, if the reformed religion got the worst of it with them, it would be likely to get the worst of it in England too; and thus, Elizabeth, though she had a high notion of the rights of Kings and Queens to do anything they liked, sent an army to Scotland to support the Reformers, who were in arms against their sovereign. All these proceedings led to a treaty of peace at Edinburgh, under which the French consented to depart from the kingdom. By a separate treaty, Mary and her young husband engaged to renounce their assumed title of King and Queen of England. But this treaty they never fulfilled.

It happened, soon after matters had got to this state, that the young French King died, leaving Mary a young widow. She was then invited by her Scottish subjects to return home and reign over them; and as she was not now happy where she was, she, after a little time, complied.

Elizabeth had been Queen three years, when Mary Queen of Scots embarked at Calais for her own rough quarrelling country. As she came out of the harbour, a vessel was lost before her eyes, and she said, "O! good God! what an omen this is for such a voyage!" She was very fond of France, and sat on the deck, looking back at it and weeping, until it was quite dark. When she went to bed, she directed to be called at daybreak, if the French coast were still visible, that she might behold it for the last time. As it proved to be a clear morning, this was done, and she again wept for the country she was leaving, and said many times, "Farewell, France! Farewell, France! I shall never see thee again!" All this was long remembered afterwards, as sorrowful and interesting in a fair young princess of nineteen. Indeed, I am afraid it gradually came, together with her other distresses, to surround her with greater sympathy than she deserved.

When she came to Scotland, and took up her abode at the palace of Holyrood in Edinburgh, she found herself among uncouth strangers and wild uncomfortable customs very different from her experiences in the court of France. The very people who were disposed to love her, made her head ache when she was tired out by her voyage, with a serenade of discordant music—a fearful concert of bagpipes, I suppose—and brought her and her train home to her palace on miserable little Scotch horses that appeared to be half starved. Among the people who were not disposed to love her, she found the powerful leaders of the Reformed Church, who were bitter upon her amusements, however innocent, and denounced music and dancing as works of the devil. John Knox himself often lectured her, violently and angrily, and did much to make her life unhappy. All these reasons confirmed her old attachment to the Romish religion, and caused her, there is no doubt, most imprudently and dangerously both for herself and for England too, to give a solemn pledge to the heads of the Romish Church that if she ever succeeded to the English crown, she would set up that religion again. In reading her unhappy history, you must always remember this; and also that during her whole life she was constantly put

forward against the Queen, in some form or other, by the
Romish party.

That Elizabeth, on the other hand, was not inclined to
like her, is pretty certain. Elizabeth was very vain and
jealous, and had an extraordinary dislike to people being
married. She treated Lady Catherine Grey, sister of the
beheaded Lady Jane, with such shameful severity, for no
other reason than her being secretly married, that she died
and her husband was ruined; so, when a second marriage
for Mary began to be talked about, probably Elizabeth
disliked her more. Not that Elizabeth wanted suitors of
her own, for they started up from Spain, Austria, Sweden,
and England. Her English lover at this time, and one
whom she much favoured too, was LORD ROBERT DUDLEY,
Earl of Leicester—himself secretly married to AMY ROBSART,
the daughter of an English gentleman, whom he was strongly
suspected of causing to be murdered, down at his country
seat, Cumnor Hall in Berkshire, that he might be free to
marry the Queen. Upon this story, the great writer, SIR
WALTER SCOTT, has founded one of his best romances. But
if Elizabeth knew how to lead her handsome favourite on,
for her own vanity and pleasure, she knew how to stop him
for her own pride; and his love, and all the other proposals,
came to nothing. The Queen always declared in good
set speeches, that she would never be married at all, but
would live and die a Maiden Queen. It was a very pleasant
and meritorious declaration, I suppose; but it has been
puffed and trumpeted so much, that I am rather tired of
it myself.

Divers princes proposed to marry Mary, but the English
court had reasons for being jealous of them all, and even
proposed as a matter of policy that she should marry that
very Earl of Leicester who had aspired to be the husband of
Elizabeth. At last, LORD DARNLEY, son of the Earl of
Lennox, and himself descended from the Royal Family of
Scotland, went over with Elizabeth's consent to try his
fortune at Holyrood. He was a tall simpleton; and could
dance and play the guitar; but I know of nothing else he
could do, unless it were to get very drunk, and eat glutton-
ously, and make a contemptible spectacle of himself in
many mean and vain ways. However, he gained Mary's
heart, not disdaining in the pursuit of his object to ally
himself with one of her secretaries, DAVID RIZZIO, who had

great influence with her. He soon married the Queen. This marriage does not say much for her, but what followed will presently say less.

Mary's brother, the EARL OF MURRAY, and head of the Protestant party in Scotland, had opposed this marriage, partly on religious grounds, and partly perhaps from personal dislike of the very contemptible bridegroom. When it had taken place, through Mary's gaining over to it the more powerful of the lords about her, she banished Murray for his pains; and, when he and some other nobles rose in arms to support the reformed religion, she herself, within a month of her wedding day, rode against them in armour with loaded pistols in her saddle. Driven out of Scotland, they presented themselves before Elizabeth—who called them traitors in public, and assisted them in private, according to her crafty nature.

Mary had been married but a little while, when she began to hate her husband, who, in his turn, began to hate that David Rizzio, with whom he had leagued to gain her favour, and whom he now believed to be her lover. He hated Rizzio to that extent, that he made a compact with LORD RUTHVEN and three other lords to get rid of him by murder. This wicked agreement they made in solemn secrecy upon the first of March, fifteen hundred and sixty-six, and on the night of Saturday the ninth, the conspirators were brought by Darnley up a private staircase, dark and steep, into a range of rooms where they knew that Mary was sitting at supper with her sister, Lady Argyle, and this doomed man. When they went into the room, Darnley took the Queen round the waist, and Lord Ruthven, who had risen from a bed of sickness to do this murder, came in, gaunt and ghastly, leaning on two men. Rizzio ran behind the Queen for shelter and protection. " Let him come out of the room," said Ruthven. " He shall not leave the room," replied the Queen; "I read his danger in your face, and it is my will that he remain here." They then set upon him, struggled with him, overturned the table, dragged him out, and killed him with fifty-six stabs. When the Queen heard that he was dead, she said, " No more tears. I will think now of revenge ! "

Within a day or two, she gained her husband over, and prevailed on the tall idiot to abandon the conspirators and fly with her to Dunbar. There, he issued a proclamation,

audaciously and falsely denying that he had any knowledge
of the late bloody business; and there they were joined by
the EARL BOTHWELL and some other nobles. With their
help, they raised eight thousand men, returned to Edinburgh,
and drove the assassins into England. Mary soon afterwards
gave birth to a son—still thinking of revenge.

That she should have had a greater scorn for her husband
after his late cowardice and treachery than she had had
before, was natural enough. There is little doubt that she
now began to love Bothwell instead, and to plan with him
means of getting rid of Darnley. Bothwell had such power
over her that he induced her even to pardon the assassins
of Rizzio. The arrangements for the christening of the
young Prince were entrusted to him, and he was one of the
most important people at the ceremony, where the child was
named JAMES: Elizabeth being his godmother, though not
present on the occasion. A week afterwards, Darnley, who
had left Mary and gone to his father's house at Glasgow,
being taken ill with the small-pox, she sent her own physician
to attend him. But there is reason to apprehend that this
was merely a show and a pretence, and that she knew what
was doing, when Bothwell within another month proposed
to one of the late conspirators against Rizzio, to murder
Darnley, "for that it was the Queen's mind that he should
be taken away." It is certain that on that very day she
wrote to her ambassador in France, complaining of him, and
yet went immediately to Glasgow, feigning to be very anxious
about him, and to love him very much. If she wanted to
get him in her power, she succeeded to her heart's content;
for she induced him to go back with her to Edinburgh, and
to occupy, instead of the palace, a lone house outside the city
called the Kirk of Field. Here, he lived for about a week.
One Sunday night, she remained with him until ten o'clock,
and then left him, to go to Holyrood to be present at an
entertainment given in celebration of the marriage of one of
her favourite servants. At two o'clock in the morning the
city was shaken by a great explosion, and the Kirk of Field
was blown to atoms.

Darnley's body was found next day lying under a tree at
some distance. How it came there, undisfigured and un-
scorched by gunpowder, and how this crime came to be so
clumsily and strangely committed, it is impossible to discover.
The deceitful character of Mary, and the deceitful character

of Elizabeth, have rendered almost every part of their joint history uncertain and obscure. But, I fear that Mary was unquestionably a party to her husband's murder, and that this was the revenge she had threatened. The Scotch people universally believed it. Voices cried out in the streets of Edinburgh in the dead of the night, for justice on the murderess. Placards were posted by unknown hands in the public places denouncing Bothwell as the murderer, and the Queen as his accomplice; and, when he afterwards married her (though himself already married), previously making a show of taking her prisoner by force, the indignation of the people knew no bounds. The women particularly are described as having been quite frantic against the Queen, and to have hooted and cried after her in the streets with terrific vehemence.

Such guilty unions seldom prosper. This husband and wife had lived together but a month, when they were separated for ever by the successes of a band of Scotch nobles who associated against them for the protection of the young Prince: whom Bothwell had vainly endeavoured to lay hold of, and whom he would certainly have murdered, if the EARL OF MAR, in whose hands the boy was, had not been firmly and honourably faithful to his trust. Before this angry power, Bothwell fled abroad, where he died, a prisoner and mad, nine miserable years afterwards. Mary being found by the associated lords to deceive them at every turn, was sent a prisoner to Lochleven Castle; which, as it stood in the midst of a lake, could only be approached by boat. Here, one LORD LINDSAY, who was so much of a brute that the nobles would have done better if they had chosen a mere gentleman for their messenger, made her sign her abdication, and appoint Murray, Regent of Scotland. Here, too, Murray saw her in a sorrowing and humbled state.

She had better have remained in the castle of Lochleven, dull prison as it was, with the rippling of the lake against it, and the moving shadows of the water on the room-walls; but she could not rest there, and more than once tried to escape. The first time she had nearly succeeded, dressed in the clothes of her own washerwoman, but putting up her hand to prevent one of the boatmen from lifting her veil, the men suspected her, seeing how white it was, and rowed her back again. A short time afterwards, her fascinating manners enlisted in her cause a boy in the Castle, called the little DOUGLAS, who, while the family were at supper, stole the keys of the great gate, went softly out with the Queen, locked the gate on the outside, and rowed her away across the lake, sinking the keys as they went along. On the opposite shore she was met by another Douglas, and some few lords; and, so accompanied, rode away on horseback to Hamilton, where they raised three thousand men. Here, she issued a proclamation declaring that the abdication she had signed in her prison was illegal, and requiring the Regent to yield to his lawful Queen. Being a steady soldier, and in no way discomposed although he was without an army, Murray pretended to treat with her, until he had collected a force about half equal to her own, and then he gave her battle. In one quarter of an hour he cut down all her hopes. She had another weary ride on horseback of sixty long Scotch miles, and took shelter at Dundrennan Abbey, whence she fled for safety to Elizabeth's dominions.

Mary Queen of Scots came to England—to her own ruin, the trouble of the kingdom, and the misery and death of many—in the year one thousand five hundred and sixty-eight. How she left it and the world, nineteen years afterwards, we have now to see.

SECOND PART.

WHEN Mary Queen of Scots arrived in England, without money and even without any other clothes than those she wore, she wrote to Elizabeth, representing herself as an innocent and injured piece of Royalty, and entreating her assistance to oblige her Scottish subjects to take her back again and obey her. But, as her character was already known in England to be a very different one from what she made it out to be, she was told in answer that she must first clear herself. Made uneasy by this condition, Mary, rather than stay in England, would have gone to Spain, or to France, or would even have gone back to Scotland. But, as her doing either would have been likely to trouble England afresh, it was decided that she should be detained here. She first came to Carlisle, and, after that, was moved about from castle to castle, as was considered necessary; but England she never left again.

After trying very hard to get rid of the necessity of

clearing herself, Mary, advised by LORD HERRIES, her best friend in England, agreed to answer the charges against her, if the Scottish noblemen who made them would attend to maintain them before such English noblemen as Elizabeth might appoint for that purpose. Accordingly, such an assembly, under the name of a conference, met, first at York, and afterwards at Hampton Court. In its presence Lord Lennox, Darnley's father, openly charged Mary with the murder of his son; and whatever Mary's friends may now say or write in her behalf, there is no doubt that, when her brother Murray produced against her a casket containing certain guilty letters and verses which he stated to have passed between her and Bothwell, she withdrew from the inquiry. Consequently, it is to be supposed that she was then considered guilty by those who had the best opportunities of judging of the truth, and that the feeling which afterwards arose in her behalf was a very generous but not a very reasonable one.

However, the DUKE OF NORFOLK, an honourable but rather weak nobleman, partly because Mary was captivating, partly because he was ambitious, partly because he was overpersuaded by artful plotters against Elizabeth, conceived a strong idea that he would like to marry the Queen of Scots—though he was a little frightened, too, by the letters in the casket. This idea being secretly encouraged by some of the noblemen of Elizabeth's court, and even by the favourite Earl of Leicester (because it was objected to by other favourites who were his rivals), Mary expressed her approval of it, and the King of France and the King of Spain are supposed to have done the same. It was not so quietly planned, though, but that it came to Elizabeth's ears, who warned the Duke "to be careful what sort of pillow he was going to lay his head upon." He made a humble reply at the time; but turned sulky soon afterwards, and, being considered dangerous, was sent to the Tower.

Thus, from the moment of Mary's coming to England she began to be the centre of plots and miseries.

A rise of the Catholics in the north was the next of these, and it was only checked by many executions and much bloodshed. It was followed by a great conspiracy of the Pope and some of the Catholic sovereigns of Europe to depose Elizabeth, place Mary on the throne, and restore

Q

the unreformed religion. It is almost impossible to doubt that Mary knew and approved of this ; and the Pope himself was so hot in the matter that he issued a bull, in which he openly called Elizabeth the "pretended Queen" of England, excommunicated her, and excommunicated all her subjects who should continue to obey her. A copy of this miserable paper got into London, and was found one morning publicly posted on the Bishop of London's gate. A great hue and cry being raised, another copy was found in the chamber of a student of Lincoln's Inn, who confessed, being put upon the rack, that he had received it from one JOHN FELTON, a rich gentleman who lived across the Thames, near Southwark. This John Felton, being put upon the rack too, confessed that he had posted the placard on the Bishop's gate. For this offence he was, within four days, taken to St. Paul's Churchyard, and there hanged and quartered. As to the Pope's bull, the people by the reformation having thrown off the Pope, did not care much, you may suppose, for the Pope's throwing off them. It was a mere dirty piece of paper, and not half so powerful as a street ballad.

On the very day when Felton was brought to his trial, the poor Duke of Norfolk was released. It would have been well for him if he had kept away from the Tower evermore, and from the snares that had taken him there. But, even while he was in that dismal place he corresponded with Mary, and as soon as he was out of it, he began to plot again. Being discovered in correspondence with the Pope, with a view to a rising in England which should force Elizabeth to consent to his marriage with Mary and to repeal the laws against the Catholics, he was re-committed to the Tower and brought to trial. He was found guilty by the unanimous verdict of the Lords who tried him, and was sentenced to the block.

It is very difficult to make out, at this distance of time, and between opposite accounts, whether Elizabeth really was a humane woman, or desired to appear so, or was fearful of shedding the blood of people of great name who were popular in the country. Twice she commanded and countermanded the execution of this Duke, and it did not take place until five months after his trial. The scaffold was erected on Tower Hill, and there he died like a brave man. He refused to have his eyes bandaged, saying that he was not at all afraid of death; and he admitted the justice of his sentence, and was much regretted by the people.

Although Mary had shrunk at the most important time from disproving her guilt, she was very careful never to do anything that would admit it. All such proposals as were made to her by Elizabeth for her release, required that admission in some form or other, and therefore came to nothing. Moreover, both women being artful and treacherous, and neither ever trusting the other, it was not likely that they could ever make an agreement. So, the Parliament, aggravated by what the Pope had done, made new and strong laws against the spreading of the Catholic religion in England, and declared it treason in any one to say that the Queen and her successors were not the lawful sovereigns of England. It would have done more than this, but for Elizabeth's moderation.

Since the Reformation, there had come to be three great sects of religious people—or people who called themselves so—in England; that is to say, those who belonged to the Reformed Church, those who belonged to the Unreformed Church, and those who were called the Puritans, because they said that they wanted to have everything very pure and plain in all the Church service. These last were for the most part an uncomfortable people, who thought it highly meritorious to dress in a hideous manner, talk through their noses, and oppose all harmless enjoyments. But they were powerful too, and very much in earnest, and they were one and all the determined enemies of the Queen of Scots. The Protestant feeling in England was further strengthened by the tremendous cruelties to which Protestants were exposed in France and in the Netherlands. Scores of thousands of them were put to death in those countries with every cruelty that can be imagined, and at last, in the autumn of the year one thousand five hundred and seventy-two, one of the greatest barbarities ever committed in the world took place at Paris.

It is called in history, THE MASSACRE OF SAINT BARTHOLOMEW, because it took place on Saint Bartholomew's Eve. The day fell on Saturday the twenty-third of August. On that day all the great leaders of the Protestants (who were there called HUGUENOTS) were assembled together, for the purpose, as was represented to them, of doing honour to the marriage of their chief, the young King of Navarre, with the sister of CHARLES THE NINTH : a miserable young King who then occupied the French throne. This dull creature was made to believe by his mother and other fierce Catholics about him that the Huguenots meant to take his life; and he was persuaded to give secret orders that, on the tolling of a great bell, they should be fallen upon by an overpowering force of armed men, and slaughtered wherever they could be found. When the appointed hour was close at hand, the stupid wretch, trembling from head to foot, was taken into a balcony by his mother to see the atrocious work begun. The moment the bell tolled, the murderers broke forth. During all that night and the two next days, they broke into the houses, fired the houses, shot and stabbed the Protestants, men, women, and children, and flung their bodies into the streets. They were shot at in the streets as they passed along, and their blood ran down the gutters. Upwards of ten thousand Protestants were killed in Paris alone; in all France four or five times that number. To return thanks to Heaven for these dia-bolical murders, the Pope and his train actually went in public procession at Rome, and as if this were not shame enough for them, they had a medal struck to commemorate the event. But, however comfortable the wholesale murders were to these high authorities, they had not that soothing effect upon the doll-King. I am happy to state that he never knew a moment's peace afterwards ; that he was continually crying out that he saw the Huguenots covered with blood and wounds falling dead before him; and that he died within a year, shrieking and yelling and raving to that degree, that if all the Popes who had ever lived had been rolled into one, they would not have afforded His guilty Majesty the slightest consolation.

When the terrible news of the massacre arrived in England, it made a powerful impression indeed upon the people. If they began to run a little wild against the Catholics at about this time, this fearful reason for it, coming so soon after the days of bloody Queen Mary, must be remembered in their excuse. The Court was not quite so honest as the people—but perhaps it sometimes is not. It received the French ambassador, with all the lords and ladies dressed in deep mourning, and keeping a profound silence. Nevertheless, a proposal of marriage which he

had made to Elizabeth only two days before the eve of
Saint Bartholomew, on behalf of the Duke of Alençon,
the French King's brother, a boy of seventeen, still went
on; while on the other hand, in her usual crafty way,
the Queen secretly supplied the Huguenots with money
and weapons.

I must say that for a Queen who made all those fine
speeches, of which I have confessed myself to be rather
tired, about living and dying a Maiden Queen, Elizabeth
was "going" to be married pretty often.   Besides always
having some English favourite or other whom she by turns
encouraged and swore at and knocked about—for the Maiden
Queen was very free with her fists—she held this French
Duke off and on through several years.   When he at last
came over to England, the marriage articles were actually
drawn up, and it was settled that the wedding should take
place in six weeks.   The Queen was then so bent upon it,
that she prosecuted a poor Puritan named STUBBS, and
a poor bookseller named PAGE, for writing and publishing
a pamphlet against it.   Their right hands were chopped off
for this crime; and poor Stubbs—more loyal than I should
have been myself under the circumstances—immediately
pulled off his hat with his left hand, and cried, "God save
the Queen!"   Stubbs was cruelly treated; for the marriage
never took place after all, though the Queen pledged herself
to the Duke with a ring from her own finger.   He went
away, no better than he came, when the courtship had lasted
some ten years altogether; and he died a couple of years
afterwards, mourned by Elizabeth, who appears to have
been really fond of him.   It is not much to her credit, for
he was a bad enough member of a bad family.

To return to the Catholics.   There arose two orders of
priests, who were very busy in England, and who were
much dreaded.   These were the JESUITS (who were everywhere in all sorts of disguises), and the SEMINARY PRIESTS.
The people had a great horror of the first, because they
were known to have taught that murder was lawful if it
were done with an object of which they approved; and
they had a great horror of the second, because they came
to teach the old religion, and to be the successors of "Queen
Mary's priests," as those yet lingering in England were
called, when they should die out.   The severest laws were
made against them, and were most unmercifully executed.

Those who sheltered them in their houses often suffered heavily for what was an act of humanity; and the rack, that cruel torture which tore men's limbs asunder, was constantly kept going. What these unhappy men confessed, or what was ever confessed by any one under that agony, must always be received with great doubt, as it is certain that people have frequently owned to the most absurd and impossible crimes to escape such dreadful suffering. But I cannot doubt it to have been proved by papers, that there were many plots, both among the Jesuits, and with France, and with Scotland, and with Spain, for the destruction of Queen Elizabeth, for the placing of Mary on the throne, and for the revival of the old religion.

If the English people were too ready to believe in plots, there were, as I have said, good reasons for it. When the massacre of Saint Bartholomew was yet fresh in their recollection, a great Protestant Dutch hero, the PRINCE OF ORANGE, was shot by an assassin, who confessed that he had been kept and trained for the purpose in a college of Jesuits. The Dutch, in this surprise and distress, offered to make Elizabeth their sovereign, but she declined the honour, and sent them a small army instead, under the command of the Earl of Leicester, who, although a capital Court favourite, was not much of a general. He did so little in Holland, that his campaign there would probably have been forgotten, but for its occasioning the death of one of the best writers, the best knights, and the best gentlemen, of that or any age. This was SIR PHILIP SIDNEY, who was wounded by a musket ball in the thigh as he mounted a fresh horse, after having had his own killed under him. He had to ride back wounded, a long distance, and was very faint with fatigue and loss of blood, when some water, for which he had eagerly asked, was handed to him. But he was so good and gentle even then, that seeing a poor badly wounded common soldier lying on the ground, looking at the water with longing eyes, he said, "Thy necessity is greater than mine," and gave it up to him. This touching action of a noble heart is perhaps as well known as any incident in history—is as famous far and wide as the blood-stained Tower of London, with its axe, and block, and murders out of number. So delightful is an act of true humanity, and so glad are mankind to remember it.

At home, intelligence of plots began to thicken every day. I suppose the people never did live under such continual terrors as those by which they were possessed now, of Catholic risings, and burnings, and poisonings, and I don't know what. Still, we must always remember that they lived near and close to awful realities of that kind, and that with their experience it was not difficult to believe in any enormity. The government had the same fear, and did not take the best means of discovering the truth—for, besides torturing the suspected, it employed paid spies, who will always lie for their own profit. It even made some of the conspiracies it brought to light, by sending false letters to disaffected people, inviting them to join in pretended plots, which they too readily did.

But, one great real plot was at length discovered, and it ended the career of Mary, Queen of Scots. A seminary priest named BALLARD, and a Spanish soldier named SAVAGE, set on and encouraged by certain French priests, imparted a design to one ANTONY BABINGTON—a gentleman of fortune in Derbyshire, who had been for some time a secret agent of Mary's—for murdering the Queen. Babington then confided the scheme to some other Catholic gentlemen who were his friends, and they joined in it heartily. They were vain weak-headed young men, ridiculously confident, and preposterously proud of their plan ; for they got a gim-crack painting made, of the six choice spirits who were to murder Elizabeth, with Babington in an attitude for the centre figure. Two of their number, however, one of whom was a priest, kept Elizabeth's wisest minister, SIR FRANCIS WALSINGHAM, acquainted with the whole project from the first. The conspirators were completely deceived to the final point, when Babington gave Savage, because he was shabby, a ring from his finger, and some money from his purse, wherewith to buy himself new clothes in which to kill the Queen. Walsingham, having then full evidence against the whole band, and two letters of Mary's besides, resolved to seize them. Suspecting something wrong, they stole out of the city, one by one, and hid themselves in St. John's Wood, and other places which really were hiding places then; but they were all taken, and all executed. When they were seized, a gentleman was sent from Court to inform Mary of the fact, and of her being involved in the discovery. Her friends have complained that she was kept in very hard and severe custody. It does not appear very likely, for she was going out a hunting that very morning.

Queen Elizabeth had been warned long ago, by one in France who had good information of what was secretly doing, that in holding Mary alive, she held "the wolf who would devour her." The Bishop of London had, more lately, given the Queen's favourite minister the advice in writing, "forthwith to cut off the Scottish Queen's head." The question now was, what to do with her? The Earl of Leicester wrote a little note home from Holland, recom-mending that she should be quietly poisoned; that noble favourite having accustomed his mind, it is possible, to remedies of that nature. His black advice, however, was disregarded, and she was brought to trial at Fotheringay Castle in Northamptonshire, before a tribunal of forty, com-posed of both religions. There, and in the Star Chamber at Westminster, the trial lasted a fortnight. She defended herself with great ability, but could only deny the con-fessions that had been made by Babington and others; could only call her own letters, produced against her by her own secretaries, forgeries; and, in short, could only deny everything. She was found guilty, and declared to have incurred the penalty of death. The Parliament met, approved the sentence, and prayed the Queen to have it executed. The Queen replied that she requested them to consider whether no means could be found of saving Mary's life without endangering her own. The Parliament rejoined, No; and the citizens illuminated their houses and lighted bonfires, in token of their joy that all these plots and troubles were to be ended by the death of the Queen of Scots.

She, feeling sure that her time was now come, wrote a letter to the Queen of England, making three entreaties; first, that she might be buried in France; secondly, that she might not be executed in secret, but before her servants and some others; thirdly, that after her death, her servants should not be molested, but should be suffered to go home with the legacies she left them. It was an affecting letter, and Elizabeth shed tears over it, but sent no answer. Then came a special ambassador from France, and another from Scotland, to intercede for Mary's life; and then the nation began to clamour, more and more, for her death.

What the real feelings or intentions of Elizabeth were, can never be known now; but I strongly suspect her of only wishing one thing more than Mary's death, and that was to keep free of the blame of it. On the first of February, one thousand five hundred and eighty-seven, Lord Burleigh having drawn out the warrant for the execution, the Queen sent to the secretary DAVISON to bring it to her, that she might sign it: which she did. Next day, when Davison told her it was sealed, she angrily asked him why such haste was necessary? Next day but one, she joked about it, and swore a little. Again, next day but one, she seemed to complain that it was not yet done, but still she would not be plain with those about her. So, on the seventh, the Earls of Kent and Shrewsbury, with the Sheriff of Northampton-shire, came with the warrant to Fotheringay, to tell the Queen of Scots to prepare for death.

When those messengers of ill omen were gone, Mary made a frugal supper, drank to her servants, read over her will, went to bed, slept for some hours, and then arose and passed the remainder of the night saying prayers. In the morning she dressed herself in her best clothes; and, at eight o'clock when the sheriff came for her to her chapel, took leave of her servants who were there assembled praying with her, and went down-stairs, carrying a Bible in one hand and a crucifix in the other. Two of her women and four of her men were allowed to be present in the hall; where a low scaffold, only two feet from the ground, was erected and covered with black; and where the executioner from the Tower, and his assistant, stood, dressed in black velvet. The hall was full of people. While the sentence was being read she sat upon a stool; and, when it was finished, she again denied her guilt, as she had done before. The Earl of Kent and the Dean of Peterborough, in their Protestant zeal, made some very unnecessary speeches to her; to which she replied that she died in the Catholic religion, and they need not trouble themselves about that matter. When her head and neck were uncovered by the executioners, she said that she had not been used to be undressed by such hands, or before so much company. Finally, one of her women fastened a cloth over her face, and she laid her neck upon the block, and repeated more than once in Latin, "Into thy hands, O Lord, I commend my spirit!" Some say her head was struck off in two blows, some say in three. However that be, when it was held up, streaming with blood, the real hair beneath the false hair she had long worn was seen to be as grey as that of a woman of seventy, though she was at that time only in her forty-sixth year. All her beauty was gone.

But she was beautiful enough to her little dog, who cowered under her dress, frightened, when she went upon the scaffold, and who lay down beside her headless body when all her earthly sorrows were over.

Third Part.

On its being formally made known to Elizabeth that the sentence had been executed on the Queen of Scots, she showed the utmost grief and rage, drove her favourites from her with violent indignation, and sent Davison to the Tower; from which place he was only released in the end by paying an immense fine which completely ruined him. Elizabeth not only over-acted her part in making these pretences, but most basely reduced to poverty one of her faithful servants for no other fault than obeying her commands.

James, King of Scotland, Mary's son, made a show likewise of being very angry on the occasion ; but he was a pensioner of England to the amount of five thousand pounds a year, and he had known very little of his mother, and he possibly regarded her as the murderer of his father, and he soon took it quietly.

Philip, King of Spain, however, threatened to do greater things than ever had been done yet, to set up the Catholic religion and punish Protestant England. Elizabeth, hearing that he and the Prince of Parma were making great preparations for this purpose, in order to be beforehand with them sent out Admiral Drake (a famous navigator, who had sailed about the world, and had already brought great plunder from Spain) to the port of Cadiz, where he burnt a hundred vessels full of stores. This great loss obliged the Spaniards to put off the invasion for a year; but it was none the less formidable for that, amounting to one hundred and thirty ships, nineteen thousand soldiers, eight thousand sailors, two thousand slaves, and between two and three thousand great guns. England was not idle in making ready to resist this great force. All the men between sixteen years old and sixty, were trained and drilled; the national fleet of ships (in number only thirty-four at first) was enlarged by public contributions and by private ships, fitted out by noblemen; the city of London, of its own accord, furnished double the number of ships and men that it was required to provide; and, if ever the national spirit was up in England, it was up all through the country to resist the Spaniards. Some of the Queen's advisers were for seizing the principal English Catholics, and putting them to death; but the Queen—who, to her honour, used to say, that she would never believe any ill of her subjects, which a parent would not believe of her own children—rejected the advice, and only confined a few of those who were the most suspected, in the fens in Lincolnshire. The great body of Catholics deserved this confidence; for they behaved most loyally, nobly, and bravely.

So, with all England firing up like one strong angry man, and with both sides of the Thames fortified, and with the soldiers under arms, and with the sailors in their ships, the country waited for the coming of the proud Spanish fleet, which was called THE INVINCIBLE ARMADA. The Queen herself, riding in armour on a white horse, and the Earl of Essex and the Earl of Leicester holding her bridle rein, made a brave speech to the troops at Tilbury Fort opposite Gravesend, which was received with such enthusiasm as is seldom known. Then came the Spanish Armada into the English Channel, sailing along in the form of a half moon, of such great size that it was seven miles broad. But the English were quickly upon it, and woe then to all the Spanish ships that dropped a little out of the half moon, for the English took them instantly! And it soon appeared that the great Armada was anything but invincible, for on a summer night, bold Drake sent eight blazing fire-ships right into the midst of it. In terrible consternation the Spaniards tried to get out to sea, and so became dispersed; the English pursued them at a great advantage; a storm came on, and drove the Spaniards among rocks and shoals; and the swift end of the Invincible fleet was, that it lost thirty great ships and ten thousand men, and, defeated and disgraced, sailed home again. Being afraid to go by the English Channel, it sailed all round Scotland and Ireland; some of the ships getting cast away on the latter coast in bad weather, the Irish, who were a kind of savages, plundered

those vessels and killed their crews. So ended this great
attempt to invade and conquer England. And I think it
will be a long time before any other invincible fleet coming
to England with the same object, will fare much better
than the Spanish Armada.

Though the Spanish king had had this bitter taste of
English bravery, he was so little the wiser for it, as still to
entertain his old designs, and even to conceive the absurd
idea of placing his daughter on the English throne. But
the Earl of Essex, SIR WALTER RALEIGH, SIR THOMAS
HOWARD, and some other distinguished leaders, put to
sea from Plymouth, entered the port of Cadiz once more,
obtained a complete victory over the shipping assembled
there, and got possession of the town. In obedience to the
Queen's express instructions, they behaved with great
humanity ; and the principal loss of the Spaniards was a
vast sum of money which they had to pay for ransom. This
was one of many gallant achievements on the sea, effected
in this reign. Sir Walter Raleigh himself, after marrying
a maid of honour and giving offence to the Maiden Queen
thereby, had already sailed to South America in search of
gold.

The Earl of Leicester was now dead, and so was Sir
Thomas Walsingham, whom Lord Burleigh was soon to
follow. The principal favourite was the EARL OF ESSEX, a
spirited and handsome man, a favourite with the people too
as well as with the Queen, and possessed of many admirable
qualities. It was much debated at Court whether there
should be peace with Spain or no, and he was very urgent
for war. He also tried hard to have his own way in the
appointment of a deputy to govern in Ireland. One day,
while this question was in dispute, he hastily took offence,
and turned his back upon the Queen ; as a gentle reminder
of which impropriety, the Queen gave him a tremendous
box on the ear, and told him to go to the devil. He went
home instead, and did not reappear at Court for half a year
or so, when he and the Queen were reconciled, though never
(as some suppose) thoroughly.

From this time the fate of the Earl of Essex and that of
the Queen seemed to be blended together. The Irish were
still perpetually quarrelling and fighting among themselves,
and he went over to Ireland as Lord Lieutenant, to the
great joy of his enemies (Sir Walter Raleigh among the rest),

who were glad to have so dangerous a rival far off. Not being by any means successful there, and knowing that his enemies would take advantage of that circumstance to injure him with the Queen, he came home again, though against her orders. The Queen being taken by surprise when he appeared before her, gave him her hand to kiss, and he was overjoyed—though it was not a very lovely hand by this time—but in the course of the same day she ordered him to confine himself to his room, and two or three days afterwards had him taken into custody. With the same sort of caprice—and as capricious an old woman she now was, as ever wore a crown or a head either—she sent him broth from her own table on his falling ill from anxiety, and cried about him.

He was a man who could find comfort and occupation in his books, and he did so for a time ; not the least happy time, I dare say, of his life. But it happened unfortunately for him, that he held a monopoly in sweet wines : which means that nobody could sell them without purchasing his permission. This right, which was only for a term, expiring, he applied to have it renewed. The Queen refused, with the rather strong observation—but she *did* make strong observations—that an unruly beast must be stinted in his food. Upon this, the angry Earl, who had been already deprived of many offices, thought himself in danger of complete ruin, and turned against the Queen, whom he called a vain old woman who had grown as crooked in her mind as she had in her figure. These uncomplimentary expressions the ladies of the Court immediately snapped up and carried to the Queen, whom they did not put in a better temper, you may believe. The same Court ladies, when they had beautiful dark hair of their own, used to wear false red hair, to be like the Queen. So they were not very high-spirited ladies, however high in rank.

The worst object of the Earl of Essex, and some friends of his who used to meet at LORD SOUTHAMPTON's house, was to obtain possession of the Queen, and oblige her by force to dismiss her ministers and change her favourites. On Saturday the seventh of February, one thousand six hundred and one, the council suspecting this, summoned the Earl to come before them. He, pretending to be ill, declined; it was then settled among his friends, that as the next day would be Sunday, when many of the citizens usually assembled at the

Cross by St. Paul's Cathedral, he should make one bold effort to induce them to rise and follow him to the Palace.

So, on the Sunday morning, he and a small body of adherents started out of his house—Essex House by the Strand, with steps to the river—having first shut up in it, as prisoners, some members of the council who came to examine him—and hurried into the City with the Earl at their head, crying out "For the Queen! For the Queen! A plot is laid for my life!" No one heeded them, however, and when they came to St. Paul's there were no citizens there. In the meantime the prisoners at Essex House had been released by one of the Earl's own friends; he had been promptly proclaimed a traitor in the City itself; and the streets were barricaded with carts and guarded by soldiers. The Earl got back to his house by water, with difficulty, and after an attempt to defend his house against the troops and cannon by which it was soon surrounded, gave himself up that night. He was brought to trial on the nineteenth, and found guilty; on the twenty-fifth, he was executed on Tower Hill, where he died, at thirty-four years old, both courageously and penitently. His step-father suffered with him. His enemy, Sir Walter Raleigh, stood near the scaffold all the time—but not so near it as we shall see him stand, before we finish his history.

In this case, as in the cases of the Duke of Norfolk and Mary Queen of Scots, the Queen had commanded, and countermanded, and again commanded, the execution. It is probable that the death of her young and gallant favourite in the prime of his good qualities, was never off her mind afterwards, but she held out, the same vain obstinate and capricious woman, for another year. Then she danced before her Court on a state occasion—and cut, I should think, a mighty ridiculous figure, doing so in an immense ruff, stomacher and wig, at seventy years old. For another year still, she held out, but, without any more dancing, and as a moody sorrowful broken creature. At last, on the tenth of March, one thousand six hundred and three, having been ill of a very bad cold, and made worse by the death of the Countess of Nottingham who was her intimate friend, she fell into a stupor and was supposed to be dead. She recovered her consciousness, however, and then nothing would induce her to go to bed; for she said that she knew that if she did, she should never get up again. There she lay for ten days, on cushions on the floor, without any food, until the Lord Admiral got her into bed at last, partly by persuasions and partly by main force. When they asked her who should succeed her, she replied that her seat had been the seat of Kings, and that she would have for her successor, "No rascal's son, but a King's." Upon this, the lords present stared at one another, and took the liberty of asking whom she meant; to which she replied, "Whom should I mean, but our cousin of Scotland!" This was on the twenty-third of March. They asked her once again that day, after she was speechless, whether she was still in the same mind? She struggled up in bed, and joined her hands over her head in the form of a crown, as the only reply she could make. At three o'clock next morning, she very quietly died, in the forty-fifth year of her reign.

That reign had been a glorious one, and is made for ever memorable by the distinguished men who flourished in it. Apart from the great voyagers, statesmen, and scholars, whom it produced, the names of BACON, SPENSER, and SHAKESPEARE, will always be remembered with pride and veneration by the civilised world, and will always impart (though with no great reason, perhaps) some portion of their lustre to the name of Elizabeth herself. It was a great reign for discovery, for commerce, and for English enterprise and spirit in general. It was a great reign for the Protestant religion and for the Reformation which made England free. The Queen was very popular, and in her progresses, or journeys about her dominions, was everywhere received with the liveliest joy. I think the truth is, that she was not half so good as she has been made out, and not half so bad as she has been made out. She had her fine qualities, but she was coarse, capricious, and treacherous, and had all the faults of an excessively vain young woman long after she was an old one. On the whole, she had a great deal too much of her father in her, to please me.

Many improvements and luxuries were introduced in the course of these five-and-forty years in the general manner of living; but cock-fighting, bull-baiting, and bear-baiting, were still the national amusements; and a coach was so rarely seen, and was such an ugly and cumbersome affair when it was seen, that even the Queen herself, on many high occasions, rode on horseback on a pillion behind the Lord Chancellor.

CHAPTER XXXII

ENGLAND UNDER JAMES THE FIRST

" Our cousin of Scotland " was ugly, awkward, and shuffling
both in mind and person. His tongue was much too large
for his mouth, his legs were much too weak for his body,
and his dull goggle-eyes stared and rolled like an idiot's. He
was cunning, covetous, wasteful, idle, drunken, greedy, dirty,
cowardly, a great swearer, and the most conceited man on
earth. His figure—what is commonly called rickety from
his birth—presented a most ridiculous appearance, dressed
in thick padded clothes, as a safeguard against being stabbed
(of which he lived in continual fear), of a grass-green colour
from head to foot, with a hunting-horn dangling at his side
instead of a sword, and his hat and feather sticking over one
eye, or hanging on the back of his head, as he happened to
toss it on. He used to loll on the necks of his favourite
courtiers, and slobber their faces, and kiss and pinch their
cheeks ; and the greatest favourite he ever had, used to sign
himself in his letters to his royal master, His Majesty's
"dog and slave," and used to address his majesty as "his
Sowship." His majesty was the worst rider ever seen, and
thought himself the best. He was one of the most imperti-
nent talkers (in the broadest Scotch) ever heard, and boasted
of being unanswerable in all manner of argument. He wrote
some of the most wearisome treatises ever read—among
others, a book upon witchcraft, in which he was a devout
believer—and thought himself a prodigy of authorship. He
thought, and wrote, and said, that a king had a right to make
and unmake what laws he pleased, and ought to be accountable to nobody on earth. This is the plain true character of
the personage whom the greatest men about the court praised
and flattered to that degree, that I doubt if there be anything
much more shameful in the annals of human nature.

He came to the English throne with great ease. The

miseries of a disputed succession had been felt so long, and so dreadfully, that he was proclaimed within a few hours of Elizabeth's death, and was accepted by the nation, even without being asked to give any pledge that he would govern well, or that he would redress crying grievances. He took a month to come from Edinburgh to London ; and, by way of exercising his new power, hanged a pickpocket on the journey without any trial, and knighted everybody he could lay hold of. He made two hundred knights before he got to his palace in London, and seven hundred before he had been in it three months. He also shovelled sixty-two new peers into the House of Lords—and there was a pretty large sprinkling of Scotchmen among them, you may believe.

His Sowship's prime Minister, CECIL (for I cannot do better than call his majesty what his favourite called him), was the enemy of Sir Walter Raleigh, and also of Sir Walter's political friend, LORD COBHAM ; and his Sowship's first trouble was a plot originated by these two, and entered into by some others, with the old object of seizing the King and keeping him in imprisonment until he should change his ministers. There were Catholic priests in the plot, and there were Puritan noblemen too ; for, although the Catholics and Puritans were strongly opposed to each other, they united at this time against his Sowship, because they knew that he had a design against both, after pretending to be friendly to each ; this design being to have only one high and convenient form of the Protestant religion, which everybody should be bound to belong to, whether they liked it or not. This plot was mixed up with another, which may or may not have had some reference to placing on the throne, at some time, the LADY ARABELLA STUART ; whose misfortune it was, to be the daughter of the younger brother of his Sowship's father, but who was quite innocent of any part in the scheme. Sir Walter Raleigh was accused on the confession of Lord Cobham—a miserable creature, who said one thing at one time, and another thing at another time, and could be relied upon in nothing. The trial of Sir Walter Raleigh lasted from eight in the morning until nearly midnight ; he defended himself with such eloquence, genius, and spirit against all accusations, and against the insults of COKE, the Attorney-General—who, according to the custom of the time, foully abused him—that those who went there detesting the prisoner, came away admiring him, and declaring that anything so wonderful and so captivating was never heard. He was found guilty, nevertheless, and sentenced to death. Execution was deferred, and he was taken to the Tower. The two Catholic priests, less fortunate, were executed with the usual atrocity ; and Lord Cobham and two others were pardoned on the scaffold. His Sowship thought it wonderfully knowing in him to surprise the people by pardoning these three at the very block ; but, blundering, and bungling, as usual, he had very nearly overreached himself. For, the messenger on horseback who brought the pardon, came so late, that he was pushed to the outside of the crowd, and was obliged to shout and roar out what he came for. The miserable Cobham did not gain much by being spared that day. He lived, both as a prisoner and a beggar, utterly despised, and miserably poor, for thirteen years, and then died in an old outhouse belonging to one of his former servants.

This plot got rid of, and Sir Walter Raleigh safely shut up in the Tower, his Sowship held a great dispute with the Puritans on their presenting a petition to him, and had it all his own way—not so very wonderful, as he would talk continually, and would not hear anybody else—and filled the Bishops with admiration. It was comfortably settled that there was to be only one form of religion, and that all men were to think exactly alike. But, although this was arranged two centuries and a half ago, and although the arrangement was supported by much fining and imprisonment, I do not find that it is quite successful, even yet.

His Sowship, having that uncommonly high opinion of himself as a king, had a very low opinion of Parliament as a power that audaciously wanted to control him. When he called his first Parliament after he had been king a year, he accordingly thought he would take pretty high ground with them, and told them that he commanded them "as an absolute king." The Parliament thought those strong words, and saw the necessity of upholding their authority. His Sowship had three children : Prince Henry, Prince Charles, and the Princess Elizabeth. It would have been well for one of these, and we shall too soon see which, if he had learnt a little wisdom concerning Parliaments from his father's obstinacy.

Now, the people still labouring under their old dread of the Catholic religion, this Parliament revived and strengthened the severe laws against it. And this so angered ROBERT CATESBY, a restless Catholic gentleman of an old family, that he formed one of the most desperate and terrible designs ever conceived in the mind of man; no less a scheme than the Gunpowder Plot.

His object was, when the King, lords, and commons, should be assembled at the next opening of Parliament, to blow them up, one and all, with a great mine of gunpowder. The first person to whom he confided this horrible idea was THOMAS WINTER, a Worcestershire gentleman who had served in the army abroad, and had been secretly employed in Catholic projects. While Winter was yet undecided, and when he had gone over to the Netherlands, to learn from the Spanish Ambassador there whether there was any hope of Catholics being relieved through the intercession of the King of Spain with his Sowship, he found at Ostend a tall dark daring man, whom he had known when they were both soldiers abroad, and whose name was GUIDO—or GUY— FAWKES. Resolved to join the plot, he proposed it to this man, knowing him to be the man for any desperate deed, and they two came back to England together. Here, they admitted two other conspirators: THOMAS PERCY, related to the Earl of Northumberland, and JOHN WRIGHT, his brother-in-law. All these met together in a solitary house in the open fields which were then near Clement's Inn, now a closely blocked-up part of London; and when they had all taken a great oath of secrecy, Catesby told the rest what his plan was. They then went up-stairs into a garret, and received the Sacrament from FATHER GERARD, a Jesuit, who is said not to have known actually of the Gunpowder Plot, but who, I think, must have had his suspicions that there was something desperate afoot.

Percy was a Gentleman Pensioner, and as he had occasional duties to perform about the Court, then kept at Whitehall, there would be nothing suspicious in his living at West-minster. So, having looked well about him, and having found a house to let, the back of which joined the Parliament House, he hired it of a person named FERRIS, for the purpose of undermining the wall. Having got possession of this house, the conspirators hired another on the Lambeth side of the Thames, which they used as a storehouse for wood, gun-powder, and other combustible matters. These were to be removed at night (and afterwards were removed), bit by bit,

to the house at Westminster ; and, that there might be some
trusty person to keep watch over the Lambeth stores, they
admitted another conspirator, by name ROBERT KAY, a very
poor Catholic gentleman.

All these arrangements had been made some months, and
it was a dark wintry December night, when the conspirators,
who had been in the meantime dispersed to avoid observation,
met in the house at Westminster, and began to dig. They
had laid in a good stock of eatables, to avoid going in and
out, and they dug and dug with great ardour. But, the wall
being tremendously thick, and the work very severe, they
took into their plot CHRISTOPHER WRIGHT, a younger brother
of John Wright, that they might have a new pair of hands
to help. And Christopher Wright fell to like a fresh man,
and they dug and dug by night and by day, and Fawkes
stood sentinel all the time. And if any man's heart seemed
to fail him at all, Fawkes said, "Gentlemen, we have abundance of powder and shot here, and there is no fear of our
being taken alive, even if discovered." The same Fawkes,
who, in the capacity of sentinel, was always prowling about,
soon picked up the intelligence that the King had prorogued
the Parliament again, from the seventh of February, the day
first fixed upon, until the third of October. When the conspirators knew this, they agreed to separate until after the
Christmas holidays, and to take no notice of each other in the
meanwhile, and never to write letters to one another on any
account. So, the house in Westminster was shut up again,
and I suppose the neighbours thought that those strange-
looking men who lived there so gloomily, and went out so
seldom, were gone away to have a merry Christmas somewhere.

It was the beginning of February, sixteen hundred and
five, when Catesby met his fellow-conspirators again at this
Westminster house. He had now admitted three more ;
JOHN GRANT, a Warwickshire gentleman of a melancholy
temper, who lived in a doleful house near Stratford-upon-
Avon, with a frowning wall all round it, and a deep moat ;
ROBERT WINTER, eldest brother of Thomas ; and Catesby's
own servant, THOMAS BATES, who, Catesby thought, had had
some suspicion of what his master was about. These three
had all suffered more or less for their religion in Elizabeth's
time. And now, they all began to dig again, and they dug
and dug by night and by day.

They found it dismal work alone there, underground, with such a fearful secret on their minds, and so many murders before them. They were filled with wild fancies. Sometimes, they thought they heard a great bell tolling, deep down in the earth under the Parliament House; sometimes, they thought they heard low voices muttering about the Gunpowder Plot; once in the morning, they really did hear a great rumbling noise over their heads, as they dug and sweated in their mine. Every man stopped and looked aghast at his neighbour, wondering what had happened, when that bold prowler, Fawkes, who had been out to look, came in and told them that it was only a dealer in coals who had occupied a cellar under the Parliament House, removing his stock in trade to some other place. Upon this, the conspirators, who with all their digging and digging had not yet dug through the tremendously thick wall, changed their plan; hired that cellar, which was directly under the House of Lords; put six-and-thirty barrels of gunpowder in it, and covered them over with fagots and coals. Then they all dispersed again till September, when the following new conspirators were admitted; Sir Edward Baynham, of Gloucestershire; Sir Everard Digby, of Rutlandshire; Ambrose Rookwood, of Suffolk; Francis Tresham, of Northamptonshire. Most of these were rich, and were to assist the plot, some with money and some with horses on which the conspirators were to ride through the country and rouse the Catholics after the Parliament should be blown into air.

Parliament being again prorogued from the third of October to the fifth of November, and the conspirators being uneasy lest their design should have been found out, Thomas Winter said he would go up into the House of Lords on the day of the prorogation, and see how matters looked. Nothing could be better. The unconscious Commissioners were walking about and talking to one another, just over the six-and-thirty barrels of gunpowder. He came back and told the rest so, and they went on with their preparations. They hired a ship, and kept it ready in the Thames, in which Fawkes was to sail for Flanders after firing with a slow match the train that was to explode the powder. A number of Catholic gentlemen not in the secret, were invited, on pretence of a hunting party, to meet Sir Everard Digby at Dunchurch on the fatal day, that they might be ready to act together. And now all was ready.

But, now, the great wickedness and danger which had
been all along at the bottom of this wicked plot, began to
show itself. As the fifth of November drew near, most of
the conspirators, remembering that they had friends and
relations who would be in the House of Lords that day,
felt some natural relenting, and a wish to warn them to
keep away. They were not much comforted by Catesby's
declaring that in such a cause he would blow up his own son.
LORD MOUNTEAGLE, Tresham's brother-in-law, was certain
to be in the house ; and when Tresham found that he could
not prevail upon the rest to devise any means of sparing
their friends, he wrote a mysterious letter to this lord and
left it at his lodging in the dusk, urging him to keep away
from the opening of Parliament, " since God and man had
concurred to punish the wickedness of the times." It contained the words " that the Parliament should receive
a terrible blow, and yet should not see who hurt them."
And it added, " the danger is past, as soon as you have
burnt the letter."

The ministers and courtiers made out that his Sowship,
by a direct miracle from Heaven, found out what this letter
meant. The truth is, that they were not long (as few men
would be) in finding it out for themselves ; and it was
decided to let the conspirators alone, until the very day
before the opening of Parliament. That the conspirators
had their fears, is certain ; for, Tresham himself said before
them all, that they were every one dead men ; and, although
even he did not take flight, there is reason to suppose that
he had warned other persons besides Lord Mounteagle.
However, they were all firm ; and Fawkes, who was a man
of iron, went down every day and night to keep watch in
the cellar as usual. He was there about two in the afternoon of the fourth, when the Lord Chamberlain and Lord
Mounteagle threw open the door and looked in. " Who
are you, friend ? " said they. " Why," said Fawkes, " I am
Mr. Percy's servant, and am looking after his store of fuel
here." " Your master has laid in a pretty good store," they
returned, and shut the door, and went away. Fawkes, upon
this, posted off to the other conspirators to tell them all was
quiet, and went back and shut himself up in the dark black
cellar again, where he heard the bell go twelve o'clock and
usher in the fifth of November. About two hours afterwards, he slowly opened the door, and came out to look

about him, in his old prowling way. He was instantly seized and bound, by a party of soldiers under SIR THOMAS KNEVETT. He had a watch upon him, some touchwood, some tinder, some slow matches; and there was a dark lantern with a candle in it, lighted, behind the door. He had his boots and spurs on—to ride to the ship, I suppose —and it was well for the soldiers that they took him so suddenly. If they had left him but a moment's time to light a match, he certainly would have tossed it in among the powder, and blown up himself and them.

They took him to the King's bed-chamber first of all, and there the King (causing him to be held very tight, and keeping a good way off), asked him how he could have the heart to intend to destroy so many innocent people? "Because," said Guy Fawkes, "desperate diseases need desperate remedies." To a little Scotch favourite, with a face like a terrier, who asked him (with no particular wisdom) why he had collected so much gunpowder, he replied, because he had meant to blow Scotchmen back to Scotland, and it would take a deal of powder to do that. Next day he was carried to the Tower, but would make no confession. Even after being horribly tortured, he con- fessed nothing that the Government did not already know ; though he must have been in a fearful state—as his signa- ture, still preserved, in contrast with his natural hand- writing before he was put upon the dreadful rack, most frightfully shows. Bates, a very different man, soon said the Jesuits had had to do with the plot, and probably, under the torture, would as readily have said anything. Tresham, taken and put in the Tower too, made confessions and unmade them, and died of an illness that was heavy upon him. Rookwood, who had stationed relays of his own horses all the way to Dunchurch, did not mount to escape until the middle of the day, when the news of the plot was all over London. On the road, he came up with the two Wrights, Catesby, and Percy; and they all galloped together into Northamptonshire. Thence to Dunchurch, where they found the proposed party assembled. Finding, however, that there had been a plot, and that it had been discovered, the party disappeared in the course of the night, and left them alone with Sir Everard Digby. Away they all rode again, through Warwickshire and Worcestershire, to a house called Holbeach, on the borders of Staffordshire. They tried to raise the Catholics on their way, but were indignantly driven off by them. All this time they were hotly pursued by the sheriff of Worcester, and a fast increasing concourse of riders. At last, resolving to defend themselves at Holbeach, they shut themselves up in the house, and put some wet powder before the fire to dry. But it blew up, and Catesby was singed and blackened, and almost killed, and some of the others were sadly hurt. Still, knowing that they must die, they resolved to die there, and with only their swords in their hands appeared at the windows to be shot at by the sheriff and his assistants. Catesby said to Thomas Winter, after Thomas had been hit in the right arm which dropped powerless by his side, "Stand by me, Tom, and we will die together!"—which they did, being shot through the body by two bullets from one gun. John Wright, and Christopher Wright, and Percy, were also shot. Rookwood and Digby were taken: the former with a broken arm and a wound in his body too.

It was the fifteenth of January, before the trial of Guy Fawkes, and such of the other conspirators as were left alive, came on. They were all found guilty, all hanged, drawn, and quartered: some, in St. Paul's Churchyard, on the top of Ludgate-hill; some, before the Parliament House. A Jesuit priest, named HENRY GARNET, to whom the dreadful design was said to have been communicated, was taken and tried; and two of his servants, as well as a poor priest who was taken with him, were tortured without mercy. He himself was not tortured, but was surrounded in the Tower by tamperers and traitors, and so was made unfairly to convict himself out of his own mouth. He said, upon his trial, that he had done all he could to prevent the deed, and that he could not make public what had been told him in confession—though I am afraid he knew of the plot in other ways. He was found guilty and executed, after a manful defence, and the Catholic Church made a saint of him; some rich and powerful persons, who had had nothing to do with the project, were fined and imprisoned for it by the Star Chamber; the Catholics, in general, who had recoiled with horror from the idea of the infernal contrivance, were unjustly put under more severe laws than before; and this was the end of the Gunpowder Plot.

Second Part.

His Sowship would pretty willingly, I think, have blown
the House of Commons into the air himself; for, his dread
and jealousy of it knew no bounds all through his reign.
When he was hard pressed for money he was obliged to
order it to meet, as he could get no money without it; and
when it asked him first to abolish some of the monopolies
in necessaries of life which were a great grievance to the
people, and to redress other public wrongs, he flew into
a rage and got rid of it again. At one time he wanted it
to consent to the Union of England with Scotland, and
quarrelled about that. At another time it wanted him to
put down a most infamous Church abuse, called the High
Commission Court, and he quarrelled with it about that.
At another time it entreated him not to be quite so fond of
his archbishops and bishops who made speeches in his
praise too awful to be related, but to have some little
consideration for the poor Puritan clergy who were persecuted for preaching in their own way, and not according
to the archbishops and bishops; and they quarrelled about
that. In short, what with hating the House of Commons,
and pretending not to hate it; and what with now sending
some of its members who opposed him, to Newgate or to
the Tower, and now telling the rest that they must not
presume to make speeches about the public affairs which
could not possibly concern them; and what with cajoling,
and bullying, and fighting, and being frightened; the House
of Commons was the plague of his Sowship's existence. It
was pretty firm, however, in maintaining its rights, and
insisting that the Parliament should make the laws, and not
the King by his own single proclamations (which he tried
hard to do); and his Sowship was so often distressed for
money, in consequence, that he sold every sort of title and
public office as if they were merchandise, and even invented
a new dignity called a Baronetcy, which anybody could buy
for a thousand pounds.

These disputes with his Parliaments, and his hunting, and
his drinking, and his lying in bed—for he was a great
sluggard—occupied his Sowship pretty well. The rest of
his time he chiefly passed in hugging and slobbering his
favourites. The first of these was Sir Philip Herbert, who
had no knowledge whatever, except of dogs, and horses, and

hunting, but whom he soon made EARL OF MONTGOMERY.
The next, and a much more famous one, was ROBERT CARR,
or KER (for it is not certain which was his right name), who
came from the Border country, and whom he soon made
VISCOUNT ROCHESTER, and afterwards, EARL OF SOMERSET.
The way in which his Sowship doted on this handsome
young man, is even more odious to think of, than the way
in which the really great men of England condescended to
bow down before him.   The favourite's great friend was
a certain SIR THOMAS OVERBURY, who wrote his love-letters
for him, and assisted him in the duties of his many high
places, which his own ignorance prevented him from dis-
charging.   But this same Sir Thomas having just manhood
enough to dissuade the favourite from a wicked marriage
with the beautiful Countess of Essex, who was to get
a divorce from her husband for the purpose, the said
Countess, in her rage, got Sir Thomas put into the Tower,
and there poisoned him.   Then the favourite and this bad
woman were publicly married by the King's pet bishop,
with as much to-do and rejoicing, as if he had been the
best man, and she the best woman, upon the face of the
earth.

But, after a longer sunshine than might have been
expected—of seven years or so, that is to say—another
handsome young man started up and eclipsed the EARL OF
SOMERSET.   This was GEORGE VILLIERS, the youngest son
of a Leicestershire gentleman: who came to Court with all
the Paris fashions on him, and could dance as well as the
best mountebank that ever was seen.   He soon danced
himself into the good graces of his Sowship, and danced the
other favourite out of favour.   Then, it was all at once discovered that the Earl and Countess of Somerset had not
deserved all those great promotions and mighty rejoicings,
and they were separately tried for the murder of Sir Thomas
Overbury, and for other crimes.   But, the King was so
afraid of his late favourite's publicly telling some disgraceful
things he knew of him—which he darkly threatened to do
—that he was even examined with two men standing, one
on either side of him, each with a cloak in his hand, ready
to throw it over his head and stop his mouth if he should
break out with what he had it in his power to tell.   So,
a very lame affair was purposely made of the trial, and his
punishment was an allowance of four thousand pounds a year

in retirement, while the Countess was pardoned, and allowed to pass into retirement too. They hated one another by this time, and lived to revile and torment each other some years.

While these events were in progress, and while his Sowship was making such an exhibition of himself, from day to day and from year to year, as is not often seen in any sty, three remarkable deaths took place in England. The first was that of the Minister, Robert Cecil, Earl of Salisbury, who was past sixty, and had never been strong, being deformed from his birth. He said at last that he had no wish to live; and no Minister need have had, with his experience of the meanness and wickedness of those disgraceful times. The second was that of the Lady Arabella Stuart, who alarmed his Sowship mightily, by privately marrying WILLIAM SEYMOUR, son of LORD BEAUCHAMP, who was a descendant of King Henry the Seventh, and who, his Sowship thought, might consequently increase and strengthen any claim she might one day set up to the throne. She was separated from her husband (who was put in the Tower) and thrust into a boat to be confined at Durham. She escaped in a man's dress to get away in a French ship from Gravesend to France, but unhappily missed her husband, who had escaped too, and was soon taken. She went raving mad in the miserable Tower, and died there after four years. The last, and the most important of these three deaths, was that of Prince Henry, the heir to the throne, in the nineteenth year of his age. He was a promising young prince, and greatly liked ; a quiet well-conducted youth, of whom two very good things are known: first, that his father was jealous of him secondly, that he was the friend of Sir Walter Raleigh, languishing through all those years in the Tower, and often said that no man but his father would keep such a bird in such a cage. On the occasion of the preparations for the marriage of his sister the Princess Elizabeth with a foreign prince (and an unhappy marriage it turned out), he came from Richmond, where he had been very ill, to greet his new brother-in-law, at the palace at Whitehall. There he played a great game at tennis, in his shirt, though it was very cold weather, and was seized with an alarming illness, and died within a fortnight of a putrid fever. For this young prince Sir Walter Raleigh wrote, in his prison in the Tower, the beginning of a History of the World : a wonderful instance how little his

448 A CHILD'S HISTORY OF ENGLAND

Sowship could do to confine a great man's mind, however
long he might imprison his .body.

And this mention of Sir Walter Raleigh, who had many
faults, but who never showed so many merits as in trouble
and adversity, may bring me at once to the end of his sad
story.   After an imprisonment in the Tower of twelve long
years, he proposed to resume those old sea voyages of his,
and to go to South America in search of gold.   His Sowship,
divided between his wish to be on good terms with the
Spaniards through whose territory Sir Walter must pass
(he had long had an idea of marrying Prince Henry to
a Spanish Princess), and his avaricious eagerness to get
hold of the gold, did not know what to do.   But, in the end,
he set Sir Walter free, taking securities for his return ; and
Sir Walter fitted out an expedition at his own cost, and, on
the twenty-eighth of March, one thousand six hundred and
seventeen, sailed away in command of one of its ships,
which he ominously called the Destiny.   The expedition
failed ; the common men, not finding the gold they had
expected, mutinied ; a quarrel broke out between Sir Walter
and the Spaniards, who hated him for old successes of his
against them ; and he took and burnt a little town called
SAINT THOMAS.   For this he was denounced to his Sowship
by the Spanish Ambassador as a pirate ; and returning
almost broken-hearted, with his hopes and fortunes shattered,
his company of friends dispersed, and his brave son (who
had been one of them) killed, he was taken—through the
treachery of SIR LEWIS STUKELY, his near relation, a scoun-
drel and a Vice-Admiral—and was once again immured in
his prison-home of so many years.

His Sowship being mightily disappointed in not getting
any gold, Sir Walter Raleigh was tried as unfairly, and with
as many lies and evasions as the judges and law officers and
every other authority in Church and State habitually practised
under such a King.   After a great deal of prevarication on
all parts but his own, it was declared that he must die under
his former sentence, now fifteen years old.   So, on the
twenty-eighth of October, one thousand six hundred and
eighteen, he was shut up in the Gate House at Westminster
to pass his last night on earth, and there he took leave of his
good and faithful lady, who was worthy to have lived in
better days.   At eight o'clock next morning, after a cheerful
breakfast, and a pipe, and a cup of good wine, he was taken

to Old Palace Yard in Westminster, where the scaffold was
set up, and where so many people of high degree were assembled to see him die, that it was a matter of some difficulty
to get him through the crowd.   He behaved most nobly,
but if anything lay heavy on his mind, it was that Earl of
Essex, whose head he had seen roll off ; and he solemnly
said that he had had no hand in bringing him to the block,
and that he had shed tears for him when he died.   As the
morning was very cold, the Sheriff said, would he come
down to a fire for a little space, and warm himself?   But
Sir Walter thanked him, and said no, he would rather it
were done at once, for he was ill of fever and ague, and in
another quarter of an hour his shaking fit would come upon
him if he were still alive, and his enemies might then
suppose that he trembled for fear.   With that, he kneeled
and made a very beautiful and Christian prayer.   Before he
laid his head upon the block he felt the edge of the axe, and
said, with a smile upon his face, that it was a sharp medicine,
but would cure the worst disease.   When he was bent down
ready for death, he said to the executioner, finding that he
hesitated, "What dost thou fear? Strike, man!"   So, the
axe came down and struck his head off, in the sixty-sixth
year of his age.

The new favourite got on fast.   He was made a viscount,
he was made Duke of Buckingham, he was made a marquis,
he was made Master of the Horse, he was made Lord High
Admiral—and the Chief Commander of the gallant English
forces that had dispersed the Spanish Armada, was displaced
to make room for him.   He had the whole kingdom at his
disposal, and his mother sold all the profits and honours of
the State, as if she had kept a shop.   He blazed all over
with diamonds and other precious stones, from his hatband
and his earrings to his shoes.   Yet he was an ignorant
presumptuous swaggering compound of knave and fool, with
nothing but his beauty and his dancing to recommend him.
This is the gentleman who called himself his Majesty's dog
and slave, and called his Majesty Your Sowship.   His Sowship called him STEENIE ; it is supposed, because that was
a nickname for Stephen, and because St. Stephen was
generally represented in pictures as a handsome saint.

His Sowship was driven sometimes to his wits'-end by his
trimming between the general dislike of the Catholic religion
at home, and his desire to wheedle and flatter it abroad, as

his only means of getting a rich princess for his son's wife : a part of whose fortune he might cram into his greasy pockets. Prince Charles—or as his Sowship called him, Baby Charles —being now PRINCE OF WALES, the old project of a marriage with the Spanish King's daughter had been revived for him; and as she could not marry a Protestant without leave from the Pope, his Sowship himself secretly and meanly wrote to his Infallibility, asking for it.   The negotiation for this Spanish marriage takes up a larger space in great books, than you can imagine, but the upshot of it all is, that when it had been held off by the Spanish Court for a long time, Baby Charles and Steenie set off in disguise as Mr. Thomas Smith and Mr. John Smith, to see the Spanish Princess ; that Baby Charles pretended to be desperately in love with her, and jumped off walls to look at her, and made a con- siderable fool of himself in a good many ways ; that she was called Princess of Wales, and that the whole Spanish Court believed Baby Charles to be all but dying for her sake, as he expressly told them he was ; that Baby Charles and Steenie came back to England, and were received with as much rapture as if they had been a blessing to it ; that Baby Charles had actually fallen in love with HENRIETTA MARIA, the French King's sister, whom he had seen in Paris ; that he thought it a wonderfully fine and princely thing to have deceived the Spaniards, all through ; and that he openly said, with a chuckle, as soon as he was safe and sound at home again, that the Spaniards were great fools to have believed him.

Like most dishonest men, the Prince and the favourite complained that the people whom they had deluded were dishonest.   They made such misrepresentations of the treachery of the Spaniards in this business of the Spanish match, that the English nation became eager for a war with them.   Although the gravest Spaniards laughed at the idea of his Sowship in a warlike attitude, the Parliament granted money for the beginning of hostilities, and the treaties with Spain were publicly declared to be at an end.   The Spanish ambassador in London—probably with the help of the fallen favourite, the Earl of Somerset—being unable to obtain speech with his Sowship, slipped a paper into his hand, declaring that he was a prisoner in his own house, and was entirely governed by Buckingham and his creatures.   The first effect of this letter was that his Sowship began to cry

and whine, and took Baby Charles away from Steenie, and
went down to Windsor, gabbling all sorts of nonsense. The
end of it was that his Sowship hugged his dog and slave,
and said he was quite satisfied.

He had given the Prince and the favourite almost un-
limited power to settle anything with the Pope as to the
Spanish marriage ; and he now, with a view to the French
one, signed a treaty that all Roman Catholics in England
should exercise their religion freely, and should never be
required to take any oath contrary thereto. In return for
this, and for other concessions much less to be defended,
Henrietta Maria was to become the Prince's wife, and was
to bring him a fortune of eight hundred thousand crowns.

His Sowship's eyes were getting red with eagerly looking
for the money, when the end of a gluttonous life came upon
him ; and, after a fortnight's illness, on Sunday the twenty-
seventh of March, one thousand six hundred and twenty-five,
he died. He had reigned twenty-two years, and was fifty-
nine years old. I know of nothing more abominable in
history than the adulation that was lavished on this King,
and the vice and corruption that such a barefaced habit of
lying produced in his court. It is much to be doubted
whether one man of honour, and not utterly self-disgraced,
kept his place near James the First. Lord Bacon, that able
and wise philosopher, as the First Judge in the Kingdom in
this reign, became a public spectacle of dishonesty and
corruption ; and in his base flattery of his Sowship, and in
his crawling servility to his dog and slave, disgraced himself
even more. But, a creature like his Sowship set upon a
throne is like the Plague, and everybody receives infection
from him.

CHAPTER XXXIII

ENGLAND UNDER CHARLES THE FIRST

BABY CHARLES became KING CHARLES THE FIRST, in the twenty-fifth year of his age. Unlike his father, he was usually amiable in his private character, and grave and dignified in his bearing; but, like his father, he had monstrously exaggerated notions of the rights of a king, and was evasive, and not to be trusted. If his word could have been relied upon, his history might have had a different end.

His first care was to send over that insolent upstart, Buckingham, to bring Henrietta Maria from Paris to be his Queen; upon which occasion Buckingham—with his usual audacity—made love to the young Queen of Austria, and was very indignant indeed with CARDINAL RICHELIEU, the French Minister, for thwarting his intentions. The English people were very well disposed to like their new Queen, and to receive her with great favour when she came among them as a stranger. But, she held the Protestant religion in great dislike, and brought over a crowd of unpleasant priests, who made her do some very ridiculous things, and forced themselves upon the public notice in many disagreeable ways. Hence, the people soon came to dislike her, and she soon came to dislike them; and she did so much all through this reign in setting the King (who was dotingly fond of her) against his subjects, that it would have been better for him if she had never been born.

Now, you are to understand that King Charles the First—of his own determination to be a high and mighty King not to be called to account by anybody, and urged on by his Queen besides—deliberately set himself to put his Parliament down and to put himself up. You are also to understand, that even in pursuit of this wrong idea (enough in itself to have ruined any king) he never took a straight course, but always took a crooked one.

He was bent upon war with Spain, though neither the House of Commons nor the people were quite clear as to the justice of that war, now that they began to think a little more about the story of the Spanish match. But the King rushed into it hotly, raised money by illegal means to meet its expenses, and encountered a miserable failure at Cadiz, in the very first year of his reign. An expedition to Cadiz had been made in the hope of plunder, but as it was not successful, it was necessary to get a grant of money from the Parliament; and when they met, in no very complying humour, the King told them, "to make haste to let him have it, or it would be the worse for themselves." Not put in a more complying humour by this, they impeached the King's favourite, the Duke of Buckingham, as the cause (which he undoubtedly was) of many great public grievances and wrongs. The King, to save him, dissolved the Parliament without getting the money he wanted; and when the Lords implored him to consider and grant a little delay, he replied, "No, not one minute." He then began to raise money for himself by the following means among others.

He levied certain duties called tonnage and poundage which had not been granted by the Parliament, and could lawfully be levied by no other power; he called upon the seaport towns to furnish, and to pay all the cost for three months of, a fleet of armed ships; and he required the people to unite in lending him large sums of money, the repayment of which was very doubtful. If the poor people refused, they were pressed as soldiers or sailors; if the gentry refused, they were sent to prison. Five gentlemen, named SIR THOMAS DARNEL, JOHN CORBET, WALTER EARL, JOHN HEVENINGHAM, and EVERARD HAMPDEN, for refusing were taken up by a warrant of the King's privy council, and were sent to prison without any cause but the King's pleasure being stated for their imprisonment. Then the question came to be solemnly tried, whether this was not a violation of Magna Charta, and an encroachment by the King on the highest rights of the English people. His lawyers contended No, because to encroach upon the rights of the English people would be to do wrong, and the King could do no wrong. The accommodating judges decided in favour of this wicked nonsense; and here was a fatal division between the King and the people.

For all this, it became necessary to call another Parliament.

The people, sensible of the danger in which their liberties were, chose for it those who were best known for their determined opposition to the King; but still the King, quite blinded by his determination to carry everything before him, addressed them when they met, in a contemptuous manner, and just told them in so many words that he had only called them together because he wanted money. The Parliament, strong enough and resolute enough to know that they would lower his tone, cared little for what he said, and laid before him one of the great documents of history, which is called the PETITION OF RIGHT, requiring that the free men of England should no longer be called upon to lend the King money, and should no longer be pressed or imprisoned for refusing to do so ; further, that the free men of England should no longer be seized by the King's special mandate or warrant, it being contrary to their rights and liberties and the laws of their country. At first the King returned an answer to this petition, in which he tried to shirk it altogether ; but, the House of Commons then showing their determination to go on with the impeachment of Buckingham, the King in alarm returned an answer, giving his consent to all that was required of him. He not only afterwards departed from his word and honour on these points, over and over again, but, at this very time, he did the mean and dissembling act of publishing his first answer and not his second—merely that the people might suppose that the Parliament had not got the better of him.

That pestilent Buckingham, to gratify his own wounded vanity, had by this time involved the country in war with France, as well as with Spain. For such miserable causes and such miserable creatures are wars sometimes made ! But he was destined to do little more mischief in this world. One morning, as he was going out of his house to his carriage, he turned to speak to a certain Colonel FRYER who was with him ; and he was violently stabbed with a knife, which the murderer left sticking in his heart. This happened in his hall. He had had angry words up-stairs, just before, with some French gentlemen, who were immediately suspected by his servants, and had a close escape from being set upon and killed. In the midst of the noise, the real murderer, who had gone to the kitchen and might easily have got away, drew his sword and cried out, "I am the man !" His name was JOHN FELTON, a Protestant and a retired officer in the army. He said he had had no personal ill-will to the Duke, but had killed him as a curse to the country. He had aimed his blow well, for Buckingham had only had time to cry out, " Villain ! " and then he drew out the knife, fell against a table, and died.

The council made a mighty business of examining John Felton about this murder, though it was a plain case enough, one would think. He had come seventy miles to do it, he told them, and he did it for the reason he had declared ; if they put him upon the rack, as that noble MARQUIS OF DORSET whom he saw before him, had the goodness to threaten, he gave that marquis warning, that he would accuse *him* as his accomplice ! The King was unpleasantly anxious to have him racked, nevertheless ; but as the judges now found out that torture was contrary to the law of England—it is a pity they did not make the discovery a little sooner—John Felton was simply executed for the murder he had done. A murder it undoubtedly was, and not in the least to be defended : though he had freed England from one of the most profligate, contemptible, and base court favourites to whom it has ever yielded.

A very different man now arose. This was SIR THOMAS WENTWORTH, a Yorkshire gentleman, who had sat in Parliament for a long time, and who had favoured arbitrary and haughty principles, but who had gone over to the people's side on receiving offence from Buckingham. The King, much wanting such a man—for, besides being naturally favourable to the King's cause, he had great abilities—made him first a Baron, and then a Viscount, and gave him high employment, and won him most completely.

A Parliament, however, was still in existence, and was *not* to be won. On the twentieth of January, one thousand six hundred and twenty-nine, SIR JOHN ELIOT, a great man who had been active in the Petition of Right, brought forward other strong resolutions against the King's chief instruments, and called upon the Speaker to put them to the vote. To this the Speaker answered, " he was commanded otherwise by the King," and got up to leave the chair—which, according to the rules of the House of Commons would have obliged it to adjourn without doing anything more— when two members, named Mr. HOLLIS and Mr. VALENTINE, held him down. A scene of great confusion arose among the members ; and while many swords were drawn and flashing about, the King, who was kept informed of all that was going on, told the captain of his guard to go down to the House and force the doors. The resolutions were by that time, however, voted, and the House adjourned. Sir John Eliot and those two members who had held the Speaker down, were quickly summoned before the council. As they claimed it to be their privilege not to answer out of Parliament for anything they had said in it, they were committed to the Tower. The King then went down and dissolved the Parliament, in a speech wherein he made mention of these gentlemen as "Vipers"—which did not do him much good that ever I have heard of.

As they refused to gain their liberty by saying they were sorry for what they had done, the King, always remarkably unforgiving, never overlooked their offence. When they demanded to be brought up before the court of King's Bench, he even resorted to the meanness of having them moved about from prison to prison, so that the writs issued for that purpose should not legally find them. At last they came before the court and were sentenced to heavy fines, and to be imprisoned during the King's pleasure. When Sir John Eliot's health had quite given way, and he so longed for change of air and scene as to petition for his release, the King sent back the answer (worthy of his Sowship himself) that the petition was not humble enough. When he sent another petition by his young son, in which he pathetically offered to go back to prison when his health was restored, if he might be released for its recovery, the King still disregarded it. When he died in the Tower, and his children petitioned to be allowed to take his body down to Cornwall, there to lay it among the ashes of his fore-fathers, the King returned for answer, "Let Sir John Eliot's body be buried in the church of that parish where he died." All this was like a very little King indeed, I think.

And now, for twelve long years, steadily pursuing his design of setting himself up and putting the people down, the King called no Parliament; but ruled without one. If twelve thousand volumes were written in his praise (as a good many have been) it would still remain a fact, impossible to be denied, that for twelve years King Charles the First reigned in England unlawfully and despotically, seized upon his subjects' goods and money at his pleasure, and punished according to his unbridled will all who ventured to oppose

him. It is a fashion with some people to think that this
King's career was cut short; but I must say myself that
I think he ran a pretty long one.

WILLIAM LAUD, Archbishop of Canterbury, was the King's
right-hand man in the religious part of the putting down of
the people's liberties. Laud, who was a sincere man, of large
learning but small sense—for the two things sometimes go
together in very different quantities—though a Protestant,
held opinions so near those of the Catholics, that the Pope
wanted to make a Cardinal of him, if he would have accepted
that favour He looked upon vows, robes, lighted candles,
images, and so forth, as amazingly important in religious
ceremonies ; and he brought in an immensity of bowing and
candle-snuffing. He also regarded archbishops and bishops
as a sort of miraculous persons, and was inveterate in the
last degree against any who thought otherwise. Accordingly,
he offered up thanks to Heaven, and was in a state of much
pious pleasure, when a Scotch clergyman, named LEIGHTON,
was pilloried, whipped, branded in the cheek, and had one
of his ears cut off and one of his nostrils slit, for calling
bishops trumpery and the inventions of men. He originated
on a Sunday morning the prosecution of WILLIAM PRYNNE,
a barrister who was of similar opinions, and who was fined
a thousand pounds ; who was pilloried ; who had his ears
cut off on two occasions—one ear at a time—and who was
imprisoned for life. He highly approved of the punishment
of DOCTOR BASTWICK, a physician ; who was also fined a
thousand pounds ; and who afterwards had *his* ears cut off,
and was imprisoned for life. These were gentle methods
of persuasion, some will tell you : I think, they were rather
calculated to be alarming to the people.

In the money part of the putting down of the people's
liberties, the King was equally gentle, as some will tell
you : as I think, equally alarming. He levied those duties
of tonnage and poundage, and increased them as he thought
fit. He granted monopolies to companies of merchants on
their paying him for them, notwithstanding the great complaints that had, for years and years, been made on the
subject of monopolies. He fined the people for disobeying
proclamations issued by his Sowship in direct violation of
law. He revived the detested Forest laws, and took private
property to himself as his forest right. Above all, he
determined to have what was called Ship Money ; that is

to say, money for the support of the fleet—not only from the seaports, but from all the counties of England: having found out that, in some ancient time or other, all the counties paid it. The grievance of this ship money being somewhat too strong, JOHN CHAMBERS, a citizen of London, refused to pay his part of it. For this the Lord Mayor ordered John Chambers to prison, and for that John Chambers brought a suit against the Lord Mayor. LORD SAY, also, behaved like a real nobleman, and declared he would not pay. But, the sturdiest and best opponent of the ship money was JOHN HAMPDEN, a gentleman of Buckinghamshire, who had sat among the "vipers" in the House of Commons when there was such a thing, and who had been the bosom friend of Sir John Eliot. This case was tried before the twelve judges in the Court of Exchequer, and again the King's lawyers said it was impossible that ship money could be wrong, because the King could do no wrong, however hard he tried—and he really did try very hard during these twelve years. Seven of the judges said that was quite true, and Mr. Hampden was bound to pay: five of the judges said that was quite false, and Mr. Hampden was not bound to pay. So, the King triumphed (as he thought), by making Hampden the most popular man in England; where matters were getting to that height now, that many honest Englishmen could not endure their country, and sailed away across the seas to found a colony in Massachusetts Bay in America. It is said that Hampden himself and his relation OLIVER CROMWELL were going with a company of such voyagers, and were actually on board ship, when they were stopped by a proclamation, prohibiting sea captains to carry out such passengers without the royal license. But O! it would have been well for the King if he had let them go!

This was the state of England. If Laud had been a madman just broke loose, he could not have done more mischief than he did in Scotland. In his endeavours (in which he was seconded by the King, then in person in that part of his dominions) to force his own ideas of bishops, and his own religious forms and ceremonies upon the Scotch, he roused that nation to a perfect frenzy. They formed a solemn league, which they called The Covenant, for the preservation of their own religious forms; they rose in arms throughout the whole country; they summoned all their men to prayers and sermons twice a day by beat of drum ; they sang psalms, in which they compared their enemies to all the evil spirits that ever were heard of; and they solemnly vowed to smite them with the sword. At first the King tried force, then treaty, then a Scottish Parliament which did not answer at all. Then he tried the EARL OF STRAFFORD, formerly Sir Thomas Wentworth ; who, as LORD WENTWORTH, had been governing Ireland. He, too, had carried it with a very high hand there, though to the benefit and prosperity of that country.

Strafford and Laud were for conquering the Scottish people by force of arms. Other lords who were taken into council. recommended that a Parliament should at last be called : to which the King unwillingly consented. So, on the thirteenth of April, one thousand six hundred and forty, that then strange sight, a Parliament, was seen at Westminster. It is called the Short Parliament, for it lasted a very little while. While the members were all looking at one another, doubtful who would dare to speak, Mr. PYM arose and set forth all that the King had done unlawfully during the past twelve years, and what was the position to which England was reduced. This great example set, other members took courage and spoke the truth freely. though with great patience and moderation. The King. a little frightened, sent to say that if they would grant him a certain sum on certain terms, no more ship money should be raised. They debated the matter for two days ; and then, as they would not give him all he asked without promise or inquiry, he dissolved them.

But they knew very well that he must have a Parliament now ; and he began to make that discovery too, though rather late in the day. Wherefore, on the twenty-fourth of September, being then at York with an army collected against the Scottish people, but his own men sullen and discontented like the rest of the nation, the King told the great council of the Lords, whom he had called to meet him there, that he would summon another Parliament to assemble on the third of November. The soldiers of the Covenant had now forced their way into England and had taken possession of the northern counties, where the coals are got. As it would never do to be without coals, and as the King's troops could make no head against the Covenanters so full of gloomy zeal, a truce was made, and a treaty with Scotland was taken into

consideration. Meanwhile the northern counties paid the
Covenanters to leave the coals alone, and keep quiet.

We have now disposed of the Short Parliament. We
have next to see what memorable things were done by the
Long one.

SECOND PART.

THE Long Parliament assembled on the third of November,
one thousand six hundred and forty-one. That day week the
Earl of Strafford arrived from York, very sensible that the
spirited and determined men who formed that Parliament
were no friends towards him, who had not only deserted
the cause of the people, but who had on all occasions opposed
himself to their liberties. The King told him, for his comfort, that the Parliament "should not hurt one hair of his
head." But, on the very next day Mr. Pym, in the House
of Commons, and with great solemnity, impeached the Earl
of Strafford as a traitor. He was immediately taken into
custody and fell from his proud height.

It was the twenty-second of March before he was brought
to trial in Westminster Hall; where, although he was very ill
and suffered great pain, he defended himself with such ability
and majesty, that it was doubtful whether he would not get
the best of it. But on the thirteenth day of the trial, Pym
produced in the House of Commons a copy of some notes
of a council, found by young SIR HARRY VANE in a red velvet
cabinet belonging to his father (Secretary Vane, who sat at
the council-table with the Earl), in which Strafford had
distinctly told the King that he was free from all rules and
obligations of government, and might do with his people
whatever he liked; and in which he had added—" You have
an army in Ireland that you may employ to reduce this
kingdom to obedience." It was not clear whether by the
words "this kingdom," he had really meant England or
Scotland; but the Parliament contended that he meant
England, and this was treason. At the same sitting of the
House of Commons it was resolved to bring in a bill of
attainder declaring the treason to have been committed: in
preference to proceeding with the trial by impeachment, which
would have required the treason to be proved.

So, a bill was brought in at once, was carried through the
House of Commons by a large majority, and was sent up to
the House of Lords. While it was still uncertain whether

the House of Lords would pass it and the King consent to it, Pym disclosed to the House of Commons that the King and Queen had both been plotting with the officers of the army to bring up the soldiers and control the Parliament, and also to introduce two hundred soldiers into the Tower of London to effect the Earl's escape. The plotting with the army was revealed by one GEORGE GORING, the son of a lord of that name: a bad fellow who was one of the original plotters, and turned traitor. The King had actually given his warrant for the admission of the two hundred men into the Tower, and they would have got in too, but for the refusal of the governor—a sturdy Scotchman of the name of BALFOUR—to admit them. These matters being made public, great numbers of people began to riot outside the Houses of Parliament, and to cry out for the execution of the Earl of Strafford, as one of the King's chief instruments against them. The bill passed the House of Lords while the people were in this state of agitation, and was laid before the King for his assent, together with another bill declaring that the Parliament then assembled should not be dissolved or adjourned without their own consent. The King—not unwilling to save a faithful servant, though he had no great attachment for him—was in some doubt what to do ; but he gave his consent to both bills, although he in his heart believed that the bill against the Earl of Strafford was unlawful and unjust. The Earl had written to him, telling him that he was willing to die for his sake. But he had not expected that his royal master would take him at his word quite so readily ; for, when he heard his doom, he laid his hand upon his heart, and said, " Put not your trust in Princes ! "

The King, who never could be straightforward and plain, through one single day or through one single sheet of paper, wrote a letter to the Lords, and sent it by the young Prince of Wales, entreating them to prevail with the Commons that " that unfortunate man should fulfil the natural course of his life in a close imprisonment." In a postscript to the very same letter, he added, " If he must die, it were charity to reprieve him till Saturday." If there had been any doubt of his fate, this weakness and meanness would have settled it. The very next day, which was the twelfth of May, he was brought out to be beheaded on Tower Hill.

Archbishop Laud, who had been so fond of having people's ears cropped off and their noses slit, was now confined in the

Tower too; and when the Earl went by his window to his death, he was there, at his request, to give him his blessing. They had been great friends in the King's cause, and the Earl had written to him in the days of their power that he thought it would be an admirable thing to have Mr. Hampden publicly whipped for refusing to pay the ship money. However, those high and mighty doings were over now, and the Earl went his way to death with dignity and heroism. The governor wished him to get into a coach at the Tower gate, for fear the people should tear him to pieces; but he said it was all one to him whether he died by the axe or by the people's hands. So, he walked, with a firm tread and a stately look, and sometimes pulled off his hat to them as he passed along. They were profoundly quiet. He made a speech on the scaffold from some notes he had prepared (the paper was found lying there after his head was struck off), and one blow of the axe killed him, in the forty-ninth year of his age.

This bold and daring act, the Parliament accompanied by other famous measures, all originating (as even this did) in the King's having so grossly and so long abused his power. The name of DELINQUENTS was applied to all sheriffs and other officers who had been concerned in raising the ship money, or any other money, from the people, in an unlawful manner; the Hampden judgment was reversed; the judges who had decided against Hampden were called upon to give large securities that they would take such consequences as Parliament might impose upon them; and one was arrested as he sat in High Court, and carried off to prison. Laud was impeached; the unfortunate victims whose ears had been cropped and whose noses had been slit, were brought out of prison in triumph; and a bill was passed declaring that a Parliament should be called every third year, and that if the King and the King's officers did not call it, the people should assemble of themselves and summon it, as of their own right and power. Great illuminations and rejoicings took place over all these things, and the country was wildly excited. That the Parliament took advantage of this excitement and stirred them up by every means, there is no doubt; but you are always to remember those twelve long years, during which the King had tried so hard whether he really could do any wrong or not.

All this time there was a great religious outcry against

the right of the Bishops to sit in Parliament; to which the Scottish people particularly objected. The English were divided on this subject, and, partly on this account and partly because they had had foolish expectations that the Parliament would be able to take off nearly all the taxes, numbers of them sometimes wavered and inclined towards the King.

I believe myself, that if, at this or almost any other period of his life, the King could have been trusted by any man not out of his senses, he might have saved himself and kept his throne. But, on the English army being disbanded, he plotted with the officers again, as he had done before, and established the fact beyond all doubt by putting his signature of approval to a petition against the Parliamentary leaders, which was drawn up by certain officers. When the Scottish army was disbanded, he went to Edinburgh in four days—which was going very fast at that time—to plot again, and so darkly too, that it is difficult to decide what his whole object was. Some suppose that he wanted to gain over the Scottish Parliament, as he did in fact gain over, by presents and favours, many Scottish lords and men of power. Some think that he went to get proofs against the Parliamentary leaders in England of their having treasonably invited the Scottish people to come and help them. With whatever object he went to Scotland, he did little good by going. At the instigation of the EARL OF MONTROSE, a desperate man who was then in prison for plotting, he tried to kidnap three Scottish lords who escaped. A committee of the Parliament at home, who had followed to watch him, writing an account of this INCIDENT, as it was called, to the Parliament, the Parliament made a fresh stir about it; were, or feigned to be, much alarmed for themselves; and wrote to the EARL OF ESSEX, the commander-in-chief, for a guard to protect them.

It is not absolutely proved that the King plotted in Ireland besides, but it is very probable that he did, and that the Queen did, and that he had some wild hope of gaining the Irish people over to his side by favouring a rise among them. Whether or no, they did rise in a most brutal and savage rebellion; in which, encouraged by their priests, they committed such atrocities upon numbers of the English, of both sexes and of all ages, as nobody could believe, but for their being related on oath by eye-witnesses. Whether one hundred thousand or two hundred thousand Protestants were murdered in this outbreak, is uncertain; but, that it was as ruthless and barbarous an outbreak as ever was known among any savage people, is certain.

The King came home from Scotland, determined to make a great struggle for his lost power. He believed that, through his presents and favours, Scotland would take no part against him ; and the Lord Mayor of London received him with such a magnificent dinner that he thought he must have become popular again in England. It would take a good many Lord Mayors, however, to make a people, and the King soon found himself mistaken.

Not so soon, though, but that there was a great opposition in the Parliament to a celebrated paper put forth by Pym and Hampden and the rest, called "THE REMONSTRANCE," which set forth all the illegal acts that the King had ever done, but politely laid the blame of them on his bad advisers. Even when it was passed and presented to him, the King still thought himself strong enough to discharge Balfour from his command in the Tower, and to put in his place a man of bad character ; to whom the Commons instantly objected, and whom he was obliged to abandon. At this time, the old outcry about the Bishops became louder than ever, and the old Archbishop of York was so near being murdered as he went down to the House of Lords—being laid hold of by the mob and violently knocked about, in return for very foolishly scolding a shrill boy who was yelping out "No Bishops!" —that he sent for all the Bishops who were in town, and proposed to them to sign a declaration that, as they could no longer without danger to their lives attend their duty in Parliament, they protested against the lawfulness of everything done in their absence. This they asked the King to send to the House of Lords, which he did. Then the House of Commons impeached the whole party of Bishops and sent them off to the Tower.

Taking no warning from this, but encouraged by there being a moderate party in the Parliament who objected to these strong measures, the King, on the third of January, one thousand six hundred and forty-two, took the rashest step that ever was taken by mortal man.

Of his own accord and without advice, he sent the Attorney-General to the House of Lords, to accuse of treason certain members of Parliament who as popular leaders were the most obnoxious to him ; LORD KIMBOLTON, SIR ARTHUR HASELRIG, DENZIL HOLLIS, JOHN PYM (they used to call him

King Pym, he possessed such power and looked so big), JOHN HAMPDEN, and WILLIAM STRODE. The houses of those members he caused to be entered, and their papers to be sealed up. At the same time, he sent a messenger to the House of Commons demanding to have the five gentlemen who were members of that House immediately produced. To this the House replied that they should appear as soon as there was any legal charge against them, and immediately adjourned.

Next day, the House of Commons sent into the City to let the Lord Mayor know that their privileges are invaded by the King, and that there is no safety for anybody or anything. Then, when the five members are gone out of the way, down comes the King himself, with all his guard and from two to three hundred gentlemen and soldiers, of whom the greater part were armed. These he leaves in the hall; and then, with his nephew at his side, goes into the House, takes off his hat, and walks up to the Speaker's chair. The Speaker leaves it, the King stands in front of it, looks about him steadily for a little while, and says he has come for those five members. No one speaks, and then he calls John Pym by name. No one speaks, and then he calls Denzil Hollis by name. No one speaks, and then he asks the Speaker of the House where those five members are? The Speaker, answering on his knee, nobly replies that he is the servant of that House, and that he has neither eyes to see, nor tongue to speak, anything but what the House commands him. Upon this, the King, beaten from that time evermore, replies that he will seek them himself, for they have committed treason; and goes out, with his hat in his hand, amid some audible murmurs from the members.

No words can describe the hurry that arose out of doors when all this was known. The five members had gone for safety to a house in Coleman-street, in the City, where they were guarded all night; and indeed the whole city watched in arms like an army. At ten o'clock in the morning, the King already frightened at what he had done, came to the Guildhall, with only half a dozen lords, and made a speech to the people, hoping they would not shelter those whom he accused of treason. Next day, he issued a proclamation for the apprehension of the five members; but the Parliament minded it so little that they made great arrangements for having them brought down to Westminster in great state, five days afterwards. The King was so alarmed now at his own imprudence, if not for his own safety, that he left his palace at Whitehall, and went away with his Queen and children to Hampton Court.

It was the eleventh of May, when the five members were carried in state and triumph to Westminster. They were taken by water. The river could not be seen for the boats on it; and the five members were hemmed in by barges full of men and great guns, ready to protect them, at any cost. Along the Strand a large body of the train-bands of London, under their commander, SKIPPON, marched to be ready to assist the little fleet. Beyond them, came a crowd who choked the streets, roaring incessantly about the Bishops and the Papists, and crying out contemptuously as they passed Whitehall, "What has become of the King?" With this great noise outside the House of Commons, and with great silence within, Mr. Pym rose and informed the House of the great kindness with which they had been received in the City. Upon that, the House called the sheriffs in and thanked them, and requested the train-bands, under their commander Skippon, to guard the House of Commons every day. Then, came four thousand men on horseback out of Buckinghamshire, offering their services as a guard too, and bearing a petition to the King, complaining of the injury that had been done to Mr. Hampden, who was their county man and much beloved and honoured.

When the King set off for Hampton Court, the gentlemen and soldiers who had been with him followed him out of town as far as Kingston-upon-Thames; next day, Lord Digby came to them from the King at Hampton Court, in his coach and six, to inform them that the King accepted their protection. This, the Parliament said, was making war against the kingdom, and Lord Digby fled abroad. The Parliament then immediately applied themselves to getting hold of the military power of the country, well knowing that the King was already trying hard to use it against them, and that he had secretly sent the Earl of Newcastle to Hull, to secure a valuable magazine of arms and gunpowder that was there. In those times, every county had its own magazines of arms and powder, for its own train-bands or militia; so, the Parliament brought in a bill claiming the right (which up to this time had belonged to the King) of appointing the Lord Lieutenants of counties, who commanded these train-bands; also, of having all the forts, castles, and garrisons in the kingdom, put into the hands of such governors as they, the Parliament, could confide in. It also passed a law depriving the Bishops of their votes. The King gave his assent to that bill, but would not abandon the right of appointing the Lord Lieutenants, though he said he was willing to appoint such as might be suggested to him by the Parliament. When the Earl of Pembroke asked him whether he would not give way on that question for a time, he said. "By God! not for one hour!" and upon this he and the Parliament went to war.

His young daughter was betrothed to the Prince of Orange. On pretence of taking her to the country of her future husband, the Queen was already got safely away to Holland, there to pawn the Crown jewels for money to raise an army on the King's side. The Lord Admiral being sick, the House of Commons now named the Earl of Warwick to hold his place for a year. The King named another gentleman; the House of Commons took its own way, and the Earl of Warwick became Lord Admiral without the King's consent. The Parliament sent orders down to Hull to have that magazine removed to London; the King went down to Hull to take it himself. The citizens would not admit him into the town, and the governor would not admit him into the castle. The Parliament resolved that whatever the two Houses passed, and the King would not consent to, should be called an ORDINANCE, and should be as much a law as if he did consent to it. The King protested against this, and gave notice that these ordinances were not to be obeyed. The King, attended by the majority of the House of Peers, and by many members of the House of Commons, established himself at York. The Chancellor went to him with the Greal Seal, and the Parliament made a new Great Seal. The Queen sent over a ship full of arms and ammunition, and the King issued letters to borrow money at high interest. The Parliament raised twenty regiments of foot and seventy-five troops of horse; and the people willingly aided them with their money, plate, jewellery, and trinkets—the married women even with their wedding-rings. Every member of Parliament who could raise a troop or a regiment in his own part of the country, dressed it according to his taste and in his own colours, and commanded it. Foremost among them all, OLIVER CROMWELL raised a troop of horse—thoroughly in earnest and thoroughly well armed—who were, perhaps, the best soldiers that ever were seen.

In some of their proceedings, this famous Parliament passed the bounds of previous law and custom, yielded to and favoured riotous assemblages of the people, and acted tyrannically in imprisoning some who differed from the popular leaders.   But again, you are always to remember that the twelve years during which the King had had his own wilful way, had gone before; and that nothing could make the times what they might, could, would, or should have been, if those twelve years had never rolled away.

Third Part.

I shall not try to relate the particulars of the great civil war between King Charles the First and the Long Parliament, which lasted nearly four years, and a full account of which would fill many large books.   It was a sad thing that Englishmen should once more be fighting against Englishmen on English ground ; but, it is some consolation to know that on both sides there was great humanity, forbearance, and honour.   The soldiers of the Parliament were far more remarkable for these good qualities than the soldiers of the King (many of whom fought for mere pay without much caring for the cause) ; but those of the nobility and gentry who were on the King's side were so brave, and so faithful to him, that their conduct cannot but command our highest admiration.   Among them were great numbers of Catholics, who took the royal side because the Queen was so strongly of their persuasion.

The King might have distinguished some of these gallant spirits, if he had been as generous a spirit himself, by giving them the command of his army.   Instead of that, however, true to his old high notions of royalty, he entrusted it to his two nephews, Prince Rupert and Prince Maurice, who were of royal blood and came over from abroad to help him. It might have been better for him if they had stayed away ; since Prince Rupert was an impetuous hot-headed fellow, whose only idea was to dash into battle at all times and seasons, and lay about him.

The general-in-chief of the Parliamentary army was the Earl of Essex, a gentleman of honour and an excellent soldier.   A little while before the war broke out, there had been some rioting at Westminster between certain officious law students and noisy soldiers, and the shopkeepers and their apprentices, and the general people in the streets. At that time the King's friends called the crowd, Roundheads, because the apprentices wore short hair ; the crowd, in return, called their opponents Cavaliers, meaning that they were a blustering set, who pretended to be very military. These two words now began to be used to distinguish the two sides in the civil war. The Royalists also called the Parliamentary men Rebels and Rogues, while the Parliamentary men called *them* Malignants, and spoke of themselves as the Godly, the Honest, and so forth.

The war broke out at Portsmouth, where that double traitor Goring had again gone over to the King and was besieged by the Parliamentary troops. Upon this, the King proclaimed the Earl of Essex and the officers serving unde.' him, traitors, and called upon his loyal subjects to meet him in arms at Nottingham on the twenty-fifth of August. But his loyal subjects came about him in scanty numbers, and it was a windy gloomy day, and the Royal Standard got blown down, and the whole affair was very melancholy. The chief engagements after this, took place in the vale of the Red Horse near Banbury, at Brentford, at Devizes, at Chalgrove Field (where Mr. Hampden was so sorely wounded while fighting at the head of his men, that he died within a week), at Newbury (in which battle LORD FALKLAND, one of the best noblemen on the King's side, was killed), at Leicester, at Naseby, at Winchester, at Marston Moor near York, at Newcastle, and in many other parts of England and Scotland. These battles were attended with various successes. At one time, the King was victorious ; at another time, the Parliament. But almost all the great and busy towns were against the King ; and when it was considered necessary to fortify London, all ranks of people, from labouring men and women, up to lords and ladies, worked hard together with heartiness and good will. The most distinguished leaders on the Parliamentary side were HAMPDEN, SIR THOMAS FAIRFAX, and, above all, OLIVER CROMWELL, and his son-in-law IRETON.

During the whole of this war, the people, to whom it was very expensive and irksome, and to whom it was made the more distressing by almost every family being divided—some of its members attaching themselves to one side and some to the other—were over and over again most anxious for peace. So were some of the best men in each cause. Accordingly, treaties of peace were discussed between commissioners from the Parliament and the King; at York, at Oxford (where the King held a little Parliament of his own), and at Uxbridge. But they came to nothing. In all these negotiations, and in all his difficulties, the King showed himself at his best. He was courageous, cool, self-possessed, and clever; but, the old taint of his character was always in him, and he was never for one single moment to be trusted. Lord Clarendon, the historian, one of his highest admirers, supposes that he had unhappily promised the Queen never to make peace without her consent, and that this must often be taken as his excuse. He never kept his word from night to morning. He signed a cessation of hostilities with the blood-stained Irish rebels for a sum of money, and invited the Irish regiments over, to help him against the Parliament. In the battle of Naseby, his cabinet was seized and was found to contain a correspondence with the Queen, in which he expressly told her that he had deceived the Parliament— a mongrel Parliament, he called it now, as an improvement on his old term of vipers—in pretending to recognise it and to treat with it; and from which it further appeared that he had long been in secret treaty with the Duke of Lorraine for a foreign army of ten thousand men. Disappointed in this, he sent a most devoted friend of his, the EARL OF GLAMORGAN, to Ireland, to conclude a secret treaty with the Catholic powers, to send him an Irish army of ten thousand men ; in return for which he was to bestow great favours on the Catholic religion. And, when this treaty was discovered in the carriage of a fighting Irish Archbishop who was killed in one of the many skirmishes of those days, he basely denied and deserted his attached friend, the Earl, on his being charged with high treason; and—even worse than this—had left blanks in the secret instructions he gave him with his own kingly hand, expressly that he might thus save himself.

At last, on the twenty-seventh day of April, one thousand six hundred and forty-six, the King found himself in the city of Oxford, so surrounded by the Parliamentary army who were closing in upon him on all sides that he felt that if he would escape he must delay no longer. So, that night, having altered the cut of his hair and beard. he was dressed up as a servant and put upon a horse with a cloak strapped behind him, and rode out of the town behind one of his own faithful followers, with a clergyman of that country who knew the road well, for a guide. He rode towards London as far as Harrow, and then altered his plans and resolved, it would seem, to go to the Scottish camp. The Scottish men had been invited over to help the Parliamentary army, and had a large force then in England. The King was so desperately intriguing in everything he did, that it is doubt- ful what he exactly meant by this step. He took it, any- how, and delivered himself up to the EARL OF LEVEN, the Scottish general-in-chief, who treated him as an honourable prisoner. Negotiations between the Parliament on the one hand and the Scottish authorities on the other, as to what should be done with him, lasted until the following February. Then, when the King had refused to the Parliament the concession of that old militia point for twenty years, and had refused to Scotland the recognition of its Solemn League and Covenant, Scotland got a handsome sum for its army and its help, and the King into the bargain. He was taken, by certain Parliamentary commissioners appointed to receive him, to one of his own houses, called Holmby House, near Althorpe, in Northamptonshire.

While the Civil War was still in progress, John Pym died, and was buried with great honour in Westminster Abbey—not with greater honour than he deserved, for the liberties of Englishmen owe a mighty debt to Pym and Hampden. The war was but newly over when the Earl of Essex died, of an illness brought on by his having over- heated himself in a stag hunt in Windsor Forest. He, too, was buried in Westminster Abbey, with great state. I wish it were not necessary to add that Archbishop Laud died upon the scaffold when the war was not yet done. His trial lasted in all nearly a year, and, it being doubtful even then whether the charges brought against him amounted to treason, the odious old contrivance of the worst kings was resorted to, and a bill of attainder was brought in against him. He was a violently prejudiced and mis- chievous person; had had strong ear-cropping and nose- splitting propensities, as you know; and had done a world of harm. But he died peaceably, and like a brave old man.

FOURTH PART.

WHEN the Parliament had got the King into their hands, they became very anxious to get rid of their army, in which Oliver Cromwell had begun to acquire great power; not only because of his courage and high abilities, but because he professed to be very sincere in the Scottish sort of Puritan religion that was then exceedingly popular among the soldiers. They were as much opposed to the Bishops as to the Pope himself; and the very privates, drummers, and trumpeters, had such an inconvenient habit of starting up and preaching long-winded discourses, that I would not have belonged to that army on any account.

So, the Parliament, being far from sure but that the army might begin to preach and fight against them now it had nothing else to do, proposed to disband the greater part of it, to send another part to serve in Ireland against the rebels, and to keep only a small force in England. But, the army would not consent to be broken up, except upon its own conditions; and, when the Parliament showed an intention of compelling it, it acted for itself in an unexpected manner. A certain cornet, of the name of JOICE, arrived at Holmby House one night, attended by four hundred horsemen, went into the King's room with his hat in one hand and a pistol in the other, and told the King that he had come to take him away. The King was willing enough to go, and only stipulated that he should be publicly required to do so next morning. Next morning, accordingly, he appeared on the top of the steps of the house, and asked Cornet Joice before his men and the guard set there by the Parliament, what authority he had for taking him away? To this Cornet Joice replied, " The authority of the army." " Have you a written commission? " said the King. Joice, pointing to his four hundred men on horseback, replied, " That is my commission." " Well," said the King, smiling, as if he were pleased, " I never before read such a commission ; but it is written in fair and legible characters. This is a company of as handsome proper gentlemen as I have seen a long while." He was asked where he would like to live, and he said at Newmarket. So, to Newmarket he and Cornet Joice and the four hundred horsemen rode; the King remarking, in the same smiling way, that he could ride as far at a spell as Cornet Joice, or any man there.

The King quite believed, I think, that the army were his
friends. He said as much to Fairfax when that general
Oliver Cromwell, and Ireton, went to persuade him to return
to the custody of the Parliament. He preferred to remain
as he was, and resolved to remain as he was. And when
the army moved nearer and nearer London to frighten the
Parliament into yielding to their demands, they took the
King with them. It was a deplorable thing that England
should be at the mercy of a great body of soldiers with arms
in their hands; but the King certainly favoured them at
this important time of his life, as compared with the more
lawful power that tried to control him. It must be added,
however, that they treated him, as yet, more respectfully
and kindly than the Parliament had done. They allowed
him to be attended by his own servants, to be splendidly
entertained at various houses, and to see his children—at
Caversham House, near Reading—for two days. Whereas,
the Parliament had been rather hard with him, and had
only allowed him to ride out and play at bowls.

It is much to be believed that if the King could have been
trusted, even at this time, he might have been saved. Even
Oliver Cromwell expressly said that he did believe that no
man could enjoy his possessions in peace, unless the King
had his rights. He was not unfriendly towards the King;
he had been present when he received his children, and had
been much affected by the pitiable nature of the scene; he
saw the King often; he frequently walked and talked with
him in the long galleries and pleasant gardens of the Palace
at Hampton Court, whither he was now removed; and in all
this risked something of his influence with the army. But,
the King was in secret hopes of help from the Scottish
people; and the moment he was encouraged to join them
he began to be cool to his new friends, the army, and to tell
the officers that they could not possibly do without him. At
the very time, too, when he was promising to make Cromwell
and Ireton noblemen, if they would help him up to his old
height, he was writing to the Queen that he meant to hang
them. They both afterwards declared that they had been
privately informed that such a letter would be found, on a
certain evening, sewed up in a saddle which would be taken
to the Blue Boar in Holborn to be sent to Dover; and that
they went there, disguised as common soldiers, and sat drinking in the inn-yard until a man came with the saddle, which

they ripped up with their knives, and therein found the letter. I see little reason to doubt the story. It is certain that Oliver Cromwell told one of the King's most faithful followers that the King could not be trusted, and that he would not be answerable if anything amiss were to happen to him. Still, even after that, he kept a promise he had made to the King, by letting him know that there was a plot with a certain portion of the army to seize him. I believe that, in fact, he sincerely wanted the King to escape abroad, and so to be got rid of without more trouble or danger. That Oliver himself had work enough with the army is pretty plain; for some of the troops were so mutinous against him, and against those who acted with him at this time, that he found it necessary to have one man shot at the head of his regiment to overawe the rest.

The King, when he received Oliver's warning, made his escape from Hampton Court; after some indecision and un-certainty, he went to Carisbrooke Castle in the Isle of Wight. At first, he was pretty free there; but, even there, he carried on a pretended treaty with the Parliament, while he was really treating with commissioners from Scotland to send an army into England to take his part. When he broke off this treaty with the Parliament (having settled with Scotland) and was treated as a prisoner, his treatment was not changed too soon, for he had plotted to escape that very night to a ship sent by the Queen, which was lying off the island.

He was doomed to be disappointed in his hopes from Scot-land. The agreement he had made with the Scottish Com-missioners was not favourable enough to the religion of that country to please the Scottish clergy; and they preached against it. The consequence was, that the army raised in Scotland and sent over, was too small to do much; and that, although it was helped by a rising of the Royalists in Eng-land and by good soldiers from Ireland, it could make no head against the Parliamentary army under such men as Cromwell and Fairfax. The King's eldest son, the Prince of Wales, came over from Holland with nineteen ships (a part of the English fleet having gone over to him) to help his father; but nothing came of his voyage, and he was fain to return. The most remarkable event of this second civil war was the cruel execution by the Parliamentary General, of Sir Charles Lucas and Sir George Lisle, two grand

Royalist generals, who had bravely defended Colchester under every disadvantage of famine and distress for nearly three months. When Sir Charles Lucas was shot, Sir George Lisle kissed his body, and said to the soldiers who were to shoot him, "Come nearer, and make sure of me." "I warrant you, Sir George," said one of the soldiers, "we shall hit you." "Ay?" he returned with a smile, "but I have been nearer to you, my friends, many a time, and you have missed me."

The Parliament, after being fearfully bullied by the army —who demanded to have seven members whom they disliked given up to them—had voted that they would have nothing more to do with the King. On the conclusion, however, of this second civil war (which did not last more than six months), they appointed commissioners to treat with him. The King, then so far released again as to be allowed to live in a private house at Newport in the Isle of Wight, managed his own part of the negotiation with a sense that was admired by all who saw him, and gave up, in the end, all that was asked of him—even yielding (which he had steadily refused, so far) to the temporary abolition of the bishops, and the transfer of their church land to the Crown. Still, with his old fatal vice upon him, when his best friends joined the commissioners in beseeching him to yield all those points as the only means of saving himself from the army, he was plotting to escape from the island; he was holding corre- spondence with his friends and the Catholics in Ireland, though declaring that he was not; and he was writing, with his own hand, that in what he yielded he meant nothing but to get time to escape.

Matters were at this pass when the army, resolved to defy the Parliament, marched up to London. The Parliament, not afraid of them now, and boldly led by Hollis, voted that the King's concessions were sufficient ground for settling the peace of the kingdom. Upon that, COLONEL RICH and COLONEL PRIDE went down to the House of Commons with a regiment of horse soldiers and a regiment of foot; and Colonel Pride, standing in the lobby with a list of the members who were obnoxious to the army in his hand, had them pointed out to him as they came through, and took them all into custody. This proceeding was after- wards called by the people, for a joke, PRIDE'S PURGE. Cromwell was in the North, at the head of his men, at the time, but when he came home, approved of what had been done.

What with imprisoning some members and causing others to stay away, the army had now reduced the House of Commons to some fifty or so. These soon voted that it was treason in a king to make war against his parliament and his people, and sent an ordinance up to the House of Lords for the King's being tried as a traitor. The House of Lords, then sixteen in number, to a man rejected it. Thereupon, the Commons made an ordinance of their own, that they were the supreme government of the country, and would bring the King to trial.

The King had been taken for security to a place called Hurst Castle : a lonely house on a rock in the sea, connected with the coast of Hampshire by a rough road two miles long at low water. Thence, he was ordered to be removed to Windsor ; thence, after being but rudely used there, and having none but soldiers to wait upon him at table, he was brought up to St. James's Palace in London, and told that his trial was appointed for next day.

On Saturday, the twentieth of January, one thousand six hundred and forty-nine, this memorable trial began. The House of Commons had settled that one hundred and thirty-five persons should form the Court, and these were taken from the House itself, from among the officers of the army, and from among the lawyers and citizens. JOHN BRADSHAW, serjeant-at-law, was appointed president. The place was Westminster Hall. At the upper end, in a red velvet chair, sat the president, with his hat (lined with plates of iron for his protection) on his head. The rest of the Court sat on side benches, also wearing their hats. The King's seat was covered with velvet, like that of the president, and was opposite to it. He was brought from St. James's to Whitehall, and from Whitehall he came by water to his trial.

When he came in, he looked round very steadily on the Court, and on the great number of spectators, and then sat down : presently he got up and looked round again. On the indictment " against Charles Stuart, for high treason," being read, he smiled several times, and he denied the authority of the Court, saying that there could be no parliament without a House of Lords, and that he saw no House of Lords there. Also, that the King ought to be there, and that he saw no King in the King's right place. Bradshaw replied, that the

Charles I taking leave of his Children

Court was satisfied with its authority, and that its authority was God's authority and the kingdom's. He then adjourned the Court to the following Monday. On that day, the trial was resumed, and went on all the week. When the Saturday came, as the King passed forward to his place in the Hall, some soldiers and others cried for "justice!" and execution on him. That day, too, Bradshaw, like an angry Sultan, wore a red robe, instead of the black robe he had worn before. The King was sentenced to death that day. As he went out, one solitary soldier said, "God bless you, Sir!" For this, his officer struck him. The King said he thought the punishment exceeded the offence. The silver head of his walking stick had fallen off while he leaned upon it, at one time of the trial. The accident seemed to disturb him, as if he thought it ominous of the falling of his own head; and he admitted as much, now it was all over.

Being taken back to Whitehall, he sent to the House of Commons, saying that as the time of his execution might be nigh, he wished he might be allowed to see his darling children. It was granted. On the Monday he was taken back to St. James's; and his two children then in England, the PRINCESS ELIZABETH thirteen years old, and the DUKE OF GLOUCESTER nine years old, were brought to take leave of him, from Sion House, near Brentford. It was a sad and touching scene, when he kissed and fondled those poor children, and made a little present of two diamond seals to the Princess, and gave them tender messages to their mother (who little deserved them, for she had a lover of her own whom she married soon afterwards), and told them that he died "for the laws and liberties of the land." I am bound to say that I don't think he did, but I dare say he believed so.

There were ambassadors from Holland that day, to intercede for the unhappy King, whom you and I both wish the Parliament had spared; but they got no answer. The Scottish Commissioners interceded too; so did the Prince of Wales, by a letter in which he offered as the next heir to the throne, to accept any conditions from the Parliament; so did the Queen, by letter likewise. Notwithstanding all, the warrant for the execution was this day signed. There is a story that as Oliver Cromwell went to the table with the pen in his hand to put his signature to it, he drew his pen across the face of one of the commissioners, who was standing near, and marked it with ink. That commissioner had not

signed his own name yet, and the story adds that when
he came to do it he marked Cromwell's face with ink in the
same way.

The King slept well, untroubled by the knowledge that it
was his last night on earth, and rose on the thirtieth of
January, two hours before day, and dressed himself carefully.
He put on two shirts lest he should tremble with the cold,
and had his hair very carefully combed.   The warrant had
been directed to three officers of the army, COLONEL HACKER,
COLONEL HUNKS, and COLONEL PHAYER.   At ten o'clock, the
first of these came to the door and said it was time to go
to Whitehall.   The King, who had always been a quick
walker, walked at his usual speed through the Park, and
called out to the guard, with his accustomed voice of
command, "March on apace !"   When he came to Whitehall,
he was taken to his own bedroom, where a breakfast was set
forth.   As he had taken the Sacrament, he would eat nothing
more ; but, at about the time when the church bells struck
twelve at noon (for he had to wait, through the scaffold not
being ready), he took the advice of the good BISHOP JUXON
who was with him, and ate a little bread and drank a glass
of claret.   Soon after he had taken this refreshment, Colonel
Hacker came to the chamber with the warrant in his hand,
and called for Charles Stuart.

And then, through the long gallery of Whitehall Palace,
which he had often seen light and gay and merry and crowded,
in very different times, the fallen King passed along, until he
came to the centre window of the Banqueting House, through
which he emerged upon the scaffold, which was hung with
black. He looked at the two executioners, who were dressed
in black and masked ; he looked at the troops of soldiers on
horseback and on foot, and all looked up at him in silence ;
he looked at the vast array of spectators, filling up the view
beyond, and turning all their faces upon him ; he looked at
his old Palace of St. James's ; and he looked at the block.
He seemed a little troubled to find that it was so low, and
asked, "if there were no place higher?"   Then, to those
upon the scaffold, he said " that it was the Parliament who
had begun the war, and not he ; but he hoped they might
be guiltless too, as ill instruments had gone between them.
In one respect," he said, " he suffered justly ; and that was
because he had permitted an unjust sentence to be executed
on another."   In this he referred to the Earl of Strafford.

He was not at all afraid to die; but he was anxious to die easily. When some one touched the axe while he was speaking, he broke off and called out, "Take heed of the axe! take heed of the axe!" He also said to Colonel Hacker, "Take care that they do not put me to pain." He told the executioner, "I shall say but very short prayers, and then thrust out my hands"—as the sign to strike.

He put his hair up, under a white satin cap which the bishop had carried, and said, "I have a good cause and a gracious God on my side." The bishop told him that he had but one stage more to travel in this weary world, and that, though it was a turbulent and troublesome stage, it was a short one, and would carry him a great way—all the way from earth to Heaven. The King's last word, as he gave his cloak and the George—the decoration from his breast—to the bishop, was, "Remember!" He then kneeled down, laid his head on the block, spread out his hands, and was instantly killed. One universal groan broke from the crowd; and the soldiers, who had sat on their horses and stood in their ranks immovable as statues, were of a sudden all in motion, clearing the streets.

Thus, in the forty-ninth year of his age, falling at the same time of his career as Strafford had fallen in his, perished Charles the First. With all my sorrow for him, I cannot agree with him that he died "the martyr of the people;" for the people had been martyrs to him, and to his ideas of a King's rights, long before. Indeed, I am afraid that he was but a bad judge of martyrs; for he had called that infamous Duke of Buckingham "the Martyr of his Sovereign."

CHAPTER XXXIV

ENGLAND UNDER OLIVER CROMWELL

BEFORE sunset on the memorable day on which King Charles the First was executed, the House of Commons passed an act declaring it treason in any one to proclaim the Prince of Wales—or anybody else—King of England. Soon afterwards, it declared that the House of Lords was useless and dangerous, and ought to be abolished; and directed that the late King's statue should be taken down from the Royal Exchange in the City and other public places. Having laid hold of some famous Royalists who had escaped from prison, and having beheaded the DUKE OF HAMILTON, LORD HOLLAND, and LORD CAPEL, in Palace Yard (all of whom died very courageously), they then appointed a Council of State to govern the country. It consisted of forty-one members, of whom five were peers. Bradshaw was made president. The House of Commons also re-admitted members who had opposed the King's death, and made up its numbers to about a hundred and fifty.

But, it still had an army of more than forty thousand men to deal with, and a very hard task it was to manage them. Before the King's execution, the army had appointed some of its officers to remonstrate between them and the Parliament; and now the common soldiers began to take that office upon themselves. The regiments under orders for Ireland mutinied; one troop of horse in the city of London seized their own flag, and refused to obey orders. For this, the ringleader was shot: which did not mend the matter, for, both his comrades and the people made a public funeral for him, and accompanied the body to the grave with sound of trumpets and with a gloomy procession of persons carrying bundles of rosemary steeped in blood. Oliver was the only man to deal with such difficulties as these, and he soon cut them short by bursting at midnight into the town of Burford, near Salisbury, where the mutineers were sheltered, taking

four hundred of them prisoners, and shooting a number of
them by sentence of court-martial. The soldiers soon found,
as all men did, that Oliver was not a man to be trifled with.
And there was an end of the mutiny.

The Scottish Parliament did not know Oliver yet; so, on
hearing of the King's execution, it proclaimed the Prince of
Wales King Charles the Second, on condition of his respecting
the Solemn League and Covenant. Charles was abroad at that
time, and so was Montrose, from whose help he had hopes
enough to keep him holding on and off with commissioners
from Scotland, just as his father might have done. These
hopes were soon at an end; for, Montrose, having raised
a few hundred exiles in Germany, and landed with them in
Scotland, found that the people there, instead of joining him,
deserted the country at his approach. He was soon taken
prisoner and carried to Edinburgh. There he was received
with every possible insult, and carried to prison in a cart,
his officers going two and two before him. He was sentenced
by the Parliament to be hanged on a gallows thirty feet
high, to have his head set on a spike in Edinburgh, and his
limbs distributed in other places, according to the old
barbarous manner. He said he had always acted under the
Royal orders, and only wished he had limbs enough to be
distributed through Christendom, that it might be the more
widely known how loyal he had been. He went to the
scaffold in a bright and brilliant dress, and made a bold end
at thirty-eight years of age. The breath was scarcely out of
his body when Charles abandoned his memory, and denied
that he had ever given him orders to rise in his behalf.
O the family failing was strong in that Charles then!

Oliver had been appointed by the Parliament to command
the army in Ireland, where he took a terrible vengeance for
the sanguinary rebellion, and made tremendous havoc,
particularly in the siege of Drogheda, where no quarter was
given, and where he found at least a thousand of the inhabitants shut up together in the great church: every one of
whom was killed by his soldiers, usually known as OLIVER'S
IRONSIDES. There were numbers of friars and priests among
them, and Oliver gruffly wrote home in his despatch that
these were "knocked on the head" like the rest.

But, Charles having got over to Scotland where the men
of the Solemn League and Covenant led him a prodigiously
dull life and made him very weary with long sermons and

grim Sundays, the Parliament called the redoubtable Oliver home to knock the Scottish men on the head for setting up that Prince.   Oliver left his son-in-law, Ireton, as general in Ireland in his stead (he died there afterwards), and he imitated the example of his father-in-law with such good will that he brought the country to subjection, and laid it at the feet of the Parliament.   In the end, they passed an act for the settlement of Ireland, generally pardoning all the common people, but exempting from this grace such of the wealthier sort as had been concerned in the rebellion, or in any killing of Protestants, or who refused to lay down their arms.   Great numbers of Irish were got out of the country to serve under Catholic powers abroad, and a quantity of land was declared to have been forfeited by past offences, and was given to people who had lent money to the Parliament early in the war.   These were sweeping measures ; but, if Oliver Cromwell had had his own way fully, and had stayed in Ireland, he would have done more yet.

However, as I have said, the Parliament wanted Oliver for Scotland ; so, home Oliver came, and was made Commander of all the Forces of the Commonwealth of England, and in three days away he went with sixteen thousand soldiers to fight the Scottish men.   Now, the Scottish men, being then —as you will generally find them now—mighty cautious, reflected that the troops they had, were not used to war like the Ironsides, and would be beaten in an open fight.   Therefore they said, " If we live quiet in our trenches in Edinburgh here, and if all the farmers come into the town and desert the country, the Ironsides will be driven out by iron hunger and be forced to go away."   This was, no doubt, the wisest plan ; but as the Scottish clergy *would* interfere with what they knew nothing about, and would perpetually preach long sermons exhorting the soldiers to come out and fight, the soldiers got it in their heads that they absolutely must come out and fight.   Accordingly, in an evil hour for themselves, they came out of their safe position.   Oliver fell upon them instantly, and killed three thousand, and took ten thousand prisoners.

To gratify the Scottish Parliament, and preserve their favour, Charles had signed a declaration they laid before him, reproaching the memory of his father and mother, and representing himself as a most religious Prince, to whom the Solemn League and Covenant was as dear as life.   He meant no sort of truth in this, and soon afterwards galloped away on horseback to join some tiresome Highland friends, who were always flourishing dirks and broadswords. He was over-taken and induced to return ; but this attempt, which was called " The Start," did him just so much service, that they did not preach quite such long sermons at him afterwards as they had done before.

On the first of January, one thousand six hundred and fifty-one, the Scottish people crowned him at Scone. He immediately took the chief command of an army of twenty thousand men, and marched to Stirling. His hopes were heightened, I dare say, by the redoubtable Oliver being ill of an ague ; but Oliver scrambled out of bed in no time, and went to work with such energy that he got behind the Royalist army and cut it off from all communication with Scotland. There was nothing for it then, but to go on to England ; so it went on as far as Worcester, where the mayor and some of the gentry proclaimed King Charles the Second straightway. His proclamation, however, was of little use to him, for very few Royalists appeared ; and, on the very same day, two people were publicly beheaded on Tower Hill for espousing his cause. Up came Oliver to Worcester too, at double quick speed, and he and his Ironsides so laid about them in the great battle which was fought there, that they completely beat the Scottish men, and destroyed the Royalist army ; though the Scottish men fought so gallantly that it took five hours to do.

The escape of Charles after this battle of Worcester did him good service long afterwards, for it induced many of the generous English people to take a romantic interest in him, and to think much better of him than he ever deserved. He fled in the night, with not more than sixty followers, to the house of a Catholic lady in Staffordshire. There, for his greater safety, the whole sixty left him. He cropped his hair, stained his face and hands brown as if they were sunburnt, put on the clothes of a labouring countryman, and went out in the morning with his axe in his hand, accompanied by four wood-cutters who were brothers, and another man who was their brother-in-law. These good fellows made a bed for him under a tree, as the weather was very bad ; and the wife of one of them brought him food to eat ; and the old mother of the four brothers came and fell down on her knees before him in the wood, and thanked God that her

S

sons were engaged in saving his life. At night, he came out of the forest and went on to another house which was near the river Severn, with the intention of passing into Wales ; but the place swarmed with soldiers, and the bridges were guarded, and all the boats were made fast. So, after lying in a hayloft covered over with hay, for some time, he came out of his place, attended by COLONEL CARELESS, a Catholic gentleman who had met him there, and with whom he lay hid, all next day, up in the shady branches of a fine old oak. It was lucky for the King that it was September-time, and that the leaves had not begun to fall, since he and the Colonel, perched up in this tree, could catch glimpses of the soldiers riding about below, and could hear the crash in the wood as they went about beating the boughs.

After this, he walked and walked until his feet were all blistered ; and, having been concealed all one day in a house which was searched by the troopers while he was there, went with LORD WILMOT, another of his good friends, to a place called Bentley, where one MISS LANE, a Protestant lady, had obtained a pass to be allowed to ride through the guards to see a relation of hers near Bristol. Disguised as a servant, he rode in the saddle before this young lady to the house of SIR JOHN WINTER, while Lord Wilmot rode there boldly, like a plain country gentleman, with dogs at his heels. It happened that Sir John Winter's butler had been servant in Richmond Palace, and knew Charles the moment he set eyes upon him ; but, the butler was faithful and kept the secret. As no ship could be found to carry him abroad, it was planned that he should go—still travelling with Miss Lane as her servant—to another house, at Trent near Sherborne in Dorsetshire ; and then Miss Lane and her cousin, MR. LASCELLES, who had gone on horseback beside her all the way, went home. I hope Miss Lane was going to marry that cousin, for I am sure she must have been a brave kind girl. If I had been that cousin, I should certainly have loved Miss Lane.

When Charles, lonely for the loss of Miss Lane, was safe at Trent, a ship was hired at Lyme, the master of which engaged to take two gentlemen to France. In the evening of the same day, the King—now riding as servant before another young lady—set off for a public-house at a place called Charmouth, where the captain of the vessel was to take him on board. But, the captain's wife, being afraid of her husband getting into trouble, locked him up and would not let him sail. Then they went away to Bridport; and, coming to the inn there, found the stable-yard full of soldiers who were on the look-out for Charles, and who talked about him while they drank. He had such presence of mind, that he led the horses of his party through the yard as any other servant might have done, and said, "Come out of the way, you soldiers ; let us have room to pass here !" As he went along, he met a half-tipsy ostler, who rubbed his eyes and said to him, "Why, I was formerly servant to Mr. Potter at Exeter, and surely I have sometimes seen you there, young man?" He certainly had, for Charles had lodged there. His ready answer was, "Ah, I did live with him once ; but I have no time to talk now. We'll have a pot of beer together when I come back."

From this dangerous place he returned to Trent, and lay there concealed several days. Then he escaped to Heale, near Salisbury ; where, in the house of a widow lady, he was hidden five days, until the master of a collier lying off Shoreham in Sussex, undertook to convey a "gentleman" to France. On the night of the fifteenth of October, accom- panied by two colonels and a merchant, the King rode to Brighton, then a little fishing village, to give the captain of the ship a supper before going on board ; but, so many people knew him, that this captain knew him too, and not only he, but the landlord and landlady also. Before he went away, the landlord came behind his chair, kissed his hand, and said he hoped to live to be a lord and to see his wife a lady ; at which Charles laughed. They had had a good supper by this time, and plenty of smoking and drinking, at which the King was a first-rate hand ; so, the captain assured him that he would stand by him, and he did. It was agreed that the captain should pretend to sail to Deal, and that Charles should address the sailors and say he was a gentleman in debt who was running away from his creditors, and that he hoped they would join him in per- suading the captain to put him ashore in France. As the King acted his part very well indeed, and gave the sailors twenty shillings to drink, they begged the captain to do what such a worthy gentleman asked. He pretended to yield to their entreaties, and the King got safe to Nor- mandy.

Ireland being now subdued, and Scotland kept quiet by

plenty of forts and soldiers put there by Oliver, the Parliament would have gone on quietly enough, as far as fighting with any foreign enemy went, but for getting into trouble with the Dutch, who in the spring of the year one thousand six hundred and fifty-one sent a fleet into the Downs under their ADMIRAL VAN TROMP, to call upon the bold English ADMIRAL BLAKE (who was there with half as many ships as the Dutch) to strike his flag.   Blake fired a raging broadside instead, and beat off Van Tromp ; who, in the autumn, came back again with seventy ships, and challenged the bold Blake —who still was only half as strong—to fight him.   Blake fought him all day ; but, finding that the Dutch were too many for him, got quietly off at night.   What does Van Tromp upon this, but goes cruising and boasting about the Channel, between the North Foreland and the Isle of Wight, with a great Dutch broom tied to his masthead, as a sign that he could and would sweep the English off the sea ! Within three months, Blake lowered his tone though, and his broom too ; for, he and two other bold commanders, DEAN and MONK, fought him three whole days, took twenty-three of his ships, shivered his broom to pieces, and settled his business.

Things were no sooner quiet again, than the army began to complain to the Parliament that they were not governing the nation properly, and to hint that they thought they could do it better themselves.   Oliver, who had now made up his mind to be the head of the state, or nothing at all, supported them in this, and called a meeting of officers and his own Parliamentary friends, at his lodgings in Whitehall, to consider the best way of getting rid of the Parliament. It had now lasted just as many years as the King's unbridled power had lasted, before it came into existence.   The end of the deliberation was, that Oliver went down to the House in his usual plain black dress, with his usual grey worsted stockings, but with an unusual party of soldiers behind him. These last he left in the lobby, and then went in and sat down.   Presently he got up, made the Parliament a speech, told them that the Lord had done with them, stamped his foot and said, "You are no Parliament.   Bring them in ! Bring them in !"   At this signal the door flew open, and the soldiers appeared.   "This is not honest," said Sir Harry Vane, one of the members.   "Sir Harry Vane !" cried Cromwell ; "O, Sir Harry Vane ! The Lord deliver me from

Sir Harry Vane!" Then he pointed out members one by one, and said this man was a drunkard, and that man a dissipated fellow, and that man a liar, and so on. Then he caused the Speaker to be walked out of his chair, told the guard to clear the House, called the mace upon the table—which is a sign that the House is sitting—"a fool's bauble," and said, "here, carry it away!" Being obeyed in all these orders, he quietly locked the door, put the key in his pocket, walked back to Whitehall again, and told his friends, who were still assembled there, what he had done.

They formed a new Council of State after this extraordinary proceeding, and got a new Parliament together in their own way: which Oliver himself opened in a sort of sermon, and which he said was the beginning of a perfect heaven upon earth. In this Parliament there sat a well-known leather-seller, who had taken the singular name of Praise God Barebones, and from whom it was called, for a joke, Barebones's Parliament, though its general name was the Little Parliament. As it soon appeared that it was not going to put Oliver in the first place, it turned out to be not at all like the beginning of heaven upon earth, and Oliver said it really was not to be borne with. So he cleared off that Parliament in much the same way as he had disposed of the other; and then the council of officers decided that he must be made the supreme authority of the kingdom, under the title of the Lord Protector of the Commonwealth.

So, on the sixteenth of December, one thousand six hundred and fifty-three, a great procession was formed at Oliver's door, and he came out in a black velvet suit and a big pair of boots, and got into his coach and went down to Westminster, attended by the judges, and the lord mayor, and the aldermen, and all the other great and wonderful personages of the country. There, in the Court of Chancery, he publicly accepted the office of Lord Protector. Then he was sworn, and the City sword was handed to him, and the seal was handed to him, and all the other things were handed to him which are usually handed to Kings and Queens on state occasions. When Oliver had handed them all back, he was quite made and completely finished off as Lord Protector; and several of the Ironsides preached about it at great length, all the evening.

SECOND PART.

OLIVER CROMWELL—whom the people long called OLD NOLL—in accepting the office of Protector, had bound himself by a certain paper which was handed to him, called "the Instrument," to summon a Parliament, consisting of between four and five hundred members, in the election of which neither the Royalists nor the Catholics were to have any share. He had also pledged himself that this Parliament should not be dissolved without its own consent until it had sat five months.

When this Parliament met, Oliver made a speech to them of three hours long, very wisely advising them what to do for the credit and happiness of the country. To keep down the more violent members, he required them to sign a recognition of what they were forbidden by "the Instrument" to do ; which was, chiefly, to take the power from one single person at the head of the state or to command the army. Then he dismissed them to go to work. With his usual vigour and resolution he went to work himself with some frantic preachers—who were rather overdoing their sermons in calling him a villain and a tyrant—by shutting up their chapels, and sending a few of them off to prison.

There was not at that time, in England or anywhere else, a man so able to govern the country as Oliver Cromwell. Although he ruled with a strong hand, and levied a very heavy tax on the Royalists (but not until they had plotted against his life), he ruled wisely, and as the times required. He caused England to be so respected abroad, that I wish some lords and gentlemen who have governed it under kings and queens in later days would have taken a leaf out of Oliver Cromwell's book. He sent bold Admiral Blake to the Mediterranean Sea, to make the Duke of Tuscany pay sixty thousand pounds for injuries he had done to British subjects, and spoliation he had committed on English merchants. He further despatched him and his fleet to Algiers, Tunis, and Tripoli, to have every English ship and every English man delivered up to him that had been taken by pirates in those parts. All this was gloriously done ; and it began to be thoroughly well known, all over the world, that England was governed by a man in earnest, who would not allow the English name to be insulted or slighted anywhere.

These were not all his foreign triumphs. He sent a fleet
to sea against the Dutch ; and the two powers, each with
one hundred ships upon its side, met in the English Channel
off the North Foreland, where the fight lasted all day long.
Dean was killed in this fight ; but Monk, who commanded
in the same ship with him, threw his cloak over his body,
that the sailors might not know of his death, and be dis-
heartened. Nor were they. The English broadsides so
exceedingly astonished the Dutch that they sheered off at
last, though the redoubtable Van Tromp fired upon them
with his own guns for deserting their flag. Soon afterwards,
the two fleets engaged again, off the coast of Holland. There,
the valiant Van Tromp was shot through the heart, and the
Dutch gave in, and peace was made.

Further than this, Oliver resolved not to bear the domineering and bigoted conduct of Spain, which country not
only claimed a right to all the gold and silver that could be
found in South America, and treated the ships of all other
countries who visited those regions, as pirates, but put
English subjects into the horrible Spanish prisons of the
Inquisition. So Oliver told the Spanish ambassador that
English ships must be free to go wherever they would, and
that English merchants must not be thrown into those same
dungeons, no, not for the pleasure of all the priests in Spain.
To this the Spanish ambassador replied that the gold and
silver country, and the Holy Inquisition, were his King's
two eyes, neither of which he could submit to have put out.
Very well, said Oliver, then he was afraid he (Oliver) must
damage those two eyes directly.

So, another fleet was despatched under two commanders,
PENN and VENABLES, for Hispaniola ; where, however, the
Spaniards got the better of the fight. Consequently, the
fleet came home again, after taking Jamaica on the way.
Oliver, indignant with the two commanders who had not
done what bold Admiral Blake would have done, clapped
them both into prison, declared war against Spain, and
made a treaty with France, in virtue of which it was to
shelter the King and his brother the Duke of York no
longer. Then, he sent a fleet abroad under bold Admiral
Blake, which brought the King of Portugal to his senses—
just to keep its hand in—and then engaged a Spanish fleet,
sunk four great ships, and took two more, laden with silver
to the value of two millions of pounds : which dazzling

prize was brought from Portsmouth to London in waggons,
with the populace of all the towns and villages through
which the waggons passed, shouting with all their might.
After this victory, bold Admiral Blake sailed away to the
port of Santa Cruz to cut off the Spanish treasure-ships
coming from Mexico. There, he found them, ten in number, with seven others to take care of them, and a big castle,
and seven batteries, all roaring and blazing away at him
with great guns. Blake cared no more for great guns than
for pop-guns—no more for their hot iron balls than for
snow-balls. He dashed into the harbour, captured and
burnt every one of the ships, and came sailing out again
triumphantly, with the victorious English flag flying at his
masthead. This was the last triumph of this great commander, who had sailed and fought until he was quite worn
out. He died, as his successful ship was coming into Plymouth Harbour amidst the joyful acclamations of the people,
and was buried in state in Westminster Abbey. Not to lie
there, long.

Over and above all this, Oliver found that the VAUDOIS,
or Protestant people of the valleys of Lucerne, were inso-
lently treated by the Catholic powers, and were even put to
death for their religion, in an audacious and bloody manner. Instantly, he informed those powers that this was
a thing which Protestant England would not allow ; and he
speedily carried his point, through the might of his great
name, and established their right to worship God in peace
after their own harmless manner.

Lastly, his English army won such admiration in fighting
with the French against the Spaniards, that, after they had
assaulted the town of Dunkirk together, the French King in
person gave it up to the English, that it might be a token
to them of their might and valour.

There were plots enough against Oliver among the frantic
religionists (who called themselves Fifth Monarchy Men),
and among the disappointed Republicans. He had a difficult game to play, for the Royalists were always ready to
side with either party against him. The " King over the
water," too, as Charles was called, had no scruples about
plotting with any one against his life ; although there is
reason to suppose that he would willingly have married one
of his daughters, if Oliver would have had such a son-in-law.
There was a certain COLONEL SAXBY of the army, once a

great supporter of Oliver's but now turned against him, who was a grievous trouble to him through all this part of his career ; and who came and went between the discontented in England and Spain, and Charles who put himself in alliance with Spain on being thrown off by France. This man died in prison at last ; but not until there had been very serious plots between the Royalists and Republicans, and an actual rising of them in England, when they burst into the city of Salisbury, on a Sunday night, seized the judges who were going to hold the assizes there next day, and would have hanged them but for the merciful objections of the more temperate of their number. Oliver was so vigorous and shrewd that he soon put this revolt down, as he did most other conspiracies ; and it was well for one of its chief managers—that same Lord Wilmot who had assisted in Charles's flight, and was now Earl of Rochester—that he made his escape. Oliver seemed to have eyes and ears everywhere, and secured such sources of information as his enemies little dreamed of. There was a chosen body of six persons, called the Sealed Knot, who were in the closest and most secret confidence of Charles. One of the foremost of these very men, a Sir Richard Willis, reported to Oliver everything that passed among them, and had two hundred a year for it.

Miles Syndarcomb, also of the old army, was another conspirator against the Protector. He and a man named Cecil, bribed one of his Life Guards to let them have good notice when he was going out—intending to shoot him from a window. But, owing either to his caution or his good fortune, they could never get an aim at him. Disappointed in this design, they got into the chapel in Whitehall, with a basketful of combustibles, which were to explode by means of a slow match in six hours ; then, in the noise and confusion of the fire, they hoped to kill Oliver. But, the Life Guardsman himself disclosed this plot ; and they were seized, and Miles died (or killed himself in prison) a little while before he was ordered for execution. A few such plotters Oliver caused to be beheaded, a few more to be hanged, and many more, including those who rose in arms against him, to be sent as slaves to the West Indies. If he were rigid, he was impartial too, in asserting the laws of England. When a Portuguese nobleman, the brother of the Portuguese ambassador, killed a London citizen in mistake for another man with whom he had had a quarrel, Oliver caused him to be tried before a jury of Englishmen and foreigners, and had him executed in spite of the entreaties of all the ambassadors in London.

One of Oliver's own friends, the DUKE OF OLDENBURGH, in sending him a present of six fine coach-horses, was very near doing more to please the Royalists than all the plotters put together.   One day, Oliver went with his coach, drawn by these six horses, into Hyde Park, to dine with his secretary and some of his other gentlemen under the trees there. After dinner, being merry, he took it into his head to put his friends inside and to drive them home : a postillion riding one of the foremost horses, as the custom was.   On account of Oliver's being too free with the whip, the six fine horses went off at a gallop, the postillion got thrown, and Oliver fell upon the coach-pole and narrowly escaped being shot by his own pistol, which got entangled with his clothes in the harness, and went off.   He was dragged some distance by the foot, until his foot came out of the shoe, and then he came safely to the ground under the broad body of the coach, and was very little the worse.   The gentlemen inside were only bruised, and the discontented people of all parties were much disappointed.

The rest of the history of the Protectorate of Oliver Cromwell is a history of his Parliaments.   His first one not pleasing him at all, he waited until the five months were out, and then dissolved it.   The next was better suited to his views ; and from that he desired to get—if he could with safety to himself—the title of King.   He had had this in his mind some time : whether because he thought that the English people, being more used to the title, were more likely to obey it ; or whether because he really wished to be a king himself, and to leave the succession to that title in his family, is far from clear.   He was already as high, in England and in all the world, as he would ever be, and I doubt if he cared for the mere name.   However, a paper, called the "Humble Petition and Advice," was presented to him by the House of Commons, praying him to take a high title and to appoint his successor.   That he would have taken the title of King there is no doubt, but for the strong opposition of the army.   This induced him to forbear, and to assent only to the other points of the petition.   Upon which occasion there was another grand show in Westminster

Hall, when the Speaker of the House of Commons formally invested him with a purple robe lined with ermine, and presented him with a splendidly bound Bible, and put a golden sceptre in his hand. The next time the Parliament met, he called a House of Lords of sixty members, as the petition gave him power to do; but as that Parliament did not please him either, and would not proceed to the business of the country, he jumped into a coach one morning, took six Guards with him, and sent them to the right-about. I wish this had been a warning to Parliaments to avoid long speeches, and do more work.

It was the month of August, one thousand six hundred and fifty-eight, when Oliver Cromwell's favourite daughter, ELIZABETH CLAYPOLE (who had lately lost her youngest son), lay very ill, and his mind was greatly troubled, because he loved her dearly. Another of his daughters was married to LORD FALCONBERG, another to the grandson of the Earl of Warwick, and he had made his son RICHARD one of the Members of the Upper House. He was very kind and loving to them all, being a good father and a good husband; but he loved this daughter the best of the family, and went down to Hampton Court to see her, and could hardly be induced to stir from her sick room until she died. Although his religion had been of a gloomy kind, his disposition had been always cheerful. He had been fond of music in his home, and had kept open table once a week for all officers of the army not below the rank of captain, and had always preserved in his house a quiet sensible dignity. He encouraged men of genius and learning, and loved to have them about him. MILTON was one of his great friends. He was good humoured too, with the nobility, whose dresses and manners were very different from his; and to show them what good information he had, he would sometimes jokingly tell them when they were his guests, where they had last drunk the health of the "King over the water," and would recommend them to be more private (if they could) another time. But he had lived in busy times, had borne the weight of heavy State affairs, and had often gone in fear of his life. He was ill of the gout and ague; and when the death of his beloved child came upon him in addition, he sank, never to raise his head again. He told his physicians on the twenty-fourth of August that the Lord had assured him that he was not to die in that illness, and that he would certainly get better. This was only his sick fancy, for on the third of September, which was the anniversary of the great battle of Worcester, and the day of the year which he called his fortunate day, he died, in the sixtieth year of his age. He had been delirious, and had lain insensible some hours, but he had been overheard to murmur a very good prayer the day before. The whole country lamented his death. If you want to know the real worth of Oliver Cromwell, and his real services to his country, you can hardly do better than compare England under him, with England under CHARLES THE SECOND.

He had appointed his son Richard to succeed him, and after there had been, at Somerset House in the Strand, a lying in state more splendid than sensible—as all such vanities after death are, I think—Richard became Lord Protector. He was an amiable country gentleman, but had none of his father's great genius, and was quite unfit for such a post in such a storm of parties. Richard's Protectorate, which only lasted a year and a half, is a history of quarrels between the officers of the army and the Parliament, and between the officers among themselves ; and of a growing discontent among the people, who had far too many long sermons and far too few amusements, and wanted a change. At last, General Monk got the army well into his own hands, and then in pursuance of a secret plan he seems to have entertained from the time of Oliver's death, declared for the King's cause. He did not do this openly ; but, in his place in the House of Commons, as one of the members for Devonshire, strongly advocated the proposals of one SIR JOHN GREENVILLE, who came to the House with a letter from Charles, dated from Breda, and with whom he had previously been in secret communication. There had been plots and counterplots, and a recall of the last members of the Long Parliament, and an end of the Long Parliament, and risings of the Royalists that were made too soon ; and most men being tired out, and there being no one to head the country now great Oliver was dead, it was readily agreed to welcome Charles Stuart. Some of the wiser and better members said—what was most true—that in the letter from Breda, he gave no real promise to govern well, and that it would be best to make him pledge him-self beforehand as to what he should be bound to do for the benefit of the kingdom. Monk said, however, it would be all right when he came, and he could not come too soon.

So, everybody found out all in a moment that the country *must* be prosperous and happy, having another Stuart to condescend to reign over it; and there was a prodigious firing off of guns, lighting of bonfires, ringing of bells, and throwing up of caps. The people drank the King's health by thousands in the open streets, and everybody rejoiced. Down came the Arms of the Commonwealth, up went the Royal Arms instead, and out came the public money. Fifty thousand pounds for the King, ten thousand pounds for his brother the Duke of York, five thousand pounds for his brother the Duke of Gloucester. Prayers for these gracious Stuarts were put up in all the churches; commissioners were sent to Holland (which suddenly found out that Charles was a great man, and that it loved him) to invite the King home; Monk and the Kentish grandees went to Dover, to kneel down before him as he landed. He kissed and embraced Monk, made him ride in the coach with himself and his brothers, came on to London amid wonderful shoutings, and passed through the army at Blackheath on the twenty-ninth of May (his birthday), in the year one thousand six hundred and sixty. Greeted by splendid dinners under tents, by flags and tapestry streaming from all the houses, by delighted crowds in all the streets, by troops of noblemen and gentlemen in rich dresses, by City companies, train-bands, drummers, trumpeters, the great Lord Mayor, and the majestic Aldermen, the King went on to Whitehall. On entering it, he commemorated his Restoration with the joke that it really would seem to have been his own fault that he had not come long ago, since everybody told him that he had always wished for him with all his heart.

CHAPTER XXXV

ENGLAND UNDER CHARLES THE SECOND, CALLED THE MERRY MONARCH

THERE never were such profligate times in England as under Charles the Second. Whenever you see his portrait, with his swarthy ill-looking face and great nose, you may fancy him in his Court at Whitehall, surrounded by some of the very worst vagabonds in the kingdom (though they were lords and ladies), drinking, gambling, indulging in vicious conversation, and committing every kind of profligate excess. It has been a fashion to call Charles the Second "The Merry Monarch." Let me try to give you a general idea of some of the merry things that were done, in the merry days when this merry gentleman sat upon his merry throne, in merry England.

The first merry proceeding was—of course—to declare that he was one of the greatest, the wisest, and the noblest kings that ever shone, like the blessed sun itself, on this benighted earth. The next merry and pleasant piece of business was, for the Parliament, in the humblest manner, to give him one million two hundred thousand pounds a year, and to settle upon him for life that old disputed tonnage and poundage which had been so bravely fought for. Then, General Monk being made EARL OF ALBEMARLE, and a few other Royalists similarly rewarded, the law went to work to see what was to be done to those persons (they were called Regicides) who had been concerned in making a martyr of the late King. Ten of these were merrily executed ; that is to say, six of the judges, one of the council, Colonel Hacker and another officer who had commanded the Guards, and HUGH PETERS, a preacher who had preached against the martyr with all his heart. These executions were so extremely merry, that every horrible circumstance which Cromwell had abandoned was revived with appalling cruelty. The hearts of the sufferers were torn out of their living bodies; their bowels were burned before their faces; the executioner cut jokes to the next victim, as he rubbed his filthy hands together, that were reeking with the blood of the last; and the heads of the dead were drawn on sledges with the living to the place of suffering. Still, even so merry a monarch could not force one of these dying men to say that he was sorry for what he had done. Nay, the most memorable thing said among them was, that if the thing were to do again they would do it.

Sir Harry Vane, who had furnished the evidence against Strafford, and was one of the most staunch of the Republicans, was also tried, found guilty, and ordered for execution. When he came upon the scaffold on Tower Hill, after conducting his own defence with great power, his notes of what he had meant to say to the people were torn away from him, and the drums and trumpets were ordered to sound lustily and drown his voice; for, the people had been so much impressed by what the Regicides had calmly said with their last breath, that it was the custom now, to have the drums and trumpets always under the scaffold, ready to strike up. Vane said no more than this: "It is a bad cause which cannot bear the words of a dying man :" and bravely died.

These merry scenes were succeeded by another, perhaps even merrier. On the anniversary of the late King's death, the bodies of Oliver Cromwell. Ireton, and Bradshaw, were torn out of their graves in Westminster Abbey, dragged to Tyburn, hanged there on a gallows all day long, and then beheaded. Imagine the head of Oliver Cromwell set upon a pole to be stared at by a brutal crowd, not one of whom would have dared to look the living Oliver in the face for half a moment! Think, after you have read this reign, what England was under Oliver Cromwell who was torn out of his grave, and what it was under this merry monarch who sold it, like a merry Judas, over and over again.

Of course, the remains of Oliver's wife and daughter were not to be spared either, though they had been most excellent women. The base clergy of that time gave up their bodies, which had been buried in the Abbey, and—to the eternal disgrace of England—they were thrown into a pit, together with the mouldering bones of Pym and of the brave and bold old Admiral Blake.

The clergy acted this disgraceful part because they hoped

to get the nonconformists, or dissenters, thoroughly put down
in this reign, and to have but one prayer-book and one
service for all kinds of people, no matter what their private
opinions were. This was pretty well, I think, for a Protestant
Church, which had displaced the Romish Church because
people had a right to their own opinions in religious matters.
However, they carried it with a high hand, and a prayer-
book was agreed upon, in which the extremest opinions of
Archbishop Laud were not forgotten. An Act was passed,
too, preventing any dissenter from holding any office under
any corporation. So, the regular clergy in their triumph
were soon as merry as the King. The army being by this
time disbanded, and the King crowned, everything was to go
on easily for evermore.

I must say a word here about the King's family. He had
not been long upon the throne when his brother the Duke
of Gloucester, and his sister the PRINCESS OF ORANGE, died
within a few months of each other, of small-pox. His
remaining sister, the PRINCESS HENRIETTA, married the DUKE
OF ORLEANS, the brother of LOUIS THE FOURTEENTH, King
of France. His brother JAMES, DUKE OF YORK, was made
High Admiral, and by-and-by became a Catholic. He was
a gloomy sullen bilious sort of man, with a remarkable
partiality for the ugliest women in the country. He married,
under very discreditable circumstances, ANNE HYDE, the
daughter of LORD CLARENDON, then the King's principal
Minister—not at all a delicate minister either, but doing
much of the dirty work of a very dirty palace. It became
important now that the King himself should be married ;
and divers foreign Monarchs, not very particular about the
character of their son-in-law, proposed their daughters to
him. The KING OF PORTUGAL offered his daughter, CATHERINE
OF BRAGANZA, and fifty thousand pounds : in addition to
which, the French King, who was favourable to that match,
offered a loan of another fifty thousand. The King of Spain,
on the other hand, offered any one out of a dozen of Princesses, and other hopes of gain. But the ready money carried
the day, and Catherine came over in state to her merry
marriage.

The whole Court was a great flaunting crowd of debauched
men and shameless women ; and Catherine's merry husband
insulted and outraged her in every possible way, until she
consented to receive those worthless creatures as her very

good friends, and to degrade herself by their companionship. A MRS. PALMER, whom the King made LADY CASTLEMAINE, and afterwards DUCHESS OF CLEVELAND, was one of the most powerful of the bad women about the Court, and had great influence with the King nearly all through his reign. Another merry lady named MOLL DAVIES, a dancer at the theatre, was afterwards her rival. So was NELL GWYN, first an orange girl and then an actress, who really had good in her, and of whom one of the worst things I know is, that actually she does seem to have been fond of the King. The first DUKE OF ST. ALBANS was this orange girl's child. In like manner the son of a merry waiting-lady, whom the King created DUCHESS OF PORTSMOUTH, became the DUKE OF RICH-MOND. Upon the whole it is not so bad a thing to be a commoner.

The Merry Monarch was so exceedingly merry among these merry ladies, and some equally merry (and equally infamous) lords and gentlemen, that he soon got through his hundred thousand pounds, and then, by way of raising a little pocket-money, made a merry bargain. He sold Dunkirk to the French King for five millions of livres. When I think of the dignity to which Oliver Cromwell raised England in the eyes of foreign powers, and when I think of the manner in which he gained for England this very Dunkirk, I am much inclined to consider that if the Merry Monarch had been made to follow his father for this action, he would have received his just deserts.

Though he was like his father in none of that father's greater qualities, he was like him in being worthy of no trust. When he sent that letter to the Parliament, from Breda, he did expressly promise that all sincere religious opinions should be respected. Yet he was no sooner firm in his power than he consented to one of the worst Acts of Parliament ever passed. Under this law, every minister who should not give his solemn assent to the Prayer-Book by a certain day, was declared to be a minister no longer, and to be deprived of his church. The consequence of this was that some two thousand honest men were taken from their congregations, and reduced to dire poverty and distress. It was followed by another outrageous law, called the Conventicle Act, by which any person above the age of sixteen who was present at any religious service not according to the Prayer-Book, was to be imprisoned three months for the first offence, six for the second, and to be transported for the third.   This Act alone filled the prisons, which were then most dreadful dungeons, to overflowing.

The Covenanters in Scotland had already fared no better. A base Parliament, usually known as the Drunken Parliament, in consequence of its principal members being seldom sober, had been got together to make laws against the Covenanters, and to force all men to be of one mind in religious matters.   The MARQUIS OF ARGYLE, relying on the King's honour, had given himself up to him ; but, he was wealthy, and his enemies wanted his wealth.   He was tried for treason, on the evidence of some private letters in which he had expressed opinions—as well he might—more favourable to the government of the late Lord Protector than of the present merry and religious King.   He was executed, as were two men of mark among the Covenanters ; and SHARP, a traitor who had once been the friend of the Presbyterians and betrayed them, was made Archbishop of St. Andrew's, to teach the Scotch how to like bishops.

Things being in this merry state at home, the Merry Monarch undertook a war with the Dutch ; principally because they interfered with an African company, established with the two objects of buying gold-dust and slaves, of which the Duke of York was a leading member.   After some preliminary hostilities, the said Duke sailed to the coast of Holland with a fleet of ninety-eight vessels of war, and four fire-ships.   This engaged with the Dutch fleet, of no fewer than one hundred and thirteen ships.   In the great battle between the two forces, the Dutch lost eighteen ships, four admirals, and seven thousand men.   But, the English on shore were in no mood of exultation when they heard the news.

For, this was the year and the time of the Great Plague in London.   During the winter of one thousand six hundred and sixty-four it had been whispered about, that some few people had died here and there of the disease called the Plague, in some of the unwholesome suburbs around London. News was not published at that time as it is now, and some people believed these rumours, and some disbelieved them, and they were soon forgotten.   But, in the month of May, one thousand six hundred and sixty-five, it began to be said all over the town that the disease had burst out with great violence in St. Giles's, and that the people were dying in great numbers. This soon turned out to be awfully true. The roads out of London were choked up by people endeavouring to escape from the infected city, and large sums were paid for any kind of conveyance. The disease soon spread so fast, that it was necessary to shut up the houses in which sick people were, and to cut them off from communication with the living. Every one of these houses was marked on the outside of the door with a red cross, and the words, Lord, have mercy upon us! The streets were all deserted, grass grew in the public ways, and there was a dreadful silence in the air. When night came on, dismal rumblings used to be heard, and these were the wheels of the death-carts, attended by men with veiled faces and holding cloths to their mouths, who rang doleful bells and cried in a loud and solemn voice, "Bring out your dead!" The corpses put into these carts were buried by torchlight in great pits: no service being performed over them; all men being afraid to stay for a moment on the brink of the ghastly graves. In the general fear, children ran away from their parents, and parents from their children. Some who were taken ill, died alone, and without any help. Some were stabbed or strangled by hired nurses who robbed them of all their money, and stole the very beds on which they lay. Some went mad, dropped from the windows, ran through the streets, and in their pain and frenzy flung themselves into the river.

These were not all the horrors of the time. The wicked and dissolute, in wild desperation, sat in the taverns singing roaring songs, and were stricken as they drank, and went out and died. The fearful and superstitious persuaded themselves that they saw supernatural sights—burning swords in the sky, gigantic arms and darts. Others pretended that at nights vast crowds of ghosts walked round and round the dismal pits. One madman, naked, and carrying a brazier full of burning coals upon his head, stalked through the streets, crying out that he was a Prophet, commissioned to denounce the vengeance of the Lord on wicked London. Another always went to and fro, exclaiming, "Yet forty days, and London shall be destroyed!" A third awoke the echoes in the dismal streets, by night and by day, and made the blood of the sick run cold, by calling out incessantly, in a deep hoarse voice, "O, the great and dreadful God!"

Through the months of July and August and September, the Great Plague raged more and more. Great fires were lighted in the streets, in the hope of stopping the infection ; but there was a plague of rain too, and it beat the fires out. At last, the winds which usually arise at that time of the year which is called the equinox, when day and night are of equal length all over the world, began to blow, and to purify the wretched town. The deaths began to decrease, the red crosses slowly to disappear, the fugitives to return, the shops to open, pale frightened faces to be seen in the streets. The Plague had been in every part of England, but in close and unwholesome London it had killed one hundred thousand people.

All this time, the Merry Monarch was as merry as ever, and as worthless as ever. All this time, the debauched lords and gentlemen and the shameless ladies danced and gamed and drank, and loved and hated one another, accord- ing to their merry ways. So little humanity did the govern- ment learn from the late affliction, that one of the first things the Parliament did when it met at Oxford (being as yet afraid to come to London), was to make a law, called the Five Mile Act, expressly directed against those poor ministers who, in the time of the Plague, had manfully come back to comfort the unhappy people. This infamous law, by for- bidding them to teach in any school, or to come within five miles of any city, town, or village, doomed them to starvation and death.

The fleet had been at sea, and healthy. The King of France was now in alliance with the Dutch, though his navy was chiefly employed in looking on while the English and Dutch fought. The Dutch gained one victory; and the English gained another and a greater; and Prince Rupert, one of the English admirals, was out in the Channel one windy night, looking for the French Admiral, with the intention of giving him something more to do than he had had yet, when the gale increased to a storm, and blew him into Saint Helen's. That night was the third of September, one thousand six hundred and sixty-six, and that wind fanned the Great Fire of London.

It broke out at a baker's shop near London Bridge, on the spot on which the Monument now stands as a remembrance of those raging flames. It spread and spread, and burned and burned, for three days. The nights were lighter than the days ; in the day-time there was an immense cloud of smoke, and in the night-time there was a great tower of fire mounting up into the sky, which lighted the whole country landscape for ten miles round. Showers of hot ashes rose into the air and fell on distant places; flying sparks carried the conflagration to great distances, and kindled it in twenty new spots at a time; church steeples fell down with tremendous crashes; houses crumbled into cinders by the hundred and the thousand. The summer had been intensely hot and dry, the streets were very narrow, and the houses mostly built of wood and plaster. Nothing could stop the tremendous fire, but the want of more houses to burn; nor did it stop until the whole way from the Tower to Temple Bar was a desert, composed of the ashes of thirteen thousand houses and eighty-nine churches.

This was a terrible visitation at the time, and occasioned great loss and suffering to the two hundred thousand burnt-out people, who were obliged to lie in the fields under the open night sky, or in hastily-made huts of mud and straw, while the lanes and roads were rendered impassable by carts which had broken down as they tried to save their goods. But the Fire was a great blessing to the City afterwards, for it arose from its ruins very much improved—built more regularly, more widely, more cleanly and carefully, and therefore much more healthily. It might be far more healthy than it is, but there are some people in it still—even now, at this time, nearly two hundred years later—so selfish, so pig-headed, and so ignorant, that I doubt if even another Great Fire would warm them up to do their duty.

The Catholics were accused of having wilfully set London in flames; one poor Frenchman, who had been mad for years, even accused himself of having with his own hand fired the first house. There is no reasonable doubt, however, that the fire was accidental. An inscription on the Monument long attributed it to the Catholics; but it is removed now, and was always a malicious and stupid untruth.

Second Part.

That the Merry Monarch might be very merry indeed, in the merry times when his people were suffering under pestilence and fire, he drank and gambled and flung away among his favourites the money which the Parliament had voted for the war. The consequence of this was that the stout-hearted English sailors were merrily starving of want,

T

and dying in the streets; while the Dutch, under their admirals DE WITT and DE RUYTER, came into the River Thames, and up the River Medway as far as Upnor, burned the guard-ships, silenced the weak batteries, and did what they would to the English coast for six whole weeks. Most of the English ships that could have prevented them had neither powder nor shot on board; in this merry reign, public officers made themselves as merry as the King did with the public money; and when it was entrusted to them to spend in national defences or preparations, they put it into their own pockets with the merriest grace in the world.

Lord Clarendon had, by this time, run as long a course as is usually allotted to the unscrupulous ministers of bad kings. He was impeached by his political opponents, but unsuccessfully. The King then commanded him to withdraw from England and retire to France, which he did, after defending himself in writing. He was no great loss at home, and died abroad some seven years afterwards.

There then came into power a ministry called the Cabal Ministry, because it was composed of LORD CLIFFORD, the EARL OF ARLINGTON, the DUKE OF BUCKINGHAM (a great rascal, and the King's most powerful favourite), LORD ASHLEY, and the DUKE OF LAUDERDALE, C. A. B. A. L. As the French were making conquests in Flanders, the first Cabal proceeding was to make a treaty with the Dutch, for uniting with Spain to oppose the French. It was no sooner made than the Merry Monarch, who always wanted to get money without being accountable to a Parliament for his expenditure, apologised to the King of France for having had anything to do with it, and concluded a secret treaty with him, making himself his infamous pensioner to the amount of two millions of livres down, and three millions more a year; and engaging to desert that very Spain, to make war against those very Dutch, and to declare himself a Catholic when a convenient time should arrive. This religious king had lately been crying to his Catholic brother on the subject of his strong desire to be a Catholic; and now he merrily concluded this treasonable conspiracy against the country he governed, by undertaking to become one as soon as he safely could. For all of which, though he had had ten merry heads instead of one, he richly deserved to lose them by the headsman's axe.

As his one merry head might have been far from safe, if these things had been known, they were kept very quiet, and

war was declared by France and England against the Dutch.
But, a very uncommon man, afterwards most important to
English history and to the religion and liberty of this land,
arose among them, and for many long years defeated the
whole projects of France. This was WILLIAM OF NASSAU,
PRINCE OF ORANGE, son of the last Prince of Orange of the
same name, who married the daughter of Charles the First
of England. He was a young man at this time, only just of
age; but he was brave, cool, intrepid, and wise. His father
had been so detested that, upon his death, the Dutch had
abolished the authority to which this son would have otherwise succeeded (Stadtholder it was called), and placed the
chief power in the hands of JOHN DE WITT, who educated
this young prince. Now, the Prince became very popular,
and John de Witt's brother CORNELIUS was sentenced to
banishment on a false accusation of conspiring to kill him.
John went to the prison where he was, to take him away to
exile, in his coach; and a great mob who collected on the
occasion, then and there cruelly murdered both the brothers.
This left the government in the hands of the Prince, who
was really the choice of the nation; and from this time he
exercised it with the greatest vigour, against the whole power
of France, under its famous generals CONDÉ and TURENNE,
and in support of the Protestant religion. It was full seven
years before this war ended in a treaty of peace made at
Nimeguen, and its details would occupy a very considerable
space. It is enough to say that William of Orange established a famous character with the whole world; and that
the Merry Monarch, adding to and improving on his former
baseness, bound himself to do everything the King of France
liked, and nothing the King of France did not like, for
a pension of one hundred thousand pounds a year, which
was afterwards doubled. Besides this, the King of France,
by means of his corrupt ambassador—who wrote accounts of
his proceedings in England, which are not always to be
believed, I think—bought our English members of Parliament, as he wanted them. So, in point of fact, during
a considerable portion of this merry reign, the King of
France was the real King of this country.

But there was a better time to come, and it was to come
(though his royal uncle little thought so) through that very
William, Prince of Orange. He came over to England, saw
Mary, the elder daughter of the Duke of York, and married

her. We shall see by-and-by what came of that marriage, and why it is never to be forgotten.

This daughter was a Protestant, but her mother died a Catholic. She and her sister ANNE, also a Protestant, were the only survivors of eight children. Anne afterwards married GEORGE, PRINCE OF DENMARK, brother to the King of that country.

Lest you should do the Merry Monarch the injustice of supposing that he was even good humoured (except when he had everything his own way), or that he was high spirited and honourable, I will mention here what was done to a member of the House of Commons, SIR JOHN COVENTRY. He made a remark in a debate about taxing the theatres, which gave the King offence. The King agreed with his illegitimate son, who had been born abroad, and whom he had made DUKE OF MONMOUTH, to take the following merry vengeance. To waylay him at night, fifteen armed men to one, and to slit his nose with a penknife. Like master, like man. The King's favourite, the Duke of Buckingham, was strongly suspected of setting on an assassin to murder the DUKE OF ORMOND as he was returning home from a dinner; and that Duke's spirited son, LORD OSSORY, was so persuaded of his guilt, that he said to him at Court, even as he stood beside the King, "My lord, I know very well that you are at the bottom of this late attempt upon my father. But I give you warning, if he ever come to a violent end, his blood shall be upon you, and wherever I meet you I will pistol you! I will do so, though I find you standing behind the King's chair; and I tell you this in his Majesty's presence, that you may be quite sure of my doing what I threaten." Those were merry times indeed.

There was a fellow named BLOOD, who was seized for making, with two companions, an audacious attempt to steal the crown, the globe, and sceptre, from the place where the jewels were kept in the Tower. This robber, who was a swaggering ruffian, being taken, declared that he was the man who had endeavoured to kill the Duke of Ormond, and that he had meant to kill the King too, but was over-awed by the majesty of his appearance, when he might otherwise have done it, as he was bathing at Battersea. The King being but an ill-looking fellow, I don't believe a word of this. Whether he was flattered, or whether he knew that Buckingham had really set Blood on to murder the Duke, is uncertain. But it is quite certain that he pardoned this thief, gave him an estate of five hundred a year in Ireland (which had had the honour of giving him birth), and presented him at Court to the debauched lords and the shameless ladies, who made a great deal of him—as I have no doubt they would have made of the Devil himself, if the King had introduced him.

Infamously pensioned as he was, the King still wanted money, and consequently was obliged to call Parliaments. In these, the great object of the Protestants was to thwart the Catholic Duke of York, who married a second time; his new wife being a young lady only fifteen years old, the Catholic sister of the DUKE OF MODENA. In this they were seconded by the Protestant Dissenters, though to their own disadvantage : since, to exclude Catholics from power, they were even willing to exclude themselves. The King's object was to pretend to be a Protestant, while he was really a Catholic ; to swear to the bishops that he was devoutly attached to the English Church, while he knew he had bargained it away to the King of France ; and by cheating and deceiving them, and all who were attached to royalty, to become despotic and be powerful enough to confess what a rascal he was. Meantime, the King of France, knowing his merry pensioner well, intrigued with the King's opponents in Parliament, as well as with the King and his friends.

The fears that the country had of the Catholic religion being restored, if the Duke of York should come to the throne, and the low cunning of the King in pretending to share their alarms, led to some very terrible results. A certain DR. TONGE, a dull clergyman in the City, fell into the hands of a certain TITUS OATES, a most infamous character, who pretended to have acquired among the Jesuits abroad a knowledge of a great plot for the murder of the King, and the re-establishment of the Catholic religion. Titus Oates, being produced by this unlucky Dr. Tonge and solemnly examined before the council, contradicted himself in a thousand ways, told the most ridiculous and improbable stories, and implicated COLEMAN, the Secretary of the Duchess of York. Now, although what he charged against Coleman was not true, and although you and I know very well that the real dangerous Catholic plot was that one with the King of France of which the Merry Monarch was himself

the head, there happened to be found among Coleman's
papers, some letters, in which he did praise the days of
Bloody Queen Mary, and abuse the Protestant religion.
This was great good fortune for Titus, as it seemed to confirm him ; but better still was in store. SIR EDMUNDBURY
GODFREY, the magistrate who had first examined him, being
unexpectedly found dead near Primrose Hill, was confi-
dently believed to have been killed by the Catholics. I
think there is no doubt that he had been melancholy mad,
and that he killed himself ; but he had a great Protestant
funeral, and Titus was called the Saver of the Nation, and
received a pension of twelve hundred pounds a year.

As soon as Oates's wickedness had met with this success,
up started another villain, named WILLIAM BEDLOE, who,
attracted by a reward of five hundred pounds offered for the
apprehension of the murderers of Godfrey, came forward and
charged two Jesuits and some other persons with having
committed it at the Queen's desire. Oates, going into
partnership with this new informer, had the audacity to
accuse the poor Queen herself of high treason. Then
appeared a third informer, as bad as either of the two, and
accused a Catholic banker named STAYLEY of having said
that the King was the greatest rogue in the world (which
would not have been far from the truth), and that he would
kill him with his own hand. This banker, being at once
tried and executed, Coleman and two others were tried and
executed. Then a miserable wretch named PRANCE, a
Catholic silversmith, being accused by Bedloe, was tortured
into confessing that he had taken part in Godfrey's murder,
and into accusing three other men of having committed it.
Then, five Jesuits were accused by Oates, Bedloe, and
Prance together, and were all found guilty, and executed
on the same kind of contradictory and absurd evidence.
The Queen's physician and three monks were next put on
their trial ; but Oates and Bedloe had for the time gone far
enough, and these four were acquitted. The public mind,
however, was so full of a Catholic plot, and so strong against
the Duke of York, that James consented to obey a written
order from his brother, and to go with his family to Brussels,
provided that his rights should never be sacrificed in his
absence to the Duke of Monmouth. The House of Commons, not satisfied with this as the King hoped, passed
a bill to exclude the Duke from ever succeeding to the

throne. In return, the King dissolved the Parliament. He had deserted his old favourite, the Duke of Buckingham, who was now in the opposition.

To give any sufficient idea of the miseries of Scotland in this merry reign, would occupy a hundred pages. Because the people would not have bishops, and were resolved to stand by their Solemn League and Covenant, such cruelties were inflicted upon them as make the blood run cold. Ferocious dragoons galloped through the country to punish the peasants for deserting the churches ; sons were hanged up at their fathers' doors for refusing to disclose where their fathers were concealed ; wives were tortured to death for not betraying their husbands ; people were taken out of their fields and gardens, and shot on the public roads without trial ; lighted matches were tied to the fingers of prisoners, and a most horrible torment called the Boot was invented, and constantly applied, which ground and mashed the victims' legs with iron wedges. Witnesses were tortured as well as prisoners. All the prisons were full ; all the gibbets were heavy with bodies ; murder and plunder devastated the whole country. In spite of all, the Covenanters were by no means to be dragged into the churches, and persisted in worshipping God as they thought right. A body of ferocious Highlanders, turned upon them from the mountains of their own country, had no greater effect than the English dragoons under GRAHAME OF CLAVERHOUSE, the most cruel and rapacious of all their enemies, whose name will ever be cursed through the length and breadth of Scotland. Archbishop Sharp had ever aided and abetted all these outrages. But he fell at last ; for, when the injuries of the Scottish people were at their height, he was seen, in his coach-and-six coming across a moor, by a body of men, headed by one JOHN BALFOUR, who were waiting for another of their oppressors. Upon this they cried out that Heaven had delivered him into their hands, and killed him with many wounds. If ever a man deserved such a death, I think Archbishop Sharp did.

It made a great noise directly, and the Merry Monarch— strongly suspected of having goaded the Scottish people on, that he might have an excuse for a greater army than the Parliament were willing to give him—sent down his son, the Duke of Monmouth, as commander-in-chief, with instructions to attack the Scottish rebels, or Whigs as they were

called, whenever he came up with them. Marching with
ten thousand men from Edinburgh, he found them, in
number four or five thousand, drawn up at Bothwell
Bridge, by the Clyde. They were soon dispersed ; and
Monmouth showed a more humane character towards them,
than he had shown towards that Member of Parliament
whose nose he had caused to be slit with a penknife. But
the Duke of Lauderdale was their bitter foe, and sent
Claverhouse to finish them.

As the Duke of York became more and more unpopular,
the Duke of Monmouth became more and more popular. It
would have been decent in the latter not to have voted in
favour of the renewed bill for the exclusion of James from
the throne ; but he did so, much to the King's amusement,
who used to sit in the House of Lords by the fire, hearing
the debates, which he said were as good as a play. The
House of Commons passed the bill by a large majority, and
it was carried up to the House of Lords by LORD RUSSELL,
one of the best of the leaders on the Protestant side. It
was rejected there, chiefly because the bishops helped the
King to get rid of it ; and the fear of Catholic plots revived
again. There had been another got up, by a fellow out of
Newgate, named DANGERFIELD, which is more famous than
it deserves to be, under the name of the MEAL-TUB PLOT.
This jail-bird having been got out of Newgate by a MRS.
CELLIER, a Catholic nurse, had turned Catholic himself, and
pretended that he knew of a plot among the Presbyterians
against the King's life. This was very pleasant to the Duke
of York, who hated the Presbyterians, who returned the
compliment. He gave Dangerfield twenty guineas, and sent
him to the King his brother. But Dangerfield, breaking
down altogether in his charge, and being sent back to
Newgate, almost astonished the Duke out of his five senses
by suddenly swearing that the Catholic nurse had put that
false design into his head, and that what he really knew
about, was, a Catholic plot against the King ; the evidence
of which would be found in some papers, concealed in
a meal-tub in Mrs. Cellier's house. There they were, of
course—for he had put them there himself—and so the tub
gave the name to the plot. But, the nurse was acquitted
on her trial, and it came to nothing.

Lord Ashley, of the Cabal, was now Lord Shaftesbury,
and was strong against the succession of the Duke of York.

The House of Commons, aggravated to the utmost extent, as we may well suppose, by suspicions of the King's conspiracy with the King of France, made a desperate point of the exclusion still, and were bitter against the Catholics generally. So unjustly bitter were they, I grieve to say, that they impeached the venerable Lord Stafford, a Catholic nobleman seventy years old, of a design to kill the King. The witnesses were that atrocious Oates and two other birds of the same feather. He was found guilty, on evidence quite as foolish as it was false, and was beheaded on Tower Hill. The people were opposed to him when he first appeared upon the scaffold; but, when he had addressed them and shown them how innocent he was and how wickedly he was sent there, their better nature was aroused, and they said, "We believe you, my Lord. God bless you, my Lord!"

The House of Commons refused to let the King have any money until he should consent to the Exclusion Bill; but, as he could get it and did get it from his master the King of France, he could afford to hold them very cheap. He called a Parliament at Oxford, to which he went down with a great show of being armed and protected as if he were in danger of his life, and to which the opposition members also went armed and protected, alleging that they were in fear of the Papists, who were numerous among the King's guards. However, they went on with the Exclusion Bill, and were so earnest upon it that they would have carried it again, if the King had not popped his crown and state robes into a sedan-chair, bundled himself into it along with them, hurried down to the chamber where the House of Lords met, and dissolved the Parliament. After which he scampered home. and the members of Parliament scampered home too, as fast as their legs could carry them.

The Duke of York, then residing in Scotland, had, under the law which excluded Catholics from public trusts, no right whatever to public employment. Nevertheless, he was openly employed as the King's representative in Scotland, and there gratified his sullen and cruel nature to his heart's content by directing the dreadful cruelties against the Covenanters. There were two ministers named CARGILL and CAMERON who had escaped from the battle of Bothwell Bridge, and who returned to Scotland, and raised the miserable but still brave and unsubdued Covenanters afresh, under the name of Cameronians. As Cameron publicly posted a declaration that the King was a forsworn tyrant, no mercy was shown to his unhappy followers after he was slain in battle. The Duke of York, who was particularly fond of the Boot and derived great pleasure from having it applied, offered their lives to some of these people, if they would cry on the scaffold " God save the King." But their relations, friends, and countrymen, had been so barbarously tortured and murdered in this merry reign, that they pre- ferred to die, and did die. The Duke then obtained his merry brother's permission to hold a Parliament in Scot- land, which first, with most shameless deceit, confirmed the laws for securing the Protestant religion against Popery, and then declared that nothing must or should prevent the succession of the Popish Duke. After this double-faced beginning, it established an oath which no human being could understand, but which everybody was to take, as a proof that his religion was the lawful religion. The Earl of Argyle, taking it with the explanation that he did not consider it to prevent him from favouring any alteration either in the Church or State which was not inconsistent with the Protestant religion or with his loyalty, was tried for high treason before a Scottish jury of which the MARQUIS OF MONTROSE was foreman, and was found guilty. He escaped the scaffold, for that time, by getting away, in the disguise of a page, in the train of his daughter, LADY SOPHIA LINDSAY. It was absolutely proposed, by certain members of the Scottish Council, that this lady should be whipped through the streets of Edinburgh. But this was too much even for the Duke, who had the manliness then (he had very little at most times) to remark that Englishmen were not accustomed to treat ladies in that manner. In those merry times nothing could equal the brutal servility of the Scottish fawners, but the conduct of similar degraded beings in England.

After the settlement of these little affairs, the Duke returned to England, and soon resumed his place at the Council, and his office of High Admiral—all this by his brother's favour, and in open defiance of the law. It would have been no loss to the country, if he had been drowned when his ship, in going to Scotland to fetch his family, struck on a sand-bank, and was lost with two hundred souls on board. But he escaped in a boat with some friends ; and the sailors were so brave and unselfish, that, when they saw him rowing away, they gave three cheers, while they themselves were going down for ever.

The Merry Monarch, having got rid of his Parliament, went to work to make himself despotic, with all speed. Having had the villainy to order the execution of OLIVER PLUNKET, BISHOP OF ARMAGH, falsely accused of a plot to establish Popery in that country by means of a French army —the very thing this royal traitor was himself trying to do at home—and having tried to ruin Lord Shaftesbury, and failed—he turned his hand to controlling the corporations all over the country; because, if he could only do that, he could get what juries he chose, to bring in perjured verdicts, and could get what members he chose, returned to Parliament. These merry times produced, and made Chief Justice of the Court of King's Bench, a drunken ruffian of the name of JEFFREYS; a red-faced swollen bloated horrible creature, with a bullying roaring voice, and a more savage nature perhaps than was ever lodged in any human breast. This monster was the Merry Monarch's especial favourite, and he testified his admiration of him by giving him a ring from his own finger, which the people used to call Judge Jeffreys's Bloodstone. Him the King employed to go about and bully the corporations, beginning with London ; or, as Jeffreys himself elegantly called it, "to give them a lick with the rough side of his tongue." And he did it so thoroughly, that they soon became the basest and most sycophantic bodies in the kingdom—except the University of Oxford, which, in that respect, was quite pre-eminent and unapproachable.

Lord Shaftesbury (who died soon after the King's failure against him), LORD WILLIAM RUSSELL, the Duke of Monmouth, LORD HOWARD, LORD JERSEY, ALGERNON SIDNEY, JOHN HAMPDEN (grandson of the great Hampden), and some others, used to hold a council together after the dissolution of the Parliament, arranging what it might be necessary to do, if the King carried his Popish plot to the utmost height. Lord Shaftesbury having been much the most violent of this party, brought two violent men into their secrets— RUMSEY, who had been a soldier in the Republican army ; and WEST, a lawyer. These two knew an old officer of Cromwell's, called RUMBOLD, who had married a maltster's widow, and so had come into possession of a solitary dwell-

ing called the Rye House, near Hoddesdon, in Hertfordshire.   Rumbold said to them what a capital place this
house of his would be from which to shoot at the King, who
often passed there going to and fro from Newmarket.   They
liked the idea, and entertained it.   But, one of their body
gave information ; and they, together with SHEPHERD, a wine
merchant, Lord Russell, Algernon Sidney, LORD ESSEX, LORD
HOWARD, and Hampden, were all arrested.

Lord Russell might have easily escaped, but scorned to do
so, being innocent of any wrong ; Lord Essex might have
easily escaped, but scorned to do so, lest his flight should
prejudice Lord Russell.   But it weighed upon his mind that
he had brought into their council, Lord Howard—who now
turned a miserable traitor—against a great dislike Lord
Russell had always had of him.   He could not bear the
reflection, and destroyed himself before Lord Russell was
brought to trial at the Old Bailey.

He knew very well that he had nothing to hope, having
always been manful in the Protestant cause against the two
false brothers, the one on the throne, and the other standing
next to it.   He had a wife, one of the noblest and best of
women, who acted as his secretary on his trial, who comforted him in his prison, who supped with him on the night
before he died, and whose love and virtue and devotion
have made her name imperishable.   Of course, he was found
guilty, and was sentenced to be beheaded in Lincoln's Inn-
fields, not many yards from his own house.   When he had
parted from his children on the evening before his death,
his wife still stayed with him until ten o'clock at night ;
and when their final separation in this world was over, and
he had kissed her many times, he still sat for a long while
in his prison, talking of her goodness.   Hearing the rain
fall fast at that time, he calmly said, "Such a rain to-
morrow will spoil a great show, which is a dull thing on
a rainy day."   At midnight he went to bed, and slept till
four ; even when his servant called him, he fell asleep again
while his clothes were being made ready.   He rode to the
scaffold in his own carriage, attended by two famous clergymen, TILLOTSON and BURNET, and sang a psalm to himself
very softly, as he went along.   He was as quiet and as
steady as if he had been going out for an ordinary ride.
After saying that he was surprised to see so great a crowd,
he laid down his head upon the block, as if upon the pillow

of his bed, and had it struck off at the second blow. His noble wife was busy for him even then ; for that true-hearted lady printed and widely circulated his last words, of which he had given her a copy. They made the blood of all the honest men in England boil.

The University of Oxford distinguished itself on the very same day by pretending to believe that the accusation against Lord Russell was true, and by calling the King, in a written paper, the Breath of their Nostrils and the Anointed of the Lord. This paper the Parliament afterwards caused to be burned by the common hangman ; which I am sorry for, as I wish it had been framed and glazed and hung up in some public place, as a monument of baseness for the scorn of mankind.

Next, came the trial of Algernon Sidney, at which Jeffreys presided, like a great crimson toad, sweltering and swelling with rage. "I pray God, Mr. Sidney," said this Chief Justice of a merry reign, after passing sentence, " to work in you a temper fit to go to the other world, for I see you are not fit for this." " My lord," said the prisoner, com-posedly holding out his arm, "feel my pulse, and see if I be disordered. I thank Heaven I never was in better temper than I am now." Algernon Sidney was executed on Tower Hill, on the seventh of December, one thousand six hundred and eighty-three. He died a hero, and died, in his own words, " For that good old cause in which he had been engaged from his youth, and for which God had so often and so wonderfully declared himself."

The Duke of Monmouth had been making his uncle, the Duke of York, very jealous, by going about the country in a royal sort of way, playing at the people's games, becoming godfather to their children, and even touching for the King's evil, or stroking the faces of the sick to cure them—though, for the matter of that, I should say he did them about as much good as any crowned king could have done. His father had got him to write a letter, confessing his having had a part in the conspiracy, for which Lord Russell had been beheaded ; but he was ever a weak man, and as soon as he had written it, he was ashamed of it and got it back again. For this, he was banished to the Netherlands ; but he soon returned and had an interview with his father, unknown to his uncle. It would seem that he was coming into the Merry Monarch's favour again, and that the Duke of

York was sliding out of it, when Death appeared to the merry galleries at Whitehall, and astonished the debauched lords and gentlemen, and the shameless ladies, very considerably.

On Monday, the second of February, one thousand six hundred and eighty-five, the merry pensioner and servant of the King of France fell down in a fit of apoplexy. By the Wednesday his case was hopeless, and on the Thursday he was told so. As he made a difficulty about taking the sacrament from the Protestant Bishop of Bath, the Duke of York got all who were present away from the bed, and asked his brother, in a whisper, if he should send for a Catholic priest ? The King replied, "For God's sake, brother, do ! " The Duke smuggled in, up the back stairs, disguised in a wig and gown, a priest named HUDDLESTON, who had saved the King's life after the battle of Worcester: telling him that this worthy man in the wig had once saved his body, and was now come to save his soul.

The Merry Monarch lived through that night, and died before noon on the next day, which was Friday, the sixth. Two of the last things he said were of a human sort, and your remembrance will give him the full benefit of them. When the Queen sent to say she was too unwell to attend him and to ask his pardon, he said, "Alas ! poor woman, *she* beg *my* pardon ! I beg hers with all my heart. Take back that answer to her." And he also said, in reference to Nell Gwyn, "Do not let poor Nelly starve."

He died in the fifty-fifth year of his age, and the twenty-fifth of his reign.

CHAPTER XXXVI

ENGLAND UNDER JAMES THE SECOND

KING JAMES THE SECOND was a man so very disagreeable, that even the best of historians has favoured his brother Charles, as becoming, by comparison, quite a pleasant character. The one object of his short reign was to re-establish the Catholic religion in England; and this he doggedly pursued with such a stupid obstinacy, that his career very soon came to a close.

The first thing he did, was, to assure his council that he would make it his endeavour to preserve the Government, both in Church and State, as it was by law established ; and that he would always take care to defend and support the Church. Great public acclamations were raised over this fair speech, and a great deal was said, from the pulpits and elsewhere, about the word of a King which was never broken, by credulous people who little supposed that he had formed a secret council for Catholic affairs, of which a mischievous Jesuit, called FATHER PETRE, was one of the chief members. With tears of joy in his eyes, he received, as the beginning of *his* pension from the King of France, five hundred thousand livres ; yet, with a mixture of meanness and arrogance that belonged to his contemptible character, he was always jealous of making some show of being independent of the King of France, while he pocketed his money. As—notwithstanding his publishing two papers in favour of Popery (and not likely to do it much service, I should think) written by the King, his brother, and found in his strong-box ; and his open display of himself attending mass—the Parliament was very obsequious, and granted him a large sum of money, he began his reign with a belief that he could do what he pleased, and with a determination to do it.

Before we proceed to its principal events, let us dispose of Titus Oates. He was tried for perjury, a fortnight after the coronation, and besides being very heavily fined, was sentenced to stand twice in the pillory, to be whipped from Aldgate to Newgate one day, and from Newgate to Tyburn two days afterwards, and to stand in the pillory five times a year as long as he lived. This fearful sentence was actually inflicted on the rascal. Being unable to stand after his first flogging, he was dragged on a sledge from Newgate to Tyburn, and flogged as he was drawn along. He was so strong a villain that he did not die under the torture, but lived to be afterwards pardoned and rewarded, though not to be ever believed in any more. Dangerfield, the only other one of that crew left alive, was not so fortunate. He was almost killed by a whipping from Newgate to Tyburn, and, as if that were not punishment enough, a ferocious barrister of Gray's Inn gave him a poke in the eye with his cane, which caused his death ; for which the ferocious barrister was deservedly tried and executed.

As soon as James was on the throne, Argyle and Monmouth went from Brussels to Rotterdam, and attended a meeting of Scottish exiles held there, to concert measures for a rising in England. It was agreed that Argyle should effect a landing in Scotland, and Monmouth in England ; and that two Englishmen should be sent with Argyle to be in his confidence, and two Scotchmen with the Duke of Monmouth.

Argyle was the first to act upon this contract. But, two of his men being taken prisoners at the Orkney Islands, the Government became aware of his intention, and was able to act against him with such vigour as to prevent his raising more than two or three thousand Highlanders, although he sent a fiery cross, by trusty messengers, from clan to clan and from glen to glen, as the custom then was when those wild people were to be excited by their chiefs. As he was moving towards Glasgow with his small force, he was betrayed by some of his followers, taken, and carried, with his hands tied behind his back, to his old prison in Edinburgh Castle. James ordered him to be executed, on his old shamefully unjust sentence, within three days ; and he appears to have been anxious that his legs should have been pounded with his old favourite the boot. However, the boot was not applied ; he was simply beheaded, and his head was set upon the top of Edinburgh Jail. One of those Englishmen who had been assigned to him was that old soldier Rumbold, the master of the Rye House. He was sorely wounded, and within a week after Argyle had suffered with great courage, was brought up for trial, lest he should die and disappoint the King. He, too, was executed, after defending himself with great spirit, and saying that he did not believe that God had made the greater part of mankind to carry saddles on their backs and bridles in their mouths, and to be ridden by a few, booted and spurred for the purpose—in which I thoroughly agree with Rumbold.

The Duke of Monmouth, partly through being detained and partly through idling his time away, was five or six weeks behind his friend when he landed at Lyme, in Dorset: having at his right hand an unlucky nobleman called LORD GREY OF WERK, who of himself would have ruined a far more promising expedition. He immediately set up his standard in the market-place, and proclaimed the King a tyrant, and a Popish usurper, and I know not what else; charging him, not only with what he had done, which was bad enough, but with what neither he nor anybody else had done, such as setting fire to London, and poisoning the late King. Raising some four thousand men by these means, he marched on to Taunton, where there were many Protestant dissenters who were strongly opposed to the Catholics. Here, both the rich and poor turned out to receive him, ladies waved a welcome to him from all the windows as he passed along the streets, flowers were strewn in his way, and every compliment and honour that could be devised was showered upon him. Among the rest, twenty young ladies came forward, in their best clothes, and in their brightest beauty, and gave him a Bible ornamented with their own fair hands, together with other presents.

Encouraged by this homage, he proclaimed himself King, and went on to Bridgewater. But, here the Government troops, under the EARL OF FEVERSHAM, were close at hand; and he was so dispirited at finding that he made but few powerful friends after all, that it was a question whether he should disband his army and endeavour to escape. It was resolved, at the instance of that unlucky Lord Grey, to make a night attack on the King's army, as it lay encamped on the edge of a morass called Sedgemoor. The horsemen were commanded by the same unlucky lord, who was not a brave man. He gave up the battle almost at the first obstacle—which was a deep drain; and although the poor countrymen, who had turned out for Monmouth, fought bravely with scythes, poles, pitchforks, and such poor weapons as they had, they were soon dispersed by the trained soldiers, and fled in all directions. When the Duke of Monmouth himself fled, was not known in the confusion; but the unlucky Lord Grey was taken early next day, and then another of the party was taken, who had confessed that he had parted from the Duke only four hours before. Strict search being made, he was found disguised as a peasant, hidden in a ditch under fern and nettles, with a few peas in his pocket which he had gathered in the fields to eat. The only other articles he had upon him were a few papers and little books: one of the latter being a strange jumble, in his own writing, of charms, songs, recipes, and prayers. He was completely broken. He wrote a miserable letter to the King, beseeching and entreating to be allowed to see him. When he was taken to London, and conveyed bound into the King's presence, he crawled to him on his knees, and made a most degrading exhibition. As James never forgave or relented towards anybody, he was not likely to soften towards the issuer of the Lyme proclamation, so he told the suppliant to prepare for death.

On the fifteenth of July, one thousand six hundred and eighty-five, this unfortunate favourite of the people was brought out to die on Tower Hill. The crowd was immense, and the tops of all the houses were covered with gazers. He had seen his wife, the daughter of the Duke of Buccleuch, in the Tower, and had talked much of a lady whom he loved far better—the LADY HARRIET WENTWORTH—who was one of the last persons he remembered in this life. Before laying down his head upon the block he felt the edge of the axe, and told the executioner that he feared it was not sharp enough, and that the axe was not heavy enough. On the executioner replying that it was of the proper kind, the Duke said, "I pray you have a care, and do not use me so awkwardly as you used my Lord Russell." The executioner, made nervous by this, and trembling, struck once and merely gashed him in the neck. Upon this, the Duke of Monmouth raised his head and looked the man reproachfully in the face. Then he struck twice, and then thrice, and then threw down the axe, and cried out in a voice of horror that he could not finish that work. The sheriffs, however, threatening him with what should be done to himself if he did not, he took it up again and

struck a fourth time and a fifth time. Then the wretched
head at last fell off, and James, Duke of Monmouth, was
dead, in the thirty-sixth year of his age. He was a showy
graceful man, with many popular qualities, and had found
much favour in the open hearts of the English.

The atrocities, committed by the Government, which
followed this Monmouth rebellion, form the blackest and
most lamentable page in English history. The poor peasants,
having been dispersed with great loss, and their leaders
having been taken, one would think that the implacable
King might have been satisfied. But no ; he let loose upon
them, among other intolerable monsters, a COLONEL KIRK,
who had served against the Moors, and whose soldiers—
called by the people Kirk's lambs, because they bore a lamb
upon their flag, as the emblem of Christianity—were worthy
of their leader. The atrocities committed by these demons
in human shape are far too horrible to be related here. It
is enough to say, that besides most ruthlessly murdering
and robbing them, and ruining them by making them buy
their pardons at the price of all they possessed, it was one
of Kirk's favourite amusements, as he and his officers sat
drinking after dinner, and toasting the King, to have
batches of prisoners hanged outside the windows for the
company's diversion ; and that when their feet quivered in
the convulsions of death, he used to swear that they should
have music to their dancing, and would order the drums
to beat and the trumpets to play. The detestable King
informed him, as an acknowledgment of these services, that
he was "very well satisfied with his proceedings." But the
King's great delight was in the proceedings of Jeffreys, now
a peer, who went down into the west, with four other judges,
to try persons accused of having had any share in the rebellion. The King pleasantly called this "Jeffreys's campaign."
The people down in that part of the country remember it
to this day as The Bloody Assize.

It began at Winchester, where a poor deaf old lady,
MRS. ALICIA LISLE, the widow of one of the judges of
Charles the First (who had been murdered abroad by some
Royalist assassins), was charged with having given shelter
in her house to two fugitives from Sedgemoor. Three times
the jury refused to find her guilty, until Jeffreys bullied
and frightened them into that false verdict. When he had
extorted it from them, he said, "Gentlemen, if I had been

one of you, and she had been my own mother, I would have found her guilty ; "—as I dare say he would. He sentenced her to be burned alive, that very afternoon. The clergy of the cathedral and some others interfered in her favour, and she was beheaded within a week. As a high mark of his approbation, the King made Jeffreys Lord Chancellor ; and he then went on to Dorchester, to Exeter, to Taunton, and to Wells. It is astonishing, when we read of the enormous injustice and barbarity of this beast, to know that no one struck him dead on the judgment-seat. It was enough for any man or woman to be accused by an enemy, before Jeffreys, to be found guilty of high treason. One man who pleaded not guilty, he ordered to be taken out of court upon the instant, and hanged ; and this so terrified the prisoners in general that they mostly pleaded guilty at once. At Dorchester alone, in the course of a few days, Jeffreys hanged eighty people ; besides whipping, transporting, imprisoning, and selling as slaves, great numbers. He executed, in all, two hundred and fifty, or three hundred.

These executions took place, among the neighbours and friends of the sentenced, in thirty-six towns and villages. Their bodies were mangled, steeped in caldrons of boiling pitch and tar, and hung up by the roadsides, in the streets, over the very churches. The sight and smell of heads and limbs, the hissing and bubbling of the infernal caldrons, and the tears and terrors of the people, were dreadful beyond all description. One rustic, who was forced to steep the remains in the black pot, was ever afterwards called "Tom Boilman." The hangman has ever since been called Jack Ketch, because a man of that name went hanging and hanging, all day long, in the train of Jeffreys. You will hear much of the horrors of the great French Revolution. Many and terrible they were, there is no doubt ; but I know of nothing worse, done by the maddened people of France in that awful time, than was done by the highest judge in England, with the express approval of the King of England, in The Bloody Assize.

Nor was even this all. Jeffreys was as fond of money for himself as of misery for others, and he sold pardons wholesale to fill his pockets. The King ordered, at one time, a thousand prisoners to be given to certain of his favourites, in order that they might bargain with them for their pardons. The young ladies of Taunton who had presented the Bible, were bestowed upon the maids of honour at court; and those precious ladies made very hard bargains with them indeed. When The Bloody Assize was at its most dismal height, the King was diverting himself with horse-races in the very place where Mrs. Lisle had been executed. When Jeffreys had done his worst, and came home again, he was particularly complimented in the Royal Gazette; and when the King heard that through drunkenness and raging he was very ill, his odious Majesty remarked that such another man could not easily be found in England. Besides all this, a former sheriff of London, named CORNISH, was hanged within sight of his own house, after an abominably conducted trial, for having had a share in the Rye House Plot, on evidence given by Rumsey, which that villain was obliged to confess was directly opposed to the evidence he had given on the trial of Lord Russell. And on the very same day, a worthy widow, named ELIZABETH GAUNT, was burned alive at Tyburn, for having sheltered a wretch who himself gave evidence against her. She settled the fuel about herself with her own hands, so that the flames should reach her quickly: and nobly said, with her last breath, that she had obeyed the sacred command of God, to give refuge to the outcast, and not to betray the wanderer.

After all this hanging, beheading, burning, boiling, mutilating, exposing, robbing, transporting, and selling into slavery, of his unhappy subjects, the King not unnaturally thought that he could do whatever he would. So he went to work to change the religion of the country with all possible speed; and what he did was this.

He first of all tried to get rid of what was called the Test Act—which prevented the Catholics from holding public employments—by his own power of dispensing with the penalties. He tried it in one case, and, eleven of the twelve judges deciding in his favour, he exercised it in three others, being those of three dignitaries of University College, Oxford, who had become Papists, and whom he kept in their places and sanctioned. He revived the hated Ecclesiastical Commission, to get rid of COMPTON, Bishop of London, who manfully opposed him. He solicited the Pope to favour England with an ambassador, which the Pope (who was a sensible man then) rather unwillingly did. He flourished Father Petre before the eyes of the people on all possible occasions. He favoured the establishment of convents in several parts of London. He was delighted to have the streets, and even the court itself, filled with Monks and Friars in the habits of their orders. He constantly endeavoured to make Catholics of the Protestants about him. He held private interviews, which he called "closetings," with those Members of Parliament who held offices, to persuade them to consent to the design he had in view. When they did not consent, they were removed, or resigned of themselves, and their places were given to Catholics. He displaced Protestant officers from the army, by every means in his power, and got Catholics into their places too. He tried the same thing with the corporations, and also (though not so successfully) with the Lord Lieutenants of counties. To terrify the people into the endurance of all these measures, he kept an army of fifteen thousand men encamped on Hounslow Heath, where mass was openly performed in the General's tent, and where priests went among the soldiers endeavouring to persuade them to become Catholics. For circulating a paper among those men advising them to be true to their religion, a Protestant clergyman, named JOHNSON, the chaplain of the late Lord Russell, was actually sentenced to stand three times in the pillory, and was actually whipped from Newgate to Tyburn. He dismissed his own brother-in-law from his Council because he was a Protestant, and made a Privy Councillor of the before-mentioned Father Petre. He handed Ireland over to RICHARD TALBOT, EARL OF TYRCONNELL, a worthless, dissolute knave, who played the same game there for his master, and who played the deeper game for himself of one day putting it under the protection of the French King. In going to these extremities, every man of sense and judgment among the Catholics, from the Pope to a porter, knew that the King was a mere bigoted fool, who would undo himself and the cause he sought to advance; but he was deaf to all reason, and, happily for England ever afterwards, went tumbling off his throne in his own blind way.

A spirit began to arise in the country, which the besotted blunderer little expected. He first found it out in the University of Cambridge. Having made a Catholic, a dean, at Oxford, without any opposition, he tried to make a monk a master of arts at Cambridge: which attempt the University resisted. and defeated him. He then went back to his favourite Oxford. On the death of the President of Magdalen College, he commanded that there should be elected to succeed him, one MR. ANTHONY FARMER, whose only recommendation was, that he was of the King's religion. The University plucked up courage at last, and refused. The King substituted another man, and it still refused, resolving to stand by its own election of a MR. HOUGH. The dull tyrant, upon this, punished Mr. Hough, and five-and-twenty more, by causing them to be expelled and declared incapable of holding any church preferment; then he proceeded to what he supposed to be his highest step, but to what was, in fact, his last plunge head-foremost in his tumble off his throne.

He had issued a declaration that there should be no religious tests or penal laws, in order to let in the Catholics more easily; but the Protestant dissenters, unmindful of themselves, had gallantly joined the regular church in opposing it tooth and nail. The King and Father Petre now resolved to have this read, on a certain Sunday, in all the churches, and to order it to be circulated for that purpose by the bishops. The latter took counsel with the Archbishop of Canterbury, who was in disgrace; and they resolved that the declaration should not be read, and that they would petition the King against it. The Archbishop himself wrote out the petition, and six bishops went into the King's bedchamber the same night to present it, to his infinite astonishment. Next day was the Sunday fixed for the reading, and it was only read by two hundred clergymen out of ten thousand. The King resolved against all advice to prosecute the bishops in the Court of King's Bench, and within three weeks they were summoned before the Privy Council, and committed to the Tower. As the six bishops were taken to that dismal place, by water, the people who were assembled in immense numbers fell upon their knees, and wept for them, and prayed for them. When they got to the Tower, the officers and soldiers on guard besought them for their blessing. While they were confined there, the soldiers every day drank to their release with loud shouts. When they were brought up to the Court of King's Bench for their trial, which the Attorney-General said was for the high offence of censuring the Government, and giving their opinion about affairs of state, they were attended by similar multitudes, and surrounded by a throng of noblemen and

gentlemen. When the jury went out at seven o'clock at
night to consider of their verdict, everybody (except the King)
knew that they would rather starve than yield to the King's
brewer, who was one of them, and wanted a verdict for his
customer. When they came into court next morning, after
resisting the brewer all night, and gave a verdict of not
guilty, such a shout rose up in Westminster Hall as it had
never heard before ; and it was passed on among the people
away to Temple Bar, and away again to the Tower. It did
not pass only to the east, but passed to the west too, until it
reached the camp at Hounslow, where the fifteen thousand
soldiers took it up and echoed it. And still, when the dull
King, who was then with Lord Feversham, heard the mighty
roar, asked in alarm what it was, and was told that it was
"nothing but the acquittal of the bishops," he said, in his
dogged way, " Call you that nothing? It is so much the
worse for them."

Between the petition and the trial, the Queen had given
birth to a son, which Father Petre rather thought was owing
to Saint Winifred. But I doubt if Saint Winifred had much
to do with it as the King's friend, inasmuch as the entirely
new prospect of a Catholic successor (for both the King's
daughters were Protestants) determined the EARLS OF
SHREWSBURY, DANBY, and DEVONSHIRE, LORD LUMLEY, the
BISHOP OF LONDON, ADMIRAL RUSSELL, and COLONEL SIDNEY,
to invite the Prince of Orange over to England. The Royal
Mole, seeing his danger at last, made, in his fright, many
great concessions, besides raising an army of forty thousand
men ; but the Prince of Orange was not a man for James
the Second to cope with. His preparations were extra-
ordinarily vigorous, and his mind was resolved.

For a fortnight after the Prince was ready to sail for
England, a great wind from the west prevented the departure
of his fleet. Even when the wind lulled, and it did sail, it
was dispersed by a storm, and was obliged to put back to
refit. At last, on the first of November, one thousand six
hundred and eighty-eight, the Protestant east wind, as it was
long called, began to blow ; and on the third, the people of
Dover and the people of Calais saw a fleet twenty miles long
sailing gallantly by, between the two places. On Monday,
the fifth, it anchored at Torbay in Devonshire, and the Prince,
with a splendid retinue of officers and men, marched into
Exeter. But the people in that western part of the country

had suffered so much in The Bloody Assize, that they had lost heart. Few people joined him; and he began to think of returning, and publishing the invitation he had received from those lords, as his justification for having come at all. At this crisis, some of the gentry joined him; the Royal army began to falter; an engagement was signed, by which all who set their hand to it declared that they would support one another in defence of the laws and liberties of the three Kingdoms, of the Protestant religion, and of the Prince of Orange. From that time, the cause received no check; the greatest towns in England began, one after another, to declare for the Prince; and he knew that it was all safe with him when the University of Oxford offered to melt down its plate, if he wanted any money.

By this time the King was running about in a pitiable way, touching people for the King's evil in one place, reviewing his troops in another, and bleeding from the nose in a third. The young Prince was sent to Portsmouth, Father Petre went off like a shot to France, and there was a general and swift dispersal of all the priests and friars. One after another, the King's most important officers and friends deserted him and went over to the Prince. In the night, his daughter Anne fled from Whitehall Palace; and the Bishop of London, who had once been a soldier, rode before her with a drawn sword in his hand, and pistols at his saddle. "God help me," cried the miserable King: "my very children have forsaken me!" In his wildness, after debating with such lords as were in London, whether he should or should not call a Parliament, and after naming three of them to negotiate with the Prince, he resolved to fly to France. He had the little Prince of Wales brought back from Portsmouth; and the child and the Queen crossed the river to Lambeth in an open boat, on a miserable wet night, and got safely away. This was on the night of the ninth of December.

At one o'clock on the morning of the eleventh, the King, who had, in the meantime, received a letter from the Prince of Orange, stating his objects, got out of bed, told LORD NORTHUMBERLAND who lay in his room not to open the door until the usual hour in the morning, and went down the back stairs (the same, I suppose, by which the priest in the wig and gown had come up to his brother) and crossed the river in a small boat: sinking the great seal of England by the

way. Horses having been provided, he rode, accompanied by
SIR EDWARD HALES, to Feversham, where he embarked in
a Custom House Hoy. The master of this Hoy, wanting
more ballast, ran into the Isle of Sheppy to get it, where the
fishermen and smugglers crowded about the boat, and informed the King of their suspicions that he was a "hatchet-
faced Jesuit." As they took his money and would not let
him go, he told them who he was, and that the Prince of
Orange wanted to take his life ; and he began to scream for
a boat—and then to cry, because he had lost a piece of wood
on his ride which he called a fragment of Our Saviour's
cross. He put himself into the hands of the Lord Lieutenant
of the county, and his detention was made known to the
Prince of Orange at Windsor—who, only wanting to get rid
of him, and not caring where he went, so that he went away,
was very much disconcerted that they did not let him go.
However, there was nothing for it but to have him brought
back, with some state in the way of Life Guards, to Whitehall. And as soon as he got there, in his infatuation, he
heard mass, and set a Jesuit to say grace at his public
dinner.

The people had been thrown into the strangest state of
confusion by his flight, and had taken it into their heads
that the Irish part of the army were going to murder the
Protestants. Therefore, they set the bells a ringing, and
lighted watch-fires, and burned Catholic Chapels, and looked
about in all directions for Father Petre and the Jesuits, while
the Pope's ambassador was running away in the dress of
a footman. They found no Jesuits ; but a man, who had
once been a frightened witness before Jeffreys in court, saw
a swollen drunken face looking through a window down at
Wapping, which he well remembered. The face was in
a sailor's dress, but he knew it to be the face of that accursed
Judge, and he seized him. The people, to their lasting
honour, did not tear him to pieces. After knocking him
about a little, they took him, in the basest agonies of terror,
to the Lord Mayor, who sent him, at his own shrieking
petition, to the Tower for safety. There, he died.

Their bewilderment continuing, the people now lighted
bonfires and made rejoicings, as if they had any reason to be
glad to have the King back again. But, his stay was very
short, for the English guards were removed from Whitehall,
Dutch guards were marched up to it, and he was told by one

of his late ministers that the Prince would enter London, next day, and he had better go to Ham. He said, Ham was a cold damp place, and he would rather go to Rochester. He thought himself very cunning in this, as he meant to escape from Rochester to France. The Prince of Orange and his friends knew that, perfectly well, and desired nothing more. So, he went to Gravesend, in his royal barge, attended by certain lords, and watched by Dutch troops, and pitied by the generous people, who were far more forgiving than he had ever been, when they saw him in his humiliation. On the night of the twenty-third of December, not even then understanding that everybody wanted to get rid of him, he went out, absurdly, through his Rochester garden, down to the Medway, and got away to France, where he rejoined the Queen.

There had been a council in his absence, of the lords, and the authorities of London. When the Prince came, on the day after the King's departure, he summoned the Lords to meet him, and soon afterwards, all those who had served in any of the Parliaments of King Charles the Second. It was finally resolved by these authorities that the throne was vacant by the conduct of King James the Second; that it was inconsistent with the safety and welfare of this Protestant kingdom, to be governed by a Popish prince; that the Prince and Princess of Orange should be King and Queen during their lives and the life of the survivor of them; and that their children should succeed them, if they had any. That if they had none, the Princess Anne and her children should succeed; that if she had none, the heirs of the Prince of Orange should succeed.

On the thirteenth of January, one thousand six hundred and eighty-nine, the Prince and Princess, sitting on a throne in Whitehall, bound themselves to these conditions. The Protestant religion was established in England, and England's great and glorious Revolution was complete.

CHAPTER XXXVII

I HAVE now arrived at the close of my little history. The events which succeeded the famous Revolution of one thousand six hundred and eighty-eight, would neither be easily related nor easily understood in such a book as this.

William and Mary reigned together, five years. After the death of his good wife, William occupied the throne, alone, for seven years longer. During his reign, on the sixteenth of September, one thousand seven hundred and one, the poor weak creature who had once been James the Second of England, died in France. In the meantime he had done his utmost (which was not much) to cause William to be assassinated, and to regain his lost dominions. James's son was declared, by the French King, the rightful King of England ; and was called in France THE CHEVALIER SAINT GEORGE, and in England THE PRETENDER. Some infatuated people in England, and particularly in Scotland, took up the Pretender's cause from time to time—as if the country had not had Stuarts enough !—and many lives were sacrificed, and much misery was occasioned. King William died on Sunday, the seventh of March, one thousand seven hundred and two, of the consequences of an accident occasioned by his horse stumbling with him. He was always a brave patriotic Prince, and a man of remarkable abilities. His manner was cold, and he made but few friends ; but he had truly loved his queen. When he was dead, a lock of her hair, in a ring, was found tied with a black ribbon round his left arm.

He was succeeded by the PRINCESS ANNE, a popular Queen, who reigned twelve years. In her reign, in the month of May, one thousand seven hundred and seven, the Union between England and Scotland was effected, and the two countries were incorporated under the name of GREAT BRITAIN. Then, from the year one thousand seven hundred and fourteen to the year one thousand eight hundred and thirty, reigned the four GEORGES.

It was in the reign of George the Second, one thousand seven hundred and forty-five, that the Pretender did his last mischief, and made his last appearance. Being an old man by that time, he and the Jacobites—as his friends were called —put forward his son CHARLES EDWARD, known as the Young Chevalier. The Highlanders of Scotland, an extremely troublesome and wrong-headed race on the subject of the Stuarts, espoused his cause, and he joined them, and there was a Scottish rebellion to make him king, in which many gallant and devoted gentlemen lost their lives. It was a hard matter for Charles Edward to escape abroad again, with a high price on his head ; but the Scottish people were extra-ordinarily faithful to him, and, after undergoing many romantic adventures, not unlike those of Charles the Second, he escaped to France. A number of charming stories and delightful songs arose out of the Jacobite feelings, and belong to the Jacobite times. Otherwise I think the Stuarts were a public nuisance altogether.

It was in the reign of George the Third that England lost North America, by persisting in taxing her without her own consent. That immense country, made independent under WASHINGTON, and left to itself, became the United States ; one of the greatest nations of the earth. In these times in which I write, it is honourably remarkable for protecting its subjects, wherever they may travel, with a dignity and a determination which is a model for England. Between you and me, England has rather lost ground in this respect since the days of Oliver Cromwell.

The Union of Great Britain with Ireland—which had been getting on very ill by itself—took place in the reign of George the Third, on the second of July, one thousand seven hundred and ninety-eight.

WILLIAM THE FOURTH succeeded George the Fourth, in the year one thousand eight hundred and thirty, and reigned seven years. QUEEN VICTORIA, his niece, the only child of the Duke of Kent, the fourth son of George the Third, came to the throne on the twentieth of June, one thousand eight hundred and thirty-seven. She was married to PRINCE ALBERT of Saxe Gotha on the tenth of February, one thousand eight hundred and forty. She is very good, and much beloved. So I end, like the crier, with

GOD SAVE THE QUEEN!